I0762091

Frat' Brats

A '60s Novel

Frat' Brats

A '60sNovel

By

Jay Dubya

Published by
Jay Dubya
Hammonton, NJ 08037

1888_PB_8

Printed in the United Stastes of America

ISBN 979-8-9949655-9-7

Other Books by Jay Dubya

Adult Literature

Black Leather and Blue Denim, A '50s Novel
The Great Teen Fruit War, A 1960 Novel
Ron Coyote, Man of La Mangia
Pieces of Eight
Pieces of Eight, Part II
Pieces of Eight, Part III
Pieces of Eight, Part IV
Nine New Novellas
Nine New Novellas, Part II
Nine New Novellas, Part III
Nine New Novellas, Part IV
So Ya' Wanna' Be A Teacher!
Fractured Frazzled Folk Fables and Fairy Farces
Fractured Frazzled Folk Fables and Fairy Farces, Part II
The Wholly Book of Genesis
The Wholly Book of Exodus
The Wholly Book of Doo-Doo-Rot-onMe
Thirteen Sick Tasteless Classics
Thirteen Sick Tasteless Classics, Part II
Thirteen Sick Tasteless Classics, Part III
Thirteen Sick Tasteless Classics, Part IV
Thirteen Sick Tasteless Classics, Part V
Mauled Maimed Mangled Mutilated Mythology
One Baker's Dozen
Two Baker's Dozen
Time Travel Tales
UFO: Utterly Fantastic Occurrences
RAM: Random Articles & Manuscripts
Modern Mythology
Prime-Time Crime Time
Snake Eyes and Boxcars
Snake Eyes and Boxcars, Part II
The Psychic Dimension
The Psychic Dimension, Part II
Shakespeare: Slammed, Smeared, Savaged & Slaughtered
Shakespeare: S, S, S, & S, Part II
First Person Stories
The Arcane Arcade

Thirteen Tantalizing Tales
PLOTS
PLOTS, Part II
THEMES
Hawthorne: Hazed, Hooked, Hammered & Hijacked
Hawthorne Hacked, Shakespeare Sacked, & Thurber Thwacked
Suite 16
The FBI Inspector
Poe: Pelted, Pounded, Pummeled & Pulverized
Twain: Tattered, Trounced, Tortured & Traumatized
London: Lashed, Lacerated, Lampooned & Lambasted
O. Henry: Obscenely and Outrageously Obliterated
HOMER'S ILL ILIAD
Homer's Odd Sea Odyssey
Homer's Ill Iliad and Odd Sea Odyssey
The Timeless Time Machine
War of the Worlds
The Invisible Man
Parody Paradise
Parody Paradise, Part II
Parody Paradise, Part III
Parody Paradise, Part IV
Bee 17, Short Stories
Bee 17, #2, Short Stories
Bee 17, #3, Short Stories
Bee 17, #4, Short Stories
Bee 17, #5, Short Stories
Bee 17, #6, Short Stories

Children's Fantasy

Pot of Gold
Enchanta
Space Bugs, Earth Invasion
The Eighteen Story Gingerbread House

Acknowledgement

Special thanks are extended to Jim Amari, a forty-three-year friend of the author and former Hammonton High School English teacher and faculty colleague, for proofreading this work *Frat' Brats, A '60s Novel*. In this literary endeavor, the fictional character Tim Amoro represents a youthful Jim Amari.

To all students that had attended *Edgewood Regional High School* before it became *Winslow Regional High*, and to all those students that had attended *Glassboro State College* before it became *Rowan University*. Your true Alma Maters have not been forgotten.

Contents

Introduction

Frat' Brats is the third book of a coming-of-age trilogy. In *Frat' Brats,* J. W. attends a South Jersey teachers' college and prepares for a professional life in the real economic world. Soon, the freshman joins an off-campus, non-sanctioned fraternity, Lambda Phi Sigma, and that's when the college student's life suddenly becomes very interesting and conflict-oriented.

In *Black Leather and Blue Denim, A '50s Novel,* J.W.'s family moves from Hammonton, New Jersey to Levittown, Pennsylvania in 1954. In '57, J. W. joins the Diablos, a street gang that has a turf war with the ruthless and racist Kenwood Kamikazes.

In *The Great Teen Fruit War, A 1960 Novel,* J.W.'s family moves back to Hammonton, NJ, an agricultural community famous for its peach and blueberry crops. The high school senior becomes a member of the Reds, a gang of peach farmers' sons that has continual conflict with the Blues, the spoiled sons of wealthy blueberry growers.

Frat Brats, A '60s Novel is author Jay Dubya's twenty-second literary endeavor.

Chapter 1
"Rowan University"

The lucky *thirteen*-mile April 1, 2004 drive from Hammonton to Glassboro, New Jersey was pleasant and almost inspirational. As my merlot-colored *Nissan Maxima* slowly passed through downtown Williamstown and onto *Route 322,* I pondered the four years I had spent at *Glassboro State College,* preparing to become an idealistic New Jersey public school teacher, a dedicated career which I had diligently pursued for thirty-four years, until my very happy retirement in June of 1999.

But many important fragments of my past have been erased by circumstances beyond my control, further adding to my general quandary that often hypothesizes whether those four incredible years between ages nineteen and twenty-three had really occurred or not, for my entire life has been dangerously lived "on the cusp". Let me explain the basis for my current rumination.

I had attended Cardinal Reagan Catholic High in Levittown, Pennsylvania from 1957-'59, but now the former parochial school is boarded-up, and its identity no longer exists. And then in 1960 I managed to finally evolve out of Edgewood Regional High School in Atco, New Jersey, but the name of that institution is now Winslow Regional High School. And consistent with that strange coincidence of my educational past being eradicated, the *Glassboro State Teachers College* of 1965 I had known and often reflect upon has now been transformed into *Rowan University.*

But for some remote, inexplicable reason, I seldom revisited my former *Glassboro State* Alma Mater, but now I felt driven by a strong compulsion to re-connect with my past escapades. Perhaps it was pure nostalgia, or maybe I was motivated by fanciful memories that still haunted my delicate psyche, or perhaps my impulse to visit Glassboro was a desperate measure to recapture the essence of my youth. 'April is symbolic of the rebirth of nature and of plant life in the *Northern Hemisphere,"* I rationally considered, 'and just like daffodils sprouting-out of the fertile ground, and deciduous trees miraculously forming splendid new green spring foliage, my soul too is being rejuvenated this *April Fools Day* by the wonderful annual spring regeneration.'

Upon crossing two-lane *Delsea Drive,* which also masquerades as *Route 47,* I ambitiously entered the small college town. I figured I would tour some exclusive sites to determine if any of my old haunts were still around and viably functioning. My curious eyes instantly recognized that Mazzeo's Bar and Lounge on High Street on my right was now the Study Hall Coffee House, a defunct boarded-up business that obviously had seen more prosperous times. Across the street and a block west was the former splendid Glassboro Movie Theater, now a mere empty bankrupt business with a huge "For Sale" sign hung in its ancient window, but back in 1964, the cinema was the site of a raucous fraternity shindig. That particular violation, along with other college high jinks, almost got my Greek brothers and me expelled from the school of higher learning for the final time, our fifth ultimatum from the beleaguered administration.

Joe's Sub Shop further down on High Street now had the creative appellation Little Beef's Hoagie Shop, a true indication that nothing is really permanent in this ephemeral life in an ever-changing world. I recalled that the Glassboro Police Station had formerly occupied the space behind the town bank, situated at the central intersection of High and Main Streets, but now I observed that a new police building occupies the corner opposite the prestigious financial institution. The town's gendarmes had moved a fantastic hundred- feet-away from the address where I had known them to operate and practice their brand of law enforcement back in the early '60s.

I felt my heart pound a little more robustly when I stopped my vehicle to study the upstairs rooms of 38 South Main Street, where Big Al Keiler, Bill Elderberry, Paul Meroski, Ralph Crenshaw, Tim Amoro, News Tomasello, and I had hibernated for three fabulous coming-of-age years. Our generally comfortable sophomore-to-senior residence was located right next to Lacy's Funeral Home, which no longer exists as a family business. 38 South Main now appeared old with its light-green siding fading as a result of four decades of wear and tear, and constant exposure to Mother Nature's indiscriminate cruelty, but nevertheless, the aging house still represented the memorable space I had shared, a little smaller than I appropriately remembered it being as my "home away from home", from September of 1962 to June of '65.

Back in the early-to-mid '60s, Seedy's Bar was a popular hangout for my unauthorized off-campus fraternity, the Lambda Phi Sigmas, which was a social group of Greek wannabe's more interested in chugging *Budweiser* and hustling pretty girls with robust busts than engrossed in the actual pursuit of academic excellence. As Timmy Amoro once said, "We're more gross than engrossed!" Ironically, Seedy's lively suds and sandwich hangout was just down the street from St. Bridget's Catholic Church, which predictably held its Sunday services on Church Street. But now, the site where Seedy's was situated back in 1965 is now a barren, vacant lot.

I slowly navigated my *Maxima* down Oakwood Avenue, which I used as a back approach to the rustic and still-handsome college campus, and while passing over the familiar railroad tracks, I noticed the old Glassboro Train Station and Depot, empty, boarded-up, and depressingly decrepit-looking. That ramshackle edifice also brought back several sentimental memories that I'll never forget as long as Alzheimer's disease doesn't completely evaporate my recollections. But the dilapidated condition of the once-vibrant train station made my heart feel melancholy and had my sixty-two-year-old body suddenly feeling worn-out and tired, too, for several great Lambda Phi Sigma early '60s adventures had taken place at that location.

I took Whitney Avenue past #501, Hollybush, the *Glassboro State College* President's residence back in 1965. But today, the structure proudly stands as a historic building dedicated to commemorate the famous 1967 *Summit Meeting* between President Lyndon Baines Johnson and the U.S.S.R. Premier Alexei B. Kosygin, which coincidentally had transpired on the *Glassboro State College Campus,* and the great international conference remains today the venerable Jersey sandstone college mansion's greatest claim to fame.

I made a right on *322,* wanting to view the historic Franklin House, which was an inn dating-back to the aristocratic fox-hunting days of the early 1790s, but I was disappointed in discovering that the building had been renovated and converted into the Landmark Americana Tap, Grill and Liquor Mart. Across from the former Franklin House was State Street, which formed a Y two blocks down at New Street, where Academy Street (the home of a rival fraternity the Tau Kappa Epsilons) began. So, being a little sad and disappointed at the Franklin House's demise, I turned-around in the Landmark Americana's parking lot and returned west on *322,* which now divides the old campus from the new building additions, most of which have been constructed since my graduation in '65.

Only *Bosshart Hall, Winans Dining Hall,* and the *Esbjornson Gymnasium* were situated on the north side of *322* my senior year, but now, a grand *Student Union Building, Robinson Hall, Mimosa Hall, Rowan Hall, Wilson Hall,* the new *Savitz Library,* along with six massive co-ed dormitories have been added to the north *322* campus scenario. Sadly, *Winans Cafeteria* has been renovated and ingeniously converted into *Winans College Bookstore,* and so, the

Glassboro State College campus (now *Rowan University*), like the rest of the universities on the planet, continues its new growth and its unique chameleon retooling of older facilities.

Glassboro's residential streets west of *Glassboro State* attempt to confirm and promote a college-town atmosphere theme. Girard Road parallels the railroad tracks that happen to form the campus's western perimeter, and the remembrance of our Lambda Phi Sigma initiation immediately surfaced from my subconscious, and managed to rekindle my flagging spirit. Princeton, Pennsylvania, Columbia, Yale, Harvard, and Lehigh Roads horizontally followed in succession to the west after Girard; and then Georgetown, Dickinson, Villanova, and Swarthmore Roads run vertically west, forming a characteristic lattice pattern with the aforementioned west-layered streets, which traditionally have housed many off-campus students from back in the '60s up to the present time. Harvard Road was the base for another Lambda Phi Sigma enemy fraternity, the Delta Alpha Omegas.

University Road is the main residential thoroughfare that parallels Dickinson and Villanova in the well-conceived interlacing pattern. Many of the University Road homes that I considered mansions back in the '60s now appear in need of repair and rather mediocre in appearance. But it was not University Road's stately oak and elm trees, nor the architectural grandeur of its aging palaces that prompted me to desire re-exploring the remainder of the very serene boulevard.

At the very end of the wide avenue was Peaks Horse, Apple and Peach Farm, which is now fenced-in and designated off-limits to strangers. But despite the three prominent "No Trespassing" signs, I felt a need to exit my *Maxima* and traverse down a familiar rural trail a hundred-feet into the nearby woods where I intended to re-discover a shallow stream. My feet rushed along the still-secluded path, now tangled in dense brush, until my trek came to the "Sacred Oak," majestically towering above me, and still deeply rooted amidst the woods' briars, thick brambles and wild vegetation.

The old severed "Tarzan jungle vine" still dangled from around the still-dignified oak's third revered limb, and the fallen-but-decomposing elm tree footbridge still spanned over the fifteen-foot-wide brook that remains today a rather imposing sight, but absolutely ravaged by time, rotted through its decayed bark and trunk. And in its ancient oak's present flimsy condition, the feeble limbs are totally incapable of holding a sixty-two-year-old male of average weight. My active mind envisioned our Lambda Phi Sigma President Bob

Abrams demonstrating his audacity, and then challenging me to duplicate his very daring heroics.

'That's the third of nine major memorable scenes I wanted to see, besides the town's railroad tracks, and 38 South Main,' I evaluated. 'The fourth-through-seventh items of interest are on the old-side of the college campus, and the eighth-and-ninth bits of nostalgia can be found two-miles south of Glassboro in Aura.'

I then carefully ambled-back to my *Nissan;* gingerly entered the vehicle; cautiously backed-up; turned around, and casually drove the mile-distance to the still-attractive countryside campus. 'I wish I had called Tim Amoro up to accompany me on this ramble,' I seriously thought. 'He would relish this nostalgia as much as I am fondly recollecting it right now.'

I halted my auto in the makeshift stone parking lot owned by the Pennsylvania Railroad. 'It's safe during the daytime,' my mind reckoned, while recalling that once; I was taking a graduate night course at the college; arrived at the campus a bit behind schedule; hastily parked my wife's green *Pontiac* in the same lot, and returned from class finding that the car's battery had been stolen. 'My brother-in-law was not too keen on driving from Hammonton to Glassboro with a replacement battery in the middle of a wicked January snowstorm,' I imagined with a naughty grin.

Although it was an early spring day, fallen leaves cushioned under my steps to the old campus buildings I wished to observe. The bright golden dome still formed a cupola above the main academic building that had been erected in 1923, then called *College Hall* up until '65, but now renamed *Bunce Hall* after a revered college dean. And then, I reviewed in a mental newsreel several fond fraternity activities associated with the gold-gilded landmark that were still deeply ingrained in my amused mind. I stopped to marvel at the majestic spectacle as students, less impressed with its essential existence, chatted and rushed to their next scheduled classes.

I detoured to where the Student Co-op snack bar used to be, which was a unique 1960s malt-shop carryover from the previous, less hostile '50s decade. The mammoth *Student Union* across *Route 322* had replaced the Co-op (and its attendant lounges in nearby *Memorial Hall)* as the campus nerve center, and the entire *Memorial Hall* complex was now a suite of specialized offices being utilized for various student organizations, clubs, the *Whit* newspaper, the *Avant Literary Magazine*, and for individual student counseling.

I passed by several groups of garrulous, preoccupied students, oblivious to my intense scrutiny of their taken-for-granted physical environment. The walkers were laughing and exchanging gossip en route to their next destinations. Four decades before, I had shared their youthful vim and vigor; their enterprise; their great expectations for individual accomplishments, and their vision for a more peaceful world, along with *their* rosy hopes and dreams for prosperous futures. But then, I felt myself' being quite out of place standing there, a realist and modern-day cynic among those dreamers that were still vulnerable to professors' unbridled entreaties and idealistic optimisms. Forty-years separated their same experience from mine as a *GSC* student, trekking down that same well-worn asphalt path, and my skeptical mind appreciated and rehashed the salient fact that I did not have to relive those same forty-years from 1965 to 2004 over again.

I next strolled to the old, magnificent dorm' Quadrangle consisting of *Laurel Hall* and *Oak Hall,* originally constructed parallel to each other in the 1920s in order to accommodate the women attending the two-year "Normal School" to earn teaching certification. And to the far end of that most beautiful sector of the scenic campus was *Linden Hall,* built in the late 1950s to complement the more distinguished twin dormitories. *Oak Hall* was just a short saunter from Hollybush, where several asphalt paths lead to *Evergreen Hall,* where Joanne Berenato and Peachy Wilcox once cheerfully resided. And next to *Evergreen* is *Mullica Hall,* a men's dormitory back in '65.

I peered across *Route 322* at the numerous building additions supplementing what I had known in '65, and the edifices now stretched all the way to Carpenter Street, which in my senior year seemed to be in another county. Behind the new dormitories and brick-faced academic buildings are numerous parking lots; tennis courts; softball; hockey; la-crosse; baseball; soccer fields; and several intramural practice fields, and finally, my perceptive eyes observed the rather outstanding *Rowan University Football Stadium.*

I cut my route back across the area next to *Memorial Hall* and jaunted through a nice, clean, pristine-looking setting that was once a student parking lot for "commuters". *Hawthorn Hall* was now altered into an administrative office building, and no longer was the men's dorm I had recalled from '65. The *Campus School,* where many of my colleagues had completed their Student Teaching and fundamental Practicum experiences, was now called *Bozarth Hall*, named after another college dean of my era. Next to the former *Campus School* was the old baseball field where Ralph Crenshaw and I used to broadcast the games for *WGLS-FM,* the college radio station, which was now housed in *Bozarth Hall,* and no longer was situated above the old *Savitz Library* building (now an administrative building) on the entrance oval, in front of what is now *Bunce Hall.*

I stood gazing at "*College Hall*" for a full minute, standing on the baseball field's pitcher's mound, as the April 1st wind swirled dust and the remains of the autumn leaves about my black leather shoes. Forty-five years had elapsed since I had played gym-class soccer for Coach Holmes on that same verdant field, and only the passage of precious time separated my present memories from those past, happy experiences that had occurred in that exact same place.

'Now that my eyes have seen the railroad tracks, the vine, the elm tree bridge, and the creek; the *College Hall Golden Dome,* the *Quadrangle,* the former Co-op, and *Evergreen Hall,* there's only two more essential memories to see on my *April Fools Day Glassboro State* excursion,' I pondered, as I gingerly stepped-around the corner of *Bunce Hall* to the oval drive before it, now blocked-off to local traffic. Arriving at my parked automobile in the all-too-familiar dirt and stone railroad parking lot, I decided to motor south two-miles to Aura to complete my day's personal itinerary.

I anxiously drove through downtown Glassboro on High to Main Street, looked left, and smiled upon seeing that Angelo's Diner was still in business. And then, I traveled south until Main became *Gloucester County Road 533.* Soon, I crossed the railroad tracks a mile from the college town, and then crossed *County 610.* Another mile or so on *County 533* I arrived at good old *Gloucester County Road 608.* After turning left, my right foot stepped more heavily on the accelerator as I wondered whether or not my fraternity's old original Lambda Phi Sigma party place was still standing.

I halted my *Nissan* to obtain a closer inspection of the structure I was so anxious to see. Yes, there it now stood, painted red, but still in the exact shape I had remembered it being. The ultimate objective of my Hammonton-to-Glassboro short excursion was Steve "Hoppy" Cassidy's infamous chicken coop, but in 1962, the commonplace farm building had been imaginatively converted into a swinging college student attraction, the infamous Lambda Phi fraternity house.

On the way back to *Delsea Drive,* following *County 608,* I passed by the picturesque *Academy Street Lake* in Clayton, which was the final item on my intended itinerary, and also, a very important part of my *Glassboro State College* coming-of-age. Feeling quite satisfied and mentally renewed, I then motored back to Hammonton.

Chapter 2
"Edgewood High"

My father drove me over to Edgewood Regional High School on Coopers Folly Road in early January of 1960 in his green and white '55 Chevy Bel Air. The Atco school was only one year old and still looked brand new. I couldn't attend Hammonton High because Dad's new business and house were in Winslow Township, Camden County, and not in Atlantic County. We had visited St. Joseph High in Hammonton where my folks really wanted me to attend, but the small parochial school did not have the same curriculum I had been taking at Levittown's Cardinal Reagan, before my family had moved back to New Jersey.

The Edgewood guidance counselors explained to Dad and me that they were going to "bump me up" from a junior to a senior, because if they didn't, I was already seventeen and would be nineteen when I would finally graduate. Pop liked the idea, but I was a little skeptical of such a radical maneuver, just because I was a year older than the normal junior happened to be. After filling-out some admissions' forms in the Edgewood Guidance Office, Pop was free to leave, and I was then a ward to public school education.

I discussed my educational background with Mr. Wilson and Mr. White, and the guidance counselors devised an individualized schedule tailored just for me. It wasn't until third period that I was able to arrive at my first class, Mrs. Murphy's American History II.

The teacher examined my "Class Admission Card," checked that I was in the right room and period on my schedule, entered my name in her roll book, and told me to sit in the back of the class. After introducing me to the Advanced College Prep group, Mrs. Murphy asked if I'd like to be called anything besides my regular name.

"Yes, you can call me J.W.," I politely replied.

"Okay, J.W. Here's your comprehensive History II text. It's quite a monster. Good luck in my class," the instructor pleasantly related. "Hope you enjoy doin' lots of homework, textbook reading, and library research."

I graciously accepted the hefty textbook with a blush on my face, as the other students snickered and giggled at my very obvious temporary discomfort. The history instructor then declared she was going to ask the class some pertinent questions about the *Civil War*. History was one of my strong suits at Cardinal Reagan High, so I thought I could impress everyone if I could accurately answer the first question.

"What important *Civil War* battle that went-on for over six weeks gave the north control of the Mississippi River?" Mrs. Murphy verbally quizzed.

That answer was definitely stored inside my mental repertoire. I proudly flung my arm up, begging for recognition. My animated solicitation was immediately acknowledged.

"I believe I'll call on our new scholar J.W. for the correct response," Mrs. Murphy indicated, as the remainder of the *CP* students silently turned their heads in the direction of my location in the last seat of the last row nearest the room's windows. Everyone was curious to hear what the new kid would say.

"It was the battle of *Vicks*burg," I enthusiastically announced, "and General Grant finally won, even without the use of cough drops!" I elaborated, deliberately attempting to be funny mentioning a brand name product while actually imitating my old Levittown pal, Bo Jalonec.

The class broke-out in a roar, not laughing at my silly pun alluding to a brand name cough drop, but becoming hysterical at me standing beside my desk. At Cardinal Reagan High, standing was required for students when either asking or answering academic matters out of respect for the priests, nuns, or lay teachers on the faculty. In my haste, I had instinctively acted out of force of habit. I was extremely embarrassed, stupidly behaving like a Catholic school kid in his new, more-liberal public-school environment.

"J.W.," Mrs. Murphy laughed. "You just have to stand in this public-school for the reciting of the *Pledge of Allegiance* during homeroom announcements. This is Edgewood Regional High School, you know. It isn't *Fort Dix* or the *Pentagon!"*

The entire class again burst-out in a boisterous roar in response to Mrs. Murphy's suave diplomatic admonishment. I sank-down in my desk with my face florid, feeling excessively naive, awkward, and very foolish.

Fourth period class was with Mr. Andrews, a stern, inflexible trigonometry teacher. His non-smiling personality-type tolerated little humor or frivolity from students. I really minded my P's and Q's during my first exposure to the austere educator. I quickly realized that I was way ahead of the public-school kids in English and social studies, but very far behind their achievement level in advanced math and science.

Fifth period was cafeteria time, so I had a chance to make some new acquaintances. I dragged my tray on the metal, waist-high ledge through the food serving line, and wound-up at the cashier with portions of meat loaf, mashed potatoes, and green peas. I saw an odd-looking kid sitting alone at a nearby table, eating a peanut butter and jelly sandwich in his left hand, and alternating bites of that with a *Three Musketeers* candy bar in his right. I paid the cashier, received my change from the Brunhilda, and then sat-down across from the strange-looking guy, and quickly started-up a conversation.

"All I need is some quiet on my tray, because I already have some peas," I laughed while again impersonating Bo Jalonec's inimitable wit. "Then, I could have *peas* and quiet!"

"Have you been a jerk-off all your life, or is it just startin' to happen right now!" the weird-looking dude loudly exclaimed so that kids three tables away could easily hear his nasty tirade. "What's the matter, Asshole? Do ya' need your goddamned diaper changed, or something?"

"Don't pay any attention to Goose," another fellow holding his tray advised. "He's always miserable and hates the world and everyone in it! Can I sit-down here?"

"Sure," I said as Goose completely ignored the new arrival. "Make yourself comfortable."

"I'm Tommy Tomasello, but my friends call me News because I know all about what's happenin' in the world. And this wise guy here is Ronald Restuccio, better known as Goose."

"Hi," I greeted the apparent discipline problem after being introduced. "Glad to make your acquaintance."

Goose looked at me with a mild grin and critically said, "Ya' look like a friggin' ankle biter to me! Bit any fuckin' ankles lately?"

"Ankle biter?" I mildly challenged. "What's that weird lingo supposed to mean?"

"Yeah, a little fuckin' kid," Goose clarified. "You're probably still wet behind the ears and dry inside your dick, too."

"Whatcha' reading?" I asked News Tomasello, trying to change the subject to avoid conflict in my new school.

"*Catcher in the Rye* by J.D. Salinger," Tommy promptly and politely answered. "I keep the book insulated in this brown book cover I made from a paper bag, so that the teachers think I'm readin' a small textbook on geometric theorems, or a scholarly collection of Shakespearean sonnets. Pretty slick, huh?"

"*Catcher in the Rye?*" I chuckled. "Is it a biography about Yogi Berra in a whiskey factory vat?" I gasped, alluding to the star *New York Yankee* catcher.

"If ya' make one more stupid-ass comment like that, I'm gonna' kick your butt good in front of all these pecker-headed kids!"

threatened Goose Restuccio, as the malcontent gestured his arm around the cafeteria table. "You and Tom-Tom here sound like Minnie Mouse and Tinker Bell havin' the dumbest of dumb fucked-up, faggot conversations."

"I really thought your joke was pretty good!" Tommy "News" Tomasello remarked while completely ignoring Goose's exaggerated protest. "The book's really pretty neat. It's about a guy named Holden Caulfield who is innocent, immature, and naïve. Young Holden Caulfield thinks that the world is messed-up, but the kid finds that the people in the world are basically evil, selfish, conniving, and sinful. They all *think* ..."

"That Holden Caulfield is fucked-up!" Goose interrupted. "I read that friggin' book when I was in fifth-grade. It's a real fuckin' doozy! Have *you* read any good fuckin' books lately?" Ronald "Goose" Restuccio haughtily asked me.

"Well, yes. Where I used to live, in Levittown, I had read D.H. Lawrence's *Lady Chatterley's Lover*. It was super cool and dirty!" I proudly exclaimed.

"J.W., that's exactly what I mean," News Tomasello excitedly articulated. "Miss Hunter, Mrs. Waldman, and the other English teachers just want us to read benign goody-goody stuff like *Silas Marner* and *Precious Bane*. They're afraid of a little controversy."

"How did you know my name?" I asked News.

"You don't remember, but I was in Mrs. Murphy's third period history class when ya' stood-up and bravely answered Vicksburg!" Tommy reminded me.

"Well, News, that history class is *ancient history* now. What's happenin' in the world?" I jovially inquired.

"Well, J.W., John H. Reynolds of the *University of California* estimates that the universe is nearly five billion years old," Tommy Tomasello stated. "His calculation is based on a meteorite found forty-one years ago in Richardton, North Dakota."

"Did he use a North *Decoder* to find it?" I asked, again paying tribute to my old Levittown friend, Bo Jalonec.

"Yes, J.W.," News nonchalantly concurred. "If Professor John H. Richardson hadn't used his North Decoder, it would've been a meteor*wrong* instead of a meteorright."

"You two guys are so fucked-up that ya' deserve each other! You two fuck-heads oughta' get married!" Goose complained as he got up and hastily moved his tray to an adjacent empty cafeteria table.

"What's with him?" I asked News. "He seems a little anti-social."

"Goose is a spoiled, temperamental, Sicilian brat," Tom-Tom said. "He's arrogant, distrustful, and has no real friends. G.R. thinks he could buy anyone with his Mafia daddy's loan-sharkin' money."

"Sounds like a kid I knew back in Pennsylvania, Bruno Popeye Messina," I related. "The two have similar traits."

News elaborated that Ronald Goose Restuccio was a bully who was resented by nearly everyone in the school. He had a brand-new white four-seater '60 Thunderbird; made fun of everyone else; had a nasty temper, and was very vindictive. Immediately, I also connected Goose's personality characteristics to those belonging to Tinker, a malicious repugnant kid back in Levittown.

Two other guys sat-down and joined our company. "J.W," News said, "I'd like ya' to meet Frankie Arena and Johnny Illiani."

"Lots of Italians in this school," I commented. "Glad to meet you guys." We shook hands, and Frankie told me his nickname was Jives, and Johnny informed me that he was often called Juice.

"Why Jives and Juice?" I inquired.

"Because Jives uses a lot of cool slang when he talks," News explained, "and Juice has all the girls wantin' his sperm."

Johnny Juice Illiani blushed upon hearing News's evaluation of *his* hypothetical, sexual prowess. Johnny had lived with the unusual nickname only because others insisted that he'd be a local male legend with the Edgewood High' girls that went goo-goo over his handsome looks.

"Juice, stop actin' like Squaresville," Jives Arena criticized. "All the chicks are eyeballin' ya' right now. They'd all like to rock and roll in the crib with ya', even the babes that are in *cherry* condition."

"Frankie means virgins," News clarified. "Did you guys know that the term rock and roll is really black slang for havin' sex in bed?"

"Yeah," I agreed. "It was invented by a Cleveland disc jockey named Alan Freed. He's broadcastin' out of New York now."

"I know," News affirmed. "Alan Freed used the term to give rock music a non-black image, so that white parents would think it was okay. The real funny irony is that rock and roll really means black sex, and white parents don't want their lily-white children to have sex at all."

I rubbernecked my head around the cafeteria and realized that a table of really cute girls was to my right. The dolls were all entranced by Johnny Juice Illiani's eminent presence at my table.

"Who's the dark-skinned girl over there sittin' at the end?" I asked Frankie. "She's got looks!"

"That's Joanne Berenato," Jives Arena informed. "She's a slick chick with a classy chassis. You ain't the first cat that's gone ape over her! I can comprende why you're hot to trot over that radioactive broad. No guy's got dibs on that bitchin' chick. She's Venus's twin sister, ya' dig?"

I soon found-out that Frankie Jives Arena and Johnny Juice Illiani were close friends and aspiring actors. The pair had been discussing the school's upcoming play competition in March between the sophomore, junior, and senior classes. The seniors were going to have tryouts for a one-act play, *There's Gold in Them Thar Hills*."

"J.W., ya' wanta' try out for the play?" Jives Arena invited. "It's gonna' be a trip and a half!"

"Yeah," Johnny Juice Illiani concurred. "Ya' have the makings of a good *thespian*."

"I think J.W. prefers being a normal male fightin' simple acne than becomin' a homosexual female wearin' retarded leotards," News laughed. "Juice, you say the queerest things. Bein' a female homo' is worse than bein' a damned neuter."

"Well, J.W., think it over," Johnny suggested. "The girls here at Edgewood that aren't *lesbians* love guys that aren't afraid to get up on stage and do their thing."

"And J.W. There's gonna' be some real cookin' babes tryin' out for the play who are hot to trot to share Cloud 9 with ya'!" Jives tempted and indicated.

I soon learned that Tommy "News" Tomasello's father was a peach farmer, Frankie Jives Arena's dad had a general store in Winslow, and Johnny Juice Illiani had excellent communications skills because his parents were teachers at Overbrook Regional, another area high school. Sal Fabian Midilli, another good-looking stud, soon joined our company at our table. The newcomer had terrific mechanical skills because, according to omniscient News, "his pop owns a popular gas/repair station in Waterford on the White Horse Pike, The Flyin' A."

The guys then gave me a little history of the Edgewood Regional High class of '60. Up until their junior year, the kids had all gone to Overbrook Regional in Lindenwold. Then, Edgewood was finally constructed, and the students from Atco, Winslow Township, and West Berlin attended Overbrook's recently constructed sister school, Edgewood High.

"So, J.W.," Jives said, "you're about as new here as the rest of us bucks and does are. My advice is just stay away from Ronald Goose Restuccio, or you'll be cruisin' for a bruisin' from most all the dudes in this here wacko, country' think hole."

I turned-around and glanced at Joanne Berenato, while News was lecturing about sixteen-year-old-boy-wonder Bobbie Fischer, who had recently successfully defended his U.S. Chess Championship in New York City.

"He was probably *jumping* for joy because he got something off of his *chess,"* I joked, as my distracted mind wandered in and out of the general conversation.

"J.W., speakin' of chess, I think ya' got your sights on *jumping* Joanne Berenato," Johnny Illiani perceptively observed and claimed as Juice saw me craning my neck toward another table.

"J.W., come on over to another *mesa* before ya' make your feelings too obvious," Juice requested. "I want ya' to meet some of the Reds."

"The Reds? Are they from Cincinnati?" I awkwardly asked, as Juice, Johnny, Frankie, and I carried our lunch trays to the cafeteria's washing and cleaning waste' window.

"No, but I'll give ya' the lowdown later on," Johnny told me. "I guarantee ya', the Reds like peaches, but they aren't *fruits,* if ya' know what I mean."

Juice brought me to a table where mostly brawny athletes were exchanging jock anecdotes about the *New Years Day* college football bowl games. I was introduced to Chickie and Charlie Calabrese, twin brothers who were district wrestling champions grappling in the 160 and 165 pounds' weight classes. Senior Jack "Hoss" Gregorio was seated next to his smaller brother, "Little Joe," an Edgewood' junior. The Gregorio brothers were tough offensive guards on the winning Edgewood High football squad.

"I guess Hoss is short for Horse," I respectfully commented.

"Ya' got that right," Johnny Illiani commended. "These two guys could be professional wrestlers and beat the stuffings out of Gorgeous George and the Butcher, if they wanted to!"

I looked at "Little Joe Gregorio", who I estimated to be around five-foot-eight and weighing about two-hundred-and twenty-pounds.

"Are ya' called Little Joe and Hoss after the Cartwright brothers on *Bonanza?"* I curiously asked.

"Yeah, that's right," Little Joe snarled. "And my older brother Hoss here is six-three and weighs in at three-fifty. I ain't never gonna' catch up to him!"

Everybody at the cafeteria table laughed and pounded the slate in front of them. That loud noise got the attention of several observant teachers on duty. The keepers of the cafeteria peace then signaled the raucous athletes to stop the ruckus by making several football referee time-out gestures.

"Hey, J.W.," Hoss bellowed. "Do ya' know who won the *Sugar Bowl* over the holidays? I missed that game on TV."

Luckily, News Tomasello had joined our company and was standing directly behind me. T.T. was ready to provide the exact answer should I falter.

"Mississippi won," I replied. "I think the score was 21-…"

"Twenty-one to zip over Louisiana State," News interrupted. "And Syracuse beat Texas in the *Cotton Bowl* 23-14; Georgia put it to Missouri in the *Orange Bowl,* 14-0, and Washington trounced Wisconsin, 44-8 in the *Rose Bowl.*"

"How do ya' remember all that stuff? I'm deeply impressed!" Hoss Gregorio stated to News Tomasello, as the teen behemoth feigned sincerity while showing a degree of admiration.

"Tommy has got a movie camera inside his' head that allows him to have a photographic mind," Juice humorously explained.

At the time, I couldn't remember the names of all the other jocks at the table, but I later would personally know them as full-fledged "Reds". Jim "Guy" Marinella was a strong-but-average-looking linebacker with a big nose, and then there was Tony Passarella, whose family owned a small peach farm next to the Silver Fox Tavern across the street from Pete's Farm Market, my parents' new business. Two other "Reds," Marty Ransom and Pete Clarke, rounded-out the remaining jocks seated at the crowded table.

Everyone laughed in response to Johnny Illiani's clever comment about the cerebral camera. I then wanted to discover why the guys at the jock table, and also News Tomasello, were called "Reds", and I was about to ask that question. Without warning, a sudden very discernible disturbance erupted at a neighboring table. I had heard a comment about a fruit war going on between Reds and Blues over in Hammonton, right before the disruption flared-up.

A black student had sat-down across from Goose Restuccio, who then apparently, had verbally insulted the colored kid. The Negro boy stood up and called Goose a "KKK racist," and then

Ronald Restuccio angrily flipped-over the cafeteria table, and the food from the black kid's tray splattered all over the tile floor.

"Shut the fuck up, ya' friggin' mool-en-yon!" Restuccio cursed. "One nigger at my table is one nigger too many!"

"I ain't afraid of you dago, even if your Daddy is in the Mafia!" the black kid yelled.

Three alarmed teachers scurried-over to quell the heightening altercation. "Now boys', just simmer-down. We'll all go down to the main office right this minute and straighten this whole thing out," the first instructor on cafeteria duty ordered.

"Right now, it's three detentions each," the second male teacher related. "Any more words from either of you two, and it'll be certain suspensions for at least a week!" the cafeteria patrolman barked at the two livid cafeteria gladiators, who still wanted to maliciously maul and cripple each other.

"Illiani, Arena, Tomasello, clean-up this mess on the floor while I escort these two offenders to the principal's office!" Math' teacher Mr. Andrews, the third teacher on the scene, commanded.

Mr. Andrews followed Goose Restuccio and the black kid out of the cafeteria. I bent-down and helped News Tomasello turn the cafeteria table right-side-up. "What's a mool-en-yon?" I asked.

"It's Italian slang for eggplant!" Tommy disgustedly explained.

News Tomasello, Goose Restuccio, along with Hoss and Little Joe Gregorio would again enter my life at *Glassboro State College.* After the Edgewood graduation, News tried attending *Rutgers University,* but became homesick at the big New Brunswick campus and went back to his family's peach farm in Elm. But then, News became my roommate at 38 South Main Street, and Goose and the Gregorio boys played vital cameo roles in conflicts that eventually arose between the Lambda Phi Sigma's and the dastardly Alpha Delta Omegas, along with the equally pugnacious Tau Kappa Epsilons. And oh, yes, coincidentally, Joanne Berenato also attended *Glassboro State College.*

Chapter 3
"A Year in Transition"

Every so often, an impact person (other than a parent) enters your life. You don't know when or where that person might appear to give guidance, until he or she shows-up and exercises influence. But that very special individual possesses dynamic qualities that have a lasting impact upon *your* perception of the world. The Godsend person will inspire the receptive beneficiary, and his or her example will dramatically affect the remainder of the lucky recipient's successful tenure upon this extraordinary planet.

In the summer of 1960, I was privileged to come into contact with a retired Hammonton High School mathematics teacher, Mr. Charles B. Sipley, who had a profound positive lasting impression upon my attitude towards the demanding world. Mr. Sipley taught me the most valuable lesson of my young life. The gentleman taught me how to overcome failure and self-imposed emotional adversity, and concurrently, the master mathematics expert injected a healthy dose of resilience and confidence into my character.

In 1959, my family had moved back to New Jersey from Levittown, Pennsylvania. My folks had an opportunity to purchase a home and a farm market, and finally, own a viable business. I had to transfer from Cardinal Reagan in Pennsylvania to Edgewood Regional High School in Tansboro/Atco, New Jersey.

Coming from a Catholic school tradition, my education had excellent background in English and also in social studies. I was very adept at grammar, spelling, vocabulary, punctuation, literature, and writing. Language arts, history, and world geography also came exceptionally easy to my learning habits.

Conversely, after I had transferred into Edgewood High, I soon discovered that I was extremely weak (compared to other students in the college' prep curriculum) in both science and in advanced math'. Each day at Edgewood seemed very paradoxical to me. I would breeze through English, history, and world cultures' classes, and then dismally suffer failure, being extremely lost through trigonometry and physics.

My mind and heart were in turbulent quandaries, and my spirit shifted several times daily from the positive end of the achievement spectrum to the negative terminal. In late May of 1960, I found-out from my guidance counselor that I had failed Trigonometry. I was not allowed to graduate on stage with my class, and that punishment greatly disturbed my psyche. I felt I had never had adequate preparation in my parochial school background in Algebra, and that I could not fairly compete with the other public-school students on a level mathematics playing field in Trigonometry.

In 1960, at Edgewood High, if a student failed one major subject, that person had to attend summer school for remedial instruction. I was extremely demoralized and confused. In my heart, I honestly believed that I was destined to be an incompetent failure for the remainder of my life and that my future had been adroitly sabotaged by Mr. Andrews, my ultra-strict Edgewood Trig' teacher. My English and social studies teachers were always touting me as one of the top students in the high school, and my very austere Science and Trig' teachers evaluated my lackluster performance as being greatly inferior, and my rank being identified as existing far below mediocre student performance.

Since I was not permitted to graduate with my classmates, I had a serious choice to make to finally obtain my Edgewood High School diploma. I could either attend summer school at Haddonfield High (twenty-miles away from my home), or I could seek-out the services of a qualified tutor. I had heard about Mr. Charles B. Sipley from a friend of News Tomasello, so I decided to give the retired teacher a call, explained my dire situation, and I was thrilled to learn that the man would accept me as his summertime student.

When I first met Mr. Sipley face to face at his home, I was deeply impressed with his congenial but no-nonsense approach. The retired teacher was not a huge man, but he possessed a strong constitution that seemed to transcend physical prowess. My soon-to-be mentor possessed a powerful inner strength that was shrouded in a rather hard, outer-mantle of Old World' values, which somehow directly and immediately communicated with my inner core being. Mr. Sipley could motivate, inspire, and influence me. Charles B. Sipley was confident that I could succeed in Trigonometry and my mentor would not accept "No, I can't do this"! as an excuse. He soon masterfully transmitted *that* extremely elusive confidence factor, along with special inspirational certainty to me.

At first, I was reluctant to open-up my soul to my Trig' guardian, trying to conceal and shield my shame and disgrace at failing high school from his scrutiny. After the first several tutorial sessions, under his calm strong demeanor, I began to finally decipher the enigmas and codes that had previously made Trigonometry a total mystery to my confused cerebrum.

With Mr. Sipley's encouragement and expertise, I soon became proficient in the fundamentals of sine, cosine, tangent, cotangent, secant, and cosecant. I soon understood the definite relationships between complicated mathematical formulas and the six vital trigonometric functions. Learning became easy, and soon it became fun. I was both happy and astonished at the definite, measurable progress I was making.

In four short weeks, I knew Trigonometry as well as the average student of that subject, and after the eight-week tutorial was over, I had a terrific command of the advanced mathematics, thanks to my sympathetic, patient-but-tough math' guru. Mr. Sipley expected me to succeed and to master Trig', and I had no alternative other than to fulfill his lofty expectation. His daily demands allowed me no wiggle room from his strict regimentation.

In early September, I made a return visit back to Edgewood Regional High School with a "Letter of Recommendation" signed by Mr. Charles B. Sipley. The neatly handwritten missive stated that I had mastered the fundamentals and the mechanics of Trigonometry and that I should "receive a minimum adjusted grade of B for the course". I proudly took the note to the main office, and a secretary showed it to Mr. Pinkerton, the no-nonsense Edgewood principal, who then shuttled me upstairs to Mr. Andrews's familiar M-Wing advanced math' classroom.

I handed the stern pedagogue Mr. Sipley's complimentary letter, and after reading its benign content, Mr. Andrews became quite skeptical and said that the note could have been a clever counterfeit and that I still had to pass his awesome final exam' "to officially graduate". The mean-spirited fellow chuckled as he directed me to park my body in the last desk near the side windows, the same seat I had occupied as a failing student up to June 15th of 1960. Then, Mr. Andrews handed me his toughest final examination as the twenty intimidated Trigonometry students under *his* dominion in the new senior advanced class chuckled and snickered at the Promethean task I was undertaking.

It took me a mere twenty-minutes to solve all of the formerly complicated mathematical riddles, and after spending an additional five-minutes checking over the more difficult and "tricky" test items, I marched-up to the teacher's desk and handed the inflexible pedagogue my exam' papers. Mr. Andrews appeared momentarily shocked by my arrogance and by the new cocky confidence that my body language was demonstrating.

The now-stunned Trig' teacher intensively scrutinized my paper, closely eyeballing every single answer with his mouth agape. Instinctively, I knew that I had gotten every problem correct, but the obstinate, disbelieving, advanced math instructor did not put any grade on my test paper. Instead, the grim-faced tyrant scribbled his name upon Mr. Sipley's letter and addressed his comment to Mr. Pinkerton, "Give this former student a final grade of C on his report card."

Andrews handed me his notation jotted on Mr. Sipley's courteous letter, which I then carefully read with an element of resentment. I looked the instructor straight in the eyes, and somehow, his former formidable dominance no longer intimidated me. I felt that I had grown into a man at that precise moment. I felt like viciously punching the uncompromising martinet in the face, but I restrained myself from committing violence and thought, 'I'm gonna' attend *Glassboro State College* and become a teacher. Then, I'll be able to help kids learn instead of trying to destroy their egos like some teacher I know!'

I accepted the altered letter from Andrews, promptly brought it downstairs to the main office, and soon a polite main office secretary inserted a "C" for Trigonometry on my report card, and then expertly typed that grade onto my Edgewood High transcript.

I shook hands with Mr. Pinkerton, who like Mr. Andrews seemed diminished in stature and in potency now that I had also escaped *his* supreme jurisdiction. I departed the high school with that chapter of my adolescence finally being closed behind me. My mind imagined a happy future at *Glassboro State Teachers College,* devoid of annoying obstacles like Mr. Andrews and Mr. Pinkerton.

In retrospect, failure was a good experience for me. It provided me with adequate determination to prove to Mr. Andrews that I could overcome the rigors associated with his most challenging subject. I believe that today's educators (including myself) are wrong when they pass undeserving students along and keep them rising on the academic escalator, while simultaneously attempting to insulate lazy kids from the reality of failure. Thanks to Mr. Charles B. Sipley, I had gained the skills I needed to effectively show Mr. Andrews that I was tougher than *his* toughest Trigonometry test items.

Mr. Sipley was definitely an impact person' who had entered my life at a most opportune time and had kindly rescued me from despair. It was because of my mentor's extraordinary example that I had vowed to become a public-school teacher and help others as he had so wonderfully assisted me. Mr. Charles B. Sipley extended to me hope, once I was able to have faith in my own ability. He had salvaged my spirit at a time when I seriously doubted my own potential and my own self-worth.

I decided to wait "a full year of maturing" before matriculating into *Glassboro State Teachers College*. During the twelve-month-interim, my father had gotten me a job as a welder's apprentice at his winter place of employment, Martin and Quade Stainless Steel Fabricating Company in Norristown, Pennsylvania. Soon, I quickly realized that I needed a good education to learn a profession, because I had no desire to breathe in nasty pungent factory welding fumes for the rest of my working life. And besides, I did not savor the long hour and fifteen-minute commute from Elm, New Jersey to Norristown every workday. Frankly, I vastly disliked laboring in a city metals' shop.

My assigned job at Martin and Quade was to operate a large seam-welding machine. Bulky stainless-steel sheets twenty-foot-long were mounted and then clamped upon my machine. The fabricating machine next folded each sheet into a circular tube, ten-inches in diameter. After polishing-off the first batch of fifty stainless steel pipes, the plant inspector came to my workstation to inspect the craftsmanship. He found many defects in the quality of the seams I had seam-welded, and my first instinct was that I had not followed directions and that I would embarrass my father and be dismissed from real-life employment. Instead, of rebuking my ineptness, the foremen told me that I had to more carefully seam-weld the tubes a second time, which I obediently did. I was thrilled when my second production easily passed the scrutiny of quality control.

In the past, American free enterprise has always emphasized quality control. When I was operating that seam-welding machine at Martin and Quade, the shop stewards didn't care how that activity was satisfying my emotional and psychological needs. One evening in December of 1960, News called me at home from his dorm' room up at *Rutgers.*

"J. W., how's welding commin' along?" Tommy began.

"Could be better," I acknowledged. "I want you to know I'm applying to attend *Glassboro State* next September. I need a profession because my father told me that right now, I have a job, and the definition of j-o-b is *j*ust *o*ver *b*roke."

"Good one!" Tommy commended. "I think I'll join ya' over at *Glassboro State*. I'm droppin' out of *Rutgers* and miss home, and also the Hammonton area guys pretty much. Maybe I'll buddy-up and room with you the next fall semester. And I hear Joanne Berenato's also goin' to *GSC* next year, too."

"That's really great news, News, about you thinkin' about goin' and Joanne also enrolling," I excitedly answered. "But my first year,

Pop says I gotta' live home and help-out around Pete's Market. We can room together durin' our sophomore year."

"It's a deal!" Tommy Tomasello instinctively replied like a TV game show host. "I feel better already!"

"Hey, Tommy," I inquired. "What is happening in the world besides John F. Kennedy beatin' Richard R. Nixon for President in the close November election?"

"Well, J. W., *Chrysler Corporation* is goin' to discontinue makin' De Soto cars," News glibly reported. "They've been manufacturin' the damned things since 1928."

"The Edsel's been scrapped, too," I lamented. "Who do you like in the *NFL Championship Game?"* Ya' gotta' go with the *Eagles* with them havin' Norm Van Brocklin and Tommy McDonald teamin' up on touchdown passes."

"I predict it's goin' to be a close contest," Tommy evasively stated. "But in the final analysis, it's gonna' be the *Eagles* over Green Bay, I'll say 17-13. But the *Packers* are gonna' be tough, no doubt about it."

"Hey, where did you get that 'in the final analysis business'?" I challenged. "I think I've heard that unique phrase somewhere else."

"President-elect Kennedy says it all the time," News confessed, "so I just incorporated it into my speakin' vocabulary."

"Sorry I asked," I hardily laughed. "Go *Eagles*. I'll see ya' over *Christmas* holidays." Click.

Mr. Andrews had actually performed a valuable favor by failing me in Trigonometry, and Mr. Charles B. Sipley did me a much bigger favor by becoming my admired mentor. The Martin and Quade shop foreman helped my development by telling me that my job performance was unsatisfactory, and then giving me a second chance to succeed. Those three men had assisted me emotionally grow and mature by being fully truthful about my inadequate performance, and by making genuine demands, and not providing false praise, the three influencers had significantly contributed to me becoming a stronger and wiser person.

On December 26, 1960, the determined *Eagles* had won the *NFL Championship Game* over the Packers at Philadelphia's *Franklin Field,* just as News had amazingly predicted, 17-13. I still remember Iron Man Chuck Bednarik tackling and then sitting on Green Bay's Jim Taylor, so that the *Packers* couldn't run another play as they were driving to within field goal/touchdown range at the end of the fourth quarter.

And then, when warm weather finally rolled-around the following spring, I remember listening to the 1961 hit songs on my 45 rpm record player, "Barbara Ann" by the Regents; "Travelin' Man" by Ricky Nelson; "Blue Moon" by the Marcels; "Runaway" by Del Shannon, and "Let's Twist Again" by Chubby Checker. The 1961 summer at Pete's Market was rather rigorous while working fifteen-hours-a-day, seven days a week non-stop. News and I had managed to break-away from our family work responsibilities for several vacation days to walk the Atlantic City, Ocean City, and Wildwood boardwalks, discussing the upcoming fall semester at *GSC.*

"What was college life like at *Rutgers?"* I asked while News and I were waiting to see the High Diving Horse and its rider plummet into its water tank at Atlantic City's famous *Steel Pier.*

"Lots of freedom, lots of term paper work and studying, and plenty of new people, girls galore, and parties to distract you from the real reason you're on campus," my pal verbally evaluated.

"I'm sure glad Goose Restuccio isn't goin' to *Glassboro State* with us," I added to the conversation. "He's all tied-up with his thrivin' gumball machine businesses and his new money launderin' operations. And besides, G.R. thinks college is for losers."

"I spoke with Goose the other day at Mr. Bill's Custard Stand over in Winslow Township," News reported. "He says he's goin' to show up at *Glassboro* once or twice just to break our stones, and after he does that, Restuccio promised me he'd grind our broken nuggets into the size of Swedish meat balls, and then feed the pulverized round tissues to hungry birds and stray cats.

Chapter 4
"Miss Sankins"

News Tomasello had known several Hammonton guys that were going to commute to *Glassboro State College* in September. In late August, Tommy introduced me to Tim Amoro, Ron Carputis and Mario DiMaris, other incoming freshmen that had been accepted to attend the teachers' preparatory school of higher learning. The five of us had agreed to commute and drive one day a week apiece from Hammonton to Glassboro in order to save on gas money and car maintenance expenses.

Tuesday, September 5th, the day after *Labor Day,* Tim Amoro picked me up at 7:15 in front of Pete's Market for the first exciting day of college. News Tomasello and Ron Carputis were in the front bench seat so that meant I had to share the back seat with Mario DiMaris, a behemoth of a man, standing five-foot-eight, but weighing three hundred-and thirty-five-pounds. I respected Mario's reputation because he was a fierce defensive guard for the awesome *Hammonton Bakers* semi-pro football team, one of the toughest maverick squads on the entire East Coast.

"Hi guys, hi Mario," I courteously began. "All ready for our first day of higher education at *Glassboro State?"* I've been thinkin' about this moment for a whole week already, and had trouble fallin' asleep last night."

"Usually, people can't sleep at night because they're constipated and have trouble shittin'," Mario laughed. "Or else, they got diarrhea and have to worry about where they're aimin' their asshole. Not like you, J.W. Ya' got constipation of the brain and diarrhea of the mouth, both conditions at the same time."

I dared not insult Mario back because the hulk was a tremendous brute, who could easily decapitate me with one ferocious swat of his immense, fat fist. Instead, I figured I would praise him before irritating him.

"I went to the *Bakers* game against the *Franklin Miners* last fall," I replied, "and Mario, I saw you make mince-meat out of that big Number 72."

"Yeah," Mario smiled with a shrug. "He was some hot shot out of *Notre Dame* who almost made the *Pittsburgh Steelers*. I got-down in my stance and snorted like a wild boar the entire fuckin' game. By the fourth quarter, the rookie punk asked his coach to take him out because I was givin' him the physical beatin' of his life, and his fuckin' pride couldn't handle it."

Everyone in the car remained mum out of both fear and respect, while Mario delivered his dissertation of exaggerated braggadocio. I figured I would break the monotonous silence that followed with a daring barb directed at the monster sitting alongside of me. I knew Mario would not hurt me, since the monster enjoyed my company, and also strangely relished my zany sense of humor. "One of these days, Mario, I'm goin' to stab you with a pin just to satisfy my curiosity, and see whether you'll deflate or not."

Mario pretended that he took umbrage with my penetrating remark. Just as Tim Amoro passed by Mr. Bill's Custard at the intersection of Winslow-Williamstown Road and *Route 73,* Mario suddenly lunged in my direction. Immediately, I avoided his feigned hostility and rolled my body into the station wagon's rear compartment. Mario somehow managed to turn his obese body over the station wagon's back seat, and duplicated my maneuver.

Tim had observed the entire sequence of events occurring in his rear-view mirror, so the driver carelessly swiveled the station wagon's steering wheel back and forth so that DiMaris and I were banging-around against the vehicle's sides and each other during the wild and woolly, madcap episode. Mario cursed and squawked the entire time, rolling and caroming like a helpless barrel of lead, with his body slamming and smashing all over the place, nearly crushing my more diminutive frame during three particular oscillations.

"You're both like ball bearings trapped in a *bell buoy* during a violent storm!" Tim shouted and laughed as my pal continued rotating the wheel left and right, while watching us collide around in his rear-view mirror. "You both remind me of two faggot hotel employees: *bell boys.* Ha, ha, ha, ha!"

"Watch out for that guardrail at the wooden bridge!" Ron Carputis cautioned while simultaneously laughing his butt off.

"Hey, Tim, cool it man!" News exclaimed. "We almost just shook hands with a pine forest and three telephone poles, and now there's a dump truck headin' our way up about a half-mile ahead."

Tim ceased his spirited wild driving activity in time for the speeding dump truck to safely pass in the opposite direction. Mario was satisfied merely chastising me after we both had awkwardly plopped-over back into the light blue station wagon's rear seat, after clumsily rolling-around within a very limited space.

"You call me fat one more time and I'll maul the livin' shit outa' ya'!" Mario very believably promised. "Next time, J.W., I'll just pretend you're that *Number 72* jerk-off outa' *Notre Dame,* and we'll play football without any fuckin' referee whistles to stop the goddamned action."

"I had only *alluded* to you being portly," I corrected. "I never called you fat!"

"Well, just don't *elude* me again," Mario insisted as the non-scholar inadvertently formulated a dumb pun that astoundingly was somewhat relevant to what had just transpired.

"Okay, I'll never call you fat again," I pledged. "I might refer to you as being corpulent, stocky, prodigious, chunky, or obese, but never as fat."

"That's better!" Mario answered as the three guys in the front proceeded to virtually cough their testicles out of their mouths from an excess of levity.

Although I liked Mario as a friend, I had trouble with his motivation for wanting to become a teacher. The brute possessed a rather lackadaisical attitude when it came to anything besides football, and DiMaris perceived the teaching profession as being an easy way of making a living after his defensive lineman days with the *Hammonton Bakers* would finally expire. But despite my low opinion of Mario's academic alacrity, I still wanted to chum-around with him, and then also be seen with him in public all over the campus, because of the awesome reputation for being a monster that preceded the local football legend everywhere he went.

"Hey, Tim, could ya' step on the gas a little more!" I suggested. "We've both got eight o'clock classes in *College Hall* and we're gonna' be late. You know how it is. Ya' always want to have the professor avoid a bad initial impression of you on the first day of class. Some profs' are known to hold grudges just like Mr. Andrews had done against me in Trigonometry class at Edgewood."

"It's a good thing that creep Andrews was only a math teacher and not the President of the United States," News jested, "or the nutcase would've flunked your ass right out of the damned country. Deported to Outer Mongolia to learn how to use an abacus, or a pubic hair bead counter, or something like that."

After going through downtown Williamstown, Tim entered *Route 322,* which would take us past the landmark Republican Club Hall to Glassboro. "Only five more miles J.W., and you'll get to meet your first professor," Timmy assured me.

"Great!" I exclaimed as I fumbled in my pants pockets for the weekly schedule I thought I had brought. "Oh crap! I can't find my schedule. I must've left it on the desk in my room in all the rush this morning."

"You probably also left a pile of shit in your toilet and forgot to flush and vomit," Mario joked. "Why worry? It's only a stupid class, man. Why are ya' so uptight about nothin' important or urgent. Cool it little daddy, and learn to relax."

"I prefer callin' it bein' conscientious and prepared," I automatically answered. "But sometimes, I'm my own worst enemy because I wind up doin' exactly what I feared doin' in the first place, if ya' know what I mean."

"J. W.," Tim stated in a very calm and reassuring voice. "Your classes are almost the same as mine. I noticed that when you had shown me your schedule last week. You got *English, Fundamentals of Communication 101,* first period, right?"

"Yes," I remembered and responded with a sigh of relief. "That's what I have on Tuesdays and Thursdays."

"Well then, you probably have *English 101* with me," Amoro persuasively maintained. "Just tag along and forget your needless damned worryin'!"

A mile outside Glassboro on *Route 322* was a commercial establishment called Glassboro Bedding. Ron Carputis yelled to Tim Amoro, "Hey, stop the damned car! We gotta' get-out and salute the idea of the bed, and all that it has contributed in terms of versatile usage, especially pertainin' to sex and jerkin-off!"

"Yeah!" Mario the group's enforcer yelled from the back seat. "Stop the damned station wagon right now, before I fart and propel the fuckin' back doors off!"

Much to my dissatisfaction and disenchantment, Tim slammed on the brakes, so that the Ford station wagon stopped in front of Glassboro Bedding. Carputis, Tomasello, and DiMaris led the charge out of the vehicle, while Tim and I reluctantly followed their goofy lead. Ron Carputis had memorized an invocation the numb-nuts had loosely organized, to sprinkle a degree of dignity to the phony, in progress, satirical liturgy. The other two clowns stood as still as statues, faking solemnity, as the farce advanced to its next phase. Then, Ron "the Chicken Hawk" Carputis pompously articulated "Ode to the Bunk", which to Tim Amoro and me sounded like plenty of bunk right from the outset. Soon, the rest of the contingent had the dis-privilege' of hearing some extraordinary and rather bizarre linguistic mumbo-jumbo.

"Glassboro Bedding, we salute your excellence in appreciation of your infinite contributions to relaxation, recreation, overpopulation, and sex education," Carputis remarkably recited from rote memory. And then, all five of us had to seriously give a military-type salute to the bedding business for a full thirty-seconds, while disgruntled *322* motorists slowed-down and gawked, cursed, scowled, and some even gave us the most supreme of pissed-off compliments, the royal middle finger. But to especially Carputis and to News, the mockery represented the imagination of immortal and invincible youth as opposed to the sterility and banality of middle-aged, middle-class, blue-collar Americans.

After the five of us hopped-back inside the powder blue Ford station wagon, Tim had some appropriate criticism to direct towards Ron Carputis and his two principal accomplices. "You, Mario, and News, don't have first-period classes on Tuesday," Tim sternly objected. "But J.W. and I do. Now he and I are gonna' be mighty lucky if we make it to *College Hall* on time and make our good impressions."

Tim parked his father's car in the commuter parking lot in the center of the campus, and he and I scurried off to *English 101* while Mario, Ron, and News chuckled at our anxiety and impetuosity. Amoro and I dashed-up the white marble steps to the building's second-floor, where the English and Speech Departments had their offices, and where the professors representing those curriculum units conducted their classes.

After seating ourselves in the crowded classroom, the professor in Room 212 took roll from his master list. I felt rather uneasy when I recognized that my name had not been called. I nervously raised my hand after the distinguished, mustached professor had asked, "Is everyone present and accounted for?"

"Are you Professor Sankins?" I worriedly inquired. "My name was not called!"

The class (with the exception of Tim Amoro) then broke-out in raucous hysteria. The abashed male professor's thick eyebrows slanted-down at almost forty-five-degree angles, expressing his general displeasure with my unorthodox inquiry. "My good fellow," the chagrined literary scholar began his admonishment. "I certainly am not Professor Sankins. I am Professor Stevens. I happen to be a man, that is, the last time I checked. Professor Sankins happens to be a member of the opposite gender. Since you are not supposed to be in this room," Professor Stevens rankled, "I strongly suggest that it would be in everybody's best interest if you proceed immediately to Room 217 and deliver yourself to the appropriate mentor!"

Boisterous laughter could be discerned as Professor Stevens terminated his deriding dissertation. I recall thinking at the time that I wished some faster mode of transportation would be available other than that provided by my two lower appendages. I rushed-out of Room 212 red-faced, slightly humiliated, and almost sweating bullets. "I'm sorry!" I clumsily apologized. "I had lost my schedule, well, I mean I misplaced my schedule this morning, and I only knew the name of the course and the Professor's name, but not the room number. Please forgive my interruption and any inconvenience I might've caused."

After feeling mortified upon leaving Dr. Stevens's sanctuary of learning, I finally located Professor Sankins's class down the second-floor *College Hall* corridor, and unfortunately, my belated entrance had interrupted the beginning of the despot's initial lecture. The class remained hush as the austere, elderly woman taciturnly surveyed the rude intruder's body from head to toe. The stern, matronly, gray-haired, very-perturbed lady motioned for me to occupy the last remaining desk next to the window, overlooking the scenic campus green and oval drive.

Professor Sankins had the distinct habit of carefully enunciating every syllable of every word she spoke. Her small, oval-shaped mouth exposed her very active tongue, continuously lubricating a *Lifesaver* wedged underneath it. The old dame had a warty face that would make any non-blind frog leap with terror. Her voice was either shrill or squawky, depending on her articulation, and when Professor Sankins hit a high pitch, a clanging burglar alarm would seem more melodious and appealing to the listener's ears.

As the first semester progressed, although I had an excellent English and writing background from Cardinal Reagan High. I found that I had to struggle to earn mostly B's and C's on Professor Sankins's labyrinthal-length objective tests. But I was extremely baffled by the professor's harsh criticism of my writing style. Throughout the first semester, the female martinet subjectively described my compositions as being too "wordy" and too "flowery", using "too many adjectives and adverbs," and I was assured of a *D* or an *F* on every essay and theme that I submitted, no matter how meticulous their organization.

"I know I have writing and language arts' talent," I confided to News one morning in the hall after English class. "Creative writing and journalism are my strong suits. Professor Sankins is trying to stifle my aspiration to someday become an author. She's deliberately breaking my balls in her *Fundamentals of Communications 101* class!" I concluded and opined.

"She doesn't like you, and I understand Sankins favors girls over male students," News disclosed. "Just hang in there and keep your nuts covered so that she doesn't disintegrate them any more than she has already. Save your tender testicles for Goose Restuccio to break and turn into sawdust or Swedish mearballs. Bite your tongue and accept her nonsensical bull-shit," News candidly advised. "Use your praiseworthy survival skills you showed during the great fruit war we had as Reds, goin' up against the Blues."

Professor Sankin's verbal and written attacks on my themes were comparable to how the *U.S. Marine Corps* trains its Parris Island soldiers. First, the recruit is broken-down to demoralize his confidence, and then, the rookie soldier is built-up according to standards practiced by the militant drill instructor. 'My creativity has to be sacrificed to allow for the rebuilding of my mastery of basic writing mechanics, which I already have,' I reckoned. "That's gotta' be Sankins's modus operandi.'

Coincidentally, as News had accurately described and predicted, the girls in Professor Sankins's freshman English class were all receiving B's and C's on their compositions, while all of the frustrated male peons were earning D's and F's. In fact, it was the two freshman year D's I had "earned" (received) from the didactical Professor Sankins first and second semesters that compelled me to have to switch my college major from High School Teacher of English to Junior High School Teacher.

'Professor Sankins isn't the first teacher trying to destroy my future with her dumb, moronic, little dictatorial power game!' I thought. 'Somehow, I'm going to graduate from this place and defy Professor Sankins out of spite, just as I had done with Mr. Andrews back at Edgewood High!'

I mentally thanked Miss Sankins for introducing me to the unwritten rules of a freshman student's survival on the perilous college frontier:

1. Never challenge the professor (even though he or she insists that he or she likes it).
2. Be courteous (falsely if necessary) and nice to the professor (color your nose brown).
3. Pretend to copy-down everything the professor utters (for he or she speaks an English dialect known as gospel).
4. Ask questions that compliment (not complement) the prof's knowledge. Don't make the professor think more than he or she actually wants to say from his or her prepared script.
5. Avoid using the naughty, self-centered pronouns *I, me,* and *my* when asking questions (be humble and subordinate).

In addition to the above academic behavioral commandments, I soon discovered that other secondary understandings would enable me to "play the cute college classroom game" and get better grades (while I exploited the "subjective factor" evident in teachers' evaluations).

1. Work or study with other students in the class, and always be cooperative (learn to kiss-up and flatter the teacher, and be compatible with his or her favorite students).
2. Buy the college companion book outline series to the course (usually authored by the professor) at the campus bookstore, and make sure the professor observes you reading his or her valuable literary contribution to the course.
3. Cheat whenever necessary, or when it is expedient.

"Well, J. W., has Professor Sankins castrated you yet?" Tim Amoro asked me outside the Co-op. "I don't see any blood drippin' outa' your trousers onto your shoes."

"Yes, she has, but I magically grow a new set of gonads every night, and bring them to her class the next morning," I smartly answered. "But Sankins is so blind to the truth that the lady dictator doesn't seem to notice or remember the odd*ball* phenomenon occurrin' and reoccurrin'."

News overheard our incredibly facetious conversation and very promptly added, "Balls said the jealous Queen, if I had them, I'd be King!"

Chapter 5
"Lambda Phi Sigma"

As a freshman at *Glassboro State,* I had the distinct privilege of studying under many erudite professors that greatly influenced me in my quest to become a teacher. I owe my gratitude to those dedicated Good Samaritan humanitarian souls, but regrettably, mixed into the academic stew were some lackluster pedagogues, some of whom used the classroom podium as a means of advancing their ultra-liberal and iconoclastic political and cultural philosophies. That malignant element has infected most college campus faculties from the late 1950's up to the present, and the myriad misfits' presence was quite apparent inside the *GSC College Hall* and *Bosshart Hall* lecture rooms.

Dr. Rolphs presumably taught Sociology and Anthropology to naïve undergraduate students. The instructor was a very restless, neurotic speaker that meandered back and forth in front of his captive audience, seldom looking directly at his listeners' faces. The paranoid professor's lectures were diatribes that advanced vitriolic condemnations of traditional American institutions and the values that the cultural pillars espoused. Each lesson would envelop some secular left-wing arguments about the existence of God, the limitations of our "breast-oriented society", and the inadequacies and selfishness associated with our American "keeping-up-with-the-Jones's materialistic culture."

Although Dr. Rolphs repeatedly indicated that his sole purpose was to "stimulate open-mindedness" among his receptive students, it was plainly obvious that the college classroom provided the pseudo-scholar with a convenient soapbox to perpetuate the suspect social doctrines of Marx, Engels, Lenin, and Rolphs. The radical professor enjoyed his self-appointed role of playing "Devil's Advocate", while the on-a-mission loon harassed the "closed-minded" beliefs of the vulnerable, impressionable neophytes his lectures were addressing. And all of his haranguing and criticisms were appropriately labeled "academic freedom" and "intellectual pursuit."

During the second-class session, Dr. Rolphs performed a series of verbal blitzkriegs on the infallibility of the Pope, the maternal instincts of women, the Divine Nature of Christ, and finally, the wacko professor deliberately attacked the virginity of the Blessed Mother. A virtuous girl in the front row challenged the maverick Sociology professor's derogatory critiques, and Rolphs chastised her with a ten-minute non-stop tongue-lashing. The pretty blonde became so upset with the disparaging remarks that she felt compelled to leave the room in tears after being the targeted victim of Rolph's insensitive, mean-spirited pragmatism.

An angered fellow also got-up and left the room, following the young lady's premature departure, apparently in an effort to comfort the aggrieved female. I wished that I had possessed the courage to follow suit, but soon realized that I lacked the emotional wherewithal to similarly abandon the grade-oriented scene in disgust. After the grueling and tension-packed class session finally concluded, I soon recognized a familiar face outside the Co-op and approached the kid that had exited the *Bosshart Hall* lecture room.

"Hi, I was in Dr. Rolphs Sociology seminar when you walked-out of his rant," I began, "and I want you to know that I thought you had done a very brave thing, steppin' out of that lecture hall. Now, I only wish I had the guts to do likewise."

"Thanks," the young freckle-faced student with thick, curly, black hair replied. "I only did what I thought I had to do. That's just the way I've always been. I guess I just have strong convictions about certain things."

"Who was that good lookin' blonde that left first?" I inquired. "Was the distressed girl a cousin or something? She really was quite bent out of shape by Rolph's tantrum."

"Her name's Patty," my new anonymous acquaintance answered. "Patty Wilcox, but her friends call her Peachy. She's a former *Miss Cape May,* ya' know? And now she's a former beauty queen with hurt feelings!"

"Is she from the same town as you're from?" I curiously inquired. "What high school did you graduate from? She's really a gorgeous knockout, when she's not cryin'."

"Lower Cape May Regional," the young handsome fellow stated. "And Peachy was in my class. I had gone to Middle Township High until my junior year, but then, my family moved to Cape May Court House where I met Peachy."

"Lower Cape May Regional," I acknowledged. "They're in the *Cape-Atlantic League* with Hammonton High. I think they have a tiger for their mascot. Well, at least a kid dressed in a tiger uniform cavortin' all around durin' basketball and football games."

"That's right," my new *GSC* chum confirmed. "Are you from Hammonton? That's really peach and blueberry territory with quite a reputation all around South Jersey."

"Sort of," I reluctantly responded. "I live in Elm, just west of Hammonton, and I know plenty of guys from *that* crazy town, but I graduated from Edgewood High."

Soon, Bob Abrams and I formally disclosed our names and then struck-up a fairly decent conversation. Bob informed me that Peachy Wilcox had been a "tiger cheerleader" in high school, and was also a very devout Catholic that took Rolphs's nasty assaults on her religion's devoted icons very personally. Then, Bob asked me something I hadn't quite expected.

"J.W., a friend and I are startin' up a new off-campus fraternity," Abrams revealed, "and we're gonna' call the new brotherhood Lambda Phi Sigma. My friend' Hoppy, well, his real name's Steve Cassidy, has a chicken coop about two-miles south of Glassboro that we're gonna' convert into a custom-made fraternity house. How would ya' like joinin' our Greek secret organization?" Bob invited. "We're goin' to be sponsored by a Lambda Phi Sigma chapter somewhere out in Southern California, and we're goin' to have an official charter, and all of the privileges that go with it."

"That sounds pretty nifty," I assessed and verbalized. "I'm getting' especially tired of wearin' this stupid brown and gold *GSC* dink on my head. Show me the nearest waste can where I can discard this hideous piece of crap."

"Yeah, J.W., it's only invitin' trouble," Bob agreed. "Everyone knows we're freshmen just waitin' to be hazed. So, let's forget all about bein' low men on the college totem pole, ready to be harassed by upperclassmen." Bob then removed my dink from my head and threw his and mine into a trash receptacle. "Do ya' have any other classes commin' up within the next two hours?"

"No, not until tomorrow morning with Miss Sankins," I honestly admitted. "I commute with four other Hammonton-area guys, but they're in class right now."

"Well then, J.W., why not take a ride with me to the other side of the railroad tracks, and I'll show ya' our initiation scheme, if that's all right with you?" Bob rhetorically asked. "Do ya' know any guys that might wanna' join Lambda Phi?"

"Well, yes, possibly," I instantly qualified with a degree of reservation. "There's News Tomasello, Tim Amoro, Ron Carputis, Big Al Keiler from my Literature Class with Mr. Ramsay, and also two guys I know from my Foundations of Education class, Tom Bell and Frank Morrissey. And oh yes," I remembered and added. "A huge guy named Mario DiMaris that plays big-time football for the *Hammonton Bakers*."

"Wow! Terrific!" my new acquaintance jubilantly exclaimed. "Now, let's take a ride out to the end of University Road where I'll show ya' the frat's initiation routine. You'll soon see that it's a real physical and mental barrier to overcome."

On the scenic fall drive out to the end of University Road, Bob provided several relevant aspects of his biography, that at first interpretation, seemed ambivalent and contradictory. But as the Lambda Phi co-founder elaborated on his perspectives, his personality became more defined to me, more likeable, and gradually, Abrams made much more sense. I listened intently to what eventually became an intriguing monologue after my initial inquiry.

"Were you offended by Rolph's comments about religion in general, the Catholic faith in particular?" I asked. "He was a little excessive, I must admit."

"My father is a Methodist minister," Bob explained as we entered his black '57 Mercury coupe. "I mean, I'm not a wet blanket or anything like that. I like beer, chicks, and havin' a blast. But I also do have core Christian values that I don't like seein' belittled. I'm not your everyday prude mind you'," Abrams mentioned, "so don't judge me by my daddy bein' a man of the cloth. I enjoy sin and temptation as much as the next guy does."

"Okay, Bob, that sounds logical," I related. "But why do ya' suppose Rolphs dwells on these controversial things that a lot of kids find offensive? Is he some kind of sadist or atheist? What's his motivation? Getting his jollies off?"

"The guy is definitely fucked-up!" Bob replied in an answer that surprised me, coming from a person of his moral background. "People that have screwed-up personal lives and poor family relationships look for causes to substitute for what they are lacking, in their own lives. Most of these environmentalists, socialists, liberals, and elite idealists have something missin' in their personal development, so they compensate by connectin' with these crazy causes," Abrams eloquently lectured. "Show me a beautiful staunch woman's rights fighter, and I'll show you one ugly lookin' female, and one even uglier soundin' bitch. That's the way it goes, J.W. That's the way of the goddamn dizzy world, always spinnin' around. People that are unhappy with themselves' latch on to these fucked-up crazy causes and hook onto goin' nowhere ideas! The dolts put faith in an abstract, secular philosophy, rather than believin' in themselves'. Do ya' get my message here?"

Bob's revelations sounded rather revolutionary in scope and content, or perhaps even conservatively counter-revolutionary to me, but his arguments also seemed fundamentally plausible and rational. I listened to more of his convincing right-wing didacticism.

"You oughta' become a lecturing psychologist," I light-heartedly recommended to my new-found amigo. "You seem to be cut out for that profession."

"Not me," Bob mildly protested with a wry smile. "My goal is to become a school superintendent, and nothin' except maybe premature death is gonna' stop me from reachin' that objective. I'm locked in on that target," Abrams elaborated, "and no damned Professor Rolphs, or anyone else on the *GSC* faculty, is gonna' deny me my dream. Sure, J.W., I'll put-up with *his* verbal bull-shit, and I've also convinced Peachy Wilcox to do likewise, but in the end, I'm gonna' be a district super' makin' three times as much as Rolphs will ever earn. That's the bottom line."

Bob stopped his black Mercury at the end of University Road, just beyond Peaks Horse, Apple and Peach Farm. We exited his vehicle, and then Abrams led me down a narrow path that eventually terminated at a serene-looking, slow-moving stream. A fallen elm tree served as a bridge over the brook. I was quite impressed with the general setting.

"A summer literature assignment recommended by the college English Department was to read *Walden Pond,"* I recalled and mentioned. "And Bob, that's exactly what this woody environment reminds me of. I think that Henry David Thoreau would *thoroughly* enjoy it," I intentionally punned.

"Well, J.W., even though I despised readin' that recommended piece of literary horse crap over the summer, here's the site of our fraternity's initiation," Bob explained. "First, we're gonna' swing from that overhead jungle vine on that tall oak tree, straight across the stream, and after that, then successfully walk blindfolded backwards on the fallen elm to this side to complete the Lambda Phi Sigma initiation rite. What do ya' think?"

"It's sort of juvenile or even adolescent, isn't it?" I contested. "I mean Bob, in all due respect, it seems like something high school kids would do before joinin' a chess club. To tell you the truth, I was hopin' for something more intellectually challengin'. I'm sorry to disappoint you, but…"

"Well again, J.W., I have several other initiation ideas I'm considerin' in reserve besides this one," Bob confidentially revealed. "But the main principle here is to test your courage. Once that's been established, we'll be able to better bond together as fraternity brothers. You already mentioned that ya' didn't have the balls to get up and walk out of Rolphs' class, didn't ya'? Now's your chance to show me what you're really made of!"

"Well, yes!" I stammered and then hesitated. "I was actually thinkin' about…"

"You were thinking about showin' some brass in Sociology class, but then fear set in, and then you worried about experiencin' the negative consequences," Bob Abrams hypothesized as the minister's son adroitly and accurately supplied the remainder of my sentence. "You gotta' demonstrate to me that ya' got some gumption, or else you're just another potential loser-cause-seeker as I see it. Are we now on the same damned page?"

I evaluated the particular circumstances and remembered my hard-earned reputation for being a daring individual with my former Diablos' gang in Levittown, and with the Reds peach guys in Hammonton. So then, I acceded to Bob's proposition and hardily endorsed his initiation strategy. "You go first, and I'll try and duplicate your feat," I voluntarily approved. "But I can't promise you perfect results."

"Okay, I'll go first," my prospective frat' brother-by-choice agreed. "Just pay attention to my technique. Show me ya' got some balls inside your scrotum sac."

Bob Abrams dexterously clambered-up to the oak tree's third limb, from which the ordinary-looking Tarzan vine dangled. He took a deep breath and then performed a Devil-may-care leap off of the limb, while tightly holding onto and clinging to the natural rope. Abrams's forward momentum swung his agile body gliding three-feet over the water, where the daring freshman soon gracefully landed in a clearing on the opposite bank.

"Not bad!" I commended. "Somewhere between amateur and professional. I know I can't beat that terrific jump, but I'll try my best to match it."

Abrams did not comment-on or brag about his near-perfect execution, but instead, focused his concentration on completing the second more difficult phase of the stunt, which his imagination had created. The gutsy kid removed a bandanna from his left back pocket and then tied it around his head to conceal his eyes. Next, after turning around with his back to me, the strong-minded young man felt for the fallen elm tree's center with his right foot, and then gently ascended onto the seemingly sturdy bridge. Abrams very deliberately took fourteen mini-steps in reverse, while marvelously maintaining his equilibrium like a circus performer entertaining on a high wire tightrope. In a matter of thirty breathtaking seconds, Bob Abrams had made it safely back to his point of origin.

"That was pretty damned fantastic!" I credited as my new pal removed his bandanna, exposing his dark brown eyes. "How many times have you done that before?"

"Never," Abrams demonstrably insisted. "That was the first time ever, and you just witnessed it happening. I believe in myself, and not in any damned social cause," Bob maintained. "Now, all *you* have to do is accomplish the same task, and you're guaranteed becomin' a Lambda Phi Sigma recruit."

I studied the dual obstacles that confronted me; grabbed the blue and white polka-dotted bandanna from Bob Abrams, and then slowly climbed-up the oak in a determined manner until my feet supported my weight upon the sturdy third limb. I latched onto the rough-surfaced vine; looked-up to the clear blue September sky; meditated a brief prayer, and then soon was air-borne, zooming-down through the massive oak. I held my breath and lifted my feet as my tennis shoes nearly skimmed the stream's surface. My pulsating heart felt only half-relieved when my feet eventually made safe contact with good old terra-firma on the opposite bank of the brook.

'Now, all I have to do is perform the second, even more-complicated miracle, and I'll finally have earned Bob's acceptance and admiration,' I concluded. I took ten deep breaths; attached the bandanna around my head; pulled the kerchief down over my eyes, and remarkably, very deliberately stepped backwards onto the fallen elm. I almost lost my balance after taking the sixth-step backwards, but after luckily regaining my center of gravity, I very meticulously stepped seven additional mini-steps in reverse. At the end, I tripped over an exposed root on the muddy bank, but managed to stay vertical. Bob immediately and excitedly congratulated me on my superb achievement. I then happily removed my blindfold.

"Welcome to the Lambda Phi Sigma brotherhood!" Bob shouted as the Frat President firmly embraced me. "Now, all *we* have to do is to perform that act one more time for keeps, when we show the other pledges exactly how it's all done!"

Chapter 6
"Mario's Great Adventures"

I was waiting in the Co-op for Mario to show-up from his late morning class, when another freshman strolled-over to the booth I was occupying. I recognized the fellow from the morning's debacle known as Dr. Rolph's Sociology class.

"Howdy," the fellow amiably began. "I'm Ken Reynolds and I believe I'm in Rolphs's class with you. That jerk really lost it that morning with that gorgeous blonde!"

I amiably introduced myself and gave Ken some pertinent background on the explosive Peachy Wilcox evacuation incident. After discussing how obnoxious and intolerable our Sociology professor was, Reynolds asked me something that immediately made me feel somewhat uncomfortable.

"Say, J.W., I'm scouting-around for some recruits into Delta Alpha Omega," Ken prefaced, "and I'm wonderin' if you'd be interested in seein' what we're all about. We have some great upperclassmen like Bob Powell, Dave Littlefield and Mike Errickson, and the Delta Alpha's are a bona fide social frat' that is fully sanctioned by the college."

I quite didn't know how to frankly answer Reynolds, so I figured I should be honest, polite, and blunt in my response. "I'm sorry Ken, but I'm gonna' join a new fraternity called Lambda Phi Sigma. Two guys named Bob Abrams and Steve Cassidy are sponsorin' me, and I've already accepted their invitation. Sorry for having to decline your offer," I regretfully stated, "but if you had asked me several before Rolphs's Sociology class, I probably would've said 'yes'."

"I heard something about that new renegade fraternity and it's gonna' soon be banned and dispersed by the administration," Ken predicted with a degree of enmity evident in his voice. "The deans don't like illegal social organizations that they can't monitor and indirectly control. I predict Lambda Phi Sigma's gonna' fold in less than a year. And besides, the Deltas have a really great frat' house on Harvard, not far from University Road."

"Thanks, anyway, Ken," I semi-apologized, "but freshman year I'm gonna' be a commuter from Hammonton and don't need to live in a frat' house. If Lambda Phi crumbles like you say it will, I'll probably take you up on your offer next year and link-up with Delta Alpha Omega."

Reynolds lost his initial suave composure and suddenly became surly and acrimonious. "Okay, Knucklehead, if that's the way ya' want it. I'm sorry I even wasted my time addressin' somebody that doesn't know their brain from their' friggin' asshole!" And then, Ken Reynolds, feeling gravely rejected, angrily left the Co-op, heading like an enraged bull in the direction of the *Memorial Hall* student lounges.

Five minutes later, I was joined in the Co-op by News Tomasello', who had just exited one of his morning classes. I was never so glad to see my old friend in all my life. "Say News, I was just asked to join Delta Alpha Omega by some guy named Ken Reynolds, but I told him I was gonna' belong to a new fraternity Lambda Phi Sigma, instead," I informed my buddy. "So then, the kid became very vindictive and nasty, and I was afraid we were goin' to have a fistfight right here in the middle of the Co-op."

"Wow, J.W. What an uncanny coincidence!" News related. "Some guy nicknamed Hoppy, I think, his last name's Cassidy, just like the famous cowboy, well anyway, he asked me to join Lambda Phi Sigma, too! Said something like convertin' a chicken coop into a frat' house. Sounds a little like a silly, low-budget operation to me, though, don't ya' think!"

"What did ya' say to the guy?" I asked with great fervor. "I hope you answered in the affirmative!"

"The kid caught me at a weak moment, just before class, so I agreed, when now I think I should've stalled for time," News casually answered. "Looks like we're gonna' be brothers, J.W. Of course, we've always been like brothers, but now it's gonna' be bona fide, and almost legal and binding."

"I'm gonna' ask Carputis, Amoro, and Mario to join, too," I ecstatically told News. "I'm sure they'll all agree. Say News, what's botherin' you?" I then asked. "You look like you've just lost a close relative or your two big toes!"

News Tomasello bit his lips for a minute and then informed me that a muscular guy named Jack Thompson had just asked him to pledge for Tau Kappa Epsilon, another *GSC* men's fraternity. "But then J.W., I told this guy Jack I had already accepted an invitation to belong to Lambda Phi Sigma, so now I guess you and I have already made some big enemies here at *GSC* while trying to be BMOC."

"BMOC?" I queried.

"Yeah, J.W., 'Big Men on Campus'. But right now, it looks like the *Glassboro State* fraternity scene is shapin' up like a college rendition of the Blues, Reds, and Ramrodders Hammonton nightmare being revisited."

Mario clumsily entered the Co-op with Tim Amoro and Ron Carputis following the "Cape Buffalo" inside, and after hearing News's and my stories, they all readily consented to the idea of becoming active in Lambda Phi Sigma, with the exception of Mario, who had his usual individual doubts, excuses, and reasons.

"Look, guys, I'm twenty-eight, married and have a kid already," DiMaris maintained. "My wife's puttin' me through college, and I gotta' live a family life. And I can't pay the bills playin' semi-pro ball for the *Bakers* the rest of my life. You jerk-offs are single and have more freedom and less fuckin' responsibility than I got."

"Look, Mario, we understand your situation and sympathize with you," News politely acknowledged, "But we need your vital protection as our main bodyguard, in addition to your cool companionship. You can belong to the fraternity, but only remotely if that's want you really prefer. In fact, Mario, you could maybe even be a distinguished Member-at-Large, and I'm not only referrin' to your tremendous bulk," News diplomatically finished.

"Okay, News, you cowardly Shit-head," DiMaris devilishly laughed. "If that's the case, I'll join this Lambs Defy Sigmans, or this Signa Fi Nothings, or whatever you call the damned group. But why don't ya' tell us what's happenin' in the world, besides this new rah-rah-rah *GSC* fraternity bull-shit?"

After receiving coaxing from the remaining friends seated in the snack bar's booth, News enunciated one of his traditional irrelevant dissertations. "Well, guys, it's a dangerous world out-there besides the threats presented by Delta Alpha Omega and Tau Kappa Epsilon. In fact," News loquaciously continued, "President Kennedy's gonna' recommend that family's build fallout shelters for protection against atomic radiation in case the Russians drop an A or an H-bomb on the United States."

"If it's a fallout shelter," Mario seriously answered while having his cerebral limits tested, "then what good is the damned shelter if everyone's gonna' fall out of it?"

Everyone laughed at Mario's creative analysis that was really sincerely stated and predicated on general ignorance of the formidable foreign atomic threat. But News was unfazed by the thunderous merriment.

"And guys, President Kennedy just signed a hijackin' bill on September 5th making air piracy a crime punishable by death or life imprisonment," Tommy related. "This action has obviously stemmed from the July 24th hijackin' to Cuba of a plane goin' from Miami to Tampa."

"Well, News, if our noble President Kennedy signed a hijackin' bill as you say he did," Tim Amoro contributed, "why is hijackin' illegal if the President signed a bill approvin' hijackin' as you've already stated?"

"And how come pirates are now hijackin' airplanes," Ron Carputis wanted to know. "Did the buccaneers run out of ships to maraud on the damned high seas? And don't give me any crap about corn bein' a damned lousy *buck an ear*."

"And what hijacker would want to get caught in the act and then have to die or be put in prison for life?" I next challenged News. "And anybody that would want to go to Cuba and live under Fidel Castro would have to be ruled psychologically insane and not have to suffer either death or life imprisonment in our American judicial system," I argued. "And besides that fact, News, livin' in Havana, even under Castro, is almost as bad as residin' in either Miami ghettoes or in Tampa slums!"

"Look, Dumb-Dumbs. I'm sorry I ever told you idiots about important developments in current events," News chastised us. "You imbeciles could visit hell and think it was a funny paradise to have barbecues! All you Creeps know how to do is sabotage and corrupt legitimate conversation, to diabolically reduce and traduce my valuable information, and then diminish my wisdom down to your moronic level. I don't know why I even friggin' bother."

"I think I was just bein' fuckin' insulted, but I don't know for goddamned sure!" yelled Mario. And then, Tim, Ron, and I broke out into a roar, much to News's chagrin. "Ridicule me in plain English next time. News. and then I'll punch your face silly!" Mario threatened with an awesome clenched right fist waving under Tomasello's delicate, glass-jawed chin.

The following morning, I drove Dad's white '61 Chevy Impala through downtown Hammonton over to Mario's modest house on Chestnut Street. Since DiMaris and I had an early U.S. History class with Dr. Martin, and Tim, Ron and News wouldn't have their first classes until 10 a.m., I had the unenviable honor of driving the obese behemoth to *Glassboro State.*

"That News is really sensitive, but I basically like the fuckin' guy," Mario related after entering the Impala's passenger side, almost breaking the right front shock absorber and exploding the tire. "He seems like he's gonna' make a good fraternity brother, even if he's basically fucked-up."

"What about me?" I interrupted. "Don't ya' think I'm gonna' be a decent guy you can depend on?"

"That goes without sayin'," Mario uncommonly qualified like a skilled politician. "And J.W., make sure ya' don't cover-up your answers on the exam'. Dr. Martin is givin' his first test today and I might need a little help to get me over the failin' level. I hate fuckin' studyin' from books more than I hate fuckin' lima beans and lima bean farts, even in the goddamned bathtub!"

"Okay, Mario, I studied pretty diligently last night and know all about the *Age of Enlightenment* and the *Age of Discovery,"* I told DiMaris, much to his relief and satisfaction. "Just be discreet when you obtain your answers. I don't want to jeopardize my average and then have to explain something embarrassin' to my folks, who both happen to think cheatin' is immoral."

"Okay, J.W., but just remember, if I get caught, you get caught too!" Mario matter-of-factly reminded me. "But that asshole Martin will never make mention of it, because he knows that I'll maul and beat the livin' shit out of him if he dares takin' our papers, or givin' *us* failin' grades we don't deserve."

I took the familiar Winslow-Williamstown Road, and was doing about sixty on "the high tension-line" two-lane highway, when Mario shouted like an asylum patient. "J.W. Slam on your brakes and back up!" I followed my bulldog companion's instruction because I preferred living to either hurting or dying. I squealed the Impala to a halt, hastily looked into the rear-view mirror, and then swiftly drove in reverse.

"Alright Jerk-weed, stop right here!" Mario demanded. "Look over on my side!" the human animal bellowed and implored. "There's a big black bull screwin' a damned brown and white cow out in that pasture! Just look at that sucker porkin' that fat porterhouse heifer to death."

"You made me risk our lives to see *that* disgustin' biological act!" I screamed. "I thought there was some sort of emergency, or we had to help somebody that crashed into a high-tension telephone pole, or something like that. This is absolutely absurd!"

"Ya' can't move the freakin' car until they're done fuckin'!" Mario ordered. "We ain't gonna' stop at Glassboro Bedding to say that stupid Ron Carputis salute bull-shit, so we can just stay here until that horny black bull pops his load!"

I put the car's right turn signal on, eased over to the side shoulder, and watched the graphic animalistic spectacle to its predictable conclusion. In the meantime, at least a dozen motorists had slowed-down while passing by. One driver, being of Mario's emotional and psychological ilk, also pulled-over to personally witness the pasture sex-exhibition in progress. "That guy's the only one else with any class!" DiMaris observed and stated while pointing at the other stopped motorist. "From now on, instead of sayin' bull-shit, I'm gonna' say bull-fuck, and J.W., you'll be the only one knowin' what the hell I'll be talkin' about."

Finally, I was able to leave the vicinity of the fenced-in grassland, animal-porno-show, and get back onto the high-tension-line road heading toward Williamstown. At the next intersection, Mario told me not to halt at the four-way Stop Sign and to "just trickle-through". I didn't know exactly what to think or say.

"We aren't blood cells flowin' around in a vein!" I adamantly balked. "Even though we're on a traffic *artery,*" I cleverly associated two remote ideas as was my bad habit, "we still gotta' abide by the rules and laws."

"Bull-fuck' J.W.!" Mario answered and lustily laughed. "I just wanted to see if ya' had any character and would do anything I told ya' to do. Ya' just passed my bull-fuckin' exam'. Now, all we gotta' do is pass Dr. Martin's bull-fuckin' history exam', and we'll be in good fuckin' shape."

After parking the white '61 in the central campus commuter student parking lot, Mario and I ambled over to *Bosshart Hall* where our first history test would be administered. We were the last two students to enter the classroom and managed to find two seats next to each other in the back. I felt rather uneasy when the distinguished Dr. Martin handed-out "Blue Composition Books," indicating that subjective essay questions would be given to supplement the objective Multiple Choice, Matching, and True and False items on his first major evaluation. I momentarily looked at Mario, but my traveling comrade seemed unperturbed by any irregularity occurring.

After distributing both sections of his examination, Dr. Martin sat at his desk in front of the room, reading and correcting papers from another class, while his thirty formerly apathetic disciples struggled with the challenging history test before our eyes. A half an hour into the exam', Mario reached-over and grabbed my stapled "objective question sheets", and without any trace of good conscience or guilt, began copying down *all* of my answers while I continued assiduously laboring and writing seven sentence paragraphs that corresponded to the very rigorous and complex subjective essay questions. And twenty-minutes after that fiasco, Mario gave me back my six-pages of Multiple Choice, Matching, and True and False items, and then without restraint, confiscated my still-uncompleted blue essay booklet. The cheater copied and scribbled-down my well-conceived answers, word for word, while I pretended that nothing extraordinary was happening or bothering me.

All the while, the seemingly aloof Dr. Martin read and corrected his other class's test papers and essay booklets, completely oblivious to Mario's blatant academic violations. And then, the final bell sounded, signaling the termination of the session. Mario stood-up, handed me my incomplete Composition Booklet, walked-up to Dr. Martin's desk and submitted both sets of his test materials to the debonair professor. I duplicated *his* shameless actions, and then met the audacious cheater outside *Bosshart Hall.*

"Are you crazy?" I vociferously began and objected. "At least six kids in that class saw you do what you did. That was a pretty disgraceful exhibition!"

"Don't sweat the small stuff!" Mario casually replied as if nothing unusual had ever transpired. "Dr. Martin never saw or cared to see it happen. That gutless wimp lives in a fuckin' artificial state of denial. None of his other goddamned students would ever dare to pull that bull-fuck on him! Nobody but me, that is!"

"Well, I didn't even have a chance to finish the last essay question because you grabbed my booklet," I protested. "Now I'll probably have to settle for a B instead of an A. I studied hard enough to earn an A on that damned exam'!"

"Don't worry, J.W.," Mario comforted. "But next time, please fuckin' write neater. I had trouble readin' and copyin' your friggin' notes. Say pal, ya' got any goddamned money on ya'? I got twenty-five bucks to burn."

"Yeah, I've got thirty-five dollars left-over from my summer job workin' at Pete's Market. I hope ya' don't need a loan," I begged. "That's my food and travelin' money for the rest of next week. In October, my weekly college expense allowance kicks in."

"Well, J.W., we're gonna' cut the rest of our worthless classes this afternoon and go over to *Atlantic City Race Track,"* DiMaris imperatively commanded. "You' ever been to the track before?"

"All the time," I fibbed in defense of my ego, while attempting to act more mature than I really was. "But I've never seen you there, not even once."

"Okay, granted J.W., but I got a super tip from my bookie so we're gonna' play the Daily-Double, Number 5 and Number 7. One problem, though. I gotta' first borrow fifteen bucks from ya' to put twenty bananas down on each horse."

"What if 5 and 7 don't come in?" I asked. "Do I gotta' throw away the rest of my money on later races?"

"No, we'll bug the hell outa' the place if my bookie's wrong," Mario promised. "He wouldn't take my bet because he gave me the confidential info' and would lose his shirt in the transaction if I put forty bucks down on the two horses he tipped me on."

At one in the afternoon, Mario and I were in the *Atlantic City Race Track* grandstand, awaiting the official trumpeter in his red foxhunting attire to summon the first group of racehorses to the starting gate. An anxious crowd of around five-thousand addicted horserace enthusiasts was on hand to watch and bet on the ten scheduled contests.

"The program states right here that Number 5 in the first race is *Land Rover,* and Number 7 in the second is *Ocean Muffin*. Mario," I said. "Aren't ya' supposed to study track conditions, the jockeys' histories, and the horses' records before plunkin' down forty bucks on a tip?"

"There ain't no damned system or science to horse racin' strategy," Mario stubbornly explained. "I've seen some real ugly women pick red and green colors for the jockey uniforms, because the horses' colors and jockeys' uniforms' fuckin' matched their negligee and lingerie that the bitches go to bed in. And ya' wanna' know something, J.W.," Mario argued. "The dames' color code method works better with horses and jockeys than most systems I've seen fuckin' used, scientific or usin' numbers or records, or fuckin' anything else."

I was fairly impressed that words like "negligee" and "lingerie" were in Mario's speaking vocabulary, although I was certain he wouldn't know where to begin spelling them to save his life. But if a reference or allusion had a sex-connotation to it, then that phraseology was most certainly in Mario's narrow perception range and verbal repertoire.

I was amazed when the illustrious favored *Land Rover* won the first race, and even more astounded when the incredible long-shot *Ocean Muffin* triumphantly flew past the *Finish Line* in the second part of the Daily-Double, even though we were nowhere near Helsinki. And when I found-out that the return on Mario's forty-dollar gamble was a fabulous bonanza of three-hundred-and-twenty-five clams, I was almost as exuberant about his good fortune as my gambling friend was.

"What are ya' gonna' do with your colossal winnings?" I asked the chronic gambler/sex maniac, after he smilingly returned from the cashier's window with a bundle of *Andrew Jacksons, Alexander Hamiltons, and Abe Lincolns* in his chubby hands.

"Here's forty-bucks for showin' your good faith in me," Mario generously offered. "Take it J.W. Now I'm gonna' be appreciative and treat us to some pizza on the way home, along with a bottle of *Southern Comfort*."

I pulled my white '61 into a Williamstown pizza parlor's parking lot on the way back to Hammonton. After Mario gave me "five clams for "grub", I got-out and ordered the Italian delight while my bad-habit companion ventured into a liquor store two doors down to purchase his "for fuckin' medicinal purposes only firewater."

My corpulent pal soon returned to the pizza palace with his most recent acquisition concealed inside a brown paper bag. The portions served were of the long, thick-dough Sicilian variety, and DiMaris virtually inhaled the first slice, shoving it horizontally into his cavernous mouth and throat, and then the contemporary caveman ravenously chewed the tomato and cheese specialty with his powerful mandible-like jaws. I sat in astonishment watching DiMaris guiltlessly devour four of the five slices in the same time it required me to consume one.

"Now let's get our asses back to Hammonton," my traveling fast-lane colleague suggested. "We'll drink the booze on the way, and if you're lucky, you'll fuckin' get the last ounce."

Upon crossing the Black Horse Pike, a fanciful thought occurred to me. "Mario," I casually addressed my Neanderthal companion. "Since we're now in Williamstown heading back to Winslow, we should call this thoroughfare Williamstown-Winslow Road instead of Winslow-Williamstown Road."

"Fuck you, J.W." Mario boomed. "Bull-fuck your ass, too!" the maniac repeated as he twisted the cap off of the quart of *Southern Comfort,* and then lifted the liquor up to his fat lips. I temporarily took my eyes off of the road to notice Mario chug almost the entire quart of the potent intoxicant down, save one or two ounces left at the bottom. "Here, Dip-shit; drink the rest before I make it fuckin' disappear, too," DiMaris advised. "I'm still thirsty, and these last two ounces won't be there too long if ya' don't indulge. And don't worry J.W. I ain't got cooties or lice, or goddamned V.D. either."

I guzzled-down the remaining two delicious ounces of the sweet bourbon blend, and then Mario rolled-down his side window and indiscriminately tossed the empty bottle outside, nearly decapitating a black man riding a bicycle. "I wish I had another fuckin' empty bottle to throw," Mario lamented. "Then, I'd have ya' turn-around so that I could knock that nigger right off of his seat and tumblin' into the goddamned woods."

"That guy might be a good man, maybe even a benign black minister, a Big Brother, or someone helpful like that," I answered. "How could you be so prejudiced without even knowin' the guy, let alone scarin' the crap out of him with a flyin' empty *Southern Comfort* bottle whizzin' by his noggin'?"

"Show me a nigger worth knowin', and I'll show ya' my house on Mars and my goddamned vacation pad on Jupiter," DiMaris bragged in an extended metaphor. "The only good niggers I've known I had played football with on the *Bakers*. But before we had the *Bakers,* we were the *Hammonton Brewers* without any damned niggers fuckin' up the team. Times are changin' for the worse, J.W. They're really fuckin' changin' for the goddamned worse! The next thing ya' know, we'll find-out that Columbus was a black fuck, and not a goddamned mixed-up Italian at all!"

Automatically, I put Mario DiMaris in the same discrimination category as Goose Restuccio, who also despised black people, despite the fact that G.R. had made a colored girl pregnant when forced to do so by the Blues, a ruthless Hammonton gang of rich sons of blueberry growers. Five minutes later, we were approaching the wooden bridge that marked the geographic boundary line between Gloucester and Camden Counties.

"Stop the freakin' car!" Mario yelled. "Stop right here and do what the hell I tell ya'!"

"Why? Do you see two blowfish havin' hot '69 sex in the stream runnin' under the bridge?" I replied in a smart-aleck reply. "Your general crudeness, Mario, could become rather borin' after a while."

"No, Asshole. It's exactly one mile from this wooden-planked bridge to the overpass goin' over the new *Atlantic City Expressway*. Since there's no damned traffic on this back country road," Mario speculated and offered, "why don't ya' see how fast you can get this Chevy up to on the speedometer. I'll bet ya' can't hit at least eighty-five in that stretch."

"Okay," I reluctantly agreed under pressure of possibly being immediately exterminated by the human cannibal sitting alongside me. I stepped on the accelerator and took-off like a falcon out of Hades. Mario was laughing his fat buttocks off as my speedometer registered eighty-miles-per-hour approaching the newly constructed *Expressway* overpass. Slickly concealed inside an opening into a wooded area on the left were three Winslow Township police cars with their accompanying officers setting-up a radar speed trap to apprehend unsuspecting motorists speeding on the isolated country road.

"Holy shit, Mario!" I boisterously yelled to my fellow *Glassboro State* passenger riding 'shotgun'. "I'll lose my damned driver's license if we get caught in this caper!" I screamed, as the white Chevy zipped-up the incline and onto the overpass's crest.

"There's a dirt trail that's used by hunters on the left, just beyond the fuckin' *Expressway* toll booth entrance!" Mario informed in a mild stupor. "Pull into the hunting trail. The damned cops don't want to get their cars dirty or fuckin' dented-up, and won't have the bull- fuck balls to speed into the damned woods after us!"

I veered the faithful Chevy left, skidded across the asphalt road, and quickly entered the sandy-white hunting trail at sixty-miles an hour. The back end of the car fishtailed as my rear tires wildly spun through the soft dirt. I had to sustain a speed of around thirty-miles-an-hour to keep going forward as the deserted trail wended left, right, and then left again. "I don't want to get stuck!" I yelled at Mario. "And I still have a trace of alcohol on my breath if *we* get caught! If that happens, I'm up I'm Shit's Creek without a paddle!"

"Without a fuckin' canoe, too!" Mario laughed while splitting a gut, wildly cackling-away in his pathetic, drunken state. "You'll be even more fucked-up than I am right now!" the nutcase added. "I'll have to visit ya' in prison and bring ya' a couple ounces of *Southern Comfort!"* Ha, ha, you dumb amateur Asshole! Ha, ha, ha. J.W.! You'll definitely be bull-fucked-up!"

A wide patch of sandy soil was situated toward the trail's exit from the woods, and much to my dissatisfaction, the Chevy's wheels pressed-down into the soft earth, and soon my driving machine could not escape its entrapment. After listening to Mario hauntingly laugh for another five minutes at my miserable discomfort, the monster finally offered to walk with me to a phone booth at Mr. Bill's Custard Stand, a half mile away on *Route 73.*

"I'll call a guy I know who owns a goddamned fuckin' gas station in Hammonton," Mario laughed as we trekked along the busy dual highway. "My friend owes me a couple favors, and he's got a tow-truck and will come-out here to haul your pop's car outa' the damned woods. Don't worry, J.W. I never renege on a good pal. But black people won't fuckin' help other black people in trouble! That's why they're called re-niggers, ha, ha, ha! Re-niggers, ha, ha, ha, ha!"

While Mario was making the necessary phone call outside Mr. Bill's, a Winslow Township cop pulled his squad car into the front parking lot and exited to buy a vanilla custard cone. I hid my face and turned my back, praying that the patrolman wouldn't come-over and interrogate us. My prayers were answered when the fuzz hopped back into his cruiser and headed south towards Williamstown, in the direction of the speed trap that had been set up.

After Mario's buddy's tow truck arrived, the mechanic then used four-wheel-drive to yank my dad's '61 Impala out of the woods. We thanked Frank "The Fat Worm" Zolda for his wonderful assistance, and then returned to the abused white automobile. "I'm gonna' drive myself home in your car!" DiMaris insisted with a stern expression, exhibited upon his bulldog face.

"But your breath's reeking with *Southern Comfort*, and we aren't *out of the woods* yet as far as the cops are concerned. They're 'vigilant' and can still get lucky and nab us by accident," I pontificated.

"I don't give a shit if they're freakin' vigilantes or not," Mario snapped back between hiccups. "If ya' don't let me drive I'm gonna' stick my fuckin' finger down my throat and vomit pizza and stinkin' booze all over your fancy fuckin' green upholstery. What do ya' have to say about that particular prospect, Mr. Fuck shit Bull fuck?"

"Okay, Mario, you win," I conceded. "Get behind the wheel and take it slow all the way back to Hammonton. I just want to get home safe, sound and unscathed."

My drunken college colleague got behind the wheel, with his fat gut overlapping and enveloping the entire steering column. When we got-out of the pine woods and advanced to the shoulder of *Route 73,* Mario turned his big skull left and noticed red flashing lights in the distance. "Look over there on my left, J.W. There's probably a real bad fuckin' accident down there. Let's go check it out!"

"Mario, I'm beggin' you to just turn right and go back to Hammonton," I maintained and pleaded. "Don't press your luck. Stop livin' on the damned edge all the time!"

DiMaris ignored my entreaty the same way the stubborn fool would obstinately eschew anyone else's plea, as was his wont. A half-mile down the four-lane highway a Winslow Township police officer raised his right hand, demanding that we stop and obey his subsequent directions. Mario rolled-down his window and held his breath as best as he could.

"Gentlemen, we're having a sobriety check stop," the officer professionally related. "Now, Sir, this is not a speed trap. You'll have to get-out and walk a straight line. Please step out of the car while I observe your gait."

Mario sighed a forced breath to demonstrate his overall frustration with the interruption of his general happiness, and the drunken imbecile cursed under his breath to express his sense of defeat. "I ain't got no *gate* for you to inspect!" Mario sincerely confessed to the cop. DiMaris easily failed the sobriety test and finally figured out too late what all of the red flashing police-car lights were all about. Three citations were written-up for drunken driving, for evading an earlier police radar trap, and for recklessly speeding without just cause. The expense was a hundred-and-ninety dollars to be paid to the Winslow Township court clerk, after Mario signed the tickets admitting guilt, thus surrendering his right to a trial. Mario DiMaris would also lose his driver's license for a three-month period as a result of his "fearless, undisciplined joyriding".

"Well, Mario," I commiserated after we got back onto the highway, "you might've passed Dr. Martin's U.S. History exam', but ya' failed the Winslow Township cops' sobriety test. I warned you to turn right on *73* toward Hammonton after ya' had to have your obstinate way and get behind the wheel. What do ya' have to say for yourself now?"

DiMaris was so pissed-off about losing most of the money he had won at the racetrack, in addition to forfeiting his driving privileges until the *New Year,* that the beast defiantly stuck his index finger down his throat and puked all over the Impala's formerly immaculate front seat. I helplessly sat there in horror, and watched the disgusting event being deliberately enacted. And the uncouth barbarian did all of that while still driving my father's white Chevy on *Route 54,* heading in the direction of Hammonton.

Chapter 7
"The Vine and the Tree Bridge"

One thing was certain in my mind. I never ever wanted to hang around with Mario DiMaris riding to or from Glassboro, unless News Tomasello, Tim Amoro, and Ron Carputis were also in our company. Our collective majority will might then be enough to negate Mario's propensity for self-destruction, and neutralize his despicable, slovenly living habits. And so, I insisted that we all ride to *Glassboro State* each morning in the same vehicle, no matter who was driving, or no matter who had later or earlier classes, since I wanted to prevent Mario from driving without a license.

I had spent nearly two-hours scrubbing-down the white '61 Chevy's front seat with disinfectant until my knuckles were bleeding from the friction. Finally, the repugnant odor had dissipated, and only the clean, dark, wet-stain remained as evidence of my toil, and as proof of eliminating Mario's repulsive digestive tract's largesse. Then, and only then, did I dare drive license plate number *FNW-701* through Al's Automatic Car Wash on the White Horse Pike, and finally home to Elm. Pop didn't use the car until the following afternoon, and never once detected any evidence of a dark stain or nauseous putrid stench.

On Monday, September 18, 1961, Ron Carputis was driving his old man's gray Chevy with his four standard passengers inside when the neurotic kid predictably stopped outside Glassboro Bedding to perform his by-now monotonous salute to the glorious bed. The other occupants were not-too-thrilled with the already hackneyed oral tradition that Carputis had unilaterally established.

"Ron, isn't this becomin' a little redundant?" I challenged in a rather bad mood. "I mean, it was cute the first couple of times, but now the novelty's worn off, don't ya' think?"

"I just like bustin' your stones, J.W., and that goes for News, Tim, and Mario as well," Ron replied with a smirk on his round, chicken-hawk face. "And besides, it'll be good practice for the Lambda Phi initiation that's set for late this afternoon. I wonder what Bob Abrams has up his sleeve?"

"Nothing but a dirty elbow," Tim briskly answered. "Let's get this travesty over with. J.W. and I have gym class with Coach Holmes first period this mornin', and the prof's already warned us twice about bein' late to the locker room to quickly change into our gym suits."

The five of us exited the car, not only because we didn't wish to be late for our early classes, and also because Ron Carputis threatened to throw his car keys onto the Glassboro Bedding roof should any of us not cooperate with his inane insane nonsense. So, we all saluted the commonplace edifice and perfunctorily recited "Ode to the Bunk" with the refrain, "Glassboro Bedding we salute you in appreciation of your infinite contributions to relaxation, recreation, overpopulation and sex education." Several critical blue-collar motorists on their way to work slowed-down, gave us the customary middle finger, and then sped-off, either east towards Williamstown, or west towards Glassboro on *Route 322*.

"That's what I like most about the salute," Ron intimated upon returning to his automobile. "I get a kick outa' pissin' the workin' people off, and then seein' their reaction. The proletariats know we're preparin' to become teachers; the idiots think educators make too much money, and then the dunces bitch about how high their damned taxes are that have to pay teachers' salaries. That's the real reason I do this Glassboro Bedding shit."

"Ron, I think you're reading a little too much into their sinister motivations," Tim corrected. "The factory workers just think we're wastin' our parents' hard-earned-money by screwin' around here on the highway, when we really should be more into studyin', and not glorifyin' dumb-ass commutin' to college."

"That's right, and I endorse Tim's opinion," I wholeheartedly chimed-in. "Those disgruntled blue-collar types resent the fact that we college kids can still enjoy ourselves, while the family providers have to go to work Monday through Friday with long faces, just to support their bitchy wives and their spoiled-rotten kids."

"Who'll' probably later in life grow-up to be Glassboro Bedding saluters, too!" News humorously added, "if not loyal employees. That's what those passin' factory and mill workers really fear the most. The jealous fools must really dread their kids growin' up to become just like us, and demandin' that their middle-class fathers pay for an expensive college education, maybe even in the elite *Poison Ivy League,* just to join fraternities and then screw-around like we're doin' right now."

Tim and I were late for the third time to Coach Holmes's eight a.m. gym class, and when I opened my' *College Hall* basement gym locker, my green Edgewood High suit was not inside. I immediately brought my dilemma to Tim Amoro's attention.

"Maybe you took it home to be washed and forgot to take it back to Glassboro," my Hammonton pal suggested. "My suit's right here in my locker, J.W. And you have a combination lock, and the only ones that know your three numbers are you and coach Holmes. And you aren't about to accuse him of stealin' your smelly decayin' jockstrap, are ya'?"

I regarded myself as being more athletic than the average eighteen-year-old, so gym class was probably my favorite freshman curricular college activity. Coach Holmes seemed to fancy me because my happy-go-lucky personality stood-out like a sore thumb; because I could take criticism without becoming aggressive, and because my revered gym mentor always called affectionately me "a good American kid".

Being late for changing into our gym suits also meant that Tim and I would consequently show-up tardy for roll call, which Dr. Holmes conducted in a military fashion, with his apostles standing in alphabetical order at attention like greenhorn *Army* recruits at *Fort Dix*. I had not yet obtained my brown and gold *GSC* gym suit, but on Monday, September 16, I had no alternative other than showing-up for class roll call wearing my civilian traveling clothes. I felt very self-conscious upon entering the college gymnasium.

"J.W., where's your gym suit? Did you buy your *Glassboro State* one yet at the campus bookstore? I'm pretty tired of that green high school outfit you've been sportin' since last week," Coach Holmes amusingly chided.

"I can't find my Edgewood High uniform anywhere, Coach," I defensively apologized. "I haven't bought the *Glassboro* one yet, and I can't seem to find my green high school one that I've been wearin', either."

"Well, J.W., by a stroke of sheer coincidence, I just happen to have found it!" Coach Holmes rankled with a sarcastic grin displayed upon his countenance. "I've recently discovered the stinkin', offensive-smellin' thing in your dirty unkempt locker. So, here's your new temporary gym uniform for today!" the Coach boomed, as the gym class instructor removed a brown and yellow *Glassboro State College* Freshman dink from a brown paper bag. "Put it on J.W., and wear it with pride! That's your special uniform for the day!"

Every freshman including Tim Amoro standing at attention laughed indulgently at Coach Holmes's successful chop busting. "Now, the class will reassemble outside on the soccer field in three minutes. Before we choose-up sides for an intramural game, I have a little ritualistic ceremony to perform in honor of J.W.'s chronic forgetfulness in regard to satisfactorily obtaining appropriate gymnasium garb."

On the soccer field that crisp and invigorating September morning, the imaginative coach showed his thoroughly entertained class my wrinkled green Edgewood gym ensemble, and then unexpectedly ignited my high school uniform with a cigarette lighter. The delighted class then began chanting in response to the pyrotechnic ritual "Up in smoke! Up in smoke!" while sounding a little like the cannibals featured in the original *King Kong* movie.

The other freshmen definitely sounded as if they were members of a primitive jungle tribe worshiping, and extolling arson and property destruction. Their dissonant melody then transformed into an improvised ceremonial dance, and the jovial classmates hopped and skipped-around my now-smoldering, forest green Edgewood High gym apparel.

Little incidents like the frenzied tribal dance, towel fights in the shower room between Tim and me and a black kid named Clayton, and the overall congenial looseness of Coach Holmes's informal gym class made his course my favorite freshman curricular enterprise. Needless to say, I had learned my moral lesson well under my gym mentor's essential tutelage. The following morning, I quickly acquired a *GSC* brown and gold gym uniform from the college store to spare myself future social embarrassment.

"Coach Holmes really did a royal number on you this mornin'," Tim Amoro told me in the Co-op an hour after the farce had occurred. "Now ya' gotta' watch your step in Dr. Rolphs's Sociology domain. Who knows what that cretin might do to you?"

"Bob Abrams and I have already made a pact that we're gonna' walk-out of his class if the idiot starts offendin' any girls in the room about their religious convictions," I related to Tim. "Over half the class will participate in the walkout, if and when Bob deems the protest bein' necessary."

News Tomasello showed-up to convey to Tim and me that the Lambda Phi pledge candidates were expected to arrive at Joe's Sub Shop on High Street at 4.p.m., a half an hour before the scheduled initiation ceremony. "What do ya' suppose Abrams is gonna' have us do?" Tomasello inquired. "Swallow a pound of live goldfish each, and then drink a gallon of scummy pond water to wash the critters down? Maybe we'll have to stuff our asses inside a midget telephone booth? Or make us all jerk-off together in a circle?"

"I haven't the slightest idea!" I lied, as I effectively preserved Bob's oak and elm tree secret. "I'll bet it'll be something special that requires poise and strength. Abrams seems to be that kind of brainy, brawny type of guy."

And then, News began prattling about how a certain Miss North Carolina contestant named Maria Beale Fletcher had won the coveted *Miss America Pageant* in Atlantic City, and then the human encyclopedia elucidated on how a *TWA* Constellation had last week crashed outside Chicago while taking-off from *Midway Airport*. "Seventy-eight people died in the horrible disaster," News reported, "and that's the largest single-plane catastrophe in aviation history."

"Wasn't there a bigger one over the *Grand Canyon* two years ago?" I asked and challenged.

"Yes, but that involved a two-plane midair collision," New clarified. "That one out West involved a *TWA* Constellation and a *United* DC-9, and ironically, both planes involved in the disaster had taken off from *Los Angeles International."*

But then, the conversation changed to baseball, my favorite sport, and a discussion ensued about the *Yankees* Roger Maris being poised to break Babe Ruth's single season home run record. "Maris has until October 1st to break Ruth's record of 60," News contributed. "I hope he does it. Records are made to be broken."

"They sure are," I concurred. "But Ruth's legendary *Yankees* only had 154 game seasons, while Maris has an unfair advantage in that respect. The '61 Yankees play 162 games, eight more than Ruth's *Yankees* played in a season. Now, News," I insisted. "It's really an unfair comparison, and also a discredit to the Babe's fantastic accomplishment, when you consider the important difference in the number of games played, and then *that* essential fact especially puts the overall statistics in perspective."

"And besides that fairly vital relevance, J.W.," News interrupted and proceeded, "the strike zone is now much smaller than it was back in the '20s and '30s, and the ball is livelier than it was back in Ruth's era. Those factors can only mean that today's hitters have it much easier to swat the ball outa' the park."

"The first Homer was somewhere in Asia Minor," I impulsively joked, referring to the generally recognized organizer of the *Iliad* and the *Odyssey*. "That's the only significant thing I've learned so far in Dr. Rolphs's controversial Sociology class."

"Don't forget guys," Tim formally reminded us. "We're gonna' meet at Joe's Sub Shop at 4 sharp. We don't want any Delta Alpha Omegas or Tau Kappa Epsilons knowin' what we're gonna' be up to. Those freaks might try and crash out initiation rite and ruin Lambda

Phi before we ever get started. We can't allow that sort of catastrophe to happen, now can we guys?"

Thirteen prospective Lambda Phi's, which constituted the nucleus of the neophyte fraternity, congregated inside Joe's Sub Shop at 4 p.m. After drinking a round of *Cokes* paid for by the gregarious Bob Abrams, our host informally took roll to ascertain that everyone invited had arrived. In addition to Steve "Hoppy" Cassidy, the pledges assembled were: News Tomasello, Tim Amoro, Ron Carputis, Mario DiMaris, Tom Bell, Frank Morrissey, Max Gunther, Big Al Keiler, Mitch Toscini, Phil Candido, and myself. "Lucky thirteen!" Bob euphorically exclaimed. "I hope none of you are superstitious! I have a supreme hunch that this is one time where thirteen is goin' to come up big!"

At four-thirty, a caravan of five cars left the curb outside Joe's Sub Shop and were driven down University Road until we reached the landmark Peaks Horse, Apple and Peach Farm. Upon exiting, we followed Bob down the narrow path through the array of dense vegetation and matured deciduous and pine trees, until we stopped near the tall oak overlooking the rustic, slow-moving stream. Bob Abrams then specifically reviewed all aspects of the all-important initial initiation rite to be individually performed.

"What is this cock suckin' bull-shit!" Mario boisterously chided. "This is some sort of high school bull-fuck crap that the *Boy Scouts,* or the fucked-up Chess Club would do! I've already heard and seen enough horse manure!"

"Thanks for your honest-but-inaccurate assessment," Bob suavely answered his new-found nemesis. "But J.W. here tells me *you* have a big reputation as a semi-pro football player for bein' tough, brave, valiant, and a true finisher. Now if the Lambda Phi's didn't attempt doin' something difficult and complicated," Bob persuasively stated, "then Mario, we'd be just like any other pussy organization on campus. Right?"

"Well, I guess ya' sort of know what you're fuckin' talkin' about," Mario stammered and paused. "And I do see your point. But I was thinking that…."

"That the vine swing and the backward blindfolded walk were absolutely too adolescent and too easy, like something Huck Finn and Tom Sawyer would have done in a Mark Twain novel," Abrams eloquently stated. "Am I right?"

"Yeah, that's kind of what I was fuckin' thinkin'," Mario conceded and stuttered. "But I couldn't right this minute think of those jerk-offs' names, or the books the shit-heads were fuckin' characters in!"

When the other guys stopped their incessant laughing, Bob continued delivering his convincing oratory. "And so, my fellow pledges, the Delta Alpha Omegas and the Tau Kappa Epsilons don't possess the imagination or the balls to do what we're about to perform. We have to prove our loyalty, trust, courage, and unity to each other by enactin' the same exceptional stunt for everyone else to witness. Do you guys all see where I'm commin' from?"

"Yes!" we all yelled in unanimity, as if we were noble Romans, and had just heard a magnificent proclamation from Cicero, or from Brutus, or from Mark Antony. "Yes!" the other pledges listening to the propaganda (including Mario) repeated with audacious intensity.

Without any further commentary, Bob Abrams climbed the stately oak to the third limb; gripped the brown vine, and then after taking a deep breath, deftly swung in a perfect arc clear across the stream. Upon making contact with the opposite side, the Lambda Phi President removed the blindfold from his back pocket, and with graceful finesse, walked backwards across the elm log-bridge without a hitch. Then, Abrams removed his blindfold and handed the black and white speckled handkerchief to Steve Cassidy. Hoppy duplicated Bob's adroit antics, and I was the third to complete the rather perfidious assignment. By 5 p.m. everyone but Mario had successfully executed the intricate series of maneuvers.

"Don't fret, even if you never played a guitar!" Bob encouraged already confused DiMaris. "We'll help you skillfully shinny-up the tree to the third limb if ya' don't mind! We feel we owe you that slight handicap!"

"Mario would rather handicap horses at the race track," I laughed. "Just like the horses, in some respects, DiMaris has a handicap, too; an addictive mental handicap."

"Don't I get some kind of exemption because I'm twenty-eight, married, have a kid, and carry around a big lard ass?" Mario pleaded almost in supplication. "I don't got no damned insurance policy to cover hospital expenses if I get fuckin' injured."

"Don't worry, I'm confident you're gonna' do just fine, and besides," Bob stipulated, "we all need you as a bodyguard against the rival frats'!" Robert Abrams compellingly argued *that* salient fact while handing the now-totally-insecure DiMaris the used spotted bandanna, which the very doubtful brawler reluctantly stuffed into his pants' left rear pocket.

We all merrily pushed and shoved Mario's chubby buttocks up the stately oak until the lard-assed climber was finally able to awkwardly clamber-up to the tree's third sturdy limb on his own extraordinary power. DiMaris stood terrified on the high limb, while fearfully contemplating the relatively complex task at hand. "I'm afraid of heights!" the pledge yelled as he tightly gripped the brown vine. "I'm afraid of fuckin' heights!" the totally frightened recruit emphatically reiterated.

Finally, the petrified, obese, degenerate allowed his tremendous body weight to leave the tree, and the fat, ungainly fool swung across the stream in a very inept and cumbersome fashion. Then, Mario's great body mass and forward momentum snapped the vine in two, and DiMaris screamed in panic as his huge frame plunged directly onto the elm-bridge, severing the object, a full five-feet away from the opposite bank. The twelve witnesses waded through the waist-deep-water, fearing that the victim had accidentally impaled himself onto the log upon which he now clung. Some blood from Mario's left thigh was discoloring the water flowing under the elm log.

"Mario, are ya' all right?" I shouted. "I'll call an ambulance! I think you'll need one!"

"Don't fuckin' bother!" DiMaris answered back. "J.W., don't fuckin' bother! Just help me up so that I can wrap this left leg with a towel, or pillowcase, or blanket, or rag, or Kotex."

Led by Big Al Keiler, the rest of us managed to manipulate the corpulent-but-pudgy Goliath into an upright position, and then ease his legs into the cold water. Immediately, we were relieved to discover that the leg wound was merely superficial, and that the minor injury had appeared a lot worse than it actually was.

"I guess you'll have to come-up with a different initiation for your new members, now that I've broken your goddamned vine and cracked your friggin' decayed log!" Mario complained to Abrams. "But it was sort of fun in a fuckin' unusual kind of way!"

"Yes, I do have a plan B on the drawing board," Bob almost robotically answered. "And in a week, when your leg heals, you'll find-out exactly what it is. Ya' still haven't passed the initiation test," Abrams informed the aggravated and disgusted Mario DiMaris, "and so, in seven days, you'll be the first candidate to officially participate in Plan B."

"Fuck you!" Mario intensely balked as his stocky anatomy ungracefully finished wading out of the cold brook. "Fuck all of ya', and while I'm at it, fuck this fuckin' fraternity, and all this other stupid high school asshole bull-fuck bull-shit, too!"

Chapter 8
"The Caboose Caper"

Friday, September 22, came around, and I was happy that Mario had gotten over his near-calamitous plummet from the oak tree vine and his dramatic severance of the elm bridge. I was between first and second period classes, and a series of Top 40 radio tunes were flashing in and out of my mind as I made the hundred-and-fifty-yard trek from *Bosshart Hall* to *College Hall.* The Everley Brothers haunting harmony to "Ebony Eyes" entered my emotions when I thought about my Italian flame, Joanne Berenato, and then Curtis Lee's melody to his smash hit "Pretty Little Angel Eyes" captured my fancy as I thought about Peachy Wilcox's sparkling light blues.

As I took the diagonal route through the campus's central commuter parking lot, my mind then sentimentally considered Ben E. King's "Stand by Me" as I contemplated the recently formed Lambda Phi Sigmas, and finally I considered the Fleetwoods' lyrics to their smash hit "Tragedy" when I recollected Mario almost impaling himself on the elm-log-bridge. 'Oh well, I have just enough time to check my mailbox before Professor Sankins's grueling English ordeal in another wicked fifteen-minutes. One grotesque session with that witch could inflict irreversible, irreparable damage upon my frail psyche.'

I entered the student mailroom in the *College Hall* basement and was immediately greeted by Bob Abrams. "Hi J.W.," the affable fraternity organizer began. "I say let's make some dust before we have to eat it!"

"What's that supposed to mean?" I asked. "You sound like you're speaking in Mother Goose riddles. Sometimes, the smarter we become, the more trouble we have communicatin' basic simple ideas. Wouldn't you agree?"

"J.W., don't you watch *Bonanza, Gunsmoke, The Rebel,* or any other popular westerns on TV? The guy leading the posse is either the sheriff or the marshal, and he's makin' dust and breathin' fresh clear air," my new friend lectured. "The other guys in the posse are swallowin' the sheriff or the marshal's dust and coughin' their lungs and tracheas out of their throats. Now do ya' literally get what I figuratively mean?"

"You want me to become either a sheriff or a marshal?" I incredulously asked with a pinch of humor sprinkled in. "As sure as death, Bob, I still don't get the dust symbolism, if there is any symbolism at all involved."

"How long have ya' been an ignoramus? Has it been only a recent phenomenon?" Bob jokingly ridiculed and scolded. "I don't want ya' to become a sheriff or a marshal. I want ya' to be a leader like I am. J.W., show your superior qualities and put your best foot forward," Abrams sermonized. "If you become a leader, then ya' can make dust and not have to eat other peoples' dust the rest of your friggin' life. That's why my ambition is I'm gonna' become a school district superintendent. The teachers under my jurisdiction will have to then eat my dust, which is really a very polite way of saying swallowin' my feces."

"I'll have to remember your unique terminology," I complimented. "Sometimes, when you explain yourself', you make more sense than Rolphs and Sankins do, put together."

Bob and I simultaneously opened our mailboxes and leafed through the various junk mail solicitations. And then we both discovered letters in official college envelopes from Dean Lang's "Campus Committee" that looked awfully official. I opened my missive to inspect the stationery's content, and Bob concurrently ripped open his. Our eyes widened and our mouths coincidentally were agape as we dually read the notifications.

"Holy shit!" Bob exclaimed. "Dean Lang wants to see me at four this afternoon in his office. It's a good thing I checked my mailbox this morning. I haven't been down here in this dungeon in the last three monotonous days."

"And Bob, Dr. Lang wants to see me at the exact same time," I informed my fellow Lambda Phi. "It states in the bottom paragraph that the purpose for the meeting is that the administration has gotten wind that half of Professor Rolphs's class got-out of their desks and defiantly walked out of Sociology. Dr. Lang further states that he wants a valid explanation for our rude interruption of the *GSC* educational process."

"Don't worry, J.W. Leave the bulk of the discussion up to me," Bob boasted. "I'll handle that college egghead at the 4 o'clock conference. And I'll gladly drive you back to Hammonton, so that the other guys you commute with don't have to be inconvenienced. How's that for friendship?"

"Thanks, Bob!" I remarked in appreciation of my fellow frat' brother's benign offer. "Where's the Administration Building located?"

"It's scattered all over the campus, but Lang's office is part of the *Savitz Library* complex on the oval, near *College Hall,"* my fraternity confederate informed. "There's a suite of deans' offices upstairs near the high-browed college radio station, WGLS-FM."

"Okay, Bob. I'll see ya' there just before four," I acknowledged. "I hope this letter doesn't lead to any severe disciplinary action. My parents actually think I've simmered-down a lot since my rowdy high school days."

All period-long, I sat as a nervous wreck in Professor Sankins's English grammar and rhetorical writing class. And after the lady martinet re-distributed the class's latest composition/essay on "What Democracy Means to Me?" I was horrified to see that my grade was an inferior D-, after I had spent three hours writing, editing, and re-writing the five-hundred-word literary masterpiece. 'If Thomas Jefferson would have ever had Miss Sankins for a professor,' I mused, 'the genius would've had such a poor self-image that our third American President would have never authored the sacred *Declaration of Independence*.'

Then, my brain reflected some more. 'This lady is tryin' to railroad me and destroy my confidence with her red-ink pen,' I conjectured. 'It's too late to transfer into another English class with a more humane and favorable instructor. Why couldn't I be lucky like Tim Amoro and have a suave professor like Dr. Stevens instead of this female horror?' I wondered. 'Tim has aspirations of becoming either a guidance counselor or principal, and is only going to use his English degree because he has to teach three years before he can evolve out of the classroom and transition into the school management echelon!'

And then, Dr. Sankins rudely interrupted my reverie by verbally quizzing me on the distinction between an adjectival and an adverbial subordinate clause, which to her disdain, I answered with impeccable proficiency while describing in detail relative pronouns and subordinating conjunctions. And next the woman nitpicker questioned me on the differentiation between restrictive and non-restrictive clauses and adjectival and adverbial prepositional phrases, and I again surprised her by providing a logical distinction between the two English elements. 'It's a good thing Mario's not in this class, or else I would have to commit suicide supporting him while trying to avoid drowning myself'!' I reckoned as I flashed an insincere smile at the Medusa-faced, male-hating pedagogue.

At precisely quarter-to-four, I met Bob Abrams outside the multifunctional *Savitz Library* building and soon accompanied him upstairs. My Lambda Phi companion seemed unruffled by the impending conference, preferring to stop in at the college radio station and momentarily consult with a DJ friend. Meanwhile, I took the liberty to fill-out and submit a brief questionnaire, and volunteered my speaking services to report the daily sports segment of the news broadcast for WGLS-FM each school day at three in the afternoon. I was told by a cute, auburn-haired secretary that I would be notified in my college mailbox in regard to an audition I first had to pass in order to qualify for dedicated on-air broadcasting and sports commentary.

"Well, maybe I'll finally get some important good news in my mailbox," I commented to the polite secretary. "I always wanted to interview somebody important over the airwaves and right now, well, I mean to say, that all I ever receive in the post are silly offers to buy stuff I don't need, or will never use."

Bob Abrams gently nudged my arm, signaling that it was time for us to meander down the hall and exchange ideas with some of the college's top brass. We entered the walnut-paneled reception room, which was indicative of the campus aristocracy's prestige, since all of the professors I knew had partial dividers separating one office from another, or one department from another. The dean's efficient, pretty brunette secretary immediately notified the important official of *our* appearance and arrival.

"Come on in, boys," Dean Lang sternly ordered with an apparent grimace on his countenance. "This is Dean Nelson, an associate of mine, who will sit in on the interrogation, or should I use the euphemistic term, our conference."

Bob and I shook hands with both eminent administrators and then were cordially asked to account for why we had boldly led a minor migration out of Dr. Rolphs's Sociology lecture. Abrams expertly handled the explanation part, while the deans patiently waited for the right moment to jump into the conversation and assert their dominance in a simulated verbal massacre.

"You two students mean to say that you were offended by what Professor Rolphs was saying, or are you maintaining that you walked-out in sympathy of a few girls that were being intellectually challenged in his class?" Dean Lang austerely asked. "Or was your premature departure a combination of both?"

"Well, sir, I suppose we walked-out because the girls' feelings were hurt," Bob courageously related. "But why are you singling J.W. and me out when at least twelve other students stepped-out of the classroom room, too?"

"Because we have information from very reliable sources that you two were the principal instigators involved in the walkout," Dr.

Lang advanced while Dr. Nelson remained reticent and jotted-down notes. "Now, I hope that you two realize that insolent and rebellious actions of this type, no matter how justified you two think they were, cannot be tolerated on this campus. Dr. Rolphs's proven instructional methods are designed to stimulate students' minds by often taking young adults' value systems to task. I have no choice but to defend our professional instructor in this particular instance."

"But why single us out?" I said echoing Bob's grievance. "All we did was follow our consciences."

"When a New Jersey State Trooper stops your car for speeding," Dean Lang stated, "and if you ask him why he's not stopping everybody else that's speeding by as he writes-out *your* ticket, he'll tell you in that particular case 'I've caught you! That's why! And that's all that really matters! And so, I'll quote a State Trooper I know by saying, 'J.W., because we caught you and Bob Abrams in the act, and that's all that really matters'!"

"But Dr. Rolphs was rudely defaming and criticizing the Pope, questioning the Virginity of the Blessed Mother, and insisting that Christ had only a human nature and not a Divine Nature," Bob angrily snapped back. "The professor was being sarcastic about values and principles that many students in the class held in great honor as being sacred!"

"It is not your job to question and evaluate Dr. Rolphs's teaching methods," Dr. Lang retorted while raising his voice. "That's the function of school administration, and I resent you even considering performing *my* job. Now then, I am warning you two hotshots. Stepping;out of a classroom against an instructor's permission is tantamount to insolence on the first offense; rebellion on the second, and anarchy on the third. And three strikes and you're out at this old ball game, Mr. Abrams! Do you now get the message loud and clear?" the red-faced, insulted dean vehemently ranted in a sudden fit of rage. "We don't like students defying teachers' authority at *Glassboro State College?* Are you two gentlemen too thick-headed to comprehend that rather elementary idea?"

"Okay, sir, I understand where you're coming from," Bob indicated, almost apologetically. "But who told you our names? I think I'm entitled to know that?"

"The administration is not obligated to divulge our reliable sources, and we don't have to share confidentialities with arrogant or disobedient students," Dr. Lang yelled and stressed. "Now, it's my distinct duty to inform the two of you anarchists that you'll be receiving disciplinary letters outlining your misdemeanors, along with subsequent consequences on successive infractions, that will be enumerated. And two more violations and I assure both of you that you'll be shortly attending another institution of higher learning, if you're lucky enough to be admitted elsewhere, based on the credentials and records that this institution will definitely forward and share."

"You both may leave now!" Dr. Nelson calmly concluded to peacefully terminate the volatile session. Bob and I left the premises in a mild state of shock.

"Who do ya' suppose ratted on us?" I asked. "Do ya' think Dr. Rolphs reported the incident? That slimy worm looks like he harbors a lot of antagonism in his black heart!"

"Maybe," Bob answered with an element of doubt. "But I think we have to ask ourselves, who didn't walk out of Sociology with us? It's all pretty crystal-clear right now J.W. I'll bet it was that clown Ken Reynolds, leader of the Delta Alpha Omegas. You already told me once that he's in Rolphs's class with you and me, and I'll bet my bottom dollar he's getting back at us for you pledgin' to join the Lambda Phi's instead of the Delta Alphas."

"Do you think the deans already know about the Lambda Phi's being an unauthorized off-campus fraternity, and also about Mario's near-death experience?" I followed up.

"Possibly," Abrams lethargically replied. "I think the Delta Alpha punks are snitches and spies for the administration. This is just the first minor battle in an upcomin' war. My hunch is that I sense that's what's been happenin'."

"Look, Bob, I've been through similar conflicts with the Diablos and Kamikaze greaser gangs back in Levittown, and with the peach and blueberry gangs in Hammonton," I cited. "But now it looks like an uneven war startin' up between the outnumbered Lambda Phi's on one side, and the powerful combined enemy of the Delta Alpha Omegas, the Tau Kappa Epsilons, and the college administration on the other. That's quite a nasty and powerful enemy we're up against. They have some heavy artillery to use against us."

"Brilliant deduction!" Bob sardonically praised. "So J.W., I want you and News, Ron, and Tim to drive-up from Hammonton tonight. Meet Hoppy, Big Al, and me at Angelo's Diner on Main Street, just before seven-thirty. I got wind of something big happenin', and we're gonna' ruin it for the damned Delta Alphas."

"What about Mario?" I inquired. "Should I ask him to come along for the ride, too?"

"That plump fatso hasn't quite passed the first-step initiation yet," Abrams assessed and conveyed. "So, we'll just let him sulk and pout until Monday afternoon when the big lunk's scheduled to endure the new secret qualifyin' procedure."

After Bob drove me back to Elm, I felt like I had been delegated a contemporary Paul Revere as I got on the horn and notified News, Tim, and Ron of a big Lambda Phi Sigma "military operation" materializing that evening. I drove the others over to Glassboro in my dependable Chevy and met Bob Abrams and Steve "Hoppy" Cassidy at Angelo's Diner at 7:30 for *Pepsis* and hamburgers. Bob was resolute in presenting his "foolproof plan" to our anxious ears.

"We Lambdas have our own intelligence sources, something like the undercover *FBI* and *CIA* agents, double agents, and espionage contacts often use," the persuasive frat' chief began. "Our latest information indicates that the Delta Alpha Omegas are jealous of us havin' an imaginative initiation rite. So, they've decided to invent one for themselves because the lame-brains don't look outmatched by us to the neutral kids on campus, who are still decidin' which fraternity to join."

"Do ya' mean that the Delta Alphas have been in operation at this college for almost thirty-years and don't have any entrance requirement like we already do?" Ron asked. "That sounds pretty unbelievable and primitive!"

"That's right Pledge Carputis. The dimwits don't, or should I say didn't, until tonight," Bob testified and confirmed. "Now here's what's goin' to happen. An English Major named Ralph Crenshaw is goin' to be *their* first inductee tonight. He's goin' to climb stark naked into the bell-tower above *College Hall,* and then sing the corny *Glassboro State* Alma Mater song as loudly as he can."

"If he's an English Major," I interrupted, "isn't he a little old to be joinin' a fraternity? Pretty soon he'll probably be an eminent three-star-General."

"Real funny, J.W., real cute!" Bob jealously responded. "But whenever we're goin' to enact one of our clandestine operations, we gotta' be serious and not humorous. Comprende Amigo?"

"How come all of the Delta Alpha Omegas aren't being initiated like we had done at the creek?" News demanded knowing in a pithy interrogative. "Why only one pledge, this Ralph guy tonight?"

"Because most of the Delta Alphas are upperclassmen and are exempt from the initiation," Abrams authoritatively answered. "That rich kid Ken Reynolds flunked Sociology two years ago, and now has to make it up in order to graduate. That's why he's in Rolphs's class with J.W. and me."

After Bob disclosed his very imaginative secret plan, I was not too enamored with having to fire-off a flare gun aimed at the *College Hall* bell tower, right beneath the majestic golden dome. But then, since I would be only one of three Lambda Phi's having to fire-off a flare into the night sky, I acceded to performing the unthinkable assignment under peer pressure and under extreme duress.

"Won't the Glassboro cops be called in to investigate?" Tim asked. "I don't want the regular law involved and then become part of an enormous interrogation. My folks will flip-out and send me to reform school, or reform college, if such an animal exists!"

"Don't worry," Hoppy Cassidy comforted Amoro. "The college has the incompetent campus cops out on patrol, which is only one level above the comic *Keystone Kops* in the old silent movies. The administration only gets the town fuzz on a case if it's too overwhelmin' for the college to handle, and that's next to never. The deans don't desire any bad publicity hittin' the newsstands. That's bad for the next year's enrollment."

I followed Bob, Hoppy, and Big Al Keiler, all seated in Abrams's black Mercury, and we parked our vehicles in the *Bosshart Hall* student lot, which was mostly full, because of several thousand graduate students taking night courses. Three Lambda Phi patrols went out on foot to different sections of the campus. Bob and Hoppy were stationed behind the *Savitz Library* on the main oval; Big Al and Ron Carputis were situated in a meadow not far from the Hollybush mansion, and Tim, News, and I had our "stake-out position" on the dark and secluded baseball diamond, next to the *Campus School*. Everything was as still as the tranquil moon, and the overall anticipation' was gnawing-away at our audacity.

According to Bob's well-conceived plan, at precisely eight p.m., the bell-tower carillon struck eight times, and then some lousy indiscernible singing could be heard coming from somewhere above stately *College Hall*. Suddenly, a bright flash illuminated the night sky, coming from the direction of *Savitz Library,* and fifteen-seconds later, another burst lit up the *College Hall* bell-tower, originating from the vicinity of *Hollybush*. I fired-off the third flare from the baseball outfield, and the overall effect was analogous to a splendid *Fourth of July* fireworks display.

My heart was still palpitating when Big Al Keiler showed-up at the pitcher's mound to repossess my flare gun. Then, Big Al gave my commando team its final instructions.

"I'm gonna' collect the flare guns from all three teams and take them back to my cousin, whose an *Army* supply manager over at the *Frankford Arsenal* in Philly'."

"I was wonderin' where we got this sophisticated military equipment," I answered. "What should we do next, Al? Chew bubble gum, read porno' mags, and whistle *Dixie?"*

"Well, guys, there's gonna' be a lot of commotion and confusion on campus for a while," Big Al predicted. "So, this gives us time to act with impunity, er, I mean act fast so that we won't get caught or noticed. I'll first collect all three guns. Hoppy's already locked the door leading-up to the bell-tower, so the inept campus cops will eventually catch trapped Ralph Crenshaw tryin' to escape his lofty embarrassin' predicament in his birthday suit."

"And what should the three of us do then?" I incredulously inquired. "Leave the country, pronto!"

"Just go to the Co-op and pretend ya' know nothin' about nothin'," Big Al suggested in the form of a command. "The campus is now in such disarray that it's like 1941 *Pearl Harbor,* or something like that," the excited History Major elaborated. "Just enjoy all of the chatter and gossip, and smile while secretly knowin' that you had partially produced all of the freakin' chaos."

Tim, News and I strolled over to the Co-op, met Ron Carputis inside, and mutually enjoyed hot fudge sundaes while acting cool and nonchalant. The bewildered school authorities were running around in general consternation, behaving like chickens without heads. Bob and Hoppy entered the college snack bar and sat-down at another booth, and we never interacted with the pair again that evening. Outside of the almost empty Co-op, red and blue lights were flashing, and at least five-hundred befuddled students were gawking at the bell tower and chattering. Next, we witnessed a bevy of inept campus cops scurrying all over the place, attempting to solve the mystery of exactly what had recently transpired.

The following Monday, the Lambda Phi's learned via the campus grapevine that a certain English Major named Ralph Crenshaw had been suspended for indecent public exposure, and that the college was thereafter going to have the "emotionally disturbed youth" subjected to a battery of psychological tests to determine the degree and nature of *his* mental instability. The Delta Alpha Omegas were privately reprimanded by the humiliated administration bureaucrats for their "unprofessional genesis of turmoil," and their *DAO* fraternity charter would be in jeopardy should similar disgraceful events materialize in the future.

Monday, September 25th, was indeed another Lambda Phi Sigma auspicious occasion. At nine p.m., Mario DiMaris was slated to pass Bob Abrams's new initiation test for admission into the esteemed brotherhood. The already pledged members all congregated in the gravel, stone and dirt railroad parking lot, located next to the college's main entrance at the beginning of University Road and its intersection with Girard.

"Okay, Mario," Bob said with a broad grin. "We badly need you in our organization, so I've designed a rather easy task for you to perform to complete your initiation."

"It better be fuckin' easy," DiMaris insisted with a shoulders shrug, before spitting an ounce of saliva from between his separated, capped two-front-teeth. "I don't want to be discriminated against, so I'm warnin' ya', don't treat me like a goddamned nigger."

"And you won't be," the Lambda Phi head honcho promised. "Tony Petters and Gil Taylor here are gonna' pledge along with ya', so that means you're not alone and havin' to feel self-conscious about doin' the initiation all by yourself."

"Well, what the fuck do we gotta' do?" Mario impatiently demanded. "Tell us right now, so I can think about how I'm goin' to accomplish the job without havin' to beat the shit outa' anybody, includin' your ass, Abrams!"

"At nine fifteen, the freight train slowly takes-off from the Glassboro Depot across the street. Your assignment is to run down Girard Road here, which as you can see, parallels the railroad track. When the train reaches the *Route 322* crossing, you, Petters, and Taylor have to leap onto the caboose and ride the sucker to the next stop, which is two-miles away in Pitman."

"How fuckin' fast do I gotta' run?" Mario nervously asked. "I've never caught a damned passenger train or a goddamned caboose before, or otherwise!"

"Look, Mario. You're supposed to be a hot-shot athlete playin' football for the *Hammonton Bakers,* and therefore, I assume you're in perfect physical condition, despite your overall slovenly appearance," Bob lampooned. "The human body can run almost twenty-five miles per hour, but you'll just have to be runnin' about fifteen-miles-an-hour when you jump onto the caboose."

"Well, I'm in good shape because of football season," Mario admitted, "but the game consists of about sixty to seventy individual battles between me and the offensive linemen tryin' to block me from pulverizin' the damned quarterback. It's got more to do with endurance with periods of rest in between each rush than it does with stamina to run a half a mile or so to catch a goddamned freight train," DiMaris complained. "I've already told ya' I've never ever run to catch a damned regular passenger train!"

"Mario, it's only a little more than a quarter of a mile to the *322* crossing," Abrams explained. "Now, the train's ready to leave the station platform right this minute, so when the caboose passes this point, be prepared to scamper after it."

The freight train chugged-out on the rails from the Glassboro Depot, and sure enough, Mario, Gil, and Tony industriously pursued the caboose as if it contained their life' savings. Three cars of Lambda Phi members then drove past the sprinting threesome as I monitored their progression inside the white Impala with Tim, Ron, and News as my loyal sidekicks. The four of us were laughing our larynxes out of our throats as the Lambda monitors observed Mario fall behind his two fellow pledges, with his chubby legs churning like pistons, and his fat buttocks wiggling back and forth like an out-of-control hyperactive *Slinky* toy.

When the trio reached the *322* crossing, Gil was first to latch on to the railing, and then the pledge assisted Tony on board the accelerating caboose. The two had to muster all the stamina the duo could manage, pulling Mario onto the train, and we all sighed with relief when we realized that the portly Sicilian had safely executed his dangerous indoctrination and was finally and officially an authentic Lambda Phi Sigma.

The three Lambda Phi cars sped-down Carpenter Street to downtown Pitman, where we awaited the arrival of the freight train at its next destination. Finally, the twenty-five-car train rumbled-up to the Pitman Depot, but instead of stopping, it barreled right on through. We all waved in shock as Mario, Gil, and Tony screamed to no avail from the rapidly moving caboose's back railing. All we could hear was Mario boisterously shouting, "Why isn't this fuckin' thing stoppin'?"

Bob Abrams leaped-out of his black Mercury and asked the Pitman Depot manager a salient question. "How come the train didn't stop?" our angry President yelled at the suddenly besieged watchman. "What's goin' on here? Is this some bizarre paranormal experience like the ones featured on the *Twilight Zone* or *Science Fiction Theater?"*

"Why's a young whippersnapper like you got your bowels all in an uproar over a simple damned freight train not stoppin' here in Pitman?" the old whiskered fellow carrying a lit lantern asked. "But if ya' really gotta' know, young fella', there's no freight cars to be attached tonight here in Pitman. That's why the damned train rambled-through town at thirty-miles-an-hour."

"Where's the next stop?" Abrams apprehensively inquired without any hesitation. "I have to know where that damned freight train makes its next spot!"

"Trenton," the old geezer winked and gently answered through his grimy beard and mustache. "Trenton."

"Trenton! That's over forty-miles away!" the Lambda Phi Sigma co-founder yelled in disbelief while holding his forehead. "I think tonight's the damned night I'll be lethally assassinated by three angry pledges, led by Mario DiMaris!"

"Nice goin' Caesar," Big Al ridiculed with a hardy laugh. "Brutus, Cassius, and Crassus are gonna' get your ass good!"

Chapter 9
"An Early Christmas Party"

Four cars sped-up to Trenton to intercept Mario, Gil, and Tony at the city rail-yard. Fortunately, Bob Abrams knew its exact location, so we didn't have to waste time stopping all over creation and inquiring about directions. Mario and his two fellow travelers hopped-off the stationary caboose's back section, as if the trio had been forced to stand on hot coals for the hour-long-excursion.

"Damn it! Ya' good-for-nothin' son-of-a-bitchin' jerk-offs'!" the infuriated *Hammonton Bakers* brute yelled. "Don't ya' know I'm fuckin' scared of the dark, and all that friggin' freight train did was go through dark scary woods and goddamned spooky pine barren forests. There ain't too much human civilization between Pitman and here, I'll say that. I oughta' beat the crap out of all of ya' stupid bastards, and then make ya' eat each other's shit! Say, where the hell are we, anyway!"

"Couldn't you guys go sit inside the caboose?" Big Al asked the three journeymen.

"No, the damn door was locked!" Gil Taylor demonstrably beefed. "And so, it was colder than Miss Sankins's ass standin' out there on the rear deck! I feel like I got friggin' ice cubes frozen up my damned rectum! And Mario must feel like he's got a freakin' iceberg lodged up his posterior!"

"Well, look on the positive side," Hoppy amicably recommended. "You're all now accepted into Lambda Phi Sigma in good standin' and you'll all be entitled to free transportation back to Glassboro in heated automobiles. And yes, Mario," Hoppy genially elaborated. "You happen to be in the paradise known as Trenton, right now. What more could ya' possibly want? The Bronx? Camden? North Philly?"

"Well, I'll tell ya'what I want. I wanna' get ripped!" Tony Petters piped-up before DiMaris could think of something dirty to say. "Yeah, after all that dog-shit freezin' my ass off in the back of the caboose, I think I'd like to get ripped really good to celebrate!"

"What a damned coincidence!" Bob Abrams exclaimed as our fearless leader adeptly took full command of the conversation. "Let's get out of this dingy railroad yard. Tonight we're gonna' christen the new frat' house down in Aura and mark the festive occasion with booze, beer, and wine. And guys, the beer's already sittin' nice and cold in the chicken coop's 'fridge."

"Now you're talkin' my fuckin' language!" Mario yelped. "But I warn ya', don't get me too drunk or I might sodomize all of ya' up your smelly assholes, way up there where the sun never shines, whether your asshole's friggin' frozen or not."

The rest of us ignored Mario's indiscreet comment, but we all feared that it might have contained some literal psychopathic truth. The pumped-up Lambda Phi's hopped into the frat' members cars, and we merrily motored back from Trenton down *Route 206* through the *Wharton Forest* pine' barrens,' where I recalled several outstanding adventures between the Reds and the Blues when we passed *Atsion Lake.* And then, after buzzing through Hammonton and later Williamstown, we were finally a small motorcade through Glassboro, and next on to somnolent Aura.

Hoppy's family's huge remodeled chicken coop was much better furnished and decorated than I had imagined, and the new recruits were all impressed with the overall stellar décor. The facility boasted a nice black leather couch; four matching chairs; a beautiful oak bar with eight stools around it; fish nets hanging from the ceiling; an ancient oriental rug; a brand new black and white remote-control television; a tiled bathroom; a stove; a 'fridge, and a terrific-looking Wurlitzer Rainbow jukebox.

"Hoppy and I did most of the carpentry and plumbin' work all by ourselves," Bob Abrams revealed. "And we both have contacts in the furniture and appliance businesses to get the refrigerator, stove, and jukebox at bargain-basement, closeout prices. In fact, the electricity and the runnin' water were just turned on yesterday."

We all stepped over to the radiant, light-pulsating rainbow jukebox, and admired the cherished mechanism. I then studied the selections and read a few of them aloud. "Look guys, this thing has over a hundred hits from the fifties and right-up to the latest chartbusters. Listen to some of these classic numbers," I implored. "We have 'Tossin' and Turnin' by Bobby Lewis; 'Hello Mary Lou' by Ricky Nelson; 'Quarter to Three' by Gary U.S. Bonds; 'Heart and Soul' by the Cleftones, and 'Pony Time' by Chubby Checker, just to name a few. This fantastic collection is next to awesome!"

"You know it, J.W.," News answered, sounding a little like a dumb parrot, that is, if a wet blanketed dumb parrot could think and speak on its own. "Rock and roll lost its edge ever since Buddy Holly died, and then the music lost some more zip with Elvis goin' into the service. It's like a big vacuum exists right now," News monotonously editorialized. "I mean, novelty songs like 'Baby Sittin' Boogie' by Buzz Clifford and 'Does Your Chewing Gum

Lose Its Flavor' by Lonnie Donnegan really don't cut it, if ya' know what I mean. It's like 'Itsy-Bitsy-Teenie-Weenie, Yellow Polka Dot Bikini' being revisited!"

"Well, News, even though Brian Hyland is not in Lambda Phi Sigma, I must admit that those ugly songs you mentioned are listed here in the juke's menu, but there's also 'Peggy Sue' by Buddy Holly; 'Don't Be Cruel' by Elvis; 'Rock Around the Clock' by Bill Haley and the Comets, and 'Great Balls of Fire' by Jerry Lee Lewis," I academically added.

"Who the hell would want their damned balls on fire in the first place?" Mario complained. "I'd then need two friggin' fire hoses and an igloo to sit on. One hose I'd use to screw my wife, and the other to keep my nuggets damp while I'm screwing my wife, or when I jerk-off, or when I take a damned hour-long piss after drinkin' half a keg of freezin' cold beer!"

Everyone ignored Mario's meaningless drivel. Bob got out the drinks, ice, and glasses, and the gathered Phi's celebrated DiMaris's and the other two new recruits' successful initiation for a solid two and a half hours. All of us were telling and sharing exaggerated stories about our oddball high school exploits. Our camaraderie was rapidly jelling, and even Mario seemed likeable and was mingling once he got over his humiliating caboose-traveling conniptions. When the booze, wine, and beer supply finally ran out, we sounded like a drunken Arabian cabal, without any veiled dancing girls or harem to entertain our fantasies. Towards the end of the first chicken coop party, we were all feeling no pain and bantering good-natured put-downs back and forth.

"Say, Mario," Big Al Keiler slurred and intrepidly remarked. "While rupturin' the elm bridge during your first initiation attempt, you almost ruptured yourself, too. I actually winced when I saw your crotch plow into the enormous tree with your freakin' legs open. It's amazin' that your nuts weren't lodged inside your damned throat after that impact!"

"Look, Shit-head," Mario jokingly and quite affectionately then bellowed. "My damned nuts are still hangin' like they're supposed to be doin'. But if ya' want to, ya' can open your big mouth and gargle them one at a time if ya' don't believe me. Then, you'll really wince, you' stupid cock-sucker!"

"That's okay," Big Al meekly compromised to DiMaris. "I believe anything ya' got to say!" To show his pleasant disposition to all eyewitnesses, Big Al plopped his derby hat on the bar along with a *Three Musketeers* candy bar, taken from his jacket's pocket. "Look here, Mario," Big Al hollered, half-inebriated. "My-hat, ma-candy! Get it Mario! Ha, ha, ha! Ma-hat, Ma-Gandhi! Ha, ha, ha! Pretty good comedy, huh?"

Mario thought that good-natured Big Al was somehow making fun of his lack of sophistication, so the Leviathan picked-up the two-hundred-and-thirty-pound Keiler; hoisted the large kid over his shoulders, and then amazingly spun Big Al around in what amounted to a dramatic, impressive, dynamic, pro-wrestling airplane-spin-maneuver. Intoxicated Mario DiMaris then hurled Big Al over the Wurlitzer jukebox, where a second later, the victim landed onto a comfortable black leather chair. "Anybody else wanna' mock me?" Mario challenged, just like Hercules might once have done. "If so, the next guy's gonna' be windin' up either in the rafters or have his head stickin' right through the goddamned roof! But that's dependin' on how damned pissed-off I get!"

"Er, no," Bob Abrams replied, trying to be a peacemaker where military police and a straight-jacket might have been a better solution. "I think we'll call it quits for tonight!"

On the drive back to Hammonton, Mario and Ron Carputis slept in the back seat while Tim Amoro and News Tomasello kept me awake and alert in the front of my white Impala coupe. I then commented on one of News's earlier dissertations.

"News, as usual, you were right, and this time it was about the recent change in rock and roll music," I praised, showing my admiration for T.T.'s infinite minutia knowledge base. "What's out there right now is too much happy bubblegum stuff."

"There are a few decent songs on the market like Chris Kenner's 'I Like It Like That', and the Shirelles' recordings of 'Dedicated to the One I Love', and the group's hit 'Soldier Boy'," Tim determined. "But the old '50s music was the best, but now it's virtually extinct!"

"Because the old cool beat is gone," News interrupted. "And now, country music is beginnin' to compete with rock and roll on the charts. I can't stand that Ferlin Husky, Johnny Cash, Conway Twitty, and that repugnant Hank Williams. Their songs are bland, and just don't have the power of Eddie Cochran's 'Summertime Blues', or Chuck Berry's 'Johnny B. Goode', and 'Sweet Little Sixteen' from the nifty '50s."

"And with this folk music fad commin' onto the scene," Tim chimed-in, "songs like 'Michael Rows the Boat to Shore' by the Highwaymen; 'Tom Dooly' by the Kingston Trio, and that Peter, Paul, and Mary trash are becomin' radio hits, and if ya' wanna' know my opinion," Amoro persisted, "I'd rather listen to David

Seville and the freakin' zany Chipmunks any day of the damned year, sober or not."

"And there's a new generation of beatniks out in San Francisco and in Greenwich Village that listen to and buy that folk garbage," News commented. "Those urban idiots are mostly dropouts, not only outa' college and outa' high school, but also kids abandonin' and droppin' outa' society. The hippies smoke marijuana all day long," News professed without a soapbox, "basically live in coffee houses; the creeps want peace and love, and the dropouts absolutely eschew the Protestant Work Ethic that's the basis for our free enterprise economy. Those damned lazy beatniks are gonna' find themselves' trapped in a dark one-way-tunnel to nowhere when it comes-around to social security time, if the parasites aren't already dead by then."

Just at that moment, a new song reminiscent of the old '50s genre' era that the three of us preferred came blasting on the car radio, "Those Oldies But Goodies" by Little Caesar and the Romans, and I felt compelled to amplify the volume as the front trio in my Chevy sang the wonderful lyrics, much to the listening dissatisfaction of the two semi-conscious, snoring Lambda Phi's slumbering in the back seats like sleeping wild boars with apnea.

Right through *Thanksgiving* of '61, the Lambda Phi's reputation gained in stature as the renegade fraternity threw one huge party after another at the old, renovated chicken coop. It got to the point where two-hundred college kids would park their posteriors in the coop's four spacious rooms; drink beer; socialize, and pair-off with opposite-sex mates. And just before *Thanksgiving,* the college threw a gala holiday dance, and only a hundred students showed-up, while over two-hundredand-fifty party-goers were hooting and hollering out in nearby Aura. The Delta Alpha Omegas, the Tau Kappa Epsilons, and the antagonized college administration were all envious of Lambda Phi Sigma's enormous prowess, and the three competing forces finally realized that *we* were a potent, respected force to be reckoned with, and the upstart Lambdas represented some very serious competition for student frat' loyalty.

But I suspected that things were going a trifle too smoothly for comfort. The Delta Alpha Omegas had not yet retaliated for Lambda Phi's enlightening intervention with, and ultimate ruination, of Ralph Crenshaw's initiation into *their* ignoble organization. Bob Abrams, Hoppy, and the rest of the 'Phi guys' felt like we were sitting on a powder keg with a short fuse ready to be ignited.

"Could it be that the Delta Alphas are so ignorant that the goons haven't figured-out that the Lambdas were responsible for sabotagin'

'The Crenshaw Golden Dome Affair'?" News asked me from the Impala's passenger seat on the evening of Saturday, December 10th. "Most of those spoiled fanatics, with the exception of Ken Reynolds, are supposed to all be Magna Cum Laude material!"

"The parties we've been throwin' at the coop have already made enough money to pay for the furniture and the renovations that Bob and Hoppy had made," I reported to News Tomasello and to Tim Amoro from the Impala's driver's seat. "And I predict that tonight's *Christmas* saturnalia is gonna' attract at least three-hundred enthusiastic *GSC* partygoers. At four dollars a head admission, plus the cost of beer, wine and whiskey, we stand to make maybe two thousand bucks in the black tonight."

"Those Delta Alphas and those Tau Kappas are bein' blown right out of the water by our fabulous success," Tim attested. "It's just like Hiroshima or Nagasaki with those cretins being mercilessly bombed by us. They're stunned out of their skulls, and don't know exactly what's hit them. They're like in suspended animation, in a weird state of shock," Tim exaggerated. "Just about every normal guy on campus that's not committed to a frat' now wants to belong to *our* noble organization."

"The other frats' are gutless," News readily agreed. "They're ratters and tattlers, and don't have the balls or the sperm to come-out and do something to us face to face, mano to mano. But the obnoxious Delta Alphas, along with the disgusting Tau Kappas, have the image-conscious deans on their side, and that worries me."

As we drove from Glassboro south on *Gloucester County Road 533* towards Aura, I thought about how much I really coveted Tim and News's friendship. Their personalities and value systems were almost mirror reflections of mine, and whenever I conversed with either of friend, it was as if I was having an erudite exchange of favorable ideas with myself. I really treasured their companionship, and to have both buddies in the white Impala at the same time was like having a double bonus being awarded.

"Hoppy and Abrams are thinkin' about adding two more rooms to the four big ones we already have at the coop," I informed my merry traveling mates. "Pretty soon our frat' house will rival that of the Deltas over on Harvard near University, and the one used by the Tau Kappas over on Academy Street."

"J.W., I just thought of a marvelous coincidence," News realized and remarked. "If ya' spell the words Co-op and coop, they're both spelled the same except for the stupid hyphen. The chicken coop is becoming the new campus Co-op!"

The three of us prided ourselves on being punctual, and we arrived early for the big Lambda Phi Sigma *Christmas* extravaganza. I parked my Chevy in a slightly muddy, fallow, grassy field, several-hundred-feet behind the now-famous remodeled structure. Tim, News, and I assisted in setting-up and preparing for the anticipated deluge of *GSC* revelers.

"This affair's gonna' be a five kegger," Bob Abrams declared to us as our chief officer pointed to a stack of metal beer containers. "It's the biggest shindig of the year, and you're all gonna' be beneficiaries. After tonight, all of the interior decoratin' will be paid for, and the Lambdas' will be profitable enough to be a legal corporation and start splittin' up the stock dividends."

News, Tim, and I were assigned to the entrance door, and we sat on metal folding chairs behind a square card table to collect the requisite admission fee. Our only minor regret was that Mario was in close proximity, for Bob had officially delegated DiMaris as the event's "chief bouncer".

"After what Mario had done to Big Al, I noticed that Keiler no longer wears his derby hat around the frat' house, and now munches his *Three Musketeers* candy bars in the bathroom, sitting on the throne," Tim whispered to News and me.

"Yeah, and every time Bob or Hoppy sees Big Al on campus," Amoro softly answered, "they' break his cashews, always saying, Ma Hat, Ma Candy. Ma Hat, Ma Candy! Ha, ha, ha!"

"Say, J.W., how come you never bring Joanne or Peachy to the coop?" News unexpectedly questioned. "Are ya' ashamed of our notorious accomplishments?"

"No, this is not a place for nice girls," I diplomatically-but-truthfully answered. "I'll take those sweet dolls out to dinner or to a family movie, but not to this sin palace," I facetiously remarked. "It's kind of like a den of inequity (iniquity), and not really a place for a lady. It's sorta' like being another Jezebel's Den over on Delilah Road in Pleasantville."

"You mean you'll take the babes out to dinner, or to a movie, separately and not together, that's what ya' meant to say," News perceptively corrected. "Stop puttin' those two pretty chicks up on a damned pedestal, J.W. They'd give their left tits and half their bushes to be invited out here!"

"Guys, I'd prefer talkin' about Mario," I replied blushing, deftly and abruptly shifting the discussion's focus. "I plan to stay-away from the volatile beast's company as much as possible. He's trouble with a Capital T, and could be embarrassin' in Joanne or Peachy's presence if he becomes drunk, rowdy, or angry. I don't even feel secure sittin' in the Co-op with him, fearing him becoming violent!"

"Mario's crazy, even when he's friggin' sober!" News asserted. "But we'd need him around if those cowardly Deltas and Tau Kappas decided to gang-up on us in a major brawl. Remember what Mario had done to Big Al, and Big Al's definitely not any damned pushover in anybody's battle league. The Wurlitzer was almost demolished, and it would've been if Mario had aimed Big Al any damned lower. But I suppose an airplane spin is safer and better any day than bein' body slammed right through the damned jukebox!"

"Yeah, those Delta Alphas and those Tau Kappas are craven knaves, no doubt about it," Timmy unanimously concurred. "Hey, here come our first guests now. Let's act professional while we're greedily acceptin' their donations to our selfish cause."

The Lambda Phi's were indeed an underground organization, brazenly doing business right out in the open, and I suspiciously feared that some unforeseen development might be imminent that would derail our success, just when we were moving full-steam ahead. Some of our more notorious exploits were frequenting strip-tease houses and reviewing and rating X-rated "smokers" at the chicken coop. Hordes of students would cram their frames through the wooden main portal, and the suds on beer mugs were often splashing-up into the air inside the four overcrowded rooms, looking much like ocean whitecaps during a nasty winter storm. I feared that soon, there was destined to be mucho trouble in paradise.

The chicken coop was really rocking that early December evening, and the Wurlitzer was ironically belting-out the refrains to Linda Scott's "I Told Every Single Star", when reality suddenly might go haywire. Pre-*Christmas* merrymaking and drinking were in full progress, which would have surely excited the Greek god Bacchus himself'. The coop was packed wall-to-wall in all four major rooms, and it would have been difficult squeezing any more male or female bodies in with a crowbar, or with an expensive shoehorn to boot. The walls were literally bulging to capacity, and only ten or so more "students" with bona fide *GSC IDs* would be allowed inside.

News and I were collecting the premium admission rate of four bucks a head, while Tim Amoro was stamping wrists with a Lambda Phi Sigma black ink seal to validate any college student, eagerly paying the very reasonable entrance fee.

"We can only service around a dozen more," News informed me. "Bob says we'll have to turn the rest away. It now officially looks like *SRO*."

"Pretty soon, we'll have to rent the college gymnasium, or maybe even *Connie Mack Stadium,"* I loudly joked. "We seem to have a lot of new faces here tonight, in addition to the normal regulars. It's hard keepin' our heads up with all of the incomin' traffic that's passin' our way."

Toward the end of the great influx, I observed an aged palm holding a five-dollar bill under my nose. Before I could scrutinize the metacarpals more in detail, Tim Amoro smacked the Lambda Phi Sigma imprint upon the guest's left wrist. Glancing upwards, I was flabbergasted to behold the stern frown of Dr. Robeson, the President of the college, who was surrounded by a phalanx of emissaries including Dean Lang and Dean Nelson, along with several New Jersey State Troopers and local county policemen.

Before I could utter a word, a half-crocked girl shrieked-out, "It's a friggin' raid! It's a goddamned college raid!" A momentary hush prevailed as everyone present in the room shockingly absorbed the significance of what was literally occurring. The *GSC* throng stood frozen for a full five-seconds, gawking in awe at the distinguished triumvirate of disgruntled deans and frightfully staring at the half dozen police officers that had accompanied the school brass to Aura.

Before I could exclaim: "You're trespassing on private property!" a mad stampede to the main exit ensued. Bodies were mercilessly ramming against and into one another to escape the premises, and Dean Lang was knocked-down in the general panic and trampled over as the horde of frenzied students herded and surged by like an aggregation of wildebeests being pursued by a hungry pride of lions. A fishing net that had been hung to ornament a sidewall somehow fell upon Dean Nelson, and the college magistrate was seen with his arms wildly flaying-away in a desperate effort to free himself from his cumbersome entanglement during the general melee. And the poor public servant, namely Dean Nelson, demonstrated motley self-satire slapstick, making Abbot and Costello's finest moment seem like rank amateur comedy.

The College President managed to maneuver to another side-wall, and began diligently copying-down the names of fraternity members from a posted list, but then News was inspired to intrepidly thrust a decorated and fully ornamented *Christmas* tree into the eminent dean's grasp, and the bulky mass, that had served as a convenient missile, sent the college official spinning-around like a spastic cyclone, his throat howling with pain. The list of Lambda Phi' names that had been stapled onto the wall disappeared like arcane magic, and the coop emptied-out quicker than a well-rehearsed Chinese fire drill. The screeching of tires could be heard as automobiles sped-off in various directions, as if everyone all of a sudden had accidentally discovered a leper colony.

My heart was incessantly palpitating throughout the entire escapade. On my hands and knees, I wriggled my body past the uninvited dignitaries, and managed to find an open window in a back room, where I could evacuate the building. I nervously waited my turn to dive through the opening and then wildly dash toward my white Chevy, which already had seven occupants, three of whom I didn't know. I frantically removed the key from my Lambda Phi Sigma jacket; turned the ignition to the "Start" position; put the Impala's gearshift in drive; fishtailed through a muddy, bumpy field, and then soon joined a very long cavalcade of speeding cars headed north toward *Glassboro State*.

Everyone in the car shared the thrill that a prey feels when escaping the clutches of a ferocious predator. The electric energy we were experiencing was a result of narrowly missing getting caught by the establishment, while we all had been deliberately engaged in performing what the college deans considered an unconventional, taboo activity. But unfortunately, my joyride to freedom proved to be short-lived.

Three days later, I found a letter from Dean Lang inside my *College Hall* mailbox. The carefully worded treatise predicted that the members of Lambda Phi Sigma would soon be suspended from the school indefinitely, until the "illegal, unsanctioned fraternity disbanded and became unincorporated in the State of New Jersey".

"I didn't know we were already a corporation," I mentioned to News and Bob Abrams outside the Co-op. "What friggin' stock exchange are we listed on, so that I can sell all my damned certificates before we go bankrupt."

"Since you're the most loquacious one in Lambda Phi," Bob very intentionally flattered, "I'm hereby appointin' you, J.W., to author the necessary letter of apology to Dr. Robeson and to Dean Lang. In it, we have to promise to return all stop signs, traffic directional signs, street signs, and various railroad signs to the appropriate organizations, authorities, clubs, and companies. And you could start with the borrowed Glassboro Lions, Rotary,

Exchange, and Kiwanis Club signs that were arrogantly tacked on the chicken coop's walls!"

"Then what?" I asked. "What's next Bob? The guillotine or the iron maiden?"

"I consulted with a cousin that's an attorney," Bob confided, "and he's been in touch with Dean Lang and with Dr. Robeson. After ya' pen the letter of apology and send it off Certified Mail, I'll provide evidence to the college bosses that our 'corporate structure has been dissolved,' to use the lawyer's fancy words. Then, we all should be legally reinstated into the college and automatically, again become meritorious students in good standing."

"Is this the end of Lambda Phi Sigma?" I inquired. "It was great while it lasted!"

"No, it isn't!" Abrams doggedly stated with a resolute expression seemingly welded upon his face. "We aren't goin' to have any more big bashes at the chicken coop that are gonna' outshine seasonal events happenin' at the college. But we are gonna' get even and then some with the Delta Alphas and with the Tau Kappa Epsilons for ruinin' our happiness. What those bastards did to us goes against the *Declaration of Independence!"*

"Why?" I asked. "What have they done now?"

"Those instigators thwarted our pursuit of happiness by jealously reportin' our Christmas Party to the holier-than-thou administration, those lousy surrogate clowns. Both frats' did squeal on us! I'm sure of it!" Bob stated with ample acrimony in his vocal inflection. "And now, the Lambda Phi's are gonna' operate as a covert, clandestine organization. We're still gonna' have fun mind you, but our main focus is gonna' be harassin' the hell out of the Delta Alpha Omegas, and out of the Tau Kappa Epsilons."

Chapter 10
"A Really Cool Ride"

On Monday afternoon, December 18th, I was pensively sitting in a Co-op booth solving a newspaper crossword puzzle when News Tomasello spied my presence and came-over to chat. I was feeling a little depressed because of the Lambda Phi Sigma chicken coop implosion; because of being guaranteed "a non-negotiable D" first semester average in English. and because of the fact that neither Peachy Wilcox nor Joanne Berenato was talking to me.

"Look, J.W., I heard from Hoppy and Bob that Dr. Robeson and your new buddies Dean Lang and Dean Nelson like your apology letter, and the missive's been approved and accepted," Tommy Tomasello declared. "We're not goin' to be suspended like poor Ralph Crenshaw was."

"It's too bad that Robeson and Lang don't teach *Fundamentals of Communications, 101* instead of that vicious faculty dragon, Sankins," I lamented. "Maybe I could wheedle a C out of one of those savants. Does Dean Nelson have a half-brother named half nelson?" I idiotically volleyed. "How come there's no Dean Martin or Dean Jerry Lewis on the faculty?"

"Stop bein' your old foolish self for a minute," News counseled. "After being attacked by the hungry *Christmas* tree, Dr. Robeson momentarily had almost as much balls as you do, J.W.," News laughed. "Now J.W., please tell me why do you suppose Mario let the rambunctious deans into the coop without first warnin' us? Not that it really mattered."

"The area football legend told me in the Co-op this morning that the cops sneaked-up on him so fast, and that our bouncer was so busy sendin' co-eds away, that he didn't have time to think or react," I dubiously related. "But in the end, ya' can't blame Mario for being overwhelmed. The Lambda Phi's would've gotten reported whether *he* was guardin' the frat' party or not."

"If Mario's so great as a defensive lineman," News speculated and advanced, "how come he doesn't play football for *Glassboro State?"* This season the beleaguered team could've used a quality defensive lineman like him cloggin' up the middle and kickin' butt all over the field."

"DiMaris told me in confidence last week that since he was a semi-pro player, he was paid money, and therefore is automatically disqualified by *NCAA* and university rules to play college ball. And besides," I continued quite snobbishly. "Mario' claims his strength would injure and brutally bruise-up too many young studs on the state conference teams, so the potent *Baker* wouldn't play by virtue of his own volition, even if he was eligible."

"Okay, J.W., but DiMaris told me he was gonna' cool it with the Lambda Phi's, and that his talents would just help us in an emergency, if he could," News reported. "I don't know if that's really goods news or bad."

"Maybe that's good news for everybody," I maintained, taking a firm stance. "That meatball-shaped Sidgy grease-ball is a little too old, seedy, and sleazy for the rest of us. It's bad enough we've committed to commute with that temperamental Sicilian. Things will be much better sophomore year, when we're both livin' somewhere in town, and Mario's drivin' back and forth from Hammonton. Hey News, how about a friendly game of 'Who Sang?' for the wager of a large *Coke*. We'll do the letter D today."

"Okay, my chummy chump," my close pal ambivalently agreed. "I'll start with the first item since you called the particular letter. Who sings 'The Wanderer'?"

"Dion without the Belmonts," I confidently answered. "That tune just came-out within the last month. Tried to sneak one by me, eh? And don't forget. Dion also came-out with 'Runaround Sue' in October. Now News, how about the singer of the now very popular 'Peppermint Twist'?"

"Joey Dee and the Starlighters," my fellow song guru correctly replied. "And what about 'Big Bad John'?"

"Jimmy Dean, not to be confused with the late James Dean," I added with a smart verbal footnote. "And what about 'Goodbye Cruel World'?"

"James Darren, who's off to join the circus," News chuckled while alluding to a key lyric in the popular song. "James Darren should've been at the chicken coop the night it was raided. Now *that* event really transformed into a real circus! Now J.W., how about the rock and roll classic 'Bristol Stomp'?"

"That's too easy and beneath my dignity, News, because I used to live in Levittown right next to Bristol," I reminded my friend. "It's the Dovells, and the hit record was just released for public consumption in September."

Our little contest prematurely ended in a stalemate when Tim Amoro entered the Co-op and hurriedly approached our booth to deliver an important message from Bob Abrams and Hoppy Cassidy. "Guys, Bob and Hoppy have commanded me to ask you two to do them a big favor."

"What's that, Tim?" I peevishly inquired. "And stop bein' so damned secretive about Lambda Phi Sigma business. Spill the beans, will ya'!"

"The night of the infamous *Christmas* party raid," Tim reviewed while relishing every word, "somebody stole our Lambda Phi Sigma banner from the main wall during all the mayhem. Bob and Hoppy think it was a Delta Alpha spy that probably crashed our hoedown, prior to the cops and the administration arrivin' in person to extinguish all the fun."

"So where do *we* fit in?" I curiously asked. "What's this unique favor you're talkin' about?"

"Abrams and Cassidy want you and me to go to Swedesboro tonight and retrieve the missin' Lambda Phi Sigma banner," Tim conveyed like an official Secret Service courier. "But it's my mom's birthday, and I've already promised the family I would go-out to dinner with them. So, I'm sorry, but I have to fink-out if the retrieval has gotta' be done tonight."

"Why can't Hoppy and Bob go and reacquire the banner themselves?" I skeptically queried. "And besides *that'* idea, how do they know where it is?"

Tim paused for a moment to collect his random thoughts and convert the theories into language equivalents. "Because J.W. Those two guys are too busy goin' to the Lions; the Soroptimists; the Kiwanis; the Exchange Club; the Railroad Company; the Glassboro Mayor's office, and to fifteen other area places, returnin' the stolen signs and other property the Lambdas had stealthily pilfered. They're both tied-up makin' important compensation for *our* past actions to keep all of us enrolled in school."

I was almost ready to decline the appointed responsibility until News presented a fact I had not considered while wallowing in my self-pity mood. "Guys, I was the fraternity's Sergeant-at-Arms, and it was *my* assigned duty to safeguard the banner during all official functions," Tom Tomasello guiltily confessed. "Since the highly coveted object was stolen in my presence, then I feel obligated to repossess the banner for the good of the fraternity."

"Alright, News, I'll buy into that," I answered, while abruptly changing my mind about my involvement in the retrieval caper. "I'll accompany *you* to get the sacred banner back since Tim is already booked with his folks for the evening. But Tim, you' still have not answered the very simple question of exactly where is the banner? And how do we know that it's somewhere in Swedesboro?"

Tim's right hand dug deep into his white with brown trim Lambda Phi Sigma linen jacket's pocket and then removed a folded piece of paper. "Here J.W., read this letter. It explains all of the vital details."

Bob Abrams
President
Lambda Phi Sigma

Bob,

I suppose you're wondering what ever happened to your illegal fraternity's prized wall banner. You'll be glad to know that it's safe and sound, and that you can send two of your stooges to Swedesboro at exactly 8 p.m. on Monday, December 18th, to get it back.

Your assigned imbeciles will find the *LPS* banner stashed inside the rear of a transportation trailer near the packinghouse of Glossy Fruit and Vegetable Farm. Your punks should take *322* west to *Route 551*. Turn south towards Swedesboro, and follow the highway until your lackeys reach Back Creek Road. Then, the Lambda Phi retards should turn left and travel until the nomads come to Glossy Fruit and Veggie Farm on the right. Lots of luck, A-holes!

Yours truly,

A Secret Admirer
October 17, 1961

"The idiot that wrote this letter never had Miss Sankins for English," I told News and Tim while shaking my head in disgust. "The date on a personal letter should always go in the upper right-hand corner, and not at the bottom under the name. And there's no damned name provided. Just a sarcastic allusion!"

"What are ya' gonna' do?" Tim wished learning and knowing. "I hate mysteries, even mysterious ones!"

"We're gonna' walk over to *Memorial Hall* and check the tri-county phone book under the payphone," I firmly advised. "Swedesboro is not that far from Glassboro, and I'm gamblin' that

Glossy Fruit and Vegetable Farm, if it exists at all, will be listed in the same phone book's white or yellow pages. There still remains the distinct possibility that we might be dealin' with a fictitious farm here! After all, the other two male fraternities are unscrupulous!"

The three amateur sleuths trekked over to *Memorial Hall* and thoroughly researched the sought after information. "Here it is gentlemen!" I exclaimed while pointing with my index finger to the desired white page in the residential section. "Glossy Fruit and Vegetable Farm, along with the phone number and Back Creek Road address are provided. But now, guys, I have to intensively pursue another major idea."

I anxiously leafed through the yellow business pages in the back of the phone directory and came-up with a tremendous clue when I looked up "Farms" in the classified advertisements section. "Glossy Fruit and Vegetable Farm is owned by a certain Wesley Reynolds, and if my guess is right, he's either Ken Reynolds father or his older brother, and I'm inclined right now to believe the former hypothesis rather than the latter."

"Great analysis, Sherlock! All those Sir Arthur Conan Doyle *Sherlock Holmes* stories and novels you read in high school are finally paying off," Tim excitedly congratulated. "But guys, please be careful that this is not some sort of sinister ,trap."

"Now, we know that the Delta Alpha Omegas have our banner, and that one of their members had purloined it during the Christmas Party raid, and then probably gave it to Ken Reynolds," News guessed and verbalized. "J.W., we're goin' to Swedesboro tonight and recover what's rightfully ours!"

News and I contrived a plausible excuse to convince our parents that we both had to do research in the *Savitz Library* for upcoming end of semester term papers, and since the peach harvest season was over for my buddy, and since the farm market was closed, we received little opposition for our reasonable, disingenuous request to return to Glassboro. When I picked-up News at his Spring Road Elm residence, I asked my Lambda associate what was occurring in the world. My normally garrulous fountain-of-information was not in a very talkative frame of mind.

"Nothin' much eventful has happened ever since the *Yankees* beat Cincinnati in the *World Series* back in October. Everything's been quiet, both on the international scene, and on the domestic front," News replied in a disappointed tone of voice. "The *AFL Championship Game* is scheduled for the day before *Christmas,* and the old guard *NFL's* classic contest is scheduled be played on December 31st."

"I hear there are negotiations in progress about the two leagues havin' a big game to decide an ultimate champion," I offered. "I can't see anybody in the *AFL* that can beat the *Green Bay Packers* like the *Eagle*s were lucky enough to do last December. I mean News," I haughtily continued, "teams like the *Houston Oilers* and the *San Diego Chargers* look alright when the squads play against each other, but the *Packers* under Vince Lombardi are in a class all by themselves. Say, News, is there' anything different playin' on *Broadway?* Maybe we'll drive-up to New York before summer work starts and catch a matinee performance."

"There's a new musical comedy that came-out in mid-October called *How to Succeed in Business without Really Trying* that's playing at the Forty-sixth Street Theater," my truly trivial colleague suavely communicated.

"Maybe we should suggest that our folks go and see that one," I mused and offered. "When our families invest in Broadway shows that make plenty of gigantic bucks, we could inherit *their* big business investments without havin' to tread water,instead of just getting by teachin' dumb-ass punk kids in public-schools for the rest of our totally doomed lives."

When I passed Mr. Bill's Custard on the Winslow-Williamstown Road, my eyes glanced at the "high-tension" telephone lines and their specially constructed heavy-duty poles, and that incidental observation made me feel uncomfortable about the Joanne Berenato and Peachy Wilcox situations; about the inevitable *D* grade I was receiving from Miss Sankins; about lying to my folks about going-out with News to the college library; about the weird-sounding, mysterious task at hand awaiting us in Swedesboro, and about everything else that engendered "high tension" in my personal life. But then the recent Lettermen's song "When I Fall in Love" came over the radio on Philadelphia's Wibbage (WIBG) Radio 99, and News was inspired to interrogate me about my faltering love life.

"J.W., I was seriously thinkin'," my fellow Impala traveler harmlessly began. "Ya' can't have it both ways and date Joanne and Peachy at the same time. I mean, you're not a damned rich Arab or wealthy Mormon, and you can't afford a harem, or more than one wife to support. I mean to say that most Catholic people like you and me are monogamous stooges, as Professor Dickinson preaches in *my* Sociology class."

"I'd rather have Dickinson than Rolphs as a prof' any day of the year," I angrily rendered my opinion. "My folks are gonna' have dual French hemorrhages when they read my report card showin' that I earned a shameful D from Sankins and a mediocre C from Rolphs. And it's all personal, spiteful and vengeful, subjective evaluation, which has nothing at all to do with actual student performance or ability."

"Maybe you could compromise a little bit and grease their gears once in a while besides studyin' more," News suggested. "That's what Rolphs and Sankins really want you to. do although the hypocrites say contrary. It's just like Mr. Andrews over again with you, J.W., but it's on the college level now. Pucker-up and kiss their royal ugly butts; surrender your stubborn independence, and wave the white flag in their middle-class, middle-aged faces," Tommy constructively enunciated. "That's all the educational tyrants really want from you, J.W., your subordination and patronage. You're unconditional allegiance, and if ya' can't give it to the demented authority figures, then simply just fake doin' it just like I do."

I didn't savor the flow of conversation and its implications pertaining to me making undesirable compromises, so I switched the discourse back to Joanne and Peachy. "Joanne's Pop doesn't like me because I'm just a farm market kid and not an authentic peach farmer," I intimated. "So right now, I'm more inclined to date Peachy. But I'm bein' sent on a guilt trip to hell because Joanne's developed a hernia from workin' in the *Memorial Hall* cafeteria, carryin' the heavy trays around, and she'll need an operation to correct the problem over the *Christmas* winter break."

News remarked that he didn't know that girls could get hernias without having any testicles, so I had to set him straight on that specific matter about women possessing weak ovaries and frail abdominal muscles and the like. And I was exceedingly glad to learn that T.T. finally didn't know something and had to be educated on the subject. And when the Wibbage DJ next played "Please Mr. Postman" by the Marvelettes, my super-nosy companion casually inquired if I had intercepted the dreadful warning letters that had been sent home by the school administration.

"Sure have," I answered in a rather relieved tone of voice. "Ya' know, News. There's too damned much detrimental daily pressure in our young lives, and we aren't even in the real adult world yet. And a lot of the stress is caused by our own bad habits. We really ought to be goin' to the college library and studyin' rather than headin' to Swedesboro to get a banned banner for Bob Abrams," I vigorously maintained. "Is he or Hoppy gonna' be around to help us twenty years from now? I don't think so. We'll both be on our own!"

When we rode through downtown Williamstown, News and I voluntarily stopped our futile quibbling and listened to the Tokens singing "The Lion Sleeps Tonight", that was then followed by Ray Charles's upbeat rendition of "Hit the Road Jack," and those numbers got me concentrating and worrying about our suspicious Swedesboro excursion.

"I feel a little uncomfortable about goin' through with this Swedesboro gig," I finally confided. "It's sorta' like we're bein' lured into a trick now that we suspect that Ken Reynolds is involved with swipin' the banner. And if you weren't the Sergeant-at-Arms assigned to protect the damned thing," I bluntly vociferated, "I'd be home callin' either Joanne or Peachy on the horn and feelin' damned good about myself."

News reminded me that we should have asked Ron Carputis and Mario to accompany us on the important mission, but I interpreted that sage advice Tomasello offered as an unwarranted insult to *our* manhood. "Look News, are we wimps or what?" I argued. "Those two turkeys would break our testicles so bad if the ballbreakers had to travel twenty-five miles just to stand there while we take a simple banner from the back of a tractor trailer. I could do without that verbal torture we'd receive from either Carputis or DiMaris, or both troublemakers!"

"You're right," News acceded. "Our freakin' balls would be broken so badly that we wouldn't even need any damned hernia operations like Joanne does! Just autopsies!"

After passing the college complex, I took *Route 322* westward, and after the highway zigzagged through Mullica Hill, the Impala next passed the *New Jersey Turnpike Interchange* connection and then zipped onto the aforementioned road to Swedesboro. Soon, we easily located Back Creek Road, and in three-minutes, were cruising up the entrance to Glossy Fruit and Vegetable Farm. I drove around an asphalt stretch to the enormous packinghouse, and we observed with relief that the place appeared to be vacated for the day. "There's the trailer over there!" I told News. "This whole process shouldn't take more than two short minutes."

"That transporter is called a reefer," my know-it-all friend immediately informed. "And that's what beatniks also call a marijuana joint. But a truck reefer has got a powerful refrigeration unit, but it's not a modified reefer already attached to a cab coordinated into one unit, but instead, this one here is a trailer reefer that has been temporarily disconnected from a tractor cab."

"I don't give two flyin' turds what it's called," I snapped-back while having my feathers ruffled by News's propensity for meaningless academics during a time of caution, or of possible crisis. "Now let's open the back doors; get what we've come to obtain, and then loyally take the banner over to Hoppy's house in Aura. Once we complete this ultra-weird project, I'm gonna' cool it for a while with the Lambda Phi's."

News and I opened the trailer's squeaky doors that sounded as if they each required a pound of grease and a quart of oil. The trailer was more than three-quarters full of apples packed in handsome shipping boxes stacked seven high, forty-nine on a skid. Tomasello was first to notice our quarry.

"There, it'is, up there, J.W.," my perceptive companion pointed-out. "The banner's folded-up, but it's too high for either of us to reach, so you can interlock your fingers, and I'll use your hands as sort of a mounting stirrup," *TNT* directed. "The banner would have to coincidentally be placed on top of the only skid that's obviously stacked nine high."

The two of us quickly clambered-up onto the trailer, and right after I boosted News up to secure the treasured banner, all of a sudden, the trailer's back doors were slammed shut and swiftly locked. We were prisoners trapped and incarcerated in total darkness, when News clumsily lost his balance, and awkwardly tumbled with a thud onto the wooden floor.

"What idiots you Lambda Phi Sigma shit heads are!" a voice sounding a lot like Ken Reynolds's yelled from outside the trailer. "Now, you're *our* special honored hostages."

"Enjoy your little junket," a second voice sounding awfully like Jack Thompson of Tau Kappa Epsilon laughed. "This trip will be our special *Christmas* present to you two buffoons!"

Soon, a diesel engine was heard coming from around the packinghouse's location, and the arriving tractor was backed-up and then expertly hooked to the reefer, which was now loaded with apples, a Lambda Phi Sigma banner, and two gullible, quixotic fools. In another five-minutes, Tomasello and I heard the highway monster rumbling onto Back Creek Road, and we were bouncing-around inside the pitch-blackness, occasionally colliding and banging into each other.

"This is consistent with our total existence ever since I've known you," News vehemently protested inside the extremely dark, moving environment. "We've both been blind to the truth and livin' in darkness all our damned lives."

"Now, you know how Ray Charles feels when he 'hits the road Jack'!" I aptly and sarcastically replied. "I knew I should've brought my damned sun glasses!"

News was even more livid about our predicament than I was. "This trailer was like a mousetrap, and the neatly folded banner was like a cheap piece of cheese used for bait. Listen, J.W.," News rambled on. "If Mario and Ron had come with us to Swedesboro as I had told you earlier tonight, then Reynolds and Thompson could've never pulled-off this insane misadventure we're experiencin'. Mario would've made those jerks into hamburger meat, dead hamburger meat, too! And Carputis could've been Mario's hamburger helper!"

"Don't blame it on me!" I yelled-back at my temporary disputer. "Pin the tail on the donkey is a silly grade-school game! Hey, wait a minute! We're stoppin' somewhere!"

"The driver's now at the Glassboro/Swedesboro toll booth entrance to the *New Jersey Turnpike!"* News realized and stated. "J.W., it looks like we're headin' either north on south right now, to somewhere in the eastern continental United States."

"Either that, or we're in some queer sort of time machine goin' back to the friggin' *Dark Ages!"* I quipped and complained, like a sulking adolescent. "Well, News. I guess that *we're* just like jungle lions caught sleepin' tonight, just as the Tokens sing about!"

"It's a good thing that we're bein' hauled somewhere with a cargo of apples and not with a damned load of peaches," my friend declared. "Then, we might be headed towards the *Ice Age* besides goin' through the *Dark Ages*."

"Why's that News?" I asked while my stomach felt a bit queasy from being unpleasantly jolted around in the dark. "Exactly why is *that* comment about apples and peaches relevant to anything?"

"Because peaches are kept and transported at a colder temperature than apples are," News authoritatively lectured. "Apples are usually transported at forty-five degrees, and peaches closer to 33 or 34, to keep them fresh for market."

"Thanks, News," I grieved in sympathy and in frustration. "You really made my nightmarish day!"

Chapter 11
"Second Semester"

Even inside the dark enclosure, News was excellent at geography, and the fact memorizer had once claimed to be an Italian descendant of Amerigo Vespucci. It came as no surprise in between my cursing and my vulgarities that my traveling fellow-captive updated where he believed we were on the *New Jersey Turnpike*. Two hours after our noisy and bouncy departure from Swedesboro, T.T. alerted me that the tractor-trailer had left the *Turnpike* and we were heading for the *George Washington Bridge* into New York City.

"Great!" I exclaimed in the very chilly darkness. "Now when we get-off, and if we're not kidnapped and held for ransom, then we could stroll on over to *Broadway* and see *How to Succeed in Business without Really Trying*. Of course," I scornfully uttered while shriveling-up on the trailer's floor and embracing my flimsy, thin Lambda Phi Sigma jacket, "we'll have to wait-around for twenty-hours or so to catch tomorrow night's performance!"

"Why the hell couldn't Big Al be the fraternity's Sergeant-at-Arms instead of me?" News bitched. "I'd rather be thrown through the center of the damned Wurlitzer by Mario than be subjected to you and this lousy simulated *Antarctica* we're now experiencin', somewhere in the *Bronx*. That lowdown skunk Ken Reynolds oughta' catch the Tinker Bell *Fairy* boat across the *Hudson*!"

"Ya' know, News, you're getting' on my damned nerves!" I yelled as the trailer's back wheels hit a nasty pothole, and I bumped my head against an apple carton. "Neither of us happens to be half as smart as we both think we are! In fact, News we're both a couple of victimized saps!"

"Yeah, wine-saps!" News giggled, referring to the apples being shipped in the stacked boxes on pallets. "We're nothin' but a couple of wine-saps, all rotten to the core!"

"Remind me to beat the crap out of you when we get back to Hammonton, if we ever first make it back to Swedesboro to repossess my car!" I threatened. "I feel sorry for your future wife. I hope she's deaf, dumb, and blind, for her sake."

The tractor-trailer pulled into some sort of yard or terminal, and then slowly was backed-up to a loading and unloading dock. Five minutes later, the rear panels were opened, and a fat man with a grimy white apron and a cigar in his mouth almost inhaled his imported *El Producto* when perceiving our surprise appearance.

"What the hell's this shit going-on inside this rig?" the old, portly, bald codger asked the driver, who was tacitly indicating general ignorance of *our* presence. "Who in God's name are these two punks?"

"Never saw them before in all my life," the anonymous bearded driver testified. "They look like a dumb-ass pair of college creeps to me, probably from *Glassboro State* in South Jersey. There's your 'Future Teachers of America' standin' there like little lost orphans on the rig's back platform, ha, ha, ha."

"Hey, where are we?" News insistently asked. "What's this place called?" Tommy imperatively demanded as he and I surveyed the new lit environment and saw stacks of fifty-pound onion bags; watermelons in bins; bushels of sweet potatoes, and all types of fruit and produce heaped up in all directions.

"You're at Hunts Point, New York City!" the stocky character puffing on the huge cigar stated. "Now you two dumbbells get the hell outa' here before I call the cops and have ya' thrown in the clinker for trespassin' and vagrancy. You're obstructin' business and interstate commerce with your crazy college bull-shit! Now hit the pike or face the cops!"

"Can't ya' give us a ride back to Swedesboro?" I politely begged the apathetic tractor-trailer driver. "We'll pay ya' thirty bucks for the trip back."

"Sorry, guys," the big-rig trucker negatively replied. "But now, after I leave here, I'm scheduled to pick-up a load of produce in Yonkers and transport it up to Albany! I won't be headin' back to Swedesboro until tomorrow night; that is, after I return another load from northern New York State, and then transport the fresh produce back-down here to Hunts Point!"

News and I exited the tractor-trailer, just when a worker piloting a forklift began unloading the numerous apple skids. We found a payphone near a crowded restaurant, called Bob Abrams at his home, and were fortunate to catch him and Hoppy at *his* residence prior to their appointment with the President of the Glassboro Rotary Club to deliver an errant road-meeting-night-sign, and to then narrate a formal apology. The pair consented to journeying-up to Hunts Point to pick News and me up, at, or near the Leaf-Brandt Produce House. TNT and I then entered the immense Food Distribution Center's main restaurant where we ate hot dogs, drank milk shakes, played pinball, and alleviated our diarrhea conditions in the greasy spoon's crummy, dirty bathroom.

Around midnight, the black '57 Mercury with Jersey tags passed by the facility's chain-link-fence, motored through the open cantilever gate, and News and I happily greeted our rescuers. While riding from midtown Manhattan to Jersey through the *Lincoln Tunnel,* News amused everyone by saying: "This famous tunnel is linkin' New York City with North Jersey. That's why this hollow tube under the *Hudson* is called the linkin'-tunnel."

On the hundred-and-thirty-mile drive south to the Swedesboro-Glassboro area, News and I reviewed our memorable tale in chronological order. I held the repossessed, folded *LPS* banner close to my chest as evidence that we had performed a paramount service for Lambda Phi Sigma, and had extraordinarily sacrificed for the benefit of its staunch membership. When we were speeding past *Turnpike Exit 5* for Mt. Holly and Burlington, Bob had some good and bad recent intelligence to report.

"Tell me the bad news first," I solemnly and soberly requested. 'Let's get that negative crap out of the way so that I don't suffer a major coronary and a simultaneous stroke listenin' to News crack any more of his pedestrian, asinine jokes."

"Well, J.W., I think your white Chevy is pretty safe," Bob confirmed from the driver's seat, with both News and me occupying the rear. "Wanta' hear the rest?"

"So, what's so *bad* about that?" I curiously asked. "That's the best bad news I've ever heard!"

"But somehow, your white '61 Impala is sittin' on top of the flat Co-op roof at the college," Abrams informed, as I nearly swallowed both my tongue and my teeth. "Hoppy and I just found-out about the problem before drivin' up to Hunts Point to salvage you two. How about those apples, and not the ones in the Big Apple, ha, ha, ha!"

"Holy Methuselah'!" I shrieked during a pregnant moment of emotional duress. "Now, Dr. Robeson and Dean Lang are really goin' to hurl my butt down the proverbial college expulsion chute! What's the good news?" I hesitantly inquired. "I now need a pound of aspirins to recover from your horribly bad announcement."

"Well, I'm delighted to report that there's two bits of good news," Bob answered as his eyes glistened in the rear-view mirror from headlights of cars behind us. "First of all, Big Al has agreed to be the new fraternity Sergeant-at-Arms. Second, J.W. I called your parents on the phone and told them that you're gonna' spend the night at my house and that we're gonna' study for a first semester final exam' together. I can't believe that your folks didn't question my integrity and ask to speak with you over the telephone about verifyin' the phony arrangement."

"How'd the pranksters get the car up on the Co-op roof?" News wondered and asked. "Forget the idea of cash. Those Delta Alpha Omegas and those Tau Kappa Epsilons must be smarter than we give them *credit* for."

"Our theory is that Reynolds's family owns a pretty large farm in Swedesboro, so the the enemy frat' must've gotten an industrial-sized fork lift; transported the white Impala over to the college in one of those flat-bed haulin' trucks, along with the forklift; pretended to be college maintenance workmen, and ingeniously got the auto' up there in maybe ten minutes. Yeah, J.W., eight to ten guys could easily slide the car off the lift's forks in ten-minutes, or so."

"And don't worry J.W.," the deans ain't gonna' suspend your ass," Hoppy insisted. "Tell me, why would any student want to put their car up on the snack bar roof? That's an insane stunt that someone mischievously does to someone else. The deans will know that it was a revenge prank," Hoppy maintained, "and since the school chieftains are in tight with the Delta Alpha Omegas and with the Tau Kappa Epsilons, the whole farce will eventually blow over. Robeson, Lang, and Nelson won't wish to see their favorite brown-nosers get into quicksand-like, disciplinary situations."

"Looks like there's gonna' be a fraternity war developin' soon," Bob warned. "Battle lines are bein' drawn, and first the chicken coop raid, followed by the banner heist, and now the kidnappin' of J.W. and News, in addition to the white Impala up on the Co-op's roof," Abrams recited and paused. "It's gonna' soon be payback time. Time for palpable retribution."

"I've seen these sorts of things before with the Levittown greaser gangs and with the 1960 Hammonton Fruit War between the Reds and the Blues," I regretfully contributed. "And believe me when I tell ya', I have lots of experience in one-upmanship when it finally comes-down to brass tacks and brass balls."

"Okay, J.W. We'll use your expertise and value your sage advice, but more importantly, war's been hereby officially declared," our main fraternity spokesman declared and affirmed. "Now let's get J.W.'s vulnerable Impala back before some lion, hyena, tiger, or other famished zoo predator attacks and devours it!"

* * * * * * * * * * * * *

Much to my relief, the white Impala had not been damaged and was removed unscathed from the Co-op roof by the Glassboro Fire Department, teaming-up with a makeshift college maintenance crew. The college billing office assessed a fee of two-hundred-dollars for the "services rendered", and the money was paid from the surplus in the Lambda Phi Sigma's secret treasury, which only Abrams and Hoppy knew the account's exact arithmetic.

Christmas came and passed, and before I knew it, the *New Year* had officially begun. I had celebrated the holiday season down at my grandparents' place in North Miami Beach, Florida, with my parents and younger brother and sister, and I joyfully returned to *Glassboro State* sporting a magnificent suntan that I knew had effectively caught the vivacious Peachy Wilcox's attention. I stood in the long matriculation line with News, Ron, and Tim, and then, before fatigued, became extremely aggravated when I discovered that Miss Sankins was again my tyrannical instructor for *Fundamentals of Communications 101, Part II.*

"I have all three credit courses," I told the guys. "I have Dr. Su for Human Behavior and Development; topinionated Professor O'Connor for Political Science; the inquisitive Mr. Silvester for Algebra; Dr. Kraft for Philosophy, and Sankins again for English. Drive a damned stake through my weak heart, will ya' Tim?"

"You aren't a pathetic vampire, but If I were you, J.W.," my fellow English Major announced, "I would strut-over to the Registrar's Office and get Sankins's class changed to Stevens's. At least Dr. S speaks normal English and acts like an American, and not like a 1890s uptight school marm havin' her period, or her friggin' menopause every damned period. Ha, ha, ha! Get it guys?" Tim inanely emphasized. "Havin' her period smeared all over J.W.'s face every damned period! Ha, ha, ha!"

"Glad you're amusin' yourself," I criticized Tim for his egregious and unsolicited remarks. "You'll never make it in either stand-up or sit-down comedy. Amoro, you're about as hilarious as a bra without any damned cups! Or as a set of sperm-less testicles on a gay sperm whale!"

"Don't waste your time J.W. tryin' to alter your schedule," the always-knowledgeable News Tomasello advised. "Whoever ya' had for *Fundamentals of Communications, 101* first semester, you automatically get second semester. It makes the schedulin' process easier for the college savants, and it also is an unwritten policy that everyone around here abides by. Otherwise, Professor Stevens would have a surplus of students, and Sankins would be all alone in *College Hall* tutorin' herself!"

My Educational Psychology professor' was Dr. Su, a petite Chinese lady' who dressed in January of 1962 as if *WWI* was still in progress, and her outdated apparel looked like the *Great Depression* had just happened. Dr. Su's class was titled Human Behavior and Development, but it would have been more appropriately titled "The Evils of Mao Tse-tung". Dr. Su spoke English with a heavy Oriental accent; despised Red Chinese Communism with a passion, and she always mispronounced my last name Wiener (as in hot dog) instead of articulating Wiessner.

One day before class, fellow student Big Al Keiler (in a moment of jocularity) scribbled on the front blackboard, "Do not erase-Dr. Wiener". Before I had a chance to erase the prosaic verse, Professor Su entered the upstairs *College Hall* classroom. The little woman automatically grabbed an eraser and then momentarily hesitated as she somberly studied the message scrawled-upon the black slate. She then innocently prattled, "Ah so, class! Dr. Wiener say I should not erase board, so I just lecture today and not write notes with chalk for you to copy." The class slipped into a minor state of pandemonium in response to the Oriental lady's shallow perception and reaction to my friend's very obvious juvenile prank.

On another occasion, Big Al and I had cut Dr. Su's class to engage in an impromptu softball catch on the baseball diamond adjacent to her corner second-floor *College Hall* classroom. Dr. Su stepped to the back of the room to open a window for some fresh air and observed me gallivanting on the baseball field below. "Wiener!" the *HB&D* teacher imperatively bellowed. "You come up here this instant to my psychology class!"

Although I had distinctly heard the charming Chinese woman's piercing soprano voice, I ignored the diminutive lady professor's command, pretending not to hear the dictum. Dr. Su re-evaluated her impetuosity and exclaimed to the already-hysterical class, "Maybe that isn't Wiener down there after all!" A thunderous burst of laughter blared-down to the baseball field from the upstairs corner classroom window.

"I guess she didn't miss *you* at all," I kidded Big Al as we engaged in our impromptu game of catch. "She just misses me!"

"Let's quit this activity and go over to *Memorial Hall* to play some four-handed pinochle with some of the guys that don't have class this period," Keiler nervously proposed. "Dr. Su is so screwed up in the head that she might open the window again and notice me down here next time, havin' an impromptu catch with you! I can't risk bein' suspended, and if I flunk-out, I'm liable to be drafted, and I'm too independent to like or to obey strict military orders and commands over in Southeast Asia."

A personal requirement of Dr. Su's *HB&D* class was that I was assigned to visit the Blackwood Elementary School and organize a case study on one of the more "challenging" (translation: discipline problem) "students" (translation: terror and menace). My task was to get records from the school's guidance and nurse's offices; from the principal's office confidential files; observe the little thug's classroom antics and semantics, and then type-up a comprehensive report to be submitted to Dr. Su by the end of January.

I watched "the child's" variety of infantile, fiendish pranks unfold the entire week, and then my left hand diligently jotted-down each and every observable example of misconduct into my spiral notebook, which was nearly filled by that Friday. The six-year-veteran male teacher was noticeably frustrated with the junior nihilist, and the instructor was also nearly at wits end. And it was precisely then and there that I realized that teaching wasn't the cake job I had imagined it to be.

"The kid was a twelve-year-old anarchist," I told News and Tim in the Co-op. "Whatever the teacher did to counter the little jerk-weed, those disciplinary measures only inspired the neurotic scoundrel to perform even crazier tricks while the instructor was tryin' to help others in the class. Now, I really appreciate most of my high school teachers and what the faculty had to go through, just to keep order and have a decent lesson goin'."

"J.W.," News answered shaking his head. "For *HB&D,* I'm observin' a similar type of kid over in the Berlin School. I suggest that the three of us Einsteins stay in college and belong to Lambda Phi Sigma the rest of our damned lives," News characteristically exaggerated. "I'd rather work eighteen-hours a day on my daddy's peach farm than to daily do arduous battle with the caliber of adolescent nutcases I've been seein' over at the Berlin School."

"The little punks aren't respectful like we were in junior-high and in high school," Tim recalled and added. "I mean, we behaved like punks outa' school at the malt shop, or at the local hamburger joint, or at the bowlin' alley, but today's spoiled, doted-on insolent rascals are rotten all the time, no matter where they are: at home, at school, or in public. The little suckers act weird all over their town all the damned time, and not only at special, more-tolerant places, where their perverted misbehavior would be acceptable."

My Political Science instructor, Professor O' Connor, was a very outspoken pedagogue who thought his essential destiny in life was to expose the myriad faults and weaknesses of our corrupt American social structure. The intellectual establishment (college deans) regarded O' Connor's attacks (like Dr. Rolphs) on U.S, on Christian religions; on government, and on social institutions as being productive and scholarly, as long as the axe-to-grind academic crusader navigated *his* intellectual anarchy through common issues like American racial prejudice and evil capitalistic exploitation, both at home and abroad.

But in January of 1962, Professor O' Connor began skating on thin ice when his fluid investigations revealed instances of homosexuality among other notable members of the college faculty. Although the cynic was one of the students' favorite profs', O' Connor soon became the object of detestation of some of his envenomed colleagues. In an incredibly short time, Professor O' Connor soon earned the disfavor of the college administration, which suddenly abhorred his inquiries into his fellow instructors' bedfellow' habits, rather than exclusively focusing his critical attention upon what was wrong with imperfect America.

O' Connor's bold muckraking and whistle-blowing activities drew big city newspaper attention to the local college campus, thus, casting a dusky pall that immediately eclipsed all of the favorable publicity that the school's deans so sanctimoniously had labored to build. O' Connor's flirtations with attempting to right all wrongs (including social injustices and sexual perversions) became an uncontrollable obsession, and the maverick professor, just like the chivalrous Lambda Phi Sigmas, did not heed the admonitions of the school's executives about O' Connor's separating what was immoral behavior both on and off of the college campus.

Professor O' Connor could best be described as a combination of Upton Sinclair and Don Quixote, and the adamant iconoclast appeared quite oblivious to the hatchet of doom ominously being held over his head. His determination to expose and expunge all evil eventually ruined the foolish man's budding career. O' Connor was soon labeled a Pariah; was denied tenure at the end of the second semester, not because of his incompetence, but because his mouth oracled bad publicity about the venerable school of higher learning.

It was perfectly all-right for Dr. O' Connor to subvert and indict the United States of America for the world's problems, but when his rants made it too personal by demonizing the college's good reputation with a faculty homosexual scandal, then the Political

Science instructor was abruptly dismissed from service. The image of the school was much more important than the professor's abundant *freedom of thought* criticisms that had been directed at America's moral decay.

"I hear some students are gonna' protest Dr. O'Connor bein' given bad evaluations by the administration," News informed the guys on a late January drive from *GSC* back to Hammonton inside Tim's blue station wagon.

"Who goes a shit?" Mario incongruously yelled from the back seat. "What did O' Connor ever do for you fuck-heads that you now wanna' stick your neck on the choppin' block for that super-asshole? Just tell me *that* answer, you dumb bull-fucks!"

"We can't have any more strikes against us, or we're evicted from the ballpark," Ron Carputis more intelligently insisted. "I had O'Connor first semester and liked the guy, but now I say let's concentrate our energy on underminin' the Delta Alpha Omegas and also trouncin' the Tau Kappa Epsilons."

"Ron's right," News compatibly added. "Let the Deltas and the Tau Kappas worry about O'Connor when the psychos really should be lookin' over their shoulders at us."

"Okay, guys, now that we're sort of all on the same page in the same chapter," I injected, "I'm gonna' now disclose a plan that Hoppy and Bob have devised to avenge the chicken coop raid; the Lambda banner being snatched, and News and me bein' taken hostage to Hunts Point New York. We nearly froze to death in the refrigeration trailer, and also, my precious Chevy windin' up on top of the Co-op's roof."

"What are ya' so pissed-off about?" News asked me. "It was because your Chevy has become a campus conversation piece that Joanne and Peachy are now again talkin' to you, because you've suddenly evolved into a BMOC!"

"Don't you mean BYOB," Mario seriously misinterpreted, "Bring Your Own Booze!"

After everyone stopped their' instant levity syndrome, I disclosed the newly-developed Lambda Phi Sigma strategy to the Hammonton crew, all of whom endorsed it's implementation wholeheartedly. "Just remember we all gotta' be at Joe's Sub Shop at seven-thirty tomorrow night," I specified.

It felt good that The Lambda Phi's were intending to administer much-needed adversity to Ken Reynolds and to Jack Thompson, co-conspirators of the reefer shenanigans that News and I had to survive, regarding the frigid ride to Hunts Point in the apple farmer's trailer. "I like everything about the plan except the Frankenstein, Dracula, and Wolfman masks," I summarized on the drive to the popular High Street hoagie and burger emporium. "Like nobody's gonna' know who Mario is wearin' any kind of disguise."

"The masks are just gonna' be used to scare the crap out of the two jerks," News logically said in defense of Bob Abrams and Steve Cassidy's ingenious plan. "We're wearin' the stupid masks in the dark to give those retards something tangible to remember and have nightmares about, should a bit of moonlight appear."

"That's right," Tim reflexively concurred. "Our contact with the Delta Alphas and with the Tau Kappas has been remote up until tonight. Now it's gonna' be physical contact, rather than just imaginative schemin' and distant pranks."

I sensed for the first time that I was a bit jealous of Bob and of Hoppy, not because they were co-founders of Lambda Phi Sigma, but because I had always prided myself on being a shrewd deviser of strategy against certain past rival factions. I knew that in the future, my expertise at gang warfare would be an indispensable asset to the Lambda Phi's when push finally would come to shove. And with *that* prospect in mind, I sustained my silence and contemplated the creative ruse that was about to go into effect.

At Joe's Sub Shop, Bob and Hoppy congenially reviewed with the guys the night's final preparations. "Wednesday night, January 26th, will be an evening that Reynolds and Thompson will want to forget!" President Abrams concluded, much to every single member's satisfaction.

The Lambda Phi surveillance network had become aware that the two fraternity honchos were cohorts and also good friends. Every Wednesday night Reynolds and Thompson drove their motorcycles to the Glass Bowl, a well patronized bar and lounge extension, which was tacked onto a successful bowling alley up on *Delsea Drive* and Pitman Road. The imaginative plan had three interesting phases.

First of all, I would drive Hoppy's dark blue pick-up into the Glass Bowl parking lot while Reynolds and Thompson were inside either bowling or hustling older women. Several carloads of Lambdas including News, Tim, Ron, Mario, Hoppy, Tom Bell, Frank Morrissey, Mitch Toscini, Phil Candido, and Gil Taylor would be furtively waiting outside to ambush the two rogues. After the two motorcycles were hoisted into the blue truck, I would drive the *Harleys* in the pick-up directly to the Glassboro Train Depot.

Hoppy was scripted to go into the Glass Bowl and start an argument with Ken Reynolds and Jack Thompson, accusing the two of the Lambda banner theft; of the dual kidnappings to Hunts Point, and of lifting and placing the white Impala onto the Co-op's roof. The two co-conspirators then would angrily chase Hoppy outside where the other Lambdas Phi's, wearing Halloween masks, would apprehend the culprits; tie the two dangerous clowns up, and then gag their mouths with a pair of of Bob's polka-dotted handkerchiefs.

Crafty Abrams knew the watchman at the Glassboro Train Depot and was aware that the sentinel was a chronic alcoholic. Bob, Tony Petters, and Max Gunther took four bottles of *Seagram's 7* to the depot and conveniently distracted the watchman by mutually sharing a few generous libations.

I was assigned to wait in the pick-up at the depot, until the rest of the Lambdas showed-up with their two enemy hostages, both then bound and gagged in two separate car trunks. The basic difficulty of the plan was that everything had to perfectly synchronize for the complicated scheme to be successful. If one aspect went slightly out of kilter, the entire ruse could result in failure.

After the *Harleys* were confiscated and my fellow *LPS* instigators deposited the expensive merchandise into the back of Hoppy's half-ton blue pickup, I fired-off the engine and made a beeline for the Glassboro Train Depot. I pulled into the gray-stone parking lot and nervously waited for another phase of the intricate operation to unravel. At around nine o'clock, four recognizable cars turned into the deserted train yard. Reynolds and Thompson were roughly removed from two auto' trunks, and then Mario and Big Al collaborated in hurling the tied and gagged hostages, one at a time, into an empty freight car's interior.

And then, Bob methodically signaled for me to drive the pick-up over to *their* location. I was ordered to stop twelve cars down from where Reynolds and Thompson had just been recently incarcerated. The two bikes were then lifted into the new freight car, and the doors were slid shut. But the worst facet of the frat' presidents tribulation was that Reynolds and Thompson had to listen to us horribly sing two verses of Gene Pitney's "Town without Pity" that must have really rusted their already-offended tin ears.

"That part with the *Harleys* bein' put into a separate freight car I never before told anybody, except Bob," Hoppy divulged to our amazement. "When this train gets to Trenton, I've assigned six new pledges to be there to un-gag the idiots, and to unfasten most of their ropes, just enough that the captured pecker-heads could work themselves free before the train, which again takes-off, headin' north."

"What about the two motorcycles twelve freight cars back?" Tim asked. "What about them?"

"After Trenton," Hoppy uttered with a grin, "this train's goin' up to Boston. I suppose that a hefty freight bill will be in order when the two frat' presidents are notified by the Boston Police that their borrowed, cherished vehicles have been located up in Bean Town, New England."

Ten minutes later, the freight train's whistle blew at the usually inactive Glassboro depot. The rest of us joined Bob, Max, Tony, and the now-drunk watchman- and jovially celebrated our secret mission by finishing off the remainder of the potent *Seagram's 7,* which Mario admitted tasted almost as good as *Southern Comfort,* just before the pot-bellied hog finished chugging-down almost an entire quart of the potent whiskey into his cavernous throat. I suspected that the corpulent swine's primitive ancestors must have either been hedonistic cannibals, or neurotic wild savages.

Chapter 12
"A Turn for the Worse"

On Friday of that late January week, News and I were sitting in the Co-op reviewing the latest conflict between the Lambda Phi's and the ruthless Delta Alpha Omegas and the dastardly Tau Kappa Epsilons. Tommy T. was laughing and telling me how the Epsilons were the "lowest class of slave idiots" in Aldous Huxley's classic novel *Brave New World,* and then my close friend vacillated to another venue of conversation as was his annoying habit. I was waiting for Tomasello to make some disparaging remarks concerning my personal life and my unrelenting travails with the bureaucratic *GSC* academic aristocracy.

"Ya' know, J.W.," News coyly prefaced. "Fifty-years from now, before you retire from teachin' to either sit in your rickety rockin' chair, or occupy your cemetery grave, you're gonna' write-down in a book all about our Lambda Phi Sigma adventures, and then Jesus is gonna' show Miss Sankins's ghost your creative manuscript and ask the dead bitch why she gave such a talented guy like youself a freakin' D in *Fundamentals of Communications, 101.*"

I was somewhat flattered at News's backhanded compliment and related to my pal how Mario had boasted that he could have chucked the two black *Harley Davidsons* into the freight car all by himself, without the assistance of Big Al and me, and how DiMaris had then threatened to hurl Big Al into the freight car when Keiler questioned the veracity of the corpulent brute's bragging. "Naturally, Big Al backed-down from the impending confrontation when faced with another airplane spin possibility and then being quickly flung into a boxcar," I concluded and opined to Tomasello.

But then, News was persistent and switched the dialogue back to me having potential as a great American writer. "*Shake*speare had trouble as an actor holdin' his sword steady on stage, because I believe that the bard had a bad case of Parkinson's disease," Tomasello frivolously said tongue-in-cheek. "So, that's why the Globe Theater actor quit the stage and became a damned British playwright, all because of Parkinson's. Poor William couldn't hold his swords, or his *spears* steady on stage withoit the *shakes.*"

I was about ready to toss my half-full cup of ice and *Pepsi* directly into the center of News's newsy face when Elaine Hill, an old Edgewood High School friend, anbled-over to our booth to share our illustrious company.

"Hi, J.W.," Elaine congenially began her gossip. "I hear you're the talk of the campus drivin' your cool white Chevy up on the Co-op roof. How did you ever manage doin' that? Did ya' have a long ramp or something?"

"It didn't really happen that way at all," I confessed with a florid face, feeling the blood surge up my neck to my cerebral cavity. "But Elaine, it was a pretty neat piece of campus scuttlebutt, you'll have to admit."

"I specifically came over to tell ya'that Joanne's doin' fine after her hernia operation and that she'll be back at the college takin' classes startin' next week," my honest female friend informed. "Her recovery is commin' along a little better than expected, and I understand she's glad oming back here to Glassboro. As you know, her father is kinda' strict and old-fashioned."

"Glad to hear that report, Elaine!" I sincerely reacted. "Joanne's a really terrific girl, the kind a guy wants to marry."

"But not to date because she's too pure, chaste, and pristine," News butted-in, much to my dismay. I gave my indiscreet companion a mean scowl and then again paid attention to Elaine.

"And J.W.," I have some more deliciously good info' for ya'," Elaine Hill teased, while fluffing her tresses over her shoulders in a very tantalizing sexy manner.

"And exactly what's that?" I asked, feigning honesty. "It's okay if you mention it in News's undistinguished presence, if it's all right with you?"

"I was talkin' to Peachy Wilcox over in *Linden Hall* this morning," Elaine continued giving me a cute wink.

"And you live over in *Evergreen Hall* where Joanne's also stayin'," I reminded Elaine, who was now a *GSC* sophomore because she had not wasted a full year like News and I had done after high school graduation. "I had thought that Peachy had been living in *Evergreen,* but apparently, she has transferred over to *Linden!"*

"That's right, J.W.," Elaine casually confirmed. "You're smarter than the average laboratory rat, I gotta' tell ya'. Well, anyway, Peachy confided that she wants to go out with you, so because that you, J.W., and *Miss Cape May* should get better emotionally acquainted. I now proposed that she and I should double-date you and News, if it's all right with you two studs."

"I'll do anything for the benefit of a dear friend," News begged me, as if the social chameleon was an incompetent thespian, flunking a monologue in drama class. "Women askin' us out! I can't believe it! The damned world's gonna' end! I just know it! Is this Sadie Hawkins Day, or something?"

"But News and Elaine, we'll have to go to the Glassboro Theater over on High Street and see Natalie Wood in *West Side Story,"* I suggested. "Elaine, Peachy and you are really nice girls and should be treated like ladies and royally wined, dined, and courted, sitting up there on your Victorian pedestals."

"That's what you think, J.W.," Elaine shockingly answered. "Peachy told me she wants ya' to get a couple of six packs of beer and we'll go to some romantic lovers' lane and party until midnight dorm' curfew."

"That's incredible news!" I exclaimed while ignoring the other News in my company. "But Elaine, truthfully, I worry because you're also good friends with Joanne Berenato besides with Peachy Wilcox, so where's your allegiance?"

"Joanne understands that you're not goin' steady with anyone and that it's an open huntin' field at the moment," Elaine surprisingly replied. "I mean, J.W., if you were engaged or married, then there could be a big dilemma, but under the present circumstances, all's fair in love and war. And besides that," my Edgewood High former classmate persuasively proceeded, "besides you bein' Peachy's big dream, after her hernia incision completely heals, Joanne wants to date you too and have a few six-packs before enjoyin' the Lovers Lane submarine races."

"Submarine races?" News undesirably injected. "That's too '50sish soundin'! Get with the times, Elaine! How about callin' the planned affair Make-out City?"

"Elaine, how about tomorrow night," I impulsively suggested, completely ignoring Tomasello's utter lunacy. "We'll all meet here at the Co-op at seven, and then we'll head-out to a placid place I've heard about over in Pitman. I'll get Bob Abrams to supply us with a case of beer, so that comes down to six bottles each."

"Okay, guys, you're on!" Elaine laughed. "Boy, what I don't do for old friends. I can't wait to tell Peachy the great news!"

"And after bein' such a great *match*maker," News commented, "then Elaine, you might eventually evolve into a fair-to-Midland cigarette lighter manufacturer."

I swiftly pulled three paper napkins from a table dispenser, rolled them into a ball, and threw the missile into News's face to demonstrate my distain for his lousy sense of humor during a critical moment in advanced mating negotiations.

When Elaine Hill sauntered-out of the snack bar, News felt a compulsion to vociferate about how earlier in January the U.S. *Army* had withdrawn tanks from the *Berlin Wall,* and how the Soviets were thinking about reciprocating the American good faith gesture to ease *Cold War* tensions, and if *that* irrelevant information wasn't bad enough, the annoying talking machine next began graphically describing how *Ranger 3* had been launched from Cape Canaveral to land scientific instruments on the moon, and then later to send color pictures back to Earth.

"But J.W., there was some kind of mix-up in technology, and *Ranger 3* passed right by the damned moon because of too much velocity, and now it's headin' straight toward the sun," my talkative Lambda colleague prattled. "What an embarrassin' failed project for our high-profile space program!"

"Look, News, two gorgeous girls just asked us out to drink beer and neck, and you're all warped-out of form by Soviet tanks four-thousand-miles-away, and by space probes two-hundred-and-fifty-thousand-miles from Earth. Maybe," I nastily continued, "well just maybe, ya' oughta' visit a damned proctologist and have him send a space probe up your big fat rectum to measure your damned *IQ!"*

Bob Abrams came through like a trooper carrying flying colors when the Lambda boss delivered the case of *Budweiser* from Mazzeo's Bar to us at the Aura chicken coop. Hoppy then felt a need to lecture News and me that the fraternity house was now "for members only", and that no outsiders, including girlfriends, fiancés, wives, former prom queens, hookers, or dates were permitted inside or anywhere on the property, unless the Lambdas were having a major group party.

"Steve, maybe you can take Dr. Rolphs's place when the bastard finally retires or gets canned, whichever comes first!" News recommended to Hoppy. "You're beginnin' to sound just like that Nazi scumbag!"

"Maybe, News, you could get laid for the first time tonight, and accidentally pop your first load, and finally advance into manhood!" Cassidy effectively retorted as Bob Abrams and I nodded our heads and laughed in total approval.

I drove my Chevy with News as my passenger back to the campus and met the alluring girls in the Co-op at the designated time. I soon conducted us out to a lake in Pitman that Bob Abrams had described as the ideal place to park and drink. Of course, News had to ruin our pleasant nocturnal rendezvous with nature with one of his absurd, ludicrous remarks.

"I hear this lake is contaminated and that all the fish and even the amoebas and other microorganism have all died from the excessive pollution," the insane idiot articulated. "This place is worse than atomic radiation!"

"News, stop tryin' to be funny and keep your big fat trap shut!" I reproached the all-too-garrulous imbecile. "Now, I know for a fact that this site is listed as the cleanest and freshest lake in all of New Jersey!" I prevaricated. "Don't listen to News's inane drivel, girls. He's still learnin' the language and can now almost talk in complete but still illogical sentences."

I parked the Chevy in a secluded dark area, News and I utilized our church keys (those were still the days before twist off bottle caps), and after three hours of chatting, singing, philosophizing, drinking delicious brew, and heterosexual embracing, Elaine then made a gruesome observation.

"J.W, I'm havin' a blast and I hate to be a party-pooper, but it's now a quarter to midnight and Peachy and I have to get back to our dorms', or else we'll get demerits and be disciplined by our cranky in-residence dorm' mothers."

"Elaine's right," Peachy amenably echoed. "And J.W., I want you to know that I had a really neat time tonight, and I'd like to do this blast again, but next time with hard liquor. I gotta' show ya' where second base is!"

I was so unnerved, excited, and neurotic by the former *Miss Cape May's* outlandish statement that I started-up the Chevy, stepped on the accelerator a trifle too hard while fantasizing an orgasm, and then the back tires wildly spun around and sunk-down into the mud as if they had been devoured by quicksand.

I responded to the emergency by having Peachy get behind the wheel while News and I pushed the trunk and back bumper with all of our might. The Impala swayed and swished back and forth and miraculously, gradually moved forward through the swampy terrain. Mud was spinning-up from the rapidly rotating back wheels, and it was being generously splattered all over Tomasello's face and mine. After several more desperate shoves, the axles were finally liberated from their sandy wet snare, and News and I were greeted as heroes when we finally reentered the car.

I drove down the dark road exit and then realized I had to turn my headlights on while fantasizing a second orgasm. All the while, I was pressured from the girls' exhortations that they had only ten-minutes left to make it from Pitman to Glassboro, and I imagined their intense screaming to be their sexual fulfillment.

A quarter moon, along with my faithful headlamps, illuminated the bumpy, soggy, winter trail on the way back to the Pitman paved road. Suddenly, the now-dirty, begrimed Impala arrived at *a fork* in the road, and News momentarily confused me by saying it should have been a large tablespoon or knife instead. My confused judgment made me make a very wrong spontaneous decision. I veered the Impala to the right, when a turn to the left would have yielded a much more satisfactory result.

"Hurry, J.W." Peachy screamed and implored. "Get us back to our dorms' before there's big trouble!"

"I can't turn around right here or even back-up," I yelled in absolute frustration, "or we might get stuck again in sand. I have to look for hard level ground, where I can do either a U-turn, or the proverbial K-turn."

"J.W., you aren't goin' for your damned driver's license test, so just turn around already," News barked. "I don't care one iota what particular letter of the alphabet you choose to turn around in; just do it for Christ's sake, if not for *our* own!"

The dirt path the Chevy was on channeled into the driveway of a country home that was situated straight ahead. As I maneuvered the Chevy around the side of the house, I noticed that there happened to be a steep embankment slanting down to the road that I wanted to enter, but that no driveway or exit led to the desired highway. I then realized that the residents of the country house used the dirt road as their sole means of access and egress to the highway.

"This damned property doesn't have any driveway leadin' to the road down there!" I shouted in exasperation. "And I'm ripping-up this guy's lawn and runnin' over his shrubs and bushes! The damage is already in the hundreds of dollars!"

"We havta' get back in seven-minutes!" Elaine loudly hollered from the back seat. "That's only four-hundred-and-twenty-seconds between now and certain disciplinary trouble for Peachy and me! Hurry J.W.! Hurry!"

"It's only three-miles back to the college! You can make it!" News screamed like a psychotic asylum patient. "Hey, J.W. This wild drama reminds me of that book I read in high school titled 'A Hundred Yards to the Outhouse!' by Willie Maykit."

"Shut the hell up, News, you simpleton fool!" I bellowed. "Can't you see I'm doin' the very best I can to navigate this machine the hell outa' here!"

The downstairs lights inside the two-story home were flicked-on, so I stepped on the gas pedal to facilitate our most difficult getaway. Adrenaline must have been liberally pumping through all our beer-infected veins, as both girls and News perpetually shrieked, sounding as if the three passengers were a dissonant trio of shrill factory whistles. Suddenly, the outline of an incensed and screaming homeowner, dressed in his pajamas, slippers, and purple bathrobe appeared in the Chevy's headlights.

"He's holdin' a damned hatchet!" News screamed. "Run him over J.W.! Run the bastard over!"

Sobriety and discretion prevailed in my thought processes as I shut-off my headlights, so that the tall, hard-hat, deer hunter-type, pissed-off resident couldn't see *FNW-701* in bold black letters emblazoned on my cream New Jersey license plates. I adroitly zoomed the Impala to the left, knocking over a masonry birdbath, and demolishing a clothesline in my frenetic mania, and when I glanced-up into my rear-view mirror, my pupils were horrified to see the livid, crazed lunatic pursuing me, with his hatchet raised-up over his bald head. In desperation, I drove over and through a flower bed and then passed through a plowed-up garden; steered around all kinds of trees, and next accidentally crashed through a fence of yew bushes as the offended hostile homeowner acted out his animosity like an aroused monster on a late-night science fiction TV movie.

"Hurry, J.W." Peachy hysterically commanded. "Please Hurry! Elaine and I have less than five-minutes to get back to *Evergreen* and to *Linden!"*

Three times I drove around the despicable landscape, with the incensed madman in violent hot pursuit, until finally, I located the dark dirt road leading back toward the paved highway.

Everyone momentarily sighed with relief after thrillingly escaping the crazed lunatic's clutches, and then I sped to Carpenter Street and soon crossed *322,* reaching the college dorm' area with not a fleeting minute to spare.

"Thanks for the most exciting date of my whole entire life!" the attractive-but-harrowed blonde beauty queen in the front seat gasped. And then Peachy kissed me on the cheek, and she and Elaine frantically exited the white Chevy, and soon scurried-off to their respective dormitories.

News had a rare mental inspiration, so we neatly placed the twenty-four empty brown beer bottles back inside the cardboard case, closed the two folding lids, and then I drove down University and cut over to Harvard Road. I dimmed the headlights, and when the coast was clear, News brashly carried the trash guilefully discarded the beer case on the Delta Alpha Omegas' front doormat.

Before I had a chance, or the desire, to study Miss Sankins's newly-assigned text The *Fundamentals of Rhetoric* for the first time, Thursday, February 1st had arrived on the 1962 calendar. Joanne Berenato was back at *GSC* and almost fully recuperated from her painful hernia surgery, but everything seemed unusually quiet on the perilous fraternity front, almost like "the calm before the storm". The Lambda Phi nucleus was discussing the general situation at the Aura chicken coop, after the guys had suffered through another week of mind-taxing academics and senseless subject matter tests.

"Well, J.W.," Bob Abrams prefaced. "I guess you'll be getting another D this semester from old lady Sankins. If that witch keeps harassin' you, we'll have to do somethin' to her and give the ninety-year-old frigid virgin a reality wake-up call, now that the Delta Alphas and the Tau Kappas have been temporarily neutralized after their recent success at kidnappin' you and News because of windin' up in Trenton in the train box car. Those two creeps will think twice before ever goin' to the Glass Bowl again."

"J.W.," Tim Amoro (also known as "the instigator") chipped-in. "What's the one single thing in life that bothers you the most?"

My mind deeply pondered for a moment to sift through my catalogue of experiences to locate, retrieve, and collate that one human condition that bugged the hell out of me more than anything else. "Well, fellas'," I finally admitted, "I really hate walkin' through a public place like a department store, or a movie theater mezzanine, or a fancy hotel lobby, and walk right through somebody's stench-laden fart. Out of all the things I detest in life, that's gotta' be the most abominable one as far as I'm concerned."

"I empathize with you," News endorsed. "Once I was in a crowded Philly' elevator and someone really cut the cheese; I mean, a real nasty broccoli-type gas bomb. Fifteen people just stood there as silent as Roman statues and sniffed-away, like we all had wicked sinus congestion, and in our minds, we all silently tried identifyin' the inconsiderate rogue without havin' either the balls or the ovaries to make an accusation to a total stranger."

"Well, guys," Bob Abrams our fearless leader interrupted. "Things have been entirely too monotonous and docile on campus to suit me. Those Delta Alphas and those Tau Kappas are too sneaky, too subversive, and too damned subtle and sinister in their furtive ways. I say that the Lambda Phi's preemptively strike first, before the other frats' realize what's hit them."

"I understand that Ken Reynolds and Jack Thompson were mauled and battered pretty good by Mario at the Glassboro Train

Depot," Tim related. "And that those turd-brains would attempt somethin' direct except they're scared shitless to try anything with DiMaris being on our side."

"I heard it cost Reynolds and Thompson over a hundred bucks each to have their *Harleys* shipped back to Jersey from Massachusetts, via commercial freight," Hoppy gleefully reported. "But it's all relative to those rich silver-spoon-in-their-mouths wick dicks. I'm with Bob, though. Let's get our rivals so pissed-off and have them publicly humbled, those two pretentious dolts!"

"I have an idea that's designed just to piss them off good," News Tomasello ("the agitator") offered. "We'll have talented J.W. here ("the aggravator") pen a contrived letter to the college newspaper. Peachy Wilcox, Paul Meroski, and Alice Crensten are on the *Whit* editorial staff, and we can use our contacts and influence to get the controversial Letter to the Editor published."

"I don't know if this is such a swell idea after all?" I instantly objected. "Miss Sankins might read my letter and feel compelled to give me another stupid D or F for the missive's journalistic content."

"J.W., you did a fantastic job puttin' together the letter of apology to the deans to get us all reinstated into *GSC,*" Bob sugar-coated. "So, this new enterprise is right up your avenue."

"I think I'd rather sleep with Godzilla's mother!" I protested. "Make that sleep with his mother and with his two ferocious aunts and their sex-addict homo' brother-in-law, too!"

"J.W., we'll all gladly contribute ideas to your essay that will be designed to piss-off our campus enemies before they can launch a spring offensive against the Lambdas," Hoppy summarized the group's sentiments. "All in favor of J.W. authorin' the *Whit* editorial literary endeavor say, 'Aye'!" A resounding extended "Aye" permeated and resonated throughout the chicken coop's main entertainment room.

"All opposed to J.W. authorin' the controversial *Whit* article say 'No!" Since I was the sole dissenter to Hoppy's second motion, I lowered my head and then weakly raised my right hand.

Chapter 13
"The Whit Letter"

Wednesday, February 14th, proved to be most memorable and significant twenty-four hours for the Lambda Phi's in general, and for me in particular. News and I were innocently sitting in the Co-op and we felt a degree of uneasiness, because some rich-kid Delta Alpha Omegas and Tau Kappa Epsilons were in the snack area, too, exhibiting public affection with certain members of their harems, which seemed repugnant and indiscreet to Tommy Tomasello and me. The Paris Sisters enchanting smash hit "I Love How you Love Me" was playing over the Co-op's static-laden sound system, and that smooth melody had my heart and mind privately thinking about romance, while News Tomasello was busy verbalizing about dumb current events that to my ears sounded like the ultimate contemporary monotony.

"President Kennedy has announced a ban on all products bein' earmarked for Cuba," News prattled. "But conversely, there's been a few positive breakthroughs evolvin' with the Russians. Do you remember that U-2 pilot Francis Gary Powers, who was shot-down while spyin' over the Soviet Union?" News rhetorically asked. "Well, he's been released and exchanged for a Soviet spy that was in U.S. custody, named Rudolph Abel."

"Did Rudolph Abel have two brothers Ready and Willing?" I sarcastically remarked. "Damn it, News! Get a friggin' life! It's *Valentine's Day* and all *you* can do is prattle-on about a guy that sounds like a red-nosed reindeer."

"To put things in clear perspective, J.W.," my nonsensical friend contended, "just look at the money we're savin' by not havin' steady girlfriends. We didn't have to buy any damned flowers or *Whitman Sampler* candy boxes. And to me, J.W., that's really being frugal and conservatively economical."

"Damn it, Tommy. Didn't you hear me the first time? I said it's freakin' *Valentine's Day!"* I ranted in a very peeved and irate voice. "Talk about luscious *GSC* co-eds instead of the screwed-up world events featured in the papers and on TV!"

"Okay, Mr. Heartthrob," my rxtremely erratic and sometimes immature friend responded. "Tonight, on television, Jacqueline Kennedy is goin' to give Charles Collingswood a personal tour of the *White House*. I can't wait to see the new First Lady. Everybody says she's a New England aristocratic snob, but I believe she's kinda' cool and aloof in her own nifty sort of way. Anyway," News expounded, "*CBS* and *NBC* are gonna' televise the tour live and simultaneously, and it's estimated that over forty-seven million proud Americans are expected to view the anticipated broadcast."

"Speakin' of broadcastin'," I quipped. "I'd like to cast those slutty broads the Deltas and the Taus are makin' out with right out of the Co-op! Now, I can't wait until the *Whit* comes-out with my letter to the editor condemnin' the ugly practice of makin' out in public."

"And also, J.W.," Tomasello continued while deviating off target as usual, "listen to this historic event. An underwater cable has been planned runnin' between Hawaii and Japan, and *Ma Bell* is gonna' install the monster right through Midway, Wake, and Guam islands in the Pacific!"

"Great news, News!" I deliberately responded. "We can now get girlfriends in Tokyo, spend the rest of our dismal lives learnin' how to speak and write Japanese, and never get laid the rest of our damned tenure on this planet because we'll always be talkin' on the phone to Japanese girls in Japan."

Henry Mancini's "Moon River" was then pumped over the Co-op's intercom, and upon seeing several of the Delta Alphas and the Tau Kappas still grossly making time with their broads across the room, I became more than a tad jealous. And so, I began discussing my college classes, when much to my sense of security, Tim Amoro came through the snack bar's portals, bought a *Pepsi* and some *Tastykake Butterscotch Krimpets* at the serving counter, and soon joined *our* illustrious company.

"Well, if it isn't the 'Duke of Earl' and the Earl of Duke-dumb!" Tim laughed as the jovial Lambda concurrently referred to News and me in reference to a recent hit record by Gene Chandler. "Ya' know J.W., the *Whit's* supposed to come-out today, and I heard from Peachy Wilcox that Alice Crensten, Paul Meroski, and the rest of the staff are gonna' publish your controversial opinion letter."

I was feeling a bit edgy and worried, so I related to my two noble associates how rampant cheating was going on in my Philosophy class. "Actually guys, last Monday three of Dr. Kraft's five freshman philosophy classes took our first major test together in *Memorial Hall* cafeteria," I explained.

"Yeah, I'll vouch for that," Tim's voice concurred. "I was there, too. Kraft was too lazy to give the exam' three times separately because he's workin' on some publish or perish project, and needed more time to make a deadline, so he put all three classes together."

"Anyway, men," I proceeded. "A hundred-and-fifty freshman Philosophy students had been massed together like a gaggle of geese.

Kraft's examination was really tough, but I managed to stumble through the hundred-and-fifty objective items, based on three nights of dire cramming."

"Wow, J.W!" News exclaimed. "I see a correlation here! A hundred-and-fifty pathetic students takin' an exam havin' a hundred-and-fifty questions! What a remarkable coincidence!"

I completely ignored Tomasello's stupid brainiac articulation while Tim thought the non-stop idiot's analysis was hilarious. "There were kids whisperin' questions and low-spoken answers among the freshmen seated at my table, as if the test's multiple choice prompts were bullets ricochetin' off the walls at the *OK Corral,"* I emphasized with disgust in my voice. "Kant, Nietzsche, a priori, Plato, and at least a hundred other correct responses were lowly traded back and forth by seven other freshmen seated at my table."

"So, what did you expect college kids to be trading, kinky women slaves for tanks and machine guns?" News commented in one of his more-quasi-intellectual statements. "They're only college kids in the cafeteria with you, J.W., not Arab princes or Indian maharajas!"

"But some of the A, B, C, D, and None of the Above answers swishin' around the table conflicted with the ones I had circled on my exam'," I truthfully stated while showing some conscience and basic morality. "And although I soon recognized that my selections were incorrect, I gallantly refused to alter my responses under my own personal honor code."

"So, what happened next?" Tim curiously asked. "I didn't cheat either, J.W. but it seemed that immorality didn't matter one iota in Kraft's Philosophy class. Now, I definitely see your damned point. Philosophy is plain, flimsy bull-shit, even without any morality or immorality connected to it."

"While the cheating disgrace was evolvin'," I proceeded with my rhetoric, "the lax professor simply sat near the cashier's register and analyzed the obituary, sports, Metro, Hollywood and editorial pages of the *Philadelphia Inquirer."*

"The same kind of cheatin' happened at my table," Tim verified. "The seven Delta and Tau pledges that were exchangin' answer received A's and B's for test grades, while I emerged with a lowly C for being honest on the exam'. Four more correct answers and I would've gotten a B on the wicked test," Amoro regretted, "but like you, J.W., I believe that the ends always don't justify the means."

At that fragile moment, I guiltily thought about how Mario had swiped my objective questions and my essay booklet in another social studies class, and the thief had copied every detail and got away with his blatant impudence. But I had kept my mouth closed and didn't want to indict myself to my friends as being an involuntary accomplice to college cheating. Before I could say anything, News began discussing Dr. Peaferm, his eccentric, egghead Economics professor.

All of us knew that Dr. Peaferm was a strange Economics professor, who appeared to be more interested in his own private stock portfolio than in the balance of international trade; the guns versus butter debate; inflation, or the rising cost-of-living index. Peaferm's notorious drowsy monotone (even during his most enthusiastic oral presentation) eventually sent even the most avid students on one-way excursions to Slumberland. Dr. Peaferm's boring lecture method could never have cut the mustard in a public high school setting, but a lecturer of his unremarkable caliber could easily flourish in a more structured, and more respectful, college classroom environment.

News stated to Tim and me that the highlight of Peaferm's Economics seminar was a raunchy skanky coed that Bob Abrams had labeled and code-named Tokyo Rose. Bob and News would sit in Peaferm's crowded lecture hall and in a trance watch Tokyo Rose systematically squeeze the pus out of at least two dozen of her facial and neck pimples. This daily ritual would make the Lambdas in attendance revel, because it added a new dimension of oddity to an otherwise very dull and dismal class session.

"At least, Peaferm is just a damned boring teacher and not out lookin' for the lost *Holy Grail* like O'Connor is, or out in front of the room denouncin' capitalism and Christianity in the name of academic freedom like Rolphs is doin'," I stated with conviction.

"Yeah, J.W.," News abruptly ascertained and replied. "But sometimes socialist instructors are better than boring robots like Peaferm. Once or twice every class period the old codger forgets what he had said in previous lectures and then declares his standard utterance: 'The propensity to save and the propensity to consume, the curve goes both ways!' And then the defective idiot points in both directions at the same time like a confused traffic cop. I don't really know what the hell that propensity stuff refers to or means," News enunciated, "but that's the only damned thing I've learned from that friggin' *Samuelson Economics* text that Peaferm keeps repeatin'."

Tim then told us about Dr. Lane, his strange-but-fascinating Speech professor, who was another living legend among the college's bizarre faculty members. Amoro related that before the first second semester Speech Class commenced, Timmy had been sedately seated in his desk, awaiting the instructor's arrival into the upstairs *College Hall* classroom. An older gentleman, whom Tim had presumed was pursuing a teaching degree, was sitting next to him. The more mature "*Korean War* veteran" decided to initiate a conversation, and Amoro soon discovered that the gentleman was very critical of the unique Speech professor, who was about to enter the room to teach the course. "The elderly man used the terms 'lousy' and 'hideous' in his depiction of Dr. Lane," Tim described with a wry smile showing on his features. "But then I explained to the old guy that I hardly knew anything about Dr. Lane, except that the Speech teacher's behavior was rumored bein' a bit on the peculiar side. Five minutes elapsed, and then the distinguished-looking *Korean War* veteran sittin' next to me arose from his desk and announced to the class that he was the inimitable Dr. Lane," Tim conveyed, as News and I sat there somewhat amused with Dr. Lane's described originality.

"On the Speech Class's second meeting," Lambda Tim anxiously continued his oratory, "Dr. Lane made what he considered to be 'a spectacular entrance'. The nutcase had scaled the tall oak tree that had grown parallel to the main campus building. The tree was coated with mid-January icicles and snow, but Lane crawled-out onto a sturdy limb, and then clumsily swung his frame inside an opened *College Hall* second-floor window, just performed to shock and astound the class."

The three of us agreed that Dr. Lane's interpretation of the word creativity was doing something excessively irregular, or something unexpectedly sensational or uncharacteristic. The Speech professor's mannerisms were predictably unpredictable, and one could only expect the unexpected from his antics. However, according to Tim's infallible evaluation, even climbing through opened second-floor windows on cold winter afternoons; standing and lecturing from atop the teacher's desk, and shouting slanderous obscenities for no apparent reason at all soon became tedious and unimpressive after the enamored classroom audience became accustomed to their constant insane enactments.

"A lot of these English, Drama, and Speech teachers are really frustrated actors that wish they could've made it big in show business," Tim aptly concluded. "Say guys, I gotta' meet someone over in *Bosshart*. See you turkeys later at the coop."

"Do ya' wanna' play some pinochle?" I asked News. "I'll scout-up a few partners."

"Why would I want anybody to pee on my knuckle, especially a freak like you!" my card playing partner ridiculously replied. I was about to rise and leave the Co-op in sheer principle when much to my delight, Joanne Berenato entered the snack bar with Loretta Sacco, a good-looking chick that had attended St. Joseph High over in Hammonton. And I was totally thrilled when the two fair young ladies graced News and me with their excellent feminine company.

"Hi Joanne, hi Loretta," I awkwardly stammered. "How's your operation Joanne? Er, I mean, how are you recoverin' and healing from your hernia operation?"

"Thanks for askin', J.W. I'm feeling much better and stronger every day," the dark-skinned Italian honey answered. "I say I'm about ninety percent right now, and in about another week, I'll be back to normal."

"So, what's up gals?" News asked. "You two girls dating Delta Alphas or Tau Kappas, or what?"

"Don't be silly!" Joanne said while flashing her pearly whites and her big brown eyes across the table in my direction. "Loretta and I would never betray the Lambda Phi's."

"Well, the frat' house out in Aura is off limits because the administration shut the coop down to college parties and girls," I reminded the dolls. "And it's too bad you two had never been there? It was pretty boss while it was happenin'."

"Guys, we have a class in ten minutes over at *Bosshart,"* Loretta explained to News and me, "so Joanne would like to ask a big favor of you J.W., especially for me?"

"Why yes! I'll do anything for you two popular ladies, anything," I prematurely guaranteed.

"Well, J.W.," Joanne took over being the speaker as her companion felt compelled to blush. "Loretta really likes a certain Lambda named Tom Bell, and would like to meet him. And since this is *Valentine's Day,* I'll just pretend that it is really Sadie Hawkins Day, instead."

"Who's Sadie Hawkins?" News asked while fully knowing all about Joanne's funny papers' *Little Abner* comic strip allusion. "Wasn't she one of those suffragettes along with Susan B. Anthony and Elizabeth Cady Stanton?"

"News is just being facetious as usual," I assured Joanne, saving the luscious babe an unnecessary explanation. "My pal reads the *Little Abner* comic strips all the time. Now Tommy, study some large estates and learn some *manor,"* I disciplined my goofy friend.

"Well, here's what Loretta and I had in mind," the gorgeous Edgewood High Prom Queen proceeded to request. "Loretta and I would like to double date Tom Bell and you. What do ya' think about that as a special favor?"

"Well, Joanne," I stuttered. "I suppose you'd two like to go to the Glassboro Theater and see *West Side Story* starring Natalie Wood? It's gonna' win a lot of Academy Awards' Oscars for music, acting and scriptwriting."

"Are you kidding?" Joanne surprisingly replied. "Elaine Hill told me all about this neat place over in Pitman near a romantic fresh water lake. Instead of *West Side Story,* you and Tom Bell can buy a couple six packs of beer, or even some hard whiskey, maybe some *Southern Comfort.* Could you do me that big favor so that I could do Loretta a small favor?"

But then, News had to open his big maw again, speaking jabberwocky. "Girls, I gotta' tell ya' that lake over in Pitman is…"

"Shut-up News!" I squawked. "Sorry Joanne and Loretta," I apologized. "But T.T. here was gonna' say that *that* lake over in Pitman is the ideal place for romance. How about if I talk to Tom and arrange the date for Sunday night, February 25th? That should give us all enough time to plan and schedule the drinkin' date on our personal agendas."

"Yeah, J.W., don't forget that on Saturday the Lambdas have rented a bus and we're goin' to take a trip out to *Lehigh University* to visit some fellow Lambdas that are co-sponsorin' us into the national organization," News reminded me. "We gotta' look legitimate, ya' know! But girls, J.W. and Tom Bell oughta' be back from *Lehigh* by late Sunday morning to take you dolls out Sunday night."

"J.W., you're a real friend," Joanne complimented as the olive-skinned chick leaned across the table and gave me a cute, firm pinch on my left cheek. "Exactly what time will you and Tom pick us up Sunday night?"

"How about if we meet right here in the Co-op around seven," I recommended in my deep mellow voice, while attempting to act being nonchalant. "I'll have to have Bob Abrams pick-up the beer that Friday night before the field trip out to *Lehigh,* because the liquor stores are closed on Sundays."

"Thanks again, J.W.," Joanne graciously acknowledged. "Let's just say I owe you one." The girls got-up and stepped-out of the Co-op, heading in the direction of *Bosshart Hall* for their next class. I couldn't believe that Joanne and Peachy were knocking my door down to go out and drink alcohol with me while parked in Pitman at that polluted lake under the twinkling stars.

I hadn't fully recovered from the *Valentine's* Sadie Hawkins phenomenon when Big Al Keiler rushed into the Co-op carrying several copies of the *Whit.* "Geez J.W.," the anxious giant gasped and panted. "The ink's not even dry yet, and your controversial 'letter to the editor' made the campus newspaper. It's the hottest thing in the whole damned tabloid. Here's a copy for you and one for you, too, News. I'll read and regurgitate it aloud while you two bungling parasites re-digest its content."

> Editor:
>
> There are inconsiderate *GSC* students among us who delight in converting our beloved Co-op into a barbarous den of iniquity. This disgusting immoral public behavior is mostly practiced by raunchy members of the Delta Alpha Omegas and by representatives of the Tau Kappa Epsilons, who all falsely think that they are Big Men On Campus.
>
> As one's eyes survey the chamber of passion (that's supposed to be an innocent snack bar), it is not uncommon to witness prolonged caresses and other erotic indecency being practiced in public by the amorous Cupids and their seemingly promiscuous Aphrodites. Perhaps the rest of us should build a viable Student Union and leave these hedonistic animals quarantined to the Co-op. The next thing these degenerates will want to do is remove snack bar booths, and then install genuine Roman baths to facilitate their lewd public orgies.
>
> Moral decay is running rampant all over America, and the debauchery of the Deltas and the Taus and their apathetic women confirms *that* very true proposition. These savages should romp and frolic in other more remote environs more compatible with their emotional lusting and with their flirtatious cravings.
>
> If the Delta Alpha Omegas and the Tau Kappa Epsilons don't respect themselves or their lady friends in public areas, then it probably is demanding too much to ask of the Don Juans to consider the emotional needs of others that have to witness and endure their daily, shameful Co-op demonstrations. It is plainly obvious that right here on the *GSC* campus the first *Ten Amendment*s of the *United States*

Constitution are cruelly undermining the traditional sanctity of the *Ten Commandments* given to Moses.

Certainly, there are more appropriate settings to release pent-up tensions and anxieties than in the almost-sacred college snack bar. Donations are now being made and accepted to rent motel rooms and beds for these egotistical, valueless, amoral cretins.

J.W.

Class of '65

"Holy crap!" Big Al whooped. "And those Deltas and those Taus and their sexy lady friends over there are still unaware of your literary accomplishment," Keiler commended me. "I mean, why don't you just throw a couple of hand grenades across the damned Co-op and blow the enemy right-away into another dimension! This article will get some definite reactions, I'll bet. J.W., I feel a massive headache commin' on."

"Just sit-down, Big Al, and eat a couple of your *Three Musketeers* bars," News snarled. "You could always use more acne on your oily face. Maybe Mario will enter into the Co-op and airplane spin and aim your ass across the snack bar, right at the other rival fraternity guys. Then, you could be used as a misguided missile in place of the damned hand grenades!"

Big Al was about to efficiently pulverize News when Bob Abrams and Hoppy Cassidy came into the snack bar all excited, and I knew that News Tomasello was mighty glad to see them arrive on the scene like White Knights, or the *U.S. Cavalry,* because next to Mario, Al Keiler was probably the toughest and most powerful Lambda Phi frat' brother.

"Well, guys, I guess you've read my poignant article in the *Whit?"* I proudly announced to the pair of revved-up Lambdas.

"How come you two are all torqued and wound-up?" News suspiciously questioned Bob and Steve. "Did you two numb-,nuts finally lose your virginities?"

Bob overlooked News's sarcasm and began telling me about the time I had described how the Diablos in Levittown and how the Reds in Hammonton efficaciously used *honey wagons* to their advantage, and how the big mobile septic trucks helped defeat both the

Kamikazes and the Blues. After his fifth energy-charged sentence, I had to interrupt the loquacious guy for specific clarification.

"So, Bob, how does the notion of honey wagons have anything at all to do with me publishin' this bizarre Letter to the Editor in the *Whit?"* I directly challenged. "There're a few missin' pieces between your excessive enthusiasm and my goin' out on a limb for the Lambdas in the paper!"

"J.W.," Bob solemnly explained, "Hoppy and I had to do some overt stuff to our proclaimed enemies in coordination with you writing the biting article, so that the Deltas and the Tau Kappas will be so crazy and so pissed-off that the degenerates won't know which end was up, and which way is left."

"Exactly, what did you two do on your own that J.W. and I didn't know about?" News asked in a suddenly prosecutorial and serious tone of voice. "Perhaps you neurotic clowns could've confided in *us* before you're both covertly goin' out on a rampage!"

Hoppy and Bob quickly sat-down in the booth and reviewed their most recent activities in detail. Soon, News and I were horrified to learn of the fierce escalation in the ever-evolving war between the Lambdas and the Deltas, the Tau Kappas, and the already inflamed school administration.

"First of all, a honey wagon is too big and noisy to be able to irritate our opponents without givin' us away to our enemies," Abrams logically stated. "And so, a septic tank distributor over in Clayton let Hoppy and me borrow a special quietly operatin' pump that works just like a damned honey wagon."

"And then," Hoppy snidely and wickedly chuckled, "Bob and I sneaked-over to Harvard Road this morning, when classes were in session, and we transferred raw sewage usin' the special pump and a long plastic tube from the backyard septic tank, spewing fecal matter straight into the Delta Alpha Omegas' empty drained swimmin' pool. What a terrific, freakin', stinkin' mess!"

"And then, Hoppy and I ventured over to Academy Street on the east side of town," Bob deftly interrupted his fellow felon, "and we duplicated the process with the Tau Kappa Epsilons' cesspool, along with their drained-for-the-winter swimmin' pool."

"Holy Vatican shit!" News ironically exclaimed and then gulped. "You guys are vandals. I think you've committed a grand felony. They're gross criminal acts that could wind you' knuckleheads up in the state penitentiary. These ain't just simple pranks you're talkin' about! You guys could go to jail."

"Not really!" Hoppy passively explained. "Then, Bob and I skillfully did the same thing to the chicken coop. Now we're gonna' blame the Deltas and the Taus for vandalism over in Aura, and they're gonna' blame each other and us for destruction to their property. Things are gonna' become chaotic around here. Mayhem will prevail! Ain't it great?"

"But can't it be traced-down through investigations that you two scholarly nincompoops cut classes just to perform all this bizarre mischief?" I considered and presented. "You two idiots don't have alibis if the police get involved, unless of course you' frivolous nimrods believe that hippos and hogs can fly."

"That's perfectly okay, J.W.," Hoppy calmly expressed. "Bob and I had a couple of brainiacs come over to *GSC* from *Drexel U.* over in Philly', and we paid them a hundred bucks each to take Dr. Peaferm's Economics exam' for us over in the big *Bosshart* lecture hall. Bob and I will no doubt get A's on the objective test. Peaferm never takes roll and doesn't know any of his students personally, and everybody in the big class doesn't really know each other or care who's sittin' next to them, or where everybody else is seated."

As Bob and Hoppy continued revealing their extraordinary complex enterprises, I sank-down inside my area of the booth, overwhelmed with despair, while News was looking-through his copy of the *Whit.* I was totally unprepared to hear the remainder of Abrams and Cassidy's exceptional narrative.

"Ya' gotta' understand J.W. that most houses in the Glassboro-Pitman area aren't hooked-up to any town sewage lines," Hoppy informed, "so most homes around here have septic tanks, cesspools, or maybe even both!"

"And finally, J.W.," Bob Abrams mentioned with more than a trace of exhilaration. "Hoppy and I took the amazin' shit-transfer machine over to Pitman and got even with your favorite instructor, Miss Sankins. The old hag didn't have a swimmin' pool, so we pumped out the septic system, pried open a basement window, and then merrily flooded her cellar with her own crap."

News bit his top lip with his bottom choppers, and instinctively, I comprehended that something big was seriously *amiss* besides a contestant competing in the *Miss America* contest. "What's the matter now, News? What else in God's name could possibly be the matter now?"

"Guys," News revealed in a very defeated and melancholy tone of voice. "There's a small notice in the *Whit's* classified ad section stating that Miss Sankins's property over in Pitman has been purchased for seventy-five-thousand-dollars by eminent and revered Dr. Albert Lang of Runnemede, who stated in the ad that he 'wanted to live closer to the college'!"

Everyone seated at the table sat there like stupefied zombies with our mouths agape. No one at that moment knew quite what to say, or even where or how to begin saying it.

Chapter 14
"The Bus to Lehigh"

The next few days in February, my spirits made pendulum swings back and forth from one end of the emotional spectrum to the other. My mind was in euphoria knowing that Joanne and Peachy both lusted for my supreme companionship, but that ecstasy would soon be replaced an hour later, feeling betrayed by Bob Abrams and by Steve "Hoppy" Cassidy, with the conniving Lambda pair acting independently and destructively against *my* avowed enemies, without my knowledge and consent. And News and Tim provided little consolation and compassion. News was pissed-off that Loretta Sacco had no desire to go out with him, and instead, the girl had hopes of partying with Lambda Tom Bell. And all Tim Amoro wished to discuss with me was the big upcoming Lambda Phi Sigma bus trip to *Lehigh University*.

News, Tim, and I didn't confide with Ron and Mario about how we genuinely felt, or about the personal stuff that was occupying our minds, because those other two Lambdas that commuted with us Monday through Friday from Hammonton to Glassboro would break our stones mercilessly if Carputis and DiMaris detected any weak chinks in *our* thin armor. And perhaps the worst fate a college freshman could endure is to be persistently harassed by well-intentioned peers, showing their admiration by making *their* preferred subject of discussion being the focal point of representing a *hurting* conversation, generally known among victimized males as "ball breaking".

On Friday afternoon, News, Tim, and I had a typical parley inside one of the four student *Memorial Hall* lounges. Several Deltas and Taus occasionally meandered in and out, but never confronted *us* about recent mischief, and this left me to believe that a major storm (that was not initiated by Mother Nature) was heading in *our* direction. Of course, I had to get News on track, because the oblivious kid was neurotically babbling about remote and insignificant domestic and international events, and about the *Cold War* that had little relevance to the imminent war flourishing between the Lambdas and their surreptitiously quiet fraternity foes.

"I forgot to tell you guys that on Wednesday John Glenn became the first American astronaut to ever circle the globe three times," News blathered in his standard South Jersey accent. "Glenn was aboard a *Project Mercury* space capsule named *Friendship 7,* and President Kennedy is really thrilled by the space program's great achievement. Could you imagine bein' up there in orbit goin' around the Earth three-times with no other human being inside the capsule to comfort you? I mean, if ya' die up there, how are they ever gonna' get you down to have a funeral and a decent burial? Now that's what I call real courage!"

"News," Tim began his predictable expected criticism. "Don't you have a litter box in another room where you can sit-down in? We're off to *Lehigh* tomorrow morning. Abrams and Cassidy hired a bus, and all you want to talk about is impractical, nauseating academic crap all the time. It's like we never leave the damned classroom with you around, even after we've already left the damned classroom. Am I communicatin' my thoughts accurately?"

"And unfortunately, Mario and Big Al can't make the trip up to Bethlehem, Pennsylvania," I glumly informed, "because DiMaris has to take his wife to a gynecologist for a tunnel check, and Keiler has to work at the Camden docks. Did you guys know that Big Al's a part-time stevedore?"

"Stevedore? Is that the guy that comes into the ring with the swords and helps the matador kill the bull?" News ludicrously joked. "Oh no, I think that's the toreador."

"Get serious for once in your damned life, will ya, News!" I loudly reacted. "The Deltas and the Taus are after my rear-end for the creative *Whit* article; thanks to Abrams and Cassidy, *their* exotic swimmin' pools have been trashed with fecal matter, and both pools have now been maliciously transformed into cesspools!"

"They're still pools, aren't they?" News obnoxiously jested. "It's just a minor dictionary difference between common swimmin' pools and utilitarian cesspools!"

"And besides that," I ranted while paying little attention to Tomasello's stupidity, "Miss Sankins is all pissed-off ever since the real estate deal with Dr. Albert Lang never came off, because of more sensational fecal theatrics performed by Bob Abrams and Steve Cassidy. And I'm afraid that sooner or later, the local authorities are gonna' get involved in the labda shenanigans, and we'll eventually be studyin' in confining prison cells, and not getting any *GSC* credits towards graduation!"

"Maybe, J.W., we could become famous biologists while we're convicted convicts without moral convictions, and studyin' the cell theory in the nearest federal pen?" News spieled.

"The administration isn't gonna' get the fuzz into the picture," Tim maintained while completely snubbing News's idiocy. "The deans will procrastinate until the bitter end, because that's their 'last resort, besides Atlantic City. Bob and Hoppy are right," Amoro determined. "The Delta Alphas and the Tau Kappas will fight when they're good and ready, and they'll wanna' settle their own problems with us on their terms. The college brass doesn't want bad publicity and just tries to threaten us with suspensions and expulsions, while acceptin' our wonderful tuition money, and with Dr. O'Connor causin' them tons of grief, the school brass doesn't need or desire any more adverse news about the college' hittin' the wire services."

"Well, I'm sure glad somebody makes some sense around here," I commended Tim while indirectly mocking News's bothersome silliness. "Tomorrow, we roll up to *Lehigh,* and then on Sunday night, I have a big date with Joanne. But first let's get the important Bethlehem excursion over and done with."

"Maybe the bus will magically convert into a time machine and we'll go back a couple of millennia and see Jesus Christ born again in Bethlehem!" News absurdly and irreverently orated. "Hey guys, we could become authentic Born-Again Christians! And then, after we tour Bethlehem and vicinity, we might have enough time to visit Jerusalem and Nazareth!"

"Shut the hell up, News!" I admonished. "I need you right now like I need three brain tumors."

"Since you already have one massive brain tumor," News cackled, "then you'll just need *two more.*"

I didn't tell Tim and News that Miss Sankins had given me an F on my latest composition "Describe and Critique a Favorite Movie." I would've been approaching suicidal if I hadn't had the mental comfort of Joanne and Peachy craving my company, and for the anticipated camaraderie of the Lambda Phi Sigmas' historic odyssey, traveling up to *Lehigh University.* Those two positive notions were favorably preserving my nearly-exhausted sanity.

Early Saturday morning, February 24th, I drove News, Tim, and Ron from Hammonton to Glassboro, and parked the white Impala in the half-full *Bosshart Hall* student lot. The Chevy had a bona fide *GSC* parking sticker, and the campus cops patrolled the lot fairly regularly, so I felt pretty safe leaving my cherished wheels in *their* incompetent custody. The bus trip to *Lehigh* had been changed from a two to a one-day affair, so that meant the itinerant Lambdas would be home late that same night, and then I would have more than sufficient time to get rested-up and be ready for the my' fantasy Pitman Lake date with Joanne Berenato.

News, Tim, Ron, and I exited the Chevy, took a short cut through *Bosshart Hall,* paced past *Hawthorn Hall* and the *Campus*

School, and then detoured to the Co-op to drink some hot coffee and grab a few stale doughnuts. After using the *Memorial Hall* lavatory facilities, the illustrious entourage took a second shortcut through *College Hall,* trekked around half of the building's oval drive, and were soon at our destination, the generally inactive Glassboro Train Depot, where our chartered bus and driver were quietly waiting for our arrival.

"Hurry-up, guys," the huge, mustached black driver, with the nameplate "George Evans" attached to his uniform, urged. "You're keepin' me off schedule! I have another run into Baltimore later this afternoon, and then have to buzz back up to *Lehigh* to transport you scholars back to *Glassboro State!"*

"Yeah, you nitwits," Bob Abrams yelled from a bus window the ballbreaker had just opened. "You're holdin' us up without any guns or dangerous weapons! You four nutcases are walkin' like you have bricks up your rear ends, instead of hundreds of little brown, circular dingle-berries."

"You're just lucky it's a nice winter day," Hoppy yelled from the same open window as the Lambda co-founder caustically alluded to the abnormally warm forty degrees temperature. "Monday there's gonna' be a severe Arctic cold blast commin' down from Canada, and we're in for some Eskimo-like weather."

We boarded the antique Vineland Transit Company Bus, and I was glad that News sat with Ron Carputis, so that the gabbler could bombard "Chicken hawk" with his "babble-lonian" rambling, while I was parked next to Tim Amoro, who would provide more rational conversation than Tomasello would while en route to Bethlehem. We impatiently waited for fledglings Tony Petters and Gil Taylor to finally hop on, and Bob Abrams told George Evans that everyone that was coming had been present and accounted for.

"Without Mario and Big Al," I shared in a disconsolate tone of voice to Tim, "we're only thirteen guys goin' on this historic visitation. I hope it turns out to be a lucky thirteen!"

"We could've easily driven-up to *Lehigh* in three cars and nicely saved a decent bundle of money," Tim critically-but-constructively mentioned. "Bob and Hoppy are spendin' greenbacks like cash is about to go outa' style, almost like it's disposable toilet paper or somethin'. But I understand J.W. that we're gonna' get some more pledges soon to beef-up our ranks, and the ambitious new guys will contribute to the good of the order."

"That's super good news, Tim," I related. "We can use some new blood in this lackluster fraternity. I know some *GSC* guys that had attended Edgewood and St. Joe's that wanna' get into the Lambdas and become brothers. The prospects bug me almost every day in the Co-op about bein' recruited."

I noticed Bob and Hoppy sitting directly behind the driver's seat in front of Tim and me, and next I turned my head and saw Tom Bell conversing with Frank Morrissey; Mitch Toscini enjoying Phil Candido's company; Tony Petters and Gil Taylor swapping words; and moody-but-loyal Max Gunther, sitting all by his lonesome. And of course, News Tomasello and Ron Carputis were seated opposite Tim and me on the right.

"We oughta' be arrivin' at *Lehigh* in about two hours," I casually said to Tim. "I hear it's a beautiful campus, even in the winter time. It's almost *Ivy League,* and many people think it is part of the *Ivy League* because of its good academic reputation."

"Just like *Rutgers* up in New Brunswick, where my cousin still goes," Tim supplemented. "Lots of people think it's also in the *Ivy League* because the first recorded college football game was between *Rutgers* and *Princeton.* And *Rutgers* is the official state university. You'd think it would be called New Jersey State just like there's *Penn State*, *Ohio State, Colorado State*, *North Carolina State*, *Florida State,* and *Michigan State*!"

George Evans boarded the bus and stated that the driver had an important announcement to make. "I just heard over the radio from my dispatcher that there's a really bad accident northbound on the *Jersey Turnpike* near Exit 5," the powerful-looking black driver courteously stated. "So, to save time, we'll be headin' over the *Delaware Memorial Bridge* into Delaware, and then up *I-95* around Philly' toward the *Northeast Extension* of the *Pennsy' Turnpike,* which we'll take up to the Bethlehem-Allentown area."

The driver's negative information announcement generated a little gossip among the Lambda Phi's, but it all seemed like a minor inconvenience, and basically, sounded like practical decision-making to save time, even though the highway to *Lehigh* would, with the route adjustment, then be around twenty-five miles longer.

"That George Evans looks like he could even give Mario a tussle in either arm wrestlin', weightliftin' or violent airplane spins," Tim perceptively commented. "I wouldn't want that dude as an enemy, or as a friend of an enemy, that's for damned sure! George looks like he could knock-out Floyd Patterson or Rocky Marciano with one lethal punch."

"You can throw a couple of professional wrestlers into the ring with either Patterson or Marciano to fiercely go against Evans," I exaggerated, "and old George could probably send the opponents to the hospital emergency ward, too, by George!" I joked. "But laconic Mr. Evans, despite his intimidating appearance, can't be all that bad of a guy. He left the heater on with the motor runnin' so that we're all warm nestled inside this primitive bus, just like caterpillars nestled in their snug little cocoons."

George Evans left his driver's seat, and again, five-minutes later, stepped onto the bus after using the train depot's pay telephone "to re-consult with my dispatcher". Evans next closed the vehicle's door, and put the bus into first gear. Soon, we had passed the main entrance to the college oval and were on Girard Road, paralleling the railroad tracks, and also the location of the new Lambda Phi Sigma "caboose initiation". And then a left onto *322* had us heading towards *New Jersey Turnpike Interchange #2,* nine-miles down the busy two-lane highway.

The Southern New Jersey landscape, in the height of winter, is very drab, with a plentitude of barren deciduous trees; flat damp ground, and gray, cloudy skies contributing to the very dreary, dismal effect. And as we rode south, I thought about how I always felt lazier in the wintertime, and how I always was brimming with motivation and incentive during spring and summer. My brain then fully fathomed that there was a definite association between the New Jersey February' mediocre cold weather and my lack of robust academic initiative at *GSC.* Sunshine was definitely an energizing force that positively charged my winter-lethargy battery.

"I don't understand why our college is named *Glassboro State,"* I mentioned to Tim, while remembering an old Bo Jalonec joke from Levittown. "Because since we're traveling on this narrow *322* road, it should be called Two-lane University, instead."

"One more wisecrack like that from you' and I'll ask News to come-over here and take your place next to me," Tim muttered with a contrived smile. "Despite his apparent mental and emotional deficiencies J.W., sometimes Tomasello actually makes more sensational sense than you do, and sometimes, the simpleton is actually more-funny to listen to than either you or I!"

Everything seemed to be going smoothly until we reached the end of the *Turnpike'*, which was really *Interchange #1* and the toll road's actual beginning, starting from south to north. The impressive tall towers of the *Delaware Memorial Bridge* that spanned the *Delaware River* from Jersey to Wilmington could be seen in the distance, when George Evans soberly and stoically announced over the bus's speakers, "My brake idiot light is blinkin' on my instrument panel, so we're gonna' have to stop at a company garage in Carney's Point and get it checked-out. There should only be a twenty-minute-or-so delay. Sorry gentlemen, for the small inconvenience."

"We'd have been better off drivin' to Bethlehem in our own damned cars," I softly complained to Tim, enough so that George Evans could not eavesdrop. "The world might end and then we'll all be baskin' and roastin' in hell before this primitive crate ever gets us up to *Lehigh*."

"This bus looks like it's a leftover from the mid-to-late '40s," Tim commiserated. "I think the Russians that use the Siberian Transit Company's buses have better equipment than Vineland Transit has. This trip's started-out on the wrong foot, J.W. And if you're superstitious like me and believe in bad omens like the Number 13, you'd believe the same damned thing."

The antiquated bus motored and sputtered through Carney's Point and kept on going. Soon, the highway narrowed, and George Evans stayed on the bumpy road that was constructed through land that showed high reeds on both sides, which indicated that we weren't far from the Delaware River. And before anyone seated could criticize George Evans's driving ability, or his sense of direction, the archaic vehicle screeched to a grinding halt, a mere fifty-feet from the *Delaware,* the vintage vehicle demonstrating that its brakes were still adequately functioning.

George Evans hopped-out of his seat and suddenly exhibited a rather reprehensible, surly demeanor, which was not evident a minute before. And when the stunned passengers looked-out of the windows, we witnessed twenty-four Delta Alphas; twenty-four Tau Kappas, and six humungous, robed Japanese Sumo wrestlers with their arms folded under their fat chests, all standing right alongside our avowed enemies. Things at that moment seemed extremely ominous and rather dooming for the almost-petrified, traveling contingent of Lambda Phi's.

"I have the keys to the bus in my pants pocket, and I'm holdin' a tear gas canister that could burn your eyes right out of their sockets," George Evans nastily addressed his shell-shocked audience. "So, if you' white college punk assholes don't cooperate and leave the bus in an orderly fashion, I'll fire-off the tear gas, and that'll get your albino butts outside in a hurry!"

Led by stunned Bob Abrams and Steve Cassidy, one by one we obediently filed past the muscular driver and gingerly and apprehensively exited the decrepit bus. Immediately, the duped

Lambda Phi's realized that we had our backs against the bus and were hopelessly surrounded by our loathed fraternity' adversaries, along with awesome George Evans, and the very intimidating half-dozen hired hands costumed as Japanese Sumo wrestlers, all of whom were staring quite menacingly at us.

"What is this?" Bob Abrams unconvincingly protested. "First, we paid good money for a first-class-quality-bus and get this rattletrap tin jalopy instead, and now we're taken here to this God-forsaken riverbank against our will! What's up?"

"First of all, Creep, and also, you other subordinate Creeps in attendance," Ken Reynolds boldly ridiculed, "my uncle is on the board of directors of the bus company you asinine jerks had hired. When I found-out about your whoopty-do field trip to *Lehigh,* I got together with my good buddy, Jack Thompson here, and we both figured our fraternities would coordinate a happy joint activity."

"That's right," Thompson verified while standing in front of his rich-kid disciples. "And Ken and I didn't appreciate our rough ride in the freight car to Trenton, or the hefty transportation bill we had to pay to get out *Harleys* back from Boston. And now, you thirteen low-life Dick-heads are gonna' feel a bit of our wrath, commin' back like a boomerang to haunt ya'."

"Just wait a cotton-pickin' minute," Abrams answered while stalling for time to compose his erratic thoughts. "O,ur frat' house was flooded with raw sewage, and we suspect that either the Delta Alpha Omegas or the Tau Kappa Epsilons had done that vandalism."

Reynolds and Thompson looked at each other with dubious suspicious eyes and shook their heads indicating their mutual total denial of any wrongdoing.

"And the Lambda Phi's also think that you guys were responsible for squealin' to the deans about the *Christmas* party over in Aura," Abrams blatantly accused our chief adversaries. "And you're also the slime-ball scoundrels that stole our banner from the chicken coop; kidnapped two of our members up to New York's Hunts Point Food Distribution Center, and then had the extreme audacity to arrogantly put the white Chevy Impala up on the Co-op roof!"

"Some of those details will be discussed by the Deltas and the Taus' executive committees, and can be ironed-out later," Reynolds boomed back, asserting his imperial authority. "But right now, you unsophisticated, uncouth morons can all strip-down to your underwear. You're just really very lucky that it's a mild winter day this late in February."

The six hired four-hundred-pound Japanese Sumo wrestlers and the Herculean George Bell all stared and glared at us, tacitly signaling their intent to cause immediate bodily injury should any or all of the Lambdas not comply with Reynolds's cruel instructions. We all reluctantly conformed to the stripping demand, while a chorus of extended irritating laughter erupted from all those sadists witnessing our general discomfort and overall frustration. I never felt so humiliated in all my life as I involuntarily stripped-off my apparel down to my socks and jockey shorts. 'We're gonna' all die of hypothermia if we don't get our clothes back within an hour,' I conjectured and stated, as I shivered with my knees knocking together. 'I'm sure that the Alphas and the Taus are aware of that horrible possibility, and you sadists don't want to spend the rest of your years in prison for deliberate aggravated manslaughter.'

Three rival fraternity guards grabbed each of us by the arms and escorted the thirteen freezing Lambdas, who were soon roughly conducted to a stretch of beach a hundred-feet away from the Vineland Transit Company bus. We were ordered like obedient robots to stop just short of a fifty-by-fifty-foot cordoned -off square patch of sandy beach that, upon first impression, appeared to be recently tampered-with by shovels and rakes.

"Okay, you grotesque Lambda Phi Sigma scumbags, here's your most intriguing assignment," implacable Ken Reynolds emphatically commanded, much to the merriment of his chuckling, snickering and giggling colleagues. "First, you Dirt balls' have to get-down on your hands and knees and await further directions."

The thirteen of us, against our wills, got-down on our hands and knees, looking as if we were children about to play and crawl around in a sandbox. Then came Reynolds's next astonishing intonation. "Let me warn you thirteen Dip-shits that this is just a sign of things to come if you persist in defyin' the awesome Delta Alphas and Tau Kappas. Now Assholes, here's your simple task!" Reynolds boomed like a *Fort Dix* basic training lieutenant. "There are two-hundred clams that have been recently buried in the beach sand. All you freaks have to do is dig them up usin' only your mouths, heads, noses, teeth, and tongues. Then when you're lucky enough to find one," Reynolds bellowed and laughed, "you'll have to crawl and grovel over to those six empty bushels ya' see fifty-yards over yonder, with the shelled mollusk in your mouth, and gently deposit the clam you had the good fortune to find inside a bushel."

And then, Jack Thompson gave the most disgusting direction of the unsolicited enemy hazing. "And none of you fraternity wannabes' are gonna' get your clothes back until all two-hundred clams have been dug-up and placed inside the bushels with your mouths," the Tau Kappa Epsilon President demanded. "We'll keep count as each clam is found and then tallied."

And so, not wanting to get our testicles frostbitten, the thirteen mortified Lambdas crawled and groveled into the cordoned-off zone and clumsily maneuvered-around the four long poles that held-up the clothesline, marking the perimeter. Phil Candido was the first to discover a clam with his mouth and then crawl fifty-yards to place the creature into one of the six bushels neatly situated in a row. The cheering Delta Alphas, Tau Kappas, and their hired thugs all cheered and yelled-out in unison, "One!"

I felt like a human bulldozer as I stuck my face and head into the wet beach sand, attempting to locate a clam and help-out the Lambda Phi Sigma survival cause. I had finally found the eighth shelled mollusk, and then suffered the indignity of crawling towards the bushels with the dirty, sandy prize between my jaws, amidst abundant jeers and heckles. As I desperately advanced on my hands and knees towards my objective, Mitch Toscini and Max Gunther passed me going in the opposite direction, heading back towards the cordoned-off mouth-digging area.

After dropping the clam into one of the round wooden containers, I heard a loud chant of "Eight!" and then moved as quickly as I could on my hands and knees back to the "mollusk excavation zone". My mind remembered a similar incident involving a comparable beach on the *Delaware* up in Tullytown, Pennsylvania, where the ruthless Kamikazes had my pal Tinker and me buried deep in sand with only our heads exposed, and then the punks kicked soccer balls front a short distance into our already battered faces, but I now believed that the torture devised by the Deltas and the Taus was far more brutal, humiliating, and irresponsible.

I also recalled as I crawled-along how I was just several hours before thinking about becoming less involved in Lambda Phi Sigma, but as I endured more and more abuse during the shameful physical and emotional persecution, I then became exceedingly spiteful and vowed to my conscience to gain a deserving retribution for the extreme anguish the unlucky thirteen were presently suffering.

My mind lost track of how many clams my grimy face and tongue had managed to dig-up, but after depositing another creature into a bushel and hearing "One-hundred and seventy-three" boisterously shouted-out, I was cognizant that the arduous labor was finally reaching its culmination. As I thrust forward like a wounded turtle back to the cordoned-off area, Jack Thompson crudely yelled at me, "I'll bet you, J.W., that you're wishin' right now you have a bearded clam in your mouth instead of that ordinary one you just contributed into the bushel! And if ya' find a pearl inside one of those damned dirty clams," the Tau Kappa Epsilon head cretin loudly yelled and snickered, "just imagine it's a nice, super-hard, aroused clit!"

I never felt such enmity towards another human being as I had that very second, when I had the presence of mind, even under great duress, to fully contemplate the wise guy's most insensitive and vicious remark.

After a hundred and ninety-nine clams had been unearthed, the thirteen Lambdas frantically shoved wet sand and silt around with our dirt-smeared faces, sand-laden noses, and grimy heads to locate the final shelled animal. All the while the roar of laughter from our thoroughly amused vindictive audience was reaching a crescendo.

"You'd all better hurry!" Ken Reynolds screamed above the ascending din. "Precious time is ticking away! High tide's coming in about an hour, and we don't care to be witnessin' any or all of you dimwits drownin'! Ha, ha, ha! And don't get too nervous, or all you' moronic retards' might all get clammy hands in addition to clammy assholes! Ha, ha, ha, ha, you stupid-ass bozos!"

Without any of the totally preoccupied Lambdas ever noticing, the Delta Alpha Omegas, the Tau Kappa Epsilons, and their retinue of hired henchmen quietly retreated to the Vineland Transit bus, and the next thing we knew, Ken Reynolds yelled-out of an opened window to us, "You stupid imbeciles! There were only a hundred and ninety-nine clams buried in the sand, and you got the total job done fifteen-minutes ago!"

And then, George Evans violently closed the bus door, started-up the sputtering engine, and pulled-out of the ordinarily secluded and deserted riverbank area with a bus-full of merry, hooting, and jeering rival fraternity passengers, along with the six immense Japanese Sumo wrestlers standing in the aisle.

The thirteen very fatigued Lambda Phi's slowly rose to our feet and then trudged back to where our clothes had been piled. Our heads were crestfallen, and our spirits were fragmented and virtually shattered. Since my body was just about frozen, I searched for my undershirt in the pile of garments, and if anyone were watching we thirteen frantic seekers, our wild futility must have appeared like a group of pathetic mendicants scouring through an incomprehensible rubbish mound.

"Our shoes and sneakers are missin'!" I heard Bob Abrams yell. "Those son-of-a-bitches have taken our shoes and our sneakers back to Glassboro with them!"

I never felt so utterly belittled and defeated in all my life. The contemptible misadventure was extremely devastating to one's heart and severely damaging to my soul. And just like my twelve exhausted fraternity brothers, I was very mentally depressed from the insulting ordeal, and *we* thirteen very depressed Lambda Phi Sigmas certainly were egregiously afflicted with deflated egos and terrible flagging spirits.

Chapter 15
"The Double Date"

The thirteen ruse victims trudged from the sandy wet *Delaware River* beach back up to the pot-holed road, and then our path meandered through the tall reeds in quest of the first semblance of civilization. Nobody had the strength or the guts to openly accuse Bob and Hoppy for the gruesome debacle we all had recently experienced. But the two fraternity co-founders felt quite guilty about the fiasco/ordeal and went through separate grievous oral examinations of conscience as if the rest of the Lambda Phi's were priests, hearing their mutual sin in an open-frigid-aired confessional.

"It was my fault for bein' too trustful and gullible," Bob lamented as a flock of seagulls flew overhead, going east towards the *Atlantic*. "When I saw that *World War II* vintage bus at the train depot, a red flag should've gone up."

"I feel like a fool, too," Hoppy remorsefully concurred. "Who would've ever thought that Reynolds's uncle was on the bus company's board of directors? If all the buses the corporation owns are like the piece of junk that hijacked us, then I'll predict that transport-company will be defunct by *Memorial Day*. On second thought," Hoppy reassessed, "make it by *Easter!"*

"It wasn't your fault, you guys," Timmy declared to the contrary. "We were all just as gullible as you were and thought we were on the way to *Lehigh*. But now, I gotta' admit we're on the way to hypothermia if we don't soon get our friggin' shoes back."

"Things are gonna' escalate and get worse," I testified from past knowledge and practice. "I've been in similar situations before in Levittown and in Hammonton, and I only hope that no one gets accidentally killed, as the outrageous conflicts and the pranks become more-fierce."

"Well, I say things could've been more punishin' and much-more-evil than they were!" News objectively insisted. "At least, the Delta Alphas and the Tau Kappas didn't force us to give them blow-jobs while we were on our knees!"

"It was too cold bein' exposed to winter weather for the faggot freaks to get and sustain erections," Ron Carputis eloquently and logically contributed. "If this travesty had happened in June or September, then News's screwed-up remark probably would've been more accurate, and right on the mark."

"Yeah, News," Hoppy agreed. "Your idiotic comment really sucked! You oughta' change your name to Phil Laychio!"

After slogging, without shoes, on the in-need-of-repair road, trudging half a mile in the direction of Carney's Point, the disheveled, struggling, nomadic group approached an old white single story clapboard house, which instantly buoyed our spirits, even though the abode looked quite ramshackle. Someone was home, because Bob and Tim had seen in the window a human silhouette standing behind the sheer curtain.

"At least the person has a telephone," Tim observed and reported as Lambda Amoro pointed to a cable line extending from the dilapidated in-need-of-paint dwelling to a utility pole. "The owner of this dump must've been the first person in New Jersey to get electricity. Some grumpy old recluse, or grouchy hermit, must live here. Don't be surprised if the person's too feeble or too afraid to answer the damned door."

As it turned-out, an eighty-year-old woman was residing in the dingy shack, and the hag had already notified the local police of our intrusion, which the spinster described in her statement to the fuzz as "trespassin'." The elderly hussy had told the Carney's Point cops over the phone that she believed that the Lambdas were a band of illegal immigrants that had been stowed-away on a merchant ship and then dropped-off on the New Jersey side of the *Delaware River*. And if it hadn't been so cold and if we hadn't been so physically and emotionally wasted, her "illegal alien" story would have been a bit humorous, because at that precise moment, the Lambda Phi's all felt as if we actually were illegal aliens from another planet, let alone illegal alien refuges from Cuba, Russia, China or Poland.

Bob and Hoppy didn't want to implicate the Delta Alpha Omegas and the Tau Kappa Epsilons into a complicated, comprehensive criminal investigation, believing as the rest of us did that the valiant Lambdas would fight the fraternity war on our own terms, and settle matters without the intervention of conventional societal authority. Remarkably, the police bought into our presentation, probably because they wanted to expedite the problem without a lot of bureaucratic red tape, and also, the patrolmen didn't intend to have the parasitic press capitalize on the sensational story and give the somnolent river community a regional bad name.

"It was simply a childish fraternity prank," Bob explained to the four amused cops that showed-up in two squad cars. "We were in the process of pledgin' into a *Glassboro State* frat' and suffered a little hazing on the beach, that's all."

"Nobody was injured or hurt," Hoppy chimed-in. "And officers, we don't mean this lady any harm. We only wanna' get back to

Glassboro, take hot showers, drink some hot chocolate and coffee, and consume some stale doughnuts just like we always usually do!"

"And we'll be willin' to pay from our treasury for any inconvenience on your part and for transportation back to the college," Bob Abrams apologetically asserted. "And officers, we've been accepted now into the fraternity because we've survived the cute little hazing, so we've all accomplished what we've desired and no one has to be hospitalized, and I assure you, no local property has been damaged."

The arguments advanced must have been convincing, or perhaps the cops didn't want to be bothered with a general nuisance originating from outside their pristine, isolated hamlet. And so, the patrolmen described the problem to their Chief from their car radios, and the head fuzz at headquarters contacted the Penns Grove Police Department several miles away, and fifteen-minutes later, a third patrol car arrived on the scene. After the Lambdas thanked the cantankerous old senile hag for her helpful assistance, we all climbed into the three fuzz cruisers and were driven to the Carneys Point station, where we impatiently waited for our mode of transportation back to Glassboro.

A half-hour later, a pale blue bus dispatched from the *New Jersey Department of Corrections* showed-up, and the thirteen fatigued and grimy Lambda Phi Sigma members were herded aboard as if we were cattle, being shuttled-off to the slaughterhouse. We were all appalled at the specific identification of our rather demeaning means of transportation.

"This is a bus used to transport chain gangs cleaning litter off the major highways," Bob Abrams mildly protested to the driver. "And it's also used to shuttle felony convicts around the State from county to county."

"Just be glad you're getting back to your college in one piece without a lot of bureaucratic hassle and law investigation," the Penns Grove Police Chief prudently cautioned. "Your parents and the deans could've been notified, and disciplinary action could've resulted from crimes your fraternity friends and sponsors had committed. Consider yourselves lucky getting away with your stupid lark without any negative consequences showing on police records, fines, or penalties. But if ya' really want to know my opinion," the Chief-of-Police remarked with a contrived frown, "all thirteen of you carefree juvenile jokesters should be spendin' the night and a few additional days thereafter in the county jailhouse."

The bus driver must have been rather parsimonious because he took all back roads instead of the *Turnpike* on the way back to Glassboro, possibly in order to save money on tolls. We traveled through Swedesboro and Tim noticed that News and I both breathed heavily and trembled a little when the bus zipped by Back Creek Road, and in the distance could be seen the packinghouse to the memorable Glossy Fruit and Vegetable Farm.

"This is the closest I ever want to bein' a convicted criminal," Timmy honestly attested with conviction. "But J.W., once I take a hot shower and drink a few shots of hard whiskey to warm-up and have nice dry shoes on my feet instead of damp socks, I might change my mind about actively creatin' some more grief for the raunchy Delta Alphas and the antagonistic Tau Kappas."

"And those cops are really gonna' have to get a cleanin' service to scrub all of that sand and dirt we left behind in their bathroom sinks and hoppers," I reminded Amoro. "And after we were done freshenin' up, News took a royal dump, and when Tomasello flushed his toilet, the *DOC* bus's bathroom throne overflowed onto the floor and made an un-majestic mess."

"Don't speak so loud," Tim advised me. "This driver might report that incident to the station, and then be ordered to turn-around and keep us in the clinker overnight to clean up the debris. Say, why's everybody in Swedesboro standin' on the sidewalks starin' at us like we're wanton criminals or something?" Amoro quipped.

The reticent, stern driver dropped us off in the *Bosshart Hall* parking lot, and we were all relieved to see that our cars were still there in good condition. We then drove in four frat' autos out to Aura to inspect the chicken coop, and after we converged on the scene, were delighted to discover our shoes heaped outside in a mound' of leather and canvas. Of course, my left shoe was knotted with News's right sneaker, and no two shoes matched that were tied together, and the aggravation required an hour of assiduous untangling. But finally, the chore was completed, and we spent the rest of the day removing the raw sewage from the smelly coop and using detergents, bleach, and cleansers all over the place to eliminate the crud and the general stench that pervaded the building.

After the tedious six-hour "housekeeping" job was done, the guys ordered carryout steak sandwiches from Joe's Sub Shop, and frankly, fast food never tasted so good. After consuming our supper, the Lambdas downed some shots of *Southern Comfort* and *Jack Daniels* and discussed recent developments. Then later, we strategically outlined some prospective future battle plans.

"If the Deltas and the Taus are mostly spoiled rich kids," I naively asked Bob and Hoppy, "why are they spinnin' their wheels at a teachers' college for middle-class students?"

"That's easy, J.W., and sometimes you're pretty wet-behind-the-ears despite your general intelligence," Bob Abrams simultaneously complimented and chastised, as was the Lambda Phi method of communicating with each other. "First of all, they're all lazy laggards, and their futures are basically secure. For example," Abrams proceeded, "Reynolds is gonna' take over his father's farm over in Swedesboro, so he's just attendin' *GSC* to fill some time in his empty life. So, to our frat' rivals, *Glassboro State* is a little less rigorous than *Harvard* or *Yale* might be. Harvard Road is the closest Reynolds will ever come to obtainin' an *Ivy League* education."

"And secondly," Hoppy verbally contributed. "There are war clouds on the horizon, especially with Communist expansion into Southeast Asia. Places like Vietnam and Cambodia are in political turmoil. And so, Reynolds, Thompson and the rest of those bratty bastards are exempt from the draft, just like we Lambdas are, as long as they're attendin' college for an education, that, in their case, they'll never need or use."

"Look, guys," I countered in defense of a very possible grave Asian conflict. "My father was in the *Army* and fought the Germans in Europe in *World War II,* and I resent you guys tryin' to get out of servin' your country and avoidin' the draft at every damned opportunity. In that respect, you're no better than the Delta Alphas and the Tau Kappas are!"

"J.W., we appreciate your idealistic patriotism," Abrams suavely answered. "But *World War II* was justified with Hitler tryin' to take over the world and takin' away our American way of life, not to mention *Pearl Harbor* also happenin' with the Japanese surprise attack. This business with the Asian Communists advancin' is more political rhetoric, and represents a lot of verbal government bull-shit than it projects a real existential threat to our country's security," Bob lectured. "It's a lot of political Democratic and Republican propaganda bein' marketed as American patriotism, and I think, J.W., that you've fallen for it, hook, line and sinker."

"And besides that reality, J.W.," Hoppy hopped-back into the political-philosophical discussion. "Would *you* go to war and fight your ass off for Deans Robeson, Lang, and Nelson? Would you fight for Rolphs or Sankins? For Reynolds and Thompson?"

"Why no!" I tersely and succinctly-fossil responded. "But I don't see the specific connection between the three deans and a potential Southeast Asian war."

"Those three administrative old-fossil deans are bureaucrats, just like the *White House* administration and the *Pentagon* are in Washington," Steve Cassidy persuasively volleyed. "And the only difference between the educational bureaucrats at *Glassboro State* and the political bureaucrats in *DC* is that the bloodsuckin' leeches in Washington are much more successful and much more powerful than the *GSC* administrative worms are."

"I hear that if there's really an Asian war," News seriously speculated and uttered, "then the college exemption might be lifted, and an age exemption like twenty-one and over will go into effect. Anyone younger than twenty-one and older than eighteen would be eligible for the draft, because the *Army* will need more warm bodies to become cold bodies in body bags."

"And then, after that," Tim piped-in and predicted, "a college guy will have to be twenty-one, married, and have at least one kid to be exempt from the damned war. And I don't know about you other fellas', but I fear the Delta Alphas and the Tau Kappas and their gigantic hired Sumo wrestlers, and George Evans, a lot more than I'm afraid of any Chinese or North Vietnamese Communists, half way around the damned world."

"I'll drink to that!" Bob Abrams saluted with his half-full glass of *Southern Comfort* on the rocks. And then, we all raised our glasses in agreement and eagerly consumed our potent sweet contents.

Phil Candido and Mitch Toscini lived in *Mullica Hall* dorm' next to *Evergreen Hall,* so Tim, News, Ron, and I left the now spic and span frat' coop and motored in my faithful Impala over to the new *GSC* building, and gladly took refreshing hot showers in the men's room. Hot water never felt so good to my weary bones and to my aching muscles.

When I eventually arrived home in Elm that Saturday evening, my father told me I should get some rest and should lead a life of moderation because I "look like crap". I was inclined to tell Dad that several hours before I had smelled like crap while scrubbing-down the floor and walls of the putrid-stench that had been corroded inside the chicken coop, but I refrained from prolonging the exchange of words and dutifully stepped upstairs, turned on my bedroom FM radio, and listened to "It's Now or Never" by Elvis; "Wild One" by Bobby Rydell, and "Everybody's Somebody's Fool" by Connie

Francis, and those three popular numbers reminded me of my scheduled date with Joanne Berenato; of the clam digging farce, and of being deviously tricked by the combined efforts of the Alpha Delta Omegas and the Tau Kappa Epsilons, respectively.

I was much more spry and energetic Sunday morning, and I even attended mass at St. Joseph's Church over in Hammonton, taking my younger brother and sister to the service. I did some research for a term paper on *Plato's Republic,* which was due the following week in Philosophy class; finished another low-grade D or F composition on "Why Human Rights Are Important!" for the never-satisfied Miss Sankins, and then finally anxiously got ready for my big drinking date with Joanne, Tom Bell, and Loretta Sacco.

I met Tom in the Co-op at a quarter to seven, and my fellow Lambda insisted that we all go-out in his dad's new blue and white *Ford Fairlane*. "My family's always preferred *Ford* products over *General Motors* or *Chrysler Corporation* cars," Tom revealed, "and the new wheels should really impress the girls."

"My dad's just the opposite, liking the *General Motors* Chevy over Fords or Dodges," I replied. "But to me, a new car is a new car. Say Tom, don't ya' think that Mario and Big Al were really lucky stayin' away from the *Lehigh U.* trip that never materialized and ended in a total social disaster for the Lambdas? Tomorrow we might be the laughin' stock of the college."

"Maybe so, J.W.," Tom expressed. "But forty-years from now, you and I will have a really cool story to tell our grandchildren about what happened on February 24th, 1962, and those two dwarf brains DiMaris and Keiler won't have anything to remember or say about the damned incident, which we had amazingly survived."

"Tom, Mario's around ten-years older than we are," I mentioned, "and the *Baker* fibber once told me he was in the *Korean War*. Somehow, the war warrior wound-up in Germany, and then in England on military assignment transfers, and when his wife was about to have her baby," I stressed, "DiMaris received special permission to come home across the *Atlantic* to New York on the *Queen Mary,* where according to the fat Sicilian, he had a ritzy first-class suite paid for by *Uncle Sam."*

"Forget buyin' the *Brooklyn Bridge* J.W. If you believe that tall tale about the *Queen Mary,"* Tom indulgently laughed, "you'd believe me tellin' ya' that I'm both Mario's biological father and his lesbian mother, and that *his* grandmother was the real Queen Mary."

"Well, anyway, Tom," I answered. "Mario told me he had heard a rumor that the Deltas and the Taus had ridden-down to Carney's

Point in a first-class luxury bus that had arrived twenty-minutes before George Evans's orange tin crate on rusty wheels got there, with us foolish victims aboard."

"I get it now," Tom suddenly realized. "Evans was really talkin' to the other bus driver on the payphone at the train depot, and not to the bus company dispatcher like he had said."

Joanne Berenato and Loretta Sacco entered the nearly empty Sunday night Co-op looking like professional models wearing sweaters and denim jeans under their furry winter coats. The chicks seemed rather anxious to be going-out with two dynamic, handsome studly Lambda Phi Casanovas.

"Hi Joanne and Loretta," I cheerfully greeted. "Maybe in the fall Tom and I can take ya' out pumpkin stealin' with us over in Mullica Hill. Last year, a farmer was shootin' buckshot pellets at our rear-ends when we made our fantastic getaway. There's nothin' like the thrill of escape from danger while havin' an excitin' college-type action-adventure scenario."

"Tom and Loretta," Joanne began, "my father doesn't like me going out with J.W.," my date disclosed much to my edification, "because he's not the son of a peach farmer, and because he's always involved in some kind of goofy controversy or conflict. But they're probably the main reasons I enjoy his company. You never know what's gonna' happen next when J.W.'s around. He doesn't find adventure. Adventure finds him!"

"Would you girls like something to eat before we meet Bob Abrams outside Mazzeo's Bar?" Tom asked. "Ya' never want to drink beer on an empty stomach!"

"Well, if you could stop somewhere and buy some clams," Loretta casually suggested. "That would be great. Fresh oysters are outa' season, so clams would be the next best thing."

I gulped three times nearly swallowing my Adam's apple upon hearing the word "clams". "Have you girls heard anything about clams involvin' the Lambda Phi's?" I asked.

"No, silly," Loretta quickly clarified. "Clams are supposed to give people more passion at the right time when oysters aren't available; that's all I was trying to say!"

"Well," Tom added while turning as beet-red as my face must have been, "maybe next time we can have clams with beer. We gotta' rush now because of your dorm' curfew, so we'll get some potato chip and pretzel bags at the counter. I mean, life would be hell without junk food."

After Tom and I made our snack bar purchases, the four of us strolled out to Bell's shiny new *Ford Fairlane,* which was parked in the student commuter lot between *Bosshart* and *College Hall.* We made small talk until Tom steered his wheels off *322* East onto Main Street; passed Angelo's Diner; then headed left on High Street, and finally two blocks down, turned into Mazzeo's Bar and Liquor Store's parking lot. A sleet-type of mixed drizzle was falling, and Joanne requested that Tom and I be careful because "there might be black ice out there on the asphalt".

Bob Abrams's familiar '57 black Mercury sedan was already in the establishment's lot to make the case-of-beer transfer to the *Fairlane.* After that elementary task had been completed, Tom and I paid Bob for the brew, thanked him for his grand favor, and after Bell closed the new Ford's trunk, we were ready to roll on out to the romantic, polluted lake over in Pitman.

"Be careful, Tom," Joanne cautiously advised. "The roads are really slick and slippery tonight. I don't want to sound like a crapehanger, but I also don't want to see anything bad happening! It's always best to be safe instead of sorry."

"Joanne, are you a soothsaying witch, or what?" Loretta laughed from the front passenger seat. "Always hope for the best, and don't ever think about or dwell on the worst. I admit; Italian girls are too superstitious! What am I sayin'? I'm Italian, too!"

Tom maneuvered his new Ford back to the liquor business's entrance/exit onto High Street, when all of a sudden, his engine made a blustering, thunderous noise. The automobile swayed and then swerved from side to side, seeming much like an out-of-control subway train going amok.

Apparently, Tom's gas pedal had gotten stuck to the floor, and the engine's power was too great for the new car's brakes to offset. Before Bell had the wherewithal to switch-off the ignition, the new *Fairlane* rocketed across High Street as the girls screamed-away like banshees. Traffic was heavily flowing in opposite directions on Glassboro's main drag, and miraculously, our car sandwiched right between two autos with honking horns approaching from the east and from the west, and both vehicles barely missed ramming the brand-new *Fairlane.* As the girls shrieked their tonsils out, the run-away *Ford* careened off of a parked station wagon; hopped a curb; skidded onto the far sidewalk, and then smashed directly into an unoccupied beauty salon, shattering the front pane-glass window. Then, two jardinières containing artificial green bushes came plopping-down and crashed onto the already-cracked windshield.

Tom frantically fumbled to shut the contraption off, while thick smoke was billowing-up from the still-whining engine. I deliberately collided my body against the left-hand-side back seat door, which much to my relief, opened after the fourth try. I leaped-out of the sedan; grabbed my date in an unmannerly emergency fashion, and pulled Joanne from the untamed machine. I then helped Tom get his door open while the Ford's back wheels furiously kept spinning-around on the wet pavement, and then Loretta hastily exited, too. But then a knowledgeable and fearless spectator stuck his head inside the car and had the presence of mind to silence the machine by reaching inside and turning off the ignition. As I regained partial sanity, I observed red flashing police beacons, and heard in the distance fire engine sirens coming east on High Street from the direction of Main.

I recall Joanne limping and hopping-about like a wounded robin, sobbing and complaining that her left ankle badly hurt, and I suggested to her to lean her weight against me while standing on her good right foot. In the meantime, Bob Abrams grabbed Tom's keys from the ignition; opened Bell's trunk, and cleverly removed the case of beer possessed by the four illegal under-twenty-one minors. Then, Abrams handed the still-stunned Bell back his keys. The entire scene was chaotic, and the weird accident event soon became cluttered with bystanders and ambulance chasers.

Paramedics administered first aid to Joanne's bleeding left foot, and then the four of us were conducted to the Glassboro Police Station situated behind the grand old brick façade bank on High and Main. The police notified Tom's father of the extensive damage inflicted by the registration owner's car, and also, Joanne's parents were contacted about her "sorely sprained left foot".

First, Tom's irate father entered the police station, raving like a maniac, and fifteen-minutes later, Joanne's strict pop duplicated Tom's dad's bellicose entrance. The infuriated adults' eyes were blazing with anger, and the Glassboro cops on duty attempted calming-down the two incensed parents, as the livid adults paced-around and peppered the entire station with a string of expletives, curse words, and uncomplimentary slang references. In fact, it was not until the fuzz threatened to arrest the two emotionally stressed parents that the fathers eventually ceased verbalizing their excessively derogatory remarks and critical vulgarities. After a very turbulent, raucous, and uncultured half-hour, things finally cooled-down, and thank goodness, reason once again prevailed as the master of out-of-control temper.

"I spoke with the ambulance attendants, and Joanne's gonna' be all right," Bob told Tom and me outside the still somewhat noisy Glassboro police station. "It's a very bad sprain. She'll need crutches, a cast and therapy for around three-to-six weeks, but then your girl's ankle should heal okay."

"Joanne's just getting over a hernia operation, and now she has to suffer this," I guiltily divulged to my friends. "Life's just not fair sometimes. That was the most-freaky auto accident I've ever seen or been involved in!"

"Well, sometimes you're right, J.W.," Tom Bell related as Bob nodded his head in complete accordance. "But this time, I believe you're dead wrong."

"What do ya' mean?" I incredulously asked. "Accidents do happen you know! I think the problem was a new car defect! A freak malfunction!"

"Not to brand new cars. They don't malfunction like that," Tom Bell declared with a bulldog-type expression upon his face. "I think that the Delta Alphas and the Tau Kappa Epsilons had sabotaged my car when we were sittin' in the Co-op, and I suspect that their wicked tinkerin' almost got the four of us killed!"

Chapter 16
"The Blame Game"

On Saturday, March 3rd, News, Tim and I were sitting in Joe's Sub Shop discussing the most recent escalation in the ongoing frat' war. Each one us admitted that we had been seriously thinking about resigning from Lambda Phi Sigma, but now that we fully understood the magnitude of the hostility being generated against us by the Delta Alphas and the Tau Kappas, the three *LPS's* had a moral obligation to hang tough and demonstrate unwavering loyalty to each other, and to the illegal fraternity during the time of crisis.

"That Mazzeo bar incident was not caused by any defect in the *Ford Fairlane,"* I concluded and assertively stated. "A skilled mechanic had to fool with Tom's car to make the accelerator stick to the floor like it did, and workin' on a farm, Ken Reynolds would certainly have acquired certain mechanical skills fixin' huge tractors and keepin' irrigation pumps, packing machines, and other equipment goin'."

"I don't like the idea of people almost getting wiped-out in a risky prank like that one," Timmy genuinely attested. "Pranks are one damned thing, but murder, homicide, and manslaughter happen to be a horse of another color."

"I've been through this sort of hostility twice before with the greaser gangs in Levittown and with the peach versus blueberry enemies in Hammonton," I soberly stated. "And I know exactly how to punish our adversaries if necessary, and it's all basically more psychological than physical pain. We' gotta' defeat the Delta Alphas and the Tau Kappas and destroy their will to fight back; make the dirt-bags doubt their assumed superiority; confuse their judgment, and compel their memberships to quarrel and revolt against both Reynolds and Thompson."

"J.W., you sound sorta' like Patrick Henry and Samuel Adams in my history text! How do we do that?" Tim wondered and asked. "It sounds like a mighty tall order."

"I have a coy scheme that we'll pull-off, just involvin' you two guys, Ron Carputis and me," I proposed. "Maybe I'll convince a few pledges to join-in, too, if they're willin' to keep a secret. Are you' two commandos game?"

"What about Bob and Hoppy?" News deductively wanted to know. "Won't they become angry and jealous if *we* do somethin' for the Lambdas without them bein' in the thick of things?"

"Yes, our chief officers will be smitten by envy," I admitted, "because they won't like clever ideas originatin' from below them in the fraternal pecking order. They're tryin' to establish their own damned bureaucracy, that's exactly what's in progress here. Generals in the *Army* don't listen to *Privates;* Superintendents of schools don't take advise from students; college deans don't listen to freshmen; and fraternity bigwigs ignore the ideas of pledges," I elaborated and orated employing admirable nomenclature. "That's the way of this screwed-up world! Every person in an organization with an ounce of ambition aspires to becomin' a damned bureaucrat and desires callin' the main shots."

"Well, J.W., what did *you* have in mind?" Tim wanted to know. "Give us the lowdown and then I'll decide if your retaliation scheme is worthy of my participation."

"I'll tell you guys the whole ball of wax Monday in the Co-op when Ron's also in our company," I frankly promised. "It's like a heavyweight boxing match. We'll jab the Harvard Road lunatics and the Academy Street punks first, just to annoy them a little, and when they're baffled and peeved, we'll pummel the Delta Alphas and the Tau Kappa freaks with a barrage of left hooks, uppercuts, and right crosses that'll send their ugly butts to the canvas."

Then Tim, being a developing intellectual, advanced a rational inquiry. "Tom Bell suspects and believes that Ken Reynolds and Jack Thompson had tampered with *his* dad's car while he was in the Co-op with Joanne, Loretta and you before the accident," Amoro rehashed in an extended preamble. "But realistically, how can we get confirmation of the tampering?"

"We have to get Baptism and Communion first before we can ever get Confirmation," News inanely added, sounding a lot like my old Levittown pal Bo Jalonec at Cardinal Reagan High. "However, plenty of people, even non-Catholics, get confirmation for their hotel rooms and for their airplane reservations, too."

Tim and I shook our heads in incredulous dissatisfaction and completely ignored Tomasello's rhetorical lunacy. And then Amoro demonstrated noteworthy maturity by adroitly elevating the dying conversation back to an even keel.

"I hear we're getting' some new members into the Lambda Phi's," my good friend said. "J.W., do you know any of these rookie pledges who will be joining?"

"Yeah, there's Hoss Gregorio I remember from the peach gang back in Hammonton. He's probably as strong as Mario and could pin Big Al in less than thirty-seconds without any big airplane spin involved," I related. "And then there's another burly guy from Perth Amboy named Ken Soblinski, a big Polish kid with a pleasant disposition whos's in several og my classes."

"That's great to learn that Ken's from Perth Amboy," News whimsically commented. "I know for a fact that Perth's in Australia and Amboy must not be too far away."

"Perth Amboy, New Jersey, you' moronic nut-job!" I chastised. "Actually, it's all pretty neat because the city's right next to Staten Island, which is a borough of New York City and…"

"And the drinkin' age anywhere in New York State is only eighteen," Timmy interrupted to finish my thought. "And so, we could visit Ken regularly and then hit the Staten Island college bar scene. That good habit would even sound kosher in Israel. But are you sure that actin' independently on the *QT* won't get Bob and Hoppy hoppin' mad?"

"It'll make them better leaders because they'll want to keep their power in the Lambdas," I maintained, while relying on past experience and knowledge. "Bob and Hoppy will be more responsive to our ideas when the two realize that we underlings could do things on our own without their input. guidance or feedback. They'll fear our competition, and eventually learn to respect us better, and besides," I cunningly added, "if ya' recall recent events, Abrams and Cassidy didn't discuss with any of us about fillin' the Deltas and the Taus swimmin' pools with fecal matter, and then doin' the same to Miss Sankins's basement to inadvertently ruin her nearly-closed real estate transaction with Dr. Lang."

"You make good *sense,"* Tim praised. "It's a wash! The Deltas, the Taus, and the Lambda Phi leaders will all hold us in higher esteem. And the conservative college deans don't want adverse publicity about their school's perverse and perverted shenanigans appearin' in the *Philadelphia Inquirer*, the *Camden Courier-Post,* and in the *Atlantic City Press."*

"But the United States mints make better 'cents' than you do J.W.," News stupidly declared, sounding like a retarded first-grader sharing the first joke he had ever heard in kindergarten.

"Hey, News," I uttered, just to get the zany numbskull back on the right track. "What do ya' think about Wilt Chamberlain scorin' a hundred points in the *Warriors* game last night played in Hershey against the *New York Knicks?* I'm pretty glad that Chamberlain's playin' his pro career in Philly'. He had attended Overbrook High, ya' know!"

"Chamberlain had thirty-six field goals and the dude remarkably made twenty-eight foul shots," Tomasello authoritatively analyzed and disclosed like a computer-robot. "And besides those excellent statistics, Wilt-the-Stilt didn't 'wilt,' and the seven-foot-tall guy scored the last bucket just in the *knicks* of time!" News ridiculously double punned.

"Let's eat our hoagies before I have to barf-up my lunch all the way from the bottom of my large intestine!" I told my faithful companions. "News, you should've lived forty-years ago because you could've been a great silent movie star. But if the movie studios had talkies back in the late twenties and early thirties, you could've never made it big in *Hollywood."*

On Monday evening, Ken Soblinski and Hoss Gregorio sprinted down Girard Road and beat the freight train's caboose to *Route 322,* where the two burly guys mounted the moving car, and the pledges fortunately wound-up in Pitman, and not in Trenton or Boston. All of the guys, including Mario and Big Al, were very ecstatic about acquiring several new Lambda Phi Sigma members, because our goal was to grow in a quick burst and become just as large, and then even bigger, than both the Deltas and the Taus. And so, the Lambdas, that evening, enthusiastically welcomed Kenny and Hoss into the fraternity with a little *Southern Comfort* and beer "boilermaker celebration party" at the reconditioned chicken coop, commemorating *their* great athletic achievement.

The next few days I spent worrying about Joanne's left ankle and visiting her convalescing in *Evergreen Hall*, hustling and flirting with Peachy Wilcox over in the *Linden Hall* dorm's public lounge area, failing another daunting Sankins' composition and contemplating my prank that was scheduled to come off on Thursday night. Most of the equipment and paraphernalia to be utilized had already been obtained from electrical suppliers that Tim knew in Hammonton and that I knew in Berlin, so the stage was now set for the prank to be perpetrated on the Delta Alphas and the Tau Kappas. And after the trick caused by six maverick Lambdas would be enacted then the subsequent "blame game" would come into effect with everyone in chaos accusing everyone else of starting a major dilemma.

On Tuesday afternoon, I checked my' *College Hall* mailbox and was excited to learn from a typed letter sent from the WGLS-FM' program director that I had passed my interview/audition and that my application had been accepted to do the nightly sports recitation. This meant that I had a good excuse to be at the college each night, with my parents believing that I was going to be the next Douglas Edwards, Walter Cronkite, or Mel Allen.

"I'll listen to you every night," Peachy pledged in the *Linden Hall* public lounge. "This could be the beginning of a wonderful career in radio and television."

And then, feeling quite cocky, I marched over to *Evergreen Hall* and informed Joanne of my sweet success into radio broadcasting, and the Edgewood babe reiterated Peachy's praise and expressed her own great expectations. I felt so thrilled, proud, and confident that my self-esteem went skyrocketing through the roof, and I couldn't wait to initiate my imaginative prank on the snooty, wealthy Deltas and the equally pompous Taus, which would involve an ingenious ruse played on the poor, unwary, out-of-shape campus cops.

The evening of Thursday, March 8th arrived, and to the rest of the *GSC* campus population, it seemed like just another ordinary dull late winter night. I knew Hoss Gregorio from my days with the Reds peach gang and got the hulk to ride back to Glassboro with me as one of my principal collaborators.

"What's that portable generator, that microphone, those speakers and that long cable wire doin' in your Chevy?" Hoss asked me as we exited his parents' farm's driveway.

"We're gonna' first meet-up with Ken Soblinski at Angelo's Diner," I told the six-foot-four, three-hundred-fifty-pound monster, "and after that, Tim, News, and Ron Carputis will show-up, and I'll review the entire scam with all of you."

"You really came-up with some gems that we played against the Blues," Hoss remembered and orally validated. "And I can't wait to hear what this sick trick's all about. I mean, J.W., college would be a hell of a lot of fun if it weren't for the problems of goin' to classes, studyin' for tests, and listenin' to some fucked-up professors! Say J.W., you ain't gonna' stop in front of Glassboro Bedding and do that asshole poem routine I've heard about, are ya'?"

I had told Hoss an emphatic "no", and the huge farmer seemed a tad pissed-off that I didn't recite the words to "Ode to the Bunk" explicitly for him. Hoss and I met Ken Soblinski at Angelo's Diner and ordered coffee and cheesecake while we waited for our three accomplices to arrive in town at the designated rendezvous point. When all six of us filled Angelo's biggest leather-seated booth, I reviewed all aspects and details of my inventive monkeyshine, which was soon unanimously endorsed and appreciated by my team of effervescent comrades.

"And when shall I get the bulldozer goin'?" Hoss excitedly inquired like a young kid about to get his first *Tonka* toy for *Christmas*. "I really love operatin' heavy equipment. I know all about highway road levelers and steam shovels, if ya' ever need one of those machines used!"

"That's alright, Hoss, and thanks for offerin' your valuable expertise and services," I answered the human mastodon. "But right now, all we require is a normal bulldozer operator. Are you guys all set to cause some mischievous havoc and make this part of the world more interestin'?"

"Let's go!" News urged and commented. "On the way, I'll tell you guys all about the first atomic energy facility openin' up in *Antarctica* at McMurdo Sound, and about Eddie Arcaro announcin' his retirement from horse racin'. Did you guys know that *that* jockey rode 4,779 winning horses and amazingly won over thirty-million-dollars in purses?"

"How much did he win in pocketbooks and in wallets?" Tim answered, employing very effective reverse psychology learned in Dr. Su's nondescript *HB&D* class. "And how come Arcaro wears boxer shorts instead of jockey shorts?"

The rest of us just raised our eyebrows in disappointment and disgust at both News and Tim's comedy act, and then after paying our coffee and dessert bills and leaving a frugal dollar tip to the disenchanted waitress, we abandoned the security of the college student eatery to bravely pursue more surreptitious, dangerous, and precarious enterprises.

I had spent all of my birthday money received from my parents and close relatives, and some savings too, investing in the equipment to be rented in the daring caper, but in my mind, the expenditure was well worthwhile in regard to the prestige I would earn among the other Lambda Phi's, especially from our obstinate, arrogant, stagnant, and complacent leadership. The six conspirators re-assembled on the baseball field next to the *Campus School* with all of our necessary gear, and I then reviewed our last-minute instructions. Hoss, Ron, and Kenny would enter *College Hall* like maintenance workers with the loud speakers, with two covered ma nikins, and with the long wire cables, which would be thrown down to ground level and attached to the portable electric generator being plugged into an outside *College Hall* socket.

The carillon in the main building's majestic Golden Dome's bell-tower chimed eight o'clock, signaling that phase one of the operation was about to commence. Tim plugged-in the speaker wires (that had been carefully draped-down from the bell tower and roof) into the generator area, along with the accompanying microphone jack.

"Thou art more than cold stone!" I chuckled and whispered to News, who stood still like a garden statue and stared at me with a very puzzled expression. "That's what it says up in the bell tower, dumkoff!" I informed my usually omniscient colleague. "Thou art more than cold stone is carved up there!"

Four unsuspecting, pot-bellied, overweight campus cops sitting in two Jeeps were heard sputtering-around the bend from the Hollybush mansion, anticipating their routine 8:05 p.m. Co-op coffee and doughnut break. News stood on one side of the dark paved road, and I was stationed on the opposite shoulder. The lead Jeep's headlights all of a sudden illuminated News and me wearing Halloween masks and counterfeit Delta Alpha and Tau Kappa jackets, and we were pulling an imaginary rope across the roadway. "*Jeepers*-creepers!" News unexpectedly yelled like a possessed imbecile. The front Jeep halted prematurely and the second vehicle, having faulty brakes, plowed directly into the first one.

News and I took-off like Olympic sprinters and dashed in opposite directions through landscaped bush thickets and assorted tree clusters. The four startled campus cops leaped-out of their Jeeps and immediately chased after us.

"Hey, you four fat lard asses!" the unobtrusive speakers situated up inside the lit-up *College Hall* bell-tower boomed-out. "The campus cops all suck! The campus cops all suck!"

The posse of four security guards halted in its tracks and fearfully shined their flashlights up at the already illuminated *College Hall* bell-tower, the astonished cops staring in wonder and amazement at the two manikins dressed in standard Delta Alpha and Tau Kappa apparel. "Can't you' incompetent fat ass creeps do anything right! You' retarded bunglers! You blunderers! You campus cop morons!" Tim very deliberately articulated into the ground-level microphone with the sound blasting out from the above bell tower.

The four idiots forgot their original quarry and then pivoted, turned direction, and scampered their corpulent buttocks in the direction of *College Hall* to arrest two manikins up in the bell tower, dressed like Alphas and Taus. In the meantime, News and I hopped into the two abandoned, slightly dented Jeeps, that already had their motors running, put the machines into gear, and peeled-out toward the student commuter parking lot in quest of *Route 322.*

Tim's dented-up campus police Jeep followed my lead down Carpenter Street to a location two-miles away in Pitman. Miss Sankins was inside *College Hall* teaching her lackluster night *Fundamentals of Communications, 101* class, and so, I dropped-off my Jeep in her driveway. News then drove us in his borrowed Jeep to the other side of Pitman where we met up with Ron, Tim, Hoss, and Kenny. The four of us zealously pushed and then rolled the second Jeep into the dirt cellar hole of a house not yet constructed. And then Hoss Gregorio started up the nearby bulldozer in that remote section of town, and pushed enough dirt into the hole to completely cover the second campus cop's Jeep.

The Lambdas hopped into my trusty Chevy Impala, which had been used by the other guys to get from the campus to the designated Pitman house construction site. On the way back through Glassboro, I drove on *Route 322,* and the normally inactive area between the Co-op and *College Hall* was teeming with gawkers who were gossiping about a peculiar series of events that had recently transpired on campus. Also quite observable were plenty of revolving red beacon police car lights and flashing campus cops' blue lights, along with plenty of spotlights shining on two immobile figures standing-up in the main building's bell-tower.

"That was absolutely tremendous, J.W." News abundantly praised. "And a little risky and flagrantly diabolical, too! You haven't lost your' magic touch, that's for damned sure!"

"Not really, News," I replied, feigning total confidence. "Campus cops aren't allowed to carry any guns or weapons. They're just hired security personnel that call the Glassboro police if anything catastrophic ever happens," I reminded my jaunty associates in mischief. "And I think that's what the morons did in this instance. The campus fuzz panicked over nothin' but was simply a well-designed charade."

"If this is what the Lambdas do for fun," Ken Soblinski loudly hooted, "I'm glad I joined this terrific fraternity. I can't wait until our next gig!"

"I'm glad you're not a *cop out* tonight," News joked to Kenny. "Especially a campus cop-out out of a job!" the zany fool uttered as if he were an unemployed Vaudeville stage reject.

In a field on Hoss's uncle's farm in Waterford, we burned the fake Delta Alpha and Tau Kappa jackets we had been wearing. The six of us laughed our royal rear-ends off in our pleasurable five-mile cruise from Waterford to Hammonton. I dropped Hoss, News, Timmy, and Ron off at their respective domiciles, and then invited

Kenny to sleep over at my place. My parents accepted him as a member of the family, and Mom and Dad thought that Soblinski was a "well-mannered, polite, young man", and Dad was pleased that Kenny like himself was "a Pollack".

On Monday, March 5th, I showed-up at Radio Station WGLS-FM to do my first sports news assignment, where I simply had to read events off of teletype-sheets that came in over the *AP* and *UPI* wire services. Jim Fagan, the assistant manager, introduced himself to me, and next the Irish kid escorted me into the adjoining room to meet my fellow co-anchor commentator that would be doing the regular international and domestic news, which was featured on the same program as the sports round-up.

"J.W., I'd like to introduce you to our news show's script narrator," Jim Fagan said, "Ralph Crenshaw. Ralph, this is J.W."

I immediately knew that Ralph was the unfortunate pledge that had been caught naked up in the *College Hall* bell-tower during the aborted Delta Alpha Omega initiation. And then, I uneasily sensed that my name seemed familiar to him, too.

"J.W., don't you belong to Lambda Phi Sigma guys?" Ralph asked very directly as my new broadcasting colleague squeezed my handshake with a fairly strong grip.

"Yes, Ralph," I admitted. "But that's no reason why we can't be friends on an individual basis here at the station. There are some decent guys in the Lambda Phi's, ya' know. Please don't generalize and judge us all by the actions of a few."

"I'm sure of that!" Ralph answered more calmly, while Jim Fagan tried to make sense out of our unusual and seemingly confrontational initial remarks. "But please, J.W., don't ask me to join your fraternity! I never want to hear that word 'fraternity' again for as long as I live, whether it be the Delta Alphas, the Tau Kappas, or the Lambda Phi Sigmas!"

Chapter 17
"Dirty Rotten Skunks"

I had detected resentment forming all around me as my friendship with non-Lambda fraternity-hater Ralph Crenshaw grew after we had done a week of news and sports shows together on WGLS-89.7 FM. Bob and Hoppy were upset about being left out of the bizarre campus cop escapade; the Deltas were pissed because the creeps were the subjects of a cursory administrative investigation into the "Jeep theft incident"; the deans were fearful of the press getting a hold of the wacky story, and last but not least, News and Tim were downright jealous of my new friendship with Ralph Crenshaw.

In 1962, *Glassboro State College* had a unique combination auditorium/gymnasium, because *College Hall* had been built during the Roaring 20s as a "Normal School", where mostly women aspiring to be public school teachers attended classes at the two-year preparatory. And so, the back curtain to the Tohill (pronounced Tow-hill) Auditorium's stage was opened for certain indoor sports' events, and students sat in the theater-type auditorium seats and watched the college basketball game being played in the gymnasium. And with the new large *Esbjornson Gymnasium* facility scheduled to open within the next year, *GSC* students only had a few more home basketball games where the local students could be fans sitting in a college auditorium.

"Say, J.W.," News addressed me in the Co-op snack line. "How about goin' with me to see the basketball game tonight between *GSC* and *Philadelphia College of Pharmacy*. I think it's the next to last home game of the season, and next year we won't be able to sit in Finger-Mountain (News's personal reference for Tohill) Auditorium to watch the contest up on the stage."

"Sorry, News," I regretted, "but Ralph Crenshaw and I have to prepare and rehearse for the upcomin' *GSC* baseball season. The station's announced that we've been assigned to do all of the *Glassboro State* home games. And we're both excited about doin' the broadcasts."

"Gee, J.W.," News babbled. "You're intentionally abandonin' your old Hammonton buddies for some stranger from Teaneck, and Bob and Hoppy and the others aren't too keen on your actin' independently with the campus cop caper, while you're also neglectin' the fraternity for the sake of this introverted clod that doesn't want to ever join *our* ranks."

"And I have another tidbit of information for you," I informed a rather stressed-out News Tomasello. "Ralph's made a commitment and is gonna' live with us our sophomore year. The student town housing office has already given him and me the address. It's 38 South Main Street, a few doors down from the police station. We'll check it out on the ride back to Hammonton."

"You're always up in that radio station hole above *Savitz Library* with Crenshaw!" News bitterly resented and remarked. "Are you two homos', or what?"

"Well, why don't ya' just come-up to the hole and check it out for yourself!" I constructively criticized. "You're actin' just like a scared woman, afraid of harmless mice."

"Why do ya' say that bull-shit?" Tomasello rankled with a grimace showing some overt disdain. "It sounds like some kind of freakin' riddle!"

"Because you're afraid to come-up to the radio station *hole* and give me credit for doin' a program, and it just so happens that women are afraid of mice because mice always run to the nearest hole!" I replied. "That's why girls cross their damned legs tight every time they see a damned hungry mouse skitterin' across the floor! And so, News, the message to you is stop actin' like a damned scared pussy!"

"Are you punkin' out on me, Tim, Ron, and the Lambdas?" News nastily asked. "Where's your damned loyalty? Evidently, it's given to a stranger named Ralph Crenshaw you've only known for a damned week!"

"I think you're overreactin' to nothin'," I answered News as politely as I could. "I'll get active again with the Lambdas in a week or so, after this baseball assignment is under control, and when I feel confident about doin' the color analysis, while Ralph does the play-by-play description of the *Glassboro Profs'* home games."

Then, I perceived the true extent of Tomasello's sense of desolation and depression. "Hey, News. Tim and I are goin' over to the Franklin House for a decent sit-down meal. Ya' wanna' join us?"

"No, J.W.," News declined. "I gotta' go over to *Savitz Library* and do some research on the Greek and Persian *Battle of Salamis* and look at some microfiche."

"I've never seen an aquarium over in *Savitz* anywhere, let alone any 'tiny micro fish' swimmin' around in it," I rudely answered, giving Tomasello a dose of his own silly, absurd, foolhardy dumb-ass medicine.

Tim and I didn't have another class until three, and we wanted to go off campus and avoid any contact with Delta Alphas or with Tau Kappas inside the neutral Co-op. Also, we despised the college's bland cafeteria food, and since the Franklin House was a historic old inn a cut above Joe's Sub Shop and Angelo's Diner, that's where we headed. My pal and I discussed News and his recent antagonism towards me, and Tim admitted that he too was somewhat resentful in that I had found a new friend at the radio station, and apparently was thinking about leaving the Lambda Phi's high and dry.

"It's only temporary, Timmy," I tenaciously claimed. "During baseball season, I'll try to get a little more active with the Lambdas. My mind's always workin' overtime, and I'll come-up with some new ideas to employ against the other frats'. Right now, Tim, I gotta' admit, I'm still gloatin' a little bit about the campus cop triumph."

I drove the white Impala past the Glassboro Theater on High Street, and Tim brought-up the general opinion that *West Side Story* was a "lead-pipe-cinch" to win the Oscar for best picture of 1961, and that supporting actors George Chakiris and Rita Moreno had been nominated for high awards, and how Mario had once said that American society was changing for the worse because "spics and niggers were making a big power move"; were being actively pushed by the record industry, and were energetically promoted by *Broadway* and *Hollywood* to suit the government's social demands."

I recollected how I had wanted to take Peachy and Joanne to see the widely acclaimed film, but those "nice girls" now preferred to go out drinking and having risky life-threatening Lambda-type adventures. That thought disturbed my delicate psyche, so I deftly channeled the discussion away from *West Side Story*. "And Blacks and Spanish are becomin' big in baseball, too!" I told Amoro. "They're finally achievin' parity in some fields, and you're right Tim," I maintained. "Even in sports like baseball, football, and especially basketball, blacks are beginnin' to earn recognition."

"You're absolutely correct about blacks and Spanish doin' well in certain fields," Tim amiably agreed. "Just look at what Willie Mays has done in centerfield for the *Giants,* and what Roberto Clemente has done in right field for the *Pirates!*" But then, Tim showed his' fickle side by becoming serious again. "J.W.," my Hammonton buddy next addressed me in a more solemn voice. "I heard where Abrams and Hoppy are gonna' get Mario, Kenny, Max, Phil, Mitch, and some of the others to pull a stunt on the Delta Alphas and on the Tau Kappas as early as this afternoon. But because of *you*r recent activities with Crenshaw and with the campus cops," Amoro austerely qualified, "the Hammonton guys are sort of on the outs with the chicken coop Lambda head honchos, all because of you."

"Timmy, what kind of stunt are you referrin' to?" I asked as I pulled into the Franklin House's parking lot at the busy intersection of *322* and State Street, which led into Academy Street at the Y, two blocks south.

"Well, J.W., I gotta' admit that Abrams and Cassidy are pretty slick and have a lot of solid connections, even out of the state," Tim prefaced. "Hoppy has obtained from an animal farmer in Delaware a hundred fully grown skunks. He's been feedin' the critters the last few days in the red barn behind the chicken coop."

"Don't his parents know that activity, and haven't they questioned Steve about havin' all those skunks around?" I asked with more than mild interest.

"No, they're vacationin' down in Florida and won't be back for a week or so," Amoro filled-in the missing puzzle piece. "And so, I've heard from Mario's chatterin' that those idiots and DiMaris, along with the other Lambdas, are gonna' cut afternoon classes and put twenty-five skunks each in the Delta Alphas home over on Harvard; in the Tau Kappa home right down Academy Street; in Miss Sankins's home over in Pitman, and the last twenty-five black and white vermin will be casually deposited inside Dean Lang's home over in Runnemede."

"Holy turmoil, Tim!" I exclaimed, slapping my forehead. "I think I just lost my appetite."

"Ya' got your fake *ID* on ya'?" Tim very sincerely asked. "I'm orderin' ya' a couple of drinks and I'll pay for the tab. You look a little unraveled, just like the Lambda Phi banner often does."

Tim and I entered the historic Franklin Inn; stepped to the bar; ordered several *Southern Comforts* on the rocks; were carded just as Tim had predicted, and then Amoro generously paid for the expensive drinks. My mind was a little addled, thinking about Abrams and Hoppy excluding not only me, but also my closest friends from *their* inner Lambda Phi Sigma circle, and also from their newly-schemed malice against *our* mutual gutless foes.

No sooner had we gulped-down our sweet potent whiskeys that bus driver George Evans swiftly entered the genteel establishment. Surprisingly, the muscular black dude looked left and right, and then rushed-over to the bar to specifically speak with Tim and me. We were both shocked out of our gourds.

"Hey, guys. I'm sorry about what happened to you out at Carneys Point, but I have a big family to support, and need any gig I can find," Evans began his commentary. "It's real hard for black guys without formal education findin' decent work, and since no one was gonna' get hurt or die, I figured…"

"That's perfectly okay, George," I replied, accepting his heartfelt apology. "What's the dire emergency?"

"There's been a bad car accident," George disclosed as his voice shifted into almost a panic state, "involvin' four girls named Joanne, Loretta, Elaine, and I think the fourth one's name, is Peachy!"

"Where George? You havta' tell me where?" I yelled as my raised voice gained the attention and alarm of other more quiet patrons standing at the bar.

"You two guys are from outa' town!" George replied. "Ya' don't know all the Glassboro side streets. It's at Poplar and Green?"

"Poplar and Green? Where's that near?" I exclaimed in an elevated, alarmed voice.

"Come and follow me!" George insisted. "I'll take ya' there rather than havin' to give ya' complicated directions."

Tim and I felt that additional questions would only be wasting vital time in an emergency crisis, so trusting George Evans's testimony, we hustled out the Franklin House's back door and rapidly descended the granite steps. No sooner had we gotten to ground level that the six Japanese Sumo wrestlers, with their pigtail-like hairdos, accosted and abducted Tim and me, and the beasts and George Evans viciously tossed us into the back of a dark blue van, and then the muscular abductor commanded us not to move or yell, or we would be increasing our misery with excruciating pain being introduced and administered into their punishment formula.

"You middle-class white boys are really stupid shits and a half!" George gleefully ridiculed. "Ya' got hard-ons for a couple of lily-white virgin chicks, and ya' both thought with your little white skinny peckers instead of with your heads, Pecker heads! Peckerwood Pecker heads! Ha, ha, ha! Now you two Peckerwood Pecker-heads are both in for a very interestin' surprise! This is so sweet! Ha, ha, ha, ha! All your blood rushed from your heads down to your dingles, ha, ha, ha!"

Tim and I were each afraid to answer the huge Afro-American and dreaded to experience pain, added to our mental misery, so we remained mum, awaiting our unknown fate. George closed the back door panels, and eagerly hopped into the dark blue van's driver's seat, while the six emotionless Japanese Sumo giants sat on two back side painted benches. Amoro and I remained lying on the floor, stunned, shocked, betrayed, and reticent, being too scared of looming consequences to even utter a syllable.

"Poplar and Green!" George Evans lustily laughed while firing-up the blue van's engine. "Really now, white boy crackers! There's no such intersection, or any such street combination, anywhere in Glassboro! Ha, ha, ha!" And then, after the sadistic driver got-over his initial levity, Evans yelled-back over his right shoulder, "Maybe *Ben Casey* and *Dr. Kildare* are gonna' do brain surgery on you two blanco loons, and then dissect your genitals and your assholes, too! Ha, ha, ha!" the black gorilla hollered as the six Sumo wrestlers sat stoically with their arms folded in front of their robes, and the awesome wrestlers were frowning like vengeful samurai warriors, staring directly at Tim and me.

"I don't think you'll be able to broadcast the sports and weather from where we're takin' you two pathetic dunces!" contemptible George laughed, as I sensed the van turning south from the town's *322'* bypass onto *Delsea Drive*. Tim and I dared not move an inch as the in-need-of-a-muffler blue van rumbled around five-miles south, and then turned left. I remember thinking, 'We're now somewhere in Clayton, not too far from the chicken coop in Aura.' Then, after several more various turns, Evans veered the van onto a bumpy dirt road that serpentined left, right, and then left again, until the run-down vehicle's bald tires slid to a halt.

My eyes only had a few seconds to scan the general environment and recognized an old one-story, boarded-up shanty that looked like the type of dwelling that summer-time farm labor migrants had once inhabited. Tim and I were roughly flung into the empty one-room shack, which weirdly featured a tall ceiling. Then, the solid wood door was slammed and locked shut.

"We're trapped!" Tim gasped in a low, neurotic-sounding voice. "I knew I should've put on two pair of jockey shorts this morning! There're no damned windows in here, J.W.! I'm claustrophobic!"

"I think we're somewhere in Clayton," I answered-back in a low tone. "We're hostages here, and I guess we'll just have to wait it out before News and some of the Lambdas eventually learn of our location and come-out to the wilderness and rescue us."

"I hope the posse arrives before the coroner and the undertaker do," Amoro anguished and lamented. "Whose idea was it to leave the Co-op and go have a damned drink at the Franklin House?"

"I think it was *our* idea by mutual consent," I argued to disguise my ostensible trepidation. "Neither of us is to blame for this setback!

So, don't point any accusin' fingers at me, Tim! I'm sick and tired of your hollow allegations and your shallow insinuations about my character, or about my good judgment!"

An overhead hatch was slid back, and the countenances of two savage-looking, stern-faced Sumo wrestlers appeared above. My first instinct was thinking, 'I hope that those fat slobs don't fall through the damned flimsy roof and crush our asses! The entire ceiling will collapse and kill Tim and me in an instant!' But then, I detected the real evil in the foreign hit men's Delta-Tau inspired modus operandi.

And before either Tim or I could scream "Viperous reptiles!", a snake with red, black, and yellow markings was dropped-down into the dilapidated room. Amoro and I separated and watched in horror, and soon five additional similar serpents were un-gently thrown-down onto the shack's dusty, planked, rotting floor. My fellow hostage and I retreated to adjacent corners in total fright as the hissing snakes coiled and uncoiled, and then began slithering-around the dark, dismal, improvised prison. And just as my horror was reaching a climax, George Evans's face appeared in the roof's temporary opening.

"Hey, you white turkeys, enjoy your stay at the Snakebite Motel!" George chuckled like a demented madman. "And I just gotta' tell ya'two suckers that my two favorite new songs are 'Twistin' the Night Away' by Sam Cooke, and 'Twist, Twist Senora' by Gary U.S. Bonds. Oh well, Peckerwood Pecker-heads, it's now reptile suppertime for the nice cold-blooded, slimy animals. Enjoy your stay at the Snakebite Motel! Ha, ha, ha!" The reprehensible bully then slid back the trap door and locked the hinge to ascertain that no one, not even a smelly, filthy, rancid-looking rat could get out.

And before either Tim or I had a chance to crap our pants, a dozen squealing brown rats were dumped-down the old stone chimney into the dismal viper pit below, and my companion and I were cruelly intimidated, watching the disgusting-rodents go pattering around the dreary enclosure, being stealthily pursued by the treacherous snakes. There were no large holes in the walls or floorboards, and the doomed vermin, along with Tim and I, were mutually confined and trapped inside the formerly unoccupied, shadowy, rectangular structure. And Amoro and I had to spend the next three horrid hours witnessing raw primitive nature in action as the voracious snakes relentlessly pursued their furry, filthy, mangy prey, in front of, and around us, until all dozen rats had finally been horribly caught, consumed, and fully devoured.

Much to our mutual consternation, Tim and I had to suffer the persecution of being confined to a small area with the six still-starving, scaly reptiles. "Snakes with colorful markings are usually poisonous," Tim related, almost sobbing out each syllable in a heightened whisper. "And poisonous snakes are called vipers, and I do believe that *these* hungry multi-colored snakes are indeed vipers!"

Just when I thought that the vile serpents would soon enjoy a change of venue and menu, my keen ears detected the sound of a car pulling-up to the shack. And then, much to *our* apprehension and dread, the sound of an axe was discerned, knocking-down the dilapidated door. "This is it!" I imagined and whimpered to Tim, who was standing and shuddering in an adjacent corner. "Death by execution!" I was thinking about taking one last whiz while I still had a live body, but then my psyche nixed the notion because a picture flashed across my mind of a viper injecting poisonous venom from its fangs into my sensitive dingle, before I would be brutally axed to death.

Sixty-seconds later, the center of the door had been smashed-in and obliterated, and I was never so happy in my life to see Mario DiMaris and News Tomasello enter the dark room.

"I keep this axe in the trunk of my car to cut firewood with at home for some extra racetrack spendin' money," Mario informed Tim and me. "Ahhhh! What the hell are those things! Jesus Christ! I'm scared shitless of snakes!" Mario shrieked.

Tim and I maneuvered-around the hissing creatures, and we considered ourselves' being blessed having the opportunity to cautiously follow News and Mario out of the deadly, shadowy despicable shack. After two-dozen or so deep breaths, I finally had the strength and the lung capacity to ask several vital questions.

"Mario, News, how did you guys ever find us?" I wondered and asked. "I thought Tim and I were gonna' be murdered by a foolproof perfect crime, and I wouldn't get to see you two guys again, until either Hell or Purgatory!"

"Your new pal Ralph Crenshaw had heard from the kid that wanted to sponsor him into the Delta Alphas that you and Tim had been singled-out for in*tim*idation experimentation," News reported. "So, Ralph gave me the precise info' and directions outside *College Hall,* and then I happened to see Mario, who was happy to have a good reason to cut his afternoon class and break-down a door with his trusty axe. J.W., you're just lucky that Ralph liked you enough to save your damned life. He's not such a bad guy after all."

"Holy shit, J.W.!" Tim finally exclaimed. "Our asses could've been filled with toxic venom, and we could've been dead by now!"

"Not really," all-knowing News Tomasello interrupted. "Coral poisonus snakes are not native to New Jersey, like the dangerous pine-barrens rattler is."

"But those creatures slitherin' around in there have colorations all over their bodies," I countered. "I remember when my high school biology teacher told his class that poisonous snakes have red, yellow and other colors warnin' potential predators to stay away!"

"J.W., that description happens to be true to a certain extent," News academically explained. "But as you know, there's an exception to most every rule, like in grammar, 'q followed by u', for example, but what about the word 'Iraq'? Iraq definitely violates the q always followed by u grammar law!"

"Well then, get to your point?" I curtly asked in close to maximum frustration. "And don't tell me that points are for pinheads!"

"Coral Snakes are native to southern states like South Carolina and Mississippi, have black snouts, and their yellow and red bands touch each other. What scared the hell out of you in there were actually Scarlet Snakes that imitate the deadly Coral Snake in appearance, to scare away their natural enemies," News expounded. "The non-venomous Scarlet Snakes have red snouts, and the yellow and red bands on their skin do not touch, but with the lethal Coral Snakes the…."

"The red and the yellow bands overlap," Tim deductively figured and described. "News, all of this extraneous knowledge in your brain has finally paid-off. From now on, I'll have more damned respect for your academic trivia! In fact, from now on, I'll treat your words as academic maxima!"

"And oh yeah, J.W.," News mechanically declared. "There's a few deadly snakes on your Chevy's front windshield."

"What!" I shouted with alarm.

"Yeah," News calmly continued his *pun*ishment. "Windshield vipers!" the aspiring stage comedian finished, as chubby Mario DiMaris nearly developed a triple hernia, laughing hysterically.

Chapter 18
"The Meeting"

It was almost April, and spring break was about to happen on the picturesque *GSC* campus. Most of the juniors and seniors were preparing to either head down to Fort Lauderdale or to Daytona Beach, Florida, but since the Lambda Phi Sigmas were a struggling upstart organization that was now an essentially bankrupt fraternity without any party revenue coming-in, we decided to hang-around South Jersey for the academic intermission.

I visited my "bad luck mailbox" in the basement of *College Hall,* mechanically turned the three-number combination, and then shuddered a little when I discovered a letter from Dean Nelson stating that the head honcho wanted to see me in his office at twelve noon the following day. And when I ran into Tim Amoro outside the same college post office, T.A. related that he had received a similar correspondence with the exact same time and place indicated for a "resolution to the matter", My suspicious mind suddenly became apprehensive of possible dual penalties being meted-out. I hoped I wouldn't be forced to testify against Ken Reynolds and Jack Thompson along with their hired surrogates for the Scarlet snakes' incident. And since I had received another D- from Professor Sankins, I was momentarily glad the old bat had to contend with her own crap floating inside her vandalized basement, and I was even further delighted to discover Joanne Berenato standing in line inside the Co-op without her crutches.

"How's the left ankle doin'?" I politely asked. 'I think about it every night!" I carefully prevaricated. "I feel responsible for your injury that night at Mazzeo's!"

"You're so sweet," Joanne replied with a huge genuine smile. "It's okay, I guess, but the ligaments and muscles still throb once in a while. I heard you had another close call with a few disgustin' snakes. You're becomin' another *Ramar of the Jungle,* J.W. And I also heard about some fascinating skunk transfers, too, that has everyone on campus talkin'," Joanne continued her compliment. "What's goin' on? I figure you'd be in the center of it all, and eventually would tell me all the exciting gory details!"

The new song "Johnny Angel" by Shelly Fabares came over the Co-op intercom, and I just sensed that Joanne had been inspired to make a salient comment about me, and she did exercise her freedom of speech, much to my chagrin.

"I just love this song!" Joanne shared. "It's now my favorite, and I just gotta' buy and play the record."

"Because 'Johnny Angel' reminds you of me?" I overconfidently inquired, feeling greatly loved.

"No, silly. Because I like the rhythm, the beat, the lyrics, the melody, and the singer's voice, too," Joanne qualified, a little too truthfully. "J.W., you look alarmed. Is everything all right?"

"Well, not really Joanne," I stated with my eyes blinking as the lids often do whenever I became nervous, horny, insecure, or unstable. "Dean Nelson wants to see Timmy and me for a big conference, and I don't know exactly what to expect at the meeting. I don't want to get kicked-out of college and wind-up weldin' sheet metal tubes in Norristown, or being recruited for duty in Southeast Asia in Vietnam or Cambodia, or one of those Buddha-forsaken countries," I sniffed and sulked. "It's not the time to be travelin' with the *Army* or with the *Marines* into dangerous, hostile territories."

The hit song "Good Luck Charm" by Elvis originated from the circular overhead ceiling speakers, and Joanne was stimulated by the lyrics to remove her birth date charm from her wrist bracelet and give it to me for good luck during the imminent meeting. "Here, take this token and keep it in your pocket during the session with Dean Nelson. It'll work like a charm!" she joked, sounding a little too deliberately corny like News Tomasello often would.

"Thanks a lot, Joanne," I blushed. "I'm sure it will bring me both *Perry Mason's* wisdom along with *Dr. Ben Casey's patience."*

I reluctantly left the Co-op after swallowing three aspirins, which Joanne had charitably provided with a tall cup of cold water. I paced to the *Savitz Library* on the *College Hall* oval and met-up with Tim Amoro outside Dean Nelson's second-floor office, right down the hall from WGLS-FM, 89.7. We slowly opened the office door, and the affable receptionist instructed us to sit-down and that the administrator would confer with us in a few minutes, after the college bureaucrat would finish discussing an important issue with Dr. Robeson on the telephone. Five-minutes later, the Dean's secretary came-out of the main office with her steno' pad, filled with cryptic notes, and the attractive middle-aged woman informed us that her boss was ready to discuss matters.

"Sit down, gentlemen," Dean Nelson sternly directed. "I presume that you two know why you're both here. There's been entirely too much juvenile conflict on campus between established fraternity organizations and a certain illegal and unsanctioned upstart named Lambda Phi Sigma, although research has surprisingly indicated that

that new group does have a national charter and affiliations on some large and rather noteworthy university campuses."

"Thank you, sir," Tim courteously confirmed, thinking that he and I had just been commended. "Thank you, sir," Amoro repeated like a stuttering myna bird with a poor memory.

"Now gentlemen, there has to be an end to this preposterous tomfoolery and a cessation to this harrowing chain of irresponsible violence," Dean Nelson directly lectured. "Dean Lang is presently suffering from heart palpitations, and is being monitored at the college infirmary for a possible coronary attack, which is directly attributed to your fraternity's persistent mischief." Dean Nelson hesitated for a moment to detect any palpable sign of guilt or remorse evident upon our callow faces.

A humorous image of Dean Nelson conversing with Dean Lang crossed my mind, and I had always thought that Dean Nelson looked like the TV cartoon character Fred Flintstone, and that Dean Lang looked almost identical to Barney Rubble, so that when the college figures ever talked and stood alongside one another, the impression appeared that Fred Flintstone and his neighbor Barney Rubble were engaged in serious consultation. And then, I had to firmly bite my tongue and feign regret for wrongdoing when I really felt like hardily laughing, since my fertile mind imagined that *Glassboro State College* should be appropriately renamed Bedrock University.

"Now, I've met with some of the other principals in this series of unfortunate events," Dr. Nelson continued, "and the principal characters have all signed contracts with the college, promising that hostilities will cease and desist, and that a permanent truce between the Delta Alpha Omegas and the Tau Kappa Epsilons on one side, and the renegade Lambda Phi Sigmas on the other, will peacefully occur, without necessary administrative repercussions ocurring."

Dean Nelson showed Tim and me copies of agreements that had already been signed by Robert Abrams, Stephen Cassidy, Kenneth J. Reynolds III, and by Jackson Aloysius Bartholomew Thompson. Tim and I examined the carefully prepared documents intensively, and after scrutinizing the legal language, we realized and comprehended that a negotiated settlement to hostilities had been brokered. I glanced at the college executive, who seemed by his facial expressions to be flustered, embarrassed, insulted, inflexible, adamant, aggrieved, and very pissed-off.

"So therefore, gentlemen," smug Dean Nelson sanctimoniously proceeded with his stern lecture, "I emphatically suggest that you both sign similar contracts promising that you'll not have any more altercations with Mr. Reynolds and Mr. Thompson's esteemed organizations," the college official strongly recommended in the honorable name of bureaucratic functionality. "I mean, there have been crazy stories abounding all over this proud campus about skunks hibernating in closets, and also in closed showers; cesspool waste being transferred into swimming pools and into basements; strange and peculiar clam expeditions along the *Delaware River;* a car on top of the Co-op, not to mention a stolen campus police Jeep buried in a cellar in a new home being constructed over in Pitman!" Dean Nelson ranted and snorted. "Do you two gentlemen consider how embarrassing such childish, infantile activity will look to the taxpaying public, once the city newspapers get possession of this disgraceful information? Where's your sense of couth and decency?" Dean Nelson raged with a fire-red face. "I urge you both to sign your contracts that represent your personal implication in the detrimental frivolities," the dean yelled, losing his cool with his old lungs desperately sucking for air. "Or the only other alternative for you' two' incorrigible, recalcitrant, delinquents is expulsion."

Tim's pupils made eye contact with mine, and without questioning any conditions at all in the prepared formal statements, we obediently applied our signatures to the two sets of contracts, copies being made to be entrusted to us for our verification that such a meeting of the minds had taken place with *our* mutual consent. Dean Nelson then called his loyal secretary into his office and she notarized the documents, making them legal, bona fide, and binding.

I felt like telling Dean Nelson about being plagued with a recent near-death kidnapping by hired scoundrels; being kept a prisoner in an abandoned farm camp shack over in Clayton, and finally, being threatened by Scarlet King Snakes that looked and behaved like venomous Coral Snakes, but I kept my mouth sealed, thinking that the revelation of those additional events would require the summoning of the campus ambulance to accommodate and attend to either Dr. Nelson's sudden stroke, or inevitable super-palsy attack, whichever happened first.

While waiting for Mario DiMaris and Ron Carputis to meet us in *Memorial Hall* for the afternoon ride back to Hammonton, Tim, News, and I had a typical meeting of the minds in the *Memorial Hall* main student lounge.

"The deans are really under a lot of political pressure to quell the escalating frat' wars," I summarized to my trustworthy associates. "Nelson mentioned that Dean Lang was under coronary arrest because the Alphas, Taus, and the Lambdas are almost daily under police scrutiny and arrest. And naturally," I resumed my pontification, "the perplexed deans are gonna' side with the established fraternities, and the way I see it, this contract business was really *their* way of resolvin' the problem, disguising the matter as an agreed-upon negotiation, which incidentally is all right by me."

"We'd be better-off having Dean Martin and Dean Jerry Lewis running this glorified high school institution," Tim amused himself and laughed. "But I'm with you, J.W. Let's have a truce with our enemies. This way nobody is gonna' seek revenge for the Scarlet Snakes lookin' like Coral Snakes' incident, which the deans apparently don't yet know about."

But as usual, because News was not directly involved in the Dean Nelson moratorium, jealous Tomasello had a contrary point of view. "I would never sign my name to anything just to get the deans off the hook," News startled Tim and me by saying. "Any time ya' sign something, it has the potential to become a legal paper. Take an *IRS* tax withholding form, for instance. If people never sign an *IRS* form, the government can't do anything to them. By signin' the first form that says your employer withholds money from your salary," News elaborated, "everyone feels pressured and surrenders their rights, and has to abide by and honor the exploitive tax laws, or else have their property seized, or be thrown into prison for government fraud."

"But if ya' don't sign the form to withhold taxes," I insisted, "then ya' can't get a job anywhere! The system is rigged against you to start with, and ya' have to go along with the flow like a Lipton Tea Bag, otherwise, you'll wind-up bein' some ghetto indigent somewhere, with aspirations of advancin' to hobo or tramp!"

"You got it right this time, J.W.," Tomasello concurred with my impeccable interpretation and analysis. "Never sign anything and you'll be liable for nothin' from traffic tickets, to apology letters, to *IRS* forms! But from what you two neophytes have told me," News maintained, "in September the contracts will be null and void."

"How come being null and void?" Timmy inquisitively asked Tomasello, the Lambda's *Perry Mason* wannabe'.

"Because Reynolds and Thompson will be graduatin' and be outa' *GSC* in June," News replied, as the 'boy wonder' perceptively discovered the always elusive loophole. "The contract is really only good until the third week in May, when those two enemy cube-heads evolve out of this hellhole. Since good old Ken and Jack signed their statements representin' the Delta Alphas and the Tau Kappas, those affidavits are only good until graduation, right?" our distinguished colleague rhetorically asked. "Well, if Reynolds and Thompson are no longer representin' their respective fraternities, then those groups will have new leadership that haven't agreed to any legal language."

"Technically, News is correct," Tim stated and conceded. "But then won't the Delta Alphas and Tau Kappas have a distinct advantage over the Lambdas after next summer with not havin' to honor the contract while the Lambdas will have to still tow the line? That's unfair! It's undemocratic! It's discrimination!"

"You're right, Tim," I commended and credited my pal. "It would be discrimination against the Lambdas because the Delta Alphas and the Tau Kappas could do things to us but since Abrams and Hoppy signed contracts as freshmen, then the Lambdas can't do anything in reciprocation. We've been hoodwinked!"

"Not really!" News contributed. "Like you say, it's definite discrimination against the Lambdas and a good lawyer could cause a lot of adverse publicity for the college in the press, which would hypothetically put all of the deans in intensive care. Secondly," Tomasello filibustered, "the Lambdas could become a democratic institution and elect new officers, thus negating the signatures of Abrams, Cassidy, Timmy and you J.W. Even though Tim and you aren't officers," Tomasello editorialized, "I don't advise either of you to become officers next year. And thirdly, if the idea of havin' new Lambda officers doesn't work out, we could always start our own non-sanctioned off campus fraternity just like Mario said and aptly called it, 'Signa Phi Nothin'!"

"I think that J.W. should type up an anonymous letter on his cousin Robert's typewriter to the deans and then I'll mail it out this summer from a remote place like Teaneck where Ralph Crenshaw lives," Tim suggested. "J.W. will masterfully put in all the points we just discussed in the rebuttal and inform the deans that the Lambdas are consultin' with legal counsel and will contact several reporters should the present agreements not be understood as null and void because of discrimination against the Lambdas in that Reynolds and Thompson are no longer students at this mental institution."

"News and Tim, you guys are geniuses, even if you happen to be raunchy evil geniuses," I commended from the heart. "I'll get the letter whipped up and ready by June and then Tim, you can mail it from Siberia or even *Tim*buktu if ya' want."

* * * * * * * * * * * * *

True to form, there was no more hostility between the Lambdas and their adversaries for the remainder of the school semester. My freshman year ended in monotony with me receiving another D from Miss Sankins, and the inferior grade forced me to change my major from Teacher of English to Junior High School Language Arts and Social Studies Teacher. The summer months were both grueling and boring, working at the retail farm market, and driving the dark blue Pete's Market Special without air-conditioning all over South Jersey and to the Food Distribution Center in Philadelphia obtaining corn, tomatoes, peaches, cucumbers, peppers, zucchini squash, blueberries and other area crops wholesale, for retail resale consumption.

I was all excited about the prospect of living with News, Tim, Big Al Keiler, Ralph Crenshaw, and new guys Paul Meroski and Bill Elderberry at 38 South Main Street for my sophomore year. But outside of the tedious work cycle, fifteen-hours a day, seven days a week, there was little time or energy for me to explore entertainment and pleasure. And it was difficult working for Dad and Mom because I was used to the idea of "college freedom", which meant I did things and made term paper deadlines at the last minute, out of absolute necessity and not "on demand".

I attended the 16th of July *Our Lady of Mt. Carmel* carnival in downtown Hammonton with News Tomasello, whom I also called "The Hammonton News" while alluding to the masthead of the local town newspaper. But News was tangental in addition to being occasionally gentle, and the gadfly would deflect-off onto another part of the enduring game-of-life playing board, once an intelligent conversation had been generated.

"News, what's playing up in New York City on *Broadway?"* I asked Tomasello at the carnival's main Italian pizza, sausage, and pepper sandwich concession stand. "You're always up on the latest trivialities and irrelevancies!"

"Well, J.W., there's a new play that opened in May at the Alvin Theater called *A Funny Thing Happened on the Way to the Forum,* starring Zero Mostel," News expounded as I gulped-down some thick-dough Sicilian pizza, regrettably listening to his petty immaterial treasury of obscure knowledge.

"That Zero Mostel will spend the rest of his life tryin' to be number one, but until then, he'll always remain a great big Zero," I jested, giving News some serious competition at being a corny, idiotic, amateur punster. "With Zero Mostel, you're either *for-em* or against him, ya' know what I mean, News?" I elucidated. "And now that I know what's playin' at the Alvin Theater, what's playin' at the Simon Theater and at the Theodore Theater?"

"Very funny, Mr. David Seville!" News reactively chided. "And also, J.W., not too long ago Malcolm Scott Carpenter became the second American astronaut to orbit the earth three times after John Glenn had accomplished that noteworthy feat. Carpenter also did the three orbits in a *Mercury* space capsule called *Aurora 7,* which sounds a lot like Aura, where Hoppy's chicken coop is located," News prattled-on with his asinine drivel. "And a powerful *Atlas Rocket* got the astronaut above the earth's atmosphere."

"I didn't know that *Ford Motor Company* made *Mercury* capsules," I busted on News, "and in fact, I never heard of either Lincoln or Edsel capsules, either. And how did Scott Carpenter survive with all that Mercury in the capsule? It must've been worse than livin' in a damned barometer or gigantic thermometer!"

News was really getting pissed at my impersonation of his thought patterns, so he elected to deftly change the subject, which was his predictable behavior when challenged or perplexed. "Well then, J.W., as you know, Jack Nicklaus won the *U.S. Open Golf Tournament* a couple of weeks ago, beatin' Arnold Palmer in a very 'intense' playoff by three strokes."

"Unbelievable news, News!" I melodramatically exclaimed. "One stroke can kill a person, let alone three, and how did Nicklaus and Palmer play the last holes *in tents* instead of on the golf course? That' must've been very awkward and unconventional," I joked as I then recalled an old Bo Jalonec pun to be expertly delivered. "And when *I* play miniature golf, News, I always wear two pairs of pants in case I get a hole in one, and as you know, I always shoot in the high eighties, besides playin' miniature golf with elves, dwarfs, midgets and Lilliputians, once in a while. If the temperature gets any damned hotter than eighty-eight degrees, which as you know is a lot of diplomas, I intentionally stay in the clubhouse and drink *Pepsi Colas* until the sultry heat wave passes."

On July 10th of that sizzling summer, I was happy that the *National League* had won the first of two summer *All-Star Games* over the *American League,* by a score of 3-1, but on July 30th, the *American League* defeated the *National*s in the second summer All-Star Game 9-4, and 1962 was to be the last year for two *All-Star Games* to be played between the two major leagues.

The only eventful thing that transpired in that summer of 1962, besides going with News to stroll the Atlantic City Boardwalk twice and visiting the world-famous *Steel Pier,* was an excursion up to

New York City on a hot, late July Saturday night with Tim, Hoss Gregorio, and another strong Italian Hammonton farm kid named Tater Bertino, to drink beer legally. I parked the car in midtown Manhattan, and we took the subway all the way out to Coney Island. Our crazy idea of fun was to use our regular *IDs* on a foreign boardwalk, instead of our fake ones we used back in Jersey.

I was amazed to hear and see the legendary Fats Domino sitting at a bar piano and singing live his greatest hits, the establishment being situated just off the renowned Coney Island Boardwalk. And then, of course, we had to sample several *Nathan's Hot Dogs* apiece; legally drink beer; pee our kidneys out, and then joyously barf over each other riding the *Cyclone Roller Coaster* seven times in a row before experiencing the incomparable *Parachute Jump Ride*. And next, we voluntarily ate more *Nathan's World-Famous Hot Dogs,* because they were so delicious, and again, the adventurers bravely rode the nauseating *Cyclone* seven more times, until we all had to incessantly regurgitate our thoroughly-abused stomachs.

After boarding the elevated train at Surf Avenue to return to downtown Manhattan, Tim, Hoss, Tater, and I rode the "Local," which eventually descended and became a subway into greater Brooklyn. A tough-looking leather jacket street gang entered the subway car, and four pugnacious street-wise punks approached and accosted us, and before I knew exactly what was happening, and before any words were ever exchanged, Hoss and Tater hoisted two of the tough guys up over their heads, and flipped the delinquents up so high that the motorcycle jacketed weirdos' hit their heads and their sideburns against the car's curved roof. And then, Hammonton farm boys Hoss and Tater hurled the two semi-conscious tough guys out at the next station, onto the concrete subway platform just before the doors closed. Their remaining two shocked companions managed to hustle through the closing doors and evacuate the subway train, just before it took off for the next Brooklyn stop.

On Sunday night, July 29th, News called me at Pete's Market, and I had just cut my right index finger while opening a wired crate of corn in order to rush to the phone. I should have known that there was no cause for an emergency.

"Guess what, J.W.!" the neurotic kid began his usual address. "Bob Feller, the pitchin' star for the *Cleveland Indians,* was inducted into the *Baseball Hall of Fame* in Cooperstown yesterday!"

"News, aren't you damned tired from workin' on the peach farm all day long?" I chastised. "Get a life, will ya'!"

"And also, J.W.," News Tomasello euphorically communicated, "the old diehard Brooklyn fans' have good reason to celebrate. Jackie Robinson of the *Dodgers* was also accepted into the *Hall of Fame,* even though their' team is now playin' out in Los Angeles."

"Now, if those baseball stars were inducted into Lambda Phi Sigma," I caustically chided, "then I think *that* ceremony would be important!" And after I told News that I had known that Bob Feller would be inducted "as fast as anyone could say Jackie Robinson," the caller became irritated and hung-up on me.

And the third Saturday night in August, I had clandestinely arranged a date with Joanne Berenato, who had left her home under the pretense of going-out with Elaine Hill. We split-up and left Bruni's Pizzeria in downtown Hammonton, with News taking Elaine up to *Palisades Park,* because he liked the song of the same name by Freddie "Boom-Boom" Cannon, and Joanne and I, in the meantime, ventured-out to *Willow Grove Amusement Park,* located just north of Philadelphia. We finally shared some quality time together, despite the fact that her father thought that I was indeed *Public Enemy Number I,* even though my photograph had not yet appeared in any United States Post Office.

On August 22nd, I received a phone call from News announcing that two U.S. nuclear submarines had made a rendezvous under the *North Pole,* and I told Tomasello not to call me and describe very ordinary, mundane events, because we would see hundreds of "atomic subs" when we would merrily rendezvous the next time at Joe's Sub Shop on High Street, and that there was nothing really extraordinary about his mediocre declaration of only two atomic subs meeting anywhere.

On August 24th, I had the deans' letters typed-up, which I entrusted to Tim, to mail the rebuttals up in Teaneck, or Paramus, or Saddle River, wherever Amoro ultimately decided. The torrid, grueling summer was nearly over, and I was fatigued from laboring long hours at Pete's Market; acquiring local produce; driving to Philadelphia and Atlantic City for loads of watermelons; selling to retail customers; and sorting fruit, and throwing-out the reject peaches and the rotting blueberries, tomatoes, and Jersey plums. I was more than anxious to get back to Glassboro and living independent of parental authority and adult domination. But deep down in my consciousness, I was very aware that the fraternity wars were not really over as the now null and void *GSC* Deans' contract had falsely stipulated

Chapter 19
"38 South Main Street"

Dad had ordered a new light green '63 Chevy Impala from Blatherwick Chevrolet over in Berlin and told me in a surprise *Labor Day* announcement that I could use the white '61 since. I had contributed to Pete's Market's success and prosperity for the past four summers that the family had owned the flourishing business. Even though the Impala's title was still in Pop's name, I sentimentally regarded the two-year-old Chevy as my own, and I was sure glad that I didn't have to drive the old (and very conspicuous) '56 dark blue Pete's Market Special Ford stake-body truck around Glassboro, trying to hustle and impress beauty queens Joanne Berenato and Peachy Wilcox.

Living with News Tomasello, Tim Amoro, Big Al Keiler, Paul Meroski, Bill Elderberry, and Ralph Crenshaw proved to be plenty of hilarity, and even sophomore Ralph had privately conceded that he might eventually be ready to join the outlawed Lambda Phi Sigmas by his senior year.

"Well, Ralph," News told the somewhat-polished WGLS-FM news broadcaster, "the 38 South Main Streeters are almost like an off-campus fraternity, so you already belong to a stealth frat', whether you know it or not. And for the rest of us Lambdas, it's like belongin' to two frats'."

On the fourth day of the fall semester, News, Tim, and I had a chance to discuss some of our "strange professors" upstairs at 38 South Main Street. Like our screwed-up freshman year instructors, many of our new teachers were eccentric, egocentric, deviant, and wifty, to say the least. I began the pertinent dissertations with a general overview of my new female nemesis replacing the reprehensible and inscrutable Professor Sankins, Dr. Attleburg.

Dr. Attleburg taught the subject of Mental Health and had a gruff- looking, square face that qualified her to enter and win any ferocious dog show, participating as a female pit bull. The woman prof's wrinkled countenance was a portrait of emotional anguish, and her tainted breath exuded an odor akin to a dried-up Manhattan. The female professor's anomalous lectures sounded very much as if her humdrum epistles were originating from the lips of a peevish tavern patron about to fall off of her wobbly barstool.

Clayton, a black student in Dr. Attleburg's nondescript seminar, sat in the fifth seat in the row to my right next to the side wall. Clayton worked nights riding around on the rear ledge of a garbage truck; was extremely fatigued during the day classes, and would always lean his body against the side wall and fall asleep during the climax of Dr. Attleburg's lecture. The lady professor, on the class's second session of the semester, was elaborating about the need for love, forgiveness, and sympathy in our interpersonal relationships as if she was giving a testament at an *Alcoholics Anonymous'* meeting. I then quite mischievously removed and opened a safety pin from my pocket and then quite methodically, mischievously pierced the "sanitation engineer's" pants and leg with the sharp object.

Clayton howled as his reflexive reaction to instant pain sent both him' and his desk crashing onto the polished wooden floor. Dr. Attleburg continued her lazy presentation as if nothing at all had happened. I wondered how such a numb person could be an authority on the manifold operations of the human mind, after the instructor had been completely oblivious to a stark reality occurring in her midst. But people of her ilk thrive in education, especially at the college level, perpetually pontificating idealistic nonsense to captive audiences. The charlatans draw lush salaries and help pollute the educational canal by supporting the advancement of non-learning.

"Well, J.W.," News joked upstairs at 38 South Main. "At least sleeping Clayton wasn't as numb as Dr. Attleburg was. She sounds like she could drink Mario under the table in a *Southern Comfort* guzzlin' contest."

"I can't wait to have Attleburg next semester," Tim facetiously quipped. "Maybe J.W. and I can take the old battleaxe to the Franklin House, get her bombed, and have the witch buy us a couple rounds of *Southern Comfort* on the rocks, and if we're lucky, George Evans will enter the establishment and tell Attleburg that her best friend was in an auto accident. The only trouble with that scenario is that Dr. Attleburg sounds more viperous than those harmless Scarlet King Snakes over in that remote Clayton farm shack. Say, J.W.," Timmy continued his lengthy narrative, "I wonder if that black kid Clayton is from Clayton?"

I told the guys that Dr. Attleburg's favorite maxim was, "There's a big difference between teaching thirty-years and teaching one year thirty-times!" The most lamentable aspect of her oratory was that Dr. Attleburg had been uttering that impressive-sounding proverb ever since her initial year of professoring, way back in 1930.

Professor Flank taught both History and Issues in United States Government, besides trying to teach the class. Right from the first session, the man's didactical, preachy lectures were as dull as an eight-inch-thick razor blade. Flank reveled in discussing American social disorganization, world chaos, and the general frailties of the culturally retarded human species. Somehow, his "blame America first" agenda always seemed devoid of integrity, sincerity, honor, truth, and courage.

During our third September class session, while delivering a vitriolic critique on the American imperialistic military/economic institutions, Dr. Flank's nose began bleeding. Feeling the slight trickle oozing out of his snout, the critical professor dabbed his nostrils with a handkerchief, but the flow of scarlet soon became even more profuse.

Flank again glanced-down in horror (as if he had been mortally wounded) at the quantity of blood inside his handkerchief, and feeling exceedingly frightened and embarrassed, the craven professor's face turned as white as a lily. The disheveled and then beleaguered pedagogue swiftly canceled the remainder of the pathetic lesson on "Dysfunctional America", dismissed the class, and hastily departed the scene, looking as if he was a wounded *Crimean War* infantryman searching for the nearest Florence Nightingale.

"It's a good thing Flank doesn't have his class at the summit of Mt. Everest," News jested, "or his nostrils would be bleedin' so often that he would need *Red Cross* blood transfusions during his entire lectures, all semester long."

"Maybe Flank was having his period through his nose," Tim imagined and comically suggested. "Or maybe each nostril was having its own individual bloody period. Sounds like his middle name should be *Kotex*. And I think I'm slated to have Flank next semester!" Tim observed and stated with a degree of amazement.

And then, it was English Major Tim Amoro's turn to discuss his most mentally-deranged sophomore-year-professor, and my close friend elected to share with us his impressions of Dr. McIntire, who according to campus chatter, did not get along too comfortably with Professor O'Connor.

Professor McIntire was an English prof' and was highly regarded as an eminent expert on William Shakespeare's works and life. Tim told us that McIntire really relished several of Paul Meroski's literary contributions that appeared in the campus newspaper, the *Whit.* and also in the school's literary magazine, the *Avant*. The fellow was a jolly sort of educator, who seemed to be knowledgeable and conversant in almost every subject, especially literature. McIntire was rumored to be a "queer instructor", and according to Tim, to listen to the Shakespearean authority's unique speech patterns, which featured a distinct feminine twinge and intonation, Amoro had good reason to place credence in the rumored *gay* hearsay. "On one occasion inside the Co-op, Dr. McIntire politely invited Paul Meroski over to his abode for cocktails to discuss romance in British literature," Tim revealed, "but Paul took a rain-check when McIntire intimated with his lisp that only the two of them would be privately romanticizin'."

"Well, Tim," I said, "now I'm sort of glad I'm no longer an English major like you are, thanks to Sankins. It's one thing to be queer, and it's another tryin' to make the whole world's male population faggots, just like McIntire is."

"Maybe McIntire drank too much *homo*-genized milk when he was a nipple suckin' little toddler," News conjectured. "But it's too bad the idiot thinks that male assholes are juicy pink female vaginas! Maybe he needs some kind of brain optometrist before McIntire ever requires the services of a licensed proctologist? Those friggin' hemorrhoids really *pile* up, ya' know! McIntire must think his dick's a *pile* driver! The amorous fool doesn't know that another man's ass is an exit and not an entrance!"

And then, we reviewed our joint 45-rpm record collection, which was perhaps our most prized 38 South Main Street possession, besides our Lambda Phi Sigma shirts and jackets.

"Hey, J.W., you really must like the new black sound," News indicated. "Ya' got 'Mashed Potatoes' by Dee Dee Sharp, who could also hit the flat notes on the piano; ya' got 'Locomotion' by Little Eva, probably because there wasn't any high commotion goin' on when ya' bought the damned warped record at the Berlin Farmers Market; ya' got 'The Wah Watusi' by the Orlons, who only wear nylon clothes and stockings, and also rayon underwear; ya' got 'Beechwood 4-5789' by the Marvelettes, because ya' ain't got no damned phone number of your own except your parents', and wow, looky here!" Tomasello exclaimed, as I resumed my facial frowning in utter disgust. "Ya' got 'Let Me In' by the Sensations. I understand that's the song you're always singin' to Joanne and Peachy!"

Tim had brought to the vinyl disk collection Gene Pitney's "Man Who Shot Liberty Valance"; Elvis Presley's "Follow That Dream"; Tommy Rowe's "Sheila"; Jimmy Clanton's "Venus in Blue Jeans"; Bobby Vinton's "Roses Are Red"; Don and Juan's "What's Your Name?", and the Duprees' immortal harmony rendition of "You Belong to Me".

"I'm beginnin' to like the new California sound with a new group I've heard on WIBG called the Beach Boys," News informed Tim and me. "A great new song just came out last month called

'Surfin' Safari', and I've never before heard anything quite like that terrific sound. The group sings a different type of four-part harmony," verbose Tomasello disclosed. "And I understand that in October they're commin' out with a new car song called *409.* I can't wait to hear that mother!"

"Guys, times are changin' and I'm afraid that Wibbage Radio 99 is goin' to go the way of the dinosaur and the saber tooth tiger," I somberly predicted.

"How come J.W.? That's been the number one radio station in Philly' since 1955! Everybody in the *Delaware Valley* listens to Joe Niagra and to Hy Lit!" Tim Amoro wondered and exclaimed.

"True, Timmy," I admitted. "But haven't you noticed that on WIP FM Color Radio that the songs sound clearer and better than on Wibbage AM. FM is definitely goin' to replace AM. I mean, even with televisions," I drew a distinct parallel, "my parents just bought an *RCA* color TV, even though there's only a couple of shows in color, and I'll tell you that I'll never watch another black and white set again if I don't have to, or have a clear choice."

Besides '50s rock and roll, News had also demonstrated an affinity for novelty songs with copies on 45s of "Ahab the Arab" by Ray Stevens, and the classic "Chantilly Lace" by the Big Bopper. To round out his favorite tunes, Tomasello had "Do You Love Me?" by the Contours; "Sherry" by the Four Seasons; "The Twist" by Chubby Checker; "Shout" by Joey Dee and the Starlighters, and finally, "Green Onions" by Booker T. and the MGs.

"You have three of Dr. McIntire's favorites in your personal record collection," Tim told News. "First the faggot prof' entices his male guest with *sherry* to drink, and then asks his prey 'Do You Love Me?' without the damned Contours ever bein' present. And then, he'll sodomize his male date up the exit highway with the horny faggot doin' the pumpin' with his Martian *green onions*."

Since 38 South Main Street was now *our* home, News, Tim, Big Al, and I spent less time at the chicken coop, and more quality time together, forming a left-wing faction to the Lambda Phi Sigmas, and leaving Bob Abrams and Steve Cassidy questioning our stealthy motives. But we did make sure that Paul Meroski and Bill Elderberry race-down Girard Road and boarded the freight train caboose with Bob and Hoppy as witnesses to confirm that *they* too were now legitimate Lambdas. But Ralph Crenshaw was stubborn about joining the insurgent fraternity, even though the other six renting residents of the upstairs 38 South Main suite all professed that we would gladly sponsor our newest resident.

News and Tim knew that I liked Ralph's mature demeanor as the plotters conspired, without my knowledge, to make him the brunt of a mischievous "Lambda Phi prank". Crenshaw worked the early morning shift every day from five-to-eight in the *Memorial Hall* cafeteria, and habitually departed for his college employment around 4:45 a.m. One night in mid-September, while Ralph was serenading himself in the shower at 11 p.m., and while I was at Angelo's Diner with Big Al and Paul, my rascally, frolicsome friends Bill Elderberry, Tim Amoro, and News Tomasello deliberately set the tiny hour and minute hands on Ralph's wind-up alarm clock to "two in the morning". So, when the buzzer went-off three-hours early, naturally Crenshaw thought it was around 4:30 (when it was still dark outside) and not around 2:00 a.m., as it really was.

Ralph exited his bed more tired than usual, stretched; shaved, and washed his face; courteously made his bed in the dark so as not to disturb his snoring roommates; carefully descended the rickety flight of stairs, and then took-off in his mediocre Nash Rambler for *Memorial Hall.* Fifteen minutes later, the downstairs door slammed shut, and loud footsteps accompanied by mumbled cursing were heard ascending up to our domicile.

Crenshaw roughly flicked-on the lights, and throughout Ralph's tirade of profanities, Tim, Bill, and News pretended to have been just awakening from their deep slumbers, just as Big Al, Paul, and I had been in reality doing. But after seeing *our* startled and confused sleepy faces, Ralph second-guessed himself and quickly apologized for his intrusion and disturbance of our sound and wonderful Sandman visitations. With some objections, the rest of us reluctantly forgave Ralph for his lack of discretion and for his annoying vituperations, and News lectured the cafeteria employee that: "You shouldn't be distrustful and inflammatory towards your fatigued Lambda Phi roommates!" But unfortunately, News, Bill, and Tim would eventually execute the exact same prank three additional times on Ralph, and were successful during every single attempt.

Bill Elderberry, in late September, also was becoming a little too big for his britches. One time I woke-up in the middle of the night, and my olfactory taste buds detected a very foul malodor. So, I flicked-on the bedside table lamp, only to discover that fresh dog feces had put placed inside the heating vent near my bed, and when the furnace would ignite about three in the morning, the lousy stench would penetrate right up my nostrils to the point where I believed, in my sleep, that my dream girls Joanne Berenato and Peachy Wilcox were both farting egregiously in my august presence, while I was simultaneously wooing the Edgewood Prom Queen and *Miss Cape May* with my abundant and inimitable charms.

And Elderberry had this crackpot fascination with the art of farting', particularly while lying in bed wearing only his scurvy jockey shorts. And when Bill felt a serious gas emission developing in his lower bowels, the nutcase clown would lift his legs above his head while lying upon his bed; flick-on his butane cigarette lighter; hold it up to his butt hole, and when Bill passed a jet of gas, a blue torch-like-streak would be emitted that would shoot-out over a foot from his rectum.

"Bill, you're goin' to start an inferno up here with that stupid-assed performance," I reprimanded. "Quit fartin' around, will ya'! You're actin' like a real asshole!"

Elderberry ignored my myriad pleas and continued to behave like a dedicated asshole until one day the blue streak somehow deflected off of his lamp table, and ignited his dirty white jockey shorts. I never saw anyone (sudden diarrhea or no sudden diarrhea) scamper so fast to the john in all my life.

And Bill had a bad influence on the rest of us, with the exception of Ralph, who never became Elderberry's disciple or supporter. The third week in September, Lacy's Funeral Home, located next door to 38 South Main, was having a night viewing. Bill convinced News, Tim, Big Al, Paul, and me to dress semi-formal and go to the event, even though we didn't know the deceased or (in this case) the grandmother's family. And after the six of us filed-by and expressed our deepest condolences, the grieving family would all look at each other and quietly ask, "Who the hell are they?"

"I can't believe we just did that sacrilege!" I yelled at Bill when we returned next door to our upstairs suite. "You're a damned pervert, do ya' know that! If ya' don't respect the dead, ya' don't respect the livin', either!"

"That's not the point!" Elderberry maintained.

"Points are for pinheads!" I yelled back.

"Well, J.W., since *you* did it, too, goin' through the grieving line," Elderberry laughed with a very sinister, macabre-type smile and snicker upon his countenance, "then like the rest of us, you're a damned pervert, too. Welcome to the club. What's wrong about mocking death? Just like taxes, it's inevitable. Isn't it?"

"Yes, it is!" I concurred on that undeniable point. "But what you orchestrated tonight was totally disrespectful to the family! Where are your scruples?"

"Are you referrin' to my family jewels?" Elderberry nonsensically asked and challenged. "I guess then that my valuable scruples are very close to my taint?"

"Your taint?" I squawked. "Where the heck is that? I never heard of a damned taint?"

"The taint is midway between your asshole and your dick!" Elderberry clarified. "It t'ain't your butt hole, and it t'ain't your testicles, either!" Wild Bill mechanically replied as everyone else in the room, with the exception of Ralph Crenshaw, laughed their dingle-berries off their anal crotch hairs. So, the other guys anonymously attended at least a dozen viewings during the next three years at Elderberry's malicious insistence, and Ralph, Tim, and I deliberately boycotted the mal-conduct by staying upstairs and discussing how juvenile and shameful Elderberry's general crudeness and insensitivity were.

A variation of the funeral viewing crashing scene was when Bill would scour the social pages of area newspapers and determine where local wedding receptions were being held. The six Lambdas from 38 South Main would dress-up and attend a large wedding reception, where the groom's family thought that we were friends of the bride, and the bride's family thought just the opposite. We would just hang-around and indulge in the hot and cold hors d' oeuvres' hour, and drink a plentitude of *Southern Comforts* and *Jack Daniels* servings at the bride's father's expense. And then, the six of us would nonchalantly vacate the catering establishment before the sit-down meal would be served.

At 3 a.m. Monday morning, October 1st, Paul Meroski and I couldn't fall soundly asleep waiting for News and Timmy to come home, so we two insomniacs walked two blocks across High Street to Angelo's Diner for a few cups of "mud" (coffee) and "crud" (cheesecake). Paul was quite different than the other 38 South Main guys, more introverted in public, but when one on one, the laconic roomate was quite garrulous and deep-minded, once I got to know his inner core. Both bizarre and mundane events interested Meroski, and Paul might one morning at 3.a.m. discuss the merits of diner table saltshakers and ashtrays as being male and female phallic symbols, and the erudite intellectual mentioned to me how my subconscious motivation was being revealed when I nervously toyed with each diner table object in a public place. And another night Mr. M. would be fully fascinated by the dire need for less cultural ethnocentrism, and less individual egomania in the world.

“I wanna’ thank ya’ for getting my nasty editorial about the Deltas and the Taus’ Co-op behavior published last year in the *Whit,”* I gratefully acknowledged to this year’s talented college newspaper’s assistant editor.

“Believe me, J.W.,” Paul answered with his typically grim expression seemingly welded on his face. “The piece was published on its own merit, and you really have nothin’ to thank me for, except usin’ good judgment and acceptin’ it. Do you like poetry J.W.? I mean to say, do you like writin’ poetry?”

“Why yes, as a matter of fact I do!” I admitted. “I would never tell News, Timmy, or Big Al, but I do get satisfaction from readin’ and from writin’ verses. Those three Neanderthals would harass the hell outa’ me if they ever found-out. The fellas’ look at poetry like they perceive music and art majors. In their pea-minds, it’s basically a faggot activity!” I regretted. “And then, Abrams, Hoppy, and the other chicken coop Lambdas would pester me too about authorin’ poetry, to no end!”

“Well, you might want to consider havin’ some of your work published in the *Avant,”* Paul suggested. “I’m also assistant editor of the literary magazine and would like to see you make several submissions. Of course, J.W., you could use a pseudonym, or even the name *Anonymous* if you don’t want the Lambdas, the Delta Alphas, or the Tau Kappas to know your actual identity.”

“Confidentially, Paul, I would someday like to be a novelist and short story author, and I’ve thought about usin’ the pen name Jay Dubya, my initials, but spelled J-a-y D-u-b-y-a. I mean William Sydney Porter was O. Henry; H.H. Munro was Saki; Samuel Langhorne Clemens became Mark Twain, and a woman named Mary Ann Evans, no relation to the black bus driver, coincidentally became George Eliot. But you’re right, Paul. I gotta’ begin somewhere, and poetry in the reputable *Avant* might be the proper writin’ vehicle for me to start out with.”

“Well, at least you aren’t exactly like the other guys we live with,” Paul commended. “I don’t have to worry about you guzzing my toothbrush up your damned rear end while I’m sleepin’, but with guys like that screwball Bill Elderberry in the house, I gotta’ always be on my damned guard.”

“I’ll share a secret with ya’, Paul!” I was about to confess. “For some reason, I trust ya’ without knowin’ ya’ too long. I guzzed Elderberry’s toothbrush real good in the bathroom a half hour ago, before we marched over here to Angelo’s.”

Meroski and I next discussed the advent of color television and we both liked the idea that *Bonanza* and *Walt Disney's Wonderful World* of *Color* were not televised in black and white, and we both concurred that black and white TV was destined to go the way of Charlie Chaplin and silent movies.

"I still watch westerns like *Gunsmoke, Rawhide,* and *Wagon Train,*" I admitted, "but I also get a kick out of corny shows like *Dobie Gillis, Dennis the Menace, Candid Camera,* and *Car 54, Where Are You?*"

"Believe it or not, J.W.," Paul disclosed as my new comrade began rendering his television preferences, "don't tell anyone, but I still derive pleasure out of viewin' *Andy Griffith, The Real McCoys,* and *Lassie*. But I can't stand TV variety and comedy shows anymore. They're too '50ish and family oriented, so in my mind, *Perry Como, Joey Bishop, Ed Sullivan, Red Skelton,* and *Sing Along with Mitch* are all on my turn-the-channel list."

"Actually, we do agree on some common ground there," I acknowledged, "even though you sound a little ambivalent in regard to *Lassie*, it being a family show and us bein' rowdy college kids lookin' for independence from parental influence. Personally, I have a dislikin' of *My Three Sons*, *Ozzie and Harriet*, *Danny Thomas, Hazel,* and *The Gary Moore Show*."

Having a lot of mutual and shared kindred perceptions of the world, Paul and I became good friends that early fall morning in '62. Meroski was intellectual, introspective, and meditative, qualities that News and Timmy sometimes demonstrated, but not all the time like Paul apparently did.

"Ya' know, J.W.," Meroski claimed in a friendly tone of voice. "I can't understand exactly how the Earth goes around the sun, and how *we* travel over seven-hundred-million-miles a year, and never once know it, or feel a goddamned thing while doin' it. I mean," Paul momentarily paused to collect his unique cerebral activity, "the ride's not bumpy or rocky, and we never realize that we're rotatin' while we're revolvin', without ever getting dizzy for one second. I mean, how come we're never jolted-around or knocked clear-off of our planet into the upper atmosphere? Why's the annual journey so damned smooth and perfect if it's so damned long?"

My pride was not to be outdone by Paul's profundity, so I advanced my own philosophical treatise. "Paul, we gotta' order another cup of mud without any more crud," I suggested with a smile as I signaled for the only Angelo's Diner waitress on duty to re-supply our empty java cups. "I'm also intrigued by how nature works. I mean, every time I go to Atlantic City or to Wildwood and walk the boardwalk, I invariably have to halt, ponder, and ask myself, 'Why does the ocean stop right here at this beach every single day of the year? How come it doesn't stop in Hammonton tomorrow, and in Philly' the next day, and drown everybody in between?' I mean, Paul, science can explain it rationally, but we can't fathom it emotionally, do ya' catch the gist of what I'm attemptin' to analyze?"

"J.W.," Paul replied with a weak grin, "that dip-shit Dr. Rolphs said something interestin' in Anthropology class. The guy claims that women evolved over time and developed large breasts', simply because humans walk erect, and lower animals walk on all fours."

"I don't quite see the connection there. What do breasts and havin' a walkin' erection have to do with each other?" I jested.

"Well, ya' see, according to Rolphs," Meroski explained, "since animals like cows, horses, and lions walk around on all fours get to see the female of the species' ass and crotch all the time, and when estrous sets in with the female, bang, copulation happens. Since humans stand and walk in an erect posture," Meroski impressively enunciated, "unless of course they have osteoporosis, men never get good glimpses of the women's sexual equipment. Men can't get a really good view of the women's ass and crotch, because they're lookin' at females vertically and not horizontally as male animals do with their mates. So, women had to develop secondary genitalia like breasts to attract men and to compensate for strollin' around the savannahs and the jungles vertically."

"Fascinating!" I complimented. "I gotta' admit Rolphs does make his students think, but the communist America-hater comes-down too heavy on religion and morality in Sociology class. Rolphs treats religion like it's nothing more than modern mythology. And speakin' of religion and morality," I persisted, "I could never comprehend why God, if He really exists, tolerates the Devil and allows an evil supernatural creature, or higher being, to harass, torment, and tempt men, ladies, teenagers, and college kids. Paul, it's a downright unfair advantage allowin' Satan to tantalize mankind with sin, greed, jealousy, and the like, when we're on the natural plane, and damned Lucifer' is existin' on the supernatural plane. It's like askin' *Little Leaguers* to play a *World Series* against the *Yankees!"*

"Wow, J.W.!" I never really thought of that relationship in that exact context," Paul praised. "I know we're gonna' be good friends, but don't expect me to be an extrovert with all of the guys. That

Lambda Phi caboose initiation was challengin' to perform, and a real traumatic experience for me to endure, I assure you."

Before any other intellectual dialogue could be exchanged, Bob Abrams unexpectedly entered Angelo's Diner, looked in both directions, and spotted me with my back to him, wearing my Lambda Phi Sigma lightweight jacket. The self-appointed renegade fraternity President hastily came-over to share some pertinent breaking news with us.

"J.W.," Bob said, not even acknowledging new member Paul. "Were News and Timmy home when you left 38 South Main?"

"No," I sincerely replied. "The two Romeos had big dates with Elaine Hill and with Loretta Sacco last night, so I figured they're really paintin' the town red."

"Listen, J.W.," Bob proceeded. "I heard from Hoppy that the girls had returned safely to their dorms', but that News and Amoro were abducted by a coalition of Delta Alphas and Taus."

"Where are they? Don't tell me the frat' wars are on again!"

"They're both handcuffed to coat rack pipes in separate first-grade and kindergarten classrooms over in the *Campus School,"* Abrams related. "It looks like the summer truce is off between the Lambda Phi's and our bitchin' enemies."

"Who's President of the Delta Alphas and the Tau Kappas this year?" I asked my Commander-in-Chief.

"Their names are Bob Powell and Lou Hiltwine," Abrams informed. "And they're just as deplorable, as sneaky, as cowardly, and as jealous as Ken Reynolds and Jack Thompson were last year!"

"What could we do? Break into the *Campus School* and try rescuin' News and Tim?" I asked.

"No, because even if we break-in," our Lambda Phi President logically began explaining, "it would take forever to file or drill the handcuffs off. We'll have to let the incompetent campus cops figure-out *that* simple law-enforcement puzzle."

"Then, we can't do anything but sit back and wait," I realized and concluded. "It looks like Armageddon is in progress on the local doomsday clock. Like you say, Bob, the peace has been broken."

"Just imagine the look on those little first-graders' faces when their teachers discover News and Timmy in those classroom closets!" Paul gasped. "Their innocence will have already been corrupted, and those little suckers are only five and six-year-olds!"

Chapter 20
"Operation Uganda"

Monday afternoon, October 1st, Big Al Keiler and I were seated in the Co-op waiting for important news about News and Tim. The two abducted Lambda Phi's had been released from their handcuffed incarceration when found by several appalled elementary grade teachers at the college's *Campus School*, and instead of summoning the Glassboro Police Department, the flustered campus cops contacted a local locksmith, who figured-out how to use a master key to release the two from the pipe coat racks in the respective kindergarten and first-grade classrooms.

"Dean Nelson is meetin' with Tim and News right now," I nervously told Big Al. "And I hear the guys are so pissed-off that they're not gonna' sign any deans' contract statin' that the frat' wars will not continue," I conveyed to my alert listener. "That kind of concession would be givin' the Deltas and the Taus a definite advantage over the Lambdas, because the deans will ultimately side with *our* enemies, and come-down heavy or us while also bein' biased against us. In short, the deans want to cover-up and hide News and Tim's abduction from the press!"

"Real heavy stuff!" Big Al determined and declared. "I hope Nelson doesn't do the 'Monster Mash' on News and Timmy," Keiler expressed, while referring to a contemporary smash hit by Bobby Boris Pickett.

The rhythm and lyrics to the Crystals "He's A Rebel" came over the Co-op speakers, and I became inspired to tell Big Al that the catchy tune's lyrics reminded Joanne and Peachy of me, and that I would be available and reliably right there at the forefront should a full-scale-war between the Lambdas versus the Delta Alphas and the Tau Kappas suddenly flares-up. And then, Brenda Lee's "All Alone Am I", and Chubby Checker's "Limbo Rock" blasted from the overhead circular ceiling speakers, and I interpreted those incidental songs as being bad omens for 'being a maverick campus rebel; for possibly being expelled from the college, and for being in Limbo as the world turns.

"And just last week News was tellin' me that *My Fair Lady* had finally closed on Broadway after 2,717 performances since 1956," Big Al nostalgically recalled. "So, how does Tomasello store all of that minuscule minutia in his tiny skull cavity? He must be a bionic kid with one of those new-fangled computers surgically being inserted inside his brain."

"Most of those computers like that experimental *Univac* model take-up as much space as the entire Co-op wall," I corrected big Al, "but ya' never know about the future. I read in a science magazine that miniaturization is now bein' achieved by the U.S. space program, so maybe someday a computer could be planted inside somebody's cerebrum. As for me. Big Al," I stated with unwavering certainty, "forget the cerebrum. I'd rather have a tiny computer buried in my cerebellum to keep my sex drive goin', and to keep me livin' longer with a better beatin' heart and better breathin' responses to brain signals that are normally received."

"Say, J.W., what do ya' think about the *Mets* losin' 120 out of 160 games this season?" Keiler asked. "Maybe Casey Stengel isn't that great of a manager after all, like we thought he was. When Stengel was with the invincible *Yankees,* he had tons of talent to carry his reputation."

"All's not happy with Casey strikin' out in *Mud*ville!" I claimed as my eyes stared into my empty paper coffee cup. But still, Al," I continued, "almost a million crazy fans showed-up at the *Polo Grounds* to watch the *Mets* play inferior baseball. Maybe they'll play better after they move to *Shea Stadium* after it's completed," I added. "And to top it off, my boyhood hero Richie Ashburn played for the horribly lousy *Mets* this past summer, and I have mixed feelings because the *Phillies* traded my favorite player away to the *Chicago Cubs* after the '59 season, and wouldn't let *their* best player finish his fabulous career in Philadelphia. I'll always hold that against the *Phils'*, always, all the way to the grave!"

Big Al saw that I was getting rather emotional and a tad petulant while speaking about News Tomasello's and Timmy Amoro's possible expulsions from *GSC,* and about Richie Ashburn's dismal season shagging centerfield fly balls with the *New York Mets.* "Well, J.W., I'm impressed by that Sonny Liston, who last week knocked-out Floyd Patterson in two-minutes-and-six-seconds of the first round," Big Al recollected and shared. "And if it wasn't for garrulous News, I would not have known *that* insignificant piece of meaningless bull-shit," Keiler reminded me. "And Patterson was the defendin' world heavyweight boxin' champion, too. Nobody's gonna' ever be able to take on Liston one on one. Not even that Ingemar Johansson brawler. Not even the notorious *Hammer of Thor* could knock-out Liston!"

"Yes, Al, you might have a major point there, despite the fact that points' are for needle heads in addition to bein' for pin heads!" I conceded. "If some disastrous administrative decision happens to

News and to Timmy, we'll have to lead a revolution against the deans to get *them* reinstated into the college's good graces. Say Big Al, do ya' know about *Operation Uganda?"*

"I never heard of it," my Lambda Phi friend conceded. "Is it some kind of new hospital surgical procedure?"

I explained to Big Al that *Operation Uganda* was designed to make the college and the administration shine in the press, getting national and international exposure, and that the project was basically humanitarian, and had been created to reflect and encourage friendship between America and Africa, especially with all of the racial strife prevalent in the U.S., particularly in the South. "The big campus event will be celebratin' Uganda's independence a week from now, on Tuesday, October 9th," I told Big Al. "There's gonna' be numerous African ambassadors and *U.N.* dignitaries and Congressmen galore all over the campus. And a huge circus tent is gonna' be erected on the baseball field next to *College Hall* to accommodate events, and also, there's gonna' be several awards ceremonies in Tohill Auditorium culminatin' with a panel discussion where students can ask questions relevant to Uganda."

"How do ya' know all this immaterial bull-shit J.W.?" Keiler inquisitively asked. "You're beginnin' to sound like News, just like I am about recitin' his remote facts and meaningless statistics!"

"If ya' remember, Al, I now do most of the sports programming over at WGLS-FM," I reminded my friend. "And that's where I get a lot of my info' about current events that are goin' to happen on campus. And the college is donatin' 50,000 books to Uganda schools as a token of *our GSC* good will and generous spirit. And the donated books will be sent to Kampala!"

"Where's Camp Allah?" Big Al inquired. "I'm in the *New Jersey National Guard,* and I never heard of such a damned *Army* camp! Must be exclusively for Muslims!"

"Kampala happens to be the capital of Uganda, Big Al," I replied with a grin, "and the entire goodwill-gesture project will put *Glassboro State* in the limelight, and as Dr. Kraft would say 'to add to your empirical knowledge', the event is bein' specifically sponsored by the *GSC* International Relations Committee. I heard Ralph Crenshaw read the text about *Operation Uganda* the other night on his radio news broadcast."

"Shit, J.W.!" Big Al exclaimed and opined. "I have enough trouble with my local sex relations right here at the college without havin' to worry about havin' complex international relations with

African women in general, and havin' foreign affairs with Uganda women in particular."

The drab, uninspiring conversation was interrupted with News and Timmy showing-up inside the crowded Co-op snack bar. My spirits were immediately lifted when I observed prodigious smiles beaming from their lower facial features.

"Actually, J.W., Tim and I had our disciplinary meeting with Dean Nelson," News began all out of breath, "and just like you had thought, *he* tried to make us sign a contract promisin' to curtail our feud with the Delta Alphas and with the Tau Kappas."

"Did you guys provide your worthless John Hancocks on the documents?" I inquired.

"Hell no!" Tim jumped into the exchange. "We both told Nelson that the old contracts that were signed were null and void because Ken Reynolds and Jack Thompson had graduated last June, and the two stooges no longer represented the Deltas and the Taus."

"And then, J.W.," News ambitiously took over Tim's revelation. "Nelson asked us if we know anything about a certain anonymous letter that Dr. Robeson, Dr. Nelson, the Board of Trustees, and he had received towards the end of the summer. And Tim and I both denied knowin' anything about such a script bein' organized and bein' sent to the four parties via the mail."

"That's super great!" I congratulated. "You guys held your ground and didn't flinch one iota! I'm really proud of both of you showin' plenty of fortitude!"

"And then, Dean Nelson complained that he was too busy with *Operation Uganda* on the horizon, and that he didn't have time to fool around with ridiculous fraternity conflict, and that News and I should definitely sign the contracts, or else it could lead to serious disciplinary action in the future," an out-of-breath Tim Amoro extemporaneously reported.

"And how did you address Dean Nelson's argument?" I anxiously queried. "Did you go tell him to find the nearest beach and start poundin' sand?"

"Well," Tim voluntarily continued after three deep inhales. "News said something wonderful and as an ideal American, and we can all be proud of Tomasello. Tommy told Dean Nelson right to his teeth that *he* and I were the ones that had been abducted by the Delta Alphas and by the Tau Kappas, and then taken as hostages to the *Campus School*. We both emphasized that the Lambdas would get a lawyer and file charges with the police against the college for not providin' us with adequate protection and security before we were molested and kidnapped."

"And also," News alternated with his charged-up colleague. "Timmy and I both accentuated the idea that we would also file charges against the *Campus School* for havin' weak security in place and allowin' us to be kidnapped and kept in custody overnight against our will, after *our* terrible hostage situation had occurred outside *Evergreen* girls' dorm'. I thought that Nelson was gonna' shit three gold bricks after we adequately defended ourselves so damned admirably."

"How did the conference end?" Big Al curiously asked. "Did Dean Nelson threaten to expel you two insurrectionists?"

"Well," News laughed and puffed-out his chest. "Dean Nelson really lost his cool and yelled like a maniac, 'I want you two wise-ass students to get the hell outa' here right now!' And then the out-of-shape guy started holdin' his chest funny-like, when we casually rose and stepped-out of his walnut-paneled office!"

* * * * * * * * * * * * *

Late Tuesday afternoon, on October 9th, just before suppertime, there was a rapping at the upstairs door at 38 South Main. I was flabbergasted to see an old Edgewood High acquaintance and a former member of the Reds Hammonton peach gang standing there, waiting to greet me, non-other than Goose Restuccio, a crude, vulgar, egotistical son of a Mafia loan shark. G.R. had a decent heart if he liked you. The street-smart kid was already a millionaire in his own right at the age of nineteen.

"J.W., how the fuck are ya' doin'?" Goose yelled as the Mafia stud warmly shook my almost-paralyzed hand. "I'm commin' up from Baltimore to Jersey on the *Turnpike,* saw the sign *Exit 2* for Glassboro/Swedesboro, and I figured I'd take *322* to look ya' up! I got your goddamned address from a Hammonton guy we both know, Mario DiMaris!"

I stared at Goose, who used obscene language whether he was happy or miserable, and I felt a trifle embarrassed having to introduce Restuccio to several of the non-Hammonton college guys I was cohabitating with. But it was good to see G.R. again, who possessed an oval head shaped like a football, looking something like a *Charlie Brown* character, except that Goose spoke-out of the left corner of his mouth, which was slanted toward his left cheek, because of either a birth defect, or a childhood paralysis. For what

Restuccio lacked in good looks, he certainly made-up for in zest, color, arrogance, flamboyancy, egomania, obscenity, vindictiveness and enviable shrewd pragmatism.

"Er, come in Goose!" I politely invited. "Of course, ya' know News Tomasello and Tim Amoro. Let me introduce ya' to Big Al Keiler and to Bill Elderberry.

"How ya' fuck-heads doin'!" my old peach gang buddy crudely greeted his new acquaintances upon meeting my co-dwellers for the first time. "What the fuck's goin' on at the freakin' college? I drove by on *322* on my way over here, and it looks like goddamned Niggerville! And there was this big circus tent next to the main building, and I figured there was a nigger carnival or somethin' like that in town, with all of these strange rug-heads walkin' around in faggot gowns and square boxes on their head," Goose remarked like a dedicated redneck racist. "I never saw so many goddamned ugly niggers in one place in all my life! Not even in the worst North Philly' slums and in Baltimore ghettoes havin' mattresses hangin' outa' upstairs windows! I fuckin' mean, I thought that Glassboro was an Italian town like Hammonton!" Restuccio typically exclaimed while astoundingly finishing a full sentence without any descriptive obscenity in it.

"Er, Goose," I said while Big Al and Bill were laughing their chubby asses off in response to my old friend's candor and deficiency in both culture and breeding. "It's called *Operation Uganda Day* at *Glassboro State,* and the college is deluged with visitors from Africa and with local and state dignitaries, along with a massive delegation commin' down from the *United Nations."*

"Call it what the fuck ya' want, J.W.," Goose verbalized. "But it still looks like a giant convention for queer niggers to me. I didn't know the college allowed shines and clouds in the Philly' *Mummers Parade* commin' over to Jersey thinkin' that it's *Mardi Gras* time in October. The next thing ya' know, these goddamned spear-chuckers are gonna' take over the entire fuckin' country, and you' stupid asshole white college kids, led by your fucked-up asshole know-nothin' professors, are gonna' help the darkies do it, and a hundred years from now, your unlucky kids will be in the minority," Restuccio seriously pontificated. "The fucked-up lazy niggers are gonna' own the plantations, and you're gonna' be their fuckin' slaves, and enjoyin' every minute of it, while my kids are gonna' be livin' in fuckin' Sicily where they really belong in the first goddamned place!"

I felt very self-conscious about Goose going on a crazed rampage, giving us his prejudiced diatribe about Afro-Americans and about black Africans, but then right when I was going to switch topics, News Tomasello had to continue the hideous dialogue with something pertinent that undistinguished Professor Rolphs had said in Tomasello's Sociology seminar.

"Goose, ya' happen to be a sort of Afro-American yourself," News indicated. "Sicily is not too far from Northern Africa, and your ancestors probably had African blood in them that was genetically transmitted into your generation. That's why most Italians like you and me have a dark complexion. And besides," News elaborated, "anthropology research has shown that all civilization on the planet, according to Dr. Rolphs, originated in Africa. And then, various migrations crossed over into what is now Europe, Asia, and next over a land-bridge between Siberia and Alaska into North America. So, in a sense Goose, we're all Afro-Americans; not just slum people in the big cities that happen to have black ancestors."

"Is that the kind of stupid bull-shit they're teachin' ya' here at *Glassboro?"* Goose countered. "Fuck ant-throw-apology! Tell me News, forget about this *Ralph* jerk-off for a minute. How much fuckin' money does a first-year teacher make?"

"Right now, about four-thousand-five-hundred dollars," my roommate answered in a little bit of a quandary at Restuccio's direct personal attack upon *his* chosen education, and upon *his* most un-favorite professor.

"Well, ya' shit brains," the spoiled and conceited Sicilian crudely proceeded. "Sometimes, I make more than that in one fuckin' day with my fuckin' eyes closed. Four-thousand-five-hundred bucks is a lousy *poultry* salary!"

"You had meant to say 'paltry'!" I corrected. "Goose, you meant to say 'paltry' when you used the homophone 'poultry'."

"No, Asshole!" Goose yelled in a fanatical tone of voice. "I mean fuckin' *poultry!"* You're gonna' fuckin' be makin' *chicken feed* when ya' finally bust your balls and graduate from that *Route 322* hellhole, and then you're gonna' spend half your salary on taxes on faggot niggers to have a goddamned jungle bunny freak show on your *Almond Mother's* (Alma Mater's) campus; and then you're gonna' help the coons make more money on welfare and unemployment than you're fuckin' makin' workin' hard, bustin' your ass with bratty *pubic* school idiots for a measly *poultry* livin'!"

"Goose may be right about makin' chicken feed," Timmy prolifically laughed. "Because our fraternity already holds its main meetings in a chicken coop."

"And let me tell ya' dumb-ass, crotch-breaths somethin' else," my jaundiced Hammonton braggart pal emphasized. "Keep helpin' mool-en-yans, both here and in Africa, and I guarantee ya' that your doomed grandsons are all gonna' be shoeshine boys in fuckin' train terminals and also in bus stations; and in hotel lobbies, and your granddaughters are all gonna' be whores and hookers and filthy sluts, and all your families are gonna' be fuckin' eatin' chitlins, grits, and watermelon every friggin' night for supper, just mark my goddamned honest words!"

I was feeling very uncomfortable having Goose interacting with my new college friends Big Al Keiler and Bill Elderberry, so I made Restuccio a reasonable suggestion that his colossal ego couldn't refuse. "Goose, I heard ya' traded in your white Thunderbird and now have a brand new black '62 Corvette. I've never been lucky enough to ever ride-around in a Corvette. How about takin' me for a little joyride around Glassboro?"

"Okay, J.W.," Restuccio readily consented. "That son-of-a-bitchin' Chevy sports car can beat the pants off of anythin' on the highway with its supercharger fuel injection system and powerful engine. Ya' know how ya' give a horny girl a beef injection, J.W.? Well, this classy-chassis 'Vette of mine gives itself fuel injections all the goddamned time!"

Goose and I said 'goodbye' to the thoroughly amused Lambdas and descended the squeaky steps to ground level. I was pleased that the 'Vette's top was down, it being a gorgeous early October day for a pleasant spin around town. I directed the driver all over Glassboro except near the college, simply because I didn't want to hear any more discriminatory diatribe against "colored people."

"Goose, how do you know Mario?" I inquired as we stopped at the Main and High Street traffic light. "I mean, he's like ten-years older than you and me."

"Well, J.W., I'll suffer acid indigestion and hemorrhoids tellin' ya' this fuckin' story, but since you insist on knowin', here it is. Last year, after graduation from Edgewood, my Pop, the dirty bastard, he wants me to learn some discipline and go out for the goddamned *Hammonton Bakers* football team, which as ya' fuckin' already know, used to be the *Hammonton Brewers,* so why the fuck am I tellin' ya' all this idiotic shit? Anyway," Restuccio continued as the signal turned to green, "on the first day of practice, Mario tells me to get-down on my fuckin' hands and knees and tie his football cleats' laces for him. I look at the Godzilla-type gorilla and figure I better do the fuckin' routine, or else, he'd kick my ass so good that I wouldn't be able to sit-down on a toilet seat and take a decent crap for at least a fuckin' month. Actually, I was afraid that I would start shittin' out of my fuckin' mouth!"

"Yeah, Goose! I wouldn't wanna' mess-around with Mario. That's one tough hombre ya' always want on your side."

"Anyway, J.W.," Goose proceeded like a contemporary uncouth bard. "I busted my ass tryin' to make third-string on the *Bakers,* and on the second day of football practice, this knucklehead jerk-off named Tater Bertino shows-up for the team. I tell Tater to get on his hands and knees to tie my football shoelaces, and the crazy monster then beats the livin' shit out of me so bad that I quit the team outa' shame and disgrace. I'll bet that fuckin' insane shit like *that* doesn't freakin' happen on your niggerized campus!"

I diplomatically described to Goose the problems that the Lambda Phi Sigma guys were having with the Delta Alpha Omegas, with the Tau Kappa Epsilons, and with the college deans, and Restuccio promised that his expertise would assist me in any way he could, should the litany of confrontations and pranks ascend to life-threatening crises. "Just stop with all the fuckin' happy Greek shit!" Restuccio requested with a grin showing out of the left side of his distorted face, which I detected when the driver turned his oval head in my direction. "J.W., believe me when I tell ya' I don't even know five fuckin' non-curse words in Italian, and I'm a fuckin' Sicilian. Boo-tana! Boo-tana, J.W. The great times we had with the son-of-a-bitchin' Hammonton Reds!"

On Carpenter Street, I inadvertently turned-around and noticed a gray Mercedes trailing us, and upon closer scrutiny, I identified Delta Alpha jackets and four rich-kid, wise-guy members seated inside the luxury sedan: Dave Littlefield, Mike Errickson, Andy Talbot, and the driver, Bob Powell. I made a crucial mistake in telling Goose about our tailgaters.

"Those fuckin' guys can never keep-up with this bad-assed street machine," Restuccio boasted as his right foot mashed the 'Vette's accelerator to the floorboard. "Any goddamned enemy of yours, J.W. is gonna' have their dicks and balls cut-off and fed to the insects, if I got anything to do with it! Eat my exhaust fumes you dirty mother-fuckers!" the wild kid yelled at his inanimate rear-view mirror.

The Mercedes pursued us through three residential streets at speeds of upwards of seventy-miles and hour, but could not keep pace with the black Corvette's maneuverability and acceleration. Goose veered right past a stop sign, and managed to get onto *Delesa Drive,* somewhere in the vicinity of nearby Hurfville, but then the gray Mercedes sedan seemed to be keeping pace with Restuccio's black Corvette, staying about ten car-lengths behind.

"Just like old times, huh J.W.!" the driver reveled in his heightened mania. "If worse comes to worst, we'll lead them to Hammonton, pull into the *Bakers* late afternoon football practice, and have Mario and his defensive linemen friends rearrange those punks' ugly faces," Goose boisterously yelled, as my long hair was blowing all over my face from the intense speeds the swift convertible was achieving. "Makin' thousands of dollars a week gets pretty fuckin' dull, so thanks to you J.W., I'm havin' a ball without even screwin' any damned expensive hooker!"

Amazingly, our antelope and cheetah chase hadn't crossed any area police patrol cars. Goose made a sharp turn off of *Delsea Drive* onto *West 322,* but the Mercedes's driver was tenacious as a bulldog in his determination to catch the Corvette and have the four occupants accost and possibly assault us. When Restuccio's black chariot reached State and Main Street, Goose swerved the wheel like an obsessed maniac, and we zoomed right past the historic Franklin House and narrowly squeezed between parked vehicles on opposite sides of the road, also just missing a third automobile approaching in the opposite direction. The Mercedes's pilot attempted to duplicate Goose's intricate manipulation, but instead, smashed into an old illegally parked dark blue van's left side back bumper.

"Ha, ha, ha!" Restuccio cackled like a mental hospital psycho. "Those son-of-a-bitches will learn not to fuck with me and my 'Vette! Ha, ha, ha!" Goose guffawed, as the fanatic slowed-down to normal speed, and then again glanced into his Vette's immaculate rear-view mirror. "You're right, J.W. I am a goddamned *racist!"*

My head turned-around out of curiosity to witness the damage that Goose had wrought on *my* bitter adversaries. I was stunned to see George Evans angrily emerge from the dark blue van and start giving his temporary in-shock employers, still sitting in the Mercedes, a good tongue-lashing.

"Ha, ha, ha, J.W.," Goose screamed in marvelous exhilaration. "It serves those asshole college bastards right! Did ya' see that? They hit right into a goddamned nigger's van! Now, those wealthy kid's ya' described will be nigger rich!

Chapter 21
"The Homecoming Parade"

Goose dropped me off at my 38 South Main residence, right after the Glassboro police converged on the Franklin House accident scene. When I told the other Lambdas at the upstairs apartment what Goose and his new shiny Corvette had done to Bob Powell, *his* Mercedes sedan, and the other three Delta Alpha Omegas at the dangerous junction of *322,* State Street, and Main Street, my "left-wing Lambda Phi fraternity brothers" were in concerted ecstasy. The guys knew that "Powell's pals" just like Deans Nelson and Lang, had only been temporarily thwarted, but we also were aware that the frat' war was heating-up again on the campus stove.

"Goose related to me that he would financially aid the Lambdas if we needed some economic assistance," I conveyed the Sicilian's promise to News, Tim, Big Al, Paul, and Bill at 38 South Main, just before suppertime over at *Memorial Hall Cafeteria.* "And despite all of his cursin', prejudice, arrogance, and bravado," I told the now-jocular fellas', "Goose Restuccio will always honor his word once it has been spoken."

My five listeners were indeed elated with the fate of Bob Powell and his cohorts, along with the knowledge of the automobile/van collision, and how it had developed and had occurred. George Evans was also punished. And when I informed Goose that Bob Powell was from a town in Middlesex County up in Central Jersey, my old Edgewood High buddy said that he had heard of homos', faggots, lesbians, and neuters, but Goose had never heard of any damned 'middle sex', and never wanted to ever meet a person of that unknown gender! And when I had told Restuccio inside his 'Vette that Dave Littlefield and Mike Errickson were from Piscataway up near New Brunswick, Restuccio had said that those guys had to drink at least a case of beer each for their kidneys to be able to 'piss a cat away, even a kitten,' but I really think Goose honestly believed what he had told me, since the cantankerous Sicilian had described himself as 'a certified expert on pussies'!

"Honestly, J.W. Regardless of what ya' say, ya' gotta' admit that Goose is certainly biased against black people," News stated. "And he's always been that way! But times are changin'. Did you guys see on the national news last week where a colored student named James H. Meredith was enrolled into the *University of Mississippi,* and U.S. marshals had to escort him around the campus and into his classrooms. And then after two men were killed in racial violence, three-thousand federal troops had to be called-in to quell the riotin'. There's been protestin', demonstrations and plenty of disruption all over the university," News reiterated, "ever since Meredith started attendin' classes October 1st."

On the all-too-familiar drive over to the college for another mediocre dinner, a new instrumental record release entitled "The Lonely Bull" by Herb Alpert had been playing on Wibbage 99, and that tune reminded News, Tim, and me of Goose Restuccio, a one-man demolition crew, who was perhaps the richest and the loneliest nineteen-year-old in South Jersey.

Inside the *Memorial Hall Cafeteria,* I was a little shocked and paranoid to see Joanne Berenato and Peachy Wilcox sitting at the same table and having a civil conversation. I dared not approach the gorgeous gals, fearing that the honeys were exchanging notes and anecdotes on their personal involvements with me, so although I desired to tell each doll separately what Goose and I had done in the black Corvette to the Delta Alphas, I decided to temporarily keep that adventure as exclusive Lambda Phi Sigma information.

"Just wave at the girls," News suggested as we carried our trays to our table. "So what, J.W., if they're conspirin' against you!" my so-called pal rubbed it in. "It's already all over campus about you in the Corvette, but the story has it that *you* were drivin' and caused Powell to impact with the blue van. You know how a tale gets distorted and twisted-around after it's re-narrated by six or seven different people."

"That's right, J.W. You're becomin' a legend, a real Big Man On Campus," Tim voluntarily divulged, instantly inflating my sagging ego on the self-esteem scale. "And your expandin' reputation makes the girls' hormones become super-active and unbearably intense, and both of 'em wanta' sleep with ya', but not together, mind you. So. they're kinda' testin' the water and evaluatin' each other's competition and personality!"

"Since when, Tim, have you' become a clinical psychologist, let alone an authority on the opposite sex?" I chided. "Mr. Amoro," I said while imitating Dr. Su. "I detect as much fraud as I do Freud in your hollow conclusions."

"This fraternity war is just like old times with the Reds goin' up against the Blues back in Hammonton," News reminisced and communicated. "Now, J.W., I'm appointin' you to arrange some kind of plan to keep the Delta Alphas off-balance before the barbarians can counterpunch us. The Homecomin' Weekend is gonna' be soon, and don't forget the annual Homecomin' Parade down Main Street, goin' all the way west to the college. Maybe you can use the parade in some way where we can sabotage the Alphas involvement in it. You're devious enough to be able to contrive such a brilliant strategy."

I was always vulnerable to praise and flattery, no matter how insincere it might have been. I pondered News's baiting proposition for a moment and then had a miraculous brainstorm. I disclosed my daring plan to News, Tim, Big Al, Paul Meroski, and Bill "Dingle" Elderberry, and the guys unanimously bought into it, and divulged their desire to participate.

"Remember, this action is gonna' be done solely by the 38 South Main division of the Lambda Phi's," I insisted. "And Bob Abrams, Steve Cassidy, and their rowdy chicken coop warriors will be just as surprised as the Delta Alphas will be after it comes off. And once *Operation Uganda* is completely outa' the picture, we'll set the stage for a glorious prank that will include the Tau Kappas, too. I just hope that nobody gets killed in the process."

"That's a terrific scheme you've concocted!" complimented Tim, whose sentiments were quickly echoed by Big Al. "And if the Corvette junket has those two beauty queens aroused and in heat, just think what an additional huge feather in your cap is gonna' do to their estrogen and progesterone production."

"Yeah, Tim," News dittoed. "Their furry pussies are gonna' be so wet and damp that their pubic hairs are gonna' drown!"

Coincidentally, the new Elvis Presley song "Return to Sender" came over the *Memorial Hall Cafeteria's* overhead circular speakers, and I worried that perhaps someday my great Lambda Phi activities would backfire on me, just like an undelivered love letter would dampen my spirits. And when Neil Sedaka's new tune release "Next Door to an Angel" was played, momentarily, my heart felt a little more attraction to Joanne than it did towards Peachy, simply because Joanne's parents' White Horse Farm was just down the *White Horse Pike* in Elm from Pete's Market.

I owed my inspiration to initiate "Operation Chains" partially to the music world; to a little bit of luck, preparation, practical application, ingenuity, and to the influence of serendipity, which I always strongly believed in. And when homogenized together, those five elements usually melded perfectly, allowing me to outsmart my enemies. And when I couldn't think-up an original tactic, I would rely on past experiences in gang warfare that I had learned with the Diablos in Levittown and with the Reds in Hammonton.

In early October, I was still helping-out on Sundays at Pete's Farm Market, and in the early morning, would drive back to Elm on the "day of non-rest" to assist my parents. The first Sunday in that month I had given Hoss Gregorio a ride from Glassboro back to his family's homestead farm, and WIP FM Color Radio was playing the 1960 hit "Chain Gang" by Sam Cooke. Then, the inspired idea hit me to incorporate chains into my being formulated Homecoming Day Parade methodology.

"Hoss," I said to my amiable, gargantuan riding companion. "I'd like you and your brother Little Joe to do me and the Lambdas livin' at 38 South Main a big favor."

"Anything ya' want!" my extremely huge passenger agreed. "I still remember those portable motorcycle ramps my brother and me had assembled for you and Goose that made those Blues and the cops go flyin' into the pit filled with rotten peaches. Now, that was the coolest project my younger brother and I have ever been involved in," Hoss claimed. "Little Joe's gonna' start at *Glassboro* next year, and he's studyin' real hard to pass the college entrance exam'. I'm sure he'll be more than willin' to help me make somethin' for you. It'll be like a real *Bonanza*, ha, ha, ha!"

"Great!" I responded and exclaimed. "But you mustn't tell anybody, especially Abrams and Hoppy and the other animal Lambdas that hang-out at the Aura chicken coop; not even Kenny Soblinski. In fact," I proceeded, "I'm gonna' tell ya'what I need manufactured, but I'm gonna' keep it a secret how the materials are gonna' be employed until after I use the equipment. It might be within a month, Hoss, or I might not use the objects ya' two guys make until my senior year. But I assure you, the things will be used."

"Okay, J.W.", Hoss Gregorio acceded without any stipulations. "You're the main man! Tell me what ya' need J.W., and if it's at all possible, Little Joe and me will put it together for ya' in our farm's shop. Peach season's over now, so we got access to the place just about all to ourselves."

"You can be like my personal Hephaestus!" I remarked, alluding to the Greek blacksmith god.

"Sure enough, J.W," Hoss verified. "My baby brother and I will work *as fest as* we can."

"Okay, Hoss. Here's what I'll need, and please have the equipment made by the third Saturday in October when I'll go to your peach farm and pick them up," I directed. "First of all, I'll need two sturdy four-foot-long metal pipes."

"No problem, there, J.W.," Hoss orally indicated. "We use pipes like that all the time as spikes on two of our tractors to skim the peach and apple orchards and scoop-up the trimmed tree branches that the migrants had just pruned."

"Excellent, Hoss!" I sincerely commended. "And then, I'll need two strong heavy chains welded to the two metal bars. The chains should be around ten-to-twelve feet-long with metal hooks on the loose ends. That means I need a set of pipes attached to two different chains havin' hooks."

"I hope ya' aren't a damned chain smoker!" Hoss laughed as the human collossus extended his mental dynamics to their fullest. "J.W., your wish is *our* command. Little Joe and me will put those pipes and chains together quicker than you can use a roll of toilet paper when sufferin' from chronic diarrhea."

My provocative plan required a very large degree of luck in order to be completely successful. There were three distinct possibilities. Half of it might succeed; all of it might be enacted, or the entire project could end in failure and disgrace. That chance, as I viewed it, was the risk that a notorious prankster gambles every time he instigates another imaginative endeavor. The Friday night before the October 20th *GSC* Homecoming Parade, I reviewed last-minute particulars with my unheralded accomplices: New Tomasello, Tim Amoro, Paul Meroski, Big Al Keiler, and "Wild Bill" Elderberry.

"Okay, men, I have the four foldin' step stools and the bars welded to chains inside the Chevy Impala's trunk," I told the guys. "At three a.m., we strike. Now, I'll shuffle this deck of cards and we'll all draw one. Whoever gets the four lowest numbers will have to go-down into the manhole pits."

"But won't those four unlucky bastards suffocate down there?" Big Al apprehensively asked. "How do we know it's safe? I mean, I might have to be one of *the casualties!"*

"First of all, Al, nothin' in life is safe or guaranteed. I mean death and taxes are certain factors, but the two realities aren't perfectly safe. But to specifically answer your minor concern," I continued, "I have a cousin that works for the Hammonton Water and Sewer Department and Jim Shaw told me that enough air will penetrate through the manhole cover and its circumference, and enough air is already down there to keep two people alive for at least twelve-hours. Whoever has to go underground is only gonna' be there a maximum of ten-hours. So, does that easy explanation satisfy your freakin' question?"

"Okay, let's pick the cards and get that task over with!" Big Al demanded. "I just need certainty in my life! That's all I want is knowin' where I stand and exactly what I have to do! I despise uncertainty and I hate suspense! That's why I never go to the damned movies or the opera!"

The five of us each selected a card facedown from the shuffled deck, and then we all simultaneously turned them over, just like we were all called at the same time while playing poker. Big Al drew a two of spades; Bill Elderberry a five of diamonds; Tim Amoro an eight of hearts; Paul Meroski a ten of clubs; News Tomasello a king of spades, and I drew a jack of clubs.

"Okay, men. Big Al and Bill will be deposited inside the manhole at High and Main at 3 a.m. with your assigned chains, metal bars and step stools," I reviewed. "And at three-ten a.m., Timmy and Paul will hop-down into the manhole at *322* and Main, just adjacent to State Street, where the Franklin House is located. Are there any further pertinent questions?"

"Isn't it dark down there?" Big Al neurotically asked. "I'm kinda' afraid of the dark. That's why the hell I sleep all night long and stay outa' damned movie houses."

"Okay, true Al, it's gonna' be dark and shadowy down there," I honestly admitted. "But you can bring food to eat and talk in low tones to Bill. And make sure you take a good dump and a long whiz in the toilet before you're existing underground, or else you'll have to leak and crap down in the hole, and nobody likes to smell anyone else's feces or urine. It's a lot worse than walkin' through the most horrendous Mario DiMaris fart imaginable," I summarized. "Now, I also have six crowbars in the trunk to pry open the manhole covers upon enterin' and exitin'."

At three a.m., while the local police were protecting their somnolent suburban community in their squad cars and eating doughnuts and drinking coffee inside the department's station, the six of us walked the block with our crowbars tucked under our jackets, and News and I toted the two cheap utilitarian step stools, while Big Al carried his metal pipe with its eleven-foot-long heavy chain wrapped twice around his neck (looking a little like Jacob Marley's Ghost) to the corner of Main and High. And when the opportunity to perform our antic was ripe, we vigorously pried -open the manhole cover and unwrapped Big Al's chain, when the paranoid Lambda verbally commented, "I hope it doesn't change into a ball and chain for life at the State Prison!"

And then, nimble Bill Elderberry, after precariously hanging from the hole's lip that met the road, plopped-down into the seven-foot-deep and nervously said: "Isn't this pit like a lost cemetery grave because it's just about as deep as one!" Big Al did likewise, and then we lowered the bar and chain along with the pair of step stools, and Tim handed the two crowbars down to the pair of intrepid Lambdas. Tim, News, Paul, and I moved the manhole cover on top of its proper place, just in the nick of time, because the headlights from several cars could be seen in the distance approaching in both directions. And when we got back onto the sidewalk and stepped past the police station, two cops on duty exited the side door, carrying coffee and doughnuts and heading towards their patrol cars.

Five minutes later, the same pattern of activities was attempted at *322* and Main, but there was more traffic at that "five-points intersection", and it took us twenty full minutes to execute that separate phase of "Operation Chains". News and I had trouble lifting-up and sliding the manhole cover-over and finally setting the heavy disk in place, but somehow, we garnered the courage and the strength to complete the challenging feat. The two of us then drove back to 38 South Main; discussed final details; climbed into our beds, and then set our alarms for eight a.m. breakfast at *Memorial Hall Cafeteria.* A lengthier than expected conversation then ensued.

"Big Al gave everyone a *Three Musketeers* candy bar for good luck!" News laughed. "Too bad he'll be missin' the standard wet scrambled eggs' breakfast at the cafeteria."

"I hope the candy bars bring us better luck than the one Big Al had gobbled-down before Mario sent him flyin' over the Wurlitzer jukebox in the chicken coop," I recalled and reminded Tomasello. "Next time the airplane spin will be followed by a DiMaris' tumultuous body slam!"

"How do ya' know the parade floats will stop directly over the manhole covers?" News asked. "Isn't there some margin for error?"

"Because last year, I had cased the Homecomin' Parade and noticed that each float in between bands and other marchin' units would be held-up at the two intersections for about three-to-four minutes, just to allow pedestrians and spectators to cross streets, buy balloons, popcorn, and souvenirs from vendors, and to be mobile for whatever reason the parade-goers might have," I explained. "And so, News, the floats usually stop directly over the two important manhole covers that our guys are now hidden inside. That's the calculated risk we're takin', that the same series of events will be employed this year as had occurred last October."

"But how do ya' know that the Delta Alpha Omegas' float and the Tau Kappa Epsilons' float will be stationary while directly over the two manholes at the same time!" News wanted to know.

"I obtained an outline of the parade and its and floats at the radio station," I described to News. "And it just so happens that the greatest time differential could be three-minutes' separation. That's where you and me come into the picture. Remember to carry your crowbar tucked under your jacket to help the guys pry themselves out of the manhole. Like I said," I emphatically reiterated, "half of the plan might come-off; none of it will occur according to design, or all of it will result in a fabulous Lambda Phi triumph. They're the three possible scenarios as I see it!"

"This is without a doubt a high-risk, dangerous commando maneuver," News attested, "but if we could pull it off without any human injury or death, or any widespread property destruction, it'll definitely be a credit to *our* reputations. The hard part is over hidin' those four guys in those two strategic manholes. I sure wouldn't want to be Big Al havin' to listen to Elderberry bitch, complain, bull-shit and fart for the next nine hours."

"Don't forget, News!" I reminded my most-of-the-time loyal chief assistant. "The parade starts at noon tomorrow! But let's synchronize our watches to the precise minute right now, before we turn out the lights and get some shuteye."

By noon on Saturday, the crowd of enthralled spectators had gathered along Main Street, beginning at High, to view the gala annual *GSC* Homecoming Parade, featuring an abundance of college and high school bands, college floats, and independent marching units. According to plan, I was stationed among the viewers at High and Main, and News was down near the Franklin House at Main and *322.* Tomasello was positioned near the start of State Street, only several blocks away from the Tau Kappa Epsilon House on Academy, which had its float listed towards the beginning of the parade, with the Delta Alpha Omega entry more in the middle of the total alignment. 'I estimate that the Tau Kappa float will be up where News is located at about 12:15 to 12:20, and with a little bit of luck and serendipity the Delta Alpha Omegas' float will be over the High and Main Street manhole at approximately the same time, give or take a few minutes,' I considered, while pretending to be just another innocent bystander to a sensational event that was about to commence.

Much to my satisfaction, the Tau Kappa float was being pulled with a *John Deere* tractor driven by Lou Hiltwine, who showed-up at the busy, crowded High and Main intersection at 12:05, and then proceeded forward as directed by police and parade officials at 12:09. At 12:20, the Delta Alpha float driven by President Bob Powell sitting upon a gray *Ford* tractor, which appeared at Main and High Street with three sorority beauty queens and five fraternity members waving to the appreciative crowd. When the pedestrians crossed the intersection, I joined the group and momentarily stopped behind the float, bent down, pretending to have dropped something, and then rolled my body underneath the suspended green-trimmed drape. I quickly located the manhole, knocked four times on the metal plate to let Big Al and Bill know I had arrived, and then the two Lambdas banged-back four times, signaling to me that they were still alive. Together, we pried the lid off and slid it over. "Hurry!" I urged. "We only have two more minutes to get the job done!"

Big Al handed me the heavy chain and hook, which would act like a sturdy cable drag. The two fellow Lambda commandos next emerged from their hollow, leaving their step stools in the pit. Bill and Big Al tossed our three crowbars into the cavity; made sure the metal bar had been securely placed inside the manhole; slid the manhole cover over the horizontal steel bar, while I attached the chain hook to the float wagon's rear axle. Then, we swiftly exited from under the float's drape, and soon blended-in with the throngs of bystanders assembled at the busy intersection.

"I hope News, Tim, and Paul have the same kind of luck up at the Franklin House, hookin' up to the undercarriage just like we did," I told my two pallid-looking co-conspirators.

"You're just lucky that neither Elderberry nor I had to take a royal dump down there," Big Al harshly stated to me. "Or else, J.W., I would've pulled your damned ears completely around both sides of your face, and then tie the two fragile body parts together."

The smiling traffic cop waved the huge gray *Ford* forward, and Bob Powell confidently put the tractor in first gear; lifted the clutch, and opened the throttle. Everything went okay for the first ten-feet, but then the metal bar served as an effective flat anchor inside the manhole, and the chain acted as a powerful resistance force. Powell increased the engine's thrust while wondering what the forward-motion difficulty was, and suddenly, the powerful tractor violently dislodged from the wobbly float, with the three sorority' queens screaming their lungs out, and the five muscle-bound Delta Alphas also simultaneously tumbling onto Main Street.

The gray tractor flipped onto its side from the "slingshot effect" that the separation from the float had caused, and Powell fell-over with the bulky Ford, and then also rolled onto the Main Street asphalt. An alert parade official turned the tractor's key off, thus preventing any further damage or injury.

No sooner had that extraordinary incident occurred when a second crowd roar was discernible two blocks north, and the distant screams distracted everyone's attention. So, Big Al, Bill, and I all immediately became aware that News, Timmy, and Paul had satisfactorily completed their part of the valiant Lambda mission. An hour later, we all celebrated our victory by polishing-off a quart of *Southern Comfort* at 38 South Main.

"That was some adventure for us and some misadventure for the Deltas and Taus!" Tim mercilessly gloated. "The dimwits must be in a state of shock while still bein' in the State of New Jersey!"

"Did you guys have any snags up at the Franklin House, News?" I asked. "Or did everything go accordin' to plan?"

"Well, the big green *John Deere* did not turn-over like you said the gray *Ford* had done at Main and High," T.T. conveyed to his amused fellow Lambdas. "But then, Lou Hiltwine panicked and lost control of the green machine, and his tractor thundered across *322* and rammed through that landmark black-painted wrought-iron-property fence at the corner. Then, the green tractor hit a massive oak tree on the old lady's pavement, and finally, the stunned Tau President had enough sense to turn-off the damned ignition."

"What happened to the beauty queens and the other Tau Kappas standin' on the float? Did the victimized broads gert hurt?"

"Well, Al, most were knocked-off when the *John Deere* tractor slammed through the fence, and the remainder were already tossed on the ground, right after Hiltwine smashed into the stately oak tree," Tomasello accurately reported. "But I was really worried when the farm machine went out of control and almost plowed into the shrieking crowd. And boy, was I relieved when the victims suffered only minor scratches and lacerations."

I raised my glass of *Southern Comfort* on the rocks upward, and proudly saluted, "Hail to the invincible Lambda Phi's!" And then, I enthusiastically clarified, "Hail to the Lambda Phi brothers livin' at 38 South Main Street!"

All of the other Lambdas joined me in the celebratory toast. But we all knew deep in our hearts that the *GSC* frat' war was indeed proliferating to a much more dangerous level.

Chapter 22
"The Republican Club"

The 38 South Main Lambda Phi's, along with Joanne Berenato, Peachy Wilcox, Elaine Hill, and Loretta Sacco, were circulating gossip and scads of rumors around the *GSC* campus that the Tau Kappas had sabotaged the Delta Alpha Omega Homecoming Float, and that the Delta Alphas had reciprocated with the Tau Kappa Epsilon's parade entry. And everyone else on campus was blaming the Lambdas for the dual travesties. Bob Abrams and Steve Hoppy Cassidy were both fuming, and in a quandary, because *they'* had suspected that I had acted unilaterally with News, Timmy, Big Al, Paul, Bill, and even Ralph Crenshaw was thrown into the mix.

Abrams contacted me on the upstairs telephone at 38 South Main and demanded that News, Hoppy, him, and me meet at Seedy's Bar for a monumental powwow, because the chicken coop was undergoing extensive renovations and was temporarily unavailable. I agreed to the confab', because I knew that News often liked playing darts and nine-ball pool at Seedy's with Max Gunther. Of course, Tomasello and I brought our false *IDs* to illegally purchase frosted mugs of beers, which somehow was always more fun than going to Staten Island, or to New York City, or to Coney Island, and drinking legally at age 18.

"What's this bull that you and the Main Street Lambdas had demolished the two rival-frat' floats during the big parade?" Abrams began his accusations, as if he was some kind of ambitious county prosecutor. "What's goin' on here?"

"That's right, *we* did pull it off," I candidly admitted. "And all of the Lambdas includin' you are gonna' get credit in the court of public opinion on campus for our success." That compromising opening salvo seemed to bring rationality to our conversation, and the two formerly steamed-up co-founders consequently toned-down their rhetoric after my persuasive introductory remark.

"Well, then, how did you guys manage to pull it off?" Hoppy curiously inquired. "You must've taken a graduate course in Advanced Destruction 102 at a much bigger and better college! Give us the essential details."

I explained to the two fascinated Lambda founders exactly how the gig had evolved, and Abrams and Cassidy gave me praise for orchestrating such a stellar method of temporarily disposing of, and humiliating, our rival fraternities. And then, News informed Bob and Hoppy how he and Timmy refused signing the offered contracts with

Dean Nelson, and then I related how I had sent the anonymous letters over the summertime to the deans and to the Board of Trustees, and suddenly Bob and Hoppy were more receptive to News and me as being vital elements of *their* prestigious organization.

"Hoppy and I wanna' get you guys directly active again in the intensifying frat' war," Bob disclosed. "The deans want to meet with *us* tomorrow in regard to the parade debacles, and we'll also decline signin' our names to any new documents givin' the two sanctioned frats' a favoritism-advantage over the Lambdas. But I'll suggest to the deans that perhaps the Delta Alphas, the Tau Kappas, and the Lambda Phi's could co-operate on some fun project to give our campus a sense of unity," Abrams added. "And finally, J.W., I want you to come-up with a financially sound idea for a Lambda Phi fundraiser outside of Glassboro, far away from Aura and the chicken coop. What do ya' say?"

"I say words just like you do, Bob," I pathetically joked. "But what about a joint frat' party? We all dress-up wearin' masks and costumes, but all of the Lambdas will wear a pink carnation that night, so that we can distinguish each other from the rest of the crowd if major trouble breaks-out. It'll be like a chicken coop party with costumed clothes on!"

"Terrific idea, J.W." Bob Abrams commended while we watched News and Max seriously engaged in a close game of darts, the loser having to buy a round of beers for all of us. "I know a couple of bigwig local politicians over in Williamstown, and we'll be able to rent the town Republican Club for less than a hundred-dollars. This party's gonna' be really big, J. W.; a five-kegger for sure, and maybe even six once we get rollin'."

"How about a masquerade party Wednesday night, November 21st, right before the *Thanksgiving* holidays, which come real early this year," I shrewdly suggested. "Everyone will need a break by then, and you can tell Roxanne, and Hoppy can tell Babs, to get the news circulatin' around campus, and we'll get Joanne, Peachy, Elaine, Loretta, and their dorm' friends to spread the word around *Evergreen, Linden, Oak,* and *Laurel*. And we'll probably get a lot of intrigued commuter kids crashin' the major event, too. But that's all right, as long as the outsiders got five bucks admission fee; a costume, and additional money to buy beer, food and whiskey."

Abrams, Hoppy, News, and I shook hands to solidify the "truce deal" that had been negotiated, but then Tomasello got pissed-off because we had interrupted his aim just before his "winning dart shot," that afterwards missed the bull's eye. So therefore, the "All-knowing one" had to buy his four mates (and also himself) a new round of drafts in frosted mugs, depleting his dwindling weekly money supply, because Tomasello had also lost five-dollars to Max Gunther in the highly-contested, unfriendly dart game.

News, Timmy, Big Al, and I had heard via the campus grapevine that Bob Powell and Lou Hiltwine had signed contracts with the deans, promising peace among the fraternities, but that Hoppy and Abrams had not acceded to a campus deal, even under intense administrative pressure. I was sitting alone in the Co-op a week before the big Williamstown Republican Club bash, when, much to my anticipated edification, Joanne Berenato came-over to my booth.

"Hi, J.W.," the dark-skinned Sicilian babe said while flashing her magnificent pearly whites. "I want ya' to know that there's really been plenty of interest in the Williamstown masquerade party, and my only concern is that people are gonna' be turned-away at the door. Do you have any experienced bouncers?"

"Er, yes, Joanne. Mario and Goose Restuccio have arranged to have some of the *Hammonton Baker* football players on hand to keep law and order," I explained to the dream girl. "Since the Republican Club affair is in the middle of the week, there's no football game scheduled over the *Thanksgiving* holidays. And if the Lambdas don't net at least two-thousand-dollars minimum profit," I proceeded while discussing the estimated net revenue, "Goose committed that he would contribute the difference, if necessary."

"Say, J.W. I ran into Bill Elderberry this morning, and your roommate told me you wanted to say something about a word I've never heard before," Joanne stated, changing gears.

"What is it?" I defensively asked. "Elderberry's not the most reliable person on the planet to listen to."

"Taint," Joanne enunciated the one syllable word. "I mean, I've heard of the word 'tainted' used in the past tense, but I'm not so sure I've ever heard it with the *ed* on the end missing."

"Er, that's all right, Joanne," I nervously replied. "But next time, ask that weirdo Elderberry the definition of that vague term. Its precise, exact elusive meaning has temporarily escaped my normally dependable memory."

"Okay, will do Handsome! See ya' around, Mr. BMOC! Gotta' run now! I have to submit a big term paper due in Earth Science for Dr. Benson!" Joanne exclaimed exhibiting a cute smile, and then with an even cuter laugh and wink.

The Co-op jukebox was playing the new song "Chains" by the Cookies, and this made me think of the intricate Homecoming

Parade ruse involving the use of Hoss Gregorio's chains, and also about Joanne's cookie existing on the north side of her taint. And next the Co-op speakers belted-out the Drifters new song "Up on the Roof", and immediately, I remembered my Chevy Impala that had been hoisted-up there by the surreptitious Delta Alphas, perhaps with the collaboration of the equally treacherous Tau Kappas.

I observed News entering the campus recreation area and advance to the snack line, and when I turned in the opposite direction, Peachy Wilcox was standing right there, waiting to be recognized. "Oh, hi Peachy!" I greeted the luscious Cape May blonde, having light facial freckles. "How's life treatin' ya'!"

"Great, J.W. Really great!" the beach beauty answered. "And I want ya' to know that most of the girls over in *Linden* are gonna' come to the big masquerade party over there in Williamstown. I hope that the Deltas and the Taus don't crash the Lambda event and start a wild brawl, just to ruin everything!"

"Don't worry, Peach. We're gonna' have some tough guys at the door guarding and protectin' the place," I replied. "And besides, the Deltas and the Taus are basically rich, spoiled, bratty cowards, and won't fight us up front, but will resort to hiring thugs and Sumo wrestlers as *their* proxy substitutes. What's up?"

"Well, J.W. I was speakin' with Bill Elderberry outside of *Bosshart* and the pervert told me that you wanted to define the word 'taint' for me. What does it mean, actually?" the Jersey surfer girl asked. "Is this one of those male-only, immoral, symbolic references or something? Like for instance, is a taint something you have that my anatomy doesn't?"

"Er, well, perhaps you can ask retarded Bill Elderberry *that* pertinent possibility, because the notorious voyeur is much more of an authority on taints than I am," I exhaled, almost out of breath as sweat beads formed all over my brow. "I'm not exactly sure if you have one of those taints, or not!" I finished in an obvious fib.

"Okay, J.W., gotta' run!" Peachy yelled in a perky tone of voice. "Maybe my English instructor Professor Donohue knows what a 'taint' is. See ya' around!"

I was gratified that News bought me a *Pepsi* with lots of ice at the counter, and so then after handing me the cold drink, Gabby sat-down and began prattling incessantly all about John Steinbeck winning the *Nobel Prize for Literature* for the famous author's classic novel *Grapes of Wrath*.

"Nobel, didn't he invent dynamite?" I asked News, who also had the nickname *TNT* for Thomas News Tomasello.

"Yes, as a matter of fact he did," News confirmed, nodding his head. "But dynamite originally was only intended to blast-out holes in mountains for tunnel expansion, and for mining purposes. But after it was used in warfare to kill human beings," Tomasello keenly clarified, "Nobel felt guilty about his lethal *dynamite invention,* that incidentally was really quite a dynamite idea, and the millionaire then donated tons of money to finance the various *Nobel Prizes,* one of which is for literary contributions."

"Didn't Steinbeck also write *East of Eden?"* I enviously asked my knowledgeable pal. "I saw James Dean in the movie version back in Levittown, right around the same time I viewed Dean and Natalie Wood in *Rebel without a Cause*. Both films were awesome!"

"Yeah, it's too bad James Dean died in that fatal auto wreck," News commiserated, "But that's the stuff that legends are made of! I mean, old coots that live to be a hundred never become damned legends in that century's time span. But getting back to John Steinbeck," *TNT* continued his acumen, "the author also wrote *Of Mice and Men*, *Cannery Ror,* and *Tortilla Flat,* which must be an apartment that looks something similar to a damned taco."

"Maybe Dr. McIntire would be thrilled to death after reading *Tortilla Flat,"* I jested to News. "The campus Shakespeare zombie supposedly thinks that a male rectum is some kind of female pink taco. And after readin' Steinbeck's story, McIntire is liable to want to sodomize every male rectum on campus, includin' yours and mine!" And before I could corrupt the dialogue any further, Tim Amoro stepped his butt into the Co-op and joined News and me for some idle conversation.

"On November 20th, President Kennedy might announce the liftin' of the Cuban Naval Blockade, if Khrushchev decides to remove all Soviet jet bombers from Cuba," News vociferated in typical fashion. "We don't need any nuclear war, although atomic subs over at Joe's Sub Shop still taste pretty good."

"The best way to relieve tensions between the damned Russians and the Americans," Timmy conjectured and declared, "is for all of the eligible American bachelors like us to go-over to Moscow and hit on the best-lookin' Soviet women. I figure that such a mass sexual fantasy would greatly relieve all the pressure and all the tension I feel from my asshole professors, and from hangin' around all the time with you two cone-headed dimwits."

"Well, thanks for sittin' here and enjoyin' our benign hospitality," News criticized Timmy. "And also, J.W.," the evasive rambler rambled. "Soon, Kennedy is gonna' sign an executive order forbiddin' racial discrimination against minorities buyin' houses when federal money and loans are involved," Tomasello revealed. "I regard *that* announcement as social progress in this country."

"That executive order ought to make Goose and Mario really pissed-off if black families moved in next door to the bigots with big guts," I declared, bringing News's declaration closer to home. "But come to think of it, guys. The Deltas, the Taus, and the Lambdas are all white Americans, even though we profess to be Greek. So, in a logical sense," I awkwardly expounded, "*we* also practice indirect discrimination by not recruitin' or pledgin' any black members."

"I think everybody, white or black, is prejudice to a certain degree, even though people say that they're not," Timmy confessed, a little too honestly. "I don't know how I would react havin' blacks in the fraternity, but I know I wouldn't want to have blacks in my immediate family! And J.W., would you marry a black girl? I mean Joanne has beautiful swarthy skin, but she's Sicilian and not black, and she doesn't have Negro features like lighter-skinned black girls do? Yet, I still would prefer to have racial justice for blacks! Am I an ambivalent hypocrite, or what?"

I skirted the difficult question by saying, "Look guys, it's all hypothetical jargon, the way I see it," I attempted expressing myself. "I feel that anyone could fall in love with a member of their own race if they keep searchin', and I believe most black people feel the same way about the sensitive subject. I mean, it's okay to mingle with blacks," I awkwardly maintained, "but that's where equality ends, as long as colored people have equal opportunity like News says about President Kennedy signin' that revolutionary housing bill. But when ya' start talkin' about bein' mixed brothers, sisters, in the same family, or marryin' someone from another race," I specified, "I think that most blacks and whites make the more comfortable choices and stay with their own kind."

* * * * * * * * * * * *

My mind often works by association, and also, by deception. For example, Southern New Jersey is rather confusing in terms of highway identity. *Route 206* quickly disappears running south at Hammonton when it meets *Route 30* (the *White Horse Pike*), and then *206* magically transforms into *Route 54*. Through downtown Hammonton, *Route 54* is also Bellevue Avenue, the town's main thoroughfare, and after Bellevue crosses the railroad tracks, it becomes Twelfth Street, which is still *Route 54* until the driver reaches Second Road, which is two-miles beyond Second Street, and then the highway again exclusively becomes *Route 54*.

Route *322* is another one of those New Jersey chameleon highways. It shares its identity with *Route 40* going west from Atlantic City. Ten-miles west of the seashore, *322* also becomes the *Black Horse Pike* when *Route 40* heads southwest towards the *Delaware Memorial Bridge* from New Jersey going into Delaware. At Williamstown, Route *322* merges with *Route 42* (which ten-miles down the road merges with *The Atlantic City Expressway,* which was built in 1960 between the *White* and *Black Horse Pikes*, (or *Routes 30* and *322*), and then *322* heads southwest towards Glassboro. Route *42* after the *Expressway* merger becomes known as the *Freeway* from Turnersville into Philadelphia.

Route 322 meets *Route 47* (also called *Delsea Drive*) at Glassboro, and the two highways are one for around a mile. Then, *322* veers left and passes *Glassboro State College* (now *Rowan University*) and remains *322* when it crosses the *Commodore Barry Bridge* into Pennsylvania, just north of Chester. So, when tourists visit Southern New Jersey, the visitors usually don't bother asking anyone for directions, because they're too hard for the average citizen, or legal or illegal alien, to ever explain in English, Spanish, Swahili, or Martian.

Now, here's where the thinking by association method comes into play. The Williamstown Republican Club is on *Route 322,* which as indicated, masquerades as many different roads. That's why when Bob Abrams mentioned to me "Williamstown Republican Club" as the setting for the humungous Lambda Phi Sigma *Thanksgiving* break party, I thought of the words "chameleon highway", and then "masquerade highway," and since it's pretty hard to have an enormous "chameleon party," the natural choice was a "masquerade party".

Subsequently, here's where the deceptive thinking aspect of my personality judiciously became a viable factor. The Lambda Phi Sigmas and our girlfriends and female acquaintances had deliberately promoted the "Masquerade Party" for an entire two weeks on campus. On the night of November 21st, three-hundred student revelers, with what looked-like bona fide *IDs,* were allowed inside the rollicking Republican Club. Goose had financed the deal for thirty-percent of the net revenues, which was equivalent to his Mafia father's loan-sharking interest rates.

Restuccio had hired two-dozen burly and surly *Hammonton Bakers* (with the exception of Mario DiMaris) to be official bouncers at the gala event. And a legitimate temporary liquor license had been officially obtained from the cooperating Williamstown City Council.

When the night of November 21st arrived, the Lambda Phi Sigmas and their dates all boycotted our own masquerade party and spent the evening socializing and frolicking at the renovated Aura chicken coop. The *Hammonton Bakers* all wore white carnations instead of pink ones to the Republican Club masquerade party, so that any other male in disguise wearing a pink carnation was automatically perceived as either a Delta Alpha Omega or a Tau Kappa Epsilon, or as one of their devious sympathizers.

By thoroughly advertising the party by word of mouth, the Lambdas knew that the deans would eventually get wind of the sensational extravaganza. The college administration, in Eliot Ness fashion, converged on the Williamstown scene, accompanied by the New Jersey State Police, and their incursion led to a big donnybrook developing between the *Hammonton Bakers* and the completely bewildered Deltas and Taus, many of whom negatively experienced a tremendous thrashing while attempting to evacuate the premises during the ineffective police raid.

In addition to having the favored Delta Alphas and the Tau Kappas get the brutal beatings of their lives from the pugnacious *Hammonton Bakers,* while fully drunk and costumed, the school administration was clobbered with a very bad publicity nightmare, looking like ridiculous slapstick comedians lost, with the college deans looking like buffoons trespassing on thin ice, without either compasses or roadmaps.

In the final tally after expenses, Goose Restuccio netted over a thousand-dollars for his impeccable planning, talent, and skills, and the Lambdas realized a wonderful two-thousand-dollar profit (for not even being at the Republican Club), thanks to the twin arts of mental association and judicious deception.

Chapter 23
"Fraternal Brotherhood"

The exasperated college deans were both embarrassed and perplexed. First of all, the academic executives had to keep the Williamstown Republican Club raid and its funny particulars out of the Philadelphia, Camden, and Atlantic City newspapers. Secondly, Lang and Nelson had to have confidential meetings with the Delta Alphas and the Tau Kappas, after the two disguised delegations had been battered by the inimitable *Hammonton Bakers;* and then detained and interrogated by the State Police; and then thirdly, the mortified deans had received a Certified Letter from a prominent South Jersey attorney (representing the Republican Club), the legal missive protesting a raid upon a legitimate, licensed event that had "all of its attendees over the legal age of twenty-one".

The *Thanksgiving* holidays had come and passed, and before the Lambda Phi's knew it, December had encroached its thirty-one dark, dank days on the 1962 college calendar. And humorously, some of the Delta Alphas and the Tau Kappas were still wearing band aids on their faces from the violent beatings that had been administered by the potent *Hammonton Bakers.*

On Saturday, December 1st, News, Tim, and I boarded a chartered bus from Glassboro to New York City for an Art Class elective we had taken with Professor Tweed. But the real reason why we had signed-up for the optional field trip was not to sample Picasso and Rembrandt masterpieces at the *Metropolitan Museum of Art* or at the *Guggenheim,* but to imbibe *Southern Comfort* on the rocks and whiskey sours at Manhattan bars, mostly found just-off of swanky Fifth Avenue. Every few hours, we would rejoin Dr. Tweed's more devoted students for a scheduled lecture tour on our itinerary, simply to make the art professor feel as if the three of us were conscientious *GSC* sophomore students with Bohemian and artistic tastes. And "the triumvirate" courteously listened to the profound oral dissertations while half-inebriated, staggering back and forth, trying to maintain our faltering equilibrium. An occasional stifled burp would be emitted now and then, but the belching was never done too loudly or obnoxiously to interfere with the art professor's pedantic lectures. And when one tour guide was speaking with passion about Vincent van Gogh, all my intoxicated mind could think about was George Evans's dark blue *van go*ing out to Clayton with Timmy and me as the apprehended Lambda hostages.

On Friday, December 7th, News' came hustling into the Co-op, and I figured the history buff wanted to tell me all about the *Pearl Harbor* anniversary, or that Tomasello was all pumped up about comparing the backfired *GSC* Deans/State Police raid on the Williamstown Republican Club as the reverse to the 1941 Japanese surprise attack.

"Hey, J.W.," my mercurial-tempered amigo began his verbal discourse. "Did ya' hear about Mario?"

"That rumor flyin' around campus that Mario's pimpin' his wife for cash is all false, and I don't want to hear about it!" I answered. "People will make-up fake stories and add and subtract from them, and then others will propagate the tales all around, and smear somebody's name or reputation. Mario is alright in my book, so don't drag DiMaris through the mud unless you're 'Ninety-nine and forty-four, a hundred percent sure' of what you're sayin'!"

"No, J.W. I heard that scuttlebutt about pimpin' his wife, too, and my brain places no credence in the campus gossip, just like you've also rejected the absurd drivel," News indicated. "This new, more-accurate story involves Mario havin' a fight with his wife, and out of anger, the brute bypassed the *Bakers* practice over in Hammonton; drove to Seedy's in town here, and met-up with Hoss, Big Al, Tony Petters, and three other Lambdas, and the whole group tied one on good and got totally ripped."

"Well, Senor TNT, what's so special about that?" I challenged. "That sort of chug fest happens all the time in small college towns like Glassboro."

"Well, J.W., Mario proceeded to lead the Lambdas on a controlled and admirable rampage all over Glassboro," News continued his rhetoric. "The booze hounds weren't loud and rowdy, but the drunkards still had the mental capacity to recognize Delta and Tau cars at the Glass Bowl; outside the Tau House on Academy Street; outside the Delta House on Harvard Road, and even a few familiar stationary autos inside the *Bosshart Hall* parkin' lot."

"News, exactly what did Mario and the others do?" I demanded. "What outside of *Webster's Dictionary* constitutes a 'controlled and admirable rampage' as you've described it?"

"The Lambdas gently picked-up autos, mostly light weight sports cars, and also those small foreign jobs like *Volkswagens,* turned the vehicles over on their roofs, and left the damaged street machines cleanly between the parking lines, so that none of the upside-down autos would be ticketed by the Glassboro Police or by the campus cops. Could you imagine that? Twelve parked cars were turned upside-down, scattered all over town!"

"You say there is little or no damage to the dozen Delta and Tau cars?" I asked. "That really does require disciplined aggression, especially on Mario's part! He's like a bull in a Peking Red China shop, even when sober."

"That's right," News insisted. "It was just a crazy prank that adds insult to injury and cruelly pours salt into the Deltas and in the Taus' wounds, especially after that Republican Club fiasco. I mean, some of those jive turkeys are still banged-up."

Tim Amoro then stepped into the Co-op with Ron Carputis, and the two new patrons also had heard a graphic report about "Mario's insane destructive antics". But then, the two Lambda co-op entrants had some other juicy news-mongering of their own to share.

"Dean Nelson and Dean Lang are puttin' pressure on the Delta Alphas and on the Tau Kappas to have a truce with the Lambdas, so that *they* could run the college's normal business affairs without always havin' to worry about the frat' war getting into the tabloids and on *Action* and *Eyewitness News*," Timmy articulated. "And the college is also getting flak from the local cops that don't wanna' get involved in student affairs off campus, or for that matter, on campus, wanting to falsely preserve Glassboro's lily-white family image."

"I'm surprised that the Deltas and the Taus haven't gotten the six Japanese sumo monsters and George Evans after our vulnerable butts," I stated. "Those rich frat' guys don't want to confront us face to face, so the connivers operate like ghosts in the night, getting hired help to do their bidding. Maybe there's a rift developin' in their organizations? Any other things to report?"

"Well, yeah, J.W.," Ron Carputis offered. "The Deltas and the Taus promised Dean Lang that they wanted to conduct a communal fraternity activity involvin' the three male college organizations. And just this morning," Carputis added before clearing his large throat, "Abrams and Hoppy met with Powell and Hiltwine, and the negotiators came-up with a joint prank to piss-off the deans even more than the college brass is fit-to-be-tied right now."

"Why a joint plan?" I wondered and then asked. "Do ya' mean to say that the Lambdas are now on friendly terms with the Deltas and with the Taus? I wouldn't trust either of those corrupt freaks as far as I could throw Mario onto Jupiter, where the gravity is at least a hundred-times greater than it is here on Earth!"

"Powell and Hiltwine are pissed because they have to kiss-up to the administration each and every day, while the Lambdas are kickin' butt all over the friggin' place, and refuse to sign any new binding contracts," Tim concluded and candidly reported from the heart. "So, they'd like to join *us* in aggravatin' the deans that aren't protectin' them from us, especially with this turned-over car destruction that wasn't authorized by Abrams, or proposed by the 38 South Main Lambda faction!"

"Okay, guys, this is hard for me to comprehend," I spoke with candor and amazement. "Mario becomes a Robin Hood-type of hero while the psycho is totally intoxicated and going on his inverted automobile binge with the other rampaging guys, and now Powell and Hiltwine want to kiss and make-up with *us,* and together want to ally against the incensed deans," I summarized. "That makes a queer sort of sense in a weird sort of way. It's what Miss Sankins usually calls an 'anomaly'."

"Truthfully, what did the three frats' agree on at their summit meeting without *our* insightful input?" News objectively queried. "What mutual plan' are we goin' to employ to further frustrate the already-livid administration?"

"Listen to this scheme I'm about to reveal, and you'll really bust a gut," Carputis promised. "Dean Lang thinks we're gonna' do a joint clothing and food drive for *Christmas* charity; or raise money for needy families and orphans with a profitable bake sale; or enact somethin' high-schoolish like that. But the furtive plan is that within the next week, on a short hour's notice, the three fraternities are gonna' unite and show their joint solidarity. We're all gonna' don *Halloween* masks. The Lambdas are gonna' run naked through *Linden Hall,* the Deltas are gonna' flash nude through *Laurel,* and the Taus are gonna' streak through *Oak,* all inside the girls' dorm' Quadrangle."

"Are you kiddin'?" I questioned with meritorious reason. "How can the Lambdas trust those other jerks after some of the nasty stunts they've pulled on us?"

"And that's not all!" Timmy butted-in to divulge insanity being piled on top of lunacy. "No one can leave their assigned dorm' and abandon the raid until the member confiscates a pair of a girl's panties. J.W., there's gonna' be shriekin' and screamin' all over the freakin' place! What a crazy, splendid battle campaign!"

"I'll say!" I admitted. "But if seventy-five or so flashers are involved in the bold escapade, then the college won't and can't do anything. The deans just like to catch one student like poor Ralph, and put him on probation, but when a huge throng of nearly a hundred streakers are flashin' around nude inside the three ladies' dorms', searchin' for panties to pilfer," I loquaciously summed-up, "then that's the kind of sensationalism that hits the front page of both the *Philadelphia Inquirer* and the *National Enquirer*. And that's the last thing in the world that Lang, Nelson, Robeson, and the rest of the hypocritical deans will ever want to see happen!"

"And don't forget, men," Tim Amoro inserted for our full understanding. "The only things we can wear are socks, tennis shoes, or sneakers to cover our feet, and masks to hide our faces. It's gonna' be a cool, smooth three-fraternity operation because it's sorta' like bein' clowns performin' in a circus. A clown is usually a shy person in public," Tim extended his graphic metaphor, "but when he puts his makeup and special face on, the normally bashful fellow suddenly becomes emboldened and brash. The same goes for us wearin' our *Halloween* masks. And we can't possibly get raped in the dorm' because we already have our damned clothes off!" Amoro snidely snickered. "And when Mario, Big Al, and Ken S. all participate in the mass flashin' episode, *that* bizarre trio has gotta' scare the crap out of every gorgeous babe, every corpulent water buffalo, and every damned hideous dragon livin' in *Linden, Oak,* and *Laurel.*"

"And don't forget," I interrupted. "The Deltas and the Taus are now givin' us parity and acceptin' us as their equals."

Monday, December 10th, I was hibernating in the downstairs basement recreation room between *Memorial Hall* and the Co-op, awaiting Big Al, Tim, and News for a late afternoon game of partners' pinochle. First, Paul Anka's vocal "Lonely Boy" was piped through the sound system, and that tune made me feel a trifle isolated and somewhat depressed without any company at my table, especially while I thought about Joanne and Peachy. But then, "Running Bear" by Billy Preston came thumping through the overhead ceiling's circular speakers, and I instinctively contemplated the anticipated surprise streaking runs through *Linden, Oak* and *Laurel Hall* by the three now-allied fraternities. And then, my sometimes-smutty, lewd mind combined ideas and imagined me playing strip poker with Joanne Berenato, Peachy Wilcox, and Elaine Hill, when my three male companions finally descended the steps from the Co-op and entered the room filled with circular tables for students to either play cards, or study. And as I looked around, six other round tables were occupied with lackadaisical students engaged in different card games.

"Geez, it's the Wheeze!" Big Al greeted me with his predictable salutation, which I totally abhorred, but nevertheless, pretended to painfully tolerate.

"Holy crap, J.W.," News hollered. "I forgot to buy ya' your standard *Pepsi* and some fries before descendin' down here into Hades to see ya'."

"Hi, guys," I officially recognized my pals. "Thanks News, but I'll just wait until suppertime at the cafeteria to grab some grub and to fill my radiator, so that my kidneys can be drained again. We're havin' pasta today as the prime entrée on the lackluster menu, and that's the only meal I actually really enjoy here."

"It's time for a new deck of pinochle cards," Tim perceptively recommended. "Pretty soon, it'll be baseball season before ya' know it J.W.," Amoro reminded me as Tim shuffled the cards, and then my playing partner News cut the deck twice. "And don't bust Ralph's stones doin' the radio play-by-play like ya' did last spring," Timmy gently admonished my offensive nature. "I was listenin' to one game, and you asked Crenshaw 'Why do baseball fields have pitchers' mounds?', and 'Why do we have dirt infields blended-in with grass on the diamond?', makin' the baseball broadcast seem like Philosophy class or somethin'. And poor nervous Ralph was put on the spot, havin' to pretend he was remotely interested in your nonsensical bull-shit, and that the teased introvert valued your facetious jargon. Get more serious this year, J.W., will ya'!"

I promised the other 38 South Main Lambdas that I would exercise more discretion by using fewer "Interrogatives" while addressing neurotic Ralph Crenshaw on the radio, and the group all chuckled at my very sterling choice of vernacular.

"Last weekend, that freak Bill Elderberry took me in his little yellow faggot Karmann Ghia out to Sweetwater over near Batsto Village, somewhere really remote, east of *206,* in the *Wharton State Forest,"* Big Al told us.

"That's *Jersey Devil* territory!" News alertly observed and mentioned. "I believe it's near Leeds Point!"

"Yeah, News, that's right!" Keiler proceeded with advancing his topic. "Anyway, somehow Bill incidentally knows this totally-queer faggot maggot that's got an opulent mansion secluded somewhere in the legendary pine forest, and there's a big party goin' on there. So, Elderberry, with me taggin' along, decides to crash the shindig."

"Was flaming Dr. McIntire one of the distinguished guests?" News intoned. "When it comes to proper sexuality, he can't see the forest for the trees."

"Will ya' shut the hell up when I'm tellin' the damned story!" Big Al shouted at News, getting the attention of other more dedicated card players at surrounding round tables. "Anyway, this rich homo', who speaks with an odd lateral lisp like some sissy faggot Castilian king ownin' a severe speech defect, has expensive harpsichords, whalebones, Gramophones and other weird paraphernalia all over his magnificent, rustic palace, secluded deep in the Jersey woods."

"So, what's your point?" News questioned Big Al. "There's plenty of rich faggots right here in Glassboro, and some pine barons livin' in pine-barrens around here, too, especially out towards Aura!"

"There's two goddamned points I wanna' make if ya' let me finish the friggin' story," Big Al fiercely chastised Tomasello. "First of all, Elderberry can get anybody to do something the person doesn't wanna' do, at least anything short of murder, like us goin' to the viewings next door at Lacy's Funeral Parlor. And secondly," Keiler editorialized, "this queer homo' out near Sweetwater has six vicious German shepherds and six ferocious Dobermans patrollin' his rustic palace to keep everybody inside drinkin' expensive whiskey and talkin' about politics and religion. The homo's mansion near the *Mullica* was some sort of modern Greek symposium, just like Professor Kraft had told us about in Philosophy class. The faggot jerk-off acted like he was some gay European duke, or baron, or somethin'," Keiler claimed, almost out of breath. "And I felt very uncomfortable bein' there bein' bored for seven long hours. And if the house wasn't near the river on the side the vicious dogs weren't patrollin', and if I could swim good, I would've escaped and desperately swam all the way to *Batsto Village*."

"But Big Al, the wealthy pansy dude gave ya' good hospitality; fed ya' like you were the Duke of Buckingham, and treated you like privileged royalty! What's your whole damned point?" News insisted. "You're ramblin' around, criticizing an odd man that treats you too-good-to-be-true, and you're soundin' a lot like a guy lookin' for his lost circumcision skin that had been surgically cut-away and disposed of, nineteen years ago!"

"The goddamned point, News, is that I never want to go back to that rich homosexual, effeminate, sissy bastard's place again, with my ass riding in any little faggot yellow sports car, despite the sumptuous foods and the expensive imported whiskey," Big Al angrily concluded in a hostile tone of voice. "And if Elderberry attempts to get me to go there again, I'm gonna' beat the shit out of the horny little prick, and then use his faggot Karmann Ghia to run the know-it-all wiseass over at least fifty-seven times, once each for every damned *Heinz Variety.*"

"Hey, J.W., any info' on the tri-frat panty' raid?" Tim inquired. "It's almost near *Christmas* break, and I imagine it's gonna' come off pretty damned soon."

"No, Tim, your guess is as good as mine," I frankly replied. "It's the best kept secret on campus, and between the four of us, I hope it never comes to fruition!"

On Tuesday night, December 18th, I was studying in the 38 South Main "Common Room" for a major test for Dr. Attleburg in Mental Health when News arrived like an 1870s Old West *Pony Express* courier with an important secret communication. "Guys, the panty raid is on for tonight. It's gonna' happen exactly ten-minutes after midnight. The temperature's gonna' be milder than usual accordin' to the weather forecast. And don't forget the rules, men," Tomasello continued his announcement. "Only wear your *Halloween* masks, socks, and footgear durin' the raid, or it'll look bad for the Lambda Phi's reputation for havin' large testicles, either in or outa' public scrutiny!"

"Okay, that confusing, warped statement was cool, News!" Tim apprehensively replied. "But where are we gonna' change. I mean to say, there isn't any available locker room or anything."

"Good question!" News snapped back. "The three fraternities are gonna' meet on the dark baseball field next to *College Hall* at midnight. At 12:05, we'll all disrobe into our birthday suits. And then seventy-five to a hundred guys are gonna' run stark naked with our masks on, dashing-around the west side of *College Hall,* past the Co-op, and then hustle straight into the girls' Quadrangle," News disclosed. "The dorms' doors will still be open until 12:30 for female curfew advocates to sign-in. The Lambdas will storm into *Linden,* and the Deltas will plow through *Oak,* and the Tau Kappas will invade *Laurel*, all participants being stark naked."

"And remember J.W.," Timmy advised and reviewed. "Nobody leaves *Linden Hall* until the Lambda steals a pair of panties, even if they're from some dragon, some hideous wildebeest, or from a tit-less lesbian broad that's the size of a damned water buffalo."

Over eighty guys from the three frats furtively assembled from all directions, standing fully clothed on the baseball diamond at midnight. The Lambdas undressed in centerfield; the Deltas around third base, and the Taus close to first. And then, we all congregated around the pitcher's mound with only our masks and our shoes on, until Bob Powell gave the command to initiate the daring raid.

Eighty naked males sprinted-up the grassy slope and around *College Hall* to the campus's main paved road. When we rushed past *Memorial Hall,* a shrill shriek was heard originating from several horrified civilian, late night black cafeteria ladies, as the strange contingent, wearing African tribal masks, came sprinting under the streetlamps in *their* direction. The three frat' house members scampered past the Co-op, and quickly entered the campus's stately Quadrangle. In another thirty-seconds, my nude body was scampering inside *Linden Hall,* and there was incredible female screaming and fearsome primitive male shouting coming to my ears from all directions.

News, Timmy, and I fled up a flight of stairs to *Linden Hall's* second floor, figuring that the bottom level had already been saturated with Lambdas in quest of various colored panties. We burst into one room, but were repelled by two screaming, horrified obese females, that must have had prehistoric woolly mammoths for parents. And when we dashed-down into the second-floor's main corridor, the overhead lights were flashing on and off in a weird psychedelic, strobe-light effect, as the fire alarm began blasting-away amidst all the mind-boggling female hysteria.

The *Linden Hall's* two matronly old hag dorm' mothers, Miss Grundell and Miss Snipes, were chasing three Lambdas in the opposite direction brandishing raised broomsticks, and I was almost castrated when one of the old spinster's poles smashed against my left thigh in passing *their* thrashing presence. I sought asylum in an upstairs room and flicked-on the lights, while three hiding and terrified your corpulent mastodons started yelling and cursing deliriously. I spotted a pair of pink panties on top of a clothes bureau, and immediately, snatched and confiscated the sought-after apparel. I was about to evacuate the dorm' room when a familiar voice yelled out, "J.W.! It's you!"

My head quickly turned to perceive through my new Watusi mask non-other than the heavenly features of a very appalled Peachy Wilcox. "Ahhh!" I shouted through the mask as I leaped-up into the air, landed on my sore feet, and then feeling excessively mortified, covered my genitalia with my hands, and also with the recently-obtained pink panties.

My feet rambunctiously exited the noisy room of shrieking females as fast as I could, and my bare legs sprinted-back down the hall the same way that I had accidentally found Peachy's room. I again encountered and passed Miss Grundell and Miss Snipes, who were vigorously pursuing (with elevated broomsticks) intimidated

Big Al wearing his Pigmy mask, the intruder desperately fleeing in the other direction in order to save both his life and his testicles.

I quickly descended the concrete steps and zipped-out of the *Linden Hall* premises' front paned doors, laughing my nude rear-end off and screaming wildly, as all kinds of rushing hormones pulsated throughout my energized body. A campus policeman lunged-out to tackle me from the right side, but I evaded his futile endeavor with a nifty twisting maneuver and a forceful football straight-arm, and then my legs bolted through the Women's Quadrangle, running past the Co-op, and finally making it to the tiny knoll next to *College Hall*.

My throbbing body excitedly descended the embankment to the pitch-black baseball field. I used an available flashlight left on the centerfield grass to find my clothes, and when I was dressing into my personal garb, I could still hear screaming, shrieking, fire alarms, and witnessing activities to my left, my eyes perceived flashing lights originating from *Linden, Oak,* and *Laurel Hall*. Five minutes later, Bob Abrams showed-up, collected my obtained pink panties, and praised my accomplishment as a "job well done".

After Big Al, News, Timmy, and Ron Carputis showed-up with their "cotton trophies", and then joined me to quickly dress, the five of us made a beeline for the railroad tracks; crossed the rails, and reentered my Chevy Impala, which was parked in front of a house on Villanova Road near Girard. I did not drive through Glassboro proper, fearing that perhaps a police road block might have been set-up to snare pernicious dormitory marauders, but instead, I sped-down Villanova, cut over to *322,* and then took the roundabout route via Carpenter Street to 38 South Main, where we triumphantly imbibed two full bottles of *Southern Comfort* to warm-up and celebrate our great hysterical turmoil.

The raid (from the Lambda Phi Sigma point of view) was a tremendous success, but the campus cops had gotten lucky and had apprehended Delta Alpha Omega pledges Russ Stillwell and Andy Talbot, and unbelievably, the local Keystone Kops had also captured Tau Kappa Epsilons Bruce Harper and Randy Irwin.

"Well, good buddy," I addressed News the following day in front of *Memorial Hall*. "The frat' war is gonna' happen some more because the deans had to suspend the four kids that had been caught during the audacious raid, and make examples out of 'em, and now the Deltas and the Taus are really pissed-off at the Lambdas, since none of our guys had been arrested," I generalized. "That means that the deans are gonna' take action against Powell's and Hiltwine's brotherhoods, but the Lambdas have temporarily, for the moment, survived and escaped the joint dorm' blitz, unscathed."

"That's what I hear, too," Tomasello verified. "But I also heard from Peachy Wilcox before first period class that some bizarre Lambda with distorted sexual paraphernalia upon his anatomy had raided her dorm' room. And ever since, your number two girl has had severe migraines about the grotesque monster havin' the repulsive, deformed fadorkenbender."

"Maybe it was Mario or Kenny," I answered, pretending to claim ignorance to the situation. "They both participated in the spectacular raid, and each managed to get three pair of panties from three horrified dragons."

"Peachy didn't say for sure," News honestly responded. "She just told me that the demented guy was disfigured and pretty horrible-lookin', but the trespasser exhibited mannerisms and body language similar to someone she knows, when he's normally wearin' clothes!"

I desired to lay low the next three days; I stayed out of the Co-op and *Memorial Hall* areas to avoid Peachy and Joanne, and only came onto the campus to attend my uninteresting classes. Then, on Friday night, during one of my more vulnerable moments, Wild Bill Elderberry accosted me with a proposition I was too weak to refuse.

"J.W., unfortunately my yellow Karmann Ghia is in the shop being repaired," Elderberry commenced his tale of woe. "And I got some pretty swift friends residin' out at *West Virginia U.* that I wanna' visit this weekend."

"Okay, Bill, but I'm runnin' a little low on cash just before *Christmas* break," I grimly replied. "I only have twenty-five bucks to my name, but I've gotten all my presents bought already. Why don't ya' give me gas, toll, and food money, and I'll drive you out there. I like to see new places. It's near Pittsburgh, right?"

"Sort of," Bill affirmed. "But J.W., I figured I would save ya' wear and tear on your car, pay for your food, and since ya' already agreed to accompany me," Elderberry reminded in his singularly devious style of communication, "we'll hitchhike together out to *West Virginia U.,* and then one of my good buddies will drive us back to Glassboro Sunday night in his car."

"In the height of December?" I yelled. "Are ya' stir-crazy Elderberry, or what?"

"My aspiration is to become as nuts as *you* already are, and J.W., ya' got a reputation and a half when it comes to insanity! That is, I mean to say for doin' insane and enjoying relatively perverted things!" Elderberry cleverly and sarcastically praised.

And so, on Saturday morning, December 22nd, one day after the Winter Solstice, Big Al drove Bill and me in *my* '61 Chevy across the *Walt Whitman Bridge* into Philadelphia, and then headed-up the *Schuylkill Expressway* to the Valley Forge toll entrance to the *Pennsylvania Turnpike,* so that Elderberry and I could hitchhike out toward Pittsburgh, over three-hundred-miles away.

"If we get a ride to Pittsburgh," Bill assured me, "the trip's gonna' be as easy as apple pie. My buddy will pick us up there."

"I get indigestion from apple pie, and also from chocolate cake!" I sarcastically commented. "And damned chronic diarrhea, too! So now, don't also tell me this trip's gonna' be as easy as cake!"

The two fools stood-out in the frigid cold for a full-hour-and-a-half, getting our thumbs frostbitten, when finally, a strange-looking guy, with his body and features appearing a little like a contemporary Ichabod Crane, stopped in an old red and black '56 Ford Crown Victoria. We gladly entered the stranger's vehicle, and although Bill and I were happy to get warm, we were disappointed to hear that the fellow could only take us as far as Harrisburg, only a hundred or so miles west of Philly'.

About fifty-miles west into our excursion, our odyssey to *West Virginia University* had to be aborted. The Ford's radio reported that "an Arctic Alberta Clipper" was heading into Pennsylvania from Canada, and that a major blizzard was scheduled to descend on Harrisburg and cities to its west, with a sizable accumulation of snow being predicted in the immediate forecast.

"Bill, didn't you check the weather before settin' out on this crazy, dimwitted Eskimo expedition?" I angrily balked. "We're gonna' need a pair of snow sleds; Sergeant Preston *RCMP* uniforms, and fresh Alaskan huskies to get back to Jersey."

"Naw, I figured everything would be fine," Elderberry remarked while shrugging his shoulders as was his bad habit when being interrogated on the spot. "You could've checked the weather, too, J.W., ya' know! Don't try to just blame me for this disaster!"

Even the rugged *Pennsy' Turnpike* was becoming treacherous and slippery with the newly arrived Yukon air pattern and snow flurries, but Elderberry remained resolute and determined to proceed as his raspy voice enunciated, "Westward Ho!" as if the quixotic ninny fancied himself as Major Seth Adams on *Wagon Train.*

The thoroughly amused driver thanked us for our glorious company, and dropped Bill and me off in metropolitan downtown Harrisburg, where we shuffled our numb feet through swirling winds, and carefully stepped-around shifting snowdrifts. The sudden intense snow accumulation had a stifling effect upon our incentive to continue our intense journey westward. Bill's idealistic quest had wonderfully been defeated, much to my great and instant joy. The powerful forces of Mother Nature had single-handedly terminated the insane "Westward Ho!" initiative.

"J.W., I see the city bus terminal up ahead, and I don't know about you," Elderberry orally conveyed almost apologetically, "but my alimentary canal needs elementary nourishment with these horrifying stomach pangs I'm sufferin', and with this intolerable growlin' I'm hearin'."

I momentarily looked-up and observed the relentless gales and felt the frigid, penetrating, cold upon my aching face. And then, my blurred eyes glanced-down at the snow-laden sidewalk. No mentally ill Harrisburg pedestrians were wandering-around anywhere in sight.

"Bill, thank goodness you're finally makin' a rational decision," I seriously noted. "We gotta' get out of this concrete Siberia and get some hot dogs and heated baked beans into our deprived systems, so that we can again think straight, and piss and crap right."

At the nearly abandoned bus terminal, Bill reluctantly paid for my ticket to Philadelphia, where Big Al finally showed-up in the '61 white Impala to transport the vanquished highway itinerants back to wonderful Glassboro.

"You're lucky you caught me on the phone at 38 South Main when you were still in Harrisburg," Big Al explained. "All of the other guys had gone home for the *Christmas* holidays, and I was about to catch a ride from Ralph to Brooklawn to my mom's place. If you had called me a half-hour later, J.W., you and Wild Bill would've been stranded in Philly'."

"It's not snowin' here, yet," Bill noticed as Big Al drove my white Chevy into Glassboro. "But that blizzard is headin' this way as sure as bones make marrow and red blood cells, and as sure as small and large intestines make fecal matter."

"I think I'd prefer attending a viewing at Lacy's Funeral Parlor, rather than go on any other screwed-up, aborted excursions with you!" I squawked to Elderberry, when Big Al finally pulled my white Chevy into the familiar 38 South Main Street driveway. "Merry *Christmas,* guys!"

Chapter 24
"Lakehurst"

I was extremely fatigued from my misadventure out to Harrisburg with numb-nuts Bill Elderberry, but I had the decency to drive the zany kid to a Glassboro repair shop to pick-up his yellow Karmann Ghia, and then a half-hour later, I took Big Al to his mom's brick home in Brooklawn, just south of Gloucester City. I was so worn-down that night, back home in Elm, I had slept longer hours and more frequently than usual, so when News called my parents' place Sunday night and inquired if I had seen the great *AFL Championship Game* where the Dallas Texans had beaten the Houston Oilers in double overtime, I had to tell him an emphatic, "no".

"J.W., it was a really excitin' game," Tomasello related over the phone. "And Tommy Brooker kicked the game winning field goal for Dallas in the second overtime quarter."

"Sorry I missed the thrilling contest, News," I feigned regretting, pretending to show interest. "But really, I'm an *NFL* fan and can't wait to see the *Packers* and the *Giants* go at it head-to-head on December 30th. I promise I'll go over to your place and watch that special game."

"Okay, J.W.," News happily began signing-off. "See ya' on the 30th. Merry *Christmas*." Click.

I did enjoy a calm *Christmas Day* at home with the family, and then on the 30th, drove over to News's house on Spring Road, situated not too far from his dad's peach farm, where we watched the mighty *Packers* defeat New York 16-7. And then, two days later, I again made it over to News's "hacienda" to view in black and white (on his parent's new color TV) LSU defeat Texas in the *Cotton Bowl;* Alabama beat Oklahoma in the *Orange Bowl;* Mississippi win a close struggle over Arkansas in the *Sugar Bowl,* and finally, watching Southern Cal coming-away victorious over the *Big Ten's* Wisconsin, 42-37, in the close-contest *Rose Bowl Game.*

"Just have another week and a half of classes, and then it's already second semester, sophomore year for us," I related to my dear friend. "Thank goodness I'll be earnin' mostly B's for the fall semester, without that witch Sankins there to vex me. I hope there's no such thing as a sophomore academic jinx for us."

"Maybe not," News attested with a degree of uncertainty. "Maybe not a sophomore jinx, but we've both done plenty of foolish sophomoric things like the crazy panty dorm' raid, and you then pickin' up and goin' on a wild gooseberry trip to Harrisburg with that pathetic scoundrel, Wild Bill Elderberry."

"Just some more terrific stories for our grandchildren to listen to," I laughed and evaluated. "Yeah, News. We now need some more tales to retell while sitting in our rickety old rockin' chairs. Anything happenin' in the papers?"

"Yeah, J.W. Leonardo DaVinci's famous *Mona Lisa* is gonna' be on loan from the *Louvre* and exhibited in New York, startin' January 8th," the human encyclopedia informed.

"Too bad that Professor Tweed's art trip wasn't a month later, or we could've stood there and watched Lisa moaning," I laughed. "But I'd rather stand in line to get into a good New York bar than to wait for a rare chance to see any historic Paris painting on loan-exhibit in downtown Manhattan."

"Well, for your information, J.W., the exhibit's gonna' later leave New York and be transported to Washington DC where they expect another million people to see the incomparable *Mona Lisa,"* Tomasello vociferated. "And if that's not enough to satisfy your aesthetic, artistic tastes, *Whistler's Mother* is gonna' be on exhibit in Atlanta during most of February. And I'm not just *whistlin' Dixie* when I tell ya' that news!"

"Gee, News, after this dull *Christmas* intermission, and after hearin' what borin' stuff's happenin' in the world, that art news could only give that faggot Dr. Tweed an immense, once-in-a-lifetime erection. To tell ya'the truth, I'll be glad to be leavin' Hammonton and getting' back to good old 38 South Main to continue my higher education, *upstairs,* inside our non-swanky humble apartment."

"Hey, J.W.," News slyly cackled like a deranged sorcerer. "Are Tweed and McIntire sleepin' together? Art and politics make strange bedfellows, ya' know."

"Don't start any more unfounded rumors about other people, particularly professors," I mildly reproached News. "But I must say the Lambdas want a monopoly on all campus rumors, whether the tales be good, bad, derogatory, scandalous, false or ten percent true."

Soon, it was January of 1963, and the guys were all happily back living at 38 South Main. On Thursday, January 10th (according to my diary, which I kept secret and only wrote inside when no one was around, or during a boring class lecture) I had finished up my morning classes and had nothing better to do, so I took a saunter through *Memorial Hall.* I discovered in the main corridor's lobby a grinning Naval Recruiter sitting at a rectangular table, and the merry fellow solicited my attention.

"You look like you could qualify to be a Naval jet pilot!" the officer boomed in a contrived genial voice. "How about sittin' down and talkin' about it? There's no obligation to explore a possible great career in aviation."

"I parked my butt and listened to all of the Naval propaganda, which incidentally didn't sound that bad with the pension and health benefits, if I could survive a twenty-year-career in a fighter plane, engaged in doing dangerous patrols and missions off of an aircraft carrier. After a half-hour's time investment, the personable recruiter had a specific proposal to make, and I seriously evaluated its content.

"We're givin' a qualifications test in the cafeteria down the hall tomorrow at two in the afternoon," the affable recruiter informed. "So, after you matriculate for your second semester classes in the morning, you can stop in and take the test to see if ya' can measure up to bein' a Naval aviator. Again, young man, I want to stress that there's no obligation, of course!"

I was flattered by the abundant praise and by the fabulous prospect of being a jet fighter pilot, so I signed the paper stating that I would take the qualifying test. The naval salesman thanked me for my cooperation and indulgence, said that I appeared to be a bright young man, and promised to see me during the testing session, scheduled for *Memorial Hall Cafeteria* the following afternoon.

The guys over at 38 South Main really razzed me over my "silly choice" because military service to them meant regimentation, blind obedience to authority, conformity to strict behavior codes, and "losing your individuality" to conduct yourself like "a programmed robot". The only one that defended my decision to take the aviator's test was Big Al, who had recently joined the *New Jersey National Guard* and had been taking summer courses to become a Second Lieutenant after graduation. "But please remember, J.W.," Keiler warned me, "there's a possible war developin' in Southeast Asia, and ya' might be eligible to be called after graduation if ya' commit to the Navy. It all depends if ya' wanna' live a long, dull, meaningless life, or a short, thrilling, adventurous, heroic one!"

The other guys continued criticizing the military life relentlessly, and I was really questioning my own credibility and decision-making capacity. Had I been duped?

"Don't let these jealous turkeys shoot ya' down when you're tryin' so hard to fly like an eagle," Big Al advised. "Because all your other roommates wanna' do is keep ya' trapped inside their cage, and existing on their same shelf. And besides, your dad was in the *Army* during *WWII,* and ya' also told me that your grandfather on your mom's side served at *Walter Reed Hospital* during *WWI,* so there's already a military tradition in your family."

"It's better that we shoot ya' down here at 38 South Main than if the friggin' Russians or the freakin' Red Chinese do, somewhere over Asia," Elderberry criticized. "I'd rather go to faggot parties in the pine-barrens with Big Al than to have to say, 'Yes sir, yes sir!' all damned day long. What if ya' get a homo' for a superior officer that insists ya' give him a blowjob every damned night? Are ya' gonna' just stand there J.W., and say, 'Yes sir, yes sir'!" Wild Bill laughed. "And I hear the doctors give lousy physicals in the Navy, and I understand that they're so lax that the examinin' medics don't even check your goddamned taint to see if it's still functionin' or not! Ha, ha, ha! The examiners only check your damned navel for Naval service! Ha, ha, ha, ha!"

I took the Navy's Naval test in the main cafeteria on Friday afternoon, along with two-dozen other gullible, idealistic *GSC* students, and a week later on January 18th, I received a letter from the Naval Commander at Lakehurst commending me on my high score, and inviting me to show-up on Friday, February 22nd, *Washington's Birthday,* for a Navy physical, since a lot of the barracks would be near empty that day, and that more time could be devoted to prospective personnel interviews and required physicals.

"Throw the damned propaganda letter away," Elderberry loudly recommended to me in the Common Room. "You've only signed your name to take the damned test. If ya' don't show-up, they'll never come to Glassboro and find your ass. The Navy can only court martial assholes that are already in the service."

"Look, Bill. It states in paragraph four of the letter that I don't have to decide until after graduation in two years whether to enlist or not, and then take their gruelin' officer training course," I argued. "And furthermore, it also states in paragraph one that I've qualified to be a jet fighter pilot."

"Yeah, J.W," Tim Amoro interrupted. "But after you enlist, they'll say they have too many jet pilot candidates and only a limited number of jet planes, and then make you a navigator on one of those bulky ancient transports that crash all the time, or maybe put you on blimps operatin' outa' Lakehurst. Say, News, isn't Lakehurst where the *Hindenburg* crashed?"

"That's right, Tim," News positively and absolutely confirmed. "On May 6th, 1937, to be exact, the German Airship *Hindenburg* exploded while mooring at Lakehurst, and then the dirigible went down like a lead zeppelin, killin' thirty-six of the ninety-seven unfortunate people aboard."

"You ain't gonna' wind-up in no supersonic jet aircraft, J.W.," Elderberry cynically chided. "So, stop bein' so damned naïve about throwin' your future, and maybe even your precious life away. You've been cleverly hoodwinked into qualifyin' to ride the next *Hindenburg* outa' Lakehurst, that's all you've freakin' qualified for."

"Do what ya' think is best for *you!"* Big Al insisted while accentuating the positive. "The last time you listened to Elderberry you both wound-up stranded in an atrocious blizzard over a hundred-miles away. And the only other place he'll lead ya' is to the funeral home next door, to view some anonymous corpse ya' never knew!"

"Don't listen to negativity, J.W.," News urged. "The U.S. Navy ceased operatin' the blimp program three years ago in 1960. And even if the Admirals still had blimps floatin' around the lower atmosphere," Tomasello reported, "the balloons would be filled with helium and not with hydrogen. Hydrogen can explode and then intensely burn-up, as was true in the dramatic *Hindenburg* tragedy. Helium is non-combustible, or non-flammable, unlike hydrogen, which easily burns."

"Thanks, News," I appreciatively commented. "I'll remember that sagacious knowledge the next time I see the *Good Year* blimp circlin' over a football or baseball stadium."

As luck would have it, the second Friday in February, I received a call from an old Edgewood High School pal, Frankie Jives Arena, inviting me up to visit him in New York City, where my old acquaintance was attending *Pace College,* the main campus being located in the lower Manhattan business district.

"Say, J.W., how's Cloud 9 treatin' your butt!" Jives began over the phone. "I mean there's only one thing worse than Dudsville in Hammonton, and that's Squaresville in Glassboro, man! That's the pits, and I an't talkin' *Indianapolis Speedway,* either!"

"Jives, how did ya' get my Glassboro phone number?" I wondered and asked. "It's pretty confidential."

"I called your Neanderthals at your pad in Elm, and your mom and dad spilled the beans, dude. It's real groovy up here in this concrete jungle, ya' dig, big daddy! You're gonna' flip when ya' escape Nowheresland down there in the Jersey sticks, where everybody and their hick granny wants to rattle your cage."

"I'll tell ya'what, Jives," I replied while efficiently coordinating dual events in my fertile mind. "I'll be up in Lakehurst on Friday,

February 22nd, *Washington's Birthday,* attendin' to some personal business. How about if I drive up the *Parkway* from Lakehurst and meet you on Saturday the 23rd somewhere in Manhattan, let's say, around noontime."

"Cool Daddio!" Frankie validated. "How about at the jive corner of 52nd Street and Park Avenue. There's a high-rise garage parko place nearby, and ya' can't miss the super-sucker blindfolded. Then, we'll both find-out what's buzzin' cuzzin'," Jives rhymed, "and J.W., ya' can tell me your entire tale, your oral nightingale startin' with 'What's the word, mockin' bird'."

"Er, cool Jives, real cool," I chuckled while awkwardly trying to imitate Maynard G. Krebs, a TV beatnik-type character on the hit *Dobie Gillis Show*.

"Tear-ass through the *Lincoln Tunnel,* J.W. And then, take *Broadway* North to 52nd Street, where you'll make a right. Catch ya' in front of the big parkin' mausoleum around noon on the 22nd. And remember J.W.," Jives imperatively added. "Don't be no party pooper. Only poop in the goddamned crapola! And don't get radioactive before I see ya', so if ya' have a blast, make sure it ain't nuclear, man! So long for now, Kookie Cat!" Click.

I woke-up very early on the 22nd, ate a *Washington's Birthday Special* breakfast alone at the Angelo's Diner's counter, and drove *322* past the Williamstown Republican Club. And then, I followed the highway (*Black Horse Pike*) east to the *Garden State Parkway,* which I proceeded on north, driving parallel to the Jersey coastline all the way up to the Lakehurst exit. I listened to some radio news about how racial strife was again showing its grotesque face in the South with a black student being enrolled in South Carolina's *Clemson University,* and then heard a commentator discussing how nuclear testing was being resumed, because negotiations had broken-down with the ever-formidable Russians.

My right hand immediately turned the car radio dial and listened to "Remember Then", a new song by the Earls being played on W-ABC out of New York, and I recalled my past in Levittown, in Hammonton, and in Glassboro. And when Skeeter Davis began singing "The End of the World", I thought considerably about my trip to the Lakehurst military base, and how jet pilots could be used to stifle Russian incursions around the free world, and how I might have to drop nerve gas or tear gas on college campuses to quell race riots and social disorder, before being gunned-out of the dangerous sky over Southeast Asia by vile North Vietnam Communists.

And when W-ABC played "Walk Right In, Sit Right Down" by the Rooftop Singers folk group, ironically, I simultaneously pulled into the Lakehurst Naval Air Station, and the gate sailor on duty saluted me when I halted my white Chevy. The guard read my letter of introduction, gave me a pass, and directed me to where my status-oriented "Officers' Barracks" was located. "Don't worry! The officers are mostly off this weekend, so you'll have the entire place all to yourself, along with several other eager college visitors."

I checked-in at the barrack's main desk, was assigned my room, ate in the mess area, met three other college guys from *Rutgers* and another idealistic upperclassman from *GSC,* and then after lunch, submitted to a battery of math and general knowledge tests before having an extensive physical at 4 p.m. I must confess that my first impression of rigid military life was negative, and I began to see significant merit in Bill Elderberry's caustic testaments.

The next morning, after a big high-calorie early breakfast, I told a recruiter during my last interview that I was still considering Navy life, and that I would ultimately decide during my senior year. Then, I packed my overnight bag, exited the barracks, and drove back to the on-duty guard's station. I surrendered my pass and saluted the sailor, who also respectfully put his right hand up to his eyebrow.

I was rather anxious to leave Lakehurst behind and chalk it up as an important coming-of-age experience. I never felt so free, so liberated and glad to again be an ordinary, civilian American citizen, as I had on the short jaunt up the *Parkway* to the *Turnpike,* and then to the *Lincoln Tunnel,* entering into midtown Manhattan. And when I motored through one of the engineering marvel's tubes toward midtown, my mind recalled the time that News and I had been kidnapped and wound-up as perishable cargo in Hunts Point, and I wondered when the *GSC* frat' war would rekindle, and once again, unconstructively dominate my already encumbered life.

I had little trouble navigating through the congested 42nd Street Theater District after turning onto *Broadway,* and at 11:45a.m., I pulled into the designated high-rise garage entrance that Jives had recommended, obtained my ticket from the courteous lady attendant, and then drove the white Impala up to the third level, where I found a suitable parking place. Remarkably, my arrival was five-minutes early for my appointment with Jives, who was impatiently standing out front of the garage when my ears detected a familiar voice.

"J.W. Welcome to the big show!" Jives Arena greeted me by shaking my gloved right hand. "It's colder than the Wicked Witch of the East's dead left tit, so let's scoot into the *Four Seasons* and have a bitchin' blast ourselves, talkin' shit about the glorious past!"

"The Four Seasons? What's that?" I innocently inquired. "Some kind of wall calendar?"

"It's the most boss bitchin'est eatery in all of the Burg, Top Cat, so what's your big tickle?" Jives jived. "Ya' still got ample smog in your noggin', J.W.! You've advanced from a square to a cube in no easy lessons! Three D daddy, three D, and breathing in livin' color, all the diggin' way!"

"They must have more than just salt, pepper, mustard, and vinegar being served in that fancy restaurant!" I joked, while alluding to the establishment's singular name. "What about some other four seasons like paprika, cinnamon, chives, and parsley?"

"Hey, dig J.W. Don't have a damned cow and get frosted over nothin'," Jives illogically jested. "You're nowhere, man! The dub *Four Seasons* pertains to the themes summer, fall, winter, spring, just like that Indian babe that used to be the lesbian princess ya' always had the hots for on the *Howdy Doody Show*. Anyway, J.W. Glad ya' can make the damned Big Aple scene. I didn't tell ya' on the horn that this neato food palace serves deluxe grub here, unlike in Hammonton, where ya' only get knuckle sandwiches done by *Bakers,* ha, ha, ha! Let's get outa' the cold before my piss freezes inside my damned radiator hose."

The *Four Seasons Restaurant,* at 9 East 52nd Street, was a really magnificent establishment that, according to Jives, had opened in 1959, and the acclaimed eatery had really exquisite dining rooms and appeared entirely too elegant, extravagant, expensive, and luxurious for my shrinking revenue flow. After a formal looking maitre d' checked Jives's lunch reservation, the snotty, tuxedoed penguin escorted us to a table inside the Grill Room, where Arena commanded me to give the accommodating fellow a five-dollar tip for seating us, and who then formally handed us two menus.

"Jives, I only have twenty-five more dollars on me. I have to pay now for my hotsy-totsy meal, I have to pay for the tunnel, and also for turnpike tolls back to Glassboro," I maintained. "And I'll be lucky if I get back with a nickel in my pocket. All I wanted to do was to pop into Gotham and say 'hello'."

"Ya' always sweat the damned small stuff, J.W.," Jives answered, as if my worried statements had fallen on deaf ears. "Just order a Bison Burger and a *Coke,* and pretend you're in paradise, dude."

"That hamburger on the menu is seven dollars!" I balked. "I can get the exact same thing served at Angelo's Diner in for a mere thirty-nine cents!"

"Everything in this metro' town is higher than anywhere in the South Jersey hinterlands," Jives informed, obviating the obvious. "I tried bookin' the Pool Room, but only the Grill was available, so cut the gas and stop fracturin' me with un-gear, cop-out-type jive negativity, man. You're giving me a bummer migraine!"

"Pool Room?" I exclaimed. "Nobody's gonna' be playin' eight ball in any back room here at a classy, ritzy, splendid restaurant like the *Four Seasons!*"

"No, Dunce-head resident," Jives corrected. "The Pool Room's a special dining box that's got a big white marble reflectin' pool in it, so stop actin' dorky and quit eyeballin' the place like it's the first time ya' got dibs on anything outside Elm, ya' big country hick."

I finally became acclimated to the fancy restaurant's decor and classy atmosphere, and decided to make the most of my dining experience by enjoying and appreciating the exquisite *ambiance,* which Jives inadvertently called "the ambulance!"

The two of us reminisced old times about the nostalgic great teen fruit war between the Hammonton area Reds and the rich-kid Blues, and I even had a chance to savor every morsel of my very delicious Bison Burger. And after recalling the best of old times, Jives Arena divulged something that really stuck in my craw.

"I was talkin' to an Edgewood dude last week who's also partyin' heavy over at *GSC,"* Frankie Jives Arena nonchalantly revealed in casual conversation. "The cat said over the telly he'd like to join us for a reunion, but then the jive turkey punked-out because the fink had to take his grungy old lady somewhere in Filthy-delphia."

A red flag automatically went-up inside my skeptical mind, and I felt compelled to ask, "What's the guy's name?"

"Sam Lista," Jives identified. "The creep never once spoke to me at Edgewood, and now the flake wants to be my amigo, and says he's good and chummy with you. Say, J.W., why ya' lookin' so uptight and pale-faced all of a sudden?"

"How did *he* get your number up here at Pace College?" I curiously asked. "How did Sam Lista find-out where you live, and where you go to school? Did he say anything about this lunch meeting we're havin'?"

"Hey, cool it, bronco," Jives defensively ordered. "Relax, man! I'm not puttin' ya' down all over town! Lista says he goes to *GSC* with ya', and ya' just did a nifty, groovy fraternity prank together, ya' dig, Senor Honcho? He thinks you're his buddyaco!"

"True, Jives. Sam Lista's in another fraternity, Delta Alpha Omega," I told my unconcerned, apathetic listener. "And *we* did cooperate in a weird caper on campus a few months ago, to mutually break the administrators' stones, just before *Christma*s. What else did that warp-headed guy tell ya'?"

"That your amigo would've liked to munch lunch with us at the *Four Seasons* today, but had to meet-up with a few frat' buds and pull a super stunt on a mean-assed enemy," Jives mentioned. "J.W., why ya' wanna' blast-off to the loony lunar surface all of a sudden?"

I just hoped my lunch hunch was wrong, and refused to discuss my premonition with Jives until I had some conclusive evidence. My distraught mind could only think about Sam Lista and his close affiliation with Bob Powell, and the dreaded Delta Alphas.

"Hey, J.W. I gotta' tell ya'about this cool freak I heard playin' over in the *Village,* a real fab' long-hair guy named Bob Dylan," Jives buoyantly chortled. "This *Greenwich Village* cat sing-talks lyrics just like he's talkin' truth, a new kind of really swell rappin' sound. Ya' gotta' hear his boss gig!"

"I'm happy to learn that you've gone from Winslow Village to *Greenwich Village.* But sorry, Jives," I apologized. "I'm familiar with a Peter, Paul, and Mary song called 'Blowin' in the Wind', and it was first recorded by your idol, Bob Dylan. Now, let's get the check and blow outa' here. I'll explain my reason for rushin', later! And I hope I'm all wrong and overreactin' to my abundant fears."

After hurriedly paying our bill, Jives demanded that I leave an eight-dollar tip, which I very reluctantly did. We "blasted" out of the swanky *Four Seasons,* and my beatnik companion and I entered the now-familiar parking garage; took the slow elevator to the third level, and then I frantically dashed like a wild maniac to my white Impala, with lard-ass Jives yelling indiscernible babble while jogging fifty-feet behind.

Arriving at my most cherished possession, the white '61 Chevy Impala, my heart dropped to my stomach, and soon Jives arrived and attempted comforting me. My wheels had four punctured tires as flat as pancakes; a windshield smashed by either a sledgehammer or a crowbar; assorted huge dents all over the hood, roof, doors, and trunk, and a totally fractured front grille. Accompanied by Jives Arena, I angrily took the narrow elevator down to the cashier, almost sobbing, and I finally had the strength and composure to describe the major vandalism.

"My car's been demolished while my friend and I were eatin' over at the exclusive *Four Seasons,"* I futilely reported. "Where do I go from here? Should I call the police?"

"Only if ya' want your insurance premiums to go sky-high through the roof!" the female attendant answered. "This sort of thing happens all the time in New York, and I don't know quite what to say to you, young man, except don't go to the cops. They'll tie you up for weeks with red-tape paperwork and interviews. Just absorb the loss," the apathetic old bag suggested to her shocked listener.

"Absorb the loss!" I desperately raved. "Are you absolutely crazy? This vandalism happened on your company's property, and your firm must be covered for vehicle losses. And you certainly have inadequate security around here, too, I must add."

"Sir, the only thing I can tell you is to carefully read the back of your ticket voucher," the elderly hussy curtly directed. "It explicitly states in black and white that the parking garage is not responsible for either theft or vandalism. Park at your own risk."

"But what am I to do?" I bellowed in an almost delirious tone of voice. "I can't drive my car back to Jersey in that condition, and I don't know if it will even start after I buy four new tires."

"I'll tell ya'what the company can do for you!" the obstinate cashier replied. "Sign this release, and we won't charge you any time for parking your vehicle here until it's removed. But you'll have only five-days to get the wreck off the premises, or else we'll have it towed and impounded by the police. So, your total cost is now only a mere six dollars. I'll report the incident to my boss."

"Great!" I yelled, almost weeping openly. "I'll see what I'll be able to do in the meantime!"

I turned to my kooky old high school chum, who for once in his life was speechless. "Jives, I can't call Dad because he's already had one coronary, and another one could kill him. There's only one person who can help me outa' this horrendous dilemma."

"*Superman?"* Arena replied in a feeble attempt to humor me up. "I mean, J.W., it's not like your parents were both wiped-out in a train wreck, or killed in an atomic explosion, or somethin' electric like that. It's sickenin' what happened, I know it is, but busted property can be fixed or replaced. People can't be friggin' reincarnated here on good old terra-firma, man!"

"You're right on target, Jives!" I sadly agreed. "Let's go to your dorm' room over at *Pace,* and then I'll call Goose on the phone, and see if he could help me out."

"Cool as a monk in a ton of junk!" Jives typically rhymed. "And I also now think that Sam Lista is on your shit lista!"

At five in the afternoon, I finally reached Goose at his Winslow residence. Th Mafia kid was actually glad to hear from me, but then his sensitive ears detected trepidation in my quivering voice.

"What's wrong, J.W.?" Restuccio keenly demanded. "Are ya' pregnant or somethin'! I know a couple of doctors that have lost their licenses that still do fuckin' abortions for college dip-shits."

"Goose, I need your help, bad," I pleaded. "I'm stuck here in New York City with my car vandalized in a parkin' garage. I need it towed and fixed, if possible, but the Chevy looks totaled to me."

"Look, J.W.!" Goose sympathetically assessed. "Don't fuckin' hit the panic button. Just give me the goddamned address where it is. I know a couple of fucked-up guys up in Hoboken and Hackensack that own chop shops, and who owe my Pop and me a few big favors. They'll get in touch with that shit-house garage where your Chevy was demolished and fuckin' safely tow your wounded white chariot back to South Jersey."

"What if I need a new car?" I asked. "What then?"

"You worry about the most stupid, goddamned, fuckin' things!" Goose reprimanded. "Look, junior Asshole. If the Chevy can't be fixed, we'll just get a fresh one that's been stolen, switch the fuckin' license plates, and use a new registration."

"But isn't that illegal?" I inquired. "I don't want to go to jail for grand larceny, or anything off the wall like that."

"Listen, J.W. The cops everywhere in the country don't even know how to wipe their asses right," Goose criticized. "Ya' gotta' forget about the fuckin' cops, and worry about the petty thieves, and the drugos, and the pimps, and the vandals. They're the ones that could snuff-out your fuckin' life in a second! They're the ones the freakin' fuzz are scared shitless of!"

"Please stop cursin', Goose!" I implored. "It makes me terribly nervous and confused!"

"Do ya' want me to fuckin' help ya', or not?" Restuccio rhetorically asked while effectively asserting his existing dominance. "Fuckin' answer me, or I'll hang-up and take a healthy shit that's commin' on! Christ, I love shittin' almost as much as I like fuckin'!"

"Well, what should I do next?" I humbly asked.

"Nothin'! Just sit tight tonight, and then take the bitchin' express train from New York to Philly'. And then, catch one of the local New Jersey Public Service buses to goddamned Glassboro. I'll send Frankie Fingers and Joe Zucchini up with a few of the boys to get your car outa' that de-luxe, fucked-up garage, and after the mother fucker's either fixed, or a duplicate auto is gotten off of the black market," Restuccio promised, "then you'll have your precious Chevy back again. Actually, I loved that cheap white car, too, J.W. And I think the son-of-a-bitch Impala deserves a better fate. Say, who did ya' fuckin' visit while up in New York?"

"Frankie Jives Arena," I related. "You must remember him from high school and bein' with the Reds gang."

"That nutcase son-of-a-bitch!" Goose cursed. "That fat fuck-face always said fucked-up things I couldn't fuckin' understand, so I couldn't give him a proper beatin' cause I never knew if the cock-sucker was insultin' me or not insultin' me with his jive bull-shit!"

"Okay, Goose. I'll tell Jives you gave him your best regards," I diplomatically fibbed. "Now here's the address of the parking garage, along with its phone number."

I sincerely thanked Goose for promising to assist me in my hour of dire need; hung-up the telephone; stared out-of Frankie Jives Arena's apartment bedroom window, and peered at New York *City's* skyscrapers. And my perplexed mind wondered why we Americans had a government if it couldn't protect common citizens and their common property from common criminals. "Hey, Jives. What should I do with my Chevy when it's finally ready for the junk yard?"

"Leave it to Beaver!" Frankie countered as the cool hipster alluded to his favorite television show. "I guess the damned answer J.W. is just like Bob Dylan sang over there in *Greenwich Village.* 'The answer is Blowin' in the Wind'!"

Chapter 25
"Cowtown"

I was afraid I didn't have enough money to catch a southbound train from New York's *Grand Central Station* to Philadelphia's *Reading Terminal* in order to follow Goose's instructions to the T, so I did the next best thing. I bade farewell to demented Frankie Jives Arena, hailed a cab, and directed the driver to conduct me to *Port Authority Bus Terminal.* Next, I caught a *Greyhound* to Filbert Street in the heart of the *Quaker City,* and then hopped-aboard a New Jersey Public Service Bus to Glassboro.

On the last leg of my trip, I thought about the erratic frat' war; about my damaged Chevy, and my wilted psyche speculated about what mysterious event could possibly happen next. 'Sam Lista had heard somewhere on campus that I was going to New York to visit Jives,' I reconstructed as if I was some sort of cheap forensics detective. 'And then the bastard obtained the *Four Seasons* and the parking lot information from Jives's parents in Winslow, who trusted Lista as being one of their hep' son's best friends. Mr. and Mrs. Arena innocuously provided the essential data to the wily Delta Alpha Benedict Arnold. Lista came-up to New York with a carload of destructive-oriented enemy "frat' brothers", and the devious scoundrels maliciously vandalized my Impala, knowing full-well that the garage would not divulge confidential information to me about a carload of college punks staying in the garage for less than an hour.'

The 38 South Main Street Lambdas were all riled and irate about what malice had transpired in Manhattan, and the guys pledged to support any endeavor I elected to employ against our yellow-bellied, clandestine, college adversaries. I didn't like being singled-out for random punishment, but *we* all concluded that the vile destruction had deliberately occurred in New York, because a police report would have been filed if the demolition had happened in Glassboro, and the local newspapers, along with the administration, would have to become involved in the crime resolution formula. Big Al, News, Timmy, Bill Elderberry and I were all in full agreement.

"That's why the Deltas went up to 52nd between Park and Lexington to commit their lousy, dastardly skullduggery," Big Al accurately asserted. "And that's supposed to be one of the wealthiest and safest parts of the city. It just shows to go ya'!" Keiler finished in a really bad play-on-words reversal.

"You're lucky Goose came to the rescue, just like Dudley Do-right of the *Royal Canadian Mounted Police,"* Timmy uselessly commented. "Despite his abrasive language and his selfish braggin', Restuccio does have a heart of gold. We oughta' have Bob Abrams make him an honorary Lambda."

"Goose is a psychopathic lone wolf," News pointed-out, using one of Dr. Su's prized, lengthy vocabulary words. "Restuccio likes bein' on the periphery when *he* himself commits crimes. And when mischief turns into malice, he's always got the Mafia and a horde of corrupt politicians to back him up."

"If it weren't for the Lambda Phi's and all our fantastic exploits," Elderberry oddly articulated, "then I would transfer from *GSC* over to *Slippery Rock* in Pennsy' and play flag football there."

I called my parents and told them that I wouldn't be coming home the following weekend because I had a big term paper deadline to meet, when actually, I didn't desire confronting my folks with news that the Impala had been savagely vandalized. But much to my surprise and delight, Goose surprisingly showed-up at 38 South Main at five p.m. on Sunday, March 3rd, with "the Impala" being in "new *Immaculate Conception* condition." I raced down the wooden steps to inspect the miraculous body and fender rehabilitation.

"Goose, I can't believe my eyes!" I happily exclaimed. "It looks just like brand-new! Thank you so much!"

"Those chop shop turkeys up in Hoboken know what the fuck they're doin'," my devilish guardian angel/savior expressed. "I know what the fuck you've suffered and gone through, J.W. Remember the time those son-of-a-bitchin' Blues destroyed my Thunderbird in the brickyard killin' (kiln)? Whenever you're ready for some 're-tally-Haitian', I wanna' get involved in this asshole frat' war, and *lit-trall-ly* break some balls and send some dick-head college fuck-heads straight to the hospital, or to the 'in-farm-merry' (infirmary)."

"Say, Goose. You and Frankie Fingers wanna' go to Angelo's Diner and have some coffee and cheesecake?" I asked. "That's the least I can do to express my appreciation!"

"No thanks, J.W. Fingers and me are goin' over to Atlantic City; hit our favorite shore whorehouse; collect some fuckin' numbers money; go back to the whorehouse, and get laid again to get all of the poisons outa' our dick systems, and then head back to goddamned Hammonton," Restuccio matter-of-factly related. "I never did take ya' to that Atlantic City whorehouse like I promised J.W., did I?"

"Maybe after I graduate, I'll take you up on that stellar offer," I indicated. "Thanks again, Goose. If I could ever help ya' in any way, just let me know!"

I thought all week about how the Lambdas and I might retaliate against the nefarious Deltas, and possibly even against the equally stealthy Taus. On Sunday night, March 10th, News, Big Al, Tim, Wild Bill Elderberry, and I were actually studying academics and organizing reports for classes when there was a gentle rapping at our upstairs door. I answered the knocks and was shocked to see none other than ongoing nemesis George Evans standing there.

"Look sir, I apologize for all the major grief I've caused you and your friends in the past," the muscular black bruiser began his narrative. "May I come in?" Evans pleasantly asked in formal, almost-sophisticated, grammatically-correct English.

I hesitated and then allowed our former menace inside, while the other four Lambdas sat there with their mouths agape, wondering, like myself, what the surprise visitation was all about. Then, George Evans continued delivering his unusual speech of contrition.

"Look, guys. I'm now off the bottle and on the wagon, and I've become a regular church goin' guy, and I even intend studyin' for the ministry down in Alabama," the reformed former rogue plausibly stated. "I wanna' sincerely apologize for any harm or aggravation I might've caused you fine young men, startin' with that rather evil bus trip to Carney's Point."

"Well, I'm not a Catholic priest, but thanks for your confession, George," I defensively and skeptically acknowledged. "But what brings you to our humble door tonight. If ya' never attacked us again, we would've surmised that something like religion or wisdom had drastically changed your criminal life! Do ya' need directions to the Franklin House?"

"Well, sir," Evans continued his tome, ignoring my sarcastic quip. "If ya' wanna' know the truth, I'm through workin' for the Deltas and for the Taus. When I heard what happened to your white Chevy up in New York," the black transgressor enunciated with almost-convincing conviction, "my three reformed brothers and I swiftly captured that Sam Lista freak, and we've brought him over to your place here on Main Street, so that you can interrogate the culprit face to face."

"You mean Lista's your prisoner, and you have him captured outside this house right now?" I incredulously asked. "Were the Taus involved in the New York vandalism, too?"

"Yes, those bonehead bozos were, my sources tell me," George claimed. "And three representatives from both fraternities drove-up to Manhattan, found your car parked in the garage, and the six felons pounded your wheels mercilessly with crowbars and sledgehammers.

Ya' wanna' come outside and acquire possession of your hostage? He's now at your disposal and mercy!"

"Let's go outside, J.W., and rough that no-good Delta Alpha creep up a bit!" Big Al volunteered his services. "I love your Chevy almost as much as you do, and Lista's gonna' suffer a severe poundin' if my fists have anything to do with it!"

"Me too!" News chimed-in. "Let's kick some enemy butt!"

"Me too!" Timmy aptly agreed.

"I'm game to make Lista lame!" Bill Elderberry hooted and rhymed, while sounding a little like Jives Arena.

The five of us rushed down the steps to have Sam Lista transferred into our custody, and when the Lambda Phi's arrived outside, the four of us were shocked to be surrounded by twelve Japanese Sumo wrestlers and by four colored behemoths that looked like *Green Bay Packer* defensive linemen.

"You really are a stupid, naïve, white-skinned sucker, along with your four simpleton duds!" George Evans hardily laughed. "Well, now two of you creeps have to get into the dark blue van with six of the Tokyo Sumo wrestlers, and the other two jerks have to get into the red van with the six other formidable Oriental brawlers."

"What about me?" I asked while still-stunned and in complete awe at being fooled by the ruse. "Where do I go?"

"Hand other your Chevy keys, you faggot Caucasian who needs persuasion," Evans cleverly commanded. "You're commin' with me and the brothers, and we're gonna' have an all-nighter watchin' you turkeys perform some fascinatin' stunts, yes, we are."

"Where ya' takin' us?" I nervously queried. "I have a right to know under the *Constitution.*"

"Oh, not too far away, cracker, I assure you," George answered, exhibiting a sinister, evil smile. "You're bein' officially transferred from *Glassboro State College* to *Bovine University.*"

"*Bovine University?*" I coughed-out those strange words. "Never heard of it. Is it in New Jersey?"

"Not too many people have ever heard of the local dump, either," Evans confessed. "But it's actually not too far from here. Now, give me your keys, or else I'll have to break your frail wrists, and then have to work on your bony shoulders, and move my pounding to injure your damned scrawny legs, too."

"Can we get our coats?" Elderberry requested. "It's a little cold out here tonight."

"Get the hell in the van, ya' disgustin' Lambda wimp!" Evans firmly yelled. "And stop makin' so much damned noise, ya' freakin' honky corn-holers. We don't wanna' disturb your landlord, or upset your nosy neighbors."

As the three-vehicle caravan drove past the Glassboro Theater and then passed Mazzeo's Bar and Liquors on High Street, I couldn't imagine what kind of abomination George Evans's definition of the plural noun "stunts" would translate into, or constitute. The lead blue van turned right onto *Route 47,* and we progressed south on *Delsea Drive* through Clayton to Malaga, where our vehicle turned onto *Route 40* (the *Harding Highway*) and soon motored past Elmer.

Just outside Woodstown, three New Jersey State Trooper cruisers zoomed-by in the opposite direction with their red beacon lights rotating and flashing, apparently to investigate an emergency or auto accident. But I truly wished that the on-a-mission police were aware of the possible horrendous crime that might soon be enacted at enigmatic *Bovine University.*

'The Deltas and the Taus have really brought in the varsity squad for this big operation,' I thought. 'Our rivals have dispatched twelve humungous Sumo wrestlers and four black weightlifters to abduct and harass five gullible Lambdas. And the vile Deltas and Taus will, as usual, delegate this assignment to their belligerent henchmen, and pretend that the plotters have no knowledge of our capture, and the scum-bags will completely disassociate from any involvement in our current, perfidious hostage situation.'

But then, a symbolic light bulb lit-up in my mind, and I remembered reading a Jack London realism story titled "Love of Life" in high school literature class. One of the vocabulary words I had to study for Mr. Mallon's English test was "bovine", meaning "pertaining to cows, cattle, or oxen".

"Are we goin' to Cowtown?" I directly asked George Evans as the monstrous captor continued driving my re-conditioned Chevy west on the *Harding Highway.* "Cowtown is just on the other side of Woodstown, and there's plenty of Brahma bulls and cattle there. The rodeo's not open yet, because it runs every Saturday from the end of May to the end of September," I remembered and related. "I used to watch the rodeo all the time on TV when I was a kid."

"Well now, junior Buffalo Bill, you're gonna' be a featured act in the rodeo, and unfortunately, nobody's gonna' see your stupidity on television," George remarked as his two confederates in the back seat and the one to my right lustily laughed. "You must be smarter than the average donkey, or brighter than any ordinary chipmunk if ya' figured-out that Cowtown is really *Bovine University!*"

Since it was only early March, Cowtown, when we finally arrived there, was like a ghost town, except for the newly settled animals that were being kept in barns and stables. A popular regional farmers' market and auction that was owned by the rodeo company was situated to the left, but the building was only frequented by area bargain-hunters on Friday and Saturday nights.

The cavalcade of two vans and one car pulled into the big asphalt parking lot; traveled-around the empty rodeo stadium, and then stopped next to a fenced-in area where a small herd of cattle was mooing and grazing away. "Okay, *junior* honky, even though I know you're only a goddamned *GSC* sophomore," George nastily directed and sinisterly laughed, "get out of the car, and we're gonna' have some *Advanced Fun, 101!"*

I soon joined News, Timmy, Big Al, and Bill Elderberry along the white painted wooden fence, and my pupils observed that our sixteen abductors had already surrounded us on the other three sides, each massive bully with an imposing, threatening frown upon his face. "Okay, you four blanco imbeciles," George cackled. "Here's five boxes filled with about a pound of grass in each. First, ya' gotta' each eat a pound of grass and pretend that you're real hungry cows. Ya' must be Jersey cows, because you're goin' to school in New Jersey! Ha, ha, ha!" Evans yelled, breaking his grimace as the other black hit-men profusely chuckled. The twelve Japanese Sumo wrestlers dressed in white karate outfits simply stood there reticent, with their huge arms folded in front of their colossal chests, showing no overt sign of emotion.

"We could choke to death on this grass if it gets stuck in our throats," I seriously objected. "This is definitely violatin' our *Constitutional Rights!"*

"Then, that's five less enemies we gotta' worry about," Evans sarcastically sneered and then giggled. "And besides, you're just lucky you ain't supposed to be horses, otherwise, we'd make ya' chew and swallow either dry hay, or long pieces of thick straw, and then you'd all choke to death for real! Now, I want you' college gringos to start eatin' grass until it all disappears from the boxes."

The five "new herbivores" were shivering from the damp cold weather, but after the first few chews and swallows, the grass really didn't taste that reprehensible, and in a half an hour, five-pounds of the common cattle food had been consumed and partially digested. I was about to say, "You've had your fun; can we go home now?" when George Evans had another extraordinary task for us to pursue, and the harasser insisted that we heed his imperative directions.

"Okay, you' cracker bovine impersonators have passed the first phase of your important assignment," the black enforcer falsely praised. "Now, all four of ya' honkies climb over the white fence, get-down on your hands and knees, and ya' cinco fools gotta' then crawl across the enclosed pasture from this side to the other, pretendin' you're tryin' to court the cows standin' and munchin' away, out in the middle of that yonder corral."

And then, Big Al, News, Timmy, Elderberry, and I obediently and awkwardly clambered-over the white fence, lowered our bodies onto our hands and knees, and began crawling like bovine creatures across the enclosed pasture. When we arrived toward the center, where a dozen cows were grazing under the pale moonlight, a side gate was opened, and a wild Brahma bull sensed that we were infringing on *his* territory and trying to mate with his harem.

All four of us leaped-up, screaming our tracheas out of our throats while making mad dashes for the fence on the opposite side of the corral. Laughter abounded behind us as we sprinted our buttocks off, while the snorting bull had its horned head down, chasing the four interlopers out of his prized domain. Luckily, all four of us clumsily leaped onto the fence, momentarily exposing our rear ends to potential catastrophe, and then we shifted our weight and rolled over the wooden wall, just as the irritated bull rushed by.

The two vans and the white Chevy had been driven to the far side of the fence, and the contingent of sixteen tormentors exited the transportation vehicles. "Not too shabby! Not too bad at all!" Evans mockingly complimented the five gasping and panting survivors. "And I don't want to see any of you jive crackers cheat by stickin' your fingers down your throats, makin' it easy to vomit-up that delicious grass you just ate before ya' all had *that* recent, good, rodio exercise! And now, Fearless One," George Evans imperatively said to me, "you'll be next to experience the thrill of phase three of today's important lesson in self-discipline!"

"What are ya' gonna' do to me next?" I demanded knowing, while my lungs sucked in all the oxygen I could inhale. "Make me chew ten-pounds of cow manure?"

"We're gonna' break your stones mighty good this time," George predicted. "But to put it more precisely, that bronco saddled-up over there is gonna' break your stones good for us, when your ass bounces up and down, crushin' and crunching your tender nuggets over and over again!"

"I've never ridden a wild horse, or even a tame one, ever before, in my entire life!" I strenuously protested. "This is human torture!

It's even worse than medieval persecution! The Marquis de Sade wouldn't even do this to his worst enemy!"

"Just be happy that as a child, you've already ridden hobby horses and have some experience at doin' it," George villainously laughed. "That beauty over there is one of Cowtown's more-tame buckin' broncos, if that's any consolation to you. And we'll even tie your feet to the stirrups; tether your legs to the saddle, and your hands and wrists to the reins so that it's impossible for you to fall off old Cannon Ball here!" George promised. "Well, gringo muchacho. Ready to ride a man's horse, lover boy?"

Two of the overweight Japanese grapplers picked me up, carried me two-hundred-feet to a nearby stable, and the ogres placed me atop the brown bronco, while its trainer tried calming the animal down. Then, my feet were secured to the stirrups by ropes; my knees were tightly tethered to the saddle's buckle, and my hands were tied to the reins, so that I wouldn't fall-off while my stones would be mercilessly breaking from the prospective, dreadful up and down repetitious banging. "Cannon Ball" and I were then led to a starting gate enclosure, and soon, the back door, sliding on channels, was abruptly closed.

Ogre George Evans next had a shocking command to yell to my four flabbergasted, totally appalled and bewildered friends. "When my three brothers begin sledgehammerin' that white Chevy Impala over there, I'll open the gate, and this here bronco will come-out wildly, leapin' and jumpin'. After around two-minutes, the horse oughta' get tired," Evans speculated and concluded. "That's when you three other clowns can hop the fence and try getting your crib brother released from his bonds, while gringo boy can still use his miniature hose to piss outa'. And if you're lucky enough to endure this very special chore," Evans said to me, "then you'll have to ride that black Brahma bull that chased ya' four nitwits outa' the cow corral, but only for two-minutes! Are ya' ready, honky?"

Before I could yell anything like curse words, or even begin to verbally object, I witnessed the first sledgehammer blows being administered to my recently re-conditioned Chevy. And then, the exit gate was thrust open, and I remember bouncing all over the place in fright with my thighs and my rump taking quite a shellacking from the repeated jolts and painful impacts. After a minute of the wild and crazy ordeal, I must have gone unconscious for a spell, because the next thing I could recall was Ralph Crenshaw leaning over me on the damp cold turf and asking if I was "Okay".

Chapter 26
"A Seafood Diet"

I noticed that Ralph was surrounded by most of the Lambda Phi Sigmas, who had somehow made the twenty-five-mile trip from Glassboro to Cowtown, in order to rescue me from additional hellish torture. The Lambdas wanted to take me to the college infirmary, which was an independent suite of rooms separate from, but attached to, *Linden Hall,* but like a stubborn fool, I refused and insisted that I could recuperate from my many lacerations and bruises with bed rest, aspirins, and *Southern Comfort* for the next two days. After I rode with Ralph Crenshaw in the front of his antique Nash Rambler back to 38 South Main, despite my abundant agony, I quickly dozed-off, thinking that slumber would heal my wounds from the inside out. I slept more soundly that night, better than I ever had snoozed before, despite my multiple body aches.

The following March morning, News and Tim assisted me out of bed, and for the first time since my bucking bronco misadventure, I was able to evaluate the extent of my "superficial injuries" to my wrists, thighs, and knees. I still felt a dull throbbing in my buttocks and found it very difficult to sit in any chair, no matter how soft it was. But it was nice being given special treatment with News pouring my *Cheerios* and milk breakfast into the table bowl, and with Tim, Big Al, Paul and even Bill Elderberry, preparing my toast and jam, coffee, and scrambled eggs. Ralph Crenshaw was still at work over in the *Memorial Hall Cafeteria,* so the other 38 South Main renters reconstructed, piece-by-piece, exactly what insanity had transpired the night before at Cowtown.

"You're lucky your taint ain't in traction," Elderberry began his *anal*ysis, without showing much-needed sensitivity to my perpetual plight. "I'll bet that even the sperm juice in your testicles was smashed, along with your indispensable epididymis."

"J.W.," News got my groggy attention. "It's too bad that we only had moonlight shinin' down at Cowtown last night. If that buckin' bronco had *saddle-lights,* we could've seen better exactly what had happened to ya'!" Tomasello jested, and when I laughed at his lousy sadistic humor, my damaged body ached all over.

But then, Tim Amoro described in detail the chronological order of detrimental events. When the dozen gargantuan Sumo wrestlers and the four muscular black desperados were shoving the Lambdas into the vehicles and into the white Impala outside 38 South Main, Ralph Crenshaw was coming home from the cafeteria, because the exploited employee had incidentally endured the late cafeteria shift while filling-in for a sick absent-from-work fellow student. Instead of pulling into the driveway and be apprehended, too, Ralph used his scruples and kept on going. The alert apartment-mate then turned around on Main and parked his Nash Rambler down the block, where the fatigued fellow patiently waited in his car next to the curb.

Crenshaw then followed the three vehicles, driving far behind the entire route from Glassboro through Woodstown, and finally onto *Route 40* to Cowtown. After learning of our ultimate destination, Ralph sped-back towards Glassboro, stopped at the chicken coop in Aura, got on the phone, rounded-up the other Lambdas, who all eventually met at Joe's Sub Shop. Then, Crenshaw intrepidly led a posse car caravan into Cowtown with his diminutive Nash Rambler.

"By that time, J.W.," Big Al proceeded to describe, "you had been untied and removed from the bucking bronco, after the obstinate animal finally ran out of steam. There was a box of your favorite cereal *Cheerios* in your smashed open trunk, which we fed to the psyched-up horse to calm-down the animal. Thank God for *Cheerios,* J.W., or ya' might've been snapped, crackled, and popped, just like *Rice Krispies!"*

"And what about my car?" I asked in a weak tone of voice. "Is the Impala again totaled?"

"Afraid so!" News solemnly related. "But at two in the mornin', I called Goose back in Hammonton and your savior said he'd get you a new Chevy if yours' is beyond salvation, er, I mean salvalgin'. That insomniac Restuccio stays-up all night and never sleeps durin' the daytime, either. I mean," Tomasello spoke, searching his mind for the appropriate verbal lexicon. "His parents are never home, and all that *that* horny toad does is stay awake all night, either counting his money, or the fanatic gets drunk or laid. But the good thing about Goose is that he can be contacted between two and five a.m. every mornin', because when he gets bored, the sex addict looks at porno' magazines, or sometimes takes different sluts home that walk Pacific Avenue over in Atlantic City."

"Did Goose say anything else?" I softly inquired, as I examined a nasty scrape on my right wrist. "He really comes through in the clutch, even if my Chevy has an automatic transmission."

"Yeah, J.W., your Mafia guardian angel sure did," News reported with a poker-expression upon his face. "Goose said to make sure you don't get bronco-itis, or it might turn into *old ammonia* before it does 'new-ammonia,' and ya' know what? I think the Sidgy wasn't tryin' to be funny when the non-scholar told me that frivolous shit! And incidentally, J.W., for your information, an automatic transmission has an automatic clutch built into it."

After the guys left the upstairs apartment to attend their morning classes, I turned-on the table radio next to my bed; found Wibbage 99 on the dial, and listened to the Cascades singing "Rhythm of the Rain". That's when my cerebrum finally realized that raindrops had been pelting against the roof most of the morning. And then, because the AM station was having some static, I switched to WIP-FM Color Radio, and heard Henry Mancini's new hit instrumental "The Days of Wine and Roses", which immediately had my wandering mind visualizing romantic restaurant dates with voluptuous Joanne Berenato, and then with vivacious Peachy Wilcox. And when the WIP disc jockey began playing the Four Seasons' new hit "Walk Like A Man", I instantly thought about the resplendent *Four Seasons Restaurant* up on 52nd Street in New York; about my damaged white Chevy, first demolished in the high-rise parking garage, and then its replacement later destroyed at Cowtown, and about my inability to stand erect and walk like a man. So, out of sheer frustration, I peevishly flicked-off the annoying song; reclined in my mediocre bed; pulled the blankets up to my chin, and quietly dozed-off.

Around noontime, I surprisingly received a visit from non-other than Joanne Berenato, who realized that I was too weak to either try or do anything in my immobile condition. But the doll with the swarthy skin showing-up at 38 South Main instantly justified my purpose, and my reason, for gratefully being alive. Then, I noticed that Loretta Sacco had faithfully accompanied the former Edgewood High Prom Queen to cheer me up.

"J.W., I heard about last night's craziness, and just had to come and see ya'," Joanne devotedly began. "I'm not used to seein' ya' confined to bed, and with a slight temperature, too," the olive-toned doll said as my dream girl blushed and gingerly felt my forehead.

"I figure I'll be outa' bed and back in classes by Wednesday," I boldly predicted. "As they say, ya' can't keep a good man down, or even keep him horizontal for long," I quipped. "Thanks for commin' to see me, too, Loretta," I candidly acknowledged to Joanne's friend.

"Bill Elderberry told me that you had something in traction," Loretta disclosed, "but I don't see any wires holdin' your leg up or anything like that."

"That's all right girls'!" I expressed with a forced grin forming on my face. "I think that Bill meant that I'm so racked-up that I almost do need traction. Sometimes, Elderberry has trouble communicating basic, simple ideas with the right words."

And much to my emotional comfort, I received a second visitation two hours later from Peachy Wilcox and Elaine Hill. Peachy commented that Elderberry had told her on campus that I might need an epididymis operation, and also that something in traction required immediate medical attention, but instinctively, I politely dismissed her statement, claiming that Bill Elderberry suffers from "illusions of grandeur that sometimes are delusions", and that the disoriented jokester often gets reality and fantasy confused and convoluted, especially while exercising his excessively defective, suspect, and notoriously disreputable vocabulary.

"Ya' gotta' get better J.W., so that we can go drinkin' again over in Pitman at that romantic lake," Peachy reminded me of the most thrilling night in her entire life. "Now that I'm no longer *Miss Cape May,* I don't have to worry anymore about havin' the perfect hourglass female body."

"Oh!" I moaned as I contemplated something excessively naughty. "Ohhhhh!" I repeated as I felt additional pain throbbing in various tender and ultra-sensitive parts of my male anatomy.

By Saturday, March 16th, I was feeling spry and rejuvenated, and ready to venture into the daily college routine once again. Being a little weak later in the day, though, I retired after supper to 38 South Main, and was escorted home by several of my concerned co-inhabitants. News had just finished a monologue about American underground nuclear testing being resumed, because test ban talks had gone sour with the scheming Russians. And then, talkative Tomasello switched gears and began expounding on President Kennedy's idea of establishing a domestic and international *Peace Corps,* when true to form, there was a rapping at the 38 South Main Street upstairs door, and upon opening it, I was quite relieved to see and greet Goose Restuccio, standing there instead of George Evans.

"J.W., how the fuck ya' doin'?" Goose affectionately prefaced. "Glad to see you're up and around, and not in bed coughin' your lungs out with bronco-itis! Ya' only got one goddamned set of friggin' air-grabbers, ya' know!"

"Come on in, Goose," I requested. "Of course, ya' know News, Timmy, Big Al, and Paul. Did ya' get the Chevy fixed?" I impetuously asked. "I had to lie again to my parents, saying that I had vital research work to do here at college, and again couldn't come home this weekend."

"Well, J.W., your jalopy was fuckin' totaled like 'Hero-she-ma', and I had to find ya' a similar hot one in South Philly'. I got it fresh from a chop shop dealer there that's a goddamned cousin of mine.

Did ya' know that Hammonton has more junk yards than any other town its size in the whole fuckin' country?" Goose disclosed a remarkable, esoteric, South Jersey fact. "I could even get an important politician a new asshole in Hammonton, if Eisenhower, Nixon, Johnson, or Kennedy needed one on the black market!"

"Does the new car look like the old Chevy?" I asked. "What about the license plates?"

"You fuckin' get constipation of the brain over nothin'!" Goose yelled as the future Mafia Don finally closed the door behind him and hit me with his typical, insulting invectives. "The car's almost the same, and you wouldn't know the difference to look at both mother-fuckers in good condition, side-by-side. And ya' got the same license plates and registration, so there's no goddamned problem there; just that the serial numbers on the dashboard are fuckin' different now!" Restuccio clarified. "Other than that, J.W., don't make toothpicks outa' any goddamned telephone poles. I'm getting fuckin' tired of fixin' your cars for ya' with the black-market contacts I have. I think there's only six more fuckin' white '61 Chevys like it on the East Coast market, so kindly show some mercy and ease-up on the goddamned demolition bull-shit."

"Care to join us for a beer?" I offered my mortal guardian angel and economic savior. "News here was just talkin' about President Kennedy's *Peace Corps* and how it's gonna' help change the world for the better."

"Piece core?" Goose shrieked. "Now we're talkin'. It's about time the government got into getting you young jerk-offs laid instead of studyin' useless 'ear-rally-vent' bull-shit and totally fucked-up ideas, over here at the hick college."

News tried explaining to our petulant guest that the *Peace Corps* initiative would be engaged in helping people in underdeveloped countries, and also helping poor sections of America like West Virginia achieve financial independence. And Tomasello stressed that the new government program would provide needy individuals better skills and opportunities in life by having young college-age students volunteer their humanitarianism to bring-about the dramatic world and national transformations.

"Ya' wanna' know somethin'? You' college jerk-offs are all fucked- up!" Restuccio arbitrarily accused. "First, ya' have a fuckin' nigger circus at your college for faggot Africans wearin' female gowns and havin' square boxes on their heads; then, ya' send books over there to those jungle bunnies that don't even know how to fuckin' read an 'alfie-bet letter', and now you dumb bastards are gonna' waste your fuckin' valuable time goin' over there and dyin' from sex diseases while you're tryin' to teach the fuckin' foreign Swahili and Watusi cannibals how to read English, when the rug-heads can't even write or think in their own stupid fucked-up language!" Restuccio bellowed. "Now, if that's not fucked-up," Goose indicted, "then I don't know what the fuck is! You' silly assholes won't be satisfied until ya' turn over the whole fuckin' world to lazy, fuckin' retarded, long-dicked, African and un-American bloodsuckin' niggers!"

I recalled at that moment how Goose, while under duress, had made a black girl Crystal Davis pregnant from *their* Hammonton Blues capture, so I figured I should get him off of the sensitive race subject, because Restuccio was in denial about having a mixed-colored son, and the biased Sicilian went absolutely ballistic whenever *that* taboo fact came-up in conversation.

And none of us wanted to wrangle with our volatile, gregarious visitor, especially me, since *he* had just provided me with an enormous favor in acquiring another '61 Chevrolet facsimile. So, I deftly eased us into briefly discussing the Deltas and the Taus, and their using surrogate hit-men to wickedly punish my four illustrious comrades and me at Cowtown. I was elated to hear Goose's extemporaneous discourse.

"Look, J.W. I'm gonna' get involved in this son-of-a-bitchin' college *maternity* war, and we're gonna' beat the fuckin' shit outa' those *mothers*. I want ya' to come-up with a cool shit-proof plan, just like ya' used to against the *mung* Blues and Ramrodders over in Hammonton. I want in. Just say the fuckin' word!"

"Thanks plenty, Goose!" I gratefully acknowledged, realizing that the Lambdas had found a solid ally who could deliver significant results when called upon. "Can I see the new Chevy now?"

"Sure. My men Frankie Fingers and Joe Zucchini are outside guardin' it," Goose informed with a smile. "That would really be fuckin' embarrassin' if the thing was destroyed again in the driveway, while I'm up here bull shittin' nonsense with you worthless, dork-headed, pathetic, college pecker-pullers!"

After the three Hammonton Mafia members left Glassboro in a shiny, new, black Cadillac, I returned upstairs to rejoin the other 38 South Mainers. My rear end still hurt from ascending the rickety stairs, and News said, in sheer imitation of Goose, that I had "too many lilies in my sack-crow-lily-axe!"

"That Goose makes Edward G. Robinson look' and sound like the Pope. He's quite a character!" Big Al summarized.

"Yeah, a character that characterizes everything in a negative way," Timmy generalized.

"What the hell is mung that Goose was talkin' about?" Big Al asked. "Did he mean to say 'among'?"

"Mung is Goose's personal vocabulary for what comes out if ya' hit a pregnant woman thirteen times in the stomach with a baseball bat," I sadly explained. "Mung is what comes out accordin' to *hi*s perverted concept and definition."

Everyone listening shook their' heads in dismay and disapproval. But then, I felt obligated to defend the weird Hammonton junior hoodlum. "Guys, how many friends do *you* have from your own town that would replace two '61 Chevy Impalas within a month for you, without askin' for a damned penny?" I demanded, bringing Restuccio's generous nature into the discussion, to form a more accurate perspective of *his* flawed but very complex personality.

The new Chevy looked and performed as well as the original did, but there just wasn't the same feel to it behind the wheel, even though the cloth interior was virtually identical to the original automobile's upholstery. I tried canceling the fraternity war out of my mind, and discovered that I was becoming a better student once the thought of the Deltas and the Taus wasn't interfering with my mental functioning. And despite Goose's low opinion of higher education, I was actually enjoying my mind becoming a veritable sponge, absorbing all of the irrelevant academic data it could. But one Thursday morning, Big Al got into a verbal altercation with Sam Lista over near *Bosshart Hall,* however, later in the day, I told my 38 South Main buddy "to cool it because *April Fools Day* (the Lambdas equivalent to *Pearl Harbor*) was just around the corner."

The first day of spring, I woke-up during a bad dream at 6:45, turned-on the radio dial, and heard the new release "Our Day Will Come" by Ruby and the Romantics. The sprightly tune had my mind focused on achieving revenge against the Delta Alphas and the Tau Kappas for certain injustices rendered upon me the second semester. And so, I recollected having my bad dream, and then coordinated its essence into my intricate retaliation scheme.

When I was seven-years-old, my family had been living in the white bungalow next to my grandparents' Square Deal Farm Market on the White Horse Pike in Hammonton. One Sunday, Uncle Frank and Aunt Josie stopped on their way to Atlantic City, along with my same-age cousin, Nicky Panachelli. The two young rascals came across a crate of twelve dozen eggs lying inside a storage shed, next to the market, and we had a brilliant idea. Not knowing too much about reproduction in humans or animals, and unaware that the eggs in the crate were unfertilized, we took a hammer from a shelf and broke-open all one-hundred-and forty-four eggs, looking for a baby chick inside. And when my father discovered our curious-but-destructive mischief, my fanny was spanked until it ached, as if I had been riding a bucking bronco for an entire day.

'That's it!' I realized, as I snapped-out of my inspiration daze. 'The Lambda Phi's will use eggs, fish, shrimp, marbles, and ball bearings to thwart the mendacious Deltas and the Taus!'

And when I told News just before breakfast in the main cafeteria about using two crates of twelve-dozen eggs each against the two targeted wise-guy fraternity factions, my pal inadvertently made some kind of humorous Freudian slip by yelling-out, "How *gross!"* How doubly gross!" And then, inspired Tomasello made one of those absolutely awfully-dumb comments that symbolically and regrettably also made plenty of sense. "And J.W., since the Lambda Phi's have been operatin' outa' a chicken coop over in Aura for two years now, it makes perfect sense and stands to reason that we oughta' use eggs as part of our retaliation salvos."

Spring break had again come and was almost over, but not before Goose and I had taken a special pilgrimage up to Manahawkin near Long Beach Island in one of his father's white box trucks, and picked-up a few bushels of disposable shrimp. Restuccio then also gladly purchased two hundred pounds of smelly fish from an elderly black man named Clyde Spellman, who operated a wholesale seafood distributorship *we* had done business with before, when Goose and I had collaborated as members of the Reds peach gang. On the way back from making his valuable Manahawkin acquisitions, G.R. stopped-off in Vineland and purchased two large crates of eggs, similar to the one my cousin Nicky and I had smashed and violated with a hammer, way back in the summer of '49.

"Tonight, we bust those other fraternities' balls while they're still down in Fort Lauderdale getting drunk and laid," Goose remarkably said to me, without even one single or married major curse word.

"The Deltas and the Taus must have some phenomenal sexual equipment if they can get laid in Florida while we're breakin' their testicles up here in New Jersey!" I quipped. "It's pretty incredible; in fact, even too fantastic for *Ripley* to believe!"

"You oughta' do some sit-down comedy on the fuckin' toilet seat before ya' think about even attemptin' stand-up at the urinal, and besides that anal-a-gee, ya' sound like a fucked-up drunken bastard!" Goose affectionately replied. "But really, I gotta' admit, J.W., that sometimes ya' say somethin' that's really fucked-up, and I actually believe it's fuckin' funny!"

"And Abrams and Hoppy will have their crew ready for action, and even Kenny Soblinski is drivin' some North Jersey Lambdas down to Glassboro early to participate in our dual raid," I told Restuccio on *Route 40,* heading from Vineland to Aura. "College resumes in just two more days, so Goose," I paused to express my emphasis, "by tomorrow night, when the Deltas and the Taus return from spring break with their Florida tans, the stench in the two frat' houses ought to be un*bear*able for even *Smokey* or *Yogi* to handle."

"Which house are *we* gonna' hit first?" Goose inquired. "The Alfie Ortegas dump, or the Toro Capa Pisalongs place?"

"Abrams and the chicken coop Lambdas are gonna' hit the Delta Alpha Omega house on Harvard Road, and you and me and the 38 South Mainers are gonna' have the second similar operation at the same time unfoldin' at the Tau Kappa Epsilon residence on Academy Street," I reviewed. "Another name for what we're doin' is called multi-taskin'."

"Well, J.W. Those fuckin' fraternity pigpens are gonna' be converted into seafood and omelette houses with lousy fuckin' food on their stinkin' menus," Goose said in a mild *eggs*aggeration. "Now let's catch some shut eye at the coop before the mission begins. I don't like bein' fuckin' *cooped-up* for too long, even in a two-door car or chicken-house!"

On *April Fools* night, around 7 p.m., twelve Lambdas plus Goose congregated at the Aura chicken coop. We partied on hard whiskey on the rocks and watched several "smokers" that Kenny Soblinski had acquired from a New Jersey State Trooper, which had been personally confiscated during a North Jersey porno' raid. By midnight, both commando teams had garnered sufficient courage to initiate the intended action.

Abrams and his crew motored out to Harvard Road in one of Hoppy's closed farm trucks to conduct their quality mischief on the absent Delta Alpha Omegas, while the 38 South Mainers had gotten into the back of Goose's white box-truck for the ride over to Academy Street, so that we could trash part of the vacated-and-doomed Tau Kappa Epsilon House.

"Just like old times," Goose reminded his lone passenger sitting inside the cab. "Now that I'm involved in this friggin' Glassboro fraternity war, your guys are gonna' fuckin' win, just as sure as assholes were made to shit out of."

"All we need is the adjustable ladder to get-up onto the roof," I reminded Restuccio. "There shouldn't be anyone home, so just pull this truck around the back of the Tau House to avoid detection from possible snoopy neighbors. But they're mostly college kids, too, not yet back from their Florida spring break."

"Maybe J.W, we'll have time to break into their place, guzz their toothbrushes, piss in their liquor bottles, and burn their porno' magazines in the fireplace!" Restuccio indulgently laughed. "I like fuckin'-up fucked-up peoples lives more than they already are fucked-up! It' gives me a sense of power, J.W., that workin' for the electric company could never fuckin' provide! And the fuckin' porno' mag' fire would make the fuckin' fish smell in the fuckin' chimney, even fuckin' worse!"

I directed Goose to make a right turn at *322,* opposite the Franklin House, and swing-down State Street to Academy, in almost a U-turn. The motivated driver pulled into the Tau House's driveway and inconspicuously parked the box-truck behind the temporarily vacated residence. And after the loud motor had been shut-off, G.R. and I exited, walked around to the back panels, and liberated News, Tim, Big Al, Bill Elderberry, and amused Paul Meroski from their dark confinement. We quickly erected the expandable ladder, and Goose and I climbed-up to the expendable chimney.

An enthusiastic bucket brigade had rapidly been formed, and Bill Elderberry, standing on the ladder, handed me the first of four bushels of smelly three-day-old fish that Clyde Spellman was about to discard over in Manahawkin. Goose held the bushel waist high, while I kept my balance and tossed stinking fish two at a time down the brick chimney.

"This is almost as much fun as loan *shark*in'!" Goose belched-out as the bizarre Sicilian incidentally manufactured a half-decent pun involving a sea-life allusion. "In two days, this Tau House is gonna' smell worse than a whorehouse with twelve dozen four-day-old dead hookers inside. That's it, J.W. I just got a fuckin' brilliant idea. I'll build a house of prostitution for white people on the White Whores Pike, and one for niggers on the Black Whores Pike. Ha, ha, ha! Pretty fucked-up, huh? Ha, ha, ha!"

"Just please be quiet before we get a neighbor's attention," I advised and pleaded. "Glassboro does have an actual police department besides the screwy campus cops, ya' know!"

"Fuck the neighbors! Fuck the fuzz! Fuck the world!" Goose laughed in his inebriated state. "Let's get-off the fish dump and start with dropping baby shrimp soon, because those 'crusty-nations' probably look like the Capa Episalongs' tiny hooked dicks!"

Finally, my intoxicated colleague and I had the opportunity to deposit twenty-five pounds of stench-laden shrimp on top of the hundred-pounds of stinking salmon, which smelled worse than "crusty-stations" (according to Goose) ever did. And after the entire bushel of shrimp had been gingerly stored inside the Delta's brick chimney, we next dropped the twelve-dozen eggs, two at a time, until all one-hundred-and-forty-four had fallen and *gross*ly split-upon impact at the chimney's base.

"Hey, those fish, shrimp, and eggs might get the flue!" Goose cackled, as the junior gangster staggered and wobbled back and forth, while holding onto the roof's brick chimney in a drunken stupor. "This sea food dump even beats loan-sharkin'!"

"Stop screwin' around, or you'll fall, and then wind-up in either the hospital or the damned morgue," I cautioned the brazen Mafia crook, who didn't really care if he got caught or not, because of his father's aegis and influence.

"Okay, mung-heads. I want all of you' college assholes to get-up on the roof, jerk-off, and pop a load down the chimney shaft," Goose boomed like an asylum patient, too demented for even a Bedlam ward. "I want all of you' cunt-lappers to fertilize those fuckin' chicken eggs down there! Ha, ha, ha, ha! And if it wasn't for you, J.W., I wouldn't know the goddamned difference between a fertilized egg and one that's not!" Goose garrulously giggled. "Ha, ha, ha, ha! You fuckin' educated me J.W. You fuckin' educated me! Ha, ha, ha, ha!" And then, crazed Restuccio yelled-down the chimney to imaginary Tau Kappa Epsilons, "*April Fools,* you goddamned, fucked-up, absent *April Fools!*"

I had to grab G.R.'s right arm, so that the intoxicated imbecile didn't tumble and roll-off of the Tau Kappa Epsilons' dark-green tiled roof. Luckily, Goose was able to find the first rung and then eventually descend the expandable ladder. We eagerly gathered-up all of the stinking bushels, and chucked them into the rear of the white box-truck. Then triumphantly, we all merrily returned to the Aura chicken coop, compared notes with the other successful Lambda Phi Sigma Harvard Road patrol, and then carefully prepared for the next evening's strategic mission.

Chapter 27
"Marbles and Ball Bearings"

On Tuesday night, April 2nd, most of the *Glassboro State* students were back in town to finish-out the arduous spring semester, including most of the Delta Alphas and the Tau Kappas, who had been doing some major league reveling down in Florida at Daytona Beach and at Fort Lauderdale. I was upstairs at 38 South Main, awaiting Goose's arrival from Berlin, where the treacherous schemer had purchased (specially ordered) seven Delta Alpha Omega and six Tau Kappa Epsilon counterfeit jackets, plus seventeen rubber Donald Duck masks to surreptitiously use during phase two of the Lambda Phi Sigma crusade against our very loathed fraternity rivals.

Five new songs were played in succession on the 38 South Main table radio, and each tune reminded me of someone or something. The Chiffons' "He's So Fine" made me think of Goose Restuccio's charity in regard to white Chevy Impalas; The Orlons' "South Street" had me thinking about arriving in Philly' with Bill Elderberry after escaping a fierce blizzard in Harrisburg, and the Drifters' "On Broadway" had my mind meditating about meeting-up with Frankie Jives Arena up at *Pace College* in New York. Lou Christie's "Two Faces Have I" set my cognitive activity contemplating how innocent I pretended to be when around my parents, and the Beach Boy's new smash hit "Surfin' USA" put my brain cells into appreciating the new "California sound" that News and Timmy had been talking about, which would fill the void in rock and roll ever since Buddy Holly had died, and ever since Elvis Presley had been drafted into the *Army*. And when the rocking beach song was half-through, News and Tim calmly entered the fairly accommodating upstairs apartment at 38 South Main.

"Hey, J.W. What do ya' think of that four-part harmony those Beach Boys are usin'?" News enthusiastically asked. "I believe it's the best innovation in teen pop' music since Bill Haley's 'Rock around the Clock'."

"I really like it," I genuinely opined. "But the song sounds a little like something else I'm familiar with, but I can't quite put my finger on it. Not the great harmony sound, mind you, but the rhythm and the beat sound almost like something else."

"That song 'Surfin' USA' sounds like a clever plagiarism on Chuck Berry's 'Sweet Little Sixteen'," Timmy chipped-in. "I'll bet there'll be a big royalty battle over whether the Beach Boys copied the melody while changin' the lyrics and the tempo," the music connoisseur assumed and contributed. "Sort of like handin' in to a professor somebody else's term paper, and then claimin' credit for developin' it yourself! But I gotta' admit. There's a tremendous difference between receivin' an A on a college term paper and securing a multi-million-dollar music settlement."

"Hey, guys, what do ya' think of the Russians havin' the audacity of flyin' their spy planes over Alaska," attention deficit News asked while deviating from the great rock and roll discussion we were having. "President Kennedy's administration and the *Pentagon* are all heated-up over the alleged sky trespassin', and all the smoke signals seem to be pointin' to war."

"As long as they're just spy planes and not loaded enemy bombers," Timmy qualified, "what's the big deal? I remember that Francis Gary Powers' pilot got caught in that U-2 snoopin' on the U.S.S.R. But I'm still more hyped-up about Loyola of Illinois beatin' Cincinnati in the *NCAA Basketball Championship Game"*

"And don't forget that Elizabeth Ann Seton is gonna' be beatified by Pope John XXIII," News added to our reaching-the-maximum empirical knowledge base. "She'll then be officially declared a saint and be canonized; the first American male or female ever to reach that distinction!"

"Yeah, News, maybe after the Pope shoots Mother Seton outa' a cannon, Dr. Robeson will name a new building after her, *Seton Hall,"* Timmy joked.

"Now you're beginnin' to sound sacrilegious, just like Goose," I reprimanded Timmy in a friendly-but-firm manner. "And now speakin' of Restuccio, the Mafia kid predicted that the classic film *Larry of Arabia* is gonna' win the Oscar for best 1962 picture on April 8th at the Academy Awards' presentations, and I do believe that Goose is right on the mark, despite his cultural deficiency. And when I told him that *Larry of Arabia* and *Ben Hur* were cousins, the Sons of Italy dolt actually believed me."

"By now, the Deltas and the Taus are smellin' something fishy in the vicinity of their fireplaces," News uttered with authentic levity. "And thanks to Goose, they're both gonna' have to pour a hundred gallons of bleach and disinfectants down their chimneys, just to neutralize the hideous smell once it intensifies to the level of stench to the tenth degree squared."

At eleven p.m., Goose showed-up at 38 South Main like a buzzard arriving at a dead carcass site, and we systematically reviewed last minute strategy, for the guys were highly-motivated to achieve full revenge on the Delta Alphas and the Tau Kappas, for what physical and psychological abuse had transpired at Cowtown, and for the vulgar vandalism administered to my cherished Chevy Impala by their ruthless, hired Oriental and black surrogates.

"Okay, ya' dumb college fuck-heads, here's the friggin' scoop," Goose began his dissertation by making us feel inferior while the conniver obviously felt dominant. "I had already delivered the six other jackets and the ten Donald Duck masks to Abrams and Hoppy over at the Aura coop. That leaves us to concentrate on givin' the local fuzz fuckin' acid indigestion and goddamned wisteria (hysteria) and brain hemorrhoids (hemorrhaging) at the same time."

"Abrams, Hoppy, Soblinski, Morrissey, Toscini, and Candido are gonna' hit the police substation over near the Glass Bowl," News capsulated. "And the 38 South Main Lambdas are gonna' clobber the local cops in their main headquarters, three doors down, wearin' our Donald Duck masks at exactly midnight, too!"

"And Lambda Agent Bell is puttin' on his Donald Duck mask, ball bearings, and marbles in the trunks of the Deltas' cars parked on Harvard," Tim Amoro summarized. "And Paul Meroski is at the coop now teaming-up with Tony Petters and Gil Taylor to stash similar phony evidence in the Taus' cars over on Academy. It's a good thing that well-connected Abrams got those car master keys from a couple of cooperative auto dealers, so that the trunks can be opened normally," Timmy declared. "Unlike J.W.'s trunk, that was brutally smashed to smithereens by those Japanese Sumo wrestlers and colored weightlifters, who went absolutely berserk with their sledgehammers after drinkin' a gallon of Saki each!"

"Okay, dork skulls. We fuckin' strike again at midnight, and let's give it really special to the local fuzz," Goose commented with conviction, sounding a little like Knute Rockne in the *Notre Dame* football team's locker room. "Make sure you're all wearin' your Donald Duck masks, and have your phony Delta Alfie Ortega jackets on, although we ain't workin' for any goddamned fancy airline company goin' to *Disneyland* out in California."

"Yeah, Goose," News interrupted, laughing incessantly. "Those cops at the stationhouse are gonna' be so disoriented that they'll think they're lost, somewhere between Alaska and Siberia, getting their ball *bearing*s *straight!"*

"What the fuck's Tomasello jabberin' about?" Goose rankled to the rest of us. "Sometimes, that babbling fuck-head Jives Arena makes more sense than you do, News! You're so full of shit you oughta' cut two new assholes to add to the one' ya' already have."

"Okay, guys, all we have to do is wait for Big Al to arrive and for the clock to approach midnight," I concluded while trying my best to preserve the peace among the expectant and overzealous instigators. "Then, we assault the cops with all our fury! And Goose, don't forget the sand and gravel we talked about."

Big Al was more punctual than he normally was and showed-up at ten of midnight. We donned our counterfeit Delta Alpha jackets; stuffed our open bags of marbles and ball bearings into our pockets; descended the wooden stairs carrying our rubber Donald Duck masks, and then Restuccio and Keiler paced to the local police station, just three doors down. Immediately, Goose and Big Al left the sidewalk, and the pair imaginatively applied their special talent for creating havoc by pouring the sand and gravel mixture through a funnel and into the gas tanks of three police cars, which had been parked behind the local station.

Four minutes later, as the distant *College Hall* bell tower carillon struck twelve, Goose's other four accomplices ambled-by the three residences to the local police headquarters, where Joanne Berenato and Tom Bell's fathers had once gone bonkers. After Big Al joined our commando party from the parking lot, we entered the building, descended the seven steps, and casually walked halfway down the hallway. Three policemen, as usual, were routinely staffing the headquarters at that inactive time of night. Tim, News, and I donned our Donald Duck masks and hustled down the remaining stretch of corridor, pacing past closed offices, slowly advancing to the main desk and booking area, where we encroached upon two unwary cops, casually chatting and drinking coffee. The third officer was seated at his desk, assiduously working on some bureaucratic forms that needed completing.

In the precious meantime, Big Al, Bill, and Paul were scattering *their* marbles and ball bearings onto *even-number* entrance-exit steps two, four, and six, and soon, the trio expeditiously stepped halfway down the long hallway.

"You' amateur cops' suck!" Tim audibly yelled through his silly Donald Duck mask.

"You lousy cops suck long, wet ones!" News imaginatively added to Amoro's acerbic remark.

"All you cops do is *cop*ulate each other's wives when ya' ain't suckin' each other!" I creatively added.

The three of us then dropped our open bags of marbles, along with three bags of small ball bearings onto the black-tiled floor, the full distance between us and the startled officers. Our eyes turned, making sure the stunned policemen got a good glimpse of our Delta Alpha Omega jackets, and then the brash intruders fled down the corridor, zipping past Big Al, Bill, and Paul, who then rolled more bags of ball bearings and marbles onto the floor to further impede the cops' futile pursuit. Tim, News, and I made sure to hop-up steps one, three, five, and seven, in order to make our safe egress, and our frenetic escape was soon followed by our fellow contemporary *GSC* pirates. When I turned around, I saw Big Al, Bill, and Paul emerge from the building, and my eyes also witnessed a patrolman (who had somehow eluded the hundreds of scattered marbles and ball bearings lying in the corridor) go flying-up into the air, and then the addled officer came dashing up the steps in a vain attempt to collar his suspected tormentors.

Goose was waiting several properties away, standing behind the station for us to exit, and promptly, the six brazen marauders removed our masks and quickly bolted through two adjoining properties to Goose's father's black *Cadillac,* which had been parked a block over. Restuccio drove us to Geet's Diner on the Black Horse Pike in Williamstown, where we eventually met-up with the Abrams' Lambdas inside the popular eatery's asphalt parking lot.

"I'll store these bogus jackets and our quacky Donald Duck masks at my place in Hammonton," Goose told Abrams and his crew, sitting in Bob's black '57 Mercury. "So, when we get to our rooms that I've rented at the motel in Atlantic City, we'll have a little party on Atlantic Avenue to complete our clever alibi. Food and *Pepsi* only, though; no fuckin' booze allowed!"

We drove to Winslow, just outside Hammonton; stored the thirteen counterfeit jackets and the remaining Donald Duck masks inside Goose's colossal bedroom closet; had a few *Southern Comforts* on the rocks at his realistic-looking club basement bar and lounge, and euphorically discussed the particulars of the latest Lambda Phi stealth operation. Tom Bell, Paul Meroski and Tony Petters had driven separately in three cars from Glassboro to Winslow, and the newcomers showed-up at Goose's house (the second strategic rendezvous point) to cheerfully inform us that their Donald Duck masks, bags of marbles and ball bearings had been successfully stashed inside the trunks of Bob Powell and Lou Hiltwine's parked automobiles.

"Everything went according to Hoyle," Bob reported for *his* Lambda commando squad. "The marbles and the ball bearings worked like a charm, just like you had predicted, J.W. The cops' substation over near the Glass Bowl was total chaos when we cautiously fled the scene."

"And with the sand and gravel formula I had poured into the two cop cars behind the substation, in addition to what you other guys did at the main headquarters," Hoppy added with a smile, "a good portion of the local police budget will be spent on cleanin' out fuel lines, car engines, and gas tanks. That was a really cool idea, Goose! You're smarter than the average *GSC* professor, that's for sure!"

"Well now," Goose laughed, after the raid's instigator chugged-down a jigger of sweet whiskey. "J.W. here helped me mastermind the whole goddamned operation. And now, the fuckin' wick-dicked Alfie Ortegas will be blamed for what happened at the main cop station; those son-of-a-bitchin' Capa Episalongs will have to answer for the *wisteria* at the substation, and some of your boys stored the extra Donald Duck masks, marbles, and ball bearings in those Alfie Ortega and Capa Episalongs' car trunks. Say, News," Goose expounded. "Did ya' know I'm almost a Capa myself' in the South Jersey Mafia? I don't know anything about that Episalong shit, but I'm almost a fuckin' Capa."

The other jubilant Lambdas all laughed in reaction to Goose's witless-but-accidentally-humorous commentary. And then, chatty News Tomasello rendered another perspective of the night's magnificent dual escapades. "The college deans are gonna' wanna' cove-upr the whole thing and smooth things out with the local cops, since *their* favored frat' boys, the Deltas and the Taus, are gonna' be facin' harassment and vandalism charges," News smartly added. "They'll probably negotiate some back-room deal with our tuition money goin' for compensation to the police, so that tonight's activities don't make the front pages of the *Inquirer, the Camden Courier-Post,* the *Atlantic City Press,* or the *Philadelphia Bulletin.*"

"Okay, jerk-offs! Let's get the fuck over to Atlantic City so that we have a good fuckin' solid alibi," Restuccio suggested. "I've rented the fuckin' *Globe Theater* at the north end of Atlantic Avenue, and the strippers are gonna' give us a private performance at 3 a.m., after their last public show, so we gotta' hurry," Goose surprised us all. "And if your college deans or the fuzz wanna' see some tits and ass, they're welcome to attend the strip-show as my fuckin' personal guests, too!"

Walking around campus the next few days, the atmosphere between the three fraternities was tense and potentially explosive. The Deltas and the Taus were catching plenty of heat and flak from the beleaguered administration, and the south end Atlantic Avenue motel owner, and the honky-tonk *Globe Theater* manager, both confirmed to the befuddled deans and to the paranoid police that the Lambdas were indeed wildly partying in Atlantic City that evening, so the college brass and the two rival frats' could only rely on suspicion of Lambda implication, without ever obtaining any concrete, direct evidence.

* * * * * * * * * * * * * *

But ever since the near-fatal Cowtown debacle, I had desired to resurrect an old ploy I had used with the Diablos back in Levittown to further thwart my Dogwood Hollow gang's enemies, the Kamikazes and the Renegades. My "new Glassboro plan" would first utilize News Tomasello and the convenient group-telephone, situated in the Common Room upstairs at 38 South Main Street. After practicing the script that I had typed-up, and with a folded handkerchief over the telephone to disguise *his* voice, News went right to work on that secret caper by first calling Bob Powell at the Delta Alpha Omega House, over on Harvard Road.

"Hello, Bob Powell?" News began quite innocently.

"Speaking. Who's this?" Powell arrogantly responded, sounding mighty aggravated and volatile.

"How's the fish fry goin' on inside your frat's chimney?" Tomasello read from his prepared text. "Have you lit the fireplace recently? I understand you need a legion of hired chimney' sweepers, all armed with detergent!"

"Who the hell are ya'!" Bob Powell shrilly yelled to the anonymous caller. "Identify yourself, you wimpy weasel!"

"Tell me, Bob. Aren't ya' interested in who put the Donald Duck mask, the marbles, and the ball bearings inside your trunk?" News further agitated. "Aren't ya' a little old to be playin' with marbles? Wanna' trade some baseball cards?"

"Look, Asshole. I'm gonna' kick your butt good once I learn your goddamned name! If ya' had any decent-sized balls, you'd tell me right now!"

News paused for a pregnant moment, following my animated hand signal. "Okay, turd brain. I'm involved with the Tau Kappas that pulled-off the stunt at the main police station, and who dumped delicious spoiled seafood down your chimney. Ya' Deltas wanna' duke it out and spill some bad blood?"

"Goddamned right!" Bob Powell boisterously thundered. "But I thought the Lambda Phi's had done the chimney stench thing, and also, the police disruption thing."

"Wrong, Idiot King!" News boomed back. "The Lambdas were in Atlantic City watchin' a striptease show, and then stayed overnight partyin' at an expensive motel. The Taus put it to you' ridiculous wick-dicks real good, and the Deltas took the entire royal salami up the ass. So, ya' dumb Dip-shit, ya' Deltas wanna' have a big brawl with us Taus?"

"Just tell us the time and place, and we'll be there to kick some serious butt," Bob Powell shouted and predicted. "I can't wait to boot your ass, right up into your intestines."

"The Deltas are the ones that are gonna' need the hospital emergency ward, because the college infirmary isn't big enough to handle all the injuries the Deltas are gonna' sustain," News skillfully read from the prepared script.

"Look, Dick Head. Get to the damned time and place!" Powell nastily scowled.

"My name's isn't Richard Head," News informed livid Bob Powell. "But anyway, Friday night at seven p.m., be at the open field on the south end of Poplar, down from Seedy's Bar. And bring along your scrotum Deltas, too, so that the cretins can experience a thorough professional beating! That's Friday night, April 12th at 7 in the field at the south end of Poplar! And remember, no weapons. I wanna' crush your ugly face at that place!" Click.

News took a dozen deep breaths, wiped some sweat off his brow, and then proceeded to dial Lou Hiltwine, leader of the Tau Kappa Epsilons, over on Academy Street.

"Hello, Lou Hiltwine, President of the Tau Capa Episalongs!" News calmly stated.

"Who the hell is this?" Hiltwine yelled. "I'm pretty torqued-up already, without any crank caller buggin' the hell outa' me!"

"This is one of the Delta Alphas that put a seafood smorgasbord down your freakin' Academy Street chimney," News lied while faithfully reading the prepared script. "And I was also involved in harassin' the cops over at the substation near the Glass Bowl and stashin' the Donald Duck mask, marbles, and ball bearings in the trunk of your exquisite Triumph Spitfire sports car. Aren't ya' a little old to be playin' with marbles? Wanna' trade some baseball cards?"

"I thought the Lambda Phi's had pulled-off that shit!" Hiltwine revealed. "Those assholes are definitely on our hit list, especially the morons that live on South Main."

"No, Idiot King. The Lambdas were in Atlantic City watchin' a striptease show, and then stayed overnight at the shore partyin' at an expensive motel," Tomasello clearly and aptly explained. "The Deltas put it to you low-I.Q. wick-dicks real good, and you took the entire royal salami up the ass. So, ya' dumb Dipshit, do the Taus wanna' have a big brawl with us Deltas?"

"You bet!" Hiltwine hollered like a desperate, possessed drugo. "Just tell us where and when, and we'll be there to thump your butts good. I believe that soon you're going to be hospitalized!"

"The Taus are gonna' be the ones that are gonna' need the hospital emergency ward, because the college infirmary isn't big enough to handle all the injuries the Taus are gonna' sustain," News expressed, while imitating an anonymous Delta Alpha caller.

"Quit the damned braggadocio and get to the friggin' time and place!" Hiltwine demanded.

"Friday night at 7 p.m. Be at the open field at the south end of Popular to receive the beatin' of your life," News further provoked. "And bring along your scrotum Tau amigos, so that the dunces can experience a professional beating, too. That's Friday night, April 12th, at 7 in the open field at the south end of Poplar. And remember, no weapons. I wanna' crush your face at that place!" Click.

That Friday night, News, Timmy, and I set-up a surveillance route as we cruised the area south of Seedy's Bar in Ralph Crenshaw's Nash Rambler to avoid suspicion and detection if riding-over in my Chevy Impala. The Deltas and the Taus congregated in a circle as Bob Powell and Lou Hiltwine, formerly best friends, met in the center of the young yeomen representing both fraternities.

First, Powell accused Hiltwine of trashing the Delta Alpha Omega chimney on Harvard Road with fish, shrimp and eggs, and then the Tau President denied all culpability and called Bob an "out-and-out liar". Then, Hiltwine advanced similar allegations against Bob Powell doing similar vandalism to the Tau Kappa Epsilon House on Academy Street, and the Delta Alpha President vehemently denied the insinuations, and falsely called Lou Hiltwine and his riled-up antagonists "blatant liars".

Soon, the acrimonious exchanges led to pushing, and pushing transformed into shoving, which then converted into punching and wrestling among the fifty or so angry occupants, thrashing-and-rolling-about upon the dusty, open field. News, Timmy, and I derived much satisfaction from witnessing the wild altercation erupt and explosively occur. But then, red beacon lights from the town cops' two remaining, still-running patrol cars, could be seen in the

Nash's rear-view mirror. And so, I stepped on the accelerator and left-behind the spectacular, evolving-and-escalating hostile battle.

"I suppose a neighbor unfortunately notified the police of the giant rumble in progress," News surmised and commented. "It's too bad the fuzz's two operational squad cars were out on patrol tonight, or the cops would've had to come-out to the end of Poplar Street on roller skates, or would have to hitchhike to the scene to break-up the damned fracas!"

"Now that we've created mucho bad blood between the Deltas and the Taus," Timmy exuberantly revealed, "we won't have to be fightin' both groups, because they'll be wastin' plenty of energy bashin' on each other."

"Maybe Goose could hire the twelve Sumo wrestlers and George Evans and his three gorilla brothers, to work for the Lambdas," News stated. "That alliance would be the ultimate in poetic justice!"

Chapter 28
"The Lambda Phi Sting"

Since the Delta Alpha Omegas and the Tau Kappa Epsilons now had a full-scale, escalating, feuding vendetta in progress, I thought-up a way to further get each organization into deeper trouble with the already-perplexed college administration. I came-up with the superb idea the following Saturday morning, April 27th, at Angelo's Diner, while shooting the breeze at 3 a.m. with Paul Meroski and with laconic Ralph Crenshaw.

"Ralph, I wanna' thank you for lendin' me your Nash Rambler to watch the Deltas and the Taus slug it out," I commended with appreciation. "And also, thanks for bringin' the guys to Cowtown to liberate me from that wicked buckin' bronco. I gotta' confess, you're really pretty dependable in an emergency."

"That's okay, J.W.," Ralph answered in a modest, dignified manner. "Anything for my broadcastin' buddy'. We have a pretty decent followin' over the local air waves, ya' know."

"Ralph, why don't ya' join the Lambda Phi's and be a member of the BMOC corps in the meantime," Paul urged. "You've already alienated the Deltas by livin' at 38 South Main with us renegades, and the ultimate response would be to snub and insult Bob Powell and his rabble by completely becomin' one of us."

"Thanks, guys," the shy cafeteria worker returned. "But I got real strict parents and don't want to offend them. They had their horns really twisted after I was suspended with my aborted Delta initiation up in the *College Hall* bell tower, which I now understand that you' fellas' were responsible for."

"Well, partly," I explained. "We were really tryin' to stymie and send a callin' card to the Delta Alphas, and you just happened to be the one that got victimized. We're sorry for the embarrassment it caused you and your strict-values family."

"I'll tell ya'what J.W.," Ralph prefaced a promise. "When I'm a senior, I'll finally become a full-fledged and pledged Lambda Phi, but first, I gotta' make sure I'm gonna' graduate from *GSC* with honors. It's sort of a dire expectation my folks have. We don't have a lot of money, and I'm the first in my clan to go to college, even if it's only a teachers' college."

"That's real noble," I wholeheartedly confessed. "Very noble, admirable, and principled, too, if I may add. You're just like Brutus, Ralph. You believe in honor above all else."

Then, my personality considered that the conversation was becoming too sentimental, and for my emotional-stability needs, I told Paul and Ralph what News had mentioned about Winston Churchill recently being proclaimed an honorary United States citizen at a *White House* ceremony, and how important honor meant in one's life; even more significant than either money or knowledge. Paul had a knack of bundling an idea's aspects properly, so that the basic principle could be adequately packaged and expressed in the most desirable context.

"Honor is definitely synonymous with integrity," Paul mentally tailored and claimed. "And a person can't buy or sell honor. The homage can only be earned, and it must be conferred on someone by others that happen to admire the individual. That's what makes honor so special," Meroski convincingly insisted. "Honor is not just any ordinary abstract word. It can't be bought, guys! And the achieved recognition received from another country, as in the case of Winston Churchill, is the ultimate respect that any one human being can ever strive to attain on this miserable planet."

"It's too bad that Goose Restuccio will never know the meanin' of honor, if the egotistical ingrate continues on his hedonistic path to Mafia wealth accumulation," I injected into the discourse. "And one time, fellas', G.R. even referred to the eminent British Prime Minister' Emeritus as Winston Church*key*, as if the distinguished gentleman, formerly livin' at 10 Downing Street, was a cheap beer tin can opener. If absolute power corrupts absolutely, as Professor Flank maintains," I iterated, "then absolute pursuit of wealth and selfishness rots-away the soul from the inside out."

"That's pretty heavy philosophical stuff," Lambda Paul readily acknowledged. "Quite eloquent, in fact. And J.W., I meant to tell you that two of your poem submissions have been accepted for publication in the *Avant*. This bull session is as good a time as any to reveal *that* particular good news development to you."

I related to Paul and to Ralph how much I enjoyed their company, because the soft-spoken friends tended to be more serious and reflective about life and academics than News, Big Al, Bill Elderberry, and even ethical Timmy Amoro. True, News was very knowledgeable, but seldom crossed the bridge from knowing information to mastering wisdom. Big Al was a "big picture guy" and had the bad habit of often overlooking supporting details. Bill Elderberry was more cynical and sarcastic than Diogenes ever was, and Timmy Amoro's personality was sort of a combination of News, Big Al's, and Bill's. And Timmy and I were like twin chameleons, blending-in with the general social environment, and on that memorable meeting sitting inside Angelo's Diner, I felt very comfortable and relaxed, just trying to be myself with Paul and with Ralph. I had temporarily found my niche in the chaotic universe.

"News was sayin' something this afternoon about Bob Cousy retirin' from the *Boston Celtics* after his team had beaten the *Lakers* in the *NBA* championship, four games to two," Ralph recalled and shared. "Tomasello's a great guy, but he doesn't stay focused and keeps meanderin' around from one topic to another. And just five minutes before rendering his statement, Tommy was yappin' about Cousy's announced retirement. Just a minute before, News was describin' how the nuclear sub *Thresher* sank in the Atlantic, killin' one-hundred-and-twenty-nine sailors, as if each mariner's life was nothin' more than a damned shallow statistic."

"And then, you have the other side of the coin," I interrupted Crenshaw. "Take Goose, for example. I've seen him hear the word nuclear and say that all the Russians should be taken to Newcombe Hospital over in Vineland, where we could *nuke 'em* so that no more American sailors would die in submarines, not realizin' that the disaster was caused by excessive floodin' that had shut-down vital electrical circuit systems on the *Thresher,"* I persuasively indicated. "Goose's whole lame-brained response had centered around two dumb word associations, Newcombe Hospital and nuke 'em."

And then, the theme of verbal interaction became more academic and erudite with Paul citing how incredible the human body is, since it could break-down any food, whether it be vegetable, meat, or dairy, and then miraculously bio-chemically transform those rudimentary compounds into energy, and successfully convert that fantastic energy into progress, civilization, music, culture, science, art, and technology.

"I know where you're commin' from, Paul," I confirmed. "It's absolutely amazin' how our brains can give billions of commands to billions of cells within our bodies, simultaneously. I mean," I tried explaining myself. "Nerve cells cause electrical impulses to happen in our bodies, and then we have other specialized cells like blood cells; reproductive cells; hormones; enzymes; antibodies; hair cells; skin cells; and fingernail and toenail cells, all behaving in concert inside our bodies," I communicated with great fervor. "And billions and billions of those microscopic entities, actin' both independently and cooperatively, are interacting while our conscious brains are concentratin' on understandin' each other at this very table inside Angelo's Diner. And our brains are orchestratin' all of this remarkable activity in our hearts; in our livers; in our lungs; in our' intestines; in our kidneys, and in all our other body functions like our eyes and ears, too. All of that amazing activity is going on inside us, while we sit here, and chew the fat, and drink coffee. Now, if that's not definite evidence of a non-religious miracle, then I don't exactly know what is!"

"But J.W., don't all animals includin' dogs, cats, and mice have similar cells performin' similar functions in their lower phylum bodies?" Ralph asked me. "Would you then consider *that* relevant fact happenin' in animals a miracle, too?"

"Probably," I replied, while still a bit confused by the depth of Crenshaw's analysis. "I mean, Ralph. I admit there is a similarity in the basic blueprint for life, and the similar way organs function in both man and in animals," I discerned and conceded. "But since man can develop culture and change his physical environment and animals can't, to the extent that humans can, then I suppose that thinkin' and inventin' are perhaps miracles on a greater scale and on a higher level with the human brain being superior. The less-dynamic animal brain merely manage's billions of cells at the same time, all throughout *their* bodies."

"Tell me, Ralph," Paul requested, extending and expanding the impromptu symposium. "If given your druthers, would you prefer livin' a long dull life or a short adventurous one?"

Crenshaw reflected deeply for several moments, and then offered a rather sophisticated reply. "I hope to live a long adventurous life," Ralph began his response. "But since that is not an option, accordin' to your question, I'd have to say I would prefer livin' a long, dull life! How about you, Paul?"

"I just like askin' questions and not answerin' them," Meroski shrewdly commented, while attempting to evade the essential issue *he* himself had generated. "Say, J.W. You said you had some sort of solution to bring peace to the campus. What is it?"

I thought about how all of the cells in the body seemed to work in unison with common interests of co-survival. That relationship got me thinking about the Lambdas, the Deltas, the Taus, and the administration, all acting as one unit with all of the various departments, or elements, cooperating simultaneously on campus (just like hearts, lungs, kidneys and livers do) for the general good of the *student body*.

"Paul, how about if I throw this notion at ya'," I carefully proposed. "The Deltas and the Taus can't have their women over to their frat' houses because of the terrible chimney stenches that are gonna' linger at least until September. As a gesture of good will," I soberly mentioned, "the Lambdas should offer the renovated chicken coop to each fraternity on consecutive Saturdays to make peace in the valley. This good will gesture could cause more harmonious relations between the three frats' and the craven administration, so that then, the college could function better as one unified unit, much the same as the heart, liver, kidneys, and lungs coexist and contribute to the body's good health."

"Your meritorious ancestors must have been Aristotle, Socrates and Plato," Paul generously commended. "That's an ingenious philosophical solution to the severe animosity problem that currently exists on our campus."

"I agree, J.W.," Ralph voluntarily pitched-in. "It's certainly worth a Lambda Phi try. It shows great concern and discretion on *your* part, J.W. Talk to Abrams and Hoppy about your unique hypothesis, and then measure their reaction."

On Friday afternoon in the Co-op, I mentioned to Bob and Steve the idea of allowing the Deltas and the Taus the use of our chicken coop on separate Saturday nights, and the Lambda brain-trust thought my proposal was an "exceptional idea". Then, Abrams and Hoppy confronted seniors Bob Powell and Lou Hiltwine about the distinct possibility, and after the rival presidents took it to their executive committees, the simple solution had been overwhelmingly accepted. The Deltas had a big shindig at "the coop" on Saturday night, May 4th, and the Taus had a super beef and beer bash on the evening of May 11th. Everything seemed to be going well without incident or conflict, until Bob Abrams and Steve Cassidy showed-up at 38 South Main Street on Saturday night, May 18th.

"Howdy, J.W., Big Al, News, Tim, Paul and Bill," Bob greeted. "Is Ralph around?"

"No, he's fillin' in tonight at the cafeteria for an absent worker," I honestly conveyed. Then, I noticed certain books in Abrams's hands. "What's with the photo albums? Are you organizin' a documentary for a class requirement?"

"Well, J.W., I meant to tell ya' sooner, but never got around to it," the Lambda Phi President coyly stated. "Just check these terrific photos we've stealthily acquired out in good old Aura. Hoppy and I had planted hidden cameras in the ceilin' of the coop, and look at these great blown-up still snapshots we got by remote control."

The assembled 38 South Main Streeters scanned and scrutinized the explicit telltale pictures, all of which depicted Bob Powell, Lou Hiltwine, and other unwary Deltas and Taus with their slutty girlfriends, all portrayed in a sex gallery portfolio featuring very damning evidence.

"My word!" Bill Elderberry gasped. "Do you guys think you're Allen Funt on *Candid Camera?* What are ya' goin' to do with 'em? Extort money from the Deltas and the Taus?"

"You mean what have I already done with the pictures would be a more accurate question," Abrams laughed in an almost-frightening, sinister manner. "I've already anonymously sent duplicates via Certified Mail to Dr. Robeson, Dean Lang, and to Dean Nelson. If these graphic photos don't change their testicles into ovaries, and blow their hemorrhoids up ten-times their normal size, then I don't know what will!"

"You had to give a return address when sending Certified Mail," Big Al pragmatically stated and argued. "I'm pretty damned sure of that! You could be legally sued for photographing others without their permission!"

"We mailed the albums from the Cherry Hill Post Office, twenty miles away," Hoppy clarified. "And we used Bob Powell's name and address on the one featurin' the Tau Kappas, and Lou Hiltwine's name and address on the album. The porn-shots were showin' the Delta Alphas and their sleazy chicks involved in some serious immoral action."

"But Bob, you never told me that you were goin' to spy on the private parties at the coop; take secret pictures, and piss-off the deans, the Deltas, and the Taus!" I angrily yelled. "Where's your decent sense of integrity?"

"Touche, J.W." Bob replied with his all-too-familiar wry grin. "But remember, you've pulled some crap unilaterally on the Deltas and the Taus without my permission or awareness, so now consider ourselves being *even* on the truth-or-consequences plateau. You never informed me of your random shenanigans, and I'm the damned President of the Lambdas," Abrams firmly emphasized with a florid face. "You should've been tried at a college court martial, or, excommunicated from *GSC* for your abominable insolence. But now, it's a wash. I think *we're* even on the balance scale. Nobody's perfect, not even you, J.W."

"But even if Powell and Hiltwine are ever lucky enough to graduate," I instinctively objected, "there will be new, upstart regimes to deal with next year, and the frat' war will continue, and perhaps even get worse. All I wanted to accomplish was to make peace, and you've stepped-in and ruined it."

"Peace is boring!" Hoppy indignantly insisted. "It's contrary to fun, adventure, and excitement!"

"Yeah, as long as no one gets paralyzed for life or killed!" I strenuously protested.

On the positive side, I had gotten all B's second semester sophomore year, had made the Dean's List (the academic one), and was ready to confidently begin my junior year in September. When I arrived home, my father remarked at how responsible I was becoming, since I had kept the white '61 Impala in "excellent, immaculate condition". I thanked Dad for his sincere compliment and pledged that I would continue to take good care of the automobile for the next two years at *Glassboro State.*

It was another grueling busy summer at Pete's Farm Market, and I drove all over South Jersey in the blue pickup truck, buying, and then transporting fresh produce to resell retail. And whenever the songs "Do Doo Ron Ron" by the Crystals, "You Can't Sit Down" by the Dovells, and "Shut Down" by the Beach Boys came on the Pete's Market Special's AM radio, their fast tempos reminded me of the hectic pace I was then involved-in with the market.

News and I had a chance to drive-up to Manhattan one Sunday night in late June; park the Chevy; take the subway out to Coney Island, and walk the boards without Hoss Gregorio and Tater Bertino to provide protection. And thank goodness we weren't accosted by any Brooklyn thugs trying to throw their weight around. I remember standing in front of *Nathan's Hot Dog Stand,* telling News about how every time I heard the melody to Little Peggy March's "I Will Follow Him", I thought about Joanne and Peachy being right behind me, giving me support, and then Tomasello would spoil my wonderful fantasy by telling me to heed the words to the new Jimmy Soul record lyrics, "If ya' wanna' be happy for the rest of your life, never make a pretty woman your wife".

"I guess 'Those Lazy-Hazy-Crazy-Days of Summer' don't pertain to peach farm and to farm market boys," I answered Tomasello, while alluding to a popular Nat King Cole song, as my leary consciousness deliberately switched the conversation away from Joanne and Peachy. "And every time I hear that wacko number 'The Bird's the Word' by the Rivingtons," I informed News, "I still recall Goose's old white Thunderbirds that were intentionally wrecked by the bullying Blues, engaging in some real ugly gang destruction."

"There's still a big void in the music sound of today," News insisted on the subway ride back to Manhattan. "The Beach Boys seem to have filled some of the vacuum, but novelty songs and teenage no-talent idols, who the vulnerable girls go goo-goo over, don't quite hit the mark. Something better in the rock and roll world has got to come-along, sooner or later. I can just feel it!"

I did manage secretly meet Joanne at the gala 16th of July *Our Lady of Mount Carmel Carnival* (Goose called it "Mt. Caramel") on 3rd Street in downtown Hammonton, that is, after we had a secret rendezvous at Bruni's Pizza, and another time we had slyly met at the Gem Teen Snack Shop on Central Avenue. Next, I drove to Atlantic City for us to walk the world-famous boardwalk, and Joanne and I attended a popular B movie. And I did date Peachy twice that summer too, driving way-down to Wildwood where she worked as a summer *Bell Telephone* operator, and then we strolled the Wildwood Boardwalk with its many concessions and amusement piers, coincidentally when Bobby Rydell's smash hit "Wildwood Days" was in full popularity on the radio stations.

And, of course, News Tomasello predictably called me too frequently every Sunday night, while business was slow at the market, because the heavy Jersey Shore traffic was mostly heading back to Philly' on the opposite side of *Route 30*. Tommy talked continuously about the *Telstar 2* satellite being able to relay color TV signals back to Earth, and about Major Gordon L. Cooper being the fourth American astronaut to orbit the planet in a space capsule dubbed *Faith 7,* as part of the last *Project Mercury* single-man space flight program.

"News, did you know that the last name Cooper refers to the barrel-making trade in colonial times," I interrupted his thought trend. "That's the only major word etymology I remember from Miss Sankins's freshman English torture chamber."

And then, News ignored my very pertinent commentary and began prattling-on about how the *American Heart Association* finally came out against cigarette and cigar smoking; and how the *National League* had been triumphant in the annual *All-Star Game* by a score of 5-3; and how President Kennedy had lectured to a crowd of West Germans, "Ich bin ein Berliner."

"What does that sentence mean when translated into English?" I requested knowing. "And by all means, don't tell me anything stupid or illogical."

"I am a Berliner!" News informed. "Yes, I'm sure it means translated into English, 'I am a Berliner'."

"Well then, News, I just gotta' tell ya', "Ich bin ein Asshole," which means 'I'm an asshole' whenever I listen to you, so I've not gonna' entertain your scatter-brained, insufferable nonsense any more this evening. Goodnight!" Click.

I was happy to see the end of August that summer of '63, but I wondered with great speculation what awaited the Lambda Phi Sigmas back at venerable *Glassboro State.* On the first drive back to the college for me to matriculate for the fall semester, News kept driveling about racial violence in Cambridge, Maryland; about Sonny Liston knocking-out Floyd Patterson again in two-minutes-and-ten-seconds of the first round, and about the Washington-Moscow hotline red phones going into effect, being implemented to reduce the possibility of nuclear war.

"News," I admonished. "Get serious for a change! You're into all of this fantasy violence between races, between boxers, and between countries, but I don't know if you're aware of it or not, but the Lambdas, includin' you and me, are in a dangerous frat' war that could get us both killed!"

"J.W., over the summer President Kennedy signed a bill requirin' equal pay for equal work for men, for women, and for blacks," Tomasello reported off-target. "What do ya' think about that? I think it's really necessary."

"I think you oughta' go back and attend Kindergarten, 101, because I honestly believe you've missed some rather important listenin' skills that you've never developed or embellished!" I angrily chastised in total disgust.

Chapter 29
"The Glassboro Theater"

My acclimation to the new fall semester was progressing smoothly. I liked most of my new junior year subjects, several of them being "Teaching Methods" courses, with one particular subject offering specifically relating to becoming a "Junior-High School Instructor". My schedule indicated that I would be spending a big portion of the second half of the year off-campus at both Clearview Regional High and at Washington Township Junior-Senior High Schools, doing my Practicum Experience where, for the first time, I would be assisting classroom teachers in mostly an aide's capacity, and even getting the chance to teach my first English and social studies lessons, being delivered to three authentic classes of students.

On the evening of Friday, September 13th, News Tomasello and Timmy Amoro were upstairs watching on the portable black and white television a taped rerun of the August 28th Martin Luther King historic "I Have A Dream!" speech, which was being broadcast on the local educational channel, *WHYY* out of Wilmington, Delaware. My buddies had been required to organize reports on the widely heralded King dissertation, while I desired watching the oration, because I had been preoccupied on August 28th working at Pete's Market when the Washington DC speech had originally been delivered on the steps of the *Lincoln Memorial,* facing the *Washington Monument's* reflecting pool.

"About a quarter of a million people listened to King's 'Freedom March' speech," News authoritatively mentioned, "even though it happened in hot August. That's approximately more than ten-times as many people' than are livin' in either metropolitan Hammonton, or in Glassboro proper."

No sooner had the *MLK* landmark speech started that the upstairs door was rapped three times, and before I could answer the heavy knocking, Goose Restuccio opened the unlocked portal and entered the shared living room.

"What the fuck' are you shit-heads watchin' that friggin' mool-en-yan for?" Goose yelled in his standard, disgusting, prejudicial mode of behavior. "That damned big-mouthed nigger wants us to be *his* fuckin' slaves. He's sayin' he has a dream, when the black bastard is a fuckin' nightmare himself!"

"Goose, we have to watch the speech and then write a report on it for a class. The assignment's due next week," News asserted. "It's a friggin' course requirement!"

"That black mother-fucker can't even think of his own ideas, or use his own goddamned words," Goose squawked to an embarrassed audience. "That arrogant black bastard's usin' George Washington's words from the Gatlinburg Address."

"Goose, first of all, Dr. King's quotin' Thomas Jefferson's sacred words from the *Declaration of Independence,"* News corrected our extremely biased visitor. And secondly, Abraham Lincoln was the one that delivered the *Gettysburg Address,* and not the Gatlinburg Address, during the culmination of the *Civil War*. If ya' remember from history, George Washington led the *Colonial Army* during the *Revolutionary War* being fought against the British."

"It doesn't fuckin' matter," Goose replied in a lesser tone of voice. "That leechin' Swahili is lookin' for something for nothin', and the scumbag wants to get his fingers into my wallet, so that I have to pay more goddamned taxes, so that the government could play Robin Hood and be the niggers' superhero. And you' simple fucks ain't gonna' be happy until ya' feel so guilty about nothin' that you've ever done, that you're gonna' go help stupid niggers in the African jungles, and then turn your own country over to other greedy, lazy niggers you're watchin' on television. I mean to say," Restuccio crazily pontificated, "science, cars, televisions, and space travel are white man's inventions that fuckin' mookers and clouds like King can only *dream* about ever achieving or doop-la-kating."."

"Goose," News piped-up to bring clarity to the discussion, "this entire Martin Luther King speech was motivated by a black man named Medgar Evers bein' shot outside his home in Jackson, Mississippi last June."

"You mean to say that a nigger was killed outside his shack in Jackson, Mississippi," Restuccio insisted with promoting his vile diatribe. "And if that nigger lived in Africa, the spear-chucker would've been killed outside his fuckin' straw hut! I mean, what's this shit that all men are created equal?" Goose petulantly yelled. "Wilt Chamberlain probably has a fuckin' dick two-foot-long! Niggers have gotten more gifts from nature between their fuckin' legs than you or I have received, but the average white man has got more intelligence inside his skull than most coon's have received, and the only half-intelligent shines have average-sized dicks, the same as white men do."

"Anyway, Goose, Medgar Evers was recently buried in *Arlington National Cemetery,* and President Kennedy has also renounced *his* shooting, and has condemned the practice of racial hatred," News academically added.

"There ya' go again!" Goose strenuously objected. "A nigger gets shot by a white guy, and its big news, but when niggers kill each other, and kill innocent whites in Philly' and New York on *Action News,* it's just an incident, and no white taxpayin' citizen being killed ever gets buried in any goddamned Allentown National Cemetery. J.W.," Restuccio continued his tirade, "your Dad was in Europe fightin' the Knot-sies in *World War II,* and he's never gonna' make it into Allentown National Cemetery for an honorable funeral. But this rug-head bastard that never did anything special in all his fuckin'life, but make a lot of goddamned noise about equal rights' bull-shit, gets blasted, and we're all supposed to have long faces extended all the way from Glassboro right into the next fuckin' county," Restuccio arrogantly maintained. "Is this country becomin' more fucked-up as each fuckin' day passes, or what?"

"Let's face it, Goose," News piped-up in defense of freedom and justice for all. "Even public-schools in Huntsville, Alabama have been desegregated. President Kennedy trumped Governor Wallace's hand by federalizin' the *Alabama National Guard,* makin' the *Guard* part of the *U.S. Army*. Integration can't be blocked anymore, anywhere in the country, so ya' might as well get used to the necessary idea, because the age of racial discrimination is finally reachin' an end."

"Do these fuckin' politicians or niggers put any money in your pocket?" Goose vehemently argued. "No, News; all they fuckin' do is take it out of your wallet. You don't realize that fact, but your' damned hard-workin', taxpayin' parents do! And you moron shit-heads are so idealistic that ya' can't see the fuckin' forest for the fuckin' shrubs!"

After Martin Luther King's educational TV speech finally ended, Goose continued his verbal rampage against unfortunate, exploited minorities. "I mean, you dumb pricks could be watchin' something good like the 'Beverly Hillbillies,' 'Route 66', 'The Lucy Show', or 'Have Gun, Will Travel', but instead, ya' prefer watchin' a nigger tell other niggers they oughta' have for free, the same as what *your* parents have struggled to earn and keep. I mean, J.W.," Restuccio summarized, "even the goddamned 'Jack Benny Show' is better than the garbage that just now poisoned your naïve minds and ruined your eyeballs. At least, Jack Benny has a polite coon chauffeur from upstate New York, Rochester, I believe, was the ugly shines' name," Goose relentlessly yelled like a demonic demagogue. "But at least Rochester was respectful and funny, unlike these niggers and clouds that make wild communist demands, and make threats if the black shits don't get what they fuckin' want by changin' the laws, and then takin' money away from you by force or threat, and what they're after for free is what you and your parents already have earned through hard fuckin' work and sacrifice. That's the niggers' definition of freedom and equality. The darkies want for free what you and your folks have worked for, without liftin' a fuckin' finger or pencil."

After listening to G.R.'s prejudicial, racial stereotypes, I decided that a change in venue was necessary, so I bluntly inquired why Goose had come and graced us with his illustrious presence. His announcement was quite intriguing, and the response caught the 38 South Main Lambdas by surprise.

"Guys, I'm pretty damned bored, and I wanna' help the Lambdas any way I can," Restuccio disclosed in a more reverent tone. "I feel like I belong to somethin' when I come here to Glassboro to see you fellas', do ya' know what the fuck I mean?" the flamboyant Italian rhetorically proceeded. "Anyway, I talked to Bob Abrams and Steve Cassidy about it over at Joe's Subshop, and the two boss men ate the poop outa' my idea."

"Which is what?" Timmy queried. "Tell us your grand scheme in ten-thousand curse words or less!"

"I'm gonna' raise money for the Lambdas by throwin' a large striptease show over at the Glassboro Theater. I've already spoken to the business manager, and the goddamned event's gonna' fuckin' come-off in two weeks at midnight, Saturday, September 28th," Restuccio surprisingly astounded us. "All that you' simple fuck-heads gotta' do is sell tickets to acne-faced college guys at six bucks apiece. If we fill the place up, I can net over three-thousand clams for you' ignorant assholes, with little effort on my part, or with no seed money bein' used."

"How about the deans, the local cops, and the city council?" Timmy smartly asked. "Won't the fuzz and the deans try and stop your show from commin' off, just like they did over at the Williamstown Republican Club masquerade party?"

"I've already checked it out. The license for the event could be easily gotten for only twenty-five bazookas," Goose maintained. "All we gotta' do is call it a 'variety show, and as long as nobody gets drunk, hospitalized, or killed, like that black, ugly gorilla-nigger in Mississippi did, then I see no problem. And if the event is legal and licensed, the local cops are gonna' lay off, because their bosses on town council already approved the fuckin' certificate."

“How about the nimrod college deans?” Timmy reiterated his unanswered interrogative. “They’ll try and shut-down your show, once Robeson and his clan get wind of your controversial plan!”

“Those gutless bastards have been so intimidated by last year’s campus panty-raid event, and also by that pathetic raid at the fuckin’ Republican Club over there in Williamstown, that they’ll pretend that the fuckin’ burlesque show ain’t happenin’,” G.R. concluded. “So, those cone-heads runnin’ your friggin’ school are too afraid to come-down heavy on the Lambdas on the night of the 28th, outa’ fear of havin’ their microscopic balls busted again, but this time, bein’ reviewed in the big city and local newspapers.”

Early every morning, before my first period class, I trekked to my *College Hall* mailbox and usually found Navy literature (mostly from Lakehurst) enticing me to join-up, and the daily event became so repetitious in the fall of ‘63 that soon I just began tossing the unopened envelopes into the trash barrel, regarding the form letter correspondence as annoying junk mail, which Timmy insisted was just “one level above blackmail,” which Goose once said “is for dark niggers only”.

Dave Littlefield was the new Delta Alpha Omega President, replacing Bob Powell, and Sal Walker became the new head honcho over at the Tau Kappa Epsilon House on Academy Street, after Lou Hiltwine and his Harvard Road counterpart amazingly graduated in August, despite the difficulties of the marbles, ball bearings, Donald Duck masks, along with the lewd chicken coop photo albums’ fiasco.

But my principal quandaries were with Joanne Berenato and with Peachy Wilcox. Both chicks had heard about the unique September 28th “Vaudeville Show” coming to the Glassboro Theater, and each doll was jealous of the idea of me admiring other attractive, well-stacked older women’ dancing-around suggestively, and then sexily stripping on the stage. The two jealous girls refused to even recognize my existence after several minor quarrels I had had with each pampered princess. And so, to defend my wounded pride, and to avoid adolescent despondency, I began dating a six-foot-tall Russian blonde babe named Alexis Terranenkov, who looked like a beautiful escapee from Jezebel’s Den over on Delilah Road in Pleasantville, just west of Atlantic City.

And Alexis had a classy, spanking new, red ‘63 Buick convertible, a heavy foot, and a physique like a muscular female weightlifter, since the broad worked-out at a local gym to keep trim and strong. But when the Russian babe would take me out parking and drinking, she could guzzle down *Southern Comfort* as well as

Mario DiMaris, without ever getting drunk, and I was afraid I would become a chronic alcoholic, while gorgeous Alexis Terranenkov intimidated me with her very outstanding feminine prowess.

One night in mid-September, Alexis and I were parked at the Academy Street Lake in Clayton, and the horny blonde began coming-on to me, talking like Mae West in the old movies. "Oh, Mighty Mouse," she said the insulting nickname she had labeled me. "Come-on over, so that I can caress your firm little body, after I polish-off the remainder of this *Southern Comfort* bottle. J.W., why don't ya' come-over to my side and see me some time!"

And after draining the last twelve-ounces of whiskey in one phenomenal chug, Alexis latched onto my left arm, dragged me down onto her car's red-rugged floor to participate in her version of the 'submarine races', and then the beautiful Amazon squeezed me so hard that I felt like farting and defecating all over her custom red-leather-upholstery. So, ever since that September 20th night, I began dating another horny blonde-haired girl named Nancy Danns, who only would squeeze the piss out of me, before I ever felt like passing gas, or emptying my aching intestines. But it was great dating, adding to my growing prestige on campus, being seen with Alexis Terranenkov and with Nancy Danns. But in truth, my troubled heart yearned for sympathy and bonding from Joanne Berenato and Peachy Wilcox, which unfortunately never materialized. All I did was piss-off the pair of gorgeous beauty queens more by increasing their resentment.

"How come you're not datin' that Russian Amazon Alexis anymore?" Timmy asked me at 3 a.m. at Angelo's Diner, the night before what Goose billed as "the Magnificent Vaudeville Show". "She's stacked, just like Liz Taylor in that new movie *Cleopatra.*"

"That flick cost thirty-seven million bucks to produce," News qualified, "and it's without a doubt the most expensive film in motion picture history. I don't know if *Twentieth Century Fox* is gonna' ever be able to recoup its lusty investment, despite the film's great advance sales."

"That Alexis is a twentieth century fox if I ever saw one," Timmy joked. "But unfortunately, you, J.W., are starrin' in *The Adventures of Mighty Mouse* instead of being featured as a leadin' man in *Cleopatra.* And if I were you, I would still go out drinkin' with that luscious blonde Russian broad with the erect big tits, and also possessing a sexy classy chassis."

"It's a good thing for the *Cleopatra* movie that Elizabeth Taylor and Richard Burton are havin' a real-life love affair off the screen that's appearin' in all the tabloids," News contributed. "And what about that track and field guy, John Pennel. He became the first human to pole vault seventeen feet, doin' seventeen-feet-three-inches, down in Miami."

"Maybe Alexis Terranenkov is really from Warsaw and not from Moscow as she claims," Timmy laughed, while effectively breaking my tender nuggets. "That means that J.W. could keep his special chick safely hidden in a Pole vault, ha, ha, ha!"

"You guys are about as funny as two submarines with screen doors and with broken screened hatches," I protested, using an old Bob Jalonec line I had recollected from Levittown. "Do you two jerks think the striptease performance at the Glassboro Theater is gonna' come-off tomorrow night as planned?"

"Standin' Room Only," Timmy answered with a wide grin. "There's only six-hundred-and-fifty seats in the place, and Goose said we had to stop sellin' tickets at eight-hundred."

"But isn't there an *Autumnal Equinox Dance* at the college tomorrow night?" I recalled and asked. "You must surely remember what the deans did, raiding the chicken coop when a competing college dance was also happening."

"Sure, but who's gonna' attend except horny eggheads and jilted wallflowers," Timmy insisted, while News was continuing his indulgent guffawing. "Maybe Goose will hire Dr. Robeson as the Master of Ceremonies for his 'Fall Vaudeville Revue', before his scheduled debacle reaches a dramatic *climax,* and I use the term lightly, ha, ha, ha!"

"Well, you two degenerate hammerheads," I squawked, "I'll be glad when the show's run its course and becomes history, so that I can again get back on good terms with Joanne and Peachy. Even Elaine Hill's been ignorin' and avoidin' me all over campus, and she and I were really close friends in high school."

"Well now, J.W. I guess that means you're a hammerhead, too," News Tomasello chortled. "Because now, Mr. B-M-O-C, you're a *lone shark,* just like Goose is a loan shark, and you're out on the *Maco* just like Timmy and me, ha, ha, ha, you' freaky hammerhead! Ya' oughta' learn to keep your friggin' jaws shut!"

"Stop *pun*ishin' me!" I hollered, getting the attention of the few Angelo's Diner patrons squandering their last dimes and nickels inside the Main Street establishment.

Saturday night, September 28th, soon arrived, and there were wall-to-wall *SRO* students packed like sardines inside the usually near-empty Glassboro Theater. Several Lambdas were exchanging opinions and observations in the movie house's lobby.

"I guess the *Autumnal Equinox Dance* at the college is a big flop tonight!" I told News, Timmy, and Ron Carputis, who had just said he was commuting to Glassboro with Mario, and had already seen twelve different bulls having sex with designated cows.

"Sex sensationally sells, and sensational sex sells even more sensationally," News declared and alliterated. "And the Lambdas are sellin' sex tonight. And all those nice girls like Joanne, Peachy, Elaine, and Loretta are at the college dance wonderin' which female they'd like to jitterbug or twist with."

"I see some Delta pledges and a few Tau sympathizers casin' the joint," Ronny Carputis suspiciously noticed and disclosed. "I hope there's not a savage brawl eruptin' in here. Somebody innocent like me is liable to get hospitalized."

"The movie theater's manager told Goose that there hadn't been so as many people inside the place since *Gone with the Wind* had debuted there, way back in the '40s," Timmy added to the conversation. "And with the advent of television, especially color TV, movie houses and drive-in theaters are really hurtin' badly, all over the country. They are two doomed American traditions that I think really need to be preserved."

After the auditorium was filled beyond capacity, a fat Master of Ceremonies, resembling Jackie Gleason, stepped-out onto the stage and announced the first stripper, Gypsy Lily Levi, who came out in a tight-fitting, blue denim outfit, strolling to David Rose's rendition of "The Stripper" being piped through the movie house's second-rate sound system. But that interesting fact about the dissonant music didn't matter. The all-male audience was receptive: rendering euphoric whistling, making catcalls, and laughing their como' se llamas off in a very exaggerated fashion.

The second act to appear when the curtains were again opened was Dixie Cups, who must have worn a *Z-bra,* and the Southern Belle was quickly and punctually followed by the Jezebel Den's one and only Mandy Titanic, who also had quite an impressive set of bouncing breasts. Everything was reaching a fabulous crescendo with the fourth act of the scheduled six that had been slated, and Ophelia Dix came struttin' out, doing a triple striptease routine with Minnie Bikini and Nicky Nochers, when the uninvited County Fire Marshal unexpectedly showed-up at the front lobby popcorn counter, accompanied by six intimidating New Jersey State Troopers.

"The capacity of this building is six-hundred-and-fifty, and you've got over a hundred people too many in here," the stoic-faced Fire Marshal informed Goose. And before Restuccio could even attempt bribing the very sober and forthright public official, an anonymous college patron pulled the fire alarm, and all hell broke loose inside the dark theater. College attendees were panicking, pushing, shoving, and punching in a wild stampede, all attempting to safely get to the exit doors, while others were leaping-over rows of seats, endeavoring to escape being incinerated and barbecued by a blazing, non-existent building inferno.

An hour later, after the false alarm had been sounded, and had yielded an out-of-control Chinese fire drill evacuation, Goose arrived at the Aura chicken coop to hand-over three thousand American dollars to the grateful Lambda Phi Sigmas. His demeanor suggested that the excessive chaos that the audience and we Lambdas had just encountered at the Glassboro Theater was merely all in an average day's work.

"It's a good thing that fuckin' Fire Warden showed-up while those three broads were dancin' to Johnny Cash's 'Ring of Fire'," Restuccio laughed. "The son-of-a-bitch Fire Warden jerk-off didn't even have time to count bodies, because the shit-face dunce was rudely knocked onto the floor by the *fan-attic* student body's bodies, ha, ha, ha! Serves the cocky, dumb bastard right!"

"That's right, Goose," Ron Carputis agreed. "If the evacuation had occurred during the openin' act, the eight-hundred sex hounds in attendance might've demanded their damned money back."

"I think the kid that pulled the alarm was a Delta Alpha Omega pledge that did it as an initiation requirement," Timmy added. "We oughta' tie the creep to a headboard over at Glassboro Bedding, so that Ronny and Mario can salute the idiot with their middle fingers every mornin' on their way to college. The imbecile probably thought it was a pretty neat prank, but somebody could've been trampled durin' the frenzy, other than that mortified Fire Marshal."

"Jesus Christ!" Goose zestily exclaimed. "Could you imagine if the theater was packed with college girls, and Pepino the Mouse, without Lou Monte, came-out on the fuckin' stage and flashed a two-foot-long hairy pecker? Those fucked-up broads would've plowed through the walls, rather than stampede to the goddamned doors."

"There's been an escalation in the frat' wars with a Delta pledge pullin' the theater's fire alarm," Timmy intelligently evaluated. "Who knows what's gonna' happen next?"

"It don't matter, and I really don't fuckin' care," Goose concluded and summarized. "All I fuckin' know is that I'm now subsudizin' the Lamp-does, just like your future federal tax dollars are gonna' subsidize the same goddamned niggers and spics you're all so fuckin' worried about on fuckin' television. The next thing they'll want is for their fuckin' straw huts in *You-gander* to be replaced by fuckin' marble mansions, all at our goddamned expense!"

Chapter 30
"The Egg Harbor River"

On Monday, October 7th, I happily exited my *Bosshart Hall* "Junior High School Teaching Methods" class, believing that I had just earned an A on the difficult objective test that Professor Zimmer had administered. I caught-up with News inside the Co-op, and joined my uptight pal for some coffee and *TastyKake Krimpets,* our favorite high-calorie snack-food treat. Tomasello was also in high spirits, thinking that he had just aced a test in his "Contemporary World Events" seminar with his favorite educational mentor, Dr. Roberts. We parked our butts in a booth and discussed some interesting current events, which News automatically knew without any prospective assistance or expertise required from either Dr. Roberts, or from any daily big city newspaper.

"Well, J.W., everything's changin' quick in the damned world, even baseball," Tomasello lamented. "Stan 'the Man' Musial is retirin' from the *St. Louis Cardinals* after playin' for the team twenty-two dedicated years. I mean, the guy had set seventeen *Major League* and thirty *National League* records."

"That's why I've been completely turned-off by the *Phillies,"* I remarked. "The *Cards* showed loyalty to *their* best player and now are makin' him a club executive, while the *Fightin' Phils* traded-off Richie Ashburn as if he were a sack of damaged potatoes. That's loyalty and gratitude for ya'. A guy of Ashburn's high caliber only comes along to a franchise once every fifty-years or so."

"It's all in the *Cards,"* News rather incompetently jested. "And speakin' of baseball, how about those *Los Angeles Dodgers* sweepin' the formerly invincible *Yankees* in four straight victories, with the last game yesterday capturing the *World Series* crown? Sandy Koufax set the tone by strikin' out fifteen Bronx Bombers in the openin' game, and then Don Drysdale pitched great, too."

"Isn't that fact something?" I marveled and claimed. "When the *Dodgers* were sluggin' away in *Brooklyn,* the team couldn't handle the *Yanks,* but after movin' out to *L.A.,* the squad treated the legendary *American League* champs like they're just another *National League* opponent. Who can figure it?"

"All I can tell ya' J.W. is that the smog out in California is horrendous and as thick as soup, because I was out there on the West Coast five years ago," Tomasello expounded. "And the way the traffic in the city is so intense, pedestrians are either *Los Angeles*

Dodgers or *Los Angeles Angels,* dependin' on how hard they might get hit when crossin' the damned streets."

"Those pedestrians must always be sufferin' from that run-down feelin', News, and also be susceptible to plenty of colds. Anything else happenin' in the doomed world?" I asked my omniscient, sometimes-annoying, trivial-fact companion.

"Why yes, J.W., there is," my Hammonton friend in Glassboro replied. "Tomorrow President Kennedy is gonna' approve sendin' over four-million metric tons of wheat, valued at over two-hundred-and-fifty-million smackers overseas, with most of the cargo bein' earmarked for Russia."

"Holy crap, News!" I artificially gasped. "If the Soviets ever learn how to make *Wheaties,* or steal the secret formula from *General Mills,* who operates the U.S. Grain Patrol, then the Russians will become as physically strong as we brave Americans are! Say, News," I proceeded. "Baseball season's over now, and pigskins are 'in vogue', or maybe even in *Esquire*. Ya' wanna' have a catch with the football out in the outfield next to *College Hall?* I have an old pigskin in the trunk of my new Impala."

"Okay, J.W.," Tomasello agreed. "But the next time I lend ya' twenty-five cents, make sure you remember to give me the friggin' 'quarter back'!"

On the campus trek to the *Bosshart* parking lot, and then on the way over to the baseball field next to *College Hall,* News and I discussed Joanne Berenato, Peachy Wilcox, Elaine Hill, Loretta Sacco, the Glassboro Theater tumult, and finally, the Delta Alpha Omegas and the Tau Kappa Epsilons. And then, on the outfield's grass, when News was demonstrating how to pass and how to even punt perfect spirals, two bone-headed freshmen Alpha pledges intruded on our personal recreation and challenged us to a four-man game of touch football.

"What are the 'stakes'?" News grumpily snorted. "You guys look so wimpy that you're probably weak vegetarians, and don't even eat hoagies, or even hamburgers!"

"If you Lambdas beat us," a kid named Vince Rogers said, "then Stu Dixon and I will take you two alcoholics over to Seedy's Bar and drink you dual clowns under the table at our' expense."

"That's an awful lot of bravado commin' from a greenhorn freshman Delta Alpha fledgling!" I gruffly asserted. "And there's no way News and I are gonna' lose to you two circus sideshow freaks, so don't bother enumeratin' what we gotta' do for you in the event you should get lucky and win. No way you two bozos are gonna' beat us, except in the stupidity category!"

As it turned out, Vince Rogers and Stu Dixon were pretty talented athletes, both being high school superstars from up in highly populated North Jersey towns. But tenacity, discipline, and experience kicked-in, and with News being the supreme quarterback and me' being his favorite and only pass receiver, we decisively trounced the wise-ass Delta Alpha Omega upstarts by a closer-than-anticipated score of 72-60.

"Okay, Salami-brains," News most excellently belittled. "Let's go over to Seedy's and see if you two Java men can drink beer as well as you can swallow-down coffee. And I hope ya' guzzle *Budweiser* better than you two hambones can play touch football."

"Okay, meet ya' two guys there in half an hour," embarrassed Vince Rogers conceded. "We wanna' go back to the Delta House over on Harvard and freshen-up a bit."

"Oh no, ya' don't!" News reacted. "You can't pull the wool or the cotton-pickin' untruth over our twenty-twenty eyes. We go together to the bar to make sure you two neophytes don't try and escape your vowed commitment."

"Okay, fellas'," Stu Dixon acceded. "My car's close by, just over the railroad tracks. How about if you Lambdas tag along and ride in the back? But don't drink too much *Bud.* I only have four-hundred bucks until I get my next allowance on Friday."

"No problemo!" News audaciously quipped. "Hope your buddy has a lot of money in his wallet too, because J.W. and I are mighty thirsty and can drink like 'camels', and I don't mean friggin' cigarettes either!"

The four of us walked to the stone, dirt, and gravel parking lot on Girard Road, which was the starting line for the imaginative Lambda Phi Sigma caboose initiation, and then News and I climbed into the rear of Dixon's big engine four-door blue Chrysler. In three minutes, we were seated inside Seedy's Bar and chugging delicious frosted mugs of cold beer, which always seemed to taste better when the 'brewskis' were free, or had been ethically won through honest and fair competition.

After an hour-and-a-half of imbibing (and actually *fraternizing)* with our avowed enemies, Vince and Stu conceded that the duo had again been vanquished and begged us to stop our drinking, because the pair felt like puking their spleens out. So, being humanitarian and empathetic, and feeling totally superior, News and I allowed the young delinquents (who like us had fake *IDs*) off the hook.

"Okay, you' totally disgusting, very atrocious, born losers," News intrepidly commanded. "Drive us over to *Bosshart Hall* to get J.W.'s impeccable white vehicle. And next time you meet a Lambda Phi, you weirdo rookies oughta' evaluate your prospective opponents better and make damned sure they're in your inferior league before recklessly challengin' a couple of Sigmas to supreme competition."

When the four of us finally exited Seedy's in rather inebriated states of mind, News and I shockingly discovered that we had been surrounded by George Evans and six diabolical-looking Japanese Sumo wrestlers.

"Glad you two loony bird Peckerwood Pecker-heads could finally make the scene," George nastily greeted us. "Now if you'll kindly once again hop into the back of the dark blue van, we're gonna' go on a little yacht cruise you'll find to be most memorable and invigoratin', especially to the soul."

"Where to?" I demanded. "There isn't any river in Glassboro. Just an occasional lake or pond."

"We're goin' to have a field trip goin' out to the Riverside Marina over in Mays Landing to board a magnificent fishin' boat," George evilly cackled. "Then, you two touch football playin', beer guzzlin' idiots are gonna' take an exquisite boat ride down the placid *Great Egg Harbor River*. And to think that you two weird honkies thought you had won a touch football game and a beer drinkin' contest besides! Ha, ha, ha, ha! Ya' two lame-brained dick-heads make me wanna' piss myself three times. Ha, ha, ha, ha!"

While in the back of the archaic, banged-up, blue van, the Japanese brutes tied News and me up with hemp, and after News asked the foreign guys if they were from *Hemp*stead, New York, the Oriental beasts next gagged our mouths with dirty handkerchiefs. And as our means of transportation proceeded out of Glassboro heading towards Williamstown on *Route 322,* ironically, the Chiffons "One Fine Day" was followed on the van's radio by the Essex's "Easier Said Than Done", which was succeeded by Rolf Harris's "Tie Me Kangaroo Down, Sport", and then Elvis Presley's "The Devil in Disguise", before the Wibbage DJ finally got to a scheduled commercial break.

But then, right before the van stopped at its Mays Landing destination, Martha and the Vandellas smash hit "Heat Wave" and Jay and the Americans classic "Only in America" were played over the Radio 99 AM air waves, as George Evans nearly laughed his tongue and well-anchored teeth out of his mouth, and the six laconic Japanese Sumo henchmen just stared and glared at News and me, with the fat brutes sitting upright upon the sturdy side-benches, as if the giants were possessed by supernatural Japanese demons.

After George Evans applied the brakes for the last time, News and I were roughly transferred from the blue van at the northern end of *Riverside Marina.* Our hands were tied in front of us, making us feel like nineteenth century prison convicts. I glanced across the serene river and my pupils saw familiar *Sugar Hill Bed and Breakfast/Restaurant,* where my parents would often take the family to dinner on special occasions, and I wished that I was then seated inside with my folks and siblings, enjoying surf and turf, instead of about to board the *Delta Alpha Queen* fishing yacht, which was snugly moored on the *Route 40* side of the popular marina.

After News and I were led down the dock ramp to the well-appointed boat, the six Sumo wrestlers and George Evans lifted us over the port side onto the expensive craft, where we were officially greeted by Dave Littlefield and Sal Walker, along with three surrogate Deltas: Russ Stillwell, Andy Talbot, and Sam Lista, accompanied by three nefarious Taus: Stan Clements, Ron Vitale, and Randy Irwin.

"Welcome aboard the fabulous *Alpha Delta Queen,"* Dave Littlefield sarcastically and insincerely laughed. "You two inept Lambda fools have been thorns in the Deltas and the Taus' sides for over two years now. I'm not John Daley or Garry Moore, but are you two South Main Street freaks ready to play *What's My Line* and *I've Got a Secret?"* Littlefield asked and ridiculed, while alluding to a pair of 1950s television shows.

"They aren't even ready for *To Tell the Truth!"* Sal Walker chuckled and opined. "These two pre-pubescent youngsters haven't yet made it past *Howdy Doody, Kukla, Fran and Ollie, Tinker Bell,* and *Romper Room!"*

"What are ya' gonna' do with us?" I demanded, while mumbling through my mouth gag. "Make us dig-up oyster with our mouths?"

"Oh, you'll find-out at four-thirty when the *Delta Alpha Queen* finally docks," the new Delta Alpha President promised. "That gives us three whole hours to pleasure cruise the river and enjoy the scenic sights. But first, gentlemen, you're gonna' have a few libations, just to show you, our fortunate guests, that the Deltas and the Taus are basically civilized, aristocratic socialites."

Littlefield motioned to George Evans, who then signaled to the Sumo wrestlers to remove our mouth gags, and quickly drop News and me onto the wooden deck face-up, where our jaws were soon forced open, and we were manipulated, slammed-around, and compelled to chug-down a half-pint of *Jack Daniels* each, which significantly added to our half-intoxicated beer condition, and made me want to barf my guts, spleen, and esophagus out.

"Now, you two bungling blunderers will be taken below to my beautifully furnished visitors' quarters," Littlefield informed, before News and I were violently raised-up to a sitting position, with our hands still bound in front of us.

"What if we have to use the bathroom?" Tomasello innocuously inquired.

"Did you mean barf room? Ha, ha, ha! Well then, you hostages have two very distinct choices!" Sal Walker gleefully exclaimed. "And I'm glad you asked. *Number One* is you can piss in your underwear, and *Number Two* is that ya' can crap your pants!"

"Thanks to you two distinguished, demented dick-lickers," Dave Littlefield interrupted the boisterous and bawdy laughter, "Vince Rogers and Stu Dixon have satisfactorily passed their prescribed Delta Alpha initiations by conning and suckering you two imbeciles into commin' here. I mean, Vince and Stu could've trounced you two dodos in touch football, and could've easily drunk your butts under the table over at Seedy's, but the pledges showed real good self-discipline and made you two piss-ant goofballs think that *you* had won both contests! Ha, ha, ha, ha! What lowlife retards!"

"And don't worry, you mentally ill Lambda goons," Sal Walker remarked. "My pal Dave here has two other boats just like this one, the *Delta Alpha II* in Cape May, and the *Delta Alpha III* down in Florida at Daytona Beach, just in case we have a navigation problem and smash into a wharf, or a jetty, or a huge, well-endowed mermaid! We have two backups to further persecute you dimwits all the way to your new frat' lodge: The Nut House, Ha, ha, ha, ha!"

News and I were hostilely escorted below and could watch the river traffic and banks from two small portholes, on the wall inside our locked-in room. The luxury cabin cruiser's dual inboard motors were started, the mooring ropes quickly un-tethered and released, and soon the sleek craft drifted away from the Riverside Marina's boarding dock. The sleek craft traveled up the river, heading east towards Somers Point and Ocean City, both towns less than twenty-miles from Mays Landing, as either the crow or the raven flies.

"I'm sure glad we took long leaks before leavin' Seedy's," I reminded News, who seemed resigned to his fate of being a victimized, bound captive. "I wonder what those turkeys above have in store for us? They're partyin' on the deck pretty heavy right now. I can hear the dip-shits hootin' like they're at some wild satanic sinners' jamboree. I hope that a *Coast Guard* river-patrol boat finds this vessel and rescues us."

"I suppose we're hostages, and I'll grant ya' *that* wish," News uttered while emphasizing the obvious. "How come I'm always a hostage with *you,* but never one when with anybody else?"

"Those idiots don't think of consequences when they engineer a prank," I protested, while ignoring News's legitimate grievance. "When my white Impala was put-up on the Co-op's roof," I continued, speaking to my nearly unconscious and now phlegmatic listener, "it could've broken through and killed a night janitor. Or when we were trapped in the tractor-trailer reefer, we could've easily been frozen to death. Gees, News," I paused to collect my random thoughts that were flitting through my troubled head like flying bats. "I sure hope the *Coast Guard* boards this yacht and finds us before we're rubbed-out by some wild, out-of-control frat' hazing!"

"You have a better chance at bein' reborn on Mars than bein' rescued!" News worriedly confided. "And ya' know what; that *Jack Daniels* tasted just about as good as *Southern Comfort* does. Say, J.W., if we don't escape this misadventure and die, the *Roman Catholic Church* is gonna' start sayin' all its masses in English, rather than in Latin, startin' in December. I want my funeral mass in Latin and not in English, so it's better that we die in October than in December. Get what I'm sayin'?"

"You *are* absolutely daft and one sick puppy!" I criticized. "Here we are, News, bein' transported to some unknown location against our wills, with our hands bound; our bladders fillin' up; our drunken nerves jangled, and all you're doin' is thinkin' about dyin'! The Pope can't save our asses, nor can the *Roman Catholic Church.* All that the priests and bishops could do is see that we're buried properly, if our bodies are even ever found! Can't ya' think of anything essential to say about our present dilemma?"

"Why certainly, yes, J.W.," Tomasello burped and replied in a psychologically frightful, drunken daze. "Mays Landing' was named after a mariner named May who first discovered Cape May, navigated up the coast, and then sailed up the *Greater Egg Harbor River* to what is now Mays…"

"News' just shut the hell up!" I bellowed. "You're givin' me a migraine on top of my migraine!"

"And this river is called the *Egg Harbor* because birds come here often to make nests and lay their'…."

"I said shut the hell up!" I screamed like a demented maniac. "Stop actin' like an absolute trite dolt! Just doze-off and sober-up before I even consider logically talkin' with you again!"

News voyaged-off at my suggestion to visit 'Mr. Sandman', without the Chordettes. My out-of-sync mental condition had me sleeping, and then awakening to glance-out the porthole, and then slumbering, and again waking-up in an intermittent pattern that seemed to warp both space and time. I remember seeing in the distance the town of Somers Point, and *Tony Mart'* and *Bay Shores*, two popular summer bars for college kids, and then cruising under the dual *Garden State Parkway Bridges,* that majestically spanned the *Greater Egg Harbor Bay,* and next seeing the historic *Tuckahoe Inn* on the south side of the river, meeting the bay, which all indicated that the *Delta Alpha Queen* had turned-around and was now heading west towards Mays Landing, and evidently the yacht, being on schedule for its 4:30 secret and mysterious rendezvous.

News woke-up from his beauty rest, just in time to witness from his porthole the fancy yacht floating-in towards a secluded dock on the northern riverbank. Everything in the picturesque environment was quiet and serene, just like the very beautiful pine barrens', which had its stately evergreens growing alongside the tranquil river, interspersed with deciduous trees in their mixed yellow, orange, green, and brown autumnal splendor. George Evans and three sour-faced Sumo wrestlers soon appeared inside the fairly large guest cabin, to conduct their hostages back up to the sun-kissed top deck.

"Hope ya' naughty honkies enjoyed your little nautical voyage," Evans cynically remarked. "Maybe someday, if ya' live through this ordeal, you wick-dicks can deposit all your savings in one of the *Egg Harbor's* many riverbanks! Ha, ha, ha!"

"Hello again!" despicable Dave Littlefield very arrogantly and facetiously greeted. "I guess it's now time for some more *Jack Daniels* chug-a-luggin' for you two nauseous worms, who aren't good enough to be hideous vermin."

News and I were rudely flung to the deck, and the impact nearly broke my coconut open. Our maws were again forced open, and generous portions of *Jack Daniels* were soon rolling-down our throats, and dripping from our unreceptive lips. But then, I was totally unprepared for the next torture that the Deltas and the Taus had arranged. Two women's nylon stockings were stretched over our tortured heads, making News and me both appear to be amateur bank robbers on the prowl. And next, to add to the mounting indignity, Tomasello and I were pulled-off the *Delta Alpha Queen* and plunked-down onto a formerly abandoned dock. Even in my groggy' state of mind, I felt like a Nazi prisoner, vulnerable and violated, and I never wanted to go out drinking or playing touch football with News Tomasello ever again.

"You duped crotch-smellers were just my *cabin* boys when you were recoverin' downstairs," Dave Littlefield declared. "So now, you're both gonna' be my official cover-boy *Log Cabin* Lambdas! Ha, ha, ha, ha! You ignoramus Lambda Phi's are livin' somewhere between the cannibal-savage level and the barbarian-warrior state of existence. Ha, ha, ha, ha!"

George Evans, the Sumo monsters, and the eight rival fraternity members, all standing on the dock, each held full bottles of sticky *Log Cabin* maple syrup, which was then generously squirted, applied, rubbed, and smeared all over our heads, facial nylons, white tee-shirts, arms, wrists, and hands, until all fifteen bottles of the gooey substance had been emptied onto the two innocent victims.

"Now, don't jerk-off, or you'll find yourselves even more sticky than ya' already are right now!" Sal Walker of the Tau Kappas hooted, as everybody, except the stoic-faced Sumo wrestlers, chuckled their rear-ends off, heckling at our encumbered presence. Then, George Evans cut our bonds with a sharp blade of his penknife; escorted News and me onto a wobbly dock, and the fifteen temporary sailors boarded the moored *Delta Alpha Queen;* the engines were restarted; the ropes untied, and the yacht eased-off the dock; turned ninety-degrees, and then headed due west in the direction of tranquil Mays Landing, the majestic *Sugar Hill Bed and Breakfast/Restaurant,* and the aforementioned *Riverside Marina.*

My eyes detected through the meshed nylon stocking a narrow dirt path that led from the shaky dock, which was nestled in a remote cove situated between thickets on both sides, and a dirt lane, which eventually led to a wider trail. 'It's too bad I'm not sober enough to enjoy this particular communion with nature,' I thought, when I finally realized that my breathing had been labored, and that I was experiencing difficulty inhaling through the tight-fitting nylon stocking, and also through the thick coating of *Log Cabin Maple Syrup*. The debilitating Draconian punishment being rendered upon News and me seemed entirely too severe and unwarranted. 'How come Soblinski and Hoppy are never subjected to this kind of barbarism from the Deltas and the Taus?' my beleaguered brain conjectured and wondered.

"Hey, J.W., slow down!" my Lambda companion panted and pleaded through his syrup-coated nylon stocking. "I feel like a wall that's just been plastered!" News logically communicated, still joking while being totally ripped. "Don't leave me *stranded,* J.W.! I'll feel like bad uncooked spaghetti! I feel like a super-brave frontiersman! 'Davy, Davy Crockett, king of the wild frontier'!" News inharmoniously sang in remembrance of Fess Parker.

"News, we'll ascend that knoll up ahead and survey the general area," I recommended. "Then, we'll try and get these damned messy, saturated nylon stockings off our abused heads. There's a painted sign up a little further that reads 'Sundown Beach'. News, we'll stop at the sign and hold it to balance our feet and attempt to get cleaned-up a bit. Pretty soon the sun will be going-down, and the temperature will really drop, so we gotta' act in a hurry," I suggested. "I just hope that there's a pay phone around here, and that the change in my pocket isn't too gooey to drop down the damned slot."

My Lambda Phi colleague and I mutually struggled and reached the top of the small hill, and just as I was about to endeavor removing Tomasello's sticky nylon head mask, three very discernible female screams were heard, and then the words "Voyeurs!" "Zombies!" "Monsters!" "Perverts!" "Molesters!" were perceived and being hollered all around and beneath *our* high vantage point. Four naked, appalled, and petrified women began throwing rocks and stones at us, as if we were ancient lepers or martyrs, while four other more modest nude damsels ran for cover into the foliage. Two chubby men dashed towards Tomasello and me with canoe paddles, and the nudist camp nutcases commenced thwacking-away, knocking both News and me off balance. And then, Tommy and I jointly tumbled-down the knoll, rolling into a cluster of sticker and briar bushes.

Feeling no pain from our alcohol, we rolled-out of our temporary entrapment and awkwardly bolted-down a side trail, until we coincidentally collided with three additional young naked women, who were rushing from their campsite to investigate the commotion that had just occurred out near the knoll.

"Ahhh!" the three skinny-dipping wenches crazily shrieked, as if the girls had just encountered human-sized Martians or Insectians.

"Ahhh!" News and I both simultaneously screamed, since we were quite shocked and frightened right out of our gooky, sticky underwear, and also right out of our syrup-stained tennis shoes, too.

Tomasello and I changed our direction, and veered to the right, staggering down a curvy dirt path, and hobbling through a pristine stretch of woods, where we unintentionally jolted into two bellicose naked men, who apparently were the constables for the exclusive

Sundown Beach Nudist Colony. Shouts abounded all over the formerly silent forest, and my companion and I clumsily, and almost blindly, scurried forth, until our bodies finally, by sheer luck, escaped the mass hysteria.

At last, the gallant, escaping Lambdas arrived at Somers Point-Mays Landing Road, and we managed to tear-off our syrup-drenched nylon stocking masks. Luckily, we located a pay phone outside of a dilapidated country gas station, and my scared voice humbly called the inimitable Goose Restuccio at his isolated Winslow mansion, and subsequently, my humble tone begged G.R. to be our "Good Samaritan", who would drive-over to Mays Landing and retrieve and deliver us from Nudist Camp evil.

"I feel like a complete asshole for lettin' those two freshman Delta pledges con us into this deplorable disaster," News sulked in the October shadows of a pine tree woods, just off the highway. "The jerkweeds really got their sweet revenge with this damned sticky syrup smeared all over our abused bodies. J.W., I never wanna' visit a damned pancake house again! Never!"

"This wouldn't have ever happened if Abrams and Hoppy hadn't taken those revealin' sex photos and mailed them to the feckless deans," I bitterly complained. "We're sufferin' revenge persecution big time, simply because Bob and Hoppy violated the peace that the chicken coop parties were supposed to create."

A half-hour later, while News and I were both freezing and commiserating, Goose showed-up in his father's green Chevy pickup truck. When we attempted to clamber inside, Restuccio chastised us for being unfit to ride up front with him while existing in *our* disheveled, unkempt, and humiliating condition.

"You stupid bastards!" Goose castigated and denigrated. "Just look at ya'! I can't understand it! Niggers wanna' become white, and you and those fuckin' asshole nudists over at Sundown Beach wanna' become tanned, dark-skinned, shit-heads. Just look' at all that fuckin' suntan lotion you two freaks have smeared all over ya'! Ya' both look worse than fuckin' asshole punk greasers!"

"Goose," I meekly answered. "It's not suntan oil that's on our skin. It's damned *Log Cabin Maple Syrup."*

"Now I know you warped jerk-offs are really fucked-up!" Restuccio chided. "First ya' wanna' save the world with all the niggers and spics abusin' it. Then, ya' wanta' waste your time in Africa tearin' down mud and straw huts, and buildin' those niggers over livin' their marble palaces. And after ya' turn the entire economy over to Martin Luther King, ya' wanna' smear yourselves with maple syrup and look like niggers, besides! And every time ya' run into that jungle gorilla George Evans, just think about what the fuck happens to ya!' What the fuck's wrong with you' dipstick, dip-shit-heads?" Goose cursed in true-blue Restuccio fashion. "There's more brains floating-around inside a fuckin' empty cesspool!"

"We'll explain everything once we get cleaned-up and into some decent clothes," I promised. "Just don't take us to a pancake house!"

"Okay, but you' daffy jungle bunny wannabe's gotta' ride in the back and sit on the tar-pullins I had laid out for ya'. Now fuckin' climb onto the tailgate and sit inside like two fuckin' embalmed mummies, putting your asses on the goddamned canvas. And don't touch anything back there, except maybe your *Log Cabin* assholes and your miniature, shrunken dicks! Then, tomorrow morning, I can take you fuck-heads over to Geets Diner in Williamstown for a delicious pancake breakfast!"

My fatigued and half-zonked companion hopped-on, and I soon obediently followed suite. Goose slammed-closed the shiny new tailgate, and our rescue hero had one final message to say.

"Now, when we get to Hammonton," Restuccio instructed, "I'm gonna' run the truck through Al's Automatic Car Wash, and you two dunces will come-out spic and span, and please look more like a couple of spics instead of like a couple of goddamned niggers, ya' stupid Watusi wanna' be's. Why don't ya' imitate Elvis Presley, or Fabian, or Frankie Avalon, or some other white nitwits, instead of lookin' like goddamned Sammy Davis Jr. and Ray Charles."

True to his word, when we reached Hammonton, Goose pulled into Al's Automatic Car Wash, paid the flabbergasted attendant the standard fee, and then drove his father's truck (with us sitting in the back cargo area) through the series of well-synchronized machines. Tomasello and I soon were being violently deluged with cold water and soap; being brutally buffered, buffeted, walloped, cleaned, and next rinsed. At the end of the lengthy car wash line, finally, News and I received really fantastic blowjobs.

After Goose returned to his parents' mansion in Winslow, News and I changed out of our syrupy clothes, and Restuccio gave us some of his knock-around-jeans and sweatshirts to wear on top of our newly-acquired clean underwear. Our tennis shoes escaped the clothes washer and dryer unscathed, and upon inspection, were in fairly good condition. And although News Tomasello and I later still frequented Seedy's Bar, we Lambda Phi's never again played another game of touch football at *Glassboro State College*.

Chapter 31
"The Toga Initiation Ceremony"

On Tuesday morning, News and I were so sore and fatigued from our horrible *Sundown Beach Nudist Colony* ordeal that we played hooky and stayed in our beds until two in the afternoon. Goose had driven us from Winslow to the *Bosshart Hall* parking lot, and after thanking Restuccio for his indispensable assistance, I drove News in the duplicate white Impala back to 38 South Main. After we ttook hot showers and shaved, we dressed into fresh apparel and shuffled-over to Angelo's Diner for an afternoon breakfast of bacon and eggs.

"I once jokingly told Miss Sankins that my two favorite British writers were Sir Francis Bacon and Sir Henry Eggs," I informed News while we were sitting at the counter. "But then, the despicable witch indignantly remarked that my brain was 'scrambled' because I probably *'poached'* on other people's property. And now, I see exactly what the old hag meant by her egg allusions, with *us* getting mauled and violated while accidentally trespassin' into that bizarre Mays Landing nudist colony."

"Don't make me laugh, J.W. Tomasello begged. "My whole body aches every time I move a muscle. And the Deltas strategy committee had their scheme all figured-out to the minute. The nudists leave their' secluded sun-bathin' area in early October, just after four in the afternoon, and that's when we were deserted in the remote cove at Sundown Beach," TNT deducted and determined. "The uninvited visitors, who just happened to be us, would *barge* in on people still paradin' around in their birthday suits, and then we would finally stumble upon the sun-bathers meandering-around in the flesh, so to speak. Pretty ingenious plan, huh?"

"Sort of ingenious, but more disingenuous on the Delta and Tau's part!" I conceded and qualified. "But News, I hate to miss Dr. Maurice Trenoff's 'Tests and Measurements' class this morning. His exams' are even worse than Sankins's were. He's gonna' put a big dent in my cumulative average this semester, because I'll be lucky to escape that academic tedium of his with a meager D. And I'm workin' my tail off just to maintain that low D average! I mean, the little nut-job has a Napoleon complex that won't quit, and the midget prof' takes his animosity out on any male or female student that's over five-foot-three-inches tall."

"His nickname is Maurie the Mole," News confidentially related, "and his physical appearance and stature seem to confirm *that* appropriate appellation and label. And J.W., you aren't the only one sweatin' that rigged course. Abrams and Hoppy have both complained to Big Al about Trenoff being a nasty tyrant. I'm sure glad I have Dr. Rankin for 'Tests and Measurements'."

"Hey News, I'm listenin' a lot to that Beach Boy song 'Little Deuce Coupe', and I'm beginnin' to like that California surfin' and car sound a lot," I commented, just to get my mind off of the cruel mental excruciation of fail-happy Maurie the Mole. "And that Jan and Dean are hittin' it big with their upbeat number 'Surf City', soundin' almost identical to the Beach Boys' four-part harmony. I guess the pair use overdubbin' to produce their unique trademark sound, bein' only the two guys doin' the vocals."

"I think you're right about that theory," Tomasello concurred. "But most music nowadays is bubblegum soundin', like Lesley Gore's 'It's My Party' and her new song 'It's Judy's Turn to Cry'. I think I'd rather have another misadventure at Sundown Beach with those loony *beach boys* beatin' us with canoe paddles than to listen to that cute *Juicy Fruit* stuff on the radio for more than ten-minutes."

"And if it's not white bubblegum lyrics, it's then gotta' be black bubblegum music played on the radio," I added. "Motown songs like 'Crossfire' and 'South Street' by the Orlons; and 'Heat Wave' by Martha and the Vandellas, and 'Please Mr. Postman' by the Marvelettes thoroughly prove my point."

"And don't forget 'Deep Purple' by Nino Tempo and April Stevens," News used as an example. "And 'Sugar Shack' by Jimmy Gilmer and the Fireballs, who aren't exactly 'Great Balls of Fire' by Jerry Lee Lewis, and'…"

"And don't forget 'Denise' by Randy and the Rainbows, and 'Candy Girl' by the Four Seasons," I contributed. "And then there's Bobby Vinton's slow numbers 'Blue on Blue' and 'Blue Velvet' that can't hold a candle to Elvis's '50s slow dance hits like 'Love Me Tender' and 'Can't Help Falling in Love with You'."

"Even Dion is turnin' bubblegum with 'Donna the Prima Donna'!" News keenly observed and honestly stated. "Say, J.W., do ya' remember that hot July night back in 1960 when we were with Jives and we drag-raced Dion and the Belmonts in their white Thunderbird all the way from Atlantic City halfway up to New York on the *Garden State Parkway*. Jives was drivin' his old black and white Plymouth, and Dion blew us off the road with his hot wheels, and we then got that flat tire goin' ninety-five!" News recalled. "If that wasn't playin' Russian Roulette' with Death, then I don't know exactly what is! Now J.W., how's your love life goin'?"

"Not too good right now, News!" I grimly confessed. "Joanne and Peachy act like they're livin' on another planet than I am. Every time I see one of the beauties, the gals look the other way. I think they hear all of this gossip about the Lambdas' exploits and then the dolls get jealous that they're 'nice girls' and can't invade nudist colonies; or pour shrimp, fish and unfertilized eggs down enemy chimneys; or sponsor sellout striptease shows at the Glassboro Theater; or effectively harass the thug Deltas and the dastardly Taus with *their* own revealing pornographic still pictures."

"So, J.W.," News interrupted my rambling speech, "Joanne and Peachy are intimidated by your legendary adventures with the Lambdas, and you're intimidated by Alexis Terranenkov and Nancy Danns, who both can easily body slam you ten-times in a row without even takin' a deep breath, by first givin' ya' an airplane spin. Frankly, it sounds like you need the services of a sex psychiatrist."

"There is one girl on campus I really think is cute, though," I divulged an intimate secret to my closest friend. "Her name is Candie Davison."

"Wow! She's in Dr. Tyler's 'World Geography' class with me," News conveyed, "and I don't think she's attached to anyone right now. I talk to her before every class session, and the luscious babe admitted to me that she truly likes the Lambdas wild and crazy, hell-bent-for-leather life style."

"Do me a mega-favor News," I requested. "Tell Candie I'd like to take her out past Pitman and do some pumpkin stealin' like I did with Joanne and with Peachy last October on separate expeditions. See what she says? And tell her you're goin' on the same exploration with Elaine Hill, after I ask her to participate for your sake. We'll double-date on a pumpkin heist mission, and the girls will get to feel what it's really like, bein' boss Lambda Phi dates."

"Okay, J.W.," News consented in an accommodating tone of voice. "It's a deal! Candie Davison might turn you down, but not turn me down askin' a date for you, and the same goes for you askin' Elaine for me, instead of me doin' it by myself. Why's everything so damned screwed-up all the time? But how about a particular date for the pumpkin pilferin'?"

"What about Saturday night, October 12rh, *Columbus Day,"* I offered. "We'll pretend we're horny country bumpkins stealin' some country pumpkins! Hey, News. I'm a poet and don't even know it. I can't wait until the next edition of the *Avant* comes out. Paul says I have two creative poems bein' published."

"Well, J.W. If ya' aspire to be an author some day," Tomasello theorized and prattled, "ya' gotta' start somewhere like publishing original poetry in the *Avant*. Poetry and teachin' junior-high English seem to be your personal springboards to the future."

Much to my elation, Candie Davison accepted my invitation through News intercession to go pumpkin-hunting, and Elaine Hill was amenable to accompanying News on the slated grand lark. On October 12th at eight p.m., I drove News and Elaine over to Candie's apartment above a hardware store on *322* (coming into Glassboro from Williamstown), and just a half-mile closer to town than Glassboro Bedding, existing on the opposite side of the highway. And I was glad that Tomasello didn't bring-up the "Ode to the Bunk" salute that had been invented by Ron Carputis, which would have had a negative impact upon Candie and Elaine. And that bit of Lambda ritualistic stupidity might've spoiled the entire evening.

The black-haired doll looked terrific in her blue jeans and black wool sweater, and it being an Indian summer evening made the crisp evening air quite enchanting, with the harvest moon rising above the horizon, displaying its autumnal splendor. News began conversing his familiar monologue about how moonlight is not moonlight at all, but simply reflected sunlight bouncing-off the lunar surface, because the moon doesn't generate its own energy, heat, and light like the sun does. So, I had to curtail Tomasello's monotonous academic eloquence and talk about the important art of pumpkin stealing.

"Now girls," I interrupted my colleague's ludicrous commentary, "and you too News, we'll obtain the pumpkins from a field I've hit before, just west of Pitman. Candie and Elaine can hold the two flashlights I've brought along, and News, you and I will cut the stems to the four largest pumpkins we can find in the patch, and then we'll transport the purloined produce back to Glassboro."

"Isn't stealin' a little risky?" Candie asked. "And aren't we takin' away from the farmer's profits?"

"Not really, Candie. News's family has a farm, and my folks have a farm market with plenty of its own pumpkins," I smartly answered. "And believe me when I say there's an excessive number of pumpkins layin' out in that field that'll never be picked, and the owner will never miss the ones we'll snare tonight."

My heart began pounding a little faster when the Wibbage DJ played Bobby Vee's "The Night Has a Thousand Eyes", suggesting that our clandestine orange-vegetable hunt might come under the grower's or the police's scrutiny, and when News brought-up the parallel between the song and what we were commencing to enact, I just knew that those feminine hormones were rushing all throughout Candie and Elaine's succulent, curvaceous bodies.

When we reached the remote country road where the selected pumpkin field had been situated, I dimmed the headlights and slowly drove down a sandy farm lane. After stopping, we carefully exited the white Impala with our four individual flashlights that I had brought along with two utilitarian penknives, and we clandestinely proceeded right to work under the gorgeous harvest moon. It did not require more than a minute to locate four nice-sized, plump pumpkins. News and I sheared the rotund objects from their vines and handed one each to Candie and to Elaine. No sooner had we performed that elementary theft that shotgun blasts were heard, originating from the vicinity of the farmer's homestead.

The girls panicked, dropped their' flashlights and pumpkins in fright, and the four trespassers swiftly sprinted back to the Chevy with News and me carrying our penknives, along with our two orange trophies. After jumping into my reliable auto' amidst great excitement and anxiety, I turned the ignition, sped backwards in reverse and escaped the premises as more shots were being fired in our direction.

"That was the most thrilling thing that ever happened to me!" Candie gasped as the well-endowed honey slid over and grabbed my right arm for security. "J.W., you really do live on the wild side!"

"J.W., you've done it again!" Elaine praised. "But Candie and I dropped and lost your two flashlights also, with our two prized pumpkins were left behind, too!"

"That's perfectly alright, Elaine!" I consoled. "I'll just buy two new flashlights tomorrow at one of the Glassboro hardware stores. And as far as the dropped pumpkins are concerned," I maintained, "you and Candie can keep the two for your rooms that News and I had bravely bagged."

It was a glorious romantic night beneath the Indian summer harvest moon and the twinkling stars, and naturally, I just happened to have a quart of *Southern Comfort* and four fresh sealed plastic cups conveniently stored in my car's trunk. And we all got a little bombed that night, and the girls were unbelievably cooperative after their emotionally draining pumpkin field tribulation, and of being fired at with a powerful shotgun, so News and I were wonderfully rewarded and treated to a fabulous "make-out city".

On Tuesday, October 15th, I was sitting in the Co-op studying my complicated "Tests and Measurements" textbook in preparation for Dr. Maurie Trenoff's next wholly incomprehensible, reprehensible examination, when News entered the most popular scene on campus. Tomasello had a wide frown on his face that immediately telegraphed forthcoming bad news.

"Why the sour puss?" I curiously asked. "Did you wash your face in vinegar?" I joked to my Lambda associate, using a classic Bo Jalonec Levittown salutation.

News reported to me some very disturbing and disconcerting information. Candie Davison, Joanne Berenato, and Peachy Wilcox were all quite disenchanted with me, and Elaine Hill and Loretta Sacco were especially pissed-off at Tomasello over recent campus-related developments. Then, News gave me the nightmarish details of the melodramatic catastrophe that could really sabotage my ongoing, complex *GSC* love life.

"Elaine Hill found-out from an anonymous Lambda that Goose Restuccio had paid-off the farmer a hundred-bucks to leave his house and come-out shootin' his shotgun, precisely when the girls stooped to pick-up their pumpkins," News divulged as my despondent buddy sucked more air into his lungs. "And then, Elaine told the story to Joanne, Peachy, to Candie, and to Loretta. And next, Joanne and Peachy compared notes with Candie and Elaine, and the five chicks soon realized that the same thing happened to all of them on different pumpkin hunting expeditions, two of which were conducted to the same farm last fall. What a friggin' ugly vexation this entire fiasco has evolved into!"

"Oh my God, News!" I gasped. "I've learned that *that* pumpkin farmer has a bad gamblin' habit and owes plenty of loan sharkin' money to Goose's father," I recollected and reviewed. "So, as a favor to Goose, the farmer goes along with the prank to get another hundred-bucks to put-down on the ponies. That farmer must be a relative of Mario, the way he's got the horse-racing fever burnin' holes inside his pockets! Last fall, I had called Goose on the horn, and I had learned that the future penitentiary occupant had set-up the previous pumpkin-theft adventures."

"So, what do we do now that the prettiest campus girls realize we've been *disingenuous* with them, all-the-while pretendin' to be courageous thieves?" News anxiously asked, while utilizing a sophisticated vocabulary word he had mastered in *Fundamentals of Communications, 101."*

"I'll bet it was that egotistical rogue, Bill Elderberry, who told Elaine about our perfect pumpkin-grabbin' scheme," I speculated and indirectly accused, risking the chance of bearing false witness.

"This seems like something that *that* garrulous scoundrel Wild Bill would do, either accidentally or intentionally."

"J.W., I can't live with a guilty conscience any longer," Tomasello confessed. "I was the one that told Elaine about Goose payin' off the farmer. She seemed to think it was funny at first, but apparently, when she talked to the others girls, and the astute dorm girls detected the same pattern in *their* past experiences, the chicks all became pissed-off and felt used."

"However, News, two damned wrongs don't make a right," I said, using a hackneyed cliché. "It was wrong for us to deceive the girls in the first place with the clever trick, and not tell the babes the truth, and it's now wrong for me to blame you for disclosin' the essence of our secret deception. You're forgiven, News," I sincerely expressed. "But my biggest problem is that I just know I'm now gonna' flunk Trenoff's freakin' test that's positively impossible to pass, even when I'm enjoyin' good mental health, without any Dr. Attleburg's special help."

I did fail Dr. Trenoff's hundred-and-fifty question conundrum, which included lengthy standard deviation formulas and perplexing hypothetical situations, all of which made the prospective teachers in his seminar want to attend undertaking school instead of *GSC*. But as I struggled with the last several Promethean-type word problems, I had a brainstorm about how the Lambdas could get retribution on the Delta Alphas and the Tau Kappas for the disastrous Mays Landing "yachting incident at Sundown Beach".

I looked-around Trenoff's classroom and noticed Bob Abrams on my left, squirming in his desk, and on my right side, I observed Dave Littlefield and Sal Walker reacting to intense emotional duress through their very evident body language. After class, I presented my strategy to Bob, and after getting Abrams's approval, I planned to confer with Goose about strategy and organization, and then along with my fellow Lambdas assistance, we would gloriously raid and ruin the Deltas and the Taus upcoming initiation dinners.

"Where did you get *that* great idea?" Timmy asked me inside the Co-op the following afternoon, as News conscientiously munched on his delectable *TastyKake Krimpets*. "You sometimes seem to be a fountain of wisdom."

"I became extremely frustrated failin' Trenoff's exam's myriad cryptograms, so I used my bottled-up mental energy to devise the classic scheme," I honestly revealed. "It all goes back to the dock at Sundown Beach," I stated to Tomasello and Amoro. "Even though I was stewed at the time, I still can remember Littlefield callin' News and me *barbarians,* along with the other non-present Lambdas, when *his* classy yacht left the dock. And when I looked-over at Littlefield and at Walker in Trenoff's house of emotional pain," I added, using an imaginative metaphor, "then it all came together in my mind. The Lambdas are gonna' really become contemporary barbarians and actively spoil the Deltas and the Taus' grandiose initiation ceremonies. And don't forget," I reminded my avid listeners, "on that night the Deltas and the Taus all dress-up in togas like Roman Senators, while they're supposed to be bona fide Greek fraternities."

"Yeah, you'd think they'd at least be historically accurate," News agreed. "But in all fairness, some ancient Greeks are portrayed in murals, on wall frescos, and on pottery, wearin' robes, in addition to others bein' shown wearin' tunics."

"And the deans divide-up on initiation banquet night, and attend both catered dinners at the Delta House on Harvard, and at the Tau House on Academy," Timmy ascertained from past memory. "And the families of all the Deltas and the Taus, and their girlfriends, also attend the separate-but-simultaneous dinner ceremonies. It's the ideal time to hit the impostors by surprise," Timmy imagined and stated. "Just like George Washington and his *Continental Army* did to the surprised British and Hessians at Trenton on *Christmas Eve.* G.W. attacked the redcoats and their German mercenaries on a holiday at night, when the enemy soldiers were all half-tuned, and when the British least expected an unbridled assault."

"And when the two marvelous Lambda Phi forays become big news on campus," News hypothesized and related, "then our reputations will be fully restored. J.W., I predict that after the dual raids are executed, Candie, Joanne, and Peachy will all go crazy over you, and Elaine and Loretta will again idolize my handsome face on enlarged photos tacked and hung on their dorm' room walls."

"Maybe you can get Alexis Terranenkov to become an honorary Lambda for one night," News mused and facetiously articulated to me. "That gorgeous Russian doll is big enough to be an Amazon, and she'd scare the hell out of Littlefield and Walker when she drops that Mae West persona, showing her true lustful, bloodthirsty, savage warrior instincts. That blonde babe could probably body slam all twelve Japanese Sumo wrestlers, and George Evan, too!"

"Stop breakin' my stones into tiny pebbles!" I threatened News with a clenched fist. "Now all we gotta' decide is whether we wanna' be barbarian Huns, Vandals, or Visigoths. That's our next essential responsibility."

The Delta Alphas and the Tau Kappas traditionally held their formal initiation dinner the second Saturday in November, and so, the Lambda Phi' clandestine activities were all secretly geared to culminate on November 9th. Goose even got Mario motivated to participate in the grand mischief, after advancing DiMaris a hundred bucks to play the ponies at the *Atlantic City Race Course*. And Goose and Bob Abrams liked the plan so much that the Lamdna Phi honchos used their contacts and commissioned four chartered bus loads to efficiently conduct the dual raids with *Hammonton Bakers* disguised as Visigoths; with *Philadelphia Mummers* clad as Huns, and with Mafia-types and Lambdas (and other Lambdas coming down from other colleges) also disguised, dressed as Huns; and with those invading groups being shuttled into Glassboro as eager bus passengers. The stage had been set for a spellbinding, chaotic, simultaneous, two-setting major disruption.

"Okay, J.W.," Goose consented at 38 South Main on Friday night, November 8th. "Two buses of *Mummers* and outside Lamp-das are gonna' raid the fuckin' Krappa Episalong House at 8:30 tomorrow night, and two buses of *Hammonton Baker*s, pro' wrestlers, and Mafia guys are gonna' dress like those fuzzy Fizzy-*golfs* (goths, Visigoths) and hit the fuckin' Delta Alphie Ortega House like a white tornado. And the 38 South Main Lamp-das are gonna' be with my group on Harvard, and the Abrams chicken coop Lamp-das are gonna' join the Academy Street craziness. Jesus Christ, J.W.!" Restuccio exclaimed. "It's like I'm goin' to fuckin' college without havin' to lift-up a goddamned borin' textbook! Maybe I'll be able to 'finish' my education and get a fuckin' hairy diploma at finishin' school?"

"What about the police?" I worried and asked. "How are we goin' to keep them out of the caper with over a hundred brawling guys, dressed as barbarians, bein' involved?"

"A few of the *Baker* football guys know a couple of your local cops here in town," Goose explained, "and the word's gonna' get-out that there's a few *ass-in-nine* college pranks commin' off tomorrow night that's not gonna' fuckin' injure or kill anybody. And the town Chief-of-Police doesn't want to get involved in any goddamned college discipline affairs, and the top-cop wants to keep his officers out of them, too, even though the two raids are gonna' happen off of your goddamned lily-white campus."

"Well, I suppose we'll need that kind of *laissez faire* situation to successfully pull-off the dual intrusions," I noted. "It's hard to effectively disguise four buses of savage-lookin' barbarians rumblin' into town to secretly conduct two separate sieges."

"Lousy fair?" Goose rankled. "What the fuck kind of jerked-off carnival is that? We might make the raids into a fuckin' wild circus, but not into any goddamned lousy fair! That fuckin' *You-Gander* nigger circus isn't commin' back to your fucked-up campus, is it?"

"No, the Africans aren't, Goose, but I value anything you say," I acquiesced, not wanting to provide a lengthy definition and explanation of the unique French/American phrase "laissez faire".

Goose promptly showed-up at 38 South Main on Saturday night, November 9th, and distributed authentic-looking Visigoth loincloths, strapped sandals, and fuzzy fur apparel that the bored rich dude had rented from a costume supplier in Philly'. "And we're gonna' wear these fuckin' ugly African masks, too, that would scare the shit outa' Sonny Liston, Jersey Joe Walcott, or even Joe Louis!" Restuccio related. "And for fifteen-minutes or so, we all can feel like Swahilis when we crash into the shit-eatin' dinner party over on Harvey, er, I meant to say, Harvard."

After we donned our primitive-looking Visigoth togs, Lambda Elderberry announced to Lambda Keiler: "Big Al, you look like Charlemagne in that furry outfit!" And Restuccio butted-in and replied, "Damn it, Wild Bill; speak fuckin' English instead of nigger Swahili. Not even American niggers over here in America know who that fuckin' Charlotte Mane was, or is!"

At 8:25, the seven 38 South Main Street Lambda Phi's entered Goose's black van, which the Junior Don had borrowed from a Mafia friend over in Berlin, and Restuccio drove back street Oakwood Avenue across the railroad tracks to University Road, and then the coy driver parked the vehicle a block away from targeted Harvard Road. Three minutes later, two chartered buses, loaded with *Hammonton Bakers* and Philadelphia Mafia members, along with a dozen second-tier professional wrestlers disguised as savage Visigoths, rumbled into town, and soon turned the corner.

When the buses' doors opened, the seven 38 South Mainers left Goose (who was dressed as an honorary Visigoth) in the black van, and we joined-up with our hundred or so fellow barbarians. After donning our hideous African masks, Mario lustily yelled, "Charge!" And in an instant, we all anxiously sprinted towards the Delta House, screaming like a contingent of carnivorous cannibals. The Deltas' front doors were flung open, and Mario blasted directly into a Japanese Sumo wrestler, knocking the astonished brute clear across the room. Shouting, shrieking, and wild exultation abounded, as the hundred-and-seven screaming plunderers interrupted the dinner ceremonies in a most hostile and ferocious fashion.

The Mafia Visigoths actualy resembled authentic raiders, carrying water pistol machine guns filled with a pepper solution that made their victims' eyes tear after *they* had been sprayed directly in the face. The face treatments had forced the recipients to stagger around the chamber like blind guests, with their hands cupped over their eyes and noses. And, of course, the second-tier professional wrestlers that had tagged along with the Philadelphia Mafia figures were applying agonizing submission holds onto Dave Littlefield, Sam Lista, Vince Rogers, Stu Dixon, and to the other designated Greek Deltas being caught wearing Roman togas.

Our grotesque African masks were also rather frightening to behold, and every woman in the raided fraternity house was absolutely terrorized, as the female guests scurried and skittered all over the main room in quest of sanctuary from the ongoing melee. Several tables were ruthlessly overturned, and at least two Sumo wrestlers flew by me after four *Baker* linemen collaborated to toss the Oriental monsters around like ordinary garden salad.

And the Mafia guys were denting jaws and chins all over the turmoil-oriented room, as the Glassboro invasion almost turned into a second *Boston Massacre,* even though Harvard Road was hundreds of miles away from Cambridge, Massachusetts. When all resistance to our frenetic aggression had ceased, the hundred and seven warriors promptly exited the Delta Alpha Omega House in a hurry, just like water flowing through a funnel, and when I turned-around before exiting the ransacked edifice, I observed George Evans hanging onto a chandelier, after being tossed-up into the rafters by several contemporary, very incensed Visigoths.

The visiting barbarians all boarded their respective buses in a jiffy, and the amused drivers soon made hasty beelines in separate directions to furtively escape the town's geographic borders. Goose drove his seven disciples to the Aura chicken coop, where we had a change of clothing waiting, and after the Abrams' Lambdas arrived and announced that their assault on the Tau Kappa Epsilon House over on Academy had also been a "devastating success", we all changed into our standard college attire and enjoyed imbibing some potent hard-whiskey shots.

"I'll take these Fizzy-golfs' outfits back to Philly' tomorrow morning," Restuccio announced to his jubilant, raucous listeners. "So tomorrow, there'll be no fuckin' link between the two slick raids and the cool-as-a-ghoul Lamp-da Phi Stigmas."

"Goose, even when you're serious, you're ten-times funnier than Bob Hope ever was!" Big Al complimented. "You're funnier than Red Skelton, Milton Berle, and Jackie Gleason all put together, and then multiplied by seven!"

"I always wondered what the fuck it would be like goin' to college," Goose remarked, "and it ain't turnin' out to be too fuckin' bad, as long as I don't have to listen to any teachers' fucked-up bull-shit! Say, how do you turkeys stay cooped-up in this *fowl* (foul) place for more than an hour? This smelly shack gives me fuckin' *cost-throw-foe-bee-ya."*

"Well, Goose," News declared to everyone's heightened delight and merriment. "We first let ya' visit here at the coop so that you can be cooped-up, and then you have to respectfully listen to all of our dumb verbal chicken shit!"

Chapter 32
"Washington and Cape May"

Monday, November 11th, News Tomasello, Timmy Amoro, Ron Carputis, and I were sitting in the Co-op at noon and chattering about the incredible dual sackings of the Delta Alpha Omega and the Tau Kappa Epsilon houses, during those fraternities most-exalted events of the year, the initiation of new pledges into the college-sanctioned Greek organizations. Evidently, our notorious Lambda prowess had also infiltrated into the student body's central gossip.

"Everyone's starin' at us as if we're immortal Olympian gods," Ron noticed and shared. "By Jupiter, if you're Zeus, J.W., and if News is the sea deity Poseidon, not living up in Neptune, New Jersey, and if mercurial Timmy here is the messenger god Hermes, then I must certainly be Apollo."

"Ron, you don't have to *apolo*gize for anything," News laughed like an inebriated hyena. "I mean, who can explain how fate operates? Saturday night we were Visigoths, and Monday morning we're now Greek gods, when all we really crave is bein' legitimate Greek fraternity brothers."

"And J.W.," Ron Carputis (alias Apollo) filled the temporary communications void, "the Deltas and the Taus are no longer destroyin' your Chevy because they think it has the ability to rein*car*nate itself. No sooner is it demolished, that a week later, it magically comes back to life in better condition than before your chariot had been reshaped twice by enemy sledgehammers."

"And the Deltas and the Tau's long faces are lookin' more and more just like the deans' frowns and grimaces every day," Timmy generalized. "It's just like the animal behavior ya' see on one of those special educational TV documentaries, mostly sponsored by *National Geographic.*"

"If most of those exotic and ferocious animals they show on television specials live in Africa, Australia, Asia, and Alaska," News ruminated, "shouldn't the shows be sponsored by International Geographic, or perhaps presented by Inter-Continental Geographic, instead of *National Geographic!*"

Everyone except me ignored Tomasello's annoying, adolescent, irresponsible remark and attempted staying focused on the subject of Deltas and Taus that was originally being discussed. "Animal behavior in what way?" I wondered and asked Timmy.

"Well," Tim Amoro chimed-in and elaborated, "we've created anarchy inside the Deltas and inside the Taus, and they've got to respect *that* salient fact. It's a matter now of who's being dominant and who's bein' subordinate. The Deltas, the Taus and the deans now lower their heads and look the other way when confronted with *our* presence, just like weaker dogs, cats, and wolves show respect to the leaders of their packs by lowerin' their heads in submission, in recognition of a superior creature of their own species."

"Great analogy, Tim," I honestly complimented. "The rival frats' heads are always crestfallen, just like the deans are, now that ya' mention it. The dolts all probably wish that they were Lambda Phi's instead of what the hell they are. Even Ralph Crenshaw wishes he was a Lambda, but out of sheer stubbornness, I believe he's gonna' honor his word and join our ranks his senior year."

"It'll be easy recruitin' new blood into the organization now," Ronnie opined. "We'll be so 'swamped' with eager applicants that we'll think we're livin' in a damned *foggy* medieval loch, or gothic marsh, without any marshmallows to gobble."

"Then, we'd have to get the *fog* outa' there!" I laughed, while quoting my old Levittown friend, Bo Jalonec.

And next, News somehow wormed his way back into the serious conversation and driveled-on about how a tremendous riot had broken out at *Roosevelt Raceway* in Westbury, Long Island after six of eight trotters in the sixth-race were involved in a massive pile-up, just the day before the great Lambda raids on the Delta and the Tau Houses had mysteriously occurred.

"And guys," Tomasello boringly added an appendix to his monotonous spiel, "racing fans that had wagered on the daily double went bananas when the winner was declared from the remainin' two horses, neither of which was the favorite. Some irate spectators that lost their money became violent out of frustration," News reported. "The upset rioters set the damned grandstand on fire. Twenty people were seriously injured in the wild imbroglio, and the battered victims had to be taken-away in ambulances to area hospitals for treatment."

"News," Timmy admonished, "we're currently talkin' about the most fantastic fraternity house invasions ever in this college's undistinguished history, and you're tellin' us about an irrelevant riot at a Long Island race track! Who was there? Were Mario and that pumpkin farmer west of Pitman there, participatin' in the scuffle, because the mental cases lost money bettin'? Why's that big immaterial altercation on Long Island so damned important to you, sittin' here in Glassboro?" Amoro challenged. "Were your parents or siblings hurt during the Long Island pandemonium? Stop livin' life so vicariously! Why don't ya' just go eat a pound of doggy-doo and wash it down with a gallon and a half of cat piss!"

And then to symbolically exhibit our mutual disgust with News's loquacious, off-subject ramblings, the three of us stood and abandoned Tomasello at that Co-op booth. And when I looked around expecting to see News sitting there dejected, all deserted, and in deep rueful meditation, I really became pissed when I noticed Alexis Terranenkov and Nancy Danns move right in and sit with Tomasello at the booth's table in our absence, and commence consoling the temporarily disenfranchised Lambda pain-in-the-ass.

For the next few weeks, my heart was disconsolate for several reasons. All I could think about was failing Dr. Trenoff's extremely demanding "Tests and Measurements" seminar, and simultaneously losing the affections of Joanne Berenato, Peachy Wilcox, and Candie Davison, in spite of the now-infamous dual Lambda Phi Sigma incursions into enemy frat' territory.

Finally, after really feeling lugubrious about failing another Maurie the Mole exam' in the early afternoon of Friday, November 22nd, I arrived at the *College Hall* basement mail room; perfunctorily utilized the three-number combination; opened the mail box, and discovered no love letters from any of my former devoted flames. Out of frustration, I removed two pieces of junk mail in the form of Navy pilot literature; ripped-up the military propaganda in anger, and tossed the scraps into a nearby waste can. Then, I decided to trudge over to *Linden Hall,* and for once be sincere and sympathetic with Peachy Wilcox, whom I knew would agree to speak with me after I took the initiative and broke the icy silence.

When I entered the common area lounge of the girls' dorm', where males were permitted to visit female acquaintances, I immediately witnessed two-dozen girls crying, sobbing, weeping, and moaning. Peachy was standing there in tears, watching the black and white television screen with her fellow residents, and I couldn't comprehend what was the genesis of their great emotional anguish. And when I finally had the urge to approach Peachy, Miss Cape May must have sensed my presence, and the tear-laden blonde beauty turned-around, hugged me with all of her precious might, and whimpered incessantly in my arms.

"What's wrong?" I innocently asked as I glanced at the black and white console television and observed a solemn Walter Cronkite addressing his national viewers.

"Haven't you heard, J.W.?" Peachy cried. "President Kennedy's been shot in Dallas. He's been rushed to a local hospital," the blonde beauty sobbed. "But from all reports, the President has massive brain damage, and if he lives, his mind's gonna' exist in a vegetable state. Oh, how horrible! It's terrible! How grossly unfair!"

At that moment, my selfish grief about failing Dr. Trenoff's exam' seemed trivial and insignificant in comparison to the terrible blow and shock *our* country had just suffered. Tears welled-up in my eyes, and Peachy led me to a couch, where we both watched a spellbinding major tragedy unfolding right before our very eyes. And events on the television screen were evolving at mind-boggling speed with each additional news dispatch that came unedited into *CBS News,* and a half-hour or so later, with great sadness, a somber Walter Cronkite and a young network correspondent, Dan Rather, announced that President John F. Kennedy had been assassinated and had died at *Parkland Memorial Hospital.*

I was in knee-weakening shock, felt terribly light-headed, and all of us gathered inside the *Linden* dorm' room were virtually mesmerized by the stunning sequence of events that ensued. It was reported that Jackie Kennedy still was wearing her bloodstained pink suit on the presidential jet airplane, still on the tarmac, ironically at *Love Air Field* in Dallas. And then minutes later, Lyndon Baines Johnson was being sworn-in as the 36th President of the United States. And there was a small consolation of hope when news was reported that Texas Governor John B. Connally was expected to live, despite the severe rifle shot wounds he had sustained.

And shortly thereafter those horrible events had occurred (amidst much mayhem and consternation in downtown Dallas), a police officer named J.D. Tippit had been shot and killed. And then, a short while later, the city's police had apprehended a short, thin suspect in a center city movie theater believed to be associated with both recent murders. And minutes after *that* scenario, the arrested individual was identified as Lee Harvey Oswald. And throughout that series of grotesque events, Peachy sat there, tightly holding my hand, and I didn't quite know how to comfort her, being temporarily mentally paralyzed myself. And like Miss Cape May, I had been basically overwhelmed with both despair and desolation.

Everyone on campus was distressed and melancholy, all walking-around like hypnotized, mechanical zombies. I noticed that the flag on top of *College Hall* had already been lowered to half-mast. Even normally jovial News Tomasello and Timmy Amoro were affected by the general depression that had powerfully descended on, and enveloped, the entire *GSC* campus. And when it was announced over intercoms that classes would be cancelled on

Monday, November 25th, no one felt inclined to cheer. Fewer words were spoken because most words seemed hollow and self-serving, but from my own private experience, I knew exactly how everyone else was feeling and thinking.

When I finally returned to 38 South Main, Timmy had something powerful to relate that amazingly connected with my saddened psyche. I didn't know how long it took him to develop and fathom the meaningful understanding, but Amoro's message made a great deal of sense when my friend had mentioned it to News and me.

"Our academic education is not in touch with the real world," distraught Tim prefaced his deduction. "What happened to President Kennedy today in Dallas is part of the way the real-world functions, and *we* can't fully comprehend our reality, since we need to learn more about it in practical terms. Goose Restuccio knows the real world much better than any of us do," Timmy honestly conceded and then continued. "And there's plenty of evil out there in the real world that we don't perceive or understand, but Goose does. College sort of insulates us from hard reality, keeping us innocent and idealistic, and today, I finally figured-out that academics is just a big smokescreen, falsely protecting us from dangers we don't want to imagine!"

"You're positively spot-on, Timmy!" News verified. "College is like those hair-growth formulas for bald men ya' see on television. Our education only works if we can somehow apply the theory to real-life practice. These hair-growing formulas out on the market work, because when men use the products, the male customers have to rub-into their scalps the magic grease with their fingers," News attempted to explain. "It's not the chemicals that make the hair grow. It's all the rubbin' that balding men do with their fingers when the fools apply the formula that seemingly makes their hair grow. The constant rubbin' stimulates the hair follicles, and not the product's formula doin' the job."

"Good analogy, but a little nebulous," Timmy commended News. "It's our motivation, our inner drive, that'll eventually determine how successful we'll be in life. What we learn here in college, and what we say, and how we say it, are really secondary in importance," Tim qualified. "When our President was assassinated today, for the first time we three are seein' the real world as Goose sees it. We now see civilization, or should I say un-civilization, as it really exists, and not how we'd like it to be."

Every problem in my life seemed to shrink in significance when weighed against the tragic Kennedy assassination. I stopped selfishly thinking about fighting the Deltas and the Taus; about inventing imaginative pranks and ruses; about dating Joanne, Peachy, Candie, Alexis, and Nancy, and about failing Dr. Trenoff's grueling and very laborious "Tests and Measurements" course. All of my personal travails paled in comparison to the great loss and tragedy that had wickedly gripped the entire nation.

On Sunday, the 38 South Main Streeters stayed home all day, and our eyes were virtually fastened to the rabbit-eared black and white television screen. And when we witnessed in real-time suspected assassin, Lee Harvey Oswald, being shot and killed while in the custody of Dallas policemen as the group left the city's main jail, we all immediately understood the danger of anarchy, and I temporarily felt guilty for practicing lawlessness with the Deltas and with the Taus. The Dallas police instantly apprehended Jack Ruby at the prison crime scene, but it really didn't matter. After Oswald gave-up the ghost and died, News, Timmy, Big Al, Bill, Paul, Ralph and I all knew that justice could never be properly served, and that the underlying truth of Lee Harvey Oswald's involvement in President Kennedy's death could never be fully learned.

After being flown from Dallas to Washington, President John F. Kennedy's casket was placed in the *Capitol* rotunda, where common Americans could pay their last respects. Mitch Toscini had a '61 white Chevy that was virtually my latest Impala's twin, except his automobile had a red stripe on both sides with the Impala insignia, and mine had a black one. Mitch and I drove two carloads of students down to Washington to be a part of the great tribute to the memory of John F. Kennedy. And the only song that made any sense on the car radio on the drive from Glassboro down to our nation's capital was the Beach Boy's new release "In My Room," suggesting a private sanctuary, a secure area, understood to be a safe haven to meditate and reflect on the recent historic event that had changed the country and its grieving people forever.

I drove Peachy, Big Al, News, Timmy, and Elaine Hill in my car, and all of us seemed to reject our artificial public personalities, since we were all genuinely sorrowful and inconsolable. When the two Chevys arrived in Washington, we parked; exited our dual white vehicles, and soon encountered the long line of silent mourners. Our entourage quietly took our place in the slow-moving procession, a full five-long-blocks from the *Capitol*. It required three-hours to finally and patiently climb the steps and enter the huge, white marble building, and then, respectfully approach the President's casket.

Just before our *GSC* contingent had finally reached the funeral bier, with its military sentinels standing as still as statues, a guard stopped our forward progress, and we and everyone else in the enormous rotunda were stunned to see Jackie Kennedy and her two children solemnly enter the immense chamber, and our captivated eyes perceived the sorrowful widow paying her last respects to her fallen husband. And Jackie's accompanying son and daughter honoring their deceased father greatly added to the mournful spectacle. That nerve-racking experience had left an indelible memory that has still remained with me, ever since witnessing the extremely emotional and heart-wrenching event.

On Monday, the 38 South Main Street Lambdas all watched with great remorse John F. Kennedy's mass at *St. Matthew's Roman Catholic Cathedral,* followed by the subsequent very sad funeral procession crossing the *Potomac Bridge* into *Arlington National Cemetery*. America, my college friends, and I had changed and grown-up those three emotionally devastating days, and I felt, and wisely knew in my heart that the carefree "Happy Days" of the late '50s and early '60s had grotesquely come to an end. Our country had massive problems that needed resolution, and mammoth wounds that required massive healing.

On November 29th, President Johnson appointed the *Warren Commission* to investigate into the Kennedy assassination, and Chief Justice Earl Warren headed the special task force committee. And even then, amidst all of the national consternation, many Americans were cynical and skeptical of any findings that would be reported, because we were all a little wiser, indeed, more defensive; more dubious of mere words, along with their hollow meaning. And our doubting minds had become more distrustful of everyone and anyone, including ourselves. But in truth, our greedy motives and egotistical inclinations had become more transparent and more identifiable to each other.

The 1963 *Thanksgiving* holidays were not as joyous as the family meal had been in the past. Mom did prepare turkey with all the trimmings, in addition to apple and pumpkin pies, but no one in my clan was abundantly cheerful or talkative. We just went about the habitual act of celebrating an annual holiday, for the sole sake of honoring tradition and our national heritage.

And when I returned to campus the following Monday, I regretted that the national tragedy of November 22nd hadn't changed Dr. Trenoff one iota. The fanatical martinet remained as didactical, dictatorial, and demanding as the strict pedagogue had appeared prior to the Kennedy assassination. Just after noon on December 9th, I left the tyrannical professor's "Tests and Measurements" class and ambled-over to the safety of the Co-op, where News Tomasello solemnly greeted me.

"Hi J.W. Why do ya' appearin' so glum and dejected? Ya' look like a combination of a cantaloupe and *Lassie!"*

"Why do you say that?" I asked in confusion. "Stop speakin' in indecipherable nomenclature!"

"Because Idiot King, your intense facial frownin' makes you look quite melon-collie!"

"Real funny, News. Remind me to laugh at my own funeral," I negatively balked, showing my discouragement with Tomasello, and also, with my true disillusionment with the real world.

"Say J.W., did you read in the *Inquire*r where Frank Sinatra Jr. was kidnapped at Lake Tahoe, and the abductors are demandin' a $240,000.00 ransom from his rich daddy?" News asked. "The elder Sinatra doesn't want the *FBI* involved on account of not wantin' to see his son hurt or killed. Money can be replaced, but not people, if ya' know what I mean."

Tomasello's comment made me think deeply about the tragic Kennedy assassination, and I instinctively replied, "Yes, News. I know exactly what you mean. What's up?"

"Well, J. W., if you'll notice Joanne is sittin' over there all by her lonesome," News pointed-out. "And I believe she wants to talk to you right now, and your lady friend asked me to come over here and intercept ya' before ya' got to the snack line. Since Timmy's not here, I'll have to take his place bein' Hermes the messenger god, and for the moment, I'll have to stop bein' Poseidon, the sea god, as Ron Carputis had dubbed and described me as the *GSC* trident wielder."

My spirits were buoyed that Joanne desired to speak with me, and I immediately thought that the Hammonton doll wanted to get back on favorable terms, because I had driven Peachy Wilcox down to Washington. I shuffled over to the Italian goddess's presence and initiated a polite conversation.

"Hi, Joanne. How have you been?" I weakly began. "Haven't seen you around for a while."

"J.W., we gotta' have a real frank talk," Joanne answered in a very stern and serious tone of voice. "You're going to graduate from *GSC* next year, and I think it's the precise time for you to make some very important decisions."

"I'm quite aware of that obvious fact!" I naively concurred. "I'll get a suitable teachin' job, don't worry about *that* not happening. I can be responsible when I need to be."

"That's not exactly what I mean!" the Sicilian prom queen austerely replied. "I'm talkin' about commitment. I'm referring specifically to *our* relationship."

"It's been good ever since high school!" I defended. "We've had plenty of great times and fun together, Joanne."

"I'm gonna' cut to the chase," Joanne imperatively insisted. "You're dating Peachy Wilcox; Alexis, whatever her name is; Nancy Danns, Candie Davison and me, too. It's about time you made a commitment to one of us, and I'm hopin' it's me."

"What do you want me to do?" I nervously responded. "I'm not ready to get married or anything permanent like that. I'm not even thinkin' about becomin' engaged."

"I think you've narrowed the field down to Peachy and me," Joanne accurately interpreted and bluntly stated. "It's now your time to make a distinct choice. You can't have both of us. It's either Peachy or me."

I pondered my dilemma for a moment, feeling cornered like a rat and trapped like a wounded bear. Which choice would I make? Prom Queen or Miss Cape May! "Okay, Joanne. I'll tell Peachy the bad news. We've known each other for nearly four-years now. Your father can't stand me, I know, but if you're willin' to make the commitment and the fidelity, then I guess I'm your man."

I didn't quite know how to break the news to the now vulnerable Peachy Wilcox, but I eventually did. I felt like a real heel making her cry outside *Linden Hall* dorm'. But the knockout blonde understood the pressure that I was under and accepted my decision with regret and emotion, which was really negative sad emotion, lingering from the November 23rd loss of our nation's President. Never before had I experienced such mixed feeling and sentimental sensations, and my soul and consciousness were grappling with each other, attempting to discern in which direction my moral compass should be pointing.

A week later, Elaine Hill discreetly informed me in a *Memorial Hall* lounge that Peachy Wilcox's father had passed-away. I felt like the world's biggest ogre, a selfish monster whose mission in life was to tinker and toy with peoples' hearts and souls, and then abandon their duress during their time of need. I had met Peachy's dad on several occasions, and her father seemed to like my humor and my spirit very much. And now, I had to endure the trauma of driving down to Mr. Wilcox's viewing in Cape May and expressing my sympathy to my former girlfriend, who I had just dumped.

Joanne rode-down to the Jersey beach resort with me, but did not go into the funeral parlor. That Promethean task I had to accomplish on my own. I somehow mustered sufficient courage to enter the dreaded mortuary, but after I stepped through the main portal, Peachy and her mom treated me with dignity and acceptance. I expressed my sincere condolences, and then left the dismal, macabre, crowded chamber, and very deliberately walked back to my white Impala. The definition of the abstract noun *sincerity* then suddenly had new meaning. I was fully aware and certain that a very ugly chapter in my life had finally concluded.

Chapter 33
"Dr. Trenoff's Final Exam"

December of '63 was waning fast, and Timmy's Darwinian behavior theory about the Deltas and the Taus becoming subordinate with the Lambda Phi's ascension to campus dominance appeared to be a valid social axiom in and around the college's gathering places. The Lambdas absorbed six new recruits into our burgeoning ranks, and we held three separate caboose-boarding initiations down Girard Road. And even though Joanne was now my steady girlfriend, I was still morose about President Kennedy's assassination, about Peachy's father's death, and my agonized heart was rather mirthless and motivationally listless concerning the dismal prospect of failing Dr. Maurice Trenoff's abominable "Tests and Measurements" crucible.

And so, the annual *Christmas* hiatus from college tedium was more gloomy than usual, and it seemingly was a dismal extension of the moribund *Thanksgiving* holidays. And as was my habit whenever besieged with sadness, I would begin pounding my typewriter keys in my upstairs' Elm bedroom, empowering my ego and attempting to elevate and liberate it out of stark pessimism. The mental technique actually was a "transfer of aggression" from my manic anxiety-depressed state of mind onto substitute targets and subjects, rather than taking my feelings of anger and aggression out on my family, my friends and myself. I preferred handling grief internally as opposed to externally.

While my parents thought I was preoccupied organizing "an essential term paper" for Dr. Maurie Trenoff, I was hitting the typewriter keys and convincing my doubting mind that I was jousting with society's gross injustices while righting the egregious wrongs that plagued contemporary American culture. I then dispatched two negative letters to the *Hammonton News,* addressing issues that concerned the inability of established channels to resolve certain local problems.

The first "Letter to the Editor" that was published involved a criticism of the local highway department's lackluster performance in removing snow from town roads, where I referred to the highways, streets, lanes, and avenues as "the *Ice Follies* of 1963". And the second poignant letter drew the ire of the local Chief-of-Police when I cited the Hammonton cops for a lack of sensitivity in dealing with Puerto Rican migrant laborers that had elected to seek year-round employment in the community, and not return to Puerto Rico for the cold winter months.

My journalistic endeavors elicited and evoked angry "Letter to the Editor" rebuttals from the agencies being bombarded by an excess of college idealism and audacity. And the Hammonton barbershops, coffee shops, taverns, bars, luncheonettes, and beauty parlors were provided with juicy tidbits to gossip and to analyze. The police department officers were particularly infuriated because I had cited them for not knowing the language, customs, and values of exploited farm labor minorities, and I had also recommended in the paper that the local cops take courses in Spanish, Sociology, and Psychology to become better equipped in their daily relationships with disadvantaged subcultures inside the community.

I must confess that my untra-liberal college education had indoctrinated me to perceive any "man-in-blue with a badge" as possessing a mass-robotic mentality, with each policeman thinking identically, since the patrolmen all wore the same uniforms, exactly like military soldiers do. 'Their similar physical appearance is symbolic of uniformity group thinking,' my firm evaluation had erroneously conjectured and falsely stereotyped. My biased thoughts concerning cops contained more potholes than a crater-infested street, and I was so blinded by my angst, that eventually, the pendulum in my conscience would swing from impugning traditional values on the liberal left point of view to later defending society's necessary institutions on the conservative right.

"Why do you have to be so outspoken about these controversial things that you wrote in the newspaper?" Dad objected. "Local people are gonna' think you're a radical and a troublemaker and buy their fruit and produce at other farm markets. Policeman and highway department employee have families in town, that might reactively boycott our business. Think about consequence before you decide to become too publicly opinionated."

"I'm sorry," I apologized, "but I just had to vent how I felt about *their* poor performance. If certain people are that thin-skinned, they oughta' protect themselves from criticism by doin' their jobs better and more skillfully."

"This is one time I have to side with your father," Mom rendered her opinion. "You've always been a good son, but now we're beginning to wonder why we ever sent you off to college and become influenced by a lot of strange, alien ideas."

News and Timmy were more empathetic to my internal turmoil and to my plethora of psychological needs, so I spent plenty of time at their homes conversing with their more sympathetic parents. And Joanne's family had taken a *Christmas* vacation away from the peach farm, journeying-down to sunny St. Augustine, Florida, so I had no compatible female companionship to assuage my damaged spirit's "internal conflicts".

On December 31st, along with News, I watched the *NFL Championship Game* at Timmy's and was somewhat happy to see the *Chicago Bears* defeat the *New York Giants,* 14-10. And then, I spent *New Years* over Timmy's place again where he, volatile News and I watched Texas beat Navy in the *Cotton Bowl,* 28-6; Illinois edge by Washington in the *Rose Bowl* by a 17-7 score, and Alabama vanquish Mississippi in the *Sugar Bowl* by a 12-7 margin.

"What are ya' gonna' do about Dr. Trenoff's student-genocide class?" News inquired toward the termination of the *Rose Bowl Game*. "I'm sure glad I don't have to be subjected to that arrogant, paranoid midget for *Tests and Measurements!"*

"Before the *Christmas* break, Bob Abrams explained that he had a good plan of action to use against Trenoff, and that the Lambda Phi Big Kahuna wanted me to directly participate. "Now News, as to the details of Bob's elaborate scheme, I'll let you know the basics when I find-out. I'm desperate and will try almost anything to get out of that excruciating torture chamber with a D."

And then, News really aggravated me when the erratic prevaricator informed that the *Broadway* musical *Hello Dolly,* starring Carol Channing, based on author Thornton Wilder's literary masterpiece *The Matchmaker,* was scheduled to open soon at the *St. James Theater* in New York. And then, following that innocent and unnecessary introduction, Tomasello declared, "J.W., you could've used that matchmaker Dolly in all of the disjointed love triangles that you're havin' back at college. At one time, you even had a love hexagon goin'; and then it was down to a love pentagon; and after that, a love rhombus, where there was no parallelogramism clickin' anywhere. And next, it really was only a love triangle involvin' Joanne, Peachy, and you, and now you're finally down to a monogamous relationship, just the way it should've been in the first damned place. And, in my estimation, you must think you're a cross between *Casanova* and *Don Juan*. Well," Tomasello persisted, "forget about *Casanova* and *Don Juan*. You're just simply a cross, and not a holy one at that!"

"First of all, News," I angrily retorted, "St. Joseph owns a lot more churches and schools than St. James does theaters, so *he* must've been plenty richer ownin' a lot more real estate. Secondly," I nastily ranted, "the next time your ass sits-down on the hopper, you won't be able to crap your brains out because your cerebral tissue has already disintegrated inside your lower intestine! I'll pick ya' up tomorrow morning at 6 a.m. sharp to drive your disintegrating torso back to Glassboro. And forget about that idiotic Carputis' 'Ode to Glassboro Bedding' crap on the way!"

Things were almost returning back to normal at 38 South Main. Ralph Crenshaw was again fooled when Bill Elderberry reset *his* alarm clock, and our fellow resident drove to the main campus cafeteria, only to find the door securely locked. Paul Meroski and I frequently wound-up at Angelo's Diner at 3 a.m. to verbally cure the world's plentiful maladies, but only between ourselves, and most importantly, all the guys rejected the idea of mocking Death by *not* attending three viewings transpiring next door at Lacy's Funeral Home, because now we finally realized that Death would always have the last laugh on each of us at its own choosing. But then, I comprehended that my principal concern was how to get an A+ on Dr. Trenoff's widely reputed "wicked final examination".

Authoritarian Dr. Trenoff demanded his students' attention during his ethereal lectures, and the academic despot seemed to exude animosity towards any male standing over five-foot-four inches in height. Although "Maurie the Mole" taught mostly Psychology classes, his students virtually and unanimously believed that the diminutive professor was the one in need of psychiatric analysis and assistance. When walking past Trenoff as I entered and exited his boot-camp classroom, I would deliberately slink-down so as not to accentuate my lankier altitude.

One day in early January, a student with sincere intentions attempted to record Professor Trenoff's "Tests and Measurements" statements on a concealed tape recorder, situated under *his* desk. Upon discovering the hidden device, the short, neurotic instructor became rather furious; grabbed the recording machine, and then also savagely confiscated the attached microphone. The mad professor scolded the petrified student for not asking permission to tape *his* profound lecture utterances. The most horrifying feature of the entire comedy was that the title of Professor Trenoff's course was designed "to make you better human beings and become more understanding prospective teachers when evaluating public-school sudents".

Trenoff had more hang-ups than the corner dry cleaners, and yet the dictator was teaching courses like "Educational Psychology in the Junior High School" in addition to the highly dreaded "Tests and Measurements boot camp. The egomaniac and his lecture method wouldn't last a marking period in the average American middle or junior high school, yet a lecturer of his caliber could flourish for decades in a regular college classroom. "The quite notorious *Peter Principle* is more evident on the university level than anywhere else in the American educational spectrum," I related to Bob Abrams inside the Co-op on that chilly afternoon of Wednesday, January 8th. "Are you failin' the Tests and Measurements class, too?" I asked Bob. "We'll both be lucky to survive Trenoff's hell-hole with D's!"

"Yeah, J.W., but I need your crucial help to bag the final exam'. We both need A+'s to earn a lowly D average from this grueling persecution we've been exposed to!"

Bob and I were fully aware that besides the professor's repulsive and affronting disposition, Dr. Trenoff prided himself' on giving his prodigies incomprehensible exams'. His true or false questions were lengthy, arbitrary, and nebulous, and his multiple-choice items were bewildering in their seemingly contradictory scope and sequence. To the beleaguered students, guessing often came nearer to the desired answers than either logic or the process of elimination.

Abrams and I knew that the bulk of the students in our "Tests and Measurements" symposium had been coming into the final exam' with D and F' averages. It was imperative for the course to be passed, or the subject would have to be made-up during the summer session, and only psycho Dr. Trenoff taught the torturous ordeal in the June-July session inside hot classrooms without air-conditioning.

On Friday's class session, deranged Dr. Trenoff attempted to exude cleverness, and I recall the maniac haughtily addressing the class, "I've heard a rumor circulating around the campus that several of you are conspiring to steal my final examination. Well, you' anonymous, amateur, failing purloiners," the very detestable Mole contemptuously continued, "I have good news for you devious potential felons. I have the exam' hidden in a safe in my home, and only my devoted wife and I know the secret combination."

As imperial Professor Trenoff spoke his intimidating oratory, I detected twenty-five other larynxes swiveling up and down as if they were hyperactive yo-yos. While Maurie Trenoff was orating his typical caustic remarks, one thought dominated my mind. 'Trenoff is unfair and his exams' are unfair,' I concluded. 'Why should I be victimized by those two inherent evils?'

Attila the Hun, in all his wicked ferocity, was probably more ethical and compassionate than either Dr. Trenoff or his diabolical tests were. And then, I glanced over at seniors Dave Littlefield of the Delta Alphas and Sal Walker of the Tau Kappas, and my alert pupils detected my nasty enemies squirming in their desks. I recalled what the two rich thugs had done to News and to me at Sundown Beach, and I was resolute in teaming-up with Bob Abrams in another highly specialized and daring Lambda Phi commando raid.

I still recollect the intense peculiar sensation I had felt on the frigid Wednesday night of January 15th, 1964. Patches of ice dotted the frozen ground near the main campus lecture building. Bob Abrams (who is now an esteemed county vocational school superintendent) and I surreptitiously used an unlocked janitor's door to sneakily enter the campus's main building. No students were allowed inside *College Hall* after 10 p.m., so our encroachment was a reprehensible breach of sacred school regulations.

Bob and I stealthily slinked and rambled from corridor to corridor to evade night custodians and watchmen, skulking around as if we were acting in a low-budget, mystery B movie. But Abrams and I couldn't have been better prepared to execute our heist if we were both honor students at the Jolly Roger Thief Academy.

My fellow conspirator and I both wore rubber-soled black sneakers, black denim trousers, black shirts and jackets, and the wily intruders carried a collection of useful tools to aid us in our covert commando mission. One of Bob's acquaintances had been a school janitor that had consented to letting him borrow the master office key as a favor returned. Abrams had duplicated the lent key at a local hardware store, and then returned the original to the custodian. With a metallic click, the office suite' lock to the college's Education and Psychology Departments was easily turned.

The self-appointed Lambda Phi test-burglar had visited Dr. Maurice Trenoff's office the day before to ask a few cursory questions, so the chief thief had a good idea of where everything was situated. Even though distrustful Trenoff had confidently claimed the exam' had been hidden in a sturdy safe at home, Bob thought that there might be a remote chance of acquiring it, or part of it, somewhere inside the coy professor's office. "Some professors are absent-minded," my fraternity friend confided, "and Trenoff is so clever that he might've unconsciously outwitted himself somewhere along the line!"

"I hope you're right," I whispered back. "If I have to take this mother-jumpin' course with *him* again, I'm immediately transferrin' to *Trenton State*. And if we get caught in this perilous escapade, we might ultimately wind-up at the State Pen instead of at *Penn State*," I theorized, honoring Bo Jalonec, my old Levittown pal whose nickname was Jokes.

The best the two interlopers had hoped for was that some useful notes relating to the final exam' might be found in a desk drawer, or possibly discarded into a metal trashcan. Two prospects were certain on that cold, dark January evening: Abrams and I were both desperate and in danger of failing the despicable professor's course, and neither of us knew what the hell we were doing masquerading as skilled thieves, searching for a long-shot lucky discovery. Bob methodically closed the squeaky door behind us; then we turned on the beams to our trusty flashlights, and hurriedly scanned the receptionist's cluttered desk inside the main office suite.

Dr. Trenoff's partitioned "Psychology cubicle" was located directly behind the first series of offices. We stood on a table and then clambered-up the flimsy barrier. Next, we crawled with our lit flashlights along the narrow dividing ledge, which separated the Psychology Department from the Educational Curriculum Department. That was the only time I ever remember praising thrift in education, for the small offices were open-roofed without any suspended acoustical tile ceiling hindering our forward mobility.

Abrams and I finally reached Trenoff's sacred enclosure, and when Bob made his descent from the elevated partition, his foot banged into a metal waste-can that rattled and then thudded repeatedly upon the floor. Sweat beads clustered on my forehead when a beam of light refracted through a glass door and into Trenoff's formerly dark office. I felt as if I was a wanton *San Quentin* fugitive on the lam, caught in an inescapable police dragnet. 'This is it! Expulsion! State Pen!' my brain frightfully speculated. My companion and I both instinctively shut and tightly held our closed flashlights in the silent darkness.

The night guard entered the office suite and paced down the narrow aisle. The watchman then turned the still-locked doorknob to Trenoff's office. Apparently satisfied with his perusal of the area, the nocturnal security guard redirected his flashlight beam, and then ambled his way back to the receptionist/secretary's desk, and much to our relief, the investigator eventually exited the office suite.

"That was too close for comfort," Abrams whispered. "I think I crapped my dungarees! I'll remember this night every single day when I become a county superintendent."

"It was too close for me, too!" I neurotically replied. "Let's see what we can discover!"

Bob and I breathed sighs of relief as if we both had been spared from being exterminated in an atomic explosion. We then proceeded with our covert *CIA*-type operation. Abrams turned-on his flashlight again, and I imitated his stellar example. Absolute astonishment immediately overcame our very-real anxiety.

To our astonishment, Dr. Trenoff's final exam's master key had been neatly placed there on his desk, appearing right before our very eyes. "Look!" Bob gasped in an amazed low voice. "The holes for the A, B, C, D and None of the Above correct answers, and the holes for the True and False questions, are punctured-out on this master grading sheet!"

"Maybe Trenoff is trying to outsmart us and set us up to be victimized and expelled!" I suspiciously answered. "Maybe this is simply a clever dummy answer sheet designed to trick us into cheatin' and puttin' down the wrong responses! It might be a treacherous trap!"

"Then, Trenoff could not only fail us, but also could have our asses booted right out of college!" Bob observed and exclaimed. "We might even have to face criminal charges for breakin' and enterin' into his cockroach-infested office and stealin' the wrong answers to his preposterous exam'! Then, I'll never have the chance of becomin' a school system superintendent!" Abrams softly uttered.

After exchanging those fearful speculations, Bob and I copied-down on blank notebook paper sheets the punched-out answers on the suspect master key, and soon we placed the pencils, papers, and master answer key back into their original positions upon Trenoff's very neat and tidy desk. We closed our flashlight beams and made our furtive and careful departure from the dark office suite; our bodies slinked and scrambled around empty hallways; our weary legs scurried-down stairwells, and finally, we slyly exited the main campus building with the utmost dispatch.

"Do you have all the answers copied-down in the right order on the notebook paper sheet?" I queried in a slightly squeaky voice, as the daring marauders paced toward the *Bosshart Hall* parking lot. "I have duplicates to verify all one-hundred-and fifty-test items."

"Yeah, let's get out of here in a jiffy, and we'll do our research at the chicken coop!" Bob advised, exhaling a deep breath. "I think I need a roll of toilet paper in a hurry."

Two days later, the "doomed class" assembled in Dr. Trenoff's musky second-floor *College Hall* classroom to suffer his formidable final exam'. Blood was surging through my neck's veins and arteries as the despotic pedagogue merrily distributed his awesome and tedious evaluation, which happened to be ten-pages in length.

Bob Abrams and I had devised an ingenious cheating method; that is to say, if the loathsome Dr. Trenoff was administering the same test that corresponded with our illegally obtained pilfered answers. On our yellow Number 2' pencils, we had made a series of tiny vertical craters on each side, representing True and False or A, B, C, D and None of the Above answers for the two major sections of the test. The correct responses to the entire exam' could be easily surveyed by rotating the yellow pencil in a clockwise direction. 'I hope Trenoff doesn't make us use *his* Number 2' pencils and not our own tampered-with ones!' I feared, as my heart wildly pulsated and pounded inside my chest.

When I initially skimmed through selected items on the comprehensive Tests and Measurements exam', I identified several problems to which I knew the correct answers. The test items appeared to harmonize and coincide perfectly with the tiny punctured pores on my yellow Number 2' writing utensil. I winked over at Bob, who then returned my tacit signal. 'How could any professor be so shrewd and yet so stupid?' I nervously mused.

True, dear old Dr. Trenoff had probably avariciously hauled the physical exams' home, and then scrupulously stashed his intellectual cache inside his airtight safe. But despite all his meticulous precaution, the mentally deranged professor neglectfully forgot *his* all-important answer key lying on his office desk. 'Bob and I didn't even have to go through the travail of researching the answers as we would have had to do if we had purloined the actual exam'!' I imagined as I easily completed the lengthy final evaluation.

The ever-alert Dr. Trenoff smelled something rotten in Denmark, but his sense of perception and his general suspicion were leading him in the opposite direction of Copenhagen. Maurie the Mole's internal compass was out of whack with our cunning strategy, but the obnoxious pedagogue couldn't detect exactly what was going wrong up on *his* battle turf.

As it turned out, Bob and I received A+'s on the final exam', and Dave Littlefield and Sal Walker failed the monstrosity, meaning that the dunces had also failed the course; would not graduate until the persistent jerks made up the subject over the summer session, and consequently, would despise and resent Abrams and me for obtaining the highest grades on the cryptic examination.

Cheating for Bob Abrams and my other Lambda Phi Sigma fraternity brothers was a lot easier and less risky during the remainder of our junior year, and also for our senior year course requirements. The savvy fraternity members had become friendly with several attractive fair damsels employed in the college's copying-machine rooms, and through our extensive contacts, we had immediate access to any test or examination issued by any mean-spirited *Glassboro State College* professor.

Chapter 34
"Practicum"

"I finally found the sound! It's arrived! Hallelujah, it's here!" News screamed as the music fanatic exuberantly burst into the Common Room at 38 South Main.

"You mean your ears just began to hear noise after nineteen years of human existence?" I sarcastically quipped. "No wonder why you always blab so damned much, News. Ya' never could hear anything anyone else was sayin', all along!"

"Get wise or get bent, J.W.!" News vitriolically replied. "Get wise, or get bent! Just listen to this new sound I've obtained on wax! It's simply amazin'!"

"Well, what is the song? Who are the artists?" I requested knowing. "Are they from this planet, from Pluto, or are the artists *radio*active space aliens from another galaxy?"

"They're a sensational group from Liverpool, England, called the Beatles!" Tomasello exclaimed, all out of breath as if the nerd had just had at least seven consecutive, lengthy orgasms. "Just listen to these spectacular songs titled 'Please, Please Me' and 'Love Me Do'! I predict that this British group is gonna' give the Beach Boys a run for their money!"

News put the pair of newly-acquired '45s on the Common Room's *RCA* record player, and we listened to the two unique-sounding tunes, which incidentally both spun around 45 times a minute. Bill, Big Al, Paul, Timmy, and even Ralph Crenshaw came out of their textbook studies to hear the fantastic new British vocals, rhythm arrangements, and lyrics. And when the second song had been played, everyone desired to hear the records again, and insisted that Tomasello spin the tunes a second time.

"And guess what guys?" News ecstatically gushed. "The Beatles are goin' to come to the States and appear on *Ed Sullivan.* They're also gonna' give a special concert at *Carnegie Hall.* Too damned bad the group isn't commin' to Finger-Mountain Auditorium (Tohill) inside *College Hall!"*

"How do we know that they're just not some two-hit wonder band that's gonna' be just another flash-in-the-pan?" Big Al rationally and negatively asked. "I mean, if they were from Tokyo, the band could be called the Japanese Beetles, or if from Germany, the singers could be the *Volkswagen* Beetles!"

"Very funny, Heir Keiler!" News sneered. "For your personal information, Beatles is spelled B-e-a-t-l-e-s! And I just read where the group acquired their name in imitation of Buddy Holly and the *Crickets!* And I've also recently read in a record magazine where the Beatles got some more groovy hits commin' out like 'She Loves You',; 'Can't Buy Me Love'; 'Do You Want to Know a Secret', and 'I Want to Hold Your Hand'."

"You wanna' hold my hand?" Big Al guffawed. "I always knew you were an undercover homo' faggot, News! Thanks for verifyin' my suspicion!"

"Big Al," News squawked. "The next time you take a crap, why don't ya' wipe your rear end with coarse sandpaper wrapped in double-edged razor blades, instead of with regular toilet paper!"

From January to mid-March of '64, I was assigned my Practicum on-the-job learning experience at Clearview Regional High School. My stint there would be for five weeks, and then my program was slated to be transferred to Washington Township High School for the following thirty school days. My responsibility at Clearview was to assist Mr. Kenner with homeroom attendance cards and lunch count; help the instructor assemble bulletin boards; aid my Cooperating Teacher with his cafeteria duty; record grades placed into the indispensable teacher roll book; write-up a dozen classroom lesson observations for my college coordinator, and then teach my first English and social studies lessons to acne-faced ninth-graders.

I'll never forget my first English teaching lesson in late January of '64. I had as my audience twenty-five fourteen-year-old ruffians, and I was rather nervous because my College Coordinator, Dr. Cowans, was present in the back of the classroom to witness my much-anticipated educational debut. As recommended in the teacher manual, I conscientiously monitored the hall traffic during the rowdy changing of classes, with the students rushing from their homerooms to their first period subject.

I then greeted the energized students as the young scholars entered the room, and I was all pumped-up about teaching the kids about helping verbs; verb phrases; direct objects following action verbs; verbs of being, and about the subtle distinctions between predicate nominatives and predicate adjectives following *linking* verbs (which of course were not invented by Abraham Link-in). After the late bell loudly rang, I entered the room and formally introduced myself to the curious, alert class.

When I turned my back to neatly print my name on the chalkboard, my ears discerned a loud thud, and immediately, my head spun-around to evaluate the noise's origin. A student's desk had been knocked-over in the center of the classroom, and two free-swinging ninth-grade gladiators were pulverizing one another; with the pair soon falling and wildly rolling-around on the tiled floor. I had been momentarily dumbfounded by the spontaneous chaos. My eyes glanced toward the back of the room at my preoccupied college professor, Dr. Cowans, and the professor was still-seated in his desk, feverishly taking notes about the frenetic battle that was transpiring in *our* midst. I had to quickly intervene in the intense altercation, or risk receiving a bad lesson evaluation, that had nothing to do with the intricate verb lesson.

I hastily moved to the center of the classroom and jumped between the pair of aggressive combatants, both of whom' were now standing and still showing plenty of antagonism towards each other. My dignified appearance in their midst was greeted with a stiff right-cross to my jaw, accompanied by an errant swift kick to my groin, which had been administered by one of the junior combatants. I finally managed to separate the crazed adversaries, using superior brute strength, and next I wisely reported the scuffle to the main office over the intercom, my voice sounding to everyone present in the room as if I desperately needed an oxygen tank.

I then intelligently sent each juvenile pugilist down to the vice-principal's office, a full three-minutes apart. My eyes glanced again to the back of the room, and my impressed college professor was still preoccupied jotting-down pertinent notes. It was then that I first realized that college coordinators and school administrators wanted teachers to break-up fights, and the system's brass had no desire to become involved as either a boxing or wrestling referee during major classroom crises.

So, after regaining my normal composure, I painfully taught my first official lesson to the jittery class, which required another ten minutes to finally settle-down. Throughout the entire grammar exercise, my jaw, groin, and right knee throbbed with pulsating pain, and I felt as if I had been a wounded war casualty. At the end of the challenging class period, my college supervisor, Dr. Cowans, commended me on effectively stopping the fight, and the college representative stated that the overall content of my first official lesson was generally satisfactory.

"Mr. Kenner says that on the average, he breaks-up eighteen fights a year, mostly in the cafeteria, in the halls, and while on bus duty!" I told News, Big Al, and Timmy back at 38 South Main Street. "Teaching can be a very dangerous occupation!"

"Maybe you should try high-wire walkin' between skyscrapers to make a livin', rather than more dangerous American education,"

Timmy laughed. "I'm over at Deptford Township High, and there's plenty of brawlin' goin' on over there, too! High school kids are becomin' more and more rebellious and pugnacious! How come the punks aren't saints like we were back at Edgewood and at St. Joe?"

"And J.W.," News sarcastically added to the discussion. "If ya' wanna' learn how to box, I suggest ya' first get a job in a cardboard factory. That's the best trainin' I can recommend for satisfactorily becomin' a boxer."

"Well, J.W., you'd better learn basic judo and karate, too, besides pugilism!" Big Al specifically inserted into the dialogue. "I understand that Dave Littlefield and Sal Walker are really pissed at Bob Abrams and you for not sharin' Dr. Trenoff's final exam' answers with them. And they're both a lot stronger than two wise-ass punk ninth-graders."

After a week of laborious classroom instruction, I also soon realized that I could not lecture fourteen-year-olds for forty-five minutes and expect my short-attention-span audience to stay focused. If I imitated the *lecture teaching method* of my college professors, especially didactical Dr. Trenoff, then my ambitious career would have been doomed to failure from the outset.

At Clearview, I quickly adopted the teaching style of discussing and introducing the general lesson the first ten-minutes of class. Next, I would walk around the room and help the pupils with their related textbook exercises. The following twenty-five minutes of the period I would assign homework, and then assist the kids with the extended learning activity the last ten-minutes of class. That teaching model was supplemented with assigning student oral reports, establishing lively panel discussions, doing explanatory blackboard work, and engaging-in library research activities.

On Tuesday night, February 25th, the 38 South Main Lambdas had the rabbit ears aimed towards Philadelphia to receive the Sonny Liston and Cassius Clay championship fight, and the guys were marveling at how the neurotic, volatile, insecure contender was giving the invincible fighting machine, Sonny Liston, a real tussle, especially with the challenger's admirable speed and evasive tactics. At the start of the second round, the upstairs door was rapped, and before anyone could respond to the annoying knocking, in stepped mercurial Goose Restuccio.

"Holy fuckin' shit!" G.R. yelled. "Now I know you fuckin' college assholes are really fucked-up!"

"Goose, you oughta' see this Cassius Clay guy escape Liston's knockout punches," I excitedly stated. "He's maneuverin' all around the ring like a graceful gazelle and is frustratin' the hell outa' Liston. Never saw anything quite like it."

"Clay's intimidatin' the bully with his awesome speed and audacity, and also frustratin' Liston with the quickness of his hands," Timmy Amoro knowledgeably added. "The big intimidator is bein' intimidated with Clay's superior leg-work, conditionin', and with his unbelievable combination punches."

"I can't fuckin' understand you jerk-off college nuts!" Goose criticized. "You' wimpy pussies are all nigger wanna' be's, wastin' your time watchin' two fuckin' rug-heads knock each other's brains out! You could be out somewhere getting laid; extortin' money; pimpin' your old ladies like Mario does; eatin' and lickin' clean pussy; shakin' down the other fraternity scumbags, or doin' somethin' else constructive like jerkin' off or takin' a healthy shit. Instead, you're all fuckin' fascinated by two spear-chuckers doin' the Watusi with each other inside a goddamned boxin' ring."

"Those guys make millions of dollars!" Big Al argued in defense of heavyweight boxers. "Liston and Clay will make more money on the canvas than van Gogh ever did when he was alive paintin'. In fact, they'll make more bread tonight than even *you* will, Goose!"

"Maybe, or maybe not!" G.R. bluntly answered without cursing, swearing, or threatening. "But I'll tell ya' what, Big Al. Niggers are niggers, and that's all there is to it. And if the coons get lucky and make a lot of bread, the dumb shits become nigger-rich and buy ten houses and ten cars, and then the government takes-away half their fuckin' money with taxes. And remember," Goose reiterated. "The niggers are still niggers, no matter how much dough they have, and then blow it all on foolish habits, and soon have to keep getting their fuckin' brains pounded-out in the ring to make the stupid blockheads dumber and dumber each fuckin' time the dumb-dicks fight! Now, with me," Restuccio elucidated and qualified, "I earn a few dollars legally, and make it appear that I'm legit'. And then, I make lots of bucks illegally that the fuckin' government' doesn't fuckin' know about. I'm even goin' to buy a Hammonton laundromat to launder my fuckin' dirty money! Ha, ha, ha, ha!"

"Are ya' gonna' stay and watch the rest of the fight?" Timmy asked Restuccio, the avowed racist. "Pardon the pun, but this boxing bout is really a knockout!"

"Naaa, I'll let you' silly, dumb fuck-heads watch the jungle bunnies *pull-veer-eyes* each other into mush!" Goose declared. "But I gotta' admit that the night we wore those goddamned Swahili masks, and when the Lamp-da teams raided the Alphie Ortega House and the Capa Episalong hide-out, it felt pretty fuckin' cool bein' and actin' like a cannibal nigger for fifteen fuckin' minutes."

"Clay has already lasted three rounds now, and Liston's really pissed and getting tired," Elderberry observed and described. "This might be one of the biggest and most stunning upsets in heavyweight boxin' history."

"Are ya' sure ya' don't want a beer?" I asked Goose. "There's a couple left in the fridge'. You're welcome to pull-up a chair and watch the match."

"Ya' know, J.W., the only worse thing than watchin' fuckin' television is watchin' fuckin' niggers on television," Restuccio profoundly objected. "And hard-working white guys that get things done and make the country wealthy don't watch television at all. That's why you' going-nowhere college assholes are just gonna' make five-thousand *poultry* dollars a year, because you're *hip-know-ties* by a stupid thing like nigger-rich ghetto creeps that don't know their dicks from their assholes," Goose chided. "And that skinny guy with the big mouth is too fuckin' arrow-gant for his own damned good. He's actually scared shitless of Liston, but he's pretendin' he's in control of the fight!"

"Well then, where are ya' off to, if you aren't gonna' stay?" I asked Goose as Round Four started.

"I came-up here to give ya' faggots my new business card!" Restuccio said, distributing to the other Lambdas and me some specific information printed on a rectangular piece of thick paper. "I just bought a tow truck, and I'm gonna' haul fuckin' stolen cars and fuckin' auto wrecks to fuckin' chop shops over in Philly', and to Hammonton junkyards, too. So, because I have to look legit'," Goose explained, "I need a few jobs from average jerk-offs like you guys, too, just to look legit!"

"What are ya' doin' tonight?" News asked Goose at the end of Round Four. "Is that a secret I'm askin' ya' to tell?"

"I'm countin' dirty money from extortion and loan' sharkin' all goddamned night with Frankie Fingers and Joe Zucchini helpin' me out," Restuccio smugly answered. "My old man and old lady are doin' the same thing up in Paramus at a classy motel tonight, so I'll be fuckin' countin' in my sleep, but instead of a herd of sheep jumpin' over fuckin' *pick-it* fences, I count fuckin' hundred-dollar bills one at a time, imaginin' the greenbacks leapin' over fuckin' tall walls! I'll be home doin' that fuckin' borin' shit for the next three days, because there's so many fuckin' greenbacks in my room, that

I'm gonna' have to buy a whole fuckin' chain of laundromats just to keep my image clean! Ha, ha, ha, ha!"

"Okay, Goose, thanks for the nice business card," I smiled and accepted. "Hope to see ya' soon! With all your marvelous income, maybe ya' need to buy an abacus?"

"No, J.W.," G.R. replied in a fairly confused state of mind. "I don't buy churches or schools with my goddamned profits."

Restuccio next walked toward the apartment's only entrance and exit door. "Good night ya' fuckin' nigger-lovin' Swahili wanna' be's!" the petulant Sicilian yelled. "And don't get your fuckin' cars stuck in the ocean, because I don't do under*tows!"* Ha, ha, ha, ha!" Restuccio's vile and filthy mouth spouted before our criminal visitor demonstrably slammed the door.

Amazingly, and much to our astonishment, Cassius Clay defeated Sonny Liston when the former champion couldn't answer the bell to box the seventh round. All of my roommates thought that the victory was an anomaly and that Liston would take Clay more seriously in a rematch that undoubtedly would erase and reverse "the fluke" we had just witnessed.

The following evening, around 11 p.m., Bob Abrams stopped by 38 South Main Street to discuss future plans for the glorious Lambda Phi's. Abrams and I were now on good terms again after the stellar "Trenoff heist", so I welcomed our President inside, and our guest chatted briefly with his fellow Lambdas. Then, Ralph Crenshaw came into the Common Room a half-hour later, since our hard-workig roommate had gotten-off early from his cafeteria stint.

"Don't forget, Ralph," Bob reminded the industrious-yet-humble 38 Main resident. "You promised to become a Lambda Phi your senior year. We want ya' to join-in as a Lambda brother!"

"Okay, Bob. I'm getting an A in Practicum, and once I'm sure I'll be on the Dean's List," Crenshaw stipulated, "I vow that I'll join-up by next February, right after my Student Teaching assignment. And as Thrasymachus said to Socrates in Plato's *Republic,* an honest man always keeps his word and pays his debts."

"Goose Restuccio would probably think that Thrasymachus is some Greek brothel outside Athens, Georgia," Timmy laughed. "Either that or a hapless *Republic*an from Athens, Georgia!"

"Well, anyway, guys," Bob proceeded with his rhetoric. "The dual barbarian raids performed on the Delta and Tau Houses went-off like clockwork, and the word around campus is that those rival fraternities are really scared of us. J.W., what do ya' say we go-out and discuss the specifics of a future enterprise in private, so that then you can share our strategy with your 38 South Main guys when ya' return home."

"Sure Bob," I reckoned. "Do ya' wanna' go for coffee and doughnuts over at Angelo's Diner?"

"No, there's always sweet-tooth cops sittin' in there this time of night, munchin' on the same greasy pastries and drinkin' java," Abrams rejected. "Let's celebrate and go have a few *Southern Comforts* over at Mazzeo's Bar on High Street. I don't know about you, but I tend to concentrate better when I'm under the influence! Or if not better, I tend to think evilly after downing some liquor!"

"Say, guys," News piped-up. "Did ya' read in the *New York Times* that President Johnson said our military program has an experimental jet aircraft called the *A-11* that'll be able to fly over two-thousand miles per hour at an altitude of over seventy-thousand feet. That's twelve-miles up in the damned stratosphere! Twelve whole miles up there, mind you, and three times the speed of sound!"

"Maybe, J.W. can pilot that baby when he gets outa' Navy pilot school at Lakehurst," Big Al frivolously suggested. "He'll do real well as a jet pilot, because he's had a 'flighty' personality ever since I've known him!"

Abrams and I left the 38 South premises with him laughing and with me frowning. We hopped into his black Mercury, and then the Lambda leader fired-up the engine and backed-out of the driveway onto Main. At the downtown traffic light, Bob turned right onto High, and two blocks down on the left we parked and entered Mazzeo's, where Tom Bell had once begun his damaging skid across High Street with Loretta Sacco, Joanne Berenato, and me as his petrified passengers. Abrams and I entered the smoky bar, ordered our *Southern Comforts* on the rocks, and began discussing a possible future prank I had in mind to further stifle the Delta Alphas and the Tau Kappas, should the frat' war spontaneously re-ignite.

"I'll tell ya', Bob, I'm so into Practicum right now that everything else is minimized in importance," I described my new adult venture into maturity land. "I wanna' get an A, but on my first lesson, a wicked fight broke-out in the classroom, and I think that *that* little fracas might've jeopardized my professional chances. School teachin' isn't as easy as everybody says it is. Times are changin', and kids are rapidly changin,' too."

"First of all, J.W.," Abrams smiled and joked, sounding a little like News Tomasello. "You aren't teaching a school, so stop callin' yourself a schoolteacher. You're teachin' young delinquent punks, who are masqueradin' around as students."

“You’re right there, Bob,” I concurred. “But I gotta’ tell you a rather peculiar story. My car needed servicin’ last week, so I brought the Impala to a mechanic over in Hammonton. I called Mario on the horn and asked the brute to take me to Clearview, because he was havin’ his Practicum program there too, for the first five-weeks as a future social studies teacher.”

“Sounds pretty routine to me so far,” Abrams assessed before sipping his double *Southern Comfort* on the rocks. “What happened next? Did ya’ stop along the way and watch two herds of cows havin’ groupy sex for twelve hours?”

“No, not exactly,” I returned. “On the way back from Clearview, Mario tells me that while the regular teacher was outa’ the room, he’s doin’ a lesson usin’ an overhead projector. After showin’ four or five photos on American Indians,” I said and paused, “Mario slides this dirty cartoon drawing that’s then projected up onto the screen.”

“What was the risque picture about?” Bob asked, showing heightened curiosity. “How did the kids react? Were there any girls in the class?”

“Whoa! One question at a time, please,” I requested. “Well, the picture showed an Apache Indian doin’ a war dance and holdin’ a patch of curly black pubic hair in one hand, and a tomahawk in the other,” I described and explained. “And on the other half of the pornographic illustration, it showed a naked white woman with a shocked expression on her face, coverin’ her bald nude crotch, since her bush had just been scalped!”

“And how did the class react?” Abrams asked. “A foolish teacher could get fired for pullin’ a crazy, indiscreet stunt like that! It only takes one incident, ya’ know, to get canned!”

“According to Mario,” I orally conveyed, “the kids all laughed their asses off, even the two retarded girls sittin’ right next to the overhead opaque projector. And Bob,” I continued. “Mario then hit me for a hundred bucks, which was my whole surplus money supply for the semester, on the drive back to Hammonton, so that the addicted gambler could go and blow *my* hard-earned money at the money-grabbin’ *A.C. Race Track.*”

Just before Bob and I were about to outline the Lambda Phi’s next outrageous prank (should it be necessary), two absolutely gorgeous, well-stacked young ladies entered smoky Mazzeo’s Bar. It was as if a pair of glamorous *Hollywood* actresses suddenly, out-of-nowhere, accidentally landed in rural Glassboro, and graced the notorious dive with their stunning presence.

"Those exotic ladies we're staring-at aren't exactly students from the college' campus, that's for damned sure!" I confided to Bob. "How are you and Roxanne getting along right now?"

"Roxanne and I are like a switch," Abrams revealed. Off and on, but right now, we're mostly off, which means I can't be on!"

The knockout blonde and the attractive brunette traipsed over to *our* side of the bar and asked us if we'd like to buy them drinks and share their company. Abrams and I immediately consented, with the blonde ordering a sloe gin fizz, and with the brunette a screwdriver. Rebecca and Janice initiated a rather intriguing conversation, and Abrams and I introduced each other to the itinerant goddesses, after which the *Miss Universe* blonde and the *Miss America* brunette adroitly took the verbal offensive.

"Ya' know, guys, we're two aspiring actresses drivin' up to New York to be auditioning for the *Broadway* show *Hello Dolly!"* Becky commented while twirling her golden tresses and blinking her fantastic blue eyes at me.

"And we're stayin' at the Glassboro Motel out on *Route 47,"* Janice voluntarily informed, flashing her tantalizing brown eyes at Bob. "And we came in here seekin' some male companionship for the night, if ya' two college studs know what we mean. Becky and I both just absolutely adore muscular college men!"

"Well, I'm a ready Teddy," Bob nervously reacted. "This all sounds too good to be true!"

"How about you, big boy?" Becky asked while gently touching me on the chin, as the flirting doll sounded a lot like either Mae West or Alexis Terranenkov. "Would ya' like to have me as your personal love machine for the next eight-hours?"

I swiftly gulped-down my *Southern Comfort* and then nearly choked to death after the potent intoxicant went down the wrong pipe, when my epiglottis temporarily became dysfunctional. "Er, I'll do almost anything to please a beautiful lady," I remarked, while deliberately clearing my clogged throat. "Especially to please a knockout lady such as yourself!"

"Okay, Big Boy," Janice coincidentally said as the stage model started rubbing Bob's leg very sensually, nearly making Abrams rise in several ways right off of his barstool and explode all the way up to the high ceiling like volcanic *Mt. Vesuvius*. "Becky and I knew you well-equipped boys would be up to the task at hand. Come on outside and hop into our van, and we'll let you ride all you want back at the motel."

The four of us impulsively finished our strong drinks, and Bob left a five-dollar tip, because he felt very lightheaded while thinking with his fadorkenbender instead of with his cerebrum. We merrily exited the dismal establishment; strolled arm and arm out to the new red Ford van, and when Bob and I were about to hop into the back, we were collared and then roughly tossed inside by six powerful Japanese Sumo wrestlers, exhibiting grim expressions upon their chunky countenances. And then, I noticed that the irrepressible, insufferable George Evans had been accompanying the antagonistic Oriental ruffians.

"You' numb-nuts college honkies didn't think that these lovely fantastic ladies want anything to do with you two clowns, now did ya'?" George aggressively berated. "How foolish and out-of-touch with reality can two Peckerwood Pecker-heads be?"

"But what about Becky and Janice?" I yelled. "Please don't hurt them. The dolls didn't do anything harmful to you!"

"You stupid horses' asses," George cackled like a demented felon. "You were so horny that ya' didn't even bother askin' the girls their last names. This here is Miss Becky Walker, and this luscious model is Miss Janice Littlefield. Now, do you two albino bozos get the big picture?" Evans rhetorically asked. "You've been cleverly duped! Set Up! Tricked! All because ya' didn't give the final exam' answers to my good friends Dave and Sal. This is what happens when you get those two nasty dudes riled."

"Where are ya' gonna' take us?" I demanded. "What's gonna' happen? I need to survive to enjoy tomorrow!"

"Well, white boy," George spoke to Bob. "Ya' wanna' ride in a motel and horse around, do ya'? And you," Evans next muttered, referring to me. "Ya' didn't have enough grief with horses over at Cowtown, so now here's your chance to make-up for lost time! Ha, ha, ha, ha!" And then Evans directed his attention to his enchanting female accomplices. "Thanks plenty, Becky and Janice. Here comes the car now to take you two beauty queens over to the Delta House for some *real* partyin'!"

After the six hired Sumo wrestlers piled-into the back of the transportation van, being assigned to guard Bob and me, one of the enormous slobs quickly slammed the rear panels shut. George Evans then climbed into the driver's seat. I noticed that Evans looked a lot like Sonny Liston in facial appearance and also in his muscular build, and soon the merry tormentor continued his obnoxious rant. "Hate to say it, white boys, but it's sorta' becomin' personal between you Lambda freaks and me, after what those two busloads of *Visti-gaffs* did to my ass over at the Delta House."

I was really pissed, being so easily hoodwinked by using classy, flirtatious, hourglass-shaped females as alluring bait. And then ironically, the hit song "I Wonder What She's Doin' Tonight" by Barry and the Tamerlanes came blasting-out on the red van's radio, and right away, I began thinking of Joanne Berenato, and why I wasn't out parked at the contaminated lake over in Pitman with her, and with us dually imbibing sweet *Southern Comfort.* And even though Bob and I were seated on our rumps, being closely scrutinized by the formidable "Tokyo Corpulent Kamikaze and Sumo Society", I knew that our point of origin was Mazzeo's Bar, and my acute mind recognized that I could figure-out our destination by piecing turns and stops together in a mental-picture-roadmap of our itinerary.

The red van exited Mazzeo's parking lot without skidding across High Street, and soon, *not* quickly plowing into the beauty parlor across the street. Lenny Welch's new release "Since I Fell for You" came over the radio, and George didn't seem to like the popular slow tune, so the fussy driver switched to WIP FM Color Radio, and coincidentally, the searcher found the Beach Boys "Be True to Your School". In my mind, the red vehicle was heading west down High in the direction of *Glassboro State College*.

And upon turning from High onto Whitney, and then crossing the railroad tracks to University Road, the Color Radio DJ began playing "Quicksand" by Martha and the Vandellas, which I considered sounded something like "Heat Wave" by the same group. I glanced at Bob's scared eyes, and his peepers reflected the same fear that my mind imagined, with us being thrown into quicksand and being swallowed-up into the earth like the nefarious villains on *Ramar of the Jungle* often were.

And when the shiny red van stopped at the end of University Road, not far from where Abrams's fractured Tarzan vine and ruptured elm tree bridge were located, Lesley Gore's "You Don't Own Me" came over the airwaves, and my petrified mind thought, 'Oh yes they do!' in relation to *my* encumbered, unenviable, van hostage predicament.

Upon being escorted out of the closed vehicle's rear compartment, my eyes confirmed my theory that we had been kidnapped and transported to Peaks Horse, Apple and Peach Farm. And then, George Evans reinforced that very accurate hypothesis.

"Now, you two annoying clowns, who have given the Deltas, the Taus, and me so much horse-shit, you're gonna' put up with some of our own manure," George disclosed and then hardily laughed. "The farm owners are on vacation in Hawaii, and one of my brothers is in charge of the operations until the elderly tourists return. Well now, you two Lambda faggots can just pretend you're A.J. Foyt winnin' the *Indianapolis 500!"* Evans yelled and cackled, guffawing so hard that the abductor had to bend-over, looking like he was vomiting in the peach orchard that we were all standing in.

"What's that supposed to mean?" I defiantly challenged.

"It means that you're both commin' in soon for a goddamned pit stop!" Evans coughed and drooled from his mouth.

And with those prophetic words, George Evans signaled the six Japanese Sumo brutes to pick-up Abrams and me, and carry us around five-hundred-feet into the farm's interior. And then, without any formal notice, we were roughly hurled into a deep pit, and in a second, were careening and tumbling-down a smelly, very slippery embankment, rolling into a waist-deep mound of fresh horse manure.

Bob and I were desperately gasping for air, with our dilemma resulting from the amount of terrible, reeking stench. For our heads had momentarily been embedded into the three-foot-deep horse crap, and our faces and foreheads were thickly coated with malodorous dung. That horrible emergency generated a great bit of amusement from George Evans, and as I wiped the lousy stinking mess from my begrimed face, and also from my irritated eyes, I glanced-up and saw that even the six Sumo brutes had smiles on their fat rotund faces.

A flat-bodied truck was soon backed-up to the inescapable pit, still quite-loaded with fresh animal manure, and George and his three big-biceped black brothers hopped-aboard, wearing rubber boots, and the quartet began shoveling hundreds of pounds of new animal feces down upon Bob and me, who both could not move, being mired up to our waists in the contemptible excrement.

"Ya' both look rather *pit*iful!" George observed and hollered much to the delight of his three muscle-bound siblings. "Instead of Lambda Phi Sigma, ya' both now belong to Horsea Krappa Enigma, which is also a synonym for Pony Poop Pumpers! Ya' stupid dip shits! Ha, ha, ha, ha! Now, you're both like a couple of veteran dip-shits! Ha, ha, ha, ha! This scene is so fuckin' hilarious! Ha, ha, ha!"

After the wagon had been scraped clean of foul-smelling horse manure, the accomplished sadists soon evacuated the scene to go party over on Harvard Road, leaving Bob and me wallowing like country pigs in chest-deep horse crap. Abrams and I cursed horses and horse racing, steeplechase jumping, and horse flies. Next, we cursed the White Horse Pike; the Black Horse Pike; horseshoes', lucky or otherwise; Cowtown; jockeys; jockey shorts, and finally, shit-stained underwear, much to our chagrin and frustration. And then Abrams and I began praying for justice and revenge against the mendacious Delta Alpha Omegas and against the repugnant Tau Kappa Epsilons, and finally, Bob and I mutually prayed for eternal salvation, should we regrettably perish before Earthly justice could be fairly implemented against our bitter rivals.

Our miraculous salvation was in the mortal forms of Joanne Berenato and Elaine Hill. The two dorm' chicks were sitting inside the Co-op discussing how exciting the Lambda Phi Sigmas were, when a girlfriend of one of the Deltas came over, and out of wonderful guilt, divulged what was concurrently happening to Abrams and me out at Peak's Horse, Apple and Peach Farm. The humanitarian *Evergreen* girls then ran six long blocks to 38 South Main and notified News, Timmy, Big Al, Paul, Bill, and Ralph of our recent misfortunes. News Tomasello called Goose on the telephone about the reported dilemma, and Restuccio volunteered to drive his new tow truck over to Glassboro in order to excavate the two dauntless Lambdas from their embarrassing, hollowed-out incarceration.

Forty-minutes elapsed, when Goose pulled into the University Road farm, accompanied by his henchmen Frankie Fingers and Joe Zucchini, who then joined-up with the 38 South Main delegation, including Ralph Crenshaw. After the nine salvagers got five-minutes of laughter out of their systems, Frankie angled the pull line down toward us, and Bob first, and I second, were dragged and hoisted one at a time from the disgusting quagmire; our grimy forms being hauled-up the pit's slippery embankment, and our cruddy bodies finally yanked-back to ground level.

"News told me all about it," Goose merrily laughed at our dire predicament. "When was the last time you two dumb bastards took baths or showers, because ya' both fuckin' smell to high heaven! You pathetic-lookin' jerk-offs smell so fuckin' bad that I'm afraid you're both gonna' rot my fuckin' dick off!"

"You two college freaks fell for the second oldest trick in the book besides ancient prostitution!" Frankie Fingers reminded us. "Remember where your damned brains are located the next time blood swiftly rushes into your swollen peckers!"

"You'd think that this shitty event would've happened in *Pit*man instead of in boring Glassboro!" amused Joe Zucchini added.

Chapter 35
"Spring Break"

After being dragged-out of the equine feces' hollow, Bob Abrams and I were really absolute messes and totally sorry sights to behold, let alone to be held. The 38 South Main Streeters had brought some old towels and rags to wipe the caked grit off of our faces, heads, necks, ankles, and crusty appendages, and fortunately, Timmy was conscientious enough to bring-along fresh underwear changes, bathrobes, and old slippers. At last, after being vigorously rubbed and scrubbed for twenty-minutes, Bob's and my filthy, ruined, stenchy clothes were hurled into the almost-full pit, laden with fresh and fresher horse manure.

"You shit-infested guys smell worse than a hundred bad fuckin' cases of halitosis bein' breathed heavily inside a city elevator, or inside a crowded closed country closet," Goose incisively slandered our dignity. "After you two take heavy-duty showers and rinse your crotches at least six times, then ya' both oughta' gargle for three hours with *Listerine,* and after that activity, smear the goddamned mouthwash all over your bodies, and balls, and everything else, and then wipe you cruddy asses and assholes with *Lysol* and with *Mr. Clean,* too. But make sure the bald detergent fucker's earring doesn't get stuck up one of your cruddy butt holes!"

Five days later, I finally got out of Clearview Regional, and then really worked hard the next several weeks at Washington Township Junior-Senior High School. But despite my dedicated alacrity, I was very disappointed at receiving a B average for my Practicum labor.

"You did well, overall," Dr. Cowans commended before deflating my ego. "But you missed too many days because of illness, and you need to develop more constructive activities for the students to learn by 'doing' instead of you lecturing to them, and simply reviewing textbook exercises, and just reading aloud, and then silently reading, and just discussing literature stories," the college evaluator cited. "And after you make those fundamental adjustments, I'm sure you'll earn an A your senior year in Student Teaching. Remember," Dr. Cowans advised. "Teachers are expected to show dedication and good punctual attendance, and only miss one or two days from their profession the entire school year."

'If I didn't require all that recovery time from wounds and injuries inflicted by the Delta Alphas and the Tau Kappa henchmen, including George Evans,' I rationalized, 'then I could've easily received an A average in Practicum. My affiliation with the Lambda

Phi's, and my connection with the ongoing frat' war had hindered my ability to excel in Practicum training.'

I realized that I had spread myself too thin doing too many activities in too many places, so I resigned my broadcasting position with radio station WGLS-FM and decided to focus on studying and battling the brutal Deltas and the ruthless Taus. I was now "angrily committed to an educational cause and to a frat' military crusade".

"That horrible horse farm travesty was quite visceral," I told News and Timmy up in the 38 South Main Common Room. "But I want to sincerely thank both you guys for commin' to my rescue with the bathrobe, which I soon had to discard into the fecal pit, along with the old towels, rags, socks, and slippers that we had to throw down there, too."

"That's perfectly alright, J.W.," Timmy amiably responded. "I would do anything for a roommate that smelled like an overflowed cesspool. That odor would force even the most brazen skunks to run-away from the vicinity. Maybe ya' oughta' put some anti-*septic* on those minor cuts and abrasions ya' have acquired, after miraculously survivin' that horrendous horse crap ordeal."

"Timmy, I'd beat the crap outa' ya' right this minute, but then you wouldn't have any puny body left for your fragile bones to support," I affectionately joked.

"Say, guys," Tomasello chattered in his dull monotone. "Jack Ruby's been convicted in Dallas. A jury has found the bar owner guilty of murderin' Lee Harvey Oswald, and Ruby got what he deserved. The TV news reports that he's been sentenced to Death."

"I guess a life 'sentence' would be much longer than ten million paragraphs, and totally impossible to read," I idiotically remarked and snickered. "Judges that believe in long sentences must not know the *laws* of good grammar."

"Where's *Ruby's* friggin' jail gonna' be located, News?" Timmy rhetorically asked. "In the *Emerald* City of Oz, or on a *Major League* baseball *diamond?"*

Tomasello did not interpret our quips as direct discouragement, so the human talking machine continued his simpleton drivel. "And that *Brotherhood of Teamsters* President Jimmy Hoffa has been found guilty of tamperin' with a federal jury back in 1962," News rehashed more who gives a crap jargon. "A Chattanooga jury sentenced Hoffa to eight-years in prison, plus a fine of ten grand."

"Maybe Jimmy Hoffa could join a weirdo prison fraternity by catchin' the caboose on the "Chattanooga Choo-Choo," Tim Amoro creatively reacted and chuckled. "But I guess the union boss can't join a damned fraternity, because he's already in a *Brotherhood* as you had just mentioned. I wouldn't be surprised if Hoffa doesn't marry the Singing Nun when the union boss gets out of the pen', and then vacations on an island somewhere in the blue Caribbean coincidentally named 'Dominique'."

"Remind me to guzz your' damned toothbrush five-times tonight, Tim!" News protested and threatened. "That might make your teeth cleaner and your breath fresher!"

"Guys," I diplomatically interrupted the escalating, silly dispute. "Goose told me in confidence that if Hoffa doesn't keep a lower profile when the thug gets out of jail, then he's gonna' wind-up cemented inside some bridge caisson, or be embedded in the tenth subbasement of a newly-constructed New York skyscraper! And Goose knows all about Mafia methodologies, and Restuccio is an expert on all kinds of gangland rules and rituals!"

And then the divergent conversation switched to contemporary music, and News informed us that a group calling themselves the 'Rip Chords' just came-out with a new California car-theme song titled "Hey Little Cobra", and that the band sounded just like the Beach Boys, and almost identical to Jan and Dean. Timmy Amoro then related to us his preference of "Be My Baby" by the Ronettes, and I related that I really enjoyed the Kingsmen's "Louie, Louie", which had lyrics that were virtually incomprehensible, but totally unique, just like the insane fraternity battles and the crazy world in which *we* were living.

And next, News really busted my chops by saying, "Well, J. W. I'll bet you also like that new Diane Renay number "Blue, Navy Blue", because you've been reconsiderin' goin' back to Lakehurst and becomin' a die (dye)-in-the-wool jet pilot, so that you can be blasted outa' the sky somewhere over North Vietnam," Tomasello articulated. "Things are heatin' up on college campuses all over the country, and it's all about the distasteful idea of President Johnson and his war-hawk cabinet startin' an unwanted conflict in Southeast Asia. The Texas politician wants to protect American democracy from communism growing in Southeast Asia. I mean, the principle just doesn't flush down most people's toilets."

I figured that I would change the subject and solicit my fellow Lambdas' opinions about an important developing matter. A new *LPS* fraternity member named Will "Blade" Barrows had a brand-new black Studebaker Lark convertible, and the pledge had asked me if I would want to get a couple of the Lambdas together to motor down to Florida for the upcoming spring break. I was really keen on

Blade's proposition, and I eagerly presented it the suggestion Timmy and to News, because we all needed a wellness break from *GSC*.

"That's a terrific idea, J.W." Timmy eagerly praised. "But in Florida, the politicians got the royal palm and the open palm, and it's the second kind of palm we gotta' worry about when tanning our regal asses down there! All chiselers don't carve statues all day long, ya' know!"

"Why don't ya' go out and steal a couple of cheap rugs and become a Carpetbagger!" News rebuked Timmy.

"My grandparents have a winter home in North Miami Beach, and they'll be back in Jersey by the start of spring break in March," I constructively informed the guys. "I'll talk the elders into lettin' us use their house if we keep the abode in good order, and don't party there. Mario owes me a hundred-bucks the gambler had borrowed, and if DiMaris pays me back with or without pimpin' his wife as the rumor goes," I qualified, "then we'll be able to drive to Miami with minimal expenses for needed transportation and housing. How about them apples?"

Tim and News immediately endorsed my Florida vacation proposition, and then Ron Carputis and Big Al said the pair also needed a change of scenery, venue, and climate, too. So, after Mario showed-up at 38 South Main with the owed hundred-dollars plus ten dollars "interest", the final trip preparations were organized.

The vernal equinox passed, and the last week in March of '64 arrived on the wall calendar. Blade Barrows pulled-up to 38 South Main, and his five Lambda Phi companions loaded his convertible's trunk to capacity with just vital necessities; two changes of clothes, three pair of underwear per guy, and one bathing suit apiece, which would see plenty of recycling at all-night North Miami Beach laundromats. News joked that his psychic brain wondered if we'd see Goose down there, laundering hundred-dollar bills, and I had to sagaciously make a significant comment.

"Restuccio says his parents have a palace down in Fort Lauderdale, built on a placid canal, just off of Las Olas Boulevard," I spilled a certain Mafia secret. "And Restuccio says he's gonna' meet me Thursday at the Elbow Room Club on South Atlantic Boulevard. Those scenic avenues I'm mentionin' are strange to us right now, but in three short days, we'll know all the streets as well, if not better than Academy, Girard, Harvard, and University Road."

The six of us gleefully piled into the small black vehicle, which featured comfortable black leather seats, and soon we were on *322*, heading west to the *New Jersey Turnpike Interchange*. And in another fifteen-minutes, the very handsome Studebaker Lark was proceeding south toward the impressive *Delaware Memorial Bridge.* The Lark's radio picked-up a hot Baltimore FM station that was playing "California Sun" by the Rivieras; "Fun, Fun, Fun" by the Beach Boys, and "Surf City" by Jan and Dean. The upbeat-tempo-music got us thinking about our semi-tropical paradise destination and mostly about beautiful, suntanned, bikini-clad, college babes arriving in Lauderdale from all over the USA.

The reliable Lark was driven non-stop through Delaware, Maryland, and Virginia, and next we made an "urgent pit stop" (without any associated horse manure) for gas and lavatory needs. Blade gladly relinquished the wheel to Timmy, and Amoro drove further south. The Lambdas rotated drivers every two-hundred-miles, with our itinerary taking us through Virginia, North Carolina, South Carolina, and Georgia.

After we sped past the Georgia-Florida line, Blade stopped the Lark, and the guys sampled our first *Burger King Whopper*s at a northern Florida franchised restaurant. News opened his big mouth and said that since four of us were Italians from Hammonton, that sampling "Whoppers for woppers" was quite appropriate, and the rest of us threatened to tie-up Tommy's hands and put masking tape over his big mouth to keep the prattler silent. And after twenty-three hours of the automobile's tires meeting *Inter-State I-95,* we finally exited the *Florida Turnpike* and entered our much-anticipated destination, North Miami Beach. The first task was to find a liquor store to buy a case of beer, but when Ron Carputis saw a bed and mattress retail outlet, the Lambda clown demanded that Blade Barrows apply the brakes, so that our comedic contingent could demonstrate to *him* our splendid Glassboro Bedding rendition of "Ode to the Bunk".

The rest of us stubbornly refused to participate, so when Ron returned from his failed lark to the stationary *Lark,* Connie Francis's '61 smash hit "Where the Boys Are?" blasted from the convertible's radio, but being full-fledged heterosexuals, we were all wondering and singing to the melody: "Where the girls are?"

It had been four-years since my last visit to my grandparents' home in North Miami Beach, and I was about as lost as the civilization of *Atlantis,* which was believed to be sunken somewhere out in the deep *Atlantic.* Having lost my geographic (but not my sexual) orientation, I pretended that I knew our exact location, and under pressure, directed Blade Barrows up and down numerous thoroughfares, pointing out sights like an effervescent tour guide would ordinarily do. "There's the fabulous *Fountainbleau;* there's the incomparable *Eden Roc;* here's famous *Collins Avenue*." But everyone else kept complaining, "Where's the goddamned house?"

"Why don't ya' have Blade stop at a gas station and ask for directions?" Big Al constructively suggested. "Well, J.W. I gotta' admit. We'd have better directions to the house if we were using a TV Guide instead of you!"

"Because that solution would be too easy and nobody around here ever goes two blocks outa' their friggin' neighborhoods!" I argued in defense of my shrinking, abused ego. "All these derelict gas station employees know about is how to pump gas; and how to pump their old ladies; and how to pump their old ladies' friends, and how to pump each other's wives and girlfriends, and nothin' more!"

After another hour of exploring the Greater Miami Area's main traffic arteries, I finally recognized the name *Biscayne Boulevard,* and eventually, we were able to arrive at our week-long residence, where the fellas' had to drink the entire case of beer for breakfast before it got warm. And then the fatigued revelers dozed-off into unconsciousness and didn't wake up until noon the next day.

The following morning, the re-energized Lambdas ate hardy ninety-nine cent breakfasts at a cheap *Biscayne Boulevard* buffet, and then anxiously climbed into the Lark with the top down. Blade took that same bustling highway north to Hallandale, and faithfully following roadway signs, the Studebaker got onto the *Federal Highway* in *Hollywood* (which somehow got moved from Southern California to Southern Florida), and then motored past Dania, which then was an area especially famous for its dog racing track and its jai alai betting arena.

And soon, the anxious college adventurers were zipping onto Las Olas Boulevard and heading directly into beautiful Fort Lauderdale. The scenic highway in several of its sections was built over a series of picturesque canals and scenic lagoons, where expensive waterfront mansions had been constructed below, several of which, according to the *GSC* gossip mill, belonged to families of wealthy Delta and Tau members who were attending the middle-class college, simply to escape the military draft along with the impending Southeast Asian War, by virtue of academic exemption.

There was something magical about being a lucky young stud thirteen-hundred-miles away from parental supervision and college expectations. That tremendous feeling of independence accounted for the joys of us being liberated from the rigors of adult authority and parental monitoring. Blade parked his black vehicle on a side street; put the top up to avoid theft or easy vandalism; locked the doors, and the guys felt that their first duty was to hit the beach. Seven hours later, we all looked and felt like broiled lobsters after basking in the resplendent Southern Florisa sunshine, even with the application of ample suntan lotion.

"I'm glad this is not a nude beach," News declared, "or otherwise, we'd all be getting our hides tanned."

"Next time you hail a damned cab', ask the driver if he's a *taxi*dermist!" Tim abruptly parried his chief instigator. "We're already doin' this terrific vacation at a *blisterin'* pace, and these water bubbles formin' on my shoulders prove my point."

The town was loaded with college kids from all over the country. Girl goddesses in bikinis abounded and kept our keen eyes occupied, and our exposed skins scorched throughout the Lauderdale beach experience. I reminded the guys that we had to buy groceries to cut-down on restaurant eating expenses, so on the way back to North Miami Beach that first full day of actual vacationing, we stopped and did some serious food shopping, and an hour later, the refrigerator was stocked with chicken pot pies and forty-eight bottles of beer.

On the way back to Fort Lauderdale that evening, Ron Carputis spotted a buffet with a flashing neon sign that read: "All you can eat for $1.00", so we made that place our supper staple after our second night in Florida, until the Lambdas got severe bouts of constipation and diarrhea, sometimes in painful combination, making our digestive stress aggravating our severe sun-poisoning condition.

Fort Lauderdale was indeed a crazy, zany scene of college-inspired high jinks. Students representing big universities from all over the country were attracted to the 'March rites" refuge during the "Easter Break", which, over the years, had somehow lost its religious significance when the week starting with Palm Sunday magically morphed into "Spring Break".

Much of the youthful excitement took on a mock religious tone, with some drunken *Michigan State* rowdies dragging palms before a drunken loon that had somehow manufactured a makeshift cross out of driftwood, tugging the quasi-religious symbol along the crowded sidewalk. There were imitation Buddha freaks and assorted nutcase Mohammed impersonators, with the impostors wearing improvised towels wrapped around their heads simulating turbans, and a few brain-dead lunatics were even giving mock preaching sermons while standing on the back seats of various convertibles. Other weirdos were standing on sidewalk ledges and lecturing non-sensical gibberish to the passing masses; giving phony blessings to the wayward pedestrian foot traffic, and usually, the height of the abundant insanity occurring at various stop lights along Lauderdale's congested Atlantic Boulevard.

Our false, authentic-looking *ID*s worked perfectly at the Elbow Room Club on South Atlantic Boulevard, which seemed to be the beach area's hot spot for the in-crowd to congregate and make romantic contacts. The Lambda Phi's met some attractive girls from *Ohio State University,* and the college cheerleaders invited us over to their motel, and when two *Ohio State* football linemen didn't like our *GSC* presence, Big Al pushed the drunken objectors fully clad into the motel's swimming pool, and the *GSC* squad instinctively decided to evacuate the dangerous scene, despite the objections of the totally gorgeous and completely enchanting *Ohio State* honeys. On the way out of the majestic motel, I witnessed two plastered *Ohio State* fugitives leap from their second-story balcony, splashing directly into the motel's swimming pool, and then the Lambdas finally realized that college kids from all over America were just as warped as those nutcases attending *Glassboro State College*.

On the flight-on-foot while fleeing the *Ohio State* swimming pool degenerates, the Lambdas scurried-back to Blade Barrows Lark convertible. Near the black car, a well-endowed girl from the *University of Texas* removed her wet tee-shirt with the familiar "Longhorn logo", and then took off her bra to proudly flash her partially suntanned, but fantastically solid breasts. Timmy must have had one beer too many at the Elbow Room, because my pal audaciously snatched the blonde babe's bra and her orange Tee-Shirt and dashed into and across a hotel's massive water fountain. Amoro incredibly climbed-up a marble pedestal; threw the bra and the tee-shirt onto a statue of Aphrodite; clambered back down, and escaped the chick's wrath while wildly wading his way through the gushing fountain's shallow water. And much to the delight of a hundred or so amused onlookers, the bare-breasted *Texas U.* doll had to ascend the water fountain's Greek mythology statue, and embarrassed out of her puzzled mind, the zany chick finally retrieved her very important article of clothing.

"Her name must be Erin, and she must be Irish," News quipped on the trek back to Blade's black Lark convertible.

"Why do ya' say that stupid remark?" I asked from my half-inebriated state of mind. "You make about as much sense as Dr. Trenoff divided by Miss Sankins!"

"Because like the natives always say in over Dublin," News jested, "Erin-go-bra!"

The guys were greatly entertained and definitely influenced by all of the frenzy and mania that had been enveloping us. And after we reentered the Lark and drove up and down Atlantic Boulevard like resurrected '50s main drag cruisers, we started to act just as nutty as those demented large university college kids sharing our lush, semi-tropical, physical environment.

At one traffic light, a carload of naughty Penn State babes sprayed three cans of shaving cream into our boss convertible, and the Lambda Phi's retaliated by squirting four tubes of handy toothpaste back at the female instigators, inadvertently ruining their car's plush cloth upholstery. And then, at another red traffic signal, a beautiful chick in a skimpy red bikini stood-up in the rear seat of a Ford convertible and tossed a lit butane lighter into our backseat, and in our wild scramble to avert being torched and incinerated, Big Al landed squarely on the lighter, nearly cauterizing his rectum, when coincidentally, a Bill Elderberry-type blue flame streaked-out from his active butt hole, as Keiler simultaneously passed an abundant blast of gas, thus extinguishing the small fire.

"Quit fartin' around, Al!" News admonished Keiler. "This is a car; not a freakin' penitentiary gas chamber!"

"If ya' keep on breakin' my sensitive stones," Big Al threatened Tomasello, "you're gonna' wind-up in the nearest swimmin' pool, just like those two *Ohio State* creeps did! But in your case, you'll be friggin' anchored-down by a block of heavy cement!"

At an asphalt recreation area, a college dance was in progress, and a DJ was playing my favorite song at the time, "Louie, Louie". Six columns of enthusiastic, half-bombed college kids were doing a new line dance titled, the "Popeye Hitchhiker", which required the completion of a complicated series of moves, jointly performed, that were fairly similar to the '50s Hand Jive pattern of consecutive gesticulations. For some arcane reason, News and Timmy jumped-out of the stopped Studebaker Lark; hustled-over to the preoccupied line dancers; and by surprise, stole several Popeye pipes right out of two massive *U. of Mass* guys' mouths. Then, the petty *GSC* thieves hurriedly fled back to the black convertible and frightfully leaped inside, just as the traffic light changed to green. The incensed *U. of Mass.* theft victims pursued us on foot for another two blocks, but then Blade Barrows detoured onto a side street, where we could more easily and safely accelerate, leaving far behind our new-found enemies, sprinting, cursing, and futilely shouting for their coveted Popeye corncob pipes.

"You guys could sleep on your stolen goods tonight and have pipe dreams!" Big Al gruffly squawked to News and to Timmy. "Now that you've stolen those punks' smokin' devices, you two loony tunes can learn how to pipe-down a bit!"

"Big Al, stop barkin' like a big Baby Huey!" News almost-mechanically retorted. "I'd call ya' retarded, but I don't want to compliment you when ya' don't really freakin' deserve it!"

When Blade eventually steered the dependable Studebaker back onto a major highway artery, Ron Carputis was feeling no pain, and the inebriated Lambda commanded the driver to stop the Lark.

"Is there a mattress and bed distribution business in the area?" Timmy loudly inquired, referring and alluding to Glassboro Bedding. "Maybe we're gonna' hear 'Ode to the Waterbed' recited this time?"

"Do ya' have to find an alley-way to relieve your kidneys?" I asked and busted on Carputis. "As Goose would say, we're a long way from Piss-cat-away!"

Ronnie stood-up and pointed to the middle of his legs and yelled, "I'm a grown adult! Do these *knees* look like they belong on a *kid?* And after uttering those rather corny and insignificant words, Carputis leaped from the convertible, dashed to a statue of Jupiter overlooking a huge shopping center; climbed-up onto the Roman god's right shoulder; lowered his green Bermudas and then his jockey shorts, and deftly mooned several hundred non-amused adults and senior citizens, who were instantly appalled and mortified by the lewd and shocking, uncivilized exhibition.

"Hey, Ronny, we're in Fort Lauderdale and not Miami!" Timmy hollered, feigning being upset. "There's no damned song titled 'Moon over Fort Lauderdale'!"

On our way southwest to connect with then-familiar Las Olas Boulevard, the Lark pulled-up to a red traffic signal with the convertible's radio blasting. When adult motorists around us turned their heads to observe the source of "Dawn", sung by Frankie Valli and the Four Seasons, the rock group's staccato voices were resonating at maximum decibels, much to the disenchanted senior citizens' dismay. The old fossils' eyes soon discovered a carload of insane college studs pretending to be playing invisible instruments while lip-syncing to accompany the radio's loud song's high-pitched lyrics. Our ostentation was specifically implemented to elicit' gasps and frowns from the older "square *WWII* generation". And when the rebellious rabble stopped and politely asked middle-aged pedestrians' directions to non-existent places, our defiant deviation from normal social conventions reached its culmination. And then,

Tim Amoro yelled-out to a motorist at a stop light, “Hey Mr., Elvis is on Q-AM,” and then Blade Barrows turned-up the volume to ‘Jailhouse Rock’ so loudly that the music had to obliterate our ears’ tympanic membranes. The stopped motorist reacted to our perverted antics and semantics by shaking his bald head in absolute disgust, accompanied by dual middle fingers.

On Wednesday morning, we returned to Fort Lauderdale and ate breakfast at what was reputed to be the world’s first *Wendy’s Restaurant*. A *Glassboro State* co-ed stopped by our table and informed us that the Deltas and the Taus had come down en masse via chartered bus from Daytona Beach, looking for some Lambdas in Lauderdale to pulverize. We thanked Carol Drake for her valuable information, and being out-manned by our avowed adversaries that were about to invade Fort Lauderdale, I suggested that we should abandon the town and spend the day down at Crandon Beach Park, where my parents and grandparents had often frequented.

“I don’t want those creeps following us back to North Miami Beach and trashin’ my grandparents’ home when we’re in Lauderdale raisin’ Cain!” I sternly exclaimed. “I don’t need those psycho lunatics ruinin’ *our* vacation and *my* life, any more than those Neanderthals have already!”

“Look, J.W.,” News facetiously answered. “This place is called Fort Lauderdale, right? All we gotta’ do is find the friggin’ fort and then we can hold off the Delta Alpha Omegas and the Tau Kappa Epsilons in a classic siege, sorta’ like the ancient *Trojans,* even without using their prophylactics defendin’ Troy for ten-years against the fierce Greek invasion!”

And so, we drove out of Lauderdale on the now-familiar and magnificent Las Olas Boulevard and enviously admired the stately mansions situated on lagoons and canals beneath the elevated highway. After getting onto *Biscayne Boulevard,* we stayed on that thoroughfare through Miami proper, and motored past the famous *MacArthur Causeway,* which led from the mainland into Miami Beach. Then, our excursion switched onto *Route 1* and took Brickell Avenue to the *Rickenbacker Causeway*, an engineering wonder that bridged-over and connected three stunning small islands, until we eventually would enter Crandon Park.

As we descended the last causeway bridge, the guys perceived what appeared to be a French film director wearing a slanted red beret over his forehead, and the producer/director was wildly waving his arms for us to stop. Of course, we didn’t honor his exaggerated gestures, and the Lark zoomed right by the agitated fellow, driving directly through an in-progress television commercial or movie trailer being filmed.

"What's that idiot doin' down here?" News yelled in total glee, with his hair blowing into his face from the car's speed and the warm Florida wind. "That movie jerk should be up the coast ten-miles in *Hollywood* doin' his stupid filmin'. That's where the French nutcase rightfully belongs!"

Blade parked the car in a remote asphalt lot, and we had a pleasant day at Crandon Park with some pretty *Arizona State* college girls coming down from Lauderdale to enjoy the more tranquil social atmosphere that the more relaxed environment provided. But at four in the afternoon, the sun-drenched Lambdas returned to the black Lark coupe to drive back up to North Miami Beach to shower, shave, and then eat at the dollar buffet to test our bodies' resistance to ptomaine poisoning, which would match our acquired sun-poisoning.

When the group arrived at Blade's automobile, which had had its top down (because we had assumed we were in a safe place), the six of us were stunned to find the Studebaker completely filled with beach sand. A note attached to the windshield stated that the prank had been executed by a combined commando team of Delta and Tau renegades, that had followed our route without our knowledge from Lauderdale down to Crandon Park. And according to the scribbled note, the Deltas and the Taus had also interrupted the enraged French director's commercial shoot two-minutes after we had.

"Well, Blade," News stupidly jested at that most inappropriate and unpropitious moment, "if ya' can crawl into the driver's seat, we'll have the only travelin' beach in all of South Florida!"

"Shut your mouth before I shove a dozen hairy coconuts down your damned throat!" Big Al threatened his chief Lambda nemesis. "This is no time for levity. Leave jocularity to the damned jocks and their athletic supporters! Can't ya' tell how upset Blade is right now? He doesn't exactly look like a happy camper sellin' ice cream as a *Good Humor* man now, does he! Grow-up and get serious, will ya'!"

Big Al volunteered to approach five little kids with red plastic sand buckets and matching red toy shovels, and the Good Samaritan bribed the "kindergarten brigade" to lend us their beach equipment for a half-hour. Keiler had given the junior entrepreneurs two-dollars apiece to go to a nearby concession and get indigestion on hot dogs, soda, popcorn, potato chips, *Good Humor* ice cream, and pretzels. After a full hour of assiduous sand removal, the exhausted Lambdas graciously returned the five red pails and shovels to the disgruntled kids, who were all holding their tender, undeveloped stomachs, and quite ready to barf all over us. Blade found a hand-held whiskbroom in the trunk, and we all took turns cleaning various sections of the rug and dashboard. By five p.m., we had corrected our "community service travail", and the Lambda Phi Sigmas were heading north to our central command base.

Thursday was business as usual at busy storefront activities in Fort Lauderdale, and after talking with some knockout *Utah State* beauties on the crowded beach, I remembered that I had an appointment to meet Goose Restuccio at the Elbow Room Club at three in the afternoon. 'Now, I know why this place is called the Elbow Room,' I finally understood. 'Even in the daytime, you're rubbing elbows with the person standing next to you at the bar, and hopefully, the person will be an unattached chick with big boobs from either *Michigan State* or *UCLA*.'

"Hey, J.W., how the fuck ya' doin'?" an all-too-familiar high-pitched voice solicited my attention. "Hey, some of these young college fillies down here in fuckin' Florida could get jobs as strippers at Jezebel's Den over on Delilah Road in Pleasantville, or as topless barmaids at the Venus Club in Mays Landing. If any of 'em are from South Jersey," my rendezvous friend proposed, "I can set the broads up."

"Er, Goose," my tongue stammered from lack of a temporary word sentence. "I don't know if any of the college dolls ya' see here are interested right now in *that* kind of questionable employment. Where are ya' stayin'?" I asked G.R., before taking a short swig from my dark brown *Budweiser* bottle.

"A couple of blocks from here at the Flamingo Motel," Restuccio reported without cursing. "And no sooner do I check in when a couple of horny *Glassboro State* broads came-over and said they had gone to a few Lambda Phi functions at the Aura chicken coop and also at the Williamstown Republican Club, and right before I was about to ask the wannabe' whores if they fuckin' wanted to get a threesome goin', one of the gabby cunts tells me that the goddamned Deltas and the mother-fuckin' Glassboro Taus have come-down from Daytona Beach to Lauderdale in two chartered buses. And the shit-heads plan on raisin' some hell with you outnumbered Lambda Phi guys. Is this fuckin' true?"

"They've already filled Blade's car with beach sand down at Crandon Park," I felt compelled to report. "And who knows what they'll attempt next. Hey, Goose, I think we'd better go and check your apartment with those *GSC* fraternity gorillas in town, and with their ugly, fat, Japanese henchmen probably on the loose."

After I had swallowed-down the last refreshing ounces of my cold beer, Goose next told me that beer wasn't good for me. "Why not?" I balked. "Beer made *Bud* wiser, didn't it!" I exclaimed using an old Bo Jalonec joke.

"Yeah," Restuccio declaratively replied. "But it makes J.W. poorer and more stupid every time he's gotta' buy a round of brew for the friggin' Lambdas over at Seedy's Bar."

When Restuccio and I arrived at the aforementioned expensive Flamingo Motel, Goose led me to his first-class suite; unlocked his metal door, and then flicked-on the lights. "It's not exactly the *Hilton* or the *Sheraton,* but what the fuck do ya' expect from a rinky-dink town like Lauderdale?"

"How come you aren't stayin' at your parents place ya' once told me about, just off of Las Olas Boulevard?" I asked in the living room area of Restuccio's de-luxe suite. "We've driven on Las Olas, going over those canals and palaces, which are sensational to admire!"

"Because Frankie Fingers and Joe Zucchini and some of the family Florida thugs are fuckin' stayin' there," G.R. complained and explained. "And my folks are now out in goddamned Vegas collectin' syndicate money, and I don't want those shit-faced Deltas and Taus discoverin' where the fuck I live down here, and then commin' over and bustin' up and trashin' the mansion, or maybe even torchin' the family yacht! It's okay if I know where *they* fuckin' live down here, but it's not fuckin' alright for those retarded assholes to know where my fuckin' place is down here. Ya' dig?"

"Well, how did ya' get to the Flamingo Motel from the *Miami Airport?"* I inquired. "Did ya' take a cab?"

"The family limo' chauffeur picked Frankie, Joe, and me up and then fuckin' dropped off the others at the Las Olas pad, while I'm fuckin' stayin' two nights here in Lauderdale, and then flyin' back to Philly' with you, J.W."

"You mean to say I'm flyin' back and not drivin' with the guys in Blade's Lark?" I asked in mild astonishment.

"That's fuckin' one-hundred percent right, J.W.," Restuccio verified. "I got a neat trick planned for the cock-suckin' Deltas and for the shit-eatin' Taus, and I want you around to help me fuckin' use my *cruise-shell* plan against the dirty, mangy, mother-fuckers."

Goose showed me his well-appointed apartment, which the spoiled Sicilian described as "a lousy dump", and when the junior millionaire opened the lights for the master bedroom, Restuccio let out a shriek that made me shudder and instantly leap backwards.

"Ahhhhh!" the Mafia heir screamed as if his life was in jeopardy. "There's two fuckin' ugly, nasty-lookin' alligators climbin' outa' my fuckin' bathroom!"

"Leapin' lizards!" I shrieked and jumped back, as Restuccio frantically slammed the door shut to separate us from the fairly huge carnivorous reptiles. "Holy crocodile eggs!" I bellowed with my tonsils vibrating. "I hope there aren't any other giant lizards around to give those two crawlin' monsters in there' gator aid."

Restuccio asked me to leaf through the yellow pages of the local phone book and contact an alligator farm, because the suspicious Don didn't want the police involved with the resolution of a dangerous fraternity prank. I located Bob's Gator Farm near Lake Okeechobee, and the congenial manager said that the business could dispatch a truck out to the designated room at the Flamingo Hotel in an hour for a minor fee of three-hundred-and-fifty-dollars, with the service call and traveling expenses all included.

"Goose, alligators *are* indigenous to this section of Florida," I reminded my still quivering pal. "You must know that the Everglades are not too far away, and I'm sure that gators like swallowing-down a few ducks, and an occasional goose, too!"

"J.W., stop talkin' about a fuckin' animal menu while I'm so fuckin' upset. I don't fuckin' know anything about fuckin' *in-digit-this* and fuckin' *in-digit-that.* All I fuckin' know how to do is count goddamned money! That's all the fuckin' math' I need to know!"

At seven a.m. on Saturday morning, Goose's black limousine showed-up at my grandparents' new North Miami Beach housing development property. Goose and I bade farewell to the vacationing Lambdas still staying there for another day, and after I reminded the guys to vacuum the floors; clean-up the place; empty the trash, and lock the doors, I put my small suitcase inside the impeccable limo'. and soon we were heading to *Miami International Airport* with Frankie Fingers driving and Joe Zucchini riding shotgun.

"Why are we takin' an airplane back to Philly'?" I curiously asked my chief benefactor. "You must really have money to burn!"

"Because fuck-head! I already told ya' that' we're both gonna' play a trick on the Ortegas and the Krappa Toros, because those sneaky shit-heads are gonna' be on the same plane flyin' north."

"How?" I inquired. "We're only two guys, and they're gonna' be at least sixty. How can we possibly play a workable prank with those kinds of stilted numbers goin' against us?"

"You'll see," Goose said with a wide grin accentuating his distorted facial features. "You'll see, J.W.! You'll wanna' give me a goddamned fuckin' blow-job after ya' see what the fuck's gonna' happen to those asshole Ortegas and Krappa Toros."

The limo' driver showed the tarmac attendant stationed at the south gate some impressive credentials, and the black omnibus had the privilege of going-out to a chartered plane, conveniently situated next to a remote terminal gate. I still couldn't figure-out the mystery behind Restuccio's ambitious, grandiose scheme.

"Okay, J.W. You and me get out, and Frankie and Joe will take the limo' back to the mansion over in Lauderdale. And guys, you two jerk-offs can use the fuckin' family yacht, but don't crack the mother-fucker up while checkin' out some of those stacked college chicks that are populatin' the Lauderdale beaches."

Restuccio accompanied me up the step-stairs that led inside the fairly new charter prop' plane. "Now, J.W., I wanna' introduce ya' to the pilot and the co-pilot, who are really employees of my Pop, who owns a majority stake in this fuckin' private airplane company."

The missing pieces of Goose's complicated strategy turned-out to be quite simple after all. G.R. and I were to ride up front and sit with the two chief air navigators. But instead of landing in Philadelphia, the pilot would tell the Delta Alpha and the Tau Kappa passengers over the plane's intercom that he was having slight mechanical problems, and that it would be best to discreetly stop in Bermuda to have the minor engine difficulty corrected, in order to ensure total safety for everyone aboard.

Several hours later, when the four-engine prop' landed at the *Georgetown Island Bermuda Airport,* the captain imperatively announced that there would be a necessary three-hour-delay, and that the passengers should all exit and wait inside the terminal for the repairs to be satisfactorily completed. Another announcement would instruct the disgruntled passengers when to again board the plane.

The disappointed and fatigued Delta Alphas and Tau Kappas descended the movable step-stairs, and as two airport employees pushed the mobile stairwell on wheels away from the aircraft, Goose yelled-out from the exit door, "You stupid Alphie Ortegas and Capa Episalong mother-fuckers! This oughta' teach ya' to fuck with the Lamp-da Phi's!" Next, Restuccio and I swiftly closed the plane's entrance and exit portal, isolating the two sets of screaming *GSC* fraternity members left outside.

Chapter 36
"The Chestnut Neck Incident"

The cooperating pilot, who had already been cleared for takeoff, fired-up the engines, and the plane began to taxi from the apron toward the runway. The livid Deltas, the incensed Taus (and their dozen Japanese Sumo henchmen) led by Dave Littlefield and Sal Walker, were cavorting and jumping all about, pleading their case to airport employees on the tarmac, who probably thought that *they* were simply involved in the middle of a frivolous college fraternity prank, and evidently, the airport personnel on the ground in Bermuda wanted no part of the ongoing, outrageous caper.

"How will the Deltas and the Taus get to *Philadelphia Airport?"* I asked G.R. I think by now, they suspect that they've been tricked."

"That's their fuckin' problem!" Restuccio matter-of-factly answered. "J.W., I believe that's their fuckin' problem!"

* * * * * * * * * * * * * *

Blade, News, Timmy, Big Al, and Ron returned to Glassboro on April 2nd, and the traveling Lambda delegation was not-at-all ready to be re-absorbed into the totally monotonous college study-test routine. We exchanged anecdotes about our separate air and land itineraries by plane back to Philadelphia, and by auto back to New Jersey, and the other 38 South Main Lambdas were thoroughly impressed with Goose's excellent airplane diversion to Bermuda.

"How was the return drive back to *GSC?"* I asked News, Big Al, Timmy, and Ron, who were visiting the upstairs 38 Main apartment to see how Goose and I had made-out with the cunning Deltas and with the volatile Taus. "Did you guys have anything out of the ordinary happen, or was it all another just-passin'-through-*Dixie* junket, without any ice-cream cups?"

"Well, J.W., first of all, somewhere in swampy southern Georgia, not far from the famous Okefenokee Swamp, it got really foggy, and Blade had trouble seein' the road, let alone the steerin' wheel," News reported. "Then, Barrows runs over somethin' round, and we were afraid it was a human head, or maybe an alligator skull. Being scared shitless, we kept on goin', not stoppin' to investigate the highway object in the dark, and leavin' that particular responsibility up to the *Georgia State Police."*

"It couldn't have been Goose Restuccio's head," I chuckled, "because the football-head was already back home in Hammonton, and because G.R.'s head is obviously oval and not round. And as you know, News, you once said, 'Goose would've had trouble livin' in England in the mid-1600s durin' their big Civil War because the guy couldn't have been one of Oliver Cromwell's Round Heads."

"You talk really big like that J.W., because Goose isn't here to beat the stuffins' outa' you," Timmy quite accurately chimed-in. "But getting back to our trip north after Blade had entered South Carolina, these small-town cops, or constables, or deputies, or whatever the hell they were, stopped us in a speed trap goin' twenty-seven in a twenty-mile an hour zone, somewhere on *Route 301,* since we had been detoured off of *I-95* because of bridge construction and highway maintenance. So then," Amoro continued his litany without hardly taking a deep breath, "the Nazi cops also accused us of passin' a tractor-trailer on the right at a stop light a mile back, when the truck should not have been in the passin' lane, and should've been in the right lane all along," Timmy continued, now-panting like an overheated puppy. "But then, Ron here goes over to the police dog growling in the one cop's car, and the mutt starts fiercely barkin', and beyin', and flashin' his sharp fangs. And then a lunatic cop threatens to lock Carputis up for obstruction of justice, or for some other trumped-up mother-humpin' false charge like that."

"And then," Lambda Ron Carputis contributed, "Big Al goes over to the two cops and tells 'em *we* all watch *The Andy Griffith Show* on television, and that we really like Mayberry RFD, even though we were in South Carolina and Mayberry is supposed to be in North Carolina. And next, I told the apathetic cops that we also liked Don Knotts as Deputy Barney Fife on the TV program, and if the two fuzz knew Barney in person, who as you know is an imaginary fictitious character livin' in Mayberry, which is also a pretend place," Carputis facetiously emphasized, "then the Lambdas would like to meet him in person some time."

"And to top that dumb-shit fabrication," Big Al vocalized, "Timmy' asked the hick town' cops if the keepers of the peace had a cash register to ring-up fines inside the patrol car to keep all the fine money they were collectin' from speedin' motorists that had been detoured off of the *Interstate* onto *301,* and the insulted cops threatened to lock-up Amoro on trumped-up charges."

"So, after that nonsense occurred," News concluded after finally catching his breath, "Big Al tells the two hick cops from the anonymous hick town that we didn't have money to pay the stupid thirty-dollar-fine; that we all wanted to go and check-out the jail, and that we all had big appetites and planned to stay in the clinker for at least ten-years, because we were all starvin' to death. But I think the clincher was when Timmy told the obstinate cops that our rich parents were all big-time lawyers and card-carrying Mafia members, and that hit teams would be invadin' their hick town, tryin' to track-down their precious children, and their promiscuous wives, and their lesbian girlfriends. And so," Tomasello elucidated, "the hick cops, being fully baffled, relented, and let us go without even issuin' Blade a warnin' ticket. But naturally, the fact that there were twenty other cars lined-up behind us that had been caught in the cop-factory speed trap might've also been a factor in the fuzz's decision to let us go on our merry way, Scot free."

News then reminded us that the *World's Fair of 1964-65* was scheduled to open on April 22nd in Flushing Meadows, New York, and that President Lyndon Baines Johnson was going to deliver the dedication speech. "And if you're interested, Flushing Meadows is not far from a twin city known as Flushing Toilets," Tomasello irrelevantly concluded.

"I know where Flushing is," I authoritatively commented. "*Shea Stadium* and the *Forrest Hills Tennis Stadium* are right next to where the *World's Fair's* amazingly bein' erected, without even the use of any juvenile Christmas set gifts."

"I'll bet plenty of anti-war demonstrators are gonna' show-up to protest and shout Johnson down," Timmy predicted without any available crystal ball or Tarot cards. "There's growin' sentiment risin' about not doin' the war, and even here on campus, some students are becomin' radical and militant, goin' against the idea of getting killed for powerful fat, sefish, bald-headed politicians in Washington, and many freshmen are droppin' out of society and turnin' into listless beatniks, believing that they're Apache Indians, or pioneers riding out West Conestoga covered wagons, and even lookin' like those pioneers, too."

"And the press is playin' it all down, of course," Ron Carputis vociferated. "But there are indications in the smaller newspapers that racial violence at the *Fair* could cause low attendance, along with the high cost of food, beer, and admissions."

"Terry Stafford, that new Elvis' sound-alike, should sing his new hit song 'Suspicion' up there in Flushing," News witlessly suggested. "And Jan and Dean could sing 'Dead Man's Curve' to give the *World's Fair* and President Johnson's speech some accurate musical accompaniment."

The Common Room phone rang, and I was almost happy to escape the meaningless 38 South Main conversation and hear Goose

Restuccio's inimitable, high-pitched voice that sounded a little like Frankie Valli's staccato speaking, rather than singing. "J.W. ya' fucked-up jerk-off, how the hell are ya'?"

"Great!" I semi-exclaimed. "But if I rode back with the guys in the Lark, then I'd probably be quite tired and too pooped to poop, like the guys are right now. What's up, Goose?"

"Not my dick!" Restuccio replied in a weak attempt at mimicking quality college humor. "I've noticed that two of those son-of-a-bitchin' Alphie Ortega fishin' boats are commin' from the *Egg Harbor* up the *Inter-coastal Waterway* to the *Mullica River,* where I fart-around once in a while with my new speedboat, and the trouble-making pricks are hangin' around outside *Chestnut Neck Marina,* where I keep my daddy's cabin cruiser. I got my fuckin' new cigarette-shaped speed boat docked down on the *Mullica* at *Sweetwater Casino,* and I want ya' to meet me there on Saturday at 11 a.m. to fuck-up the snoopin' Delta Alphie Ortega bastards, once and for all!"

"Okay, Goose!" I agreed, making a mental note of the prescribed time and place. "*Sweetwater Casino,* across the river from historic *Batsto Village* at 11 in the morning on Saturday, April 5th."

"That's right, you' moron college mool-en-yan lover!" Restuccio loudly indicted, effectively busting my delicate testicles. "And get to the fuckin' casino early, so that we can drink and gargle some goddamned red vino!" Click.

"Dave Littlefield and Sal Walker are really pissed because they've failed Trenoff's 'Tests and Measurements' class, and can't graduate out on the lawn in front of *College Hall,* I told the guys. "The ingrates gotta' make-up the credits over the summer time, and only Trenoff teaches the F-trap course in July and August."

"So, what's your point?" Ronnie challenged. "We already know from experience those elementary particulars."

"My point is that those two fraternity creeps are gonna' wanna' pressure Abrams and me for the answers to Trenoff's final when the two numbskulls have to take that exam a second time," I related. "And if the molesters can't obtain the correct responses by persuasion or by bribes, then they'll probably resort to intimidation and force. What I'm sayin' is that the frat' war is not over by a long shot, as evidenced by what happened with the beach sand to Blade Barrows's Lark down in Crandon Park, and with the non-docile alligators deliberately stashed inside Goose's pink bathtub at the Flamingo Motel."

On Saturday morning, according to schedule, I met Goose at the indicated time and at the designated place, and immediately, Restuccio began bragging about his new red speedboat, *Goose's Gadget II*. "J.W., this sucker can do over fifty-five on the water if it has to ever escape the Coast Guard Patrol. The salesman over at *Egg Harbor Boat Company* says this baby has around sixty-five fuckin' horse power."

"Wow! It sure is a dream machine!" I marveled and complimented. "Could I navigate it with minimal instruction?"

"Ain't nothin' much to it," G.R. bluntly answered, feigning nonchalance. "If ya' can drive a fuckin' motorcycle, or shit in a toilet shaped to match your ass, ya' can easily drive this goddamned thing. It's easy as smellin' and eatin' pussy blindfolded. I'd show ya' how to do that, too, but there aren't any nice-lookin' cunts or boo-tanas walkin' around on the dock right now."

My erratic host and I climbed into *Goose's Gadget II* right where the speed boat had been tightly moored. My river mentor activated the powerful outboard motor; we untied the bow and stern ropes, and the Italian stallion then put the *Gadget II* in gear. G.R. gently guided the sleek wave-cutter away from the Sweetwater dock, and then we gingerly drifted-out of the *Casino Marina* into the *Mullica's* main channel.

"Exactly how much did this expensive baby cost?" I curiously inquired. "I would need a full piggy bank as high as the *Empire State Building* just to buy one of these gems."

"More than your' friggin' house and farm market are worth combined," the self-appointed navigator boasted. "Cigarette-shaped *Fiberglas* speedboats don't come as prizes in *Crackerjack*' boxes, ya' know. They're a little more expensive than white '61 Chevy Impalas on the goddamned black market."

"I know that ya' told me about the river laws a couple of years ago on our last trip up the *Mullica*," I mentioned to avoid more unwarranted insults. "Could ya' please review them for me?"

"All ya' gotta' know is ya' pass other boats commin' the other way on the right, and they fuckin' pass your ass on their left," my mentor related. "It's sorta' like drivin' a car on the fuckin' highway."

"You mean saying *by left,* on the port side," I clarified.

"J.W., what the fuck's the matter with ya'?" my *Mullica River* tour-guide strenuously objected. "There's ports on the left side, and ports on the goddamned right side, all along this damned curvy river, and all over the whole shiteatin' coastline. Didn't we have this same fuckin' conversation on this same river back in high school?"

"In other words," I suggested and recalled, "ya' always keep to the right, no matter which way you're goin'."

"That's right, Jerk-weed!" G.R. chastised. "Not like in fuckin' England where the fools drive cars, and boats, and buses, and their dicks ass-backwards! If you give me any more dumb shit, J W., I'll slice your dick-off and send your tiny boner to Oscar Mayer!"

Goose then gave me a vital brief refresher lesson on channel markers, claiming that certain parts of the *Mullica* up near Sweetwater were shallow, and that amateur and professional sailors had to stay in the center of the river to avoid shoals, or else, their boats would scrape the bottom. "Notice the markers on those long poles planted in the river. They're called 'day markers'," my cruise director lectured, without even once cursing or swearing. "Notice Dip-shit, that the red markers are on the left, and the fuckin' green ones are on the goddamned right. The poles mark where the main river channel is, and we gotta' safely keep between those goddamned markers, or this here fuckin' wild-ass speedboat might just become a fuckin' death anchor."

"I get it," I understood. "Ya' gotta' keep closer to the green marker to stay to the right, and the red markers are probably green on the other side, for traffic goin' toward Sweetwater."

"J.W.," G.R. admitted and shook his head. "You oughta' manage a sewer plant, because you really know your brown shit from your fuckin' yellow piss!"

"Where are we headin' now?" I wondered and asked. "Didn't you say something about a Walnut and a Throat?" I jested, simply to intentionally to elicit and egg a vitriolic reaction out of my guide.

"No, you' stupid dick slapper! We're goin' down to *Chestnut Neck Marina,* just past the *Parkway' Bridge*," Restuccio informed. "It'll be a nice ride for an amateur boats' man like yourself, and if you're lucky, you'll get tangled-up in a couple of crab traps, and tumble overboard when we're goin' fifty-miles an hour."

"*Chestnut Neck!*" I pondered and exclaimed. "Isn't that where the Hammonton Blues used to keep all their boats?"

"Boats!" Goose yelled. "Ya' fuckin' mean yachts. Those guys run cunt-grabbin' cabin cruisers with huge dual inboard motors. The rich blueberry farm jerk-offs don't fart-around with lousy penny-ante speedboats, like this red piece of shit is in comparison. But now they've moved their yachts fuckin' south to Wildwood and to Cape May. But it's not the Blues I'm worried about on this special cruise, J.W. It's those fuckin' Delta Alphie Ortegas and those fart-faced Capa Krappa Episalongs."

"*Chestnut Neck* was the scene of a *Revolutionary War'* battle," I said, as I shifted into my academic gear, since News Tomasello was not present to fully elucidate on the historic matter. "American privateers had a warehouse at *Chestnut Neck* and auctioned-off goods the patriots stole from British ships. The cargo thieves advertised the auctions in Philly' and New York newspapers," I related to apathetic deaf ears. "The British got angry and leveled the town, but the Redcoats never made it down to *Batsto* to torch the bog-iron cannon ball factory."

"J.W., who gives three turkey turds about what the fuck happened at *Chestnut Neck,* or at Walnut Throat in your little kid's fuckin' history book ya' study at college," Goose criticized. "I wanta' know about why the ass-wipin' Deltas have come-up from Mays Landing on the *Egg Harbor* to the *Oyster Creek* and *Chestnut Neck* areas on the *Mullica* to scope-out my private activities."

"Say Goose, what are those bobbing barrels doin' floatin' on the river?" I inquired.

"This is a goddamned 'No Wake Zone' on the *Mullica,"* G.R. confidently stated. "You're only supposed to go fuckin' five-miles-an-hour under this here shit-eatin' bridge, and just as slow while floatin' by the asshole houses on both sides of the river."

"No wake zone. Is everybody sleepin'?" I stupidly joked. "Is there a funeral parlor viewing around here to attend? Where are we now?" I asked and bantered, just trying to make idle discussion about an already known fact.

"This here shittin' place is called Green Bank, and there's another bridge just like this one five-miles or so down the goddamned river at Lower Bank. Then, the channel gets deeper and wider as we move out closer to the bay, and finally to the mother-fuckin' *Atlantic.*"

"Look at the forests and the sky," I remarked, appreciating the river's resplendent aesthetics. "It's all really marvelously beautiful out here. It's sort of like communion with nature. It's like the dysfunctional world has stopped, and we're the only two livin' creatures enjoyin' this terrific river, all to ourselves."

"J.W., you're a goddamned dreamer," Goose correctly derived and derided. "And ya' gotta' make big bucks out there in the real world to be able to have the fuckin' luxury of cruisin' this river and getting away from friggin' *syphilis-zation.* But maybe someday you'll advance from a dreamer to a white dreamer, and you'll know when that particular change happens; when you'll find all yellow stains on your white jockey shorts."

"You're far too materialistic," I argued and accused. "There's more to life than money and sex for money, and racketeerin'."

"You're right, J.W., there's power and influence, too!" Goose yelled as the speedboat throttled-up to twenty-miles per hour as we sped beyond Green Bank. "Have ya' ever been in a big city department store?"

"Yeah, it's easy once ya' get beyond the revolvin' door," I answered. "My folks used to take me to Gimbels and Wanamaker's on Markt Street in Philly."

"Well, J.W., life's full of fuckin' revolvin' doors, and your dull life is now stuck in a maze of 'em. Revolvin' doors are power objects," G.R. declared.

"Power objects? How?" I queried.

"Listen. Everybody tries to trap you in their own fuckin' revolvin' door, which just make themselves feel more powerful," Goose logically indicated. "Mr. Andrews had ya' trapped in his spinning door back in high school; Joanne Berenato in hers; your parents in theirs, and the fuckin' Delta Alphie Ortegas and the son-of-a-bitchin' Capa Krappa Episalongs now want to intimidate us into their friggin' revolvin' door," Restuccio stated and insisted. "If ya' learn how to stay outa' other people's revolvin' doors, ya' can then trap your enemies in your own revolvin' door, and then learn how to fuckin' become rich and famous off of the trapped assholes."

I assessed the insights that Ronald Goose Restuccio had conveyed, and I saw a degree of merit in his hypothesis and in his logic. The speedboat again slowed-down for the *Lower Bank Bridge,* and the accompanying 'No Wake Zone', and several signs and barrels anchored and bobbing in the river alerted us to that fact.

"I think I remember News sayin' somethin' about an International Waterway Code," I mentioned, "and this 'No Wake Zone' business must be part of it."

"Only seven or eight more miles to the friggin' *Garden State Parkway Bridge,* and then we'll hit *Chestnut Neck,"* Goose laughed and informed. "But don't worry, J.W. I'm not gonna' pull into that goddamned marina. I know that the Delta Alphie Ortega taco boats are patrolin' around there. I just wanta' open this baby up when we get near the *Parkway Bridge* and then…"

"The *Parkway Bridge!"* Say Goose, that's where Jives began racin' Dion and the Belmonts," I interrupted. I began describing to Restuccio how Edgewood High buddies Jives Arena, Fabian Midilli, News Tomasello, Juice Illiani and I had gotten involved racing with Dion and the Belmonts on the *Garden State Parkway* when my astute eyes perceived two pleasure yachts on the *Mullica* heading our way at intense speeds. As the small armada approached, I had a funny feeling that some significant problem was about to occur.

"Yeah, J.W.," G.R. proceeded with his river lecture. "Right here is about where the goddamned fresh water line ends and the fuckin' salt water from the ocean begins. It's sorta' like the point of no return. Comprende, Amigo?"

"Er, Goose," I gagged with a lump forming in my throat. "Aren't those two boats commin' towards us a little too fast?"

"Jesus Christ!" Goose loudly shouted. "That's Littlefield's two yachts I was tellin' ya' about, commin' right towards us."

Restuccio swung his new red cigarette-shaped speedboat around, and quickly turned the craft's lever to full throttle. The two pleasure cruisers had to momentarily slow-down because of the *about-face* wake that *Goose's Gadget II* had created, which gave us a temporary advantage in the ensuing chase.

"Those wicked mother-fuckers ain't gonna' ever catch me!" Goose screamed like a complete lunatic. "If they do, I'll have *you* suck all of their dicks as a ransom deal."

"Watch-out ahead! We're trapped!" I yelled as my right hand pointed to a boat coming through the closed *Lower Bank Bridge*.

"You're as fuckin' stupid as those clowns chasin' after us are!" Restuccio reprimanded. "Now, I'll do a complete three-sixty around those warped mother-fuckers, and then slow-down enough to have them fuckin' chase me all the way up to *Chestnut Neck* on the bay!"

"What do ya' have planned?" I yelled back as the early April wind blew my long hair into my face. I was holding on for dear life, fearing that Goose was going to capsize the speedboat, but centripetal force, which I had learned about in Mr. Jenkins's high school physics class, came into play, and *it* kept me from falling out of the speeding, circling speed boat.

Goose made the rotation around the *Delta Alpha* piloted by Dave Littlefield and the *Delta Alpha II* being steered by Sal Walker. Pernicious half-dozen Sumo wrestlers were standing on each boat, along with six or seven fraternity members being visible on each of the two yachts, all vehemently cursing and yelling while sporting raised clenched fists in reaction to the enactment of *our* daring circling maneuver. G.R. had to safely navigate a series of five serpentine bends in the meandering river, in order to finally have a fairly straight run to *Chestnut Neck*.

The *Goose's Gadget II* sped under the *Garden State Parkway Bridge,* but Restuccio made certain that his right hand kept his speed at thirty knots, so that the two pursuing yachts could keep pace with him. “I don’t wanna’ discourage those mother-fuckers too soon, or else my secret plan might short-circuit!” Goose hollered above the roar of the powerful outboard motor’s whining. “Keep your eyes peeled on those four guys in that anchored fishin’ boat to the left, where the red channel marker is.”

“So what?” I hollered, quickly becoming more concerned at being stalked by the pair of impressive cabin cruisers. “It’s only four guys fishin’ from an anchored dingey that’s gonna’ rock and roll from our wakes, when the three speeding boats pass by!”

“You fuckin’ dumb ass nitwit!” Goose shrieked and then cackled. “That’s Frankie Fingers and Joe Zucchini pretendin’ to be fishin’, along with two professional scuba divers that I’ve hired!”

No sooner had Restuccio bellowed those decisive words from his long vertical throat that we slowed-down, and then zipped right by the four men occupying the small fishing boat. The two yachts slowed-down, too, but the first one scraped bottom and opened-up its hull from the huge impact, and the second luxury cruiser harshly plowed into the first, doing around fifteen knots.”

“What the hell happened?” I gasped in amazement. “What did *you* make happen?”

“Ha, ha, ha!” Goose laughed like an asylum patient possessed with ninety-nine and a half demons. “Those two scuba divers and Frankie and Joe had moved the green channel marker over fifty-feet, so that when the first ship slowed-down, it scraped against a few jagged reefs or rocks, located on the bottom at low tide. If they had fuckin’ continued at their regular high speed without slowin’ down, Littlefield’s stern woulda’ stayed higher in the water, and the two son-of-a-bitchin’ collisions wouldn’t have ever fuckin’ occurred.”

“You mean to say that those four guys pretendin’ to be fishin’ had illegally moved the channel marker, and when you slowed-down this speedboat, you were able to safely navigate over the shoals,” I panted and gasped. “And the Deltas and the Taus weren’t the ones causin’ two separate accidents within a matter of five seconds?”

“That’s fuckin’ right, J.W.!” Goose lustily laughed. “You’re smarter than the average fart shootin’ outa’ Einstein’s fat ass!”

Chapter 37
"A Real Dive"

"But what happens now?" I asked. "I mean, what will Littlefield and Walker have to do with their damaged boats? I don't think anyone was injured in the crash, thank goodness!" I stated, just as G.R. turned north into the main bay, heading toward Mystic Island.

"Well, J.W. First of all, they'll send out an *SOS*. Some salvage river-rats from the marina and the *Coast Guard* will come-out to fuckin' investigate' the accident, which was fuckin' really a cleverly schemed incident. Then, the salvage guys will fuckin' plug-up the hull in the first boat, and then tow the two goddamned wounded cruisers into *Chestnut Neck*."

"How much will the repairs cost?" I inquired. "Big bucks!"

"Ha, ha, ha!" Goose continued laughing his buttocks off. "The salvage for the two yachts will come to around ten-thousand each. And that's not countin' the fuckin' huge damage to the twin cabin cruisers, that I figure will come to around thirty-grand more."

"Won't insurance cover the losses?" I asked.

"That's the funny fuckin' part!" Restuccio indulgently laughed, nearly busting-out of his tight white cotton pants. "When the *Coast Guard* and the salvage old salts tow the two crippled boats into *Chestnut Neck,* the divers and Frankie and Joey go right back to goddamned work and move the buoy back to where it belongs in the goddamned channel. And then, when the *Coast Guard* comes-out again to measure the water depth, they'll find…"

"They'll find that the markers were in the right place, and that the first boat captain was not payin' attention, and maybe even drunk, and that the frat' navigator went out of the channel and scraped bottom," I concluded in astonishment. "So, at low tide your speedboat could pass over the shoal, but when the *Delta Alpha* slowed-down, its rear went lower into the river and the luxury cruiser scraped bottom."

"Exactly, you champion shit!" Goose laughed and snorted until the "Mullica River Admiral" loudly farted twice while bending-over from suffering accumulated intestinal gas pains. "And the fuckin' State investigation will show that Dave Littlefield was outside the goddamned channel and was fuckin' negligent, or some legal bull-shit term like that. And the insurance company won't pay for the fuckin' damages because the captain wasn't payin' attention to the fuckin' river rules and markers! Ha, ha, ha, J.W. Ya' don't mind if I fuckin' fart again out loud do ya'! Ha, ha, ha, ha! I hope my balls and ass don't fuckin' propel right off my goddamned bony body! Ha, ha, ha!"

* * * * * * * * * * * * * *

Several weeks passed on the *GSC* campus without any major incidents occurring between the Lambda Phi's and the humiliated and now boat-less Delta Alphas and the vanquished Tau Kappas. On Tuesday night, April 21st, Timmy Amoro and I walked at 3 a.m. from 38 South Main to Angelo's Diner to have some coffee and apple pie, and next discuss the general situation of events in and around campus. I always enjoyed sharing Amoro's company because besides News, Tim was the one Lambda Phi who had a personality and personal interests parallel to mine.

"Every time I see Peachy," I intimated to my pal, "I feel guilty as sin about dumpin' her right before her father died. And every time I see Alexis Terranenkov," I admitted, "I go the other way before she starts tossin' me around like a pet *Raggedy Andy Doll* and contemplates either rapin' or body slammin' my ass in public. And Candie Davison is definitely outa' the romance scenario because the doll knows Joanne too well, but another problem I have is that my girl wants me to get more involved with her and not with the adventurous Lambdas, so my disheveled mind and my ambitious heart are always intensely battlin' each other."

"Why don't ya' just get Joanne involved with a major Lambda Phi project?" Timmy shrewdly suggested. "Then, Hercules, you can kill two eagles with one boulder."

"Good solution-oriented idea, Tim!" I commended. "I'll file that nugget away for future reference. But getting back to Goose callously destroyin' the two Delta Alpha yachts near *Chestnut Neck,"* I returned staying on task, "on the way back to *Sweetwater Casino'* Restuccio says he wants to learn a little Shakespeare and has the audacity to ask me to recite some verses for him, so that the academic dunce could repeat the lines and act sophisticated when he's impressin' Frankie Fingers and Joe Zucchini."

"Well, that's mighty odd and kinda' on the strange side of peculiar!" Lambda Amoro attested, knowing full well Goose's abhorrence and contempt of higher education. "Was the attitude sincere, or was the insecure turk tryin' to mock and ridicule you and your academic knowledge, as is G.R.'s singular style?"

"I can't tell for sure," I honestly confessed. "But the only lines I could think of as an example from Shakespeare were from *Romeo and Juliet,* I think. So, Timmy, I pretended that I was a faggot thespian on stage at the *Globe Theater,* the one in medieval England, and not the striptease joint on North Atlantic Avenue in Atlantic City, and I imagined that I was dressed in tight leotards, and I melodramatically recited to Goose, 'She sleeps with hope in her soul. I'll snatch a kiss and flee into the night'."

"Dr. McIntire would've gotten a huge erection just listenin' to your discourse that sounded a lot like male-to-male intercourse, if ya' just substitute the pronouns *he* and *his* for *she* and *her*. So, J.W., did Restuccio capably repeat those simple basic lines?" Amoro curiously inquired before sipping more coffee.

"Yes, well anyway, the Romeo impersonator attempted to orate the words," I related with a wry smile. "Goose said in a very serious way while recklessly steerin' the speedboat all over the damned river, 'She sleeps with soap in her hole. I'll kiss her snatch and pee into the night, until I piss directly into the wind.' And I'll tell ya' quite sincerely, Timmy," I mirthfully related, "I laughed so damned hard that I nearly lost my equilibrium sittin' inside the *Gadget II,* and my ass almost tumbled into the murky *Mullica* while Goose was doin' around forty-five knots around a bend, which is far more dangerous than forty-five Don Knotts appearin' as Deputy Barney Fife on *The Andy Griffith Show,* which Big Al habitually watches all the friggin' time."

"Where's Paul Meroski tonight?" Tim wondered and asked. "Usually, the *Avant* editor comes to Angelo's with you. Ya' always tell me he's real good intellectual company here at the diner."

"He's spendin' some time with his new girlfriend at Sunset Cabins over on *Route 47,* you know, between here and Runnemede," I divulged and informed. "Paul's goin' for his mattress and spring testin' certification, and needs a few more trainin' sessions to officially qualify for pussy plowin' honors."

When Tim and I departed Angelo's Diner, we turned left to cross High Street in the direction of 38 South, but a hundred-feet ahead, near the corner of Main and High, burly surly George Evans and his three pugnacious brothers were standing there, waiting to snare us into their perilous custody. I grabbed Timmy's arm and lowly said, "Let's take off the other way towards the Franklin House. Those black dudes wanna' capture our butts and take you and me as doomed hostages."

Amoro and I did a radical one-eighty, and when the four black dudes quickened their pace and were only fifty or so feet behind us, we decided to flee their approaching presence, and subsequently, endeavored to outrun the sprinters. A hundred-feet up North Main, six immovable Sumo wrestlers popped-out of the foliage, and the dastardly villains intercepted and captured us. Then, I noticed the familiar dark blue van parked along the curb, and I restlessly related to Tim, "Okay, we're gonna' be tortured, so say some prayers for salvation, because it might already be too late for redemption."

"News is right about you!" Timmy yelled as the maverick vainly struggled, attempting to escape the clutches of three gigantic, hippo-type Sumo wrestlers. "Anyone who goes anywhere with you at night either gets kidnapped, or molested, or both. Why didn't I friggin' listen to Tomasello and avoid you as if you were small pox, or the *Blue Bonnet* (bubonic) plague, or something lethal like that?"

By that time, villainous George Evans and his three mean-spirited henchmen had arrived on the assault scene, and my livid friend and I were flung like two *Raggedy Andy Dolls* (without the assistance of Alexis Terranenkov) into the rear of the dark blue van.

"Where are ya' takin' us this time?" I vociferously shouted to Evans. "Back to Peaks Horse, Apple and Peach Farm to enjoy another stenchy pit visit?"

"Ha, ha, ha!" George indulgently laughed, along with his three muscular siblings. "Your wild guess was pretty close to the damned truth, but your skinny lily-white ass is gonna' soon find-out our destination in about fifteen-minutes. Have you two bozos ever been visitors to the world-famous *Steel Pier* near Virginia Avenue, over on the Atlantic City Boardwalk?"

"Sure, many times," I acknowledged. "I've seen Fabian, Frankie Avalon, Ricky Nelson, and Dion and the Belmonts perform there. And I've been to several *General Motors* car exhibits, and I've also been inside the *Diving Bell,* and not to mention…."

"That's enough horse-shit from you, ya' talkative, fucked-up college honky," George nastily interrupted my Homeric litany monologue. "You'll be visitin' the *Steel Pier* in about fifteen damned minutes! Ha, ha, ha, ha!"

"But that's illogical!" I squawked. "Atlantic City is about fifty miles from Glassboro, and it's impossible to get to the north end of the boardwalk in less than an hour!" I defiantly debated my chief captor's veracity.

"Well, white honky, you'll have to relearn your goddamned geography, ya' snow-white dough boy," Evans hollered, as the tough guy and his belligerent brothers actively demonstrated their not-too-hilarious laughing reaction. "We're friggin' rewriting the area's South Jersey map tonight!"

The six humungous Sumo wrestlers predictably piled into the rear of the used blue van, nearly rupturing the ancient mode of transportation's shock absorbers and suspension system with their ton-and-a-half of prime porterhouse. And then, George drove us off of Main, made a left onto *322,* and I knew from the imaginary map inside my head that we were in the process of soon passing by the college. The Reflections new tune "Just Like Romeo and Juliet" was being played on the AM radio, and instantly, I thought about the Shakespeare lesson I had given to Goose Restuccio on the *Mullica River* junket, and about my vacillating romance with the enchanting Joanne Berenato. And next, Mary Wells's popular new number "My Guy" came over the airwaves, and I wondered if "my girl" would ever again see me alive.

"You' wet-behind-the-ears crackers hang-out at Angelo's Diner?" Evans yelled-back to Timmy and me, seated on the van's oil-stained rug. "That place is a real dive. But where we're takin' ya' both right now, that place is an even bigger dive! Ha, ha, ha, ha!"

"Stop talkin' in evasive riddles!" I adamantly protested. "Where are ya' really takin' us?"

"I promise that you're both gonna' get tanked while horsin' around again," George guffawed in enigmatic lingo. "But you're not gonna' get tanked at Mazzeo's Bar this time, that's for damned sure! Ha, ha, ha, ha!"

The dark blue van rumbled west past the village of Mullica Hill on *322,* heading-out towards Bridgeport, a Jersey town situated on the *Delaware*. My mind figured that around three-miles past the *I-295* exit, Evans had steered the vehicle to the right, and we traveled for ten-minutes on a secluded country road, unfamiliar to my mental map. Then, the diabolical driver again turned right onto a bumpy dirt trail, and two-minutes later, Evans applied the brakes.

"We're here!" George enthusiastically announced to his un-captivated captives. "Are ya' two retards ready for your audition for the *Steel Pier?* Mr. Littlefield and Mr. Walker didn't exactly relish *one bit* what the hell happened to them out at *Chestnut Neck,* and so the two honchos figured that they're due for some sweet revenge."

Timmy and I were forcefully pushed-out of the van and were lucky to land on our feet. Before us was a twenty-five-foot-high ramp that served as a pathway to a fairly large wooden box constructed at the top of the incline, which extended-out like a wide diving board, existing over a huge water tank.

"Okay, you Peckerwood pecker-heads," un-Gorgeous George unsympathetically belittled. "This here is the official trainin' camp for the high divin' horses that perform every summer at the end of the *Steel Pier*. Now, one of you' crackers is gonna' get on a white stallion, and then the trap door at the bottom of the box opens," Evans commanded. "The horse with the lucky rider mounted on its back will zoom down the fifteen-foot-long metal slide, and then dive the remainin' fifteen-feet smack-dab into the middle of the water tank. Not bad entertainment, huh?"

"But it takes a highly-skilled rider to perform such an incredibly difficult stunt!" I strenuously objected. "Timmy or I could get killed, without either of us bein' expert equestrians! This prank is entirely too dangerous, and could result in sudden death!"

"Well, worried white wonder boy," Evans racially ridiculed. "It looks like you've just volunteered to be Mr. Godiva with your clothes on! Hope your family has good health insurance! Let me know the next time you get a decent boner. I'll slice your erect dangle off and send it First Class Mail to Bob Evans!"

A handsome white stallion was taken-out of a nearby red barn by one of the imposing Sumo servants, and the obedient horse and me were led-up the diagonal incline to the starting box's launching position. Soon, I was hoisted-up by a mechanically cranked crane onto the magnificent animal's back, without any saddle to sit upon. And then, the restive beast was eased into the small rectangular corral, before the rear wooden gate was slammed shut and locked.

"Hold tight to the reins, white boy, because that's your only control mechanism. This is the first time I've ever seen a horse's ass sittin' on top of a horse's ass! Ha, ha, ha, ha!" George Evans bellowed and hardily laughed, as the culprit's three brutal brothers relentlessly giggled and snickered.

I sat like Napoleon atop the impressive white stallion, until a release pin was detached, and the trap door at the bottom of the wooden corral opened, which instantly sent the white horse and me swooshing-down the stainless-steel ramp like we had been thrust out of a medieval catapult. Before I could close my eyes and start screaming for dear life, I was flung off the plummeting horse and went hurtling, and soon plunging into the eight-foot-deep water tank, which upon my splash entering, I was surprised to discover that the giant tub had contained salt water.

And then a formidable Sumo wrestler paced-down a planked side-ramp and grabbed the horse's reins, and the thoroughly wet animal was guided up the incline and safely escorted back onto ground level, where an exit door was soon opened.

"I can't swim that well!" I shouted-up to my tormentors. "I'll drown in another few minutes with all of these wet, heavy clothes I'm wearing!"

"Don't worry, you' stupid Italian stallion!" Evans hollered and laughed down at my predicament. "My brother Marvin, who's not gay, likes horses, so that's why he was over at Peaks Farm for the memorable horse crap caper. He'll-drain three feet of *agua* out of the damned metal aquarium, once we do one more spectacular thing!"

And the next event that occurred was Timmy being hurled into the tank without even being given the choice of riding a trained diving horse. Marvin turned a valve, and luckily, within three-minutes, the enormous vat had only five-foot-deep water left inside it, so that Timmy and I could actually stand without needing to either swim or float.

"Are you' circus assholes ready for a little more fun?" George Evans persisted in badgering Timmy and me. "Well, let's see how crabby you idiots can get after we throw two-hundred live crawlers and two-hundred hungry lobsters into the salt water. Ya' better keep your hands over your peckers, because it hurts a lot more when your tender dingle gets caught in a crab or lobster claw than when one of your fingers does! Ha, ha, ha, ha!"

My Lambda Phi companion and I were absolutely petrified as two-dozen-bushels of voracious, ravenous crabs along with famished lobsters were ambitiously dumped into the shallow saltwater tank, and my loyal friend and I defensively covered our dingles and our shriveled-up testicles, praying that only our fingers would be severed and devoured. We stood erect without erections, trembling and afraid to take a step, hoping that the excessively starved, crustaceans would think that we were seascape decorations, rather than human bait, or their edible *chums.*

"What's God's phone number?" I asked my dumbfounded and flabbergasted Sigma associate. "I need to get on the heaven hotline right away."

"It can't be 'Et cum spiri, tu tuo'," Timmy replied, "because that's the Pope's phone number. Why don't ya' try C-l-o-u-d-9, but it really doesn't matter J.W., because we don't have any phones here in this alien, dank tank! You'll just have to try advanced mental telepathy, commonly known as prayer!"

It was a most terrible and an extremely unbearable psychological anguish, standing there in five-foot-deep salt water, accompanying by greedy lobsters and crabs, flitting around our ankles, knees, and vulnerable legs. Several of the mobile creatures were crawling all over our tennis shoes and pants. I prayed for a sudden, swift, and painless death, and hoped that my body would be discovered in short time, in order for a proper embalming and burial before the crabs and the lobsters consumed all of my organs, tissues, and valued dingle.

"These distasteful crawfish are like hyperactive crawl-fish," Timmy neurotically lamented. "News was right about you! You carry the damned Devil's curse all throughout your damned body!"

The Delta Alpha Omegas and the Tau Kappa Epsilons had made one strategic mistake in the calculation of their imaginative torture-chamber tank. The larger lobsters were ignoring Timmy and me and were feasting off of the smaller crabs, but Timmy and I knew that if we weren't soon rescued from our punishment in twenty-four hours, the larger crustaceans would eventually figure-out to start taking chunks of flesh off of our torsos, rather than committing marine cannibalism, and consuming and devouring each other.

"I'll never go to the damned *Steel Pier* again!" Timmy nervously reckoned and uttered. "And if I ever escape this horrible ordeal, I'm gonna' file a complaint to the *SPCA* for animal cruelty, the way the owners of this camp or farm treats horses and humans."

"How about grievin' your case to the *SPCH?"* I corrected my encumbered, incarcerated friend. "That would be more appropriate!"

"SPCH?" Timmy questioned.

"Yeah, the *Society for the Prevention of Cruelty to Humans!"* I testily answered. "It's not in the damned phone book's yellow pages, and it's not even in the damned white pages, either!"

Thank goodness for the female heroines Elaine Hill and Joanne Berenato. The "good girls" picked-up some relevant gossip the following morning inside the Co-op about what had happened, and what *was* happening to Timmy and me. And the two humanitarian *Evergreen* chicks immediately conveyed the vital information to Big Al, News, Mario, Hoss Gregorio, and Ron Carputis. The five crusading Lambdas accosted the nearest available Delta, a kid named Russ Stillwell, and after Mario threatened to conduct the kid to a nearby hog farm, cut off his tender fadorkenbender and testicles, and then toss the severed organs into the nearest convenient swine trough, so that Russ could watch slimy pigs consume his sexual equipment, while simultaneously bleeding to death, Stillwell under immense duress, told the Lambda Phi cavalry the exact location of the diving horses' *Steel Pier* training grounds.

Chapter 38
"Clementon Lake Park"

The posse showed-up just as Tim was about to collapse, and just as I was about to faint from general fatigue and from overexposure to the cold April night' elements. And after the two of us were successfully rescued using sturdy ropes, and next tugged from our horrendous persecution, Mario performed a most ungraceful belly flop into the saltwater tank, and found anf grabbed a half-dozen healthy lobsters to take back to Hammonton.

"Ironically," News chortled, "DiMaris, when translated from Italian into English, means something like 'of the sea'."

"Mario, when you smacked your huge bod into the water, three lobsters flew-up directly toward us, and we had to duck our heads in a hurry!" Ron Carputis hollered-down to the colossal behemoth.

Tommy Tomasello also had some eccentric words to deliver to the *Hammonton Baker*. "Mario, make sure there's no peanut butter and jelly-fish in that salt water tank, because the toxic jelly-fish could sting and shrink your testicles with their poisonous tentacles!" News yelled-down to DiMaris, who looked a little like *Orca* the whale, or *Moby Dick* appearing in human disguise.

"I'm gonna' give a couple of these big suckers to Goose Restuccio when I get back to Hammonton," Mario yelled-up and promised. "He once told me that he likes eatin' crusty-stations!"

* * * * * * * * * * * * *

"Did you guys see Mario belly flop into that saltwater tank like a pregnant sperm whale?" News eloquently exclaimed to Timmy and me on Wednesday afternoon, as we judiciously conferred upstairs at 38 South Main. "I'll bet DiMaris emptied more water outa' that horse pool than Marvin Evans had drained after turnin'-on the damned valve! And J.W., you had said you think that George's younger brother had let about three-to-four-feet of water out of the massive tank, right?"

"That's a good guess-timation," I automatically agreed. "And on the way back from the diving horse farm to the college this morning, Mario tried cheerin' me up, so the gargantuan Leviathan tells me a weird story about him goin' into a mom and pop convenience store on Fairview Avenue in Hammonton, and when the football lineman checked-out with only two purchased items, the clerk asked DiMaris if he wanted a bag, and Mario answered, 'No thanks, I'm already married to one!' Now if that isn't a classic put-down line, guys, then I don't' know exactly what is!"

"J.W.," News rather sarcastically remarked, "before ya' fart in the bathtub the next time, make sure ya' got a cork up your ass and keep all your damned stagnant gas to yourself. You're nothin' but talk, all gas! That's why your ideas are so damned ethereal."

"News is as right as Republican Senator Barry Goldwater from Arizona," Timmy jested. "What Joanne sees in you, J.W., defies all hospital x-rays! But just like Goldwater, in her heart, your sweetheart knows she's right."

I had just received my Student Teaching assignment for the fall semester, and was rather disappointed that I would be learning and mastering the art of instruction in the rural, four-room Folsom Elementary School just outside Hammonton, with a class of twenty-four students, grades six-to-eighth-graders, all mixed together. I was hoping to be placed into a large system like Clearview, Washington Township, Williamstown, Overbrook, or Sterling, but I had to adjust mentally for the mammoth Promethean task that would confront me the following September. I protested the placement with Dr. Ash, my Student Teacher adviser, but the erudite professor's position on my situation was that I should take the assignment with a grain of salt, and that I should perceive the responsibility as "a challenge" instead of as "a hassle".

And on the positive side, I had received some exceptionally good news at the end of April from Goose Restuccio. Through *his* influence throughout South Jersey, and by virtue of the crazy guy's many unethical contacts, the twelve Japanese Sumo wrestlers, along with George Evans and his three delinquent brothers, had been brought (bought) over to the Lambda Phi Sigma side, and were now in Goose's employ at the discretion of the Lambdas, especially the ones living at 38 South Main Street. And so having the upper-hand in our fraternity grudge poker game, Bob Abrams, Goose, and I met to contrive a foolproof plan to further thwart the diabolical Deltas and the satanic Taus once and for all.

"J.W.," Goose began as we conferred in a Joe's Sub Shop booth. "Joanne says she wants to fuckin' get involved in some Lamp-da Phi Stigma mischief before she graduates from *Glassboro State*. What the fuck did ya' have in mind? News and Tim told me that you are *a-fairy-yell (ethereal)* and can fuckin' communicate with Tom Bell's sister *Tinker Bell*."

"Well, as you're fully aware, Goose," I responded without addressing Restuccio's grammar, diction, distorted vocabulary, or perverted allusions, “the Deltas and the Taus both have their myriad moral *deficiencies.*”

“J.W.,” Goose seriously interrupted. “What the hell do fish in the oceans fuckin’ have to do with your fuckin’ plan? And ya’ sometimes say that I fuckin’ talk in twisted riddles when ya’ often sound like one of those double-talkin’ queer-bait invaders’from Mars, or like some cock-suckin’ low I.Q. homo’ space alien!”

“Well, Goose,” I commenced in my defense. “I’m not too happy about my ridin’ the *Steel Pier* white stallion into the water tank, and then getting pinched and bitten by a colony of bad-tempered lobsters and crabs,” I peevishly indicated. “And I also didn’t enjoy bein’ thrown into the foul horse manure pit at the Peaks Farm; or ridin’ that insane buckin’ bronco over at Cowtown; or bein’ dropped-off at the nudist colony at Sundown Beach; or bein’ tortured by snakes in Clayton; or bein’ kidnapped in a reefer in Swedesboro, and then coincidentally windin’-up at Hunts Point Food Distribution Center in the Bronx, or collectin’ with my mouth putrid, infected clams, buried in sand at Carneys Point!”

“So, what’s your big point you’re tryin’ to make?” Bob Abrams asked while begging for clarity. “But more importantly J.W., what’s your innovative plan involvin’ Joanne?”

“Okay, we’ll not only get Joanne involved in this classic operation, but also Elaine Hill, who can be trusted to the max’,” I emphatically answered. “Now guys, we’ll divide-up into two teams to jointly perform the incomparable trick. Goose, you and Bob can capture next year’s Delta and Tau Presidents, Fred Patton and Randy Irwin, right here in Glassboro. In the meantime, take along the new Lambda Phi pledges Nicky La Sasso and Joe Sacci, so that the recruits can enjoy a little excitement outside of academics. And then,” I added, “the 38 South Main guys will take care of Dave Littlefield and Sal Walker, usin’ Joanne and Elaine’s charms as alluring bait. Now here’s what I have in mind.”

The assembled leadership unanimously endorsed my scheme wholeheartedly, and the complicated trap would be set for, or before Saturday, May 9th, with the implementation of the creative ruse being enacted the following Saturday night, May 16th. I intended for the bizarre strategy to unfold just prior to the end of the spring semester, and a month before the much-anticipated advent of summer vacation. We all shook hands on enacting the deal, and Goose generously picked-up the tab for our Italian hoagies, Philadelphia-style cheese steaks, and for our *Pepsis.*

"J.W.," Restuccio concluded and promised. "I know a couple of fucked-up flunkies that work over at *Clementon Lake Amusement Park* that owe me and my Pop some bookie debts. I'll erase those goddamned *IOU's* if the ass-suckin', lowlife grease monkeys cooperate with your plan. I gotta' tell ya', though; I need a fuckin' urinal right now, because your fuckin' scheme is a real pisser!"

I had made-up a script for Joanne to read over the telephone from the 38 South Main Street Common Room, and her call would be addressed to Dave Littlefield over at the Delta Alpha Omega House on Harvard. Elaine Hill tagged along to provide my calendar girl moral support, should Joanne falter in her well-rehearsed presentation. On Saturday night, May 9th, at six p.m., Joanne dialed the Delta House and requested to speak with Dave Littlefield.

"Hello, is this that Delta Alpha Omega hunk, Dave Littlefield?" Joanne began her introduction while demonstrating a very sexy and alluring phone voice.

"Speakin' and in person. Who's this?" the vile Delta head honcho inquired. "Do I know you?"

"My name is Joanne Berenato. I used to date one of the major Lambda Phi's, you know, that freaky jerk cruisin' around in a white '61 Chevy Impala."

"The divin' horse creep?" At least lame-brain Littlefield knew the identity of one of his professed enemies.

"Yeah, him. We broke-up about a week ago after a big argument," Joanne fibbed in a feigned depressed tone, as the amateur actress read from the prepared text. "And I understand that you and Sal Walker also broke-up with your main women, too."

"Wow! Now I know who you are!" Littlefield realized and jubilantly exclaimed. "You're that luscious Sicilian broad with the pearly white teeth; and the radiant jet-black hair, and the terrific big brown eyes. How ya' doin', Gorgeous? My envious eyes check ya' out at every opportunity."

"Just great!" Joanne convincingly exclaimed. "Now Dave, I want you to know that I quiver whenever I think of your huge biceps and your totally masculine broad shoulders. You're what the other girls call 'a real hunk'."

"Yeah," Littlefield vainly agreed with ample conceit. "They're really my pride and joy, and my entire body is worthy of both male and female admiration."

"And Dave, I want ya' to know that my panties get real moist whenever I think about how big and strong you must be in all the right places," Joanne competently lied, rather radically contrary to her normal, shy, lady-like demeanor.

"Er, thanks for the fantastic compliment," the non-graduating Delta President responded to the phony, flowery flattery. "Most girls are afraid to express or show their appreciation of my awesome strength and power. You must need a new boyfriend!"

"As a matter of fact, that's why I'm specifically callin' ya'," my true-blue girlfriend replied. "But I wanna' tell ya', Dave, I'm really horny and very lonely lately. How would ya' like to take me out for a get-acquainted date?"

Dave Littlefield seemed stunned at being propositioned and solicited over the telephone by a promiscuous, super-sexy co-ed named Joanne Berenato. "Er, tremendous Joanne. Where to? When should we meet? Er, where should we meet?" the outgoing Delta Alpha Omega President anxiously stammered.

The swarthy-skinned Italian dish then told Littlefield that she had a close girlfriend named Elaine Hill, who was totally disgusted with News Tomasello, and who was dying to meet Tau Kappa Epsilon President Sal Walker. Joanne aptly explained that News had recently dumped Elaine for a weirdo bisexual, and my girl wanted to arrange a get-even double-date with the Delta and Tau Presidents to make J.W. and News jealous and exceptionally pissed-off.

Littlefield quickly agreed to Joanne's seemingly innocuous-but-treacherous request, and then my true-blue girlfriend suggested that the four should meet at the Co-op at six p.m. on Saturday, May 16th for a "fantastic double-date *to Clementon Lake Amusement Park,* between Berlin and Blackwood.

"See ya' about six, just before it gets dark," Joanne promised the arrogant, self-centered creep. "And don't forget to bring Sal along to the Co-op, or my best girlfriend Elaine will become very disappointed, and that might ruin *our* excitin' evening together, too. Ya' got your rear in gear, and ready for no fear?"

Dave Littlefield couldn't believe what his *Dumbo*-like ears were hearing. "We'll split-up into two cars after Sal and me get to take you through the famous Clementon *Tunnel of Love,* and then the four of us will drive back to Glassboro, right?" Littlefield boldly 'proposed' to his vivacious caller, with no intention of getting engaged.

Joanne was anxious to bring closure to the set-up conversation. "Exactly, Dave. Then, we could rock and roll like there's no tomorrow," my woman persuasively predicted. "I wanna' see your face at that place. And Dave, if you're really lucky, you might even get to visit a second love tunnel, if' ya' know what I mean? Ya' might even have to change your name to Dave Bigfield after *I* get done with you."

"Er, sure thing," intrigued Littlefield stuttered, showing his great nervousness and anticipation at Joanne's very audacious and scintillating statement. "Sal and I will see you and Elaine in the Co-op next Saturday at six. Thanks for callin' Sweets." Click.

Joanne Berenato and Elaine Hill had skillfully set-up Dave Littlefield and Sal Walker, just like Janice Littlefield and Becky Walker had effectively double-crossed and hoodwinked Bob Abrams and me at Mazzeo's Bar, right before *our* breathtaking expedition and grueling misadventure. It was a good thing that most of Littlefield's head blood had drained from his cerebrum to some other smaller appendage of his muscle-bound body, because under normal thinking conditions, the nitwit would have recognized that my plan was merely a devious Delta Alpha/Tau Kappa ruse in reverse.

Joanne and Elaine met the two horny legends in their own minds at the Co-op, and then Littlefield drove the twenty-minutes out to *Clementon Lake Amusement Park* in his four-seat red Thunderbird. The couples rode the *Jackrabbit* roller coaster; the *Giant Ferris Wheel,* and enjoyed some caroms and collisions on the vintage *Bumping Car Ride*. After playing some games of chance and eating pizza and French fries, washed-down with *Cokes,* according to plan, Joanne and Elaine pleaded with Littlefield and Walker to escort them through the park's popular *Haunted House* before finally taking a gondola ride through the dark and romantic *Tunnel of Love*.

After experiencing the fun house's tilted room; the space distortion room; the hall of mirrors, and awkwardly walking-over the rolling, bouncing barrels, the *Haunted House* maze-like passages became dark and scary, until the fun house's midway juncture, where the two pair of revelers plopped-down at ten-second intervals onto the phenomenal *Magic Carpet,* which was a rotating eight-foot-wide rug that served as a human conveyor belt, taking the enthralled riders for an exhilarating seventy-five-foot diagonal, downward trip. Just as the four thrill-seekers exited the *Magic Carpet* area and entered a infamous dark haunted labyrinth, Mario DiMaris, Big Al, Hoss Gregorio, News, Timmy, Wild Bill Elderberry, Ron Carputis, Paul Meroski and myself were waiting to separate the two stooges from the much-relieved Lambda Phi chicks.

An employee that had been notified by Goose of the 9:10 p.m. operation had shown *us* a well-concealed side maintenance door, where we eventually dragged Littlefield and Walker, who at first actually believed that they were being abducted and mugged in the dark by bellicose total strangers. Inside the "interrogation closet", Timmy flicked-on a light, and it was then that the two shocked and frightened-out-of-their-minds fraternity big wigs finally realized the true nature of their custody.

"You could've screamed and shouted all you wanted back there in the three dark corridors," News lectured to our two captured adversaries, "and no one would've paid any attention to you two idiots because you were only doin' what you're supposed to be doin' in a damned haunted house, screamin' and yellin'!"

"What are you goin' to do with us?" Littlefield stammered while still suffering from emotional trauma and duress. "I think we have a *right* to know."

"Even though it's not specifically stated in the *U.S. Constitution,* after the park closes at eleven," I explained, "you'll find-out the essential facts then. Until that time, *your* two disloyal dates are goin' to enjoy News's and my exquisite company in the *Tunnel of Love,* while the other Lambdas in your presence will make sure that no harmful injuries happen to you," I curtly commanded. "Just make yourselves comfortable in this miniature custodial closet and think about what might just happen to you and your testicles right after midnight!"

I knew that people fear the unknown much more than even the horrid realization of knowing their doomed fate, so the mental torture that accompanies extreme apprehension would plague the two isolated imbeciles' minds and emotions for the next three hours. Joanne and I, along with Elaine and News, merrily toured the remainder of the *Haunted House;* went through the *Tunnel of Love* seven consecutive times; checked-out the weekly dance inside the amusement park's main pavilion, and then at eleven o'clock sharp, walked to the parking lot; hopped into my Impala, and then News and I escorted the fine young ladies back to *Glassboro State* before the looming midnight curfew.

"That was really great fun," Elaine told News, Joanne and me. "At last, I've been involved in a historic Lambda Phi fantastic prank, and I loved every second of it."

"I'm sure glad *you* were in the *Haunted House* with me, Joanne sighed. "It would've been horrible goin' into the *Tunnel of Love* gondola with that disgusting egomaniac freak. You're a brilliant diamond J.W., when compared to that conceited artificial chunk of Delta quartz who took me to Clementon!"

That same evening, Abrams and Goose's commando squad (that included Hoppy, Nicky LaSasso, Joe Sacci, George Evans, and three very corpulent Japanese Sumo monsters now on Restuccio's father's payroll) had deftly kidnapped the next year's Delta and Tau Presidents, Fred Patton and Randy Irwin, outside of *Evergreen* dorm'. The two prospective chief executives were then conducted to the back employee entrance to *Clementon Lake Amusement Park,* that was off limits to the general public.

At twelve midnight, exactly when News and I were returning from *GSC* to the scenic amusement park, three speedboats conducted the second Lambda Phi entourage across the large lake, which was positioned at the posterior section of *CLAP.* Then, the group walked several-hundred-feet, directly to *Clementon's* most sickening ride, the infamous *Salt and Pepper Shaker*. The park had been evacuated of visitors for a full hour, and so, and only a skeleton maintenance crew loyal to Goose's authority was around to check-out and work on ride adjustments, and perform basic early season chain and equipment greasing.

The two Lambda teams met-up in front of the *Salt and Pepper Shaker* with our four apprehensive captives, who were within the grasps of Hoss Gregorio and Mario DiMaris, and George Evans and the biggest of the three Japanese wrestlers, respectively. Everyone was staring at the popular park attraction that was to be imaginatively utilized by the Lambda Phi Sigmas under Goose's sterling direction.

The daunting *Salt and Pepper Shaker* wild ride consisted of two oval compartments on either end of a huge vertical shaft, which was anchored into the ground, serving as the thrill ride's base. Each oval compartment contained two sub-compartments that were attached back-to-back. The *Salt and Pepper Shaker* ride would first rotate around like a *Ferris Wheel,* and then gradually change angles from three-sixty to one-eighty, and then back to three-sixty again. After two-minutes of turbulent and crazy revolving, while simultaneously vacillating from side-to-side in two separate-bu-concurrent motions, the zany ride would then grind to a halt, and then perform the same motion patterns backwards for two additional minutes, making the passengers want to vomit, belch, fart, choke, spit, sneeze, curse, shit, piss and gag.

"Okay, you dunce-like fuck-heads," Goose commanded to the two Deltas and the pair of Taus in our secure custody. "I wanna' see Littlefield and Walker get fuckin' back-to-back in the first two cages, and when the goddamned *Salt and Pepper Shaker* rotates to its change positions, I wanna' see the other two fuckin' clowns climb back-to-back into the second set of compartments. Now, do what the fuck I say," Restuccio menacingly threatened our prisoners, "or else we'll drown you four assholes in the fuckin' lake over there, and then stuff your remains down a sewer somewhere in fuckin' South Africa, or maybe in fuckin' Tim-Buck-Tooth!"

Littlefield and Walker reluctantly entered the first compartments facing back-to-back, and then the friendly operator of the ride rotated the "two eggs", with the one having the two "human yolks" a full hundred-and-eighty-degrees, with Littlefield and Walker now being thirty-feet up above the ground. Then, Fred Patton and Randy Irwin were forcefully deposited inside the second set of back-to-back compartments; the egg's two doors were slammed shut, and the riders were advised to fasten their seat belts.

"How long are we gonna' be in this damned thing?" Patton asked with much anxiety evident in his voice. "I get motion sickness pretty easy on long trips."

"Well, it's twelve thirty-five right now, and the day crew shows up at the park at nine to eventually open the gates at noon, so I imagine you'll experience only around nine delightful hours of twistin', twirlin', rotatin', and barfin'!" I proudly announced.

"J.W.," Goose remembered and spoke-up. "Did ya' bring-along that fuckin' new 45 record ya' was tellin' me all about? These lucky clowns will enjoy havin' the privilege of listenin' to the goddamned swingin' lyrics for the next nine fuckin' hours."

I handed Restuccio a copy of the Beach Boys latest hit, "I Get Around", and G.R. gave the 45rpm record to one his major park contacts, who incidentally owed the Sicilian Don massive gambling debts. The Beach Boys' lively four-part-harmony song came over the ride's sound system, and I yelled to all four passenger in their four respective *Salt and Pepper Ride* egg compartments, "The bad guys know you, but they *won't* leave you alone!", deliberately adding a negative contraction while referring to a certain verse in the song that had been masterfully manipulated to especially accommodate the ever-vigilant Lambdas present needs. Everyone except Fred Patton and Randy Irwin laughed in response to my exceptional good humor, which seemed to get better results at *amusement* parks than inside the Co-op; inside Angelo's Diner; inside Joe's Sub Shop; inside Mazzeo's Bar; inside Seedy's; inside the Franklin House, or inside 38 South Main.

After about an hour of hearing the Beach Boys sing "Round, Round, Get Around, I Get Around" and "The Bad Guys Know Us But Leave Us Alone", the assembled Lambdas and their hired henchmen became bored and tired with the *Clementon Lake*

Amusement Park festivities, and so we left the popular facility via separate exoduses, while listening to the four sick, nauseous, rotating passengers hoarsely screaming and shrieking, as our tortured victims puked their guts all over themselves, and all over their respective, revolving amusement cages.

* * * * * * * * * * * * *

Summer vacation arrived upon the college calendar, with classes finally ending May 18th. I was happy that I once again had made the "Good Dean's List", and I was emotionally maturing, and becoming more serious about studying, and about finding future public-school employment as a professional Junior-High-School English/social studies instructor.

News and I got together over the hot '64 summer and exchanged some 45s that had become popular: namely "Memphis" by Johnny Rivers; "My Boy Lollipop" by Millie Small; "Viva Las Vegas" by Elvis, and "Under the Boardwalk" by the Drifters, all of which I initially had lent Tomasello. And News reciprocated by giving me his copies of "Rag Doll" by the Four Seasons; "The Little Old Lady from Pasadena" by Jan and Dean; "Come on and Swim" by Bobby Freeman, and the classic "Dancing in the Street" by fabulous Martha and the Vandellas.

In the sports world that summer, News and I were elated watching the *Phillies* Jim Bunning pitch a no-hit-perfect-game (allowing no walks or base runners) against the hapless *New York Mets* on June 21st at *Shea Stadiuw,* with the Phils' winning by a score of 6-0, and the pitcher's remarkable achievement was the first regular season "perfect game" since 1922. And, of course, Timmy, News, and I were happy that the *National League* had again defeated the *American League* in the annual *All-Star Game*, 7-4.

And redundantly, I worked the Pete's Market routine sixteen-hours a day, mostly seven days a week; attended the July 16th *Our Lady of Mt. Carmel Carnival* with Joanne; secretly met the olive-skinned Prom Queen three times at Bruni's Pizza for Atlantic City and Ocean City boardwalk dates; traveled with News and Timmy once each to Coney Island and Wildwood, and generally couldn't wait for my senior year at *GSC* to commence.

Some neat records came-out in August of '64 like "I Like Bread and Butter" by the Newbeats; "Pretty Woman" by Roy Orbison, and a Beach Boy sound-alike car song titled "G.T.O." by Ronny and the

Daytonas. But the innocence of the wonderful leftover '50s culture that Tim, News and I loved so much was in grave jeopardy.

Storm clouds were on the horizon. The summer of '64 also had many draft-age kids nervous about war drums beating in the news headlines. and the eligible candidates were aware of the war development prospects constantly being communicated on television newscasts. On August 2nd, three North Vietnamese PT boats attacked the U.S. destroyer *Maddox* in the *Gulf of Tonkin,* in what was regarded as international waters. U.S. jet fighters were dispatched from the aircraft carrier *Ticonderoga* and fought-off the PT boats' aggression, and I imagined myself being a Naval pilot out of Lakehurst participating in the raging battle, incessantly strafing the enemy patrol vessels. And then, three days later, President Johnson ordered U.S. planes to bomb North Vietnamese naval bases as retaliation for what had become known and comprehensively described as the "*Gulf of Tonkin* incident".

Anti-war sentiment was rapidly growing on college campuses all over America, and beatniks were gaining influence and notoriety, and the "Flower Children" were creating a new generation of dropout anti-war rebels known as "hippies", who were mostly rebellious youths that loved folk music, as opposed to good old-time rock and roll.

"Well, J.W.," News declared on the way back to Glassboro after *Labor Day.* "The developin' war in Southeast Asia along with the beatnik culture is expandin' all over the country. And those August 28th race riots in Philly' are all combinin' to make colleges hotbeds for active political protests against the military, and against the federal government," Tomasello academically summarized. "Things are lookin' bleaker now than they ever did."

"You're generally right," I agreed with my companion and roommate. "Mayor Tate had to seal-off a hundred-and-twenty-five blocks of Philly' to put a stop to the vandalism, arson, and the widespread lootin'. And Goose is goin' to attribute the destruction to the fact that black people are getting' equal rights and are lookin' for something for nothing. And Restuccio called me an ignor-*anus* over the telephone for stickin' up for and defendin' black rights."

"Well, if ever the *National Guard's* services were needed, it's right now," News plausibly opined. "More than five-hundred people were hurt in the violent Philly' riots, and over three-hundred-and-fifty anarchists have been arrested and booked. Times are changin' for the worse, J.W., and I do believe it all began when President Kennedy was assassinated on November 22nd of '63."

"And besides, News," I stated, "that lousy folk music is becomin' more popular, and that guy Bob Dylan is makin' headway with his talk-singin'! We grew-up in the best of times back in the '50s when everything, including rock and roll, was innocent, pure fun, and simple."

"And that Peter, Paul, and Mary song 'Puff the Magic Dragon' is not a kiddy tune after all as everybody thinks it is," Tomasello declared. "It's all about beatniks smokin' marijuana and getting higher than kites."

"On the positive side, News, we still have Joanne and Elaine at our comfort to give us moral support," I reminded my friend as I drove through downtown Williamstown and then veered towards Glassboro on *322*. "And I'm beginnin' to think that you and the guys were right about me stupidly, becomin' a Navy jet pilot."

"Well, J.W.," News chuckled as we passed the all-too-familiar Williamstown Republican Club. "Democrats in office usually means war for the country, and Republicans usually means recession, at least that's what my Pop says," T.T. reminded me. "But in your particular case, be careful. If the North Vietnamese don't shoot ya' down in your Navy jet fighter, then Joanne, or her cantankerous father, might perform *that* task when ya' least expect it."

Chapter 39
"Student Teaching"

After arriving back at mediocre-but-comfortable 38 South Main, I was glad to be reunited with my fellow Lambda colleagues and Ralph Crenshaw, and I felt a need to rehash old times and unique adventures that we had commonly shared in the past. I explained to the fellows that I would be having Student Teaching in Folsom until January, and that I would not be too active with the fraternity, unless a sudden emergency developed on campus involving renewed conflict between the ruthless Delta Alphas, the volatile Tau Kappas, and the inimitable Lambda Phi's.

"I'm also havin' Student Teaching first semester," Ralph matter-of-factly announced to his fraternity co-residents. "But as soon as I ace the course, I'll be virtually guaranteed graduatin' with Summa Cum Laude honors, and when that's an absolute certainty, I hereby promise I'll be joinin' the Lambda Phi's in late January, or no later than mid-February."

"Goose told me after the *Steel Pier* horse tank rescue that the evil genius would like to become an honorary Lambda when Ralph finally joins our rank-ranks," I mirthfully indicated. "Restuccio can't be a regular fraternity member because he doesn't attend the college, even though we're illegitimate and illegal to start with. Does that make any damned sense at all?"

"Hey guys," T.T. piped-in like a high-pitched circus calliope. "Did ya' know that the *Broadway* musical *Fiddler on the Roof* is gonna' open in two weeks at the Imperial Theater, just off *Times Square*. Zero Mostel just had 'a funny thing happen' to him' on the way to the forum', and now he's gonna' star in *Fiddler."*

"Maybe when that Zero is 'Up on the Roof' with the Drifters," Timmy speculated and feigned with a serious facial expression, "the actor could then accompany the singin' group the Drifters 'Under the Boardwalk'. Those damned Drifters really know a lot of damned prepositional phrases, and constantly use them for song titles."

"How about Goose hiring the twelve Japanese Sumo wrestlers and George Evans, with *his* three gorilla brothers, to work for the Mafia as shake-down debt collectors and rules enforcers," I mentioned. "That betrayal's gotta' be a big blow to the Deltas and the Taus' prestige and confidence. And after that *Clementon Lake Park Salt and Pepper Shaker* nine-hour marathon, I don't see those other frats' challengin' us too soon, especially with what happened to Littlefield, Walker, Patton, and Irwin."

"That would be certain *frat*ricide if the Deltas or the Taus try anything drastic!" Timmy laughed. "Mario, Hoss, the Japanese goons and the Evans brothers will use uppercuts and karate chops to knock all fifty-eight Deltas and Taus gliding 'up on the roof', so that our recent enemies could then be with the Drifters, and with that Fiddler musician, in *zero* time."

"Blow it out your ear, Timmy!" Big Al lividly yelled at Amoro. "And if that doesn't work, you could blow it out your lint-filled navel, or you could just implode your ass right into another damned science-fiction dimension!"

News must have related the word "implode" with the word *explode,* so then naturally, TNT characteristically bored everyone to death describing how astronomers were discovering "Blue Galaxies" on the fringes of the known universe, and that those revolutionary new findings were supporting the controversial *Big Bang Theory,* explaining the creation of our *Milky Way Galaxy,* and consequently, the eventual formation of our own solar system, including our special native planet, Earth.

"Goose probably thinks that Blue Galaxies are where blue movies originate from," News sputtered-out like a daffy imbecile. "And Restuccio also probably thinks that the *Big Bang* phenomenon is really a mass orgy materializin' at his favorite naughty hangout, Jezebel's Den over on Delilah Road in Pleasantville."

My senior year objectives certainly placed a large degree of stress upon my fragile mind. Thanks to Miss Sankins and to Dr. Trenoff's unrealistic grading methods, I had to struggle to raise my cumulative average to a respectable B+ level by doing exceptionally well in my final academic subjects, including Student Teaching. And I was under a great deal of pressure from my parents to secure a public-school teaching position, and finally become a productive member of society, so it was my obligation to industriously fulfill my family's high expectations.

My Student Teaching stint was very unique when contrasted to my Junior/Senior High School junior year Practicum at Clearview. I was assigned to a small rural country schoolhouse, which was a throwback to the early 1900s. I had a class of twenty-four pupils in Folsom, just south of Hammonton, but one-third of the country students were immature sixth-graders, a third self-centered seventh-graders, and the remaining eight were wired eighth-graders.

My cooperating teacher was rather old-fashioned in appearance and also in practicing classroom discipline, and the old dame was on the last leg of a lengthy teaching career. Her ultra-strict teaching style seemed as archaic as cuneiform writing, and the elderly woman's appearance and dress habits would have qualified her to pose for a Mathew Brady *Civil War* photograph. Mrs. Miller was not the easiest person to get along with, and she ruled her classroom domain with martinet austerity. The distrustful lady was very suspicious and paranoid about a novice male student-teacher bringing to her rural three-level-classroom foreign knowledge and dangerous alien ideas.

Mrs. Miller was quite reluctant to turn the classroom reins over to me, and she nearly fell-out of her girdle when one day I gave the class a small lecture on the increasing widespread use of marijuana among vulnerable U.S. teenagers, and the drugs inherent dangers and ramifications. After apparently mentally suffering while listening to *that* particular trauma, Mrs. Miller made certain that my every lesson was under her doubting authoritarian surveillance. The woman did not want her clan of backwoods angels corrupted by some wet-behind-the-ears radical college student, exploring sensitive subject matter of debatable ethical propriety.

Whenever my college coordinator would arrive to observe and evaluate a lesson, the two-dozen kids in the Folsom class would try their' hardest to be attentive and receptive. The cooperative students and I had devised *our* special internal communications system, especially designed for when my college mentor, Dr. Ash, came to assess my performance and competency. When students in the class knew the correct answer to a question, the kids would raise their left hands, and if the classmates didn't know the correct response, then they would raise their right arms.

My college coordinator believed that I was doing a tremendous job, motivating the kids because all of the students had their hands up all of the time throughout each observation period. My questions were eliciting fantastic and amazing correct answers. "You appear to be quite effective, and your enthusiasm has definitely aroused the students' interest and curiosity," Dr. Ash noticed and attested. "But you should try to promote inductive thinking rather than deductive thinking. Try to get your students to think divergently, rather than answering questions that engender simple convergent thinking and factual responses."

Of course, Dr. Ash's suggestion was diametrically opposed to Mrs. Miller's antiquated teaching strategy and philosophy, so if I loyally employed the college professor's recommendation, then I was destined to receive a C or less from Mrs. Miller, which was part of my final Student Teaching grade. If I employed Mrs. Miller's strict rote-memory, old-fashioned methods, the obvious repercussion would be Dr. Ash giving me a C for not being innovative and modernistic. It was a terrible dilemma that made me feel quite uncomfortable and consistently frustrated during that first-half of the college year, struggling at the rural four-room, square Folsom Elementary School.

I did drive to 38 South Main several times for mental health reasons to stay overnight; date Joanne, and drink beer and *Southern Comforts* with the fellows to promote male bonding. But I could tell that graduation, full time teaching, and the prospect of marriage were slowly-but-surely tugging me away from the rebellious spirit and brotherhood of rebellious Lambda Phi Sigma.

Bill Elderberry had again changed the time on Ralph Crenshaw's alarm clock, and Ralph for the sixth time, unfortunately showed-up at *Memorial Hall Cafeteria* at three a.m., only to find the doors locked. And to add insult to misery, the future Lambda was also exposed to doggie dung mischievously placed inside the heating vent next to his bed, with the rancid odor also waking Crenshaw up at three in the morning on two additional occasions.

But Ralph confidentially informed me that he was definitely receiving an A in Student Teaching at Clayton High School, and that the very serious student was still working in the cafeteria before and after his high school teaching placement. But Bill Elderberry had to get new Lambda recruits to accompany him to Lacy's Funeral Home to falsely and insincerely visit wakes that were occurring next door to 38 South; however, the rest of the campus residents, including Big Al, refused to attend viewings, simply to mock Death, and much to *his* admirable credit, Ralph never ever went next door once to pay phony last respects to someone he didn't know.

"What's goin' to happen to the Lambdas after we graduate?" Timmy asked me one night in early October. "Have ya' ever thought about that? The fraternity might just go extinct!"

"I don't know, and I really don't care!" I vehemently answered. "I mean, I care about the 38 South Main Street' Lambdas, but I don't think Hoppy is gonna' let others use the chicken coop after Cassidy graduates, and also Tim," I continued my analysis, "Bob Abrams is so adamant about becomin' a superintendent that he'll probably within a year lose all interest and loyalty in the organization that he and Hoppy had co-founded."

"And Goose is gonna' become more involved in his father's illicit businesses; you'll marry Joanne, and I'll probably teach in Fort Lauderdale after what I saw of the chaotic place," Timmy facetiously said and laughed. "But we'd better enjoy ourselves now, because next year this time, J.W., we'll be tossed to the wolves, huntin' fame and fortune out there in the evil real world. And we'd better get married soon, because I hear that the college exemption from the draft is gonna' be lifted, but that married teachers won't be drafted," Timmy elaborated, "especially married teachers with a newborn baby in the house. I feel a big ugly war commin' our way, J.W., and I'm sure glad you're not goin' back to Lakehurst to learn jet pilotin' after you and me finally evolve outa' *GSC.*"

And then Timmy and I listened to some more recent 45s, and remarkably, each song had some major significance exclusively to me, that I discreetly kept my thoughts all to myself and did not share any of my ruminations in further conversation with my close friend. The Shangri-Las "Leader of the Pack" had reminded me of Bob Abrams; and the Kinks' "You Really Got Me" made me think of George Evans at the Peaks Horse, Apple and Peach Farm; at Cowtown; at the dilapidated Clayton shack, and at the *Steel Pier* white stallion farm. Bobby Vinton's "Mr. Lonely" brought reclusive Ralph Crenshaw to the forefront of my mind, and for some obscure reason, Manfred Mann's crazy-sounding "Do Wah Diddy Diddy" had my fertile imagination focused on Bill Elderberry's notorious behaviors and stranger-than-strange misbehaviors.

And then, some other recordings being played brought additional fond and not so fond memories, acutely rising from my subconscious into my cerebral consideration. The Animals' "House of the Rising Sun" had me thinking about Goose's implication in prostitution (Restuccio once told me he never needed any *African-dizzy-yak* (aphrodisiac) to become aroused), and G.R.'s profiteering in gambling and loan sharking were also of an illicit nature. And next, Dusty Springfield's smash hit "Wishin' and Hopin" had my active imagination concentrating on Timmy's noble aspirations and ambitions in a future career, and in a happy prospective marriage; Herman's Hermits' "I'm Into Something Good" had me appreciating the 38 South Main Street' guys; the Beach Boys' "Dance, Dance, Dance" had me contemplating News and his preferred California sound, and the Zombies haunting rendition of "She's Not There" put my guilty mind onto the resurfaced memory of rejected Patricia "Peachy" Wilcox.

And before I left Timmy's company that night in our upstairs' suite at 38 South, the Beatles "A Hard Day's Night" made me consider dating Joanne at the college, and then having to do Student Teaching the next day at Folsom, feeling very fatigued and dragging;

the Dave Clark Five's "Bits and Pieces" had me assessing the probable breakup of the Lambda Phi Sigmas after June graduation; the Dixie Cups "Chapel of Love" made me speculate about marrying Joanne despite her father's vociferous objections, and the Rolling Stones' "Time Is on My Side" made me wonder about what would happen for the rest of my life after leaving the protective halls of *Glassboro State College.*

And then, News Tomasello came into the Common Room and started, out-of-context, prattling about how the *United Auto Workers* had been tying-up production at many *General Motors* plants across the country, because there was a delay in negotiating a new three-year-contract. And next, News was explaining how the *Warren Commission* had released a report on the John F. Kennedy assassination, which concluded that no national or international conspiracy had been determined in the late President's murder, and that Lee Harvey Oswald and Jack Ruby had each acted independently. And somehow, I still blamed Oswald for causing all of the social turmoil that was perpetually happening throughout the country, because just like Timmy and News, I believed that President Kennedy's game-changing assassination had triggered widespread social disorganization along with reactive anti-Americanism on college and university campuses across the United States.

But during my senior year, I was more skeptical of some of the college's left-wing professors like Rolphs and Flank that attempted to "blame America first" for the ills of society, and for the debilitating conditions of the world global community. And I found more solace in the country's traditional values and patriotic heritage, despite the grotesque existence of widespread poverty, racism, communism, socialism, corruption, decadence, crime, anarchy, drugs, violence and industrial pollution. But despite all of the national adversity, I refused to be alienated from my country; from my religious values; from my American culture and civic pride; from my knowledge of American history, and finally, from my strong feelings of American ethnocentrism, despite the inevitability of the approaching *Southeast Asian War.*

Even News Tomasello's priorities were changing, as my long-time friend adopted a more adult-mentality about establishing his future in education and simultaneously averting the draft. News and I never discussed the *'64 World Series* where the *St. Louis Cardinals* had beaten the legendary *New York Yankees* four games to three, and where the *Cards'* fantastic pitcher, Bob Gibson, had struck-out thirty-one batters in three games, setting a *Fall Classic* record. And despite Mickey Mantle breaking Babe Ruth's home run record, hitting his 16th *World Series* blast, Tomasello and I remained mum about the annual baseball tournament, probably because the '64 *Phillies* had had the *National League Pennant* won that year, but then collapsed (like the *Hindenburg* at Lakehurst in 1937) and blew an eight game lead in September, when the *Cardinals* were surging to the top, just like quality cream in coffee.

And News and I were so depressed after the *Phillies* horrendous implosion that we never once discussed that debacle ever again when in each other's company, nor did we talk about the daring jewel robbery at New York's *Museum of Natural History,* where the 565 karat *Star of India Sapphire* and the 100 karat *DeLong Ruby* had been heisted by clever thieves. And we never even once discussed the grand opening of the *Verrazano-Narrows Bridge* connecting Staten Island and Brooklyn, even though we both knew it was the longest suspension bridge in the world, being over a mile long at 6,690 feet in length. I had wanted to drive over the span just to experience its magnificent design and construction, but never once drove my white Chevy Impala anywhere near Staten Island during my crucial senior year at *GSC.* And all of *our* apparent reticence and disdain had been directly attributable to those hapless '64 *Philadelphia Phillies* panicking in the clutch and giving-away the coveted *National League Crown* to the more aggressive, more-hungry, and more worthy *St. Louis Cardinals.*

Just before the *Christmas* break, I was inspired to participate in one last adolescent rebellion against adult authority and the college's "petty bureaucratic administration". Like many other students, including those that were into the hippie movement phenomenon, folk music, and protesting the upcoming war, I believed that students at the college lacked power and essential input about the school government in relation to college management; input about the obsolete midnight curfew for girls, and input about the lousy cafeteria food, among other petty grievances that, at the time, seemed pretty major and paramount.

The Lambdas got involved in a symbolic protest rally around the *College Hall* oval just before *Christmas* break, and the now-meek Delta Alphas and the now-docile Tau Kappa frats' had become relatively domesticated, and did not participate in the campus protests. And I deliberately played "hooky" from my Student Teaching obligation at Folsom School to participate in the student militancy that had generally been Lambda inspired. Girls in the *Evergreen, Oak, Laurel,* and *Linden* dorms' configured nifty placards with catchy slogans, and our general dissent culminated in a grand march on the administrators' perch, which was situated above *Savitz Library*. Several hundred brave students (including beatniks and hippies rebelling against the war) joined our monotonous ambulation around the *College Hall* oval, showing *our* common-ground dissatisfaction with almost everything and anything that the deans had been advocating to keep strict discipline among the disenchanted-but-restless student ranks.

The deans reluctantly invited into their administrative offices Bob Abrams, Frank Morrissey, a new Lambda named Joe Wallers, and myself. We stepped-out of the bleak, cold drizzle that had been falling that inclement January day. We were summoned to "negotiate and alleviate" our complaints before the newspapers got wind of the mounting "grass-roots demonstration". Our specific grievances were heard, discussed, considered, put on hold, but never resolved. But we all felt tired of submitting to adult dominion transcending over our humble student lives, and we needed to get one final protest and rebellion out of our systems before the real world, with its real pressures and intimidating responsibilities, enveloped us, as we were gradually becoming more removed from our idealistic, academic campus environment.

* * * * * * * * * * * * *

I had completed Student Teaching in early January of '65 with the grade of B, which was mutually agreed upon by Mrs. Miller and Dr. Ash. I found some consolation in Dr. Ash's testament, "The best public-school teachers were B and C students when they had attended college. Eggheads with A' averages usually don't and can't relate their stilted lingo too well to public school kids!" Dr. Ash claimed. "B and C students have more balanced personalities than A' college seniors do!"

Over the span of my senior year's fall semester, I traveled the length and breadth of New Jersey, going to job interviews in Hammonton, East Orange, Haddonfield, Edgewood High School, Sparta, and in Pitman. I finally received a "Position Offering" in the mail, but the invitation had come from Edgewood Junior/Senior High, which needed a seventh-grade social studies/English teacher. "I don't really want to teach on the same faculty as Mr. Andrews, who had failed me in algebra II and also in trigonometry!" I told my disappointed parents. "I'll wait a week or so before I respond to the superintendent. I still have more time to decide."

Even though I was nearly hitting the panic button, I judiciously elected to wait seven additional days for hopefully a more enticing "Position Proposal". My eligibility for the *Vietnam War,* which had been rapidly escalating, was a real consideration and a definite factor in my thinking and worrying, and I would be exempt from military service if I could secure a teaching position and then get married.

Luckily, I had received a second offering, this time from the Hammonton School District, and I hastily signed the contract to teach a self-contained sixth-grade class seven' different subjects. And over the summer time (my last one at Pete's Market) I received a notice from the Hammonton School System's Board of Education that my salaried first year contract of $4,900.00 had been generously raised to $5,050.00.

"Wow!" I excitedly exclaimed to Mom and Dad. "Teaching's really a terrific profession! I haven't even done anything yet in a Hammonton classroom, and already, I'm getting a hundred and fifty dollar raise!"

But when January 1, 1965 rolled in, my heart and mind were geared to returning to *Glassboro State College* one final time. The Lambda Phi Sigmas were ready to party, and if the Delta Alpha Omegas and the Tau Kappa Epsilons desired to resurrect the fraternity war, then News, Timmy, Big Al, and I were ready to accommodate their whim.

And Ralph Crenshaw and Goose Restuccio had pledged that they wanted to officially join Lambda Phi Sigma, and Bob Abrams and Steve Cassidy had already approved their applications, and the two candidates were primed for initiation. Things were going super between Joanne and me. I already had a teaching contract for the following school year, and I really savored and enjoyed the company of the 38 South Main Streeters (including eccentric Bill Elderberry). In January of 1965, life indeed seemed like a bed of roses, without any irksome thorns penetrating my sensitive skin.

Chapter 40
"Ralph and Goose"

On the Monday, January 4th drive from Hammonton to Glassboro, News was boringly reviewing for me from his "*Univac* brain" the scores of the big *New Year's Eve* and *New Year's Day* college bowl games. I wished that my pal would talk about things more relevant and practical, like our futures; our girlfriends; the Lambda Phi's; or even the Delta Alphas or the Tau Kappas; but Tomasello, as usual, was robotically enumerating the various winners and losers of the annual college football contests from rote memory.

"And J.W.," my talkative companion declared, just before we crossed the *Black Horse Pike* into downtown metropolitan Williamstown, "as you know, my favorite comrade, Arkansas beat Nebraska 10-7 in the *Cotton Bowl;* Texas had trouble but squeaked by Alabama 21-17 in the *Orange Bowl;* LSU inched by Syracuse 13-10 in the *Sugar Bowl….* "

"Hold your horses right there, News," I blew my top at my boring and garrulous passenger. "How could two college football teams like Texas and Alabama ever fit in an orange bowl, and two other teams like LSU and Syracuse ever fit inside a sugar bowl to play football games, even if there wern't any sugar or oranges in the damned bowls. What you're sayin' is not logical, according to the bizarre laws of physics, which you and I both study every time we sit on the toilet and take a decent crap!"

Tom Tomasello ignored my verbal wit and continued with his standard monologue of lackluster TV news events, which in reality, were quite remote to our lives, but especially significant for some unknown reason to him. "And in the *Rose Bowl* classic, J.W., which I know, according to your inane thinking, should've been played in a vase instead of a bowl," T.T. annoyingly qualified, "Michigan pounded Oregon State 34-7, and in the…"

"I know all the scores and statistics, too, so please stop obviating the obvious, and please start talkin' about something more important and directly connected to our lives," I strongly chastised. "Don't ya' have any essential information stored in that computer brain ya' carry-around on your neck all the time? Damn it! I almost veered off the road and wound-up in a ditch!"

"Well, J.W., Lyndon Baines Johnson will be officially inaugurated as the 36th President of the United States after he finishes-out the late John F. Kennedy's term," Tomasello mundanely communicated. "And the pompous and elite political ceremony will take place as usual on the *Capitol* steps at…"

"Damn it, News! Cut it out!" I screamed, as we drove past the all-too-familiar Williamstown Republican Club on *Route 322*. "Ya' never told me what ya' got in Student Teaching! Are you ashamed to disclose your grade?"

"Do I have to?" my loyal companion asked, almost whimpering. "I really don't want to!"

"Damn it, yes, you do!" I emphatically challenged. "We're good friends, News, aren't we? I mean, we gotta' trust each other's character through thick and thin."

"Okay, then, here it goes," Tomasello hesitantly volleyed. "I received an A, and Big Al, Timmy, Ron Carputis, Paul, Ralph, Bob Abrams, Hoppy and even Wild Bill Elderberry all got A's in Student Teaching, too. Only you and Mario, among the Lambda Phi seniors, earned B's, and all the while, I was tryin' to shield and protect your damned ego from *that* hurtful truth, but after ya' screamed at me twice like a maniac, J.W.," News Tomasello softly commented with regret and remorse, "well, then I just had to tell you the facts as I know them. That's why none of the other guys ever mentioned their grades to you, despite their own personal happiness, because the gang didn't want to hurt your damned sensitive feelings!"

I felt like crying and repeatedly punching myself in the face for being so damned stupid and demanding in regard to my close friend. I sat there driving the white Impala all the way to Glassboro, angry at the world, because I knew that everyone else News had mentioned wanted to become a school administrator, a guidance counselor, or had aspirations of transferring from the educational world into the business realm, except me. I had wanted to make teaching my career. Our only common threads were not wanting to be drafted into the army, and belonging to the notorious Lambda Phi Sigmas.

Since the atmosphere was then quiet inside the car, with neither News nor I knowing exactly what to say next, I angrily turned the volume up on the radio to fill the ice-cold void. And not even Stan Getz's lively "Girl from Ipanema"; the Hondells upbeat "Little Honda"; the Supremes quick tempo to "Baby Love", or the Beatles energetic "Twist and Shout" could adequately cheer me up. And when we eventually entered Glassboro, finally crossing *Delsea Drive,* the Temptations catchy "The Way You Do the Things You Do", followed by the Kinks driving rhythm of "You Really Got Me", made me so exasperated that I flicked-off the radio dial with such ferocity that I twisted the knob right off of its mounting.

The following day, everything on campus seemed back to normal. My courses appeared fairly easy, and now that the important parts of my professional preparation, being Practicum and Student Teaching, were behind me, I had signed-up (after final exams' in mid-January) to matriculate into and take several less-difficult electives for my final *GSC* spring semester.

World Geography with Dr. Cramer was a wise choice, but *Ancient Civilizations and Literature* was my favorite selection, and when Dr. Fletcher stipulated that half of the class's grades would be determined by some major student project, like building a six-foot-high Egyptian pyramid model, or making duplicates of the *Dead Sea Scrolls,* or manufacturing an authentic-looking scale miniature of the Athenian *Parthenon,* then my mind was really inspired, especially since the task could be a joint effort, with as many as two other students in the class involved in its development.

"Listen to what I have in mind," I lectured to Timmy and News, who were the other two Lambdas in Dr. Fletcher's elective class. "Fred Patton, Sam Lista, and Russ Stillwell from the Delta Alphas are in the class, too. Now, I have a terrific idea."

"What's that?" News and Timmy simultaneously asked. "A triple homicide followed by a triple suicide?" Timmy finished.

"We'll have a contest, a boat buildin' contest, between the Lambda Phi's in the class and those three incompetent Delta Alphas," I recommended. "It'll be a matter of pride as to which fraternity could construct the best ancient Greek fightin' ship!"

"I have an associated idea!" Timmy boldly offered. "After we build the ancient fightin' ships and get our A grades, we could then have a naval battle right after graduation to get all of the bad blood between the Delta Alphas and us out of our systems. We could build both boats on opposite shores of the same lake, let's say Academy Street Lake over in Clayton, and then we could stage a re-creation of the Battle of…."

Timmy couldn't right then and there think of any particular ancient Greek naval battles, so News authoritatively chimed-in, "We could have the *Battle of Salamis,* that is, the second *Battle of Salamis,* enacted on the *placid* Academy Street Lake, which is nowhere near Lake Placid."

"That's a positively great idea!" I commended my two zany friends. "The Lambdas could be the good-guy Greeks, and the Deltas could be the bad-guy Persians tryin' to get to Athens to attack and sack the *Acropolis*. Let's see, if I remember now," I proceeded, "Salamis was an island in the…."

"It was a horseshoe-shaped island in the Saronic Gulf approximately ten-miles west of Athens," News finished my thought much better' than I possibly could. "After the *Battle of Thermopylae* in 480 BC, where incidentally, there were hot springs nearby to explain the *thermo* part of the proper noun *Thermopylae,* the three-hundred *Spartans,* under the leadership of their king, Leonidas, valiantly staved-off the Persians, who outnumbered the Greeks over a hundred to one."

"Okay, men," I interrupted. "We'll discuss this matter with Dr. Fletcher and see what the prof' says. If our professor likes the general idea, then we'll approach the Deltas and mull it over with the degenerates to reach an agreement. If everything plays out accordin' to plan," I conjectured and declared, "we'll have the second glorious major *Battle of Salamis* occur on Academy Street Lake, just down the road from the Aura Lambda Phi Sigma chicken coop."

Dr. Fletcher euphorically approved the idea of two separate ships (one Greek and one Persian) for dual group project grades, and so did the three Delta Alpha Omegas in the class. But Dr. Fletcher was unaware that the two ships would be manned, and would later, right after graduation, have a decisive sea battle on Clayton's Academy Street Lake at high noon on Friday, May 28th, the day after the senior commencement exercises.

The Delta Alphas and the Lambda Phi's agreed on an intricate ship design, with both war vessels holding a crew of twenty-five; twelve oarsmen on either side, and a captain on each vessel, and we used a prototype model of a *bireme* that had been illustrated in our *Ancient Civilizations and Literature* textbook (from the Greek invasion of Troy in 1184 BC) as the official standard.

The Deltas agreed to put Persian markings on their version of the same Greek-designed ship, and although the *Battle of Salamis* was around six-hundred years later than Homer's *Trojan War,* historical accuracy wasn't the prime consideration as far as the two fraternities were concerned. Dr. Fletcher thought that if the ships were authentic in their construction and somewhat operable on water, then those were *his* vital criteria in determining *our* group grades.

Goose Restuccio had heard of our major shipbuilding project and claimed that the deal-maker knew highly skilled boat-builders at the Leeks Boatyard in Lower Bank on the *Mullica,* who could expertly construct the vessel for us "so that the Lambdas wouldn't have to waste their time and effort". And Goose said to me over the phone, "J.W., don't worry about a fuckin' thing. I'll float the money for your fuckin' boat to float on Academy Street Lake, so that ya' can fight the goddamned Alphie Ortegas and beat-up on the mother-fuckin' creeps once and for all. In fact, I have enough goddamned money to float a fuckin' academy on Academy Lake, if I wanted to. But there's gotta' be one damned *step-pew-lay-shin!"*

"What's that?" I asked. "Do ya' wanna' hold the anchor during the battle? You might even become a news anchor!"

"If I'm payin' for the son-of-a-bitchin' ship to win the Battle of Salamander, then I've gotta' be the fuckin' honorary captain for the not-too-bright Lamp-das."

"Okay, Goose. I'm sure that Bob and Hoppy will go along with *that* reasonable request," I confidently replied. "Since you're payin' the freight, the bosses should have no special objections!"

"Fuck those two nobody assholes!" Goose nastily rankled. "I'm payin' the fuckin' freight, like ya' say, to have the goddamned *buy-ream* built, ain't I? If those two ignor-*anuses* don't like it, the lowlife shits can fuckin' fight for the Persian rug mother-fuckers instead, and we'll fuckin' bust *their* asses, too!"

"But if we have our boat built on the *Mullica* and then transported to Academy Street Lake in Clayton," I worriedly answered, "wouldn't that be considered cheatin' if we didn't build the damned boat all by ourselves?"

"J.W., were you fuckin' born tomorrow?" Goose screamed in his staccato shriek. "The goddamned Alphie Ortegas are gonna' have their *ain't-shit* boat built by another company located on the *Egg Harbor River*. They're gonna' cheat the same fuckin' way we're gonna'! I found-out that info' while talkin' to some old fucks over at the *Sweetwater Casino Marina,* and then speakin' with some even older fucks over at *Chestnut Neck!"*

"But isn't the name *Leaks* Boatyard kinda' sound funny and *prophetic* for a reputable boat-buildin' company?" I wondered and inquired. "Now an old salt leaks the enemy's secret to you!"

"J.W., ya' know that sometimes you're really a stupid, three asshole, retarded bastard!" Restuccio yelled over the phone. "First of all, there's nothin' *pathetic* about it. If it wasn't for fuckin' leaks, then you would have fuckin' exploded over ten-years-ago for havin' too much fuckin' piss in all four of your fuckin' kidneys!"

On Wednesday evening, February 24th (according to my diary) News, Timmy, Paul, and I were sitting in our upstairs Common Room, and Cicero Tomasello was loquaciously communicating to us in a lackluster manner how a hundred-and-five cadets at the *United States Air Force Academy* in Colorado had been compelled to resign from that prestigious institution for cheating on exams' and for breaking the school's rigid honor code. And then, nutcase News described how other cadets were still in hot water because the acquaintances knew about the unmeritorious conduct, and had not reported the obvious violations to their military superiors.

"But unlike *GSC,* the *Air Force Academy* is a military school with strict disciplinary standards," esoteric Lambda Paul M. intellectually evaluated and contributed. "I don't believe, News, that you'd see anything similar or so drastic happenin' here at *GSC.*"

"But sometimes cheatin' is warranted and justified," Timmy A. pitched-in. "Let's say ya' pull a class with a crazy, demented professor like Sankins, Flank, Rolphs, or Trenoff, just to name a few. Their tests and exams are abominable and highly unfair. Do ya' remember when we were freshmen?" Amoro rhetorically asked. "There were eleven-hundred-students in our class, but now we've been whittled-down to only five-hundred. The system is designed to weed-out deadwood and make big money for the college, but part of that scam is conducted by professors who just want to bust students' chops, and bust their testicles and deflate their tits, too!"

"Timmy's right for a change," News assessed and concurred. "If Trenoff was fair and decent, then J.W. and Abrams would've never felt compelled to steal the answers to the creep's final examination. Cheating happens everywhere. The big question in my mind is, 'Did the cadets at the *Air Force Academy* have some deranged biased teachers like Sankins, Trenoff, Rolphs, Peaferm or Flank? To me, that's the central issue of debate."

"How about cheatin' on your girlfriend?" I asked, while enjoying being in a humorous mood. "How would that form of cheating be handled at the *Air Force Academy?"*

Tomasello, Paul, and News momentarily ignored my nonsensical statement, but then TNT soon deftly incorporated my comment into *their* profound discussion. "Then, even the damned professors are cheatin' as well when the instructors hop in bed with their fellow professors' wives and husbands!" News very smartly remarked. There was a three-second pause that ensued, and then Tomasello continued expounding his random rambling.

"And also in the headlines," News proceeded with his rhetoric because our television had been turned-off all day, since several of us had major term paper reports to organize. "Four people in New York were arrested, includin' leaders of a group called the *Black Liberation Front*. Those insurrectionists were plottin' to dynamite the *Statue of Liberty;* the *Liberty Bell,* the *Lincoln Memorial,* and the *Washington Monument*. Forget what's happenin' over there in

Vietnam," Tomasello argued and maintained. "Things are getting' mighty insane, hairy, and hectic, right here in America."

Just then the door was rapped, and before I could answer the knocking, Goose Restuccio strutted and bopped-into the Common Room. "Did you guys see where those fuckin' niggers wanted to blow-up the Liberty Bell Statue, the Lincoln Monument, and the Washington Memorial?" G.R. said, getting his D.C. architectural terminology slightly convoluted. "Why don't those communist mother-fuckin' mool-en-yans just blow themselves up and dynamite each other's asses?"

"They can't blow themselves up because they're not inflatable!" News joked. "Do you think that they're balloons or car tires?"

Paul didn't want to hear any more of Goose's defamation and slandering of an entire race simply because of the actions of a few of its members, so Meroski rose from his chair and then flicked-on the television, before futilely adjusting the rabbit-ears to achieve better reception. "Hey guys! Check this news out! There's been another damned assassination!"

All attention turned to the television monitor, where a news reporter was commenting on Malcolm X being assassinated while addressing a group of followers at the Audubon Ballroom in Washington Heights, New York. "Malcolm X was born Malcolm Little, and had been prominent in the Black Muslim movement in the United States until 1964," the news commentator prefaced. "But then, the black leader became active in the Black Nationalist cause, which was another movement the dissident had founded. Police suspect that radical elements of the Black Muslims had assassinated the now Black Nationalist for changing his allegiance to the newer cause. We'll have more specific details later in this broadcast, as more facts about motives are gleaned, and when possible' murder suspects are discovered and accurately identified."

"That fancy news reporter is just a *common-tater!* Who really gives a shit about that ugly *arrow-gent* alphabet nigger kickin' the bucket?" Goose argued to no one, yet to everyone in the room. "It's just niggers killin' niggers, just like on *Action News* in Philly', every fuckin' night! We oughta' be fuckin' glad that those rug-heads stay most of the time in the goddamned cities," Restuccio continued his prolific tirade. "If those mookers ever find-out where the fuckin' suburbs are, then we're all in fuckin' trouble. The *Air Force* would do the country a big fuckin' favor if they stopped kickin' ambitious white guys outa' their school in Collie-rotto, and use their planes to bomb every fuckin' nigger neighborhood in the big cities," Restuccio orated. "Then, you' *i-deal-list-tic* college jerk-offs could have a good life without havin' a lousy fuckin' future, and also, you confused dick-pullers won't have to pay half your fucked-up, meager salaries just to keep the fuckin' lazy niggers alive and on welfare."

"Goose," Paul intrepidly challenged. "You're a total, absolute narrow-minded bigot. There are plenty of decent black people in the world. Your discrimination is based on stereotypes, and on *KKK*-type biases, dating back to the *Civil War* era. You have to be more tolerant and open-minded."

"Yeah Paul, you'll be fuckin' real open-minded if some nigger shoots ya' in the fuckin' head with a high-powered rifle," Goose loudly countered. "And my *incrimination* against mool-en-yans is based on fact and experience, and that's more than *you* can fuckin' say for yourself and your dumb-ass, high-brow *college-inn* classes!"

"What do ya' mean by that?" Paul defensively insisted. "You're talkin' in generalities without specific references. I've had good relations with black kids on the college's *Whit* newspaper staff, and our school's *Avant* literary magazine."

"Okay, wise-ass," Father Goose stubbornly proceeded. "Niggers are merchant-terries (mercenaries), and they'll turn on you in a second if they can get more money outa' somebody else than the shines can fuckin' steal, or rob, or threaten from you. Take George Evans for a good fuckin' example," Restuccio screamed like a demented madman. "That dark shadow now works for me, because I pay him more than the fuckin' Alphie Ortegas and Capa Episalongs did, but if those goddamned jerk-offs we sent fuckin' whirlin' around in the *Salt and Pepper Shaker* ever decide to pay that nigger more dough than I do, then those black bastards have no goddamned loyalty. They'll leave us high and dry and work for the fuckin' Alphie Ortegas and the Capa Krappa Episalongs! And I should *men-shin* that I fuckin' hate the term *salt and pepper* because that's when ya' see a white-trash trailer park woman with a black wanna'-be-white-nigger!"

"That's called capitalism, free enterprise!" Paul aptly returned, sounding a little like Dr. Peaferm. "Most white Americans will work for somebody else, or transfer to another company that's willin' to pay more than what their old company was payin' for *their* needed services. You gotta' understand, Goose, that freedom of choice and free enterprise often go hand-in-hand here in America."

"Just remember my words after ya' bust your balls workin' for the next forty-years and goin' nowhere with your life, because of high taxes you'll have to pay to support lazy fuckin' niggers and *lack-a-daisy-kill spics,"* Goose verbally rankled. "And when there's no more fuckin' money left for social security, you'll finally understand what the fuck caused ya' to have nothin' in the first place. You'll then lose what the fuck *you* were entitled to in the second fuckin' place."

"Guys, maybe we can continue this intellectual debate at another more appropriate time," I interrupted and suggested, trying to act as a UN peacemaker. "Tell us Goose, is there a reason you've come to pay us an unexpected visit tonight?"

"Why yes, there is," Restuccio replied in a softer tone, since our mercurial guest was speaking to me and not to Paul. "I stopped by the chicken coop over in Aura before commin' here, and the initiation for Ralph and me is set to go off two fuckin' evenings from now, on fuckin' Friday, when everybody gets laid."

"That's really great, Goose!" I instantly congratulated our erratic-tempered pledge. "Then, you'll officially become a Lambda Phi Sigma honorary member on Friday night."

"Just as long as there aren't any son-of-a-bitchin' niggers ridin' for free on that caboose'," Goose stated, while trying to get the last word in on Paul. "It's bad enough that my white tax money's gotta' pay the fuckin' freight for most of those stupid black bastards to ride the gravy train for free, all their fuckin' lives."

"I wish you would just call them blacks rather than usin' that redundant racial slur!" Paul declared.

"Well Paul, let me tell ya' some-thing' pretty *relly-vent,"* Restuccio sneered and scowled, attempting to impress us with his distorted nomenclature. "There are some blacks that buy into the goddamned culture, and I sorta' respect them," Goose clarified. "Those coons think and behave like normal white *peep-hole* do. But the rest of the race are still niggers that commit crime; kill white people; murder each other; rape white girls; and collect welfare from Uncle Sam, which is really *your* fuckin' tax money bein' wasted. Those lowlife clouds will fuckin' rob and murder you, or anybody else, for a goddamned dollar or a penny cigarette butt. And those son-of-a-bitches that commit serious crimes are the felons ya' see every fuckin' night on *Action News.* Those crazy niggers lack respect for people and property, and they'll always be nothing better than fuckin' *get-toe* niggers!"

"Then, you're making a basic distinction between upper and middle-class college-educated blacks and deprived ghetto dwellers with no normal future," Paul interpreted and recognized. "That does put your arguments into a slightly different perspective!"

"Fuckin' A!" Goose haughtily replied. "And if *you, Paul,* kill, rob, murder, steal, rape, mug people, take lethal drugs, and collect welfare when ya' can work all along, then I'll go so far as sayin' that you're a goddamned fuckin' white nigger, Mur-saki!"

On Friday night at 9 p.m., a dozen Lambda Phi members showed-up to watch Goose Restuccio and Ralph Crenshaw be officially initiated into our noble fraternity. The freight train was, as usual, scheduled to depart the Glassboro depot at 9:15, and Goose and Ralph were all pumped-up about running down Girard Road and then catching the slow-moving caboose at the *322* railroad-crossing. It was a cold, bleak, winter night, and patches of ice-covered Girard Road, making footing slippery, and running on asphalt treacherous in some separate areas.

"Ralph," Bob Abrams mentioned with concern, "it's a real cold night and the road's a little icy. Are ya' sure ya' wanna' go through with this initiation?"

"If Goose is gonna' go," the quietest of my roommates declared, "then I'm game, too! I was an offensive lineman at Teaneck High and always considered myself an athlete, and since I'm still in excellent physical shape, I should be able to catch and board the caboose with no problem whatsoever."

"What about you, Goose?" I asked our most generous supporter. "Do ya' wanna' go tonight, or postpone your dash? You don't have to do it tonight, if you'd rather not attempt the stunt."

"I'll have to go, even though I'm no fuckin' athlete like Ralph is!" Restuccio honestly insisted. "I'm fuckin' flyin' out to Palm Springs from New York with Frankie and Joey tomorrow, and then meetin' up with my folks to go over next month's goddamned family secret West Coast business. I'm caught in a fuckin' time window."

"Okay, guys," Hoppy confirmed. "But my advice is please be careful. There're only eight cars and a caboose tonight, and the train's only half as long as it usually is. That means it'll probably be goin' a few miles an hour faster than normal when it crosses *322,* Lambda Vice-President Steve Cassidy indicated. "But a normal human can easily run over fifteen-miles-an-hour, so that variance shouldn't be any major problem. Just watch-out for a slippery piece of ice here and there on the road, especially on asphalt, which some people call black ice!"

The locomotive's shrill whistle sounded at the Glassboro Depot, and Ralph and Goose got ready at the starting line for their "cooperative competition". Everyone else entered four Lambda cars to form a procession line that would slowly follow the participants scampering down Girard Road to complete their initiation task. Then, Abrams yelled one final instruction to the two eager pledges.

"If you guys feel like quittin', then we'll do it again in a couple of weeks when the spring weather arrives," our fraternity President yelled. "We'll all understand why you changed your mind, so don't hesitate to do so. And Goose, that goes for you, too! You can join-up after ya' return home from Vegas and Palm Springs!"

The red flashing railroad lights came on; the road crossing gates descended, and the black locomotive began chugging its way out of the ramshackle Glassboro Depot. When the shorter-than-usual train passed the University Road tracks, Ralph and Goose took-off hustling down Girard Road from the crossroads' intersection. The dual pledges had no problem keeping-up with the orange-painted caboose, but the two sprinters still would have to have their timing perfect when latching onto to the last car's railing upon reaching the *322* crossing, still a quarter-mile ahead.

Ralph was certainly much more agile and coordinated than Restuccio, but Goose demonstrated tenacious determination and was only ten-or-so feet behind his fellow recruit. And Ralph was sort of a guide for Goose, weaving left and right every so often to avoid the occasional ice patches, so that Restuccio knew when to change direction in performing his imitation dash.

"They look like dashing young men!" News humorously quipped at the initiation's halfway mark.

"You oughta' be wearin' either Elaine or Loretta's nylon stockings," Timmy laughed to News from the Impala's back seat. "Then, you could have your own two runners!"

And when Ralph had nearly gotten to *322,* slightly before Goose, our Lambda Phi roommate waved to Restuccio to have the Sicilian pass him and reach the caboose's railing first, in order to easily hop aboard. G.R. easily passed Ralph after Crenshaw, who had deliberately slowed-down, and remarkably, the feisty Italian grabbed the railing and pulled himself-up onto the caboose's moving deck.

When Ralph attempted to duplicate the same maneuver two seconds later, something quite extraordinary happened. Crenshaw had his head down to compensate for an adjustment in needed speed, and when the pledge lifted his neck up at the last second, the train's whistle blew, temporarily distorting the pursuer's perception and his sense of judgment. The engineer suddenly applied the brakes, and instead of Ralph's hands making contact with the vertical parallel bars, Crenshaw's head impacted with the railing, and then became wedged between two of the orange caboose's vertical bars. And unfortunately, the poor victim was instantly and horribly dragged forward by his neck.

Safely aboard the caboose, Goose was hysterically screaming as the freight train picked-up speed. G.R. desperately held onto the railing, and used his right foot, endeavoring to push against Ralph's head in order to free Crenshaw from his terrible entrapment. Crenshaw's limp legs dragged and bounced against each successive railroad tie as the terrible accident progressed. We all watched in horror as Restuccio finally liberated Crenshaw several-hundred-feet down the track. Ralph's body fell between the parallel rails, and when we hurriedly exited our cars and ran to the tragic scene, Restuccio leaped-off of the caboose, and then, the Sicilian's forward momentum had his body rolling and tumbling down an incline. Meanwhile, the unaware engineer inside the locomotive kept the train moving and heading towards Pitman.

When I arrived at the horrendous scene, instinct told me to first descend down to Goose, for I knew that my benefactor was moving-around and still alive, and also, I intensely feared what Ralph's horrible fate might have been. Restuccio was stunned, but too frightened to say a word, and when I assisted my friend to his feet, and directed his path up the embankment heading towards the other Lambdas, I could see Abrams hustling back to his black '57 Mercury to get help on *322*.

"He's barely breathing!" We need an ambulance fast!" Hoppy helplessly hollered.

"This is terrible!" I yelled as the shock of what had actually occurred finally sunk in. "Absolutely hideous!"

"Ralph slowed-down to let me go first!" Goose sniffed and sobbed. "That *could* be me layin' there! I hate to say it, but that *should* be me layin' there!"

Fifteen-minutes later, the Glassboro Rescue Squad finally arrived upon the scene. A stretcher was hastily brought to where Ralph lay motionless, as if my roommate had been permanently paralyzed. "He's still barely breathing," a concerned paramedic reported. "But his injuries are so bad that we'll have to take him to Underwood Hospital in Woodbury. He definitely has a broken neck!"

"And your friend certainly has severe injuries scattered all over his body, and is bleeding from many areas," the second rescue squad member confirmed. "But I don't believe it's from superficial cuts! This poor kid is also suffering from serious internal bleeding! I can tell you that from thirty-years of on-the-job training!"

Chapter 41
"A Funeral and A Graduation"

The Lambda Phi's did not abandon Ralph Crenshaw during his hour of need. After our friend had been placed upon the stretcher with a neck brace, we loyally followed the Glassboro ambulance north on *Delsea Drive,* and then Route *47* led us to *Underwood Hospital* in Woodbury, ten-miles up from the Glassboro campus. But our fidelity and concern produced very futile results, because our introverted 38 South Main roommate was pronounced dead an hour later, while still on the emergency surgery ward's operating table.

"We did all we could!" Dr. Porter told us with a grim expression on his face. "Your friend had ruptured several key neck arteries and lost too much blood in his vital organs from the time of the accident to the time of his arrival here at Underwood. Your companion was a Glassboro State student, wasn't he? We're very sorry that we could not save him."

I looked at News, Timmy, Goose, Bob, and Hoppy, and the other six Lambdas sobbing in the emergency ward's waiting room, and none of us could say anything of merit, but we all knew exactly how terrible, miserable, and disconsolate each other felt. It was the most horrific moment of our lives, of *my* life.

"Thank you, Dr.!" I finally was able to answer with a shaky, weak voice. "Ralph was from Teaneck up in North Jersey. Have you notified his family?"

"Dr. Stokes is working on that detail right now," Dr. Porter, the head surgeon replied. "Your close friend's home number and his emergency contacts were all found inside his wallet. But you won't be able to leave the hospital until you all are questioned and released by the police."

A few minutes later, the County Sheriff, the Glassboro Chief-of-Police, along with two patrolmen entered the Woodbury hospital and wanted to interrogate the Lambda Phi's about the nature of Ralph's shocking accident. After the authorities learned that the tragedy had occurred during a college initiation requirement, and how the task was to be completed involving leaping onto the moving caboose at the *322* railroad-crossing, all four law enforcement officers shook their heads in dismay and disgust.

"Do you boys know that the twelve of you can be held and tried in court for involuntary manslaughter?" the Sheriff grimly disclosed. "Some of it all depends on how hard the victim's family wants to prosecute the matter."

"Has the railroad been contacted about the accident?" News asked. "It happened on their property. I think that they oughta' know about the circumstances, too."

"Yes, the railroad has been contacted!" the Chief-of-Police tersely replied. "We're still tryin' to piece all of the moving parts of the puzzle together in order to file as accurate a report as we can, since a human life has been taken. But we do know from the railroad that the engineer had hit the brakes because a deer was standing on the tracks, probably blinded by the locomotive's bright light, so that's when he blew his whistle," the Chief divulged. "The change in speeds must've distracted and confused your friend momentarily, and when he lifted his head, he was closer to the caboose's railing then he had expected. But it was too late for him to stop, and his head collided with the bars and got stuck in between two of them. That's the way we see it, right now!"

"Then, the train's engineer might be accused of involuntary manslaughter, too, for slowin' down the locomotive!" Paul Meroski deducted and suggested his non-influential legal opinion. "That's a distinct possibility, too, because if Ralph's family sues, they'll get more money from the railroad and its insurance company than they will ever get from middle-class college kids."

"That remains to be seen," the Sheriff growled. "Remember that the engineer was just doin' his job, unaware that a running young man was tryin' to climb onto the caboose. But if you kids had been studyin' like you were supposed to be doin', then this unnecessary tragedy could've definitely been averted."

An hour later, the twelve of us were seated inside the Glassboro Police Headquarters, located behind the bank at High and Main, and each Lambda Phi witness had been conducted one-by-one into an interrogation room to provide independent answers to an assigned detective's pertinent questions. Two hours thereafter, the police thanked us for our cooperation, and the no-nonsense Chief verified that the department would get back to the involved Lambdas as soon as the detectives discussed matters in depth with Ralph's family; with railroad officials; with the college deans, and with the county prosecutor's administrative personnel.

The next several days, everyone at 38 South Main just kind of hibernated, reflected on reality, and seriously meditated about what had happened. I took a drive to the intersection of *322* and Girard Road, and just gazed at the railroad tracks, near where the unforgettable disaster had occurred. The Sounds Orchestral's newly-released rendition of "Cast Your Fate to the Wind" was being played on WIP FM, Color Radio, so I nervously switched to Wibbage 99 AM and became even more neurotic when Little Anthony and the Imperials' "Hurt So Bad", followed by "Tears on My Pillow", came over the airwaves. I snapped the radio's dial to the left, aggressively shutting-off the source of my ascending grief.

Ralph's family insisted that their son's viewing be held in Glassboro to accommodate his campus friends who might wish to pay their final tribute, and ironically, Lacy's Funeral Home, next door to 38 South Main Street, was the mortuary chosen by Mr. and Mrs. Crenshaw. And it was a most difficult thing for the Lambdas (and especially for Bill Elderberry) to attend Ralph's viewing, introducing our identities to our deceased friend's mom, dad, and two younger sisters, and to genuinely grieve with the family, truly expressing our very candid and heartfelt condolences. And after frivolously mocking Death so many times at the same funeral parlor, Ralph's passing reminded the saddened Lambdas of exactly how ephemeral and mortal we all really are; and how abundantly powerful Death was; and how futile it was for frail, fragile creatures like the next-door fraternity members to foolishly consider ridiculing the deadly Grim Reaper ever again, because then, we finally understood and fathomed *His* awesome dominion over us.

Many students from the college attended Ralph's wake on Tuesday evening March 2nd, and the line was like an endless slow procession from seven p.m. until 10 that night. And just about everyone we knew came to the viewing except the Delta Alpha Omegas and the Tau Kappa Epsilons, who either boycotted the viewing out of spite, or were too afraid to express sincere feelings to a fallen enemy and his beleaguered family.

And Goose Restuccio was also absent from Ralph's very sad viewing, flying out to Palm Springs to escape the reality of what he had been a part of, and *we* consented to *his* going out to the western resort because all of us realized that Restuccio would carry the emotional burden with him out to California, and never have complete closure as most of us that had attended the viewing might eventually have. We all comprehended that Goose could change his physical location from New Jersey to Palm Springs, but the mental anguish could not be erased anywhere in the world.

On Wednesday morning, twenty-five Lambda Phi's attending the college drove-up to Teaneck in five cars, all following the black hearse up the *New Jersey Turnpike* to *Exit 11,* and then going west past Orange on the congested *Garden State Parkway,* until we eventually crossed the *Passaic River,* and slowly exited onto the

Garfield ramp. Then, the funeral procession traveled several more miles to *St. Anastasia's Roman Catholic Church,* and listened to a fine eulogy delivered by the pastor, who had remembered Ralph as one of *hi*s "finest and most honest altar boys". And then, we attended Ralph's grim burial, five-miles away in *St. Joseph Cemetery* on Hackensack Road, in Hackensack.

Six of the Lambdas had volunteered being pallbearers, and the grateful family acceded to our request. News, Timmy, Big Al, Paul, Bill and myself performed the dutiful responsibility, since we had lived with Ralph for almost three whole years. Besides going to Peachy Wilcox's father's viewing in Cape May, Ralph's burial in Hackensack was the hardest thing I ever had to do up until that moment in my short life. Tears welled-up in my eyes, and when I looked at my grieving roommates, the same reaction was happening to them, no matter how hard the guys attempted camouflaging their true feelings by sniffing and looking the other way. And when Ralph's casket was lowered into its concrete vault, I felt that two parts of me had also died with him: my youthful innocence and my immense immaturity.

After the very sad interment, Mr. Crenshaw invited the twelve Lambdas to attend a reception at a local restaurant, but feeling very uncomfortable, guilty, and insecure, we sincerely declined the polite offer, saying that we had to return back to Glassboro to again be interviewed by the local and state police.

"We want you boys to know that my wife and I really appreciate you attending our son's viewing, and then driving way up here to North Jersey to attend his mass and burial, and then be his pallbearers," Mr. Crenshaw said with tears in his eyes. "Our son often mentioned your names to us over the past few summers. So, over the span of these last few heart-wrenching days, you've shown my wife and me that his roommates really cared about Ralph by volunteering to carry him to his final resting place," Mr. Crenshaw stated. "And now we're convinced that the entire incident was a freak accident, and that our son had participated in it at his own volition. My wife and I want you all to know that we don't hold you responsible in any way for our son's death, and we will not press charges or sue any of you, when we're again contacted by the Gloucester County Prosecutor's Office! Again, thank you so much for attending your roommate's funeral!"

All I could think of saying was, "Thank you, Mr. Crenshaw! This has been the saddest day of my life! God bless you!" And then, the other Lambda Phi Sigmas present had the decency to also express their final sympathies to Mr. and Mrs. Franklin Crenshaw, standing in front of Ralph's *St. Joseph Cemetery* gravesite.

* * * * * * * * * * * *

Right through the first week of spring and into April, 38 South Main Street seemed as much a mortuary as did Lacy's Funeral Parlor next door. Even normally radical Bill Elderberry ceased his frivolous high jinks, because the clownish prankster had been greatly affected by Ralph Crenshaw's tragic death; by his very sad viewing, and by his soul-stirring church mass and burial. And News, Timmy, Big Al, Paul, and myself all felt despondent, with our hearts filled with pathos and grief, just like some of the ancient Greek plays of Sophocles, Aeschylus, and Euripides portrayed. And I then realized that even News had too much decency and too much compunction to say his classic overdone Greek tailor joke, "You rippa' these, you menna' these pants, too!"

And during our overwhelming grief, sportive jocularity seemed not to be our purpose or desire. Plenty of national and world disruption happened in the outside world during the next two months, but our minds remained steadfastly on four principal goals: getting the Homeric-era fighting boat onto Academy Street Lake in Clayton; receiving A's from the amenable Dr. Fletcher for our intense labor; graduating from *Glassboro State Teacher College* on May 27th; and finally, dedicating the May 28th *Second Battle of Salamis* to Ralph Crenshaw, and then thoroughly taking-out our angst and frustration on the doomed Delta Alpha Omegas.

And certain historic events transpired between March 4th and May 27th, but News remained reticent about their impact and influence, all out of solemn respect for "Ralph's ghost". UCLA had defeated Michigan 91-80 on March 20th to win the *NCAA Basketball Tournament,* and on March 23rd, the *Gemini* 3, nicknamed *Molly Brown,* had blasted-off from Cape Kennedy, Florida, and not even the names of its pilots Major Virgil Grissom and Lt. Commander John Young, Jr., or their three-orbit flight, was ever once mentioned from News Tomasello's normally hyperactive lips. When the annual *Hollywood Academy Awards* were given, none of us watched or cared that Rex Harrison had received his Oscar for the Best Actor Award for his major role in *My Fair Lady,* or that Julie Andrews had won best actress for her beloved part in *Mary Poppins.* And any other year besides 1965, News would have been both glib and obnoxious, recounting the trivial particulars of those major-but-nevertheless-commonplace newsworthy events.

By April 9th, when the marvelous *Houston Astrodome* opened with an exhibition game between the *Houston Astros* and the *New York Yankees,* a little talk about current events was finally generated amongst the 38 South Main Street Lambdas. And several days later, I did mention that the *Phillies* Richie Allen was the first player to hit a home run in the Houston Astrodome architectural wonder, where baseball was being played on a new green synthetic material called *Astro-Turf,* and where the indoor temperature remained a perfect 72 degrees *Fahrenheit* without any rain or wind ever changing the perfect field conditions.

On May 15th, the Homeric-style *Trojan War* boats had arrived in sections, and being transported and assembled on Clayton's Academy Street Lake. But, of course, the competing fraternities had to receive bureaucratic permission from the small town's mayor and council to launch the vessels at both ends of the springs-fed body of water. Dr. Fletcher had viewed and boarded both the Greek and the Persian fighting ships, and instantly declared that each vessel looked authentic and fantastically well-made and seaworthy, and the results of his inspections were A's for the three Lambda Phi's, and also for the three Delta Alpha students enrolled in the professor's popular *Ancient Civilizations and Literature* seminar.

After receiving his A, News finally broke his two-month penance of silence and related to Timmy and me off subject, "Yesterday Queen Elizabeth dedicated a monument at Runnymede, England to the memory of President John F. Kennedy."

"Why at a place named Runnymede?" I curiously asked. "I'll bet that Runnemede, New Jersey, over near Woodbury on *Route 47,* had been named after this Runnymede in England you're citing. Isn't it coincidental, News, that you're talkin' about John F. Kennedy's death, and with Underwood Hospital, where Ralph had died, being located right near Runnemede here in Jersey? I'm no soothsayer or auger, or anything else like that, but I find *that* word relationship pretty damned fascinatin'!" I remarked. "It's almost an omen from the supernatural world that we're gonna' emerge victorious over the Delta Alphas in the upcoming *Second Battle of Salamis."*

"Well, J.W.," News asserted, while my roommate was finally returning to his standard, traditional, boring form of dictatorial conversation. "Runnymede, England is where King John had signed the *Magna Carta* in 1215, which was the first government document guaranteein' the property rights of common citizens be protected under law. An inscription at the site reads: 'This acre of English ground was given to the United States of America by the people of Great Britain in memory of John Fitzgerald Kennedy."

"That's quite a really wonderful, inspirational tribute," Timmy candidly acknowledged. "That's why *we* have to soundly defeat the Delta Alpha Omegas on May 28th in the *Second Battle of Salamis*. It's a real test of wills and character. But first, let's all concentrate on finally graduatin' on May 27th."

On the evening of Tuesday, May 25th, Goose Restuccio (after a near two-month absence) showed-up at 38 South Main to discuss final preparations for the scheduled Greek and Persian sea battle on Academy Street Lake. Apparently, Goose's guilt associated with Ralph's lamentable death had been erased from *his* conscience, and Restuccio's period of mourning had evidently abruptly ended. Unfortunately, G.R. showed-up just before the start of the second Sonny Liston-Cassius Clay fight, and the black, loud-mouthed, arrogant, bragging heavyweight champion had recently changed his official name to Muhammad Ali.

"Just like a fuckin' nigger!" Goose immediately criticized and discriminated. "The fuckin' guy makes a couple of million bucks as Cassius Clay, and then rejects his country's free enter-*prize* system; forgets all about bein' a goddamned Christian, and tells the whole damned country and every white person in it to go fuck themselves usin' slightly different words! Now, if that's not fuckin' nigger gratitude, then I don't know what the hell is, the black bastard!"

"Goose, the fight's about to begin, so please keep it down a bit, will ya'?" the *Whit* and *Avant* editor commented and pleaded. "This is the first excitement or entertainment we've been able to enjoy since Ralph's funeral. And Ralph said that he really liked Cassius Clay's, or excuse me, Muhammad Ali's style and grace in the ring."

"Well, J.W., I can't understand any of you fuckin' not-too-brilliant Lamp-da guys," Restuccio continued his diatribe. "You' college assholes not only like when fuckin' niggers shit on your heads, but then ya' love it when their crap rolls down your goddamned faces, moves around your eyes, and goes directly into your shit-eatin' mouths and noses. Any nigger commin' out of the slums without any goddamned education isn't fuckin' worth his weight in horse-shit, J.W.; especially the quality horse-shit that George Evans and his fuckin' black *u-rang-a-tangs* had shoveled on Abrams' and your heads out at Peaks Farm! Now, just try tellin' me to my face that I'm a goddamned liar!"

The much-anticipated and heralded rematch between Muhammad Ali and Sonny Liston began, and everyone in the room watching the black and white television (which incidentally corresponded with Goose's values) was stunned when Liston hit the canvas, only a minute into the first round.

"I didn't see any punch thrown!" Timmy exclaimed. "Liston looked like he just tripped! What the hell happened? There was no damned punch thrown!"

"He fuckin' took a dive!" Goose alleged and accused. "Just like J.W. did on that goddamned white *Steel Pier* horse. And I don't feel one bit sorry for all those stupid white mother-fuckers in the audience that paid five-hundred dollars or more for decent seats, only to watch a dumb ghetto nigger fall-down without even bein' fuckin' bein' punched by a mouthy, goddamned nigger, who now thinks he's a fuckin' Arab. What a fuckin' joke!"

The referee dramatically counted Sonny Liston out and raised Muhammad Ali's right hand to boos, jeers, and catcalls being generated from the irate and incensed mostly white fans in ringside attendance. The TV announcer, amidst the raucous hysteria and chaos, tried interviewing the champion, who was a little too flamboyant and filled with braggadocio to suit our Sicilian guest.

"When we fuckin' knock those fuckin' Alphie Ortegas' lights-out over there in Clayton on Friday, I guarantee ya' that it's not gonna' be as fuckin' easy as the boxin' joke we just saw on television," Restuccio predicted. "I only wish that those goddamned sneaky Alphie Ortegas were niggers, so that I could be more excited about beatin' the shit outa' the grubbing assholes. But I'll just pretend that they're the next best thing," Goose announced and decreed. "I'll just pretend that those gay homo Alphie Ortegas are educated black men instead of being uncivilized cannibal-get-toe-gorilla-niggers."

And then, before Goose Restuccio left the property, the perturbed visitor had to hammer Paul one final time for recent disagreements between the two. "Hey, Mur-cow-ski, was your mother ever pregnant?" and before Paul could respond to the insult, Goose rose from his chair, slammed the door shut, and hustled-down the wooden, rickety stairs.

The Thursday May 27th *Graduation Day* eventually arrived for the *Glassboro State College Class of '65.* Lengthy speeches were delivered by Dr. Robeson and by Dr. Lang, and then several local Congressmen had to remind the graduates of their important mission in life as being the "educators of tomorrow's hopes, our precious children". The five-hundred-and-fifty surviving candidates receiving

Bachelor of Arts Degrees, along with their bona fide New Jersey Teaching Certificates, took turns by rows, standing in line, and the litany of our names were boringly and individually announced. I was sitting next to News Tomasello, who had also become a Junior-High English/social studies teacher. News had brought along a pint of *Southern Comfort,* and we Lambdas shared swigs during the long hot introductions and rambling, meaningless, idealistic orations.

"Those pompous graduation speakers think we're all *B.S.ers* instead of B.A.ers," News joked. "But I really wish that Ralph was here to be receivin' his Summa Cum Laude honors that he had earned! Sometimes, both life and nature are cruel!"

"News, the kids graduatin' with science teaching degrees are the real *B.S.ers!"* I jested back. "Now please remember, good buddy; you get in line and grab my diploma, and I'll follow and snatch yours. Big Al and Bill Elderberry are doin' the same trick we are by switchin' places in line, and so are Bob and Hoppy, and Mario and Timmy. It's sort of our last act of defiance directed at the repulsive deans, and our final campus tribute to Ralph. I sure hope he's smilin' down on us when we enact our final respects to his memory, in the form of Lambda Phi *tom*-foolery, even without any damned male turkeys anywhere in sight."

When News and I received each other's diplomas, Dr. Lang recognized what had just transpired, but the coward refused to stop the ceremony and then have to explain to the crowd *our* final prank directed upon the besieged college administration. And after the impressive, lengthy ceremony in the hot noonday sun had finally terminated, the proud graduates of the *GSC* class of '65 all let out a boisterous "Whoop!" ,and we merrily tossed our cap' tassels into the air, as if we had just evolved out of the *Army Military Academy at West Point,* or the *Naval Academy at Annapolis*.

Mom and Dad never knew about the fraternity wars between the Lambda Phi's and the Delta Alphas and the Tau Kappas, and the many near-death experiences I had quite fortunately escaped. And also, my parents never learned about Ralph Crenshaw's horrendous death, which the feckless administration had skillfully kept out of the local and city newspapers. But despite those truths, nevertheless, my folks were absolutely thrilled at my fairly extraordinary *GSC* academic achievement.

"Congratulations, son!" Dad commended while warmly shaking my hand. "Your mother and I are very proud and excited about your accomplishment. You're the first member of our family to ever graduate from college. Good luck to you!"

And Mom showed her happiness too, but wondered why News had received my diploma and I had received his up on the makeshift, temporary, wooden platform.

"The deans got everything mixed up as usual!" I creatively explained by establishing blame outside myself. "But when we returned to our seats, News and I just exchanged our diplomas and teaching certificates."

But my disheveled mind really wasn't simply focused on the joy of graduating *GSC*. Like my fellow Lambdas, my angry heart was set on taking-out my animosit and my frustrations on the Delta Alpha Omegas, who, like the ancient Persians, were destined to lose an important Salamis Sea Battle.

Chapter 42
"The Second Battle of Salamis"

Paul and I were suffering from our usual chronic insomnia, so we descended the all-too-familiar rickety wooden stairs and stepped-out of 38 South Main, crossed High Street, and then slowly paced the remaining block north to cozy Angelo's Diner. Neither of us had ever admitted it to each other, but pensively thinking to myself, I was then, at that moment, smitten by nostalgia, leaving the security of *GSC,* and having the massive task of boldly venturing-out into the treacherous real world that was patiently awaiting to stifle me. My perception was analogous to me jumping out of an airplane, having faith in my parachute, knowing full-well that I wasn't going back up into the air without first landing safely somewhere on the ground.

Paul and I both realized that we were now autonomous adults and no longer under the deans' austere protection and their arbitrary jurisdiction. And so were most of the other Lambda Phi's, Delta Alphas, and Tau Kappas. Graduation had ascended us to a higher adult plateau, a new, more-formidable echelon that needed to be addressed and adjusted-to by each of us recently created *GSC* alumni. The 38 South Lambdas were evolving out of the old constraints, and into the new ones, just like awkward drab caterpillars are gradually morphing into colorful, graceful butterflies.

"I understand you've signed a contract to teach," I commended Paul. "Nice goin'! I suppose you're lookin' forward to the real-world next September."

"Yeah, J.W. I'll be teachin' high school English at Washington Township," Paul matter-of-factly related. "It's sorta' a funny feeling leavin' the predictability and the artificial freedom of *GSC,* and havin' to sit behind the teacher's desk representin' the damned establishment that we've both been fighting in our own ways these last four years. Maybe after the Vietnam conflict is over, I'll wind-up doin' something else more profitable than teachin'. Perhaps I'll try my hand at newspaper journalism? Who knows what the nebulous future portends for you and for me?"

"You're right, Paul," I acceded. "The newspapers report that the war's expandin' all the time; kids are droppin' out of college and out of society, all over the country, and everything American seems to be the genesis of evil throughout the world, accordin'. to the mediocre television and press accounts. And Paul," I fearfully stressed, "those rebellious and obnoxious kids we'll be teachin' are gonna' be affected by all the mania that's goin' on, so if we model our methods after those of all the teachers we had admired in high school and here at *GSC,* I worry we're in the process of authorin' our own future problems. As Rolphs once said in *Sociology* class: 'Either change or be affected by change'."

"It's sort of Darwinian in scope and sequence, wouldn't you say!" Lambda Phi Paul Meroski hypothesized and verbalized. "I mean J.W., we'll have to evolve and adapt and become stronger willed than our students are. It's definitely survival of the fittest, so to speak, on an educational plane, and we can't be too convivial with the kids we teach, or else we're askin' for colossal trouble," Paul reckoned. "And economics is exactly that same way with everyone wantin' to get rich; and government is that same way with the Democrats tryin' to get stronger than the Republicans, and vice-versa; and the military is that same conflict-oriented way tryin' to defeat communism all over the world, and now we'll have to be that same way in classrooms, clampin' down on the more challengin' discipline-problem anarchists masquerading as students. Everything is Darwinian when ya' actually think about it, J.W."

"Flank had an interesting theory in my Political Science elective," I commented. "That space cadet psycho case is either off the wall or on the toilet!"

"And what was Flank's enlightening hypothesis?" Meroski asked before slowly sipping his black coffee.

"Everything, as you say, Paul, is survival of the fittest, but everything must evolve outa' something, and then transform into something else to keep thrivin'. For example," I continued, mentally groping for the exact right words, "government first started as aristocracy, with noblemen running the show; and after a few centuries, *aristocracy* evolved into *monarchy,* when the need for a central power among the feuding nobleman class arose; which then evolved into *democracy,* where the common man ascended to power and influence; which was next interpreted by Hitler to evolve into *fascism;* and by Lenin into *socialism;* and socialism was manipulated by Stalin to transform and evolve into *communism.* And if you apply that reasonin' to Ralph," I maintained, "he has…."

"In a religious sense, our former roommate has evolved from Earth into Heaven!" Paul concluded and finished my thought. "In that case, J.W., religion actually has beaten social science to the punch, and remarkably, faith wins the culture-war competition over political and social science, by nearly two-thousand-years."

I was absolutely speechless by Paul's profundity. Then, Meroski pondered for a moment and masterfully collected his thoughts. "Do ya' think that the Lambdas are gonna' continue operatin' here at *Glassboro State* after we move on to greener pastures?" my Angelo's Diner companion contemplated and asked. "I mean, we've been around for four-years now, without any change in leadership, and we've always been like a renegade, orphaned fraternity on campus, not to mention the deans' greatest vexation. The Lambdas, at best, are an unsanctioned bastard fraternity, with no legitimacy, if ya' read me. Our name will be forgotten at *GSC* in less than five-years!"

"I think that either Blade Barrows or Nicky LaSasso would be good leaders somewhere down the line," I stated. "But only time will tell for sure. And I also think that once Abrams and Cassidy ascend into real-life teachers and go on to become superintendents, still super-intending their wills on others, then their college experiences will all be left far behind, ghosting as mere sentimental memories to be publicly denied and ignored, and with no fraternity house or legitimate recognition by the almighty deans," I elaborated, "then I think three-years from now, that Lambda Phi Sigma here at *GSC* will simply become a vague legend, a fading myth."

"And speakin' of mythology and ancient history," Paul extended our cordial Platonic conversation, "What about the *Second Battle of Salamis?* I'm really not a fighter J.W., but then again, I'm not a pacifist or a freakin' lazy, lethargic, defiant beatnik, either. I'm kind of trapped in a disarrayed Darwinian twilight zone, if ya' know what I mean. The entire outside world is nothing but gross mayhem!

"Very true, Paul," I strongly agreed. "But I've never felt such animosity welled-up in me that needs releasin' as I do right now. It's all quite primitive and Neanderthal," I admitted and confided. "Just like survival of an endangered species in Darwinian terms. Paul, we're presently fightin' for the prestige and for the survival of the Lambda Phi Sigmas, and our noble cause is the memory of Ralph Crenshaw, because we aren't manly enough to admit that we're responsible for his sickening death, and not the Delta Alphas that we're takin' his death out on," I adamantly contended. "It's ruthless anger bein' inflicted as violence. We're transferrin' blame from our own consciences to the Deltas, and in the final analysis, we're fightin' for an organization that will go extinct, just like the saber-toothed tiger and the mastodon, but in just three or four more years."

"That's really deep-dive thinking and totally accurate," Paul conceded. "You should've been President of the Philosophy Club, or the Forensics Club, J.W., rather than wastin' your spare time at the radio station readin' the sports off of the wire service teletypes, or partying at the chicken coop, or wasting your college experience at 38 South Main."

"You're wrong in one respect," I challenged Meroski. "At the radio station I got to know Ralph really well, and we became good friends, once we got beyond the Lambda Phi business and his aborted Delta Alpha initiation in the *College Hall* bell-tower," I clarified. "And once *ou*r ego facades had been stripped-away, Ralph and I really had a lot in common. And I hope his soul can look-down on us at noon today, and as the priest had recited at *his* gravesite," I paraphrased: 'And let perpetual light shine down upon *us'*."

"Wow! Paul exclaimed with an honest opened mouth. "You've inspired me to want to actually fight the Delta Persian rich-creeps now. I was really reluctant about the idea of brawling on a lake with the gruesome Deltas," Paul sincerely intimated, "because Deltas usually belong at the mouth of a river and not at the beginning of a lake," Meroski facetiously joked. "But now, I feel like the beatniks and the anti-war demonstrators, or like the white Freedom Bus Riders bringin' justice to blacks in the South. And for once in my life, J.W.," Paul pontificated, "I feel inspired by a *cause,* Ralph's cause, and the Lambda Phi cause, as ridiculous as that might sound. And we might all wind-up ten-hours from now in the hospital, or in the morgue, but we will have the satisfaction of dyin' knowin' that life was worth livin' and sacrificin' for, and our existence had a certain purpose, simply because we were swept into active insanity by a damned cause!"

While our erudite academic/intellectual discussion, like Darwin's impactful theory, had *evolved,* the Angelo's Diner jukebox was quite active, playing various popular tunes of the time, and each particular song reminded me of something that was then relevant to my habitation on this conflict-oriented planet. The Detergents "Leader of the Laundromat" reminded me of Bob Abrams; the Ad Libs "The Boy from New York City" made me think of Ralph coming from Teaneck across the *Hudson* from Manhattan; and next, the Beach Boys "Help Me Rhonda" made me consider certain helpful female assistance I had received in the past from both Joanne Berenato and benevolent Elaine Hill.

And then Johnny Rivers's "Mountain of Love" had my mind again fantasizing about Joanne; Sam the Sham and the Pharaohs' "Wooly Bully" somehow got my mind wondering about the ever-flamboyant Goose Restuccio; the Dixie Cups' "Iko, Iko" had a primeval rhythm and beat, which made me want to again feel like a barbarian Visigoth raiding the Delta House, or like severely bashing Delta Alpha Omega heads at the impending *Second Battle of Salamis;* and finally, Barbara Mason's slow ballad "Yes I'm Ready" made me realize that I was fully prepared to get all of my bad blood for the Deltas Alpha Omegas out of my system, even if my blood was to be shed because of wounds administered to me; but more importantly, the shedding of blood would ultimately be dedicated to the memory of Ralph Crenshaw.

* * * * * * * * * * * *

At 11:30 a.m., the on-a-mission Lambda Phi's all arrived in our various automobiles at our designated staging area, as we assembled in front of the popular Aura chicken coop. Goose had appeared at the rendezvous point with Frankie Fingers and Joe Zucchini in one of his father's white box trucks, which was ordinarily used to conduct official Mafia business.

"Hi, J.W., how's it hangin'?" Restuccio enthusiastically greeted. "Usually, I would come to a fuckin' event like this driven in a limo'. That's the fuckin' way that my Pop regularly conducts his debt collections from goddamned gamblers and from fucked-up loan sharkin' customers," egocentric Restuccio nonchalantly related. "And we always rent limos' up here in Jersey, so that the goddamned police and the meddlin' *Feds* have trouble followin' us to and from our fuckin' secret destinations. Why don't those asshole government bastards just mind their own fuckin' business? I'm *fed* up with the always-snoopin' *Feds!* Ha, ha, ha! All *Uncle Sam* wants to fuckin' do is *steal* my hard-earned syndicate money and then give it to fuckin' lazy niggers and deadhead spics! So, in my opinion, Uncle Sam is the biggest crook of all!"

Goose then directed Bob Abrams and Hoppy to open the white truck's rear panels, and inside the large cube were twenty-five ancient Greek uniforms that Restuccio had somehow clandestinely obtained on the black market. Naturally, G.R. had to elucidate on the uniforms and their particular significance. "I bought the gaudy mother-fuckers instead of rentin' them, figurin' that the costumes might get fuckin' ruined in the big *Salamander Battle,"* Restuccio informed his very un-impressed listeners. "The salesman told me when I put one of the battle outfits on that I fuckin' looked just like some fuckin' dead, purple guy named Alexander the Grape, whoever the fuck he was! Sounds like he was probably a big *typhoon* in the wine business. Anyway, here they fuckin' are."

After we all tried on our ancient Greek uniforms, helmets, sandals, simulated bronze breast plates, and all the other archaic apparel, Timmy made a rather pertinent statement concerning our spectacular paraphernalia, when Amoro distinctly yelled-out, "We all look like the friggin' *University of Southern California Trojan Marching Band,* without any damned heavy musical instruments to carry into the friggin' battle."

"Just as long as we don't have to lead a *Spartan* existence the rest of our damned lives," News Tomasello imaginatively quipped, alluding to the *Michigan State University* mascot and logo. "Then, who gives a hefty shit if we look like used leftover *Trojan* rubbers, just as long as we win the friggin' sea battle."

"Are ya' sure we're ready for any secret tricks the Deltas may have up their sleeves?" Bob Abrams asked Goose and me. "They're notorious for bein' slippery and deceitful. I would trust Satan before I would ever trust any of those delusional crazies."

"Those fuckin' Alphie Ortegas are gonna' get crushed and *ob-litter-rated,* no matter what the fuck those assholes try!" Restuccio adamantly vowed. "We're gonna' kick their asses so bad that they're all gonna' have to shit outa' their elbows and outa' their goddamned *navels* after we get through with 'em in this fuckin' *naval* battle! Ha, ha, ha! How about that one, J.W. Pretty fuckin' clever, huh? I'm as full of shit as you and News are! Ha, ha, ha, ha!"

"Don't worry, Bob," I confidently declared while completely ignoring Goose's rather amateur emulation of News and me. "All contingencies are in place should the nefarious Deltas deviate from the rules. Remember men," I yelled-out to my proud, stout fraternity brothers. "Here are the rules. You can only clobber the enemy with your oars, your fists, your hands, and your feet. Anything else is illegal and could cost us the fair and square victory that we're fightin' for, in honor of Ralph."

Adams then checked to see if all twenty-five participating members were present and accounted for, and all the selected Lambda Phi members' names were read-off a list: "Bob Abrams, Steve "Hoppy" Cassidy, Ron Carputis, Tom Bell, Big Al Keiler, Bill Elderberry, Paul Meroski, J.W., Thomas News Tomasello, Tim Amoro, Mario DiMaris, Ken Soblinski, Frank Morrissey, Max Gunther, Mitch Toscini, Phil Candido, Tony Petters, Gil Taylor, Blade Barrows, Nicky LoSasso, Joe Sacci, Hoss Gregorio, Little Joe Gregorio, Joe Wallers, and distinguished honorary member Admiral Ronald Goose Restuccio."

And I almost cracked-up towards the end of the roll call, laughing my guts out when I noticed Mario DiMaris, Big Al Keiler, and Hoss Gregorio standing together, all looking like oversized "gorilla Goliaths" in their ancient bronze breastplates, sandals and dull bronze helmets, which featured authentic-looking red plumes sticking-out on top.

The Lambda Phi's all clambered-up into the large box truck's interior, and Frankie Fingers and Joe Zucchini, still dressed as Mafia civilians, closed and locked the rear doors. Soon, the two mean-looking hit-men joined Goose in the cab; the truck's ignition was turned-on, and in a Glassboro second we were heading a mile down the road to Clayton's Academy Street Lake. After driving to the lake's east side, the box-truck's brakes were applied; the back panels were quickly swung-open, and the Lambda gladiators exited our confinement and purposefully walked down a small dock. One by one, the mariner/warriors climbed onto our Homeric-age bireme battleship, similar to the fighting vessels used in 1184 BC by Achaean kings: Odysseus, Achilles, Menelaus, and Agamemnon, during the famous siege of Troy.

I looked towards the highway and observed that several-hundred anxious *GSC* students had already gathered to witness the prodigious *Second Battle of Salamis,* soon to be enacted, and among the more concerned spectators were Joanne Berenato, Elaine Hill, and Loretta Sacco. I gratefully waved to the three faithful girls, all having apprehensive and worried expressions on their faces that were very visible, even from our Achaean boat, several-hundred-feet away from *their* excellent vantage point.

At precisely twelve o'clock, Admiral Goose, sounding a little like Mother Goose, gave the signal to push-off from the pier; the moorings were untied, and the boat eased-away from the small dock it had been resting against. And when our Achaean ship rounded a bend in the lake, our eyes observed a similar floating object with Persian markings and a fierce crew of Delta Alpha Omegas aboard, all dressed in full battle attire. Immediately, my keen perception noticed that the enemy was advancing and directly approaching our vessel from the lake's western shore.

In another minute, the two vessels had moved side by side, and all two-dozen Lambda Phi's and the twenty-four bellicose enemy combatants aboard the Deltas' ship instantly unfastened our oars from their locks; stood-up, and began whacking and pummeling each other with our crude wooden weapons. But after ten-seconds of savagely thwacking-away, the Delta Alpha Omegas deviated from the well-defined rules, and lowered their oars simultaneously, while amazingly, absorbing some very powerful thrusts and blows from the puzzled Lambda Phi Greeks. And as expected, the diabolical Persian impersonators shoved and pushed our vessel with their oars, so that *we* Greeks were now seven or eight feet distant from their wooden Persian ship.

My eyes glanced-down to my right and recognized a plethora of air bubbles rising-up to the water's surface, and before I could scream and warn everyone else of imminent danger, twenty-five Tau Kappa Epsilons rose from the murky depths, all wearing scuba gear, and the frightful frogmen, all together, pushed-up in unison, succeeding in capsizing our canoe-shaped ship, and their sneak-attack sending twenty-five courageous Lambdas turbulently plunging into the Academy Street Lake.

"Help! Help!" Goose screamed and exclaimed in desperation. "I'm gonna' drown! I can't fuckin' swim! J.W., fuckin' save my ass! I can't fuckin' swim to save my goddamned life!"

The Deltas were relentlessly hammering and pounding us, chaotically bobbing up and down in the water; and the Taus were wrestling with certain Lambdas in the lake, and because the aquatic attackers were wearing their oxygen tanks and scuba masks, the Kappa Epsilons were better equipped for lake combat, and for going underwater and grabbing our legs than *we* were. Dueling heads were bobbing up and down in the lake, as if the Lambdas were mallards in a carnival duck pond with snapper turtles pulling us under. And poor Goose was screaming his tonsils out during the wild tumult, but then I received a violent blow to my head that nearly knocked me into unconsciousness on Weird Street.

I next gazed at the lake's eastern shore, several-hundred-feet away, and saw George Evans and his brothers scampering on the beach, dashing towards the water in bathing suits, and next I noticed the twelve almost naked Japanese Sumo wrestlers accompanying the black foursome, awkwardly wading into the fray. I tried propping the now-delirious Goose Restuccio up in the water, and in a minute that seemed like an hour, George and Marvin swam over to Goose and began tugging him towards the beach. Meanwhile, the monstrous Sumo wrestlers and the remaining Evans brothers pushed over the Deltas' Persian boat, so that the battle was now more evenly matched, with everybody now flailing-away in the water, frenetically slugging, splashing, flaying, fighting, and pulverizing each other.

The Deltas and the Taus sensed a stalemate at best, so the antagonists began swimming towards Academy Street Lake's western shore, where the retreating cowards reached land before us. But when the craven fools got to the beach, fifteen *Hammonton Bakers,* wearing their football jerseys, emerged out of the woods and intercepted *their* frantic, hurried exit. The infuriated Lambdas, including still-hysterical Goose Restuccio, reached the beach, along with the invincible Sumo wrestlers and the muscular Evans brothers, and instantly, a land brawl of epic proportions was initiated.

Bodies were flying all over the recreation area, as the devious and conniving Delta Alpha Omegas, and the equally abominable and dastardly Tau Kappa Epsilons, were receiving the royal beating of their delinquent lives. And after smashing Sam Lista in the face, and sending the punk sprawling onto the sand, I glanced-up at the sky, and a shaft of sunlight emerged from behind a thick cloud. Immediately, my superstitious mind theorized that Ralph Crenshaw was using his celestial influence and shining-down perpetual light upon the Lambda Phi Sigmas' finest hour.

I looked-around in full amazement and witnessed indispensable Mario and Big Al randomly pummeling two hurting Deltas, and Hoss and Little Joe Gregorio were clobbering several Taus, and the entire scenario was one of absolute chaos and pandemonium. I snapped-out of my daze and re-entered the wild altercation, and punched Fred Patton in the jaw, making the belligerent jerk collapse to the ground with blood squirting out of his already abused mouth and nose.

Three minutes or so later, a dozen police cars pulled into the vicinity, and excited officers jumped-out and hustled towards the mammoth in-progress donnybrook. The running cops had their nightsticks in hand to use against any and all rival combatants. Everything' happening at that wild moment seemed blurred and hazy, and was rapidly transpiring in an accelerated state of ascending flux and agitation.

Seeing the sudden police incursion, the cowardly Delta Alphas and the equally craven Tau Kappas' all hightailed it into the woods, escaping the embarrassment of aristocratic college graduates being arrested, but more importantly, *their* principal motivation was to flee and escape the wrath of the still-highly inspired Lambda Phi Sigmas and our tenacious confederates. And it was good to see the deplorable creeps, led by Fred Patton and Randy Irwin, retreat like timid field mice into the dense thickets.

"What the hell's goin' on here?" a county sheriff's deputy yelled in sheer astonishment. "What the hell's goin' on?" the constable repeated. "It looks like Armageddon was about to break lose!"

"Just a last fling at college fun time!" News Tomasello reported as T.T. wiped some excessive blood and mud away from his mouth and nose. "Just celebratin' graduation from *Glassboro State* with a little party, and then things got a bit out of hand. Nothin' was done intentionally, Officer. It just all happened."

"Is this some kind of damned masquerade party? Why are ya' all dressed-up in those wet ancient war costumes?" an astonished officer asked, referring to a very evident anachronism being quite prevalent before his gaping eyes. "Have we gone back in history without my knowledge, or what?"

"We were just a few frisky Greek fraternities tryin' to outdo one another," a wet Timmy Amoro explained. "And then, a couple of guys got into arguments, and fights over girlfriends ignited, and the next thing we knew, we began throwin' punches and splashin' all over in the water, and then thank goodness, the police arrived just like the valiant *United States Cavalry* in those old western movies, right before matters got out of hand. And it's a good thing you fine officers showed-up, just in the nick of time," Timmy emphasized, "because a major massacre has been averted, which would've been just as shockin' as the one that happened to General George Armstrong Custer at *Little Big Horn,* which indeed sounds like a definite oxymoron."

"Well, gentlemen, it's a good thing we did arrive to quell the anarchy," a Clayton sergeant proudly-but-sternly concluded and admitted. "Otherwise, you young hooligans woulda' maimed and killed each other as sure as God made little green apples and purple plums. Has anybody here been hurt?"

"Only Goose here, but he's much better now! He's just suffered superficial cuts that band aids could easily cover," I chipped-in. "No one's really been seriously injured, and it would be grossly unfair pressin' charges against *us,* because we were the ones that didn't run-away from the police like the other guys that had instigated the brawl had done."

"Your name is Goose?" the sergeant incredulously asked my Mafia-associated friend. "Your last name wouldn't happen to be Restuccio from Hammonton, now, would it?"

"That's right, officer!" Goose cavalierly admitted while rising-up off the beach and dusting some of the loose sand from his wet arms, face, and legs. "My father's full name is Dante Antonio 'the Brute' Restuccio. Have ya' ever heard of him? He's internationally known to law enforcement all over the world."

A look of alarm instantly appeared on all of the cops' faces. The sergeant gulped and uttered, "Well, all right, Mr. Restuccio, as long as nobody was hurt or killed, and as long as you college punks clean-up the beach and get rid of the general mess ya' made," the cop in change strictly stipulated, "then we aren't gonna' press charges for disturbin' the peace, because there aren't any neighbors in the vicinity to disturb, and because the other kids you were fightin' with all ran-away. And before you leave here," the by-the-book sergeant starkly stated, "don't forget to turn those two boats right side up and tie them up to the docks where they rightfully belong."

Goose Restuccio thankfully shook George and Marvin's hands, and expressed his gratitude to the mercenary Evans' brothers for miraculously rescuing the future Mafia czar from almost certain drowning. "I wanna' thank you men for what ya' did," Goose genuinely and gratefully stated without a trace of racism, or discrimination, or cursing in his voice. "I owe you guys my life!"

"Thanks for employin' us, boss!" George answered. "Now my brothers and I can travel all over the world workin' for the Italian Mafia! No more Glassboro, Clayton, Cowtown, Carneys Point, or Mays Landing, small time stuff, no sir-ee! I see Sicily, Florida, the Bronx, and Vegas on the horizon, yes-sir-ee! And Boss, as long as my brothers and me are on your payroll, ya' don't have to worry one bit about drownin' anywhere in the whole-wide world. No sir-ee!"

Joanne ran-up to me and threw her arms around my chest, and Elaine did the same to News, and Loretta surprisingly did the same to Timmy, and at last we all felt completely removed and severed from *Glassboro State College,* and our hearts were at total peace with ourselves and with the turbulent adult world.

I pointed to a charm dangling-down from a gold chain I was wearing around my neck, and Joanne recognized the object as the good luck token she had removed from her bracelet and had given me in the Co-op prior to my important administrative meeting with Dean Nelson. My best girl smiled, and then we again embraced. I then realized that Ralph Crenshaw's friendship had been validated, and his honor vindicated, and that the four-year-long acrimonious *Glassboro State College* "frat' brats' war" had finally come to a dramatic end.

About the Author

Jay Dubya is author John Wiessner's initials (J.W.) and also his pen name. John is a retired New Jersey public school English teacher and he had taught the subject for thirty-four years. John lives in southern New Jersey with wife Joanne and the couple has three grown sons.

Jay Dubya has written many adult fiction works. *Fractured Frazzled Folk Fables and Fairy Farces. Nine New Novellas*, *Nine New Novellas Part II, So Ya' Wanna' Be A Teacher, The Wholly Book of Genesis, Black Leather and Blue Denim, A '50s Novel* and its sequel, *The Great Teen Fruit War, A 1960' Novel* are adult-oriented literary endeavors. *Pieces of Eight, Pieces of Eight, Part II, Pieces of Eight Part III and Pieces of Eight, Part IV* are short story/novella collections featuring science fiction, paranormal and humorous plots and themes. *Ron Coyote, Man of La Mangia* is adult humor and the work is an imaginative satire/parody on Miguel Cervantes *Don Quixote,* published in 1605. *The Wholly Book of Exodus* is also adult satirical humor. *Thirteen Sick Tasteless Classics, Thirteen Sick Tasteless Classics, Part II, Thirteen Sick Tasteless Classics, Part III* and *Thirteen Sick Tasteless Classics, Part IV* are adult satirical rewrites of famous short fiction.

John has also authored a trilogy of young adult fantasy novels. Besides *Space Bugs, Earth Invasion, Enchanta* and *Pot of Gold* complete the set of three young adult novels. *The Eighteen Story Gingerbread House* is a new collection of eighteen diverse and creative children's stories.

Jay Dubya likes '50s rock and roll music, and he also enjoys pop songs by the Beach Boys, Fleetwood Mac, the Eagles, the Rolling Stones, ELO and by John Fogerty. When not writing stories or listening to music, Jay Dubya likes watching *76ers* basketball and *Phillies* and *Yankees* television baseball games.

Author Biography

Born in Hammonton, NJ in 1942, John Wiessner had attended St. Joseph School up to and including Grade 5. After his family moved from Hammonton to Levittown, Pa in 1954, John attended St. Mark School in Bristol, Pa. for Grade 6, St. Michael the Archangel School in Levittown for Grades 7 and 8 and then Immaculate Conception School, Levittown, Pa. for Grade 9. Bishop Egan High School, Levittown PA. was John's educational base for Grades 10 and 11, and later in 1960, the aspiring author graduated from Edgewood Regional High, Tansboro, NJ. John then next attended Glassboro State College, where he was an announcer for the school's baseball games and also read the nightly news and sports over WGLS, GSC's radio station.

John Wiessner had been primarily an English teacher in the Hammonton Public School System for 34 years, specializing in the instruction of middle school language arts. Mr. Wiessner was quite active in the Hammonton Education Association, loyally serving in the capacities of Vice-President, then building representative, and finally, teachers' head negotiator for a period of 7 years. During his lengthy teaching career, John had been nominated into "Who's Who among American Teachers" three times. He also was quite active giving professional workshops at schools around South Jersey on the subjects of creative writing and the use of movie videos to motivate students to organize their classroom theme compositions.

In addition, John Wiessner was very active in community service, being a past President of the Hammonton Lions Club, where he also functioned for many years as the club's Tail-Twister, Vice-President and Liontamer. John had been named Hammonton Lion of the Year in 1979 and in 2009 received the prestigious Melvin Jones Fellow Award, the highest honor a Lion can receive.

John also was a successful businessman, starting with being a Philadelphia Bulletin newspaper delivery boy for two-years in the late 1950s in Levittown, Pennsylvania. After his family moved back to New Jersey in 1959, John worked at his grandparents and his parents' farm markets, Square Deal Farm (now Ron's Gardens in Hammonton) and Pete's Farm Market in Elm, respectively. He later managed his wife's parents' farm market, White Horse Farms in Elm for three summers.

Also in a business capacity, for 16 summers starting in 1967 John Wiessner had co-owned Dealers Choice Amusement Arcade on the Ocean City, Maryland boardwalk and also co-owned the New

Horizon Tee-Shirt Store for eight summers (1973-‘81) on the Rehoboth Beach, Delaware boardwalk. In addition, “Jay Dubya” was a co-owner of Wheel and Deal Amusement Arcade, Missouri Avenue and Boardwalk, Atlantic City. And then, for 18 summers beginning in 1986, John had been the Field Manager in charge of crew-leaders for Atlantic Blueberry Company (the world’s largest cultivated blueberry farm), both the Weymouth and Mays Landing Divisions.

After retiring from teaching in 1999, writing under the pen name Jay Dubya (his initials), John Wiessner became the author of 75 books in the genre Action/Adventure Novels, Sci-Fi/Paranormal Story Collections, Adult Satire, Young Adult Fantasy Novels and also Non-Fiction Books. His books exist in hardcover, in paperback and in popular Kindle and Nook e-book formats.

In January of 2022, John Wiessner (Jay Dubya) was nominated into Marquis Who’s Who in America, and in April of that same year, was one of nine distinguished Who’s Who in America members honored with receiving Lifetime Achievement Awards, all nine sharing a news article of recognition appearing in the Wall Street Journal.

Google: Jay Dubya books

Google: Walmart, Jay Dubya

www.ingramcontent.com/pod-product-compliance
Lightning Source LLC
Chambersburg PA
CBHW020556310726
48979CB00008B/1239/J